DAME AGATHA ABROAD
A Mystery Guild Lost Classics Omnibus

DAME AGATHA ABROAD:

MURDER ON THE ORIENT EXPRESS

MURDER IN MESOPOTAMIA

THEY CAME TO BAGHDAD

by
Agatha Christie

Mystery Guild
Garden City, New York

Contents

MURDER ON THE ORIENT EXPRESS

To M.E.L.M. Arpachiya, 1933

Contents

Part 3
Hercule Poirot Sits Back and Thinks

Cast of Characters

The Inspector   Hercule Poirot
The Belgian sleuth illustrates the efficiency of his methods when he comes face-to-face with a murderer on an international express.

The Director   M. Bouc
Representing Compagnie Internationale des Wagons Lits—shunts his friend Poirot onto the track of a discomfiting crime.

The Conductor   Pierre Michel
Fixes the criminal's wagon.

The Doctor   Dr. Constantine
Diagnoses that the right hand of the assassin did not know what the left hand was doing to the victim.

The Victim and the Suspects

Mary Debenham
An English governess whose manner was as calm and unruffled as her coiffure.

Colonel Arbuthnot
His French was limited, but his verbal defense in his duel with the Belgian is adroit.

Hector MacQueen
A secretary deluxe who speaks in many tongues.

M. Ratchett
This pseudophilanthropist was more malevolent than benevolent.

Antonio Foscarelli
Information gushed out of this swarthy, menacing Italian like the blood from the victim.

Edward Henry Masterman
A spare, neat, noncommunicative valet who has the haughtily disapproving face of the well-trained British servant.

Cyrus Hardman
An American commercial traveler who knows more than he tells and tells more than he knows.

Princess Dragomiroff
A Russian *grande dame* whose pearls were so large they were as improbable as her story.

Greta Ohlsson
This Swedish-trained nurse with the sheeplike face was the last suspect to see the victim alive.

Mrs. Hubbard
Stereotype of an American matron—she never stopped talking, but her acting spoke louder than her words.

Hildegarde Schmidt
Lady's-maid to the Russian princess, deeply involved in the murderous game of *chemin de fer*.

Count Andrenyi
More attached to the Hungarian Embassy than it is to him.

Countess Andrenyi
The youngest, prettiest snowbound suspect.

Part 1
The Facts

Chapter 1

An Important Passenger on the Taurus Express

It was five o'clock on a winter's morning in Syria. Alongside the platform at Aleppo stood the train grandly designated in railway guides as the Taurus Express. It consisted of a kitchen and dining-car, a sleeping-car and two local coaches.

By the step leading up into the sleeping-car stood a young French lieutenant, resplendent in uniform, conversing with a small man muffled up to the ears of whom nothing was visible but a pink-tipped nose and the two points of an upward-curled moustache.

It was freezingly cold, and this job of seeing off a distinguished stranger was not one to be envied, but Lieutenant Dubosc performed his part manfully. Graceful phrases fell from his lips in polished French. Not that he knew what it was all about. There had been rumours, of course, as there always were in such cases. The General's—*his* General's—temper had grown worse and worse. And then there had come this Belgian stranger—all the way from England, it seemed. There had been a week—a week of curious tensity. And then certain things had happened. A very distinguished officer had committed suicide, another had suddenly resigned, anxious faces had suddenly lost their anxiety, certain military precautions were relaxed. And the General, Lieutenant Dubosc's own particular General, had suddenly looked ten years younger.

Dubosc had overheard part of a conversation between him and the stranger. "You have saved us, *mon cher*," said the General emotionally, his great white moustache trembling as he spoke. "You have saved the honour of the French Army—you have averted much bloodshed! How can I thank you for acceding to my request? To have come so far—"

To which the stranger (by name M. Hercule Poirot) had made a fitting reply including the phrase—"But indeed, do I not remember that once you saved my life?" And then the General had made another fitting reply to that, disclaiming any merit for that past service; and with more mention of France, of Belgium, of glory, of honour and of such kindred things they had embraced each other heartily and the conversation had ended.

As to what it had all been about, Lieutenant Dubosc was still in the dark, but to him had been delegated the duty of seeing off M. Poirot by the Taurus Express, and he was carrying it out with all the zeal and ardour befitting a young officer with a promising career ahead of him.

"To-day is Sunday," said Lieutenant Dubosc. "To-morrow, Monday evening, you will be in Stamboul."

It was not the first time he had made this observation. Conversations on the platform, before the departure of a train, are apt to be somewhat repetitive in character.

"That is so," agreed M. Poirot.

"And you intend to remain there a few days, I think?"

"*Mais oui*. Stamboul, it is a city I have never visited. It would be a pity to pass through—*comme ça*." He snapped his fingers descriptively. "Nothing presses—I shall remain there as a tourist for a few days."

"La Sainte Sophie, it is very fine," said Lieutenant Dubosc, who had never seen it.

A cold wind came whistling down the platform. Both men shivered. Lieutenant Dubosc managed to cast a surreptitious glance at his watch. Five minutes to five—only five minutes more!

Fancying that the other man had noticed his glance, he hastened once more into speech.

"There are few people travelling this time of year," he said, glancing up at the windows of the sleeping-car above them.

"That is so," agreed M. Poirot.

"Let us hope you will not be snowed up in the Taurus!"

"That happens?"

"It has occurred, yes. Not this year, as yet."

"Let us hope, then," said M. Poirot. "The weather reports from Europe, they are bad."

"Very bad. In the Balkans there is much snow."

"In Germany, too, I have heard."

"*Eh bien*," said Lieutenant Dubosc hastily as another pause seemed to be about to occur. "Tomorrow evening at seven-forty you will be in Constantinople."

"Yes," said M. Poirot, and went on desperately, "La Sainte Sophie, I have heard it is very fine."

"Magnificent, I believe."

Above their heads the blinds of one of the sleeping-car compartments was pushed aside and a young woman looked out.

Mary Debenham had had little sleep since she left Baghdad on the preceding Thursday. Neither in the train to Kirkuk, nor in the Rest House at Mosul, nor last night on the train had she slept properly. Now, weary of lying wakeful in the hot stuffiness of her overheated compartment, she got up and peered out.

This must be Aleppo. Nothing to see, of course. Just a long, poorly lighted platform with loud, furious altercations in Arabic going on some-where. Two men below her window were talking French. One was a French officer, the other was a little man with enormous moustaches. She smiled faintly. She had never seen anyone quite so heavily muffled up. It must be very cold outside. That was why they heated the train so terribly. She tried to force the window down lower, but it would not go.

The Wagon Lit conductor had come up to the two men. The train was about to depart, he said. Monsieur had better mount. The little man re-moved his hat. What an egg-shaped head he had! In spite of her preoccu-pations Mary Debenham smiled. A ridiculous-looking little man. The sort of little man one could never take seriously.

Lieutenant Dubosc was saying his parting speech. He had thought it out beforehand and had kept it till the last minute. It was a very beautiful, polished speech.

Not to be outdone, M. Poirot replied in kind. . . .

"*En voiture, Monsieur*," said the Wagon Lit conductor.

With an air of infinite reluctance M. Poirot climbed aboard the train. The conductor climbed after him. M. Poirot waved his hand. Lieutenant Dubosc came to the salute. The train, with a terrific jerk, moved slowly forward.

"*Enfin!*" murmured M. Hercule Poirot.

"*Brrrrrrr,*" said Lieutenant Dubosc, realising to the full how cold he was.

"*Voilà, Monsieur!*" The conductor displayed to Poirot with a dramatic gesture the beauty of his sleeping compartment and the neat arrangement of his luggage. "The little valise of Monsieur, I have put it *here*."

His outstretched hand was suggestive. Hercule Poirot placed in it a folded note.

"*Merci, Monsieur.*" The conductor became brisk and business-like. "I have the tickets of Monsieur. I will also take the passport, please. Monsieur breaks his journey in Stamboul, I understand?"

M. Poirot assented. "There are not many people travelling, I imagine?" he said.

"No, Monsieur. I have only two other passengers—both English. A Colonel from India and a young English lady from Baghdad. Monsieur requires anything?"

Monsieur demanded a small bottle of Perrier.

Five o'clock in the morning is an awkward time to board a train. There were still two hours before dawn. Conscious of an inadequate night's sleep, and of a delicate mission successfully accomplished, M. Poirot curled up in a corner and fell asleep.

When he awoke it was half-past nine and he sallied forth to the restaurant car in search of hot coffee.

There was only one occupant at the moment, obviously the young English lady referred to by the conductor. She was tall, slim and dark—perhaps twenty-eight years of age. There was a kind of cool efficiency in the way she was eating her breakfast and in the way she called to the attendant to bring her more coffee, which bespoke a knowledge of the world and of travelling. She wore a dark-coloured travelling dress of some thin material eminently suitable for the heated atmosphere of the train.

M. Hercule Poirot, having nothing better to do, amused himself by studying her without appearing to do so.

She was, he judged, the kind of young woman who could take care of herself with perfect ease wherever she went. She had poise and efficiency. He rather liked the severe regularity of her features and the delicate pallor of her skin. He liked the burnished black head with its neat waves of hair, and her eyes—cool, impersonal and grey. But she was, he decided, just a little too efficient to be what he called *"jolie femme."*

Presently another person entered the restaurant car. This was a tall man of between forty and fifty, lean of figure, brown of skin, with hair slightly grizzled round the temples.

"The Colonel from India," said Poirot to himself.

The newcomer gave a little bow to the girl. "Morning, Miss Debenham."

"Good morning, Colonel Arbuthnot."

The Colonel was standing with a hand on the chair opposite her.

"Any objections?" he asked.

"Of course not. Sit down."

"Well, you know, breakfast isn't always a chatty meal."

"I should hope not. But I don't bite."

The Colonel sat down. "Boy," he called in peremptory fashion.

He gave an order for eggs and coffee.

His eyes rested for a moment on Hercule Poirot, but they passed on indifferently. Poirot, reading the English mind correctly, knew that he had said to himself: "Only some damned foreigner."

True to their nationality, the two English people were not chatty. They exchanged a few brief remarks and presently the girl rose and went back to her compartment.

At lunch time the other two again shared a table and again they both completely ignored the third passenger. Their conversation was more animated than at breakfast. Colonel Arbuthnot talked of the Punjab and occasionally asked the girl a few questions about Baghdad where, it became clear, she had been in a post as governess. In the course of conversation they discovered some mutual friends, which had the immediate effect of making them more friendly and less stiff. They discussed old Tommy Somebody and old Reggie Someone Else. The Colonel inquired whether she was going straight through to England or whether she was stopping in Stamboul.

"No, I'm going straight on."

"Isn't that rather a pity?"

"I came out this way two years ago and spent three days in Stamboul then."

"Oh! I see. Well, I may say I'm very glad you are going right through, because I am."

He made a kind of clumsy little bow, flushing a little as he did so.

He is susceptible, our Colonel, thought Hercule Poirot to himself with some amusement. "The train, it is as dangerous as a sea voyage!"

Miss Debenham said evenly that that would be very nice. Her manner was slightly repressive.

The Colonel, Hercule Poirot noticed, accompanied her back to her compartment. Later they passed through the magnificent scenery of the Taurus. As they looked down towards the Cilician Gates, standing in the corridor side by side, a sigh came suddenly from the girl. Poirot was standing near them and heard her murmur:

"It's so beautiful! I wish—I wish—"

"Yes?"

"I wish I could enjoy it!"

Arbuthnot did not answer. The square line of his jaw seemed a little sterner and grimmer.

"I wish to Heaven you were out of all this," he said.

"Hush, please. Hush."

"Oh! it's all right." He shot a slightly annoyed glance in Poirot's direction. Then he went on: "But I don't like the idea of your being a governess—at the beck and call of tyrannical mothers and their tiresome brats."

She laughed with just a hint of uncontrol in the sound.

"Oh! you mustn't think that. The downtrodden governess is quite an exploded myth. I can assure you that it's the parents who are afraid of being bullied by *me*."

They said no more. Arbuthnot was, perhaps, ashamed of his outburst.

"Rather an odd little comedy that I watch here," said Poirot to himself thoughtfully.

He was to remember that thought of his later.

They arrived at Konya that night about half-past eleven. The two English travellers got out to stretch their legs, pacing up and down the snowy platform.

M. Poirot was content to watch the teeming activity of the station through a window pane. After about ten minutes, however, he decided that a breath of air would not perhaps be a bad thing after all. He made careful preparations, wrapping himself in several coats and mufflers and encasing his neat boots in goloshes. Thus attired, he descended gingerly to the platform and began to pace its length. He walked out beyond the engine.

It was the voices which gave him the clue to the two indistinct figures standing in the shadow of a traffic van. Arbuthnot was speaking.

"Mary—"

The girl interrupted him.

"Not now. Not now. When it's all over. When it's behind us—*then*—"

Discreetly M. Poirot turned away. He wondered. . . .

He would hardly have recognised the cool, efficient voice of Miss Debenham. . . .

"Curious," he said to himself.

The next day he wondered whether, perhaps, they had quarrelled. They spoke little to each other. The girl, he thought, looked anxious. There were dark circles under her eyes.

It was about half-past two in the afternoon when the train came to a halt. Heads were poked out of windows. A little knot of men was clustered by the side of the line looking and pointing at something under the dining-car.

Poirot leaned out and spoke to the Wagon Lit conductor who was hurrying past. The man answered, and Poirot drew back his head and, turning, almost collided with Mary Debenham who was standing just behind him.

"What is the matter?" she asked rather breathlessly in French. "Why are we stopping?"

"It is nothing, Mademoiselle. It is something that has caught fire under the dining-car. Nothing serious. It is put out. They are now repairing the damage. There is no danger, I assure you."

She made a little abrupt gesture, as though she were waving the idea of danger aside as something completely unimportant.

"Yes, yes, I understand that. But the *time!*"

"The time?"

"Yes, this will delay us."

"It is possible—yes," agreed Poirot.

"But we can't afford delay! This train is due in at 6.55, and one has to cross the Bosphorus and catch the Simplon Orient Express on the other side at nine o'clock. If there is an hour or two of delay we shall miss the connection."

"It is possible, yes," he admitted.

He looked at her curiously. The hand that held the window bar was not quite steady; her lips, too, were trembling.

"Does it matter to you very much, Mademoiselle?" he asked.

"Yes. Yes, it does. I—I *must* catch that train."

She turned away from him and went down the corridor to join Colonel Arbuthnot.

Her anxiety, however, was needless. Ten minutes later the train started again. It arrived at Haydapassar only five minutes late, having made up time on the journey.

The Bosphorus was rough and M. Poirot did not enjoy the crossing. He was separated from his travelling companions on the boat and did not see them again.

On arrival at the Galata Bridge he drove straight to the Tokatlian Hotel.

Chapter 2

The Tokatlian Hotel

At the Tokatlian, Hercule Poirot asked for a room with bath. Then he stepped over to the concierge's desk and inquired for letters.

There were three waiting for him and a telegram. His eyebrows rose a little at the sight of the telegram. It was unexpected.

He opened it in his usual neat, unhurried fashion. The printed words stood out clearly.

> *Development you predicted in Kassner case has come unexpectedly. Please return immediately.*

"*Voilà ce qui est embêtant,*" muttered Poirot vexedly. He glanced up at the clock. "I shall have to go on to-night," he said to the concierge. "At what time does the Simplon Orient leave?"

"At nine o'clock, Monsieur."

"Can you get me a sleeper?"

"Assuredly, Monsieur. There is no difficulty this time of year. The trains are almost empty. First-class or second?"

"First."

"*Très bien, Monsieur.* How far are you going?"

"To London."

"*Bien, Monsieur.* I will get you a ticket to London and reserve your sleeping-car accommodation in the Stamboul-Calais coach."

Poirot glanced at the clock again. It was ten minutes to eight. "I have time to dine?"

"But assuredly, Monsieur."

The little Belgian nodded. He went over and cancelled his room order and crossed the hall to the restaurant.

As he was giving his order to the waiter, a hand was placed on his shoulder.

"Ah, *mon vieux*, but this is an unexpected pleasure!" said a voice behind him.

The speaker was a short, stout, elderly man, his hair cut *en brosse*. He was smiling delightedly.

Poirot sprang up.

"M. Bouc!"

"M. Poirot!"

M. Bouc was a Belgian, a director of the Compagnie Internationale des Wagons Lits, and his acquaintance with the former star of the Belgian police force dated back many years.

"You find yourself far from home, *mon cher*," said M. Bouc.

"A little affair in Syria."

"Ah! and you return home—when?"

"To-night."

"Splendid! I, too. That is to say, I go as far as Lausanne, where I have affairs. You travel on the Simplon Orient, I presume?"

"Yes. I have just asked them to get me a sleeper. It was my intention to remain here some days, but I have received a telegram recalling me to England on important business."

"Ah!" sighed M. Bouc. "*Les affaires—les affaires*! But you, you are at the top of the tree nowadays, *mon vieux*!"

"Some little success I have had, perhaps." Hercule Poirot tried to look modest but failed signally.

M. Bouc laughed.

"We will meet later," he said.

Hercule Poirot addressed himself to the task of keeping his moustaches out of the soup.

That difficult task accomplished, he glanced round him whilst waiting for the next course. There were only about half a dozen people in the restaurant, and of those half dozen there were only two that interested Hercule Poirot.

These two sat at a table not far away. The younger was a likeable-looking young man of thirty, clearly an American. It was, however, not he but his companion who had attracted the little detective's attention.

He was a man perhaps of between sixty and seventy. From a little distance he had the bland aspect of a philanthropist. His slightly bald head, his domed forehead, the smiling mouth that displayed a very white set of false teeth—all seemed to speak of a benevolent personality. Only the eyes belied this assumption. They were small, deep-set and crafty. Not only that. As the man, making some remark to his young companion, glanced across the room, his gaze stopped on Poirot for a moment and just for that second there was a strange malevolence, an unnatural tensity in the glance.

Then he rose.

"Pay the bill, Hector," he said.

His voice was slightly husky in tone. It had a queer, soft, dangerous quality.

When Poirot rejoined his friend in the lounge, the other two men were just leaving the hotel. Their luggage was being brought down. The younger was supervising the process. Presently he opened the glass door and said:

"Quite ready now, Mr. Ratchett."

The elder man grunted an assent and passed out.

"*Eh bien*," said Poirot. "What do you think of those two?"

"They are Americans," said M. Bouc.

"Assuredly they are Americans. I meant what did you think of their personalities?"

"The young man seemed quite agreeable."

"And the other?"

"To tell you the truth, my friend, I did not care for him. He produced on me an unpleasant impression. And you?"

Hercule Poirot was a moment in replying.

"When he passed me in the restaurant," he said at last, "I had a curious impression. It was as though a wild animal—an animal savage, but savage! you understand—had passed me by."

"And yet he looked altogether of the most respectable."

"*Précisément!* The body—the cage—is everything of the most respectable—but through the bars, the wild animal looks out."

"You are fanciful, *mon vieux*," said M. Bouc.

"It may be so. But I could not rid myself of the impression that evil had passed me by very close."

"That respectable American gentleman?"

"That respectable American gentleman."

"Well," said M. Bouc cheerfully, "it may be so. There is much evil in the world."

At that moment the door opened and the concierge came towards them. He looked concerned and apologetic.

"It is extraordinary, Monsieur," he said to Poirot. "There is not one first-class sleeping berth to be had on the train."

"*Comment?*" cried M. Bouc. "At this time of year? Ah, without doubt there is some party of journalists—of politicians—?"

"I don't know, sir," said the concierge, turning to him respectfully. "But that's how it is."

"Well, well." M. Bouc turned to Poirot. "Have no fear, my friend. We will arrange something. There is always one compartment, the No. 16, which is not engaged. The conductor sees to that!" He smiled, then glanced up at the clock. "Come," he said, "it is time we started."

At the station M. Bouc was greeted with respectful empressement by the brown-uniformed Wagon Lit conductor.

"Good evening, Monsieur. Your compartment is the No. 1."

He called to the porters and they wheeled their load halfway along the carriage on which the tin plates proclaimed its destination:

ISTANBUL TRIESTE CALAIS

"You are full up to-night, I hear?"

"It is incredible, Monsieur. All the world elects to travel to-night!"

"All the same you must find room for this gentleman here. He is a friend of mine. He can have the No. 16."

"It is taken, Monsieur."

"What? The No. 16?"

A glance of understanding passed between them, and the conductor smiled. He was a tall sallow man of middle age.

"But yes, Monsieur. As I told you, we are full—full—everywhere."

"But what passes itself?" demanded M. Bouc angrily. "There is a conference somewhere? It is a party?"

"No, Monsieur. It is only chance. It just happens that many people have elected to travel to-night."

M. Bouc made a clicking sound of annoyance.

"At Belgrade," he said, "there will be the slip coach from Athens. There will also be the Bucharest-Paris coach. But we do not reach Belgrade until to-morrow evening. The problem is for to-night. There is no second-class berth free?"

"There is a second-class berth, Monsieur—"

"Well, then—"

"But it is a lady's berth. There is already a German woman in the compartment—a lady's maid."

"Là là, that is awkward," said M. Bouc.

"Do not distress yourself, my friend," said Poirot. "I must travel in an ordinary carriage."

"Not at all. Not at all." He turned once more to the conductor. "Everyone has arrived?"

"It is true," said the man, "that there is one passenger who has not yet arrived." He spoke slowly, with hesitation.

"But speak then!"

"No. 7 berth—a second-class. The gentleman has not yet come, and it is four minutes to nine."

"Who is it?"

"An Englishman," the conductor consulted his list. "A M. Harris."

"A name of good omen," said Poirot. "I read my Dickens. M. Harris, he will not arrive."

"Put Monsieur's luggage in No. 7," said M. Bouc. "If this M. Harris arrives we will tell him that he is too late—that berths cannot be retained so long—we will arrange the matter one way or another. What do I care for a M. Harris?"

"As Monsieur pleases," said the conductor. He spoke to Poirot's porter, directing him where to go. Then he stood aside from the steps to let Poirot enter the train.

"Tout à fait au bout, Monsieur," he called. "The end compartment but one."

Poirot passed along the corridor, a somewhat slow progress, since most of the people travelling were standing outside their carriages.

His polite "Pardons" were uttered with the regularity of clockwork. At last he reached the compartment indicated. Inside it, reaching up to a suitcase, was the tall young American of the Tokatlian.

He frowned as Poirot entered.

"Excuse me," he said. "I think you've made a mistake." Then, laboriously in French: *"Je crois que vous avez un erreur."*

Poirot replied in English. "You are Mr. Harris?"

"No, my name is MacQueen. I—"

But at that moment the voice of the Wagon Lit conductor spoke from over Poirot's shoulder—an apologetic, rather breathless voice.

"There is no other berth on the train, Monsieur. The gentleman has to come in here."

He was hauling up the corridor window as he spoke and began to lift in Poirot's luggage.

Poirot noticed the apology in his tone with some amusement. Doubtless the man had been promised a good tip if he could keep the compartment for the sole use of the other traveller. However, even the most munificent of tips lose their effect when a Director of the Company is on board and issues his orders.

The conductor emerged from the compartment, having swung the suitcases up onto the racks.

"*Voilà, Monsieur*," he said. "All is arranged. Yours is the upper berth, the No. 7. We start in one minute."

He hurried off down the corridor. Poirot reentered the compartment.

"A phenomenon I have seldom seen," he said cheerfully. "A Wagon Lit conductor himself puts up the luggage! It is unheard of!"

His fellow traveller smiled. He had evidently gotten over his annoyance—had probably decided that it was no good to take the matter otherwise than philosophically. "The train's remarkably full," he said.

A whistle blew, there was a long melancholy cry from the engine. Both men stepped out into the corridor.

Outside a voice shouted, *"En voiture!"*

"We're off," said MacQueen.

But they were not quite off. The whistle blew again.

"I say, sir," said the young man suddenly. "If you'd rather have the lower berth—easier and all that—well, that's all right by me."

A likeable young fellow.

"No, no," protested Poirot. "I would not deprive you—"

"That's all right—"

"You are too amiable—"

Polite protests on both sides.

"It is for one night only," explained Poirot. "At Belgrade—"

"Oh! I see. You're getting out at Belgrade—"

"Not exactly. You see—"

There was a sudden jerk. Both men swung round to the window, looking out at the long, lighted platform as it slid slowly past them.

The Orient Express had started on its three-day journey across Europe.

Chapter 3

Poirot Refuses a Case

M. Hercule Poirot was a little late in entering the luncheon-car on the following day. He had risen early, had breakfasted almost alone, and had spent the morning going over the notes of the case that was recalling him to London. He had seen little of his travelling companion.

M. Bouc, who was already seated, gesticulated a greeting and summoned his friend to the empty place opposite him. Poirot sat down and soon found himself in the favoured position of being at the table which was served first and with the choicest morsels. The food, too, was unusually good.

It was not till they were eating a delicate cream cheese that M. Bouc allowed his attention to wander to matters other than nourishment. He was at the stage of a meal when one becomes philosophic.

"Ah!" he sighed. "If I had but the pen of a Balzac! I would depict this scene." He waved a hand.

"It is an idea, that," said Poirot.

"Ah, you agree? It has not been done, I think? And yet—it lends itself to romance, my friend. All around us are people, of all classes, of all nationalities, of all ages. For three days these people, these strangers to one another, are brought together. They sleep and eat under one roof, they cannot get away from each other. At the end of three days they part, they go their several ways, never perhaps to see each other again."

"And yet," said Poirot, "suppose an accident—"

"Ah, no, my friend—"

"From your point of view it would be regrettable, I agree. But nevertheless let us just for one moment suppose it. Then, perhaps, all these here are linked together—by death."

"Some more wine," said M. Bouc, hastily pouring it out. "You are morbid, *mon cher*. It is, perhaps the digestion."

"It is true," agreed Poirot, "that the food in Syria was not perhaps quite suited to my stomach."

He sipped his wine. Then, leaning back, he ran his eye thoughtfully round the dining-car. There were thirteen people seated there and, as M. Bouc had said, of all classes and nationalities. He began to study them.

At the table opposite them were three men. They were, he guessed, single travellers graded and placed there by the unerring judgment of the restaurant attendants. A big swarthy Italian was picking his teeth with gusto. Opposite him a spare neat Englishman had the expressionless disapproving face of the well-trained servant. Next to the Englishman was a big American in a loud suit—possibly a commercial traveller.

"You've got to put it over *big*," he was saying in a loud, nasal voice.

The Italian removed his toothpick to gesticulate with it freely.

"Sure," he said. "That whatta I say alla de time."

The Englishman looked out of the window and coughed.

Poirot's eye passed on.

At a small table, sitting very upright, was one of the ugliest old ladies he had ever seen. It was an ugliness of distinction—it fascinated rather than repelled. She sat very upright. Round her neck was a collar of very large pearls which, improbable though it seemed, were real. Her hands were covered with rings. Her sable coat was pushed back on her shoulders. A very small and expensive black toque was hideously unbecoming to the yellow, toad-like face beneath it.

She was speaking now to the restaurant attendant in a clear, courteous, but completely autocratic tone.

"You will be sufficiently amiable to place in my compartment a bottle of mineral water and a large glass of orange juice. You will arrange that I shall have chicken cooked without sauces for dinner this evening—also some boiled fish."

The attendant replied respectfully that it should be done.

She gave a slight gracious nod of the head and rose. Her glance caught Poirot's and swept over him with the nonchalance of the uninterested aristocrat.

"That is Princess Dragomiroff," said M. Bouc in a low tone. "She is a Russian. Her husband realised all his money before the Revolution and invested it abroad. She is extremely rich. A cosmopolitan."

Poirot nodded. He had heard of Princess Dragomiroff.

"She is a personality," said M. Bouc. "Ugly as sin but she makes herself felt. You agree?"

Poirot agreed.

At another of the large tables Mary Debenham was sitting with two other women. One of them was tall and middle-aged, in a plaid blouse and tweed skirt. She had a mass of faded yellow hair unbecomingly arranged in a large bun, wore glasses, and had a long mild amiable face rather like a sheep. She was listening to the third woman, a stout, pleasant-faced, elderly person who was talking in a slow clear monotone which showed no signs of pausing for breath or coming to a stop.

"—and so my daughter said, 'Why,' she said, 'you just can't apply American methods in this country. It's natural to the folks here to be indolent,' she said. 'They just haven't got any hustle in them—' But all the same you'd be surprised to know what our college there is doing. They've got a fine staff of teachers. I guess there's nothing like education. We've got to apply our Western ideals and teach the East to recognise them. My daughter says—"

The train plunged into a tunnel. The calm, monotonous voice was drowned.

At the next table, a small one, sat Colonel Arbuthnot—alone. His gaze was fixed upon the back of Mary Debenham's head. They were not sitting together. Yet it could easily have been managed. Why?

Perhaps, Poirot thought, Mary Debenham had demurred. A governess learns to be careful. Appearances are important. A girl with her living to get has to be discreet.

His glance shifted to the other side of the carriage. At the far end, against the wall, was a middle-aged woman dressed in black with a broad, expressionless face. German or Scandinavian, he thought. Probably the German lady's-maid.

Beyond her were a couple leaning forward and talking animatedly together. The man wore English clothes of loose tweed, but he was not English. Though only the back of his head was visible to Poirot, the shape of it and the set of the shoulders betrayed him. A big man, well made. He turned his head suddenly and Poirot saw his profile. A very handsome man of thirty-odd with a big fair moustache.

The woman opposite him was a mere girl—twenty at a guess. A tight-fitting little black coat and skirt, white satin blouse, small chic black toque perched at the fashionable outrageous angle. She had a beautiful foreign-looking face, dead white skin, large brown eyes, jet black hair. She was smoking a cigarette in a long holder. Her manicured hands had deep red nails. She wore one large emerald set in platinum. There was coquetry in her glance and voice.

"Elle est jolie—et chic," murmured Poirot. "Husband and wife—eh?" M. Bouc nodded. "Hungarian Embassy, I believe," he said. "A handsome couple."

There were only two more lunchers—Poirot's fellow traveller MacQueen and his employer, Mr. Ratchett. The latter sat facing Poirot, and for the second time Poirot studied that unprepossessing face, noting the false benevolence of the brow and the small, cruel eyes.

Doubtless M. Bouc saw a change in his friend's expression.

"It is at your wild animal you look?" he asked.

Poirot nodded.

As his coffee was brought to him, M. Bouc rose to his feet. Having started before Poirot he had finished some time ago.

"I return to my compartment," he said. "Come along presently and converse with me."

"With pleasure."

Poirot sipped his coffee and ordered a liqueur. The attendant was passing from table to table with his box of money, accepting payment for bills. The elderly American lady's voice rose shrill and plaintive.

"My daughter said: 'Take a book of food tickets and you'll have no trouble—no trouble at all.' Now, that isn't so. Seems they have to have a ten per cent tip, and then there's that bottle of mineral water—and a queer sort of water too. They didn't have any Evian or Vichy, which seems queer to me."

"It is—they must—how do you say?—serve the water of the country," explained the sheep-faced lady.

"Well, it seems queer to me." She looked distastefully at the heap of small change on the table in front of her. "Look at all this peculiar stuff he's given me. Dinars or something. Just a lot of rubbish, it looks like! My daughter said—"

Mary Debenham pushed back her chair and left with a slight bow to the other two. Colonel Arbuthnot got up and followed her. Gathering up her despised money the American woman followed suit, followed by the other one like a sheep. The Hungarians had already departed. The restaurant car was empty save for Poirot and Ratchett and MacQueen.

Ratchett spoke to his companion, who got up and left the car. Then he rose himself, but instead of following MacQueen he dropped unexpectedly into the seat opposite Poirot.

"Can you oblige me with a light?" he said. His voice was soft—faintly nasal. "My name is Ratchett."

Poirot bowed slightly. He slipped his hand into his pocket and produced a matchbox which he handed to the other man, who took it but did not strike a light.

"I think," he went on, "that I have the pleasure of speaking to Mr. Hercule Poirot. Is that so?"

Poirot bowed again. "You have been correctly informed, Monsieur."

The detective was conscious of those strange shrewd eyes summing him up before the other spoke again.

"In my country," he said, "we come to the point quickly. Mr. Poirot, I want you to take on a job for me."

Hercule Poirot's eyebrows went up a trifle.

"My *clientèle*, Monsieur, is limited nowadays. I undertake very few cases."

"Why, naturally, I understand that. But this, Mr. Poirot, means big money." He repeated again in his soft, persuasive voice, "Big money."

Hercule Poirot was silent a minute or two. Then he said: "What is it you wish me to do for you, Monsieur—er—Ratchett?"

"Mr. Poirot, I am a rich man—a very rich man. Men in that position have enemies. I have an enemy."

"Only one enemy?"

"Just what do you mean by that question?" asked Ratchett sharply.

"Monsieur, in my experience when a man is in a position to have, as you say, enemies, then it does not usually resolve itself into one enemy only."

Ratchett seemed relieved by Poirot's answer. He said quickly:

"Why, yes, I appreciate that point. Enemy or enemies—it doesn't matter. What does matter is my safety."

"Safety?"

"My life has been threatened, Mr. Poirot. Now I'm a man who can take pretty good care of himself." From the pocket of his coat his hand brought a small automatic into sight for a moment. He continued grimly. "I don't think I'm the kind of man to be caught napping. But, as I look at it, I might as well make assurance doubly sure. I fancy you're the man for my money, Mr. Poirot. And remember—*big* money."

Poirot looked at him thoughtfully for some minutes. His face was completely expressionless. The other could have had no clue as to what thoughts were passing in that mind.

"I regret, Monsieur," he said at length, "that I cannot oblige you."

The other looked at him shrewdly. "Name your figure, then," he said.

Poirot shook his head.

"You do not understand, Monsieur. I have been very fortunate in my profession. I have made enough money to satisfy both my needs and my caprices. I take now only such cases as—interest me."

"You've got a pretty good nerve," said Ratchett. "Will twenty thousand dollars tempt you?"

"It will not."

"If you're holding out for more, you won't get it. I know what a thing's worth to me."

"I, also, M. Ratchett."

"What's wrong with my proposition?"

Poirot rose. "If you will forgive me for being personal—I do not like your face, M. Ratchett," he said.

And with that he left the restaurant car.

Chapter 4

A Cry in the Night

The Simplon Orient Express arrived at Belgrade at a quarter to nine that evening. It was not due to depart again until 9.15, so Poirot descended to the platform. He did not, however, remain there long. The cold was bitter, and though the platform itself was protected, heavy snow was falling outside. He returned to his compartment. The conductor, who was on the platform stamping his feet and waving his arms to keep warm, spoke to him.

"Your valises have been moved, Monsieur. To the compartment No. 1, the compartment of M. Bouc."

"But where is Monsieur Bouc, then?"

"He has moved into the coach from Athens which has just been put on."

Poirot went in search of his friend. M. Bouc waved his protestations aside.

"It is nothing. It is nothing. It is more convenient like this. You are going through to England, so it is better that you should stay in the through coach to Calais. Me, I am very well here. It is most peaceful. This coach is empty save for myself and one little Greek doctor. Ah! my friend, what a night! They say there has not been so much snow for years. Let us hope we shall not be held up. I am not too happy about it, I can tell you."

At 9.15 punctually the train pulled out of the station, and shortly afterwards Poirot got up, said good night to his friend, and made his way along the corridor back into his own coach which was in front next to the dining-car.

On this, the second day of the journey, barriers were breaking down.

Colonel Arbuthnot was standing at the door of his compartment talking
to MacQueen. When MacQueen saw Poirot he broke off something he
was saying. He looked very much surprised.

"Why," he cried, "I thought you'd left us. You said you were getting
off at Belgrade."

"You misunderstood me," said Poirot, smiling. "I remember now, the
train started from Stamboul just as we were talking about it."

"But, man, your baggage. It's gone."

"It has been moved into another compartment, that is all."

"Oh! I see."

He resumed his conversation with Arbuthnot, and Poirot passed on
down the corridor.

Two doors from his own compartment, the elderly American, Mrs.
Hubbard, was standing talking to the sheep-like lady, who was a Swede.
Mrs. Hubbard was pressing a magazine on the other.

"No, do take it, my dear," she said. "I've got plenty of other things to
read. My, isn't the cold something frightful?" She nodded amicably to
Poirot.

"You are most kind," said the Swedish lady.

"Not at all. I hope you'll sleep well and that your head will be better in
the morning."

"It is the cold only. I make now myself a cup of tea."

"Have you got some aspirin? Are you sure now? I've got plenty. Well,
good night, my dear."

She turned to Poirot conversationally as the other woman departed.

"Poor creature, she's a Swede. As far as I can make out she's a kind of
missionary. A teaching one. A nice creature, but doesn't talk much English. She was *most* interested in what I told her about my daughter."

Poirot, by now, knew all about Mrs. Hubbard's daughter. Everyone on
the train who could understand English did! How she and her husband
were on the staff of a big American college in Smyrna, and how this was
Mrs. Hubbard's first journey to the East, and what she thought of the
Turks and their slipshod ways and the condition of their roads.

The door next to them opened and the thin pale manservant stepped
out. Inside, Poirot caught a glimpse of Mr. Ratchett sitting up in bed. He
saw Poirot and his face changed, darkening with anger. Then the door
was shut.

Mrs. Hubbard drew Poirot a little aside.

"You know, I'm dead scared of that man. Oh! not the valet—the other.
His master. Master, indeed! There's something *wrong* about that man.
My daughter always says I'm very intuitive. 'When Mamma gets a
hunch, she's dead right,' that's what my daughter says. And I've got a

hunch about that man. He's next door to me and I don't like it. I put my grips against the communicating door last night. I thought I heard him trying the handle. Do you know, I shouldn't be a bit surprised if that man turned out to be a murderer—one of these train robbers you read about. I daresay I'm foolish, but there it is. I'm absolutely scared to death of the man! My daughter said I'd have an easy journey, but somehow I don't feel happy about it. It may be foolish, but I feel as if anything might happen—anything at all. And how that nice young fellow can bear to be his secretary, I can't think."

Colonel Arbuthnot and MacQueen were coming towards them down the corridor.

"Come into my carriage," MacQueen was saying. "It isn't made up for the night yet. Now what I want to get right about your policy in India is this—"

The two men passed and went on down the corridor to MacQueen's carriage.

Mrs. Hubbard said good night to Poirot. "I guess I'll go right to bed and read," she said. "Good night."

"Good night, Madame."

Poirot passed into his own compartment, which was the next one beyond Ratchett's. He undressed and got into bed, read for about half an hour and then turned out the light.

He awoke some hours later, awoke with a start. He knew what it was that had wakened him—a loud groan, almost a cry, somewhere close at hand. At the same moment the ting of a bell sounded sharply.

Poirot sat up and switched on the light. He noticed that the train was at a standstill—presumably at a station.

That cry had startled him. He remembered that it was Ratchett who had the next compartment. He got out of bed and opened the door just as the Wagon Lit conductor came hurrying along the corridor and knocked on Ratchett's door. Poirot kept his door open a crack and watched. The conductor tapped a second time. A bell rang and a light showed over another door farther down. The conductor glanced over his shoulder. At the same moment a voice from within the next compartment called out: *"Ce n'est rien. Je me suis trompé."*

"Bien, Monsieur." The conductor scurried off again, to knock at the door where the light was showing.

Poirot returned to bed, his mind relieved, and switched off the light. He glanced at his watch. It was just twenty-three minutes to one.

Chapter 5

The Crime

He found it difficult to go to sleep again at once. For one thing he missed the motion of the train. If it *was* a station outside, it was curiously quiet. By contrast the noises on the train seemed unusually loud. He could hear Ratchett moving about next door—a click as he pulled down the wash-basin, the sound of the tap running, a splashing noise, then another click as the basin shut to again. Footsteps passed up the corridor outside, the shuffling footsteps of someone in bedroom slippers.

Hercule Poirot lay awake staring at the ceiling. Why was the station outside so silent? His throat felt dry. He had forgotten to ask for his usual bottle of mineral water. He looked at his watch again. Just after a quarter past one. He would ring for the conductor and ask for some mineral water. His finger went out to the bell, but he paused as in the stillness he heard a ting. The man couldn't answer every bell at once.

Ting. . . . Ting. . . . Ting. . . .

It sounded again and again. Where was the man? Somebody was getting impatient.

Ti-i-i-ing!

Whoever it was, was keeping a finger solidly on the push-button.

Suddenly with a rush, his footsteps echoing up the aisle, the man came. He knocked at a door not far from Poirot's own.

Then came voices—the conductor's, deferential, apologetic; and a woman's, insistent and voluble.

Mrs. Hubbard!

Poirot smiled to himself.

The altercation—if it was one—went on for some time. Its proportions were ninety per cent of Mrs. Hubbard's to a soothing ten per cent of the conductor's. Finally the matter seemed to be adjusted. Poirot heard distinctly a *"Bonne nuit, Madame,"* and a closing door.

He pressed his own finger on the bell.

The conductor arrived promptly. He looked hot and worried.

"De l'eau minérale, s'il vous plaît."

"Bien, Monsieur." Perhaps a twinkle in Poirot's eye led him to unburden himself. *"La dame américaine—"*

"Yes?"

He wiped his forehead. "Imagine to yourself the time I have had with her! She insists—but *insists*—that there is a man in her compartment! Figure to yourself, Monsieur. In a space of this size." He swept a hand round. "Where would he conceal himself? I argue with her. I point out that it is impossible. She insists. She woke up, and there was a man there. And how, I ask, did he get out and leave the door bolted behind him? But she will not listen to reason. As though there were not enough to worry us already. This snow—"

"Snow?"

"But yes, Monsieur. Monsieur has not noticed? The train has stopped. We have run into a snowdrift. Heaven knows how long we shall be here. I remember once being snowed up for seven days."

"Where are we?"

"Between Vincovci and Brod."

"Là-là," said Poirot vexedly.

The man withdrew and returned with the water.

"Bon soir, Monsieur."

Poirot drank a glass of water and composed himself to sleep.

He was just dropping off when something again woke him. This time it was as though something heavy had fallen with a thud against the door.

He sprang up, opened it and looked out. Nothing. But to his right, some distance down the corridor, a woman wrapped in a scarlet kimono was retreating from him. At the other end, sitting on his little seat, the conductor was entering up figures on large sheets of paper. Everything was deathly quiet.

"Decidedly I suffer from the nerves," said Poirot and retired to bed again. This time he slept till morning.

When he awoke the train was still at a standstill. He raised a blind and looked out. Heavy banks of snow surrounded the train.

He glanced at his watch and saw that it was past nine o'clock.

At a quarter to ten, neat, spruce and dandified as ever, he made his way to the restaurant car, where a chorus of woe was going on.

Any barriers there might have been between the passengers had now quite broken down. All were united by a common misfortune. Mrs. Hubbard was loudest in her lamentations.

"My daughter said it would be the easiest way in the world. Just sit in the train until I got to Parrus. And now we may be here for days and days," she wailed. "And my boat sails day after to-morrow. How am I going to catch it now? Why, I can't even wire to cancel my passage. I'm just too mad to talk about it!"

The Italian said that he had urgent business himself in Milan. The large American said that that was "too bad, Ma'am," and soothingly expressed a hope that the train might make up time.

"My sister—her children wait me," said the Swedish lady, and wept. "I get no word to them. What they think? They will say bad things have happen to me."

"How long shall we be here?" demanded Mary Debenham. "Doesn't anybody *know*?"

Her voice sounded impatient, but Poirot noted that there were no signs of that almost feverish anxiety which she had displayed during the check to the Taurus Express.

Mrs. Hubbard was off again.

"There isn't anybody knows a thing on this train. And nobody's trying to *do* anything. Just a pack of useless foreigners. Why, if this were at home, there'd be someone at least *trying* to do something!"

Arbuthnot turned to Poirot and spoke in careful British French.

"Vous êtes un directeur de la ligne, je crois, Monsieur. Vous pouvez nous dire—"

Smiling, Poirot corrected him.

"No, no," he said in English. "It is not I. You confound me with my friend, M. Bouc."

"Oh! I'm sorry."

"Not at all. It is most natural. I am now in the compartment that he had formerly."

M. Bouc was not present in the restaurant car. Poirot looked about to notice who else was absent.

Princess Dragomiroff was missing, and the Hungarian couple. Also Ratchett, his valet, and the German lady's-maid.

The Swedish lady wiped her eyes.

"I am foolish," she said. "I am bad to cry. All is for the best, whatever happen."

This Christian spirit, however, was far from being shared.

"That's all very well," said MacQueen restlessly. "We may be here for days."

"What is this country anyway?" demanded Mrs. Hubbard tearfully.

On being told it was Jugo-Slavia, she said: "Oh! one of these Balkan things. What can you expect?"

"You are the only patient one, Mademoiselle," said Poirot to Miss Debenham.

She shrugged her shoulders slightly. "What can one do?"

"You are a philosopher, Mademoiselle."

"That implies a detached attitude. I think my attitude is more selfish. I have learned to save myself useless emotion."

She was speaking more to herself than to him. She was not even looking at him. Her gaze went past him, out of the window to where the snow lay in heavy masses.

"You are a strong character, Mademoiselle," said Poirot gently. "You are, I think, the strongest character amongst us."

"Oh! no. No, indeed. I know one far, far stronger than I am."

"And that is—?"

She seemed suddenly to come to herself, to realise that she was talking to a stranger and foreigner, with whom, until this morning, she had exchanged only half a dozen sentences.

She laughed, a polite but estranging laugh.

"Well—that old lady, for instance. You have probably noticed her. A very ugly old lady but rather fascinating. She has only to lift a little finger and ask for something in a polite voice—and the whole train runs."

"It runs also for my friend M. Bouc," said Poirot. "But that is because he is a director of the line, not because he has a strong character."

Mary Debenham smiled.

The morning wore away. Several people, Poirot amongst them, remained in the dining-car. The communal life was felt, at the moment, to pass the time better. He heard a good deal more about Mrs. Hubbard's daughter, and he heard the lifelong habits of Mr. Hubbard, deceased, from his rising in the morning and commencing breakfast with a cereal to his final rest at night in the bed-socks that Mrs. Hubbard herself had been in the habit of knitting for him.

It was when he was listening to a confused account of the missionary aims of the Swedish lady that one of the Wagon Lit conductors came into the car and stood at his elbow.

"Pardon, Monsieur."

"Yes?"

"The compliments of M. Bouc, and he would be glad if you would be so kind as to come to him for a few minutes."

Poirot rose, uttered excuses to the Swedish lady and followed the man out of the dining-car. It was not his own conductor, but a big fair man.

He followed his guide down the corridor of his own carriage and along the corridor of the next one. The man tapped at a door, then stood aside to let Poirot enter.

The compartment was not M. Bouc's own. It was a second-class one—chosen presumably because of its slightly larger size. It certainly gave the impression of being crowded.

M. Bouc himself was sitting on the small seat in the opposite corner. In the corner next to the window, facing him, was a small dark man looking out at the snow. Standing up and quite preventing Poirot from advancing any farther were a big man in blue inform (the *chef de train*) and his own Wagon Lit conductor.

"Ah! my good friend," cried M. Bouc. "Come in. We have need of you."

The little man in the window shifted along the seat, and Poirot squeezed past the other two men and sat down facing his friend.

The expression on M. Bouc's face gave him, as he would have expressed it, furiously to think. It was clear that something out of the common had happened.

"What has occurred?" he asked.

"You may well ask that. First this snow—this stoppage. And now—"

He paused—and a sort of strangled gasp came from the Wagon Lit conductor.

"And now what?"

"And now a passenger lies dead in his berth—stabbed."

M. Bouc spoke with a kind of calm desperation.

"A passenger? Which passenger?"

"An American. A man called—called—" he consulted some notes in front of him. "Ratchett. That is right—Ratchett?"

"Yes, Monsieur." The Wagon Lit man gulped.

Poirot looked at him. He was as white as chalk.

"You had better let that man sit down," he said. "He may faint otherwise."

The *chef de train* moved slightly and the Wagon Lit man sank down in the corner and buried his face in his hands.

"Brr!" said Poirot. "This is serious!"

"Certainly it is serious. To begin with, a murder—that in itself is a calamity of the first water. But not only that, the circumstances are unusual. Here we are, brought to a standstill. We may be here for hours—and not only hours—days! Another circumstance—passing through most countries we have the police of that country on the train. But in Jugo-Slavia, no. You comprehend?"

"It is a position of great difficulty," said Poirot.

"There is worse to come. Dr. Constantine—I forgot, I have not introduced you. Dr. Constantine, M. Poirot."

The little dark man bowed, and Poirot returned the bow.

"Dr. Constantine is of the opinion that death occurred at about 1 A.M."

"It is difficult to speak exactly in these matters," said the doctor, "but I think I can say definitely that death occurred between midnight and two in the morning."

"When was this M. Ratchett last seen alive?" asked Poirot.

"He is known to have been alive at about twenty minutes to one, when he spoke to the conductor," said M. Bouc.

"That is quite correct," said Poirot. "I myself heard what passed. That is the last thing known?"

"Yes."

Poirot turned toward the doctor, who continued.

"The window of M. Ratchett's compartment was found wide open, leading one to suppose that the murderer escaped that way. But in my opinion that open window is a blind. Anyone departing that way would have left distinct traces in the snow. There were none."

"The crime was discovered—when?" asked Poirot.

"Michel!"

The Wagon Lit conductor sat up. His face still looked pale and frightened.

"Tell this gentleman exactly what occurred," ordered M. Bouc.

The man spoke somewhat jerkily.

"The valet of this M. Ratchett, he tapped several times at the door this morning. There was no answer. Then, half an hour ago, the restaurant car attendant came. He wanted to know if Monsieur was taking *déjeuner*. It was eleven o'clock, you comprehend.

"I open the door for him with my key. But there is a chain, too, and that is fastened. There is no answer and it is very still in there, and cold—but cold. With the window open and snow drifting in. I thought the gentleman had had a fit, perhaps. I got the *chef de train*. We broke the chain and went in. He was—Ah! *c'était terrible!*"

He buried his face in his hands again.

"The door was locked and chained on the inside," said Poirot thoughtfully. "It was not suicide—eh?"

The Greek doctor gave a sardonic laugh. "Does a man who commits suicide stab himself in ten—twelve—fifteen places?" he asked.

Poirot's eyes opened. "That is great ferocity," he said.

"It is a woman," said the *chef de train*, speaking for the first time. "Depend upon it, it was a woman. Only a woman would stab like that."

Dr. Constantine screwed up his face thoughtfully.

"She must have been a very strong woman," he said. "It is not my desire to speak technically—that is only confusing; but I can assure you that one or two of the blows were delivered with such force as to drive them through hard belts of bone and muscle."

"It was clearly not a scientific crime," said Poirot.

"It was most unscientific," returned Dr. Constantine. "The blows seem to have been delivered haphazard and at random. Some have glanced off, doing hardly any damage. It is as though somebody had shut his eyes and then in a frenzy struck blindly again and again."

"*C'est une femme,*" said the *chef de train* again. "Women are like that. When they are enraged they have great strength." He nodded so sagely that everyone suspected a personal experience of his own.

"I have, perhaps, something to contribute to your store of knowledge," said Poirot. "M. Ratchett spoke to me yesterday. He told me, as far as I was able to understand him, that he was in danger of his life."

" 'Bumped off'—that is the American expression, is it not?" asked M. Bouc. "Then it is not a woman. It is a 'gangster' or a 'gunman.' "

The *chef de train* looked pained at seeing his theory come to nought.

"If so," said Poirot, "it seems to have been done very amateurishly." His tone expressed professional disapproval.

"There is a large American on the train," said M. Bouc, pursuing his idea. "A common-looking man with terrible clothes. He chews the gum, which I believe is not done in good circles. You know whom I mean?"

The Wagon Lit conductor to whom he had appealed nodded.

"*Oui, Monsieur,* the No. 16. But it cannot have been he. I should have seen him enter or leave the compartment."

"You might not. You might not. But we will go into that presently. The question is, what to do?" He looked at Poirot.

Poirot looked back at him.

"Come, my friend," said M. Bouc. "You comprehend what I am about to ask of you. I know your powers. Take command of this investigation! No, no, do not refuse. See, to us it is serious—I speak for the Compagnie Internationale des Wagons Lits. By the time the Jugo-Slavian police arrive, how simple if we can present them with the solution! Otherwise delays, annoyances, a million and one inconveniences. Perhaps, who knows, serious annoyance to innocent persons. Instead—*you* solve the mystery! We say, 'A murder has occurred—*this* is the criminal!' "

"And suppose I do not solve it?"

"Ah, *mon cher!*" M. Bouc's voice became positively caressing. "I know your reputation. I know something of your methods. This is the ideal case for you. To look up the antecedents of all these people, to discover their *bona fides*—all that takes time and endless inconvenience. But have I not heard you say often that to solve a case a man has only to lie back in his chair and think? Do that. Interview the passengers on the train, view the body, examine what clues there are, and then—well, I have faith in you! I am assured that it is no idle boast of yours. Lie back and think—use (as I have heard you say so often) the little grey cells of the mind—and you will *know*!"

He leaned forward, looking affectionately at the detective.

"Your faith touches me, my friend," said Poirot emotionally. "As you say, this cannot be a difficult case. I myself last night—but we will not speak of that now. In truth, this problem intrigues me. I was reflecting, not half an hour ago, that many hours of boredom lay ahead whilst we are stuck here. And now—a problem lies ready to my hand."

"You accept then?" said M. Bouc eagerly.

"*C'est entendu.* You place the matter in my hands."

"Good—we are all at your service."

"To begin with, I should like a plan of the Istanbul-Calais coach, with a note of the people who occupied the several compartments, and I should also like to see their passports and their tickets."

"Michel will get you those."

The Wagon Lit conductor left the compartment.

"What other passengers are there on the train?" asked Poirot.

"In this coach Dr. Constantine and I are the only travellers. In the coach from Bucharest is an old gentleman with a lame leg. He is well known to the conductor. Beyond that are the ordinary carriages, but these do not concern us, since they were locked after dinner had been served last night. Forward of the Istanbul-Calais coach there is only the dining-car."

"Then it seems," said Poirot slowly, "as though we must look for our murderer in the Istanbul-Calais coach." He turned to the doctor. "That is what you were hinting, I think?"

The Greek nodded. "At half an hour after midnight we ran into the snowdrift. No one can have left the train since then."

M. Bouc said solemnly, *"The murderer is with us—on the train now. . . ."*

Chapter 6

A Woman

"First of all," said Poirot, "I should like a word or two with young Mr. MacQueen. He may be able to give us valuable information."

"Certainly," said M. Bouc. He turned to the *chef de train*. "Get Mr. MacQueen to come here."

The *chef de train* left the carriage.

The conductor returned with a bundle of passports and tickets. M. Bouc took them from him.

"Thank you, Michel. It would be best now, I think, if you were to go back to your post. We will take your evidence formally later."

"Very good, Monsieur," said Michel, and in his turn left the carriage.

"After we have seen young MacQueen," said Poirot, "perhaps M. *le docteur* will come with me to the dead man's carriage."

"Certainly."

"After we have finished there—"

But at this moment the *chef de train* returned with Hector MacQueen.

M. Bouc rose. "We are a little cramped here," he said pleasantly. "Take my seat, Mr. MacQueen. M. Poirot will sit opposite you—so."

He turned to the *chef de train*. "Clear all the people out of the restaurant car," he said, "and let it be left free for M. Poirot. You will conduct your interviews there, *mon cher*?"

"It would be the most convenient, yes," agreed Poirot.

MacQueen had stood looking from the one to the other, not quite following the rapid flow of French.

"*Qu'est-ce qu'il y a?*" he began laboriously. "*Pourquoi—?*"

With a vigorous gesture Poirot motioned him to the seat in the corner. He took it and began once more.

"*Pourquoi—?*" Then checking himself and relapsing into his own tongue: "What's up on the train? Has anything happened?"

He looked from one man to another.

Poirot nodded. "Exactly. Something has happened. Prepare yourself for a shock. *Your employer, M. Ratchett, is dead!*"

MacQueen's mouth pursed itself into a whistle. Except that his eyes grew a shade brighter, he showed no signs of shock or distress.

"So they got him after all," he said.

"What exactly do you mean by that phrase, Mr. MacQueen?"

MacQueen hesitated.

"You are assuming," said Poirot, "that M. Ratchett was murdered?"

"Wasn't he?" This time MacQueen did show surprise. "Why, yes," he said slowly. "That's just what I did think. Do you mean he just died in his sleep? Why, the old man was as tough as—as tough—"

He stopped, at a loss for a simile.

"No, no," said Poirot. "Your assumption was quite right. M. Ratchett was murdered. Stabbed. But I should like to know why you were so sure it *was* murder, and not just—death."

MacQueen hesitated. "I must get this clear," he said. "Who exactly are you? And where do you come in?"

"I represent the Compagnie Internationale des Wagons Lits." Poirot paused, then added, "I am a detective. My name is Hercule Poirot."

If he expected an effect he did not get one. MacQueen said merely, "Oh! yes?" and waited for him to go on.

"You know the name, perhaps?"

"Why, it does seem kind of familiar. Only I always thought it was a woman's dressmaker."

Hercule Poirot looked at him with distaste. "It is incredible!" he said.

"What's incredible?"

"Nothing. Let us advance with the matter in hand. I want you to tell me, M. MacQueen, all that you know about the dead man. You were not related to him?"

"No. I am—was—his secretary."

"For how long have you held that post?"

"Just over a year."

"Please give me all the information you can."

"Well, I met Mr. Ratchett just over a year ago when I was in Persia—"

Poirot interrupted.

"What were you doing there?"

"I had come over from New York to look into an oil concession. I don't suppose you want to hear all about that. My friends and I had been let in rather badly over it. Mr. Ratchett was in the same hotel. He had just had a row with his secretary. He offered me the job and I took it. I was at a loose end and glad to find a well-paid job ready made, as it were."

"And since then?"

"We've travelled about. Mr. Ratchett wanted to see the world. He was hampered by knowing no languages. I acted more as a courier than as a secretary. It was a pleasant life."

"Now tell me as much as you can about your employer."

The young man shrugged his shoulders. A perplexed expression passed over his face.

"That's not so easy."

"What was his full name?"

"Samuel Edward Ratchett."

"He was an American citizen?"

"Yes."

"What part of America did he come from?"

"I don't know."

"Well, tell me what you do know."

"The actual truth is, Mr. Poirot, that I know nothing at all! Mr. Ratchett never spoke of himself or of his life in America."

"Why do you think that was?"

"I don't know. I imagined that he might be ashamed of his beginnings. Some men are."

"Does that strike you as a satisfactory solution?"

"Frankly, it doesn't."

"Has he any relatives?"

"He never mentioned any."

Poirot pressed the point.

"You must have formed *some* theory, Mr. MacQueen."

"Well, yes, I did. For one thing, I don't believe Ratchett was his real name. I think he left America definitely in order to escape someone or something. I think he was successful—until a few weeks ago."

"And then?"

"He began to get letters—threatening letters."

"Did you see them?"

"Yes. It was my business to attend to his correspondence. The first letter came a fortnight ago."

"Were these letters destroyed?"

"No, I think I've got a couple still in my files—one I know Ratchett tore up in a rage. Shall I get them for you?"

"If you would be so good."

MacQueen left the compartment. He returned a few minutes later and laid down two sheets of rather dirty notepaper before Poirot.

The first letter ran as follows:

Thought you'd double-cross us and get away with it, did you? Not on your life. We're out to GET you, Ratchett, and we WILL get you!

There was no signature.

With no comment beyond raised eyebrows, Poirot picked up the second letter.

We're going to take you for a ride, Ratchett. Some time soon. We're going to GET you—see?

Poirot laid the letter down.

"The style is monotonous!" he said. "More so than the handwriting."

MacQueen stared at him.

"You would not observe," said Poirot pleasantly. "It requires the eye of one used to such things. This letter was not written by one person, M. MacQueen. Two or more persons wrote it—each writing one letter of a word at a time. Also, the letters are printed. That makes the task of identifying the handwriting much more difficult." He paused, then said: "Did you know that M. Ratchett had applied for help to me?"

"To *you*?"

MacQueen's astonished tone told Poirot quite certainly that the young man had not known of it.

The detective nodded. "Yes. He was alarmed. Tell me, how did he act when he received the first letter?"

MacQueen hesitated.

"It's difficult to say. He—he—passed it off with a laugh in that quiet way of his. But somehow"—he gave a slight shiver—"I felt that there was a good deal going on underneath the quietness."

Poirot nodded. Then he asked an unexpected question.

"Mr. MacQueen, will you tell me, quite honestly, exactly how you regarded your employer? Did you like him?"

Hector MacQueen took a moment or two before replying.

"No," he said at last. "I did not."

"Why?"

"I can't exactly say. He was always quite pleasant in his manner." He paused, then said: "I'll tell you the truth, Mr. Poirot. I disliked and distrusted him. He was, I am sure, a cruel and dangerous man. I must admit, though, that I have no reasons to advance for my opinion."

"Thank you, Mr. MacQueen. One further question: when did you last see Mr. Ratchett alive?"

"Last evening about"—he thought for a minute—"ten o'clock, I should say. I went into his compartment to take down some memoranda from him."

"On what subject?"

"Some tiles and antique pottery that he bought in Persia. What had been delivered was not what he had purchased. There has been a long, vexatious correspondence on the subject."

"And that was the last time Mr. Ratchett was seen alive?"

"Yes, I suppose so."

"Do you know when Mr. Ratchett received the last threatening letter?"

"On the morning of the day we left Constantinople."

"There is one more question I must ask you, Mr. MacQueen. Were you on good terms with your employer?"

The young man's eyes twinkled suddenly.

"This is where I'm supposed to go all goosefleshy down the back. In the words of a best seller, 'You've nothing on me.' Ratchett and I were on perfectly good terms."

"Perhaps, Mr. MacQueen, you will give me your full name and your address in America."

MacQueen gave his name—Hector Willard MacQueen—and an address in New York.

Poirot leaned back against the cushions.

"That is all for the present, Mr. MacQueen," he said. "I should be obliged if you would keep the matter of Mr. Ratchett's death to yourself for a little time."

"His valet, Masterman, will have to know."

"He probably knows already," said Poirot drily. "If so, try to get him to hold his tongue."

"That oughtn't to be difficult. He's a Britisher and, as he calls it, he 'keeps to himself.' He has a low opinion of Americans, and no opinion at all of any other nationality."

"Thank you, Mr. MacQueen."

The American left the carriage.

"Well?" demanded M. Bouc. "You believe what he says, this young man?"

"He seems honest and straightforward. He did not pretend to any affection for his employer, as he probably would have done had he been involved in any way. It is true, Mr. Ratchett did not tell him that he had tried to enlist my services and failed, but I do not think that that is really a suspicious circumstance. I fancy Mr. Ratchett was a gentleman who kept his own counsel on every possible occasion."

"So you pronounce one person at least innocent of the crime," said M. Bouc jovially.

Poirot cast on him a look of reproach.

"Me, I suspect everybody till the last minute," he said. "All the same, I must admit that I cannot see this sober, long-headed MacQueen losing his head and stabbing his victim twelve or fourteen times. It is not in accord with his psychology—not at all."

"No," said M. Bouc thoughtfully. "That is the act of a man driven almost crazy with a frenzied hate—it suggests rather the Latin temperament. Or else it suggests, as our friend the *chef de train* insisted—a woman."

Chapter 7

The Body

Followed by Dr. Constantine, Poirot made his way to the next coach and to the compartment occupied by the murdered man. The conductor came and unlocked the door for them with his key.

The two men passed inside. Poirot turned inquiringly to his companion.

"How much has been disarranged in this compartment?"

"Nothing has been touched. I was careful not to move the body in making my examination."

Poirot nodded. He looked round him.

The first thing that struck the senses was the intense cold. The window was pushed down as far as it would go, and the blind was drawn up.

"Brrr," observed Poirot.

The other smiled appreciatively.

"I did not like to close it," he said.

Poirot examined the window carefully.

"You are right," he announced. "Nobody left the carriage this way. Possibly the open window was intended to suggest that somebody did; but if so, the snow has defeated the murderer's intention."

He examined the frame of the window carefully. Taking a small case from his pocket he blew a little powder over the frame.

"No fingerprints at all," he said. "That means it has been wiped. Well, if there had been fingerprints they would have told us very little. They would have been those of Mr. Ratchett or his valet or the conductor. Criminals do not make mistakes of that kind nowadays.

"And that being so," he added cheerfully, "we might as well shut the window. Positively it is the cold storage in here!"

He suited the action to the word and then turned his attention for the first time to the motionless figure lying in the bunk.

Ratchett lay on his back. His pyjama jacket, stained with rusty patches, had been unbuttoned and thrown back.

"I had to see the nature of the wounds, you see," explained the doctor.

Poirot nodded. He bent over the body. Finally he straightened himself with a slight grimace.

"It is not pretty," he said. "Someone must have stood there and stabbed him again and again. How many wounds are there exactly?"

"I make it twelve. One or two are so slight as to be practically scratches. On the other hand, at least three would be capable of causing death."

Something in the doctor's tone caught Poirot's attention. He looked at him sharply. The little Greek was standing staring down at the body with a puzzled frown.

"Something strikes you as odd, does it not?" he asked gently. "Speak, my friend. There is something here that puzzles you?"

"You are right," acknowledged the other.

"What is it?"

"You see these two wounds—here and here—" He pointed. "They are deep. Each cut must have severed blood vessels—and yet the edges do not gape. They have not bled as one would have expected."

"Which suggests?"

"That the man was already dead—some little time dead—when they were delivered. But that is surely absurd."

"It would seem so," said Poirot thoughtfully. "Unless our murderer figured to himself that he had not accomplished his job properly and came back to make quite sure—but that is manifestly absurd! Anything else?"

"Well, just one thing."

"And that?"

"You see this wound here—under the right arm—near the right shoulder. Take this pencil of mine. Could you deliver such a blow?"

Poirot poised his hand.

"*Précisément,*" he said. "I see. With the *right* hand it is exceedingly difficult, almost impossible. One would have to strike backhanded, as it were. But if the blow were struck with the *left* hand—"

"Exactly, M. Poirot. That blow was almost certainly struck with the *left* hand."

"So that our murderer is left-handed? No, it is more difficult than that, is it not?"

"As you say, M. Poirot. Some of these other blows are just as obviously right-handed."

"Two people. We are back at two people again," murmured the detective. He asked abruptly: "Was the electric light on?"

"It is difficult to say. You see, it is turned off by the conductor every morning about ten o'clock."

"The switches will tell us," said Poirot.

He examined the switch of the top light and also the roll-back, bed-head light. The former was turned off. The latter was closed.

"Eh bien," he said thoughtfully. "We have here a hypothesis of the First and the Second Murderer, as the great Shakespeare would put it. The First Murderer stabbed his victim and left the compartment, turning off the light. The Second Murderer came in in the dark, did not see that his or her work had been done, and stabbed at least twice at a dead body. *Que pensez-vous de ça?"*

"Magnificent!" said the little doctor with enthusiasm.

The other's eyes twinkled.

"You think so? I am glad. It sounded to me a little like the nonsense."

"What other explanation can there be?"

"That is just what I am asking myself. Have we here a coincidence, or what? Are there any other inconsistencies, such as would point to two people being concerned?"

"I think I can say yes. Some of these blows, as I have already said, point to a weakness—a lack of strength or a lack of determination. They are feeble, glancing blows. But this one here—and this one—" Again he pointed. "Great strength was needed for those blows. They have penetrated the muscle."

"They were, in your opinion, delivered by a man?"

"Most certainly."

"They could not have been delivered by a woman?"

"A young, vigorous, athletic woman might have struck them, especially if she were in the grip of a strong emotion; but it is in my opinion highly unlikely."

Poirot was silent a moment or two.

The other asked anxiously, "You understand my point?"

"Perfectly," said Poirot. "The matter begins to clear itself up wonderfully! The murderer was a man of great strength—he was feeble—it was a woman—it was a right-handed person—it was a left-handed person. *Ah! c'est rigolo, tout ça!"* He spoke with sudden anger. "And the victim—what does he do in all this? Does he cry out? Does he struggle? Does he defend himself?"

He slipped his hand under the pillow and drew out the automatic pistol which Ratchett had shown him the day before.

"Fully loaded, you see," he said.

They looked round them. Ratchett's day clothing was hanging from the hooks on the wall. On the small table formed by the lid of the wash basin were various objects. False teeth in a glass of water. Another glass, empty. A bottle of mineral water. A large flask. An ashtray containing the butt of a cigar and some charred fragments of paper; also two burnt matches.

The doctor picked up the empty glass and sniffed it.

"Here is the explanation of the victim's inertia," he said quietly.

"Drugged?"

"Yes."

Poirot nodded. He picked up the two matches and scrutinised them carefully.

"You have a clue then?" demanded the little doctor eagerly.

"Those two matches are of different shapes," said Poirot.

"One is flatter than the other. You see?"

"It is the kind you get on the train," said the doctor. "In paper covers."

Poirot was feeling in the pockets of Ratchett's clothing.

Presently he pulled out a box of matches. He compared them carefully with the burnt ones.

"The rounder one is a match struck by Mr. Ratchett," he said. "Let us see if he had also the flatter kind."

But a further search showed no other matches.

Poirot's eyes were darting about the compartment. They were bright and sharp like a bird's. One felt that nothing could escape their scrutiny.

With a little exclamation he bent and picked up something from the floor.

It was a small square of cambric, very dainty. In the corner was an embroidered initial—H.

"A woman's handkerchief," said the doctor. "Our friend the *chef de train* was right. There is a woman concerned in this."

"And most conveniently she leaves her handkerchief behind!" said Poirot. "Exactly as it happens in the books and on the films—and to make things even easier for us, it is marked with an initial."

"What a stroke of luck for us!" exclaimed the doctor.

"Is it not?" said Poirot.

Something in his tone surprised the doctor, but before he could ask for elucidation Poirot had made another dive onto the floor.

This time he held out on the palm of his hand—a pipe cleaner.

"It is perhaps the property of Mr. Ratchett?" suggested the doctor.

"There was no pipe in any of his pockets, and no tobacco or tobacco pouch."

"Then it is a clue."

"Oh! decidedly. And again dropped most conveniently. A masculine clue, this time, you note! One cannot complain of having no clues in this case. There are clues here in abundance. By the way, what have you done with the weapon?"

"There was no sign of any weapon. The murderer must have taken it away with him."

"I wonder why," mused Poirot.

"Ah!" The doctor had been delicately exploring the pyjama pockets of the dead man.

"I overlooked this," he said. "I unbuttoned the jacket and threw it straight back."

From the breast pocket he brought out a gold watch. The case was dented savagely, and the hands pointed to a quarter past one.

"You see?" cried Constantine eagerly. "This gives us the hour of the crime. It agrees with my calculations. Between midnight and two in the morning is what I said, and probably about one o'clock, though it is difficult to be exact in these matters. *Eh bien*, here is confirmation. A quarter past one. That was the hour of the crime."

"It is possible, yes. It is certainly possible."

The doctor looked at him curiously. "You will pardon me, M. Poirot, but I do not quite understand you."

"I do not understand myself," said Poirot. "I understand nothing at all. And, as you perceive, it worries me."

He sighed and bent over the little table examining the charred fragment of paper. He murmured to himself, "What I need at this moment is an old-fashioned woman's hatbox."

Dr. Constantine was at a loss to know what to make of this singular remark. In any case Poirot gave him no time for questions. Opening the door into the corridor, he called for the conductor.

The man arrived at a run.

"How many women are there in this coach?"

The conductor counted on his fingers.

"One, two, three—six, Monsieur. The old American lady, a Swedish lady, the young English lady, the Countess Andrenyi, and Madame la Princesse Dragomiroff and her maid."

Poirot considered.

"They all have hatboxes, yes?"

"Yes, Monsieur."

"Then bring me—let me see—yes, the Swedish lady's and that of the lady's-maid. Those two are the only hope. You will tell them it is a customs regulation—something—anything that occurs to you."

"That will be all right, Monsieur. Neither lady is in her compartment at the moment."

"Then be quick."

The conductor departed. He returned with the two hatboxes. Poirot opened that of the maid, and tossed it aside. Then he opened the Swedish lady's and uttered an exclamation of satisfaction. Removing the hats carefully, he disclosed round humps of wire netting.

"Ah, here is what we need! About fifteen years ago hatboxes were made like this. You skewered through the hat with a hatpin on to this hump of wire netting."

As he spoke he was skillfully removing two of the attached humps. Then he repacked the hatbox and told the conductor to return both boxes where they belonged.

When the door was shut once more he turned to his companion.

"See you, my dear doctor, me, I am not one to rely upon the expert procedure. It is the psychology I seek, not the fingerprint or the cigarette ash. But in this case I would welcome a little scientific assistance. This compartment is full of clues, but can I be sure that those clues are really what they seem to be?"

"I do not quite understand you, M. Poirot."

"Well, to give you an example—we find a woman's handkerchief. Did a woman drop it? Or did a man, committing the crime, say to himself: 'I will make this look like a woman's crime. I will stab my enemy an unnecessary number of times, making some of the blows feeble and ineffective, and I will drop this handkerchief where no one can miss it'? That is one possibility. Then there is another. Did a woman kill him, and did she deliberately drop a pipe cleaner to make it look like a man's work? Or are we seriously to suppose that two people, a man and a woman, were separately concerned, and that each was so careless as to drop a clue to his or her identity? It is a little too much of a coincidence, that!"

"But where does the hatbox come in?" asked the doctor, still puzzled.

"Ah! I am coming to that. As I say, these clues—the watch stopped at a quarter past one, the handkerchief, the pipe cleaner—they may be genuine, or they may be faked. As to that I cannot yet tell. But there is one clue here which—though again I may be wrong—I believe has not been faked. I mean this flat match, *M. le docteur. I believe that that match was used by the murderer, not by Mr. Ratchett.* It was used to burn an incriminating paper of some kind. Possibly a note. If so, there was something in that note, some mistake, some error, that left a possible clue to the assailant. I am going to try to discover what that something was."

He went out of the compartment and returned a few moments later with a small spirit stove and a pair of curling-tongs.

"I use them for the moustaches," he said, referring to the latter.

The doctor watched him with great interest. Poirot flattened out the two humps of wire, and with great care wriggled the charred scrap of paper on to one of them. He clapped the other on top of it and then, holding both pieces together with the tongs, held the whole thing over the flame of the spirit-lamp.

"It is a very makeshift affair, this," he said over his shoulder. "Let us hope that it will answer our purpose."

The doctor watched the proceedings attentively. The metal began to glow. Suddenly he saw faint indications of letters. Words formed themselves slowly—words of fire.

It was a very tiny scrap. Only three words and part of another showed.

—member little Daisy Armstrong

"Ah!" Poirot gave a sharp exclamation.

"It tells you something?" asked the doctor.

Poirot's eyes were shining. He laid down the tongs carefully.

"Yes," he said. *"I know the dead man's real name. I know why he had to leave America."*

"What was his name?"

"Cassetti."

"Cassetti?" Constantine knitted his brows. "It brings back to me something. Some years ago. I cannot remember. . . . It was a case in America, was it not?"

"Yes," said Poirot. "A case in America."

Further than that Poirot was not disposed to be communicative. He looked round him as he went on:

"We will go into all that presently. Let us first make sure that we have seen all there is to be seen here."

Quickly and deftly he went once more through the pockets of the dead man's clothes but found nothing there of interest. He tried the communicating door which led through to the next compartment, but it was bolted on the other side.

"There is one thing that I do not understand," said Dr. Constantine. "If the murderer did not escape through the window, and if this communicating door was bolted on the other side, and if the door into the corridor was not only locked on the inside but chained, how then did the murderer leave the compartment?"

"That is what the audience says when a person bound hand and foot is shut into a cabinet—and disappears."

"You mean—?"

"I mean," explained Poirot, "that if the murderer intended us to believe that he had escaped by way of the window, he would naturally make it appear that the other two exits were impossible. Like the 'disappearing person' in the cabinet, it is a trick. It is our business to find out how the trick is done."

He locked the communicating door on their side—"In case," he said, "the excellent Mrs. Hubbard should take it into her head to acquire first-hand details of the crime to write to her daughter."

He looked round once more.

"There is nothing more to do here, I think. Let us rejoin M. Bouc."

Chapter 8

The Armstrong Kidnapping Case

They found M. Bouc finishing an omelet.

"I thought it best to have lunch served immediately in the restaurant car," he said. "Afterwards it will be cleared and M. Poirot can conduct his examination of the passengers there. In the meantime I have ordered them to bring us three some food here."

"An excellent idea," said Poirot.

None of the three men was hungry, and the meal was soon eaten; but not till they were sipping their coffee did M. Bouc mention the subject that was occupying all their minds.

"*Eh bien?*" he asked.

"*Eh bien*, I have discovered the identity of the victim. I know why it was imperative he should leave America."

"Who was he?"

"Do you remember reading of the Armstrong baby? This is the man who murdered little Daisy Armstrong. Cassetti."

"I recall it now. A shocking affair—though I cannot remember the details."

"Colonel Armstrong was an Englishman—a V.C. He was half American, his mother having been a daughter of W. K. Van der Halt, the Wall Street millionaire. He married the daughter of Linda Arden, the most famous tragic American actress of her day. They lived in America and had one child—a girl whom they idolized. When she was three years old she was kidnapped, and an impossibly high sum demanded as the price of her return. I will not weary you with all the intricacies that followed. I will come to the moment when, after the parents had paid over the enormous sum of two hundred thousand dollars, the child's dead body was discovered; it had been dead for at least a fortnight. Public indignation rose to fever point. And there was worse to follow. Mrs. Armstrong was expecting another baby. Following the shock of the discovery, she gave birth prematurely to a dead child, and herself died. Her broken-hearted husband shot himself."

"*Mon Dieu*, what a tragedy. I remember now," said M. Bouc. "There was also another death, if I remember rightly?"

"Yes, an unfortunate French or Swiss nursemaid. The police were convinced that she had some knowledge of the crime. They refused to believe her hysterical denials. Finally, in a fit of despair the poor girl threw herself from a window and was killed. It was proved afterwards that she had been absolutely innocent of any complicity in the crime."

"It is not good to think of," said M. Bouc.

"About six months later, this man Cassetti was arrested as the head of the gang who had kidnapped the child. They had used the same methods in the past. If the police seemed likely to get on their trial, they killed their prisoner, hid the body, and continued to extract as much money as possible before the crime was discovered.

"Now, I will make clear to you this, my friend. Cassetti was the man! But by means of the enormous wealth he had piled up, and owing to the secret hold he had over various persons, he was acquitted on some technical inaccuracy. Notwithstanding that, he would have been lynched by the populace had he not been clever enough to give them the slip. It is now clear to me what happened. He changed his name and left America. Since then he has been a gentleman of leisure, travelling abroad and living on his *rentes*."

"*Ah! quel animal!*" M. Bouc's tone was redolent of heartfelt disgust. "I cannot regret that he is dead—not at all!"

"I agree with you."

"*Tout de même*, it is not necessary that he should be killed on the Orient Express. There are other places."

Poirot smiled a little. He realised that M. Bouc was biased in the matter.

"The question we have now to ask ourselves is this," he said. "Is this murder the work of some rival gang whom Cassetti had double-crossed in the past, or is it an act of private vengeance?"

He explained his discovery of the few words on the charred fragment of paper.

"If I am right in my assumption, then, the letter was burnt by the murderer. Why? Because it mentioned the name 'Armstrong,' which is the clue to the mystery."

"Are there any members of the Armstrong family living?"

"That, unfortunately, I do not know. I think I remember reading of a younger sister of Mrs. Armstrong's."

Poirot went on to relate the joint conclusions of himself and Dr. Constantine. M. Bouc brightened at the mention of the broken watch.

"That seems to give us the time of the crime very exactly."

"Yes," said Poirot. "It is very convenient."

There was an indescribable something in his tone that made both the other two look at him curiously.

"You say that you yourself heard Ratchett speak to the conductor at twenty minutes to one?" asked M. Bouc.

Poirot related just what had occurred.

"Well," said M. Bouc, "that proves at least that Cassetti—or Ratchett, as I shall continue to call him—was certainly alive at twenty minutes to one."

"Twenty-three minutes to one, to be precise."

"Then at twelve thirty-seven, to put it formally, Mr. Ratchett was alive. That is one fact, at least."

Poirot did not reply. He sat looking thoughtfully in front of him.

There was a tap on the door and the restaurant attendant entered.

"The restaurant car is free now, Monsieur," he said.

"We will go there," said M. Bouc, rising.

"I may accompany you?" asked Constantine.

"Certainly, my dear doctor. Unless M. Poirot has any objection?"

"Not at all. Not at all," said Poirot.

After a little politeness in the matter of precedence—"Après vous, Monsieur"—"Mais non, après vous"—they left the compartment.

Part 2
The Evidence

Chapter 1

The Evidence of the Wagon Lit Conductor

In the restaurant car all was in readiness.

Poirot and M. Bouc sat together on one side of a table. The doctor sat across the aisle.

On the table in front of Poirot was a plan of the Istanbul-Calais coach with the names of the passengers marked in red ink. The passports and tickets were in a pile at one side. There was writing paper, ink, pen, and pencils.

"Excellent," said Poirot. "We can open our Court of Inquiry without more ado. First, I think, we should take the evidence of the Wagon Lit conductor. You probably know something about the man. What character has he? Is he a man on whose word you would place reliance?"

"I should say so, most assuredly. Pierre Michel has been employed by the company for over fifteen years. He is a Frenchman—lives near Calais. Thoroughly respectable and honest. Not, perhaps, remarkable for brains."

Poirot nodded comprehendingly. "Good," he said. "Let us see him."

Pierre Michel had recovered some of his assurance, but he was still extremely nervous.

"I hope Monsieur will not think that there has been any negligence on my part," he said anxiously, his eyes going from Poirot to M. Bouc. "It is a terrible thing that has happened. I hope Monsieur does not think that it reflects on me in any way?"

Having soothed the man's fears, Poirot began his questions. He first elicited Michel's name and address, his length of service, and the length of time he had been on this particular route. These particulars he already knew, but the routine questions served to put the man at his ease.

"And now," went on Poirot, "let us come to the events of last night. M. Ratchett retired to bed—when?"

"Almost immediately after dinner, Monsieur. Actually before we left Belgrade. So he did on the previous night. He had directed me to make up the bed while he was at dinner, and I did so."

"Did anybody go into his compartment afterwards?"

"His valet, Monsieur, and the young American gentleman, his secretary."

"Anyone else?"

"No, Monsieur, not that I know of."

"Good. And that is the last you saw or heard of him?"

"No, Monsieur. You forget he rang his bell about twenty to one—soon after we had stopped."

"What happened exactly?"

"I knocked at the door, but he called out and said he had made a mistake."

"In English or in French?"

"In French."

"What were his words exactly?"

"Ce n'est rien. Je me suis trompé."

"Quite right," said Poirot. "That is what I heard. And then you went away?"

"Yes, Monsieur."

"Did you go back to your seat?"

"No, Monsieur, I went first to answer another bell that had just rung."

"Now, Michel, I am going to ask you an important question. Where were you at a quarter past one?"

"I, Monsieur? I was at my little seat at the end—facing up the corridor."

"You are sure?"

"Mais oui—at least—"

"Yes?"

"I went into the next coach, the Athens coach, to speak to my colleague there. We spoke about the snow. That was at some time soon after one o'clock. I cannot say exactly."

"And you returned—when?"

"One of my bells rang, Monsieur—I remember—I told you. It was the American lady. She had rung several times."

"I recollect," said Poirot. "And after that?"

"After that, Monsieur? I answered your bell and brought you some mineral water. Then, about half an hour later, I made up the bed in one of

WAGON RESTAURANT

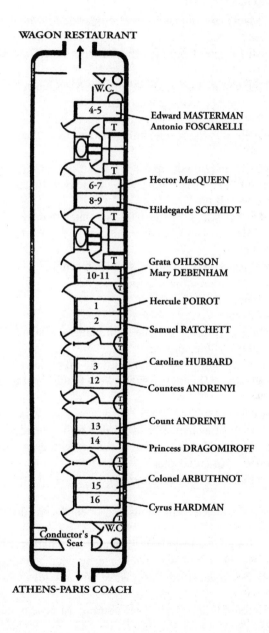

Edward MASTERMAN
Antonio FOSCARELLI

Hector MacQUEEN

Hildegarde SCHMIDT

Grata OHLSSON
Mary DEBENHAM

Hercule POIROT

Samuel RATCHETT

Caroline HUBBARD

Countess ANDRENYI

Count ANDRENYI

Princess DRAGOMIROFF

Colonel ARBUTHNOT

Cyrus HARDMAN

Conductor's
Seat

ATHENS-PARIS COACH

the other compartments—that of the young American gentleman, Mr. Ratchett's secretary."

"Was Mr. MacQueen alone in his compartment when you went to make up his bed?"

"The English Colonel from No. 15 was with him. They had been sitting talking."

"What did the Colonel do when he left Mr. MacQueen?"

"He went back to his own compartment."

"No. 15—that is quite close to your seat, is it not?"

"Yes, Monsieur, it is the second compartment from that end of the corridor."

"His bed was already made up?"

"Yes, Monsieur. I had made it up while he was at dinner."

"What time was all this?"

"I could not say exactly, Monsieur. Not later than two o'clock certainly."

"And after that?"

"After that, Monsieur, I sat in my seat till morning."

"You did not go again into the Athens coach?"

"No, Monsieur."

"Perhaps you slept?"

"I do not think so, Monsieur. The train being at a standstill prevented me from dozing off as I usually do."

"Did you see any of the passengers moving up or down the corridor?"

The man reflected. "One of the ladies went to the toilet at the far end, I think."

"Which lady?"

"I do not know, Monsieur. It was far down the corridor and she had her back to me. She had on a kimono of scarlet with dragons on it."

Poirot nodded. "And after that?"

"Nothing, Monsieur, until the morning."

"You are sure?"

"Ah, pardon—you yourself, Monsieur, opened your door and looked out for a second."

"Good, my friend," said Poirot. "I wondered whether you would remember that. By the way, I was awakened by what sounded like something heavy falling against my door. Have you any idea what that could have been?"

The man stared at him. "There was nothing, Monsieur. Nothing, I am positive of it."

"Then I must have had the *cauchemar*," said Poirot philosophically.

"Unless," put in M. Bouc, "it was something in the compartment next door that you heard."

Poirot took no notice of the suggestion. Perhaps he did not wish to before the Wagon Lit conductor.

"Let us pass to another point," he said. "Supposing that last night an assassin joined the train. Is it quite certain that he could not have left it after committing the crime?"

Pierre Michel shook his head.

"Nor that he can be concealed on it somewhere?"

"It has been well searched," said M. Bouc. "Abandon that idea, my friend."

"Besides," said Michel, "no one could get on to the sleeping-car without my seeing them."

"When was the last stop?"

"Vincovci."

"What time was that?"

"We should have left there at 11.58, but owing to the weather we were twenty minutes late."

"Someone might have come along from the ordinary part of the train?"

"No, Monsieur. After the service of dinner, the door between the ordinary carriages and the sleeping-cars is locked."

"Did you yourself descend from the train at Vincovci?"

"Yes, Monsieur. I got down onto the platform as usual and stood by the step up into the train. The other conductors did the same."

"What about the forward door—the one near the restaurant car?"

"It is always fastened on the inside."

"It is not so fastened now."

The man looked surprised; then his face cleared. "Doubtless one of the passengers opened it to look out on the snow."

"Probably," said Poirot.

He tapped thoughtfully on the table for a minute or two.

"Monsieur does not blame me?" said the man timidly.

Poirot smiled on him kindly.

"You have had the evil chance, my friend," he said. "Ah! one other point while I remember it. You said that another bell rang just as you were knocking at M. Ratchett's door. In fact I heard it myself. Whose was it?"

"It was the bell of Madame la Princesse Dragomiroff. She desired me to summon her maid."

"And you did so?"

"Yes, Monsieur."

Poirot studied the plan in front of him thoughtfully. Then he inclined his head.

"That is all," he said, "for the moment."

"Thank you, Monsieur."

The man rose. He looked at M. Bouc.

"Do not distress yourself," said the latter kindly. "I cannot see that there has been any negligence on your part."

Gratified, Pierre Michel left the compartment.

Chapter 2

The Evidence of the Secretary

For a minute or two Poirot remained lost in thought.

"I think," he said at last, "that it would be well to have a further word with Mr. MacQueen, in view of what we now know."

The young American appeared promptly.

"Well," he said, "how are things going?"

"Not too badly. Since our last conversation, I have learnt something— the identity of Mr. Ratchett."

Hector MacQueen leaned forward interestedly. "Yes?" he said.

" 'Ratchett,' as you suspected, was merely an alias. The man 'Ratchett' was Cassetti, who ran the celebrated kidnapping stunts—including the famous affair of little Daisy Armstrong."

An expression of utter astonishment appeared on MacQueen's face. Then it darkened. "The damned skunk!" he exclaimed.

"You had no idea of this, Mr. MacQueen?"

"No, sir," said the young American decidedly. "If I had, I'd have cut off my right hand before it had a chance to do secretarial work for him!"

"You feel strongly about the matter, Mr. MacQueen?"

"I have a particular reason for doing so. My father was the district attorney who handled the case, Mr. Poirot. I saw Mrs. Armstrong more than once—she was a lovely woman. So gentle and heartbroken." His face darkened. "If ever a man deserved what he got, Ratchett—or Cassetti—is the man. I'm rejoiced at his end. Such a man wasn't fit to live!"

"You almost feel as though you would have been willing to do the good deed yourself?"

"I do. I—" He paused, then added rather guiltily, "Seems I'm kind of incriminating myself."

"I should be more inclined to suspect you, Mr. MacQueen, if you displayed an inordinate sorrow at your employer's decease."

"I don't think I could do that even to save myself from the chair," said MacQueen grimly. Then he added: "If I'm not being unduly curious, just how did you figure this out? Cassetti's identity, I mean."

"By a fragment of a letter found in his compartment."

"But surely—I mean—that was rather careless of the old man?"

"That depends," said Poirot, "on the point of view."

The young man seemed to find this remark rather baffling. He stared at Poirot as though trying to make him out.

"The task before me," said Poirot, "is to make sure of the movements of everyone on the train. No offence need be taken, you understand. It is only a matter of routine."

"Sure. Get right on with it and let me clear my character if I can."

"I need hardly ask you the number of your compartment," said Poirot, smiling, "since I shared it with you for a night. It is the second-class compartment Nos. 6 and 7, and after my departure you had it to yourself."

"That's right."

"Now, Mr. MacQueen, I want you to describe your movements last night from the time of leaving the dining-car."

"That's quite easy. I went back to my compartment, read a bit, got out on the platform at Belgrade, decided it was too cold, and got in again. I talked for a while to a young English lady who is in the compartment next to mine. Then I fell into conversation with that Englishman, Colonel Arbuthnot—as a matter of fact I think you passed us as we were talking. Then I went in to Mr. Ratchett and, as I told you, took down some memoranda of letters he wanted written. I said good night to him and left him. Colonel Arbuthnot was still standing in the corridor. His compartment was already made up for the night, so I suggested that he should come along to mine. I ordered a couple of drinks and we got right down to it. Discussed world politics and the Government of India and our own troubles with Prohibition and the Wall Street crisis. I don't as a rule cotton to Britishers—they're a stiff-necked lot—but I liked this one."

"Do you know what time it was when he left you?"

"Pretty late. Nearly two o'clock, I should say."

"You noticed that the train had stopped?"

"Oh, yes. We wondered a bit. Looked out and saw the snow lying very thick, but we didn't think it was serious."

"What happened when Colonel Arbuthnot finally said good night?"

"He went along to his compartment and I called to the conductor to make up my bed."

"Where were you whilst he was making it?"

"Standing just outside the door in the corridor smoking a cigarette."

"And then?"

"And then I went to bed and slept till morning."

"During the evening did you leave the train at all?"

"Arbuthnot and I thought we'd get out at—what was the name of the place?—Vincovci—to stretch our legs a bit. But it was bitterly cold—a blizzard on. We soon hopped back again."

"By which door did you leave the train?"

"By the one nearest to our compartment."

"The one next to the dining-car?"

"Yes."

"Do you remember if it was bolted?"

MacQueen considered.

"Why, yes, I seem to remember it was. At least there was a kind of bar that fitted across the handle. Is that what you mean?"

"Yes. On getting back into the train did you replace that bar?"

"Why, no—I don't think I did. I got in last. No, I don't seem to remember doing so." He added suddenly, "Is that an important point?"

"It may be. Now, I presume, Monsieur, that while you and Colonel Arbuthnot were sitting talking the door of your compartment into the corridor was open?"

Hector MacQueen nodded.

"I want you, if you can, to tell me if anyone passed along that corridor *after* the train left Vincovci up to the time you parted company for the night."

MacQueen drew his brows together.

"I think the conductor passed along once," he said, "coming from the direction of the dining-car. And a woman passed the other way, going towards it."

"Which woman?"

"I couldn't say. I didn't really notice. You see I was arguing a point with Arbuthnot. I just seem to remember a glimpse of some scarlet silk affair passing the door. I didn't look, and anyway I wouldn't have seen the person's face. As you know, my carriage faces the dining-car end of the train, so a woman going along the corridor in that direction would have her back to me as soon as she'd passed."

Poirot nodded. "She was going to the toilet, I presume?"

"I suppose so."

"And you saw her return?"

"Well, no, now that you mention it, I didn't notice her returning, but I suppose she must have done so."

"One more question. Do you smoke a pipe, Mr. MacQueen?"

"No, sir, I do not."

Poirot paused a moment. "I think that is all at present. I should now like to see the valet of Mr. Ratchett. By the way, did both you and he always travel second-class?"

"He did. But I usually went first—if possible in the compartment adjoining Mr. Ratchett's. Then he had most of his baggage put in my compartment and yet could get at both it and me easily whenever he chose. But on this occasion all the first-class berths were booked except the one that he took."

"I comprehend. Thank you, Mr. MacQueen."

Chapter 3

The Evidence of the Valet

The American was succeeded by the pale Englishman with the inexpressive face whom Poirot had already noticed on the day before. He stood waiting very correctly. Poirot motioned to him to sit down.

"You are, I understand, the valet of M. Ratchett."

"Yes, sir."

"Your name?"

"Edward Henry Masterman."

"Your age?"

"Thirty-nine."

"And your home address?"

"21 Friar Street, Clerkenwell."

"You have heard that your master has been murdered?"

"Yes, sir. A very shocking occurrence."

"Will you now tell me, please, at what hour you last saw M. Ratchett?"

The valet considered.

"It must have been about nine o'clock, sir, last night. That or a little after."

"Tell me in your own words exactly what happened."

"I went in to Mr. Ratchett as usual, sir, and attended to his wants."

"What were your duties exactly?"

"To fold or hang up his clothes, sir, put his dental plate in water and see that he had everything he wanted for the night."

"Was his manner much the same as usual?"

The valet considered a moment.

"Well, sir, I think he was upset."

"In what way—upset?"

"Over a letter he'd been reading. He asked me if it was I who had put it in his compartment. Of course I told him I hadn't done any such thing, but he swore at me and found fault with everything I did."

"Was that unusual?"

"Oh, no, sir. He lost his temper easily—as I say, it just depended what had happened to upset him."

"Did your master ever take a sleeping draught?"

Dr. Constantine leaned forward a little.

"Always when travelling by train, sir. He said he couldn't sleep otherwise."

"Do you know what drug he was in the habit of taking?"

"I couldn't say, I'm sure, sir. There was no name on the bottle—just *'The Sleeping Draught to be taken at bedtime.'* "

"Did he take it last night?"

"Yes, sir. I poured it into a glass and put it on top of the toilet table ready for him."

"You didn't actually see him drink it?"

"No, sir."

"What happened next?"

"I asked if there was anything further, and also asked what time he would like to be called in the morning. He said he didn't want to be disturbed till he rang."

"Was that usual?"

"Quite usual, sir. When he was ready to get up he used to ring the bell for the conductor and then send him for me."

"Was he usually an early or a late riser?"

"It depended, sir, on his mood. Sometimes he'd get up for breakfast, sometimes he wouldn't get up till just on lunch time."

"So that you weren't alarmed when the morning wore on and no summons came?"

"No, sir."

"Did you know that your master had enemies?"

"Yes, sir." The man spoke quite unemotionally.

"How did you know?"

"I had heard him discussing some letters, sir, with Mr. MacQueen."

"Had you an affection for your employer, Masterman?"

Masterman's face became, if possible, even more inexpressive than it was normally.

"I should hardly like to say that, sir. He was a generous employer."

"But you didn't like him?"

"Shall we put it that I don't care very much for Americans, sir?"

"Have you ever been in America?"

"No, sir."

"Do you remember reading in the paper of the Armstrong kidnapping case?"

A little colour came into the man's cheeks.

"Yes, indeed, sir. A little baby girl, wasn't it? A very shocking affair."

"Did you know that your employer, Mr. Ratchett, was the principal instigator in that affair?"

"No, indeed, sir." The valet's tone held positive warmth and feeling for the first time. "I can hardly believe it, sir."

"Nevertheless, it is true. Now, to pass to your own movements last night. A matter of routine, you understand. What did you do after leaving your master?"

"I told Mr. MacQueen, sir, that the master wanted him. Then I went to my own compartment and read."

"Your compartment was—"

"The end second-class one, sir. Next to the dining-car." Poirot was looking at his plan.

"I see—and you had which berth?"

"The lower one, sir."

"That is No. 4?"

"Yes, sir."

"Is there anyone in with you?"

"Yes, sir. A big Italian fellow."

"Does he speak English?"

"Well, a kind of English, sir." The valet's tone was deprecating. "He's been in America—Chicago, I understand."

"Do you and he talk together much?"

"No, sir. I prefer to read."

Poirot smiled. He could visualize the scene—the large, voluble Italian, and the snub direct administered by the gentleman's gentleman.

"And what, may I ask, are you reading?" he inquired.

"At present, sir, I am reading *Love's Captive*, by Mrs. Arabella Richardson."

"A good story?"

"I find it highly enjoyable, sir."

"Well, let us continue. You returned to your compartment and read *Love's Captive* till—when?"

"At about ten thirty, sir, this Italian wanted to go to bed. So the conductor came and made the beds up."

"And then you went to bed and to sleep?"

"I went to bed, sir, but I didn't sleep."

"Why didn't you sleep?"

"I had the toothache, sir."

"Oh, là-là—that is painful."

"Most painful, sir."

"Did you do anything for it?"

"I applied a little oil of cloves, sir, which relieved the pain a little, but I was still not able to get to sleep. I turned the light on above my head and continued to read—to take my mind off, as it were."

"And did you not go to sleep at all?"

"Yes, sir, I dropped off about four in the morning."

"And your companion?"

"The Italian fellow? Oh, he just snored."

"He did not leave the compartment at all during the night?"

"No, sir."

"Did you?"

"No, sir."

"Did you hear anything during the night?"

"I don't think so, sir. Nothing unusual, I mean. The train being at a standstill made it all very quiet."

Poirot was silent a moment or two. Then he spoke.

"Well, I think there is very little more to be said. You cannot throw any light upon the tragedy?"

"I'm afraid not. I'm sorry, sir."

"As far as you know, was there any quarrel or bad blood between your master and Mr. MacQueen?"

"Oh! no, sir. Mr. MacQueen was a very pleasant gentleman."

"Where were you in service before you came to Mr. Ratchett?"

"With Sir Henry Tomlinson, sir, in Grosvenor Square."

"Why did you leave him?"

"He was going to East Africa, sir, and did not require my services any longer. But I am sure he will speak for me, sir. I was with him some years."

"And you have been with Mr. Ratchett—how long?"

"Just over nine months, sir."

"Thank you, Masterman. By the way, are you a pipesmoker?"

"No, sir. I only smoke cigarettes—gaspers, sir."

"Thank you, that will do."

Poirot gave him a nod of dismissal.

The valet hesitated a moment.

"You'll excuse me, sir, but the elderly American lady is in what I might describe as a state, sir. She's saying she knows all about the murderer. She's in a very excitable condition, sir."

"In that case," said Poirot, smiling, "we had better see her next."

"Shall I tell her, sir? She's been demanding to see someone in authority for a long time. The conductor's been trying to pacify her."

"Send her to us, my friend," said Poirot. "We will listen to her story now."

Chapter 4

The Evidence of the American Lady

Mrs. Hubbard arrived in the dining-car in such a state of breathless excitement that she was hardly able to articulate her words.

"Now just tell me this—who's in authority here? I've got some very important information, *very* important indeed, and I'm going to tell it to someone in authority just as soon as I can. If you gentlemen—"

Her wavering glance fluctuated between the three men. Poirot leaned forward.

"Tell it to me, Madame," he said. "But first, pray be seated."

Mrs. Hubbard plumped heavily down on to the seat opposite to him.

"What I've got to tell you is just this. There was a murder on the train last night, and the murderer was *right there in my compartment*!"

She paused to give dramatic emphasis to her words.

"You are sure of this, Madame?"

"Of course I'm sure! The idea! I know what I'm talking about. I'll tell you everything there is to tell. I'd gotten into bed and gone to sleep, and suddenly I woke up—everything was dark—and I knew there was a man in my compartment. I was just so scared I couldn't scream, if you know what I mean. I just lay there and thought, 'Mercy, I'm going to be killed!' I just can't describe to you how I felt. These nasty trains, I thought, and all the outrages I'd read of. And I thought, 'Well, anyway, he won't get my jewellery'—because, you see, I'd put that in a stocking and hidden it under my pillow—which isn't any too comfortable, by the way; kinda bumpy, if you know what I mean. But that's neither here nor there. Where was I?"

"You realised, Madame, that there was a man in your compartment."

"Yes, well, I just lay there with my eyes closed, and wondered what I'd do. And I thought, well, I'm just thankful that my daughter doesn't know the plight I'm in. And then, somehow, I got my wits about me and I felt about with my hand and I pressed the bell for the conductor. I pressed it and I pressed it, but nothing happened—and I can tell you, I thought my heart was going to stop beating. 'Mercy,' I said to myself, 'maybe they've murdered every single soul on the train.' It was at a standstill anyhow and there was a nasty quiet feel in the air. But I just went on pressing that bell and oh! the relief when I heard footsteps coming running down the corridor and a knock on the door! 'Come in,' I screamed, and I switched on the lights at the same time. And would you believe it, there wasn't a *soul* there!"

This seemed to Mrs. Hubbard to be a dramatic climax rather than an anticlimax.

"And what happened next, Madame?"

"Why, I told the man what had happened and he didn't seem to believe me. Seemed to imagine I'd dreamed the whole thing. I made him look under the seat, though he said there wasn't room for a man to squeeze himself in there. It was plain enough that the man had got away—but there *had* been a man there, and it just made me mad the way the conductor tried to soothe me down! I'm not one to imagine things, Mr.—I don't think I know your name?"

"Poirot, Madame; and this is M. Bouc, a director of the company, and Dr. Constantine."

Mrs. Hubbard murmured, "Pleased to meet you, I'm sure," to all three of them in an abstracted manner and then plunged once more into her recital.

"Now I'm just not going to pretend I was as bright as I might have been. I got it into my head that it was the man from next door—the poor fellow who's been killed. I told the conductor to look at the door between the compartments, and sure enough it wasn't bolted. Well, I soon saw to that. I told him to bolt it then and there, and after he'd gone out I got up and put a suitcase against it to make sure."

"What time was this, Mrs. Hubbard?"

"Well, I'm sure I can't tell you. I never looked to see. I was so upset."

"And what is your theory now?"

"Why, I should say it was just as plain as plain could be. The man in my compartment was the murderer. Who else could he be?"

"And you think he went back into the adjoining compartment?"

"How do I know where he went? I had my eyes tight shut."

"He might have slipped out through the door into the corridor."

"Well, I couldn't say. You see, I had my eyes tight shut."

Mrs. Hubbard sighed convulsively.

"Mercy, I was scared! If my daughter only knew—"

"You do not think, Madame, that what you heard was the noise of someone moving about next door—in the murdered man's compartment?"

"No, I do not, Mr.—what is it?—Poirot. The man was *right there in the same compartment with me*. And what's more I've got proof of it."

Triumphantly, she hauled a large handbag into view and proceeded to burrow in its interior.

She took out in turn two large clean handkerchiefs, a pair of horn-rimmed glasses, a bottle of aspirin, a packet of Glauber's Salts, a celluloid tube of bright green peppermints, a bunch of keys, a pair of scissors, a book of American Express cheques, a snapshot of an extraordinarily plain-looking child, some letters, five strings of pseudo-Oriental beads, and a small metal object—a button.

"You see this button? Well, it's not one of my buttons. It's not off anything I've got. I found it this morning when I got up."

As she placed it on the table, M. Bouc leaned forward and gave an exclamation. "But this is a button from the tunic of a Wagon Lit attendant!"

"There may be a natural explanation for that," said Poirot.

He turned gently to the lady.

"This button, Madame, may have dropped from the conductor's uniform, either when he searched your cabin or when he was making the bed up last night."

"I just don't know what's the matter with all you people. Seems as though you don't want to do anything but make objections. Now listen here. I was reading a magazine last night before I went to sleep. Before I turned the light out, I placed that magazine on a little case that was standing on the floor near the window. Have you got that?"

They assured her that they had.

"Very well then. The conductor looked under the seat from near the door, and then he came in and bolted the door between me and the next compartment, but he never went near the window. Well, this morning that button was lying right on top of the magazine. What do you call that, I should like to know?"

"That, Madame, I call evidence," said Poirot.

The answer seemed to appease the lady.

"It makes me madder than a hornet to be disbelieved," she explained.

"You have given us most interesting and valuable evidence," said Poirot soothingly. "Now may I ask you a few questions?"

"Why, certainly."

"How was it, since you were nervous of this man Ratchett, that you hadn't already bolted the door between the compartments?"

"I had," returned Mrs. Hubbard promptly.

"Oh, you had?"

"Well, as a matter of fact I asked that Swedish creature—a pleasant soul—if it was bolted, and she said it was."

"How was it you couldn't see for yourself?"

"Because I was in bed and my spongebag was hanging on the door-handle."

"What time was it when you asked her to do this for you?"

"Now let me think. It must have been round about half-past ten or a quarter to eleven. She'd come along to see if I had an aspirin. I told her where to find it and she got it out of my grip."

"You yourself were in bed?"

"Yes."

Suddenly she laughed. "Poor soul—she was so upset! You see, she'd opened the door of the next compartment by mistake."

"Mr. Ratchett's?"

"Yes. You know how difficult it is as you come along the train and all the doors are shut. She opened his by mistake. She was very distressed about it. He'd laughed, it seemed, and I guess he said something not quite nice. Poor thing, she certainly was upset. 'Oh! I make mistake,' she said. 'I ashamed make mistake. Not nice man,' she said. 'He say, "You too old." ' "

Dr. Constantine sniggered, and Mrs. Hubbard immediately froze him with a glance.

"He wasn't a nice kind of man," she said, "to say a thing like that to a lady. It's not right to laugh at such things."

Dr. Constantine hastily apologised.

"Did you hear any noise from Mr. Ratchett's compartment after that?" asked Poirot.

"Well—not exactly."

"What do you mean by that, Madame?"

"Well—" She paused. "He snored."

"Ah!—he snored, did he?"

"Terribly. The night before, it kept me awake."

"You didn't hear him snore after you had had the scare about a man being in your compartment?"

"Why, Mr. Poirot, how could I? He was dead."

"Ah, yes, truly," said Poirot. He appeared confused.

"Do you remember the affair of the Armstrong kidnapping, Mrs. Hubbard?" he asked.

"Yes, indeed I do. And how the wretch that did it escaped scot-free! My, I'd have liked to get my hands on him."

"He has not escaped. He is dead. He died last night."

"You don't mean—?" Mrs. Hubbard half rose from her chair in excitement.

"But yes, I do. Ratchett was the man."

"*Well*! Well, to think of that! I must write and tell my daughter. Now, didn't I tell you last night that that man had an evil face? I was right, you see. My daughter always says: 'When Mamma's got a hunch you can bet your bottom dollar it's O.K.' "

"Were you acquainted with any of the Armstrong family, Mrs. Hubbard?"

"No. They moved in a very exclusive circle. But I've always heard that Mrs. Armstrong was a perfectly lovely woman and that her husband worshipped her."

"Well, Mrs. Hubbard, you have helped us very much—very much indeed. Perhaps you will give me your full name?"

"Why, certainly. Caroline Martha Hubbard."

"Will you write your address down here?"

Mrs. Hubbard did so, without ceasing to speak. "I just can't get over it. Cassetti—on this train. I had a hunch about that man, didn't I, Mr. Poirot?"

"Yes, indeed, Madame. By the way, have you a scarlet silk dressing gown?"

"Mercy, what a funny question! Why, no. I've got two dressing gowns with me—a pink flannel one that's kind of cosy for on board ship, and one my daughter gave me as a present—a kind of local affair in purple silk. But what in creation do you want to know about my dressing gowns for?"

"Well, you see, Madame, someone in a scarlet kimono entered either your or Mr. Ratchett's compartment last night. It is, as you said just now, very difficult when all the doors are shut to know which compartment is which."

"Well, no one in a scarlet dressing gown came into my compartment."

"Then she must have gone into Mr. Ratchett's."

Mrs. Hubbard pursed her lips together and said grimly: "That wouldn't surprise me any."

Poirot leaned forward. "So you heard a woman's voice next door?"

"I don't know how you guessed that, Mr. Poirot. I don't really. But—well—as a matter of fact, I *did*."

"But when I asked you just now if you heard anything next door, you only said you heard Mr. Ratchett snoring."

"Well, that was true enough. He *did* snore part of the time. As for the other—" Mrs. Hubbard got rather embarrassed. "It isn't a very nice thing to speak about."

"What time was it when you heard a woman's voice?"

"I can't tell you. I just woke up for a minute and heard a woman talking, and it was plain enough where she was. So I just thought, 'Well, *that's* the kind of man he is! I'm not surprised'—and then I went to sleep again. And I'm sure I should never have mentioned anything of the kind to three strange gentlemen if you hadn't dragged it out of me."

"Was it before the scare about the man in your compartment, or after?"

"Why, that's like what you said just now! He wouldn't have had a woman talking to him if he were dead, would he?"

"*Pardon.* You must think me very stupid, Madame."

"I guess even you get kinda muddled now and then. I just can't get over its being that monster Cassetti. What my daughter will say—"

Poirot managed adroitly to help the good lady to replace the contents of her handbag, and he then shepherded her towards the door.

At the last moment, he said:

"You have dropped your handkerchief, Madame."

Mrs. Hubbard looked at the little scrap of cambric he held out to her.

"That's not mine, Mr. Poirot. I've got mine right here."

"*Pardon.* I thought as it had the initial H on it—"

"Well, now, that's funny, but it's certainly not mine. Mine are marked C.M.H., and they're sensible things—not expensive Paris fal-lals. What good is a handkerchief like that to anybody's nose?"

None of the three men seemed to have an answer to this question and Mrs. Hubbard sailed out triumphantly.

Chapter 5

The Evidence of the Swedish Lady

M. Bouc was handling the button that Mrs. Hubbard had left behind her.

"This button. I cannot understand it. Does it mean that after all, Pierre Michel is involved in some way?" he asked. He paused, then continued, as Poirot did not reply. "What have you to say, my friend?"

"That button, it suggests possibilities," said Poirot thoughtfully. "Let us interview next the Swedish lady before we discuss the evidence that we have heard."

He sorted through the pile of passports in front of him.

"Ah! here we are. Greta Ohlsson, age forty-nine."

M. Bouc gave directions to the restaurant attendant, and presently the lady with the yellowish grey bun of hair and the long, mild, sheep-like face was ushered in. She peered short-sightedly at Poirot through her glasses, but was quite calm.

It transpired that she understood and spoke French, so the conversation took place in that language. Poirot first asked her the questions to which he already knew the answers—her name, age, and address. He then asked her her occupation.

She was, she told him, matron in a missionary school near Stamboul. She was a trained nurse.

"You know, of course, of what took place last night, Mademoiselle?"

"Naturally. It is very dreadful. And the American lady tells me that the murderer was actually in her compartment."

"I hear, Mademoiselle, that you were the last person to see the murdered man alive?"

"I do not know. It may be so. I opened the door of his compartment by mistake. I was much ashamed. It was a most awkward mistake."

"You actually saw him?"

"Yes. He was reading a book. I apologised quickly and withdrew."

"Did he say anything to you?"

A slight flush showed on the worthy lady's cheek.

"He laughed and said a few words. I—I did not quite catch them."

"And what did you do after that, Mademoiselle?" asked Poirot, passing from the subject tactfully.

"I went in to the American lady, Mrs. Hubbard. I asked her for some aspirin and she gave it to me."

"Did she ask you whether the communicating door between her compartment and that of Mr. Ratchett was bolted?"

"Yes."

"And was it?"

"Yes."

"And after that?"

"After that I went back to my own compartment, took the aspirin, and lay down."

"What time was all this?"

"When I got into bed it was five minutes to eleven. I know because I looked at my watch before I wound it up."

"Did you go to sleep quickly?"

"Not very quickly. My head got better, but I lay awake some time."

"Had the train come to a stop before you went to sleep?"

"I do not think so. We stopped, I think, at a station just as I was getting drowsy."

"That would be Vincovci. Now your compartment, Mademoiselle, is this one?" He indicated it on the plan.

"That is so, yes."

"You had the upper or the lower berth?"

"The lower berth, No. 10."

"And you had a companion?"

"Yes, a young English lady. Very nice, very amiable. She had travelled from Baghdad."

"After the train left Vincovci, did she leave the compartment?"

"No, I am sure she did not."

"Why are you sure if you were asleep?"

"I sleep very lightly. I am used to waking at a sound. I am sure that if she had come down from the berth above I should have awakened."

"Did you yourself leave the compartment?"

"Not until this morning."

"Have you a scarlet silk kimono, Mademoiselle?"

"No, indeed. I have a good comfortable dressing gown of Jaeger material."

"And the lady with you, Miss Debenham? What colour is her dressing gown?"

"A pale mauve aba such as you buy in the East."

Poirot nodded. Then he asked in a friendly tone: "Why are you taking this journey? A holiday?"

"Yes, I am going home for a holiday. But first I am going to Lausanne to stay with a sister for a week or so."

"Perhaps you will be so amiable as to write me down the name and address of your sister?"

"With pleasure."

She took the paper and pencil he gave her and wrote down the name and address as requested.

"Have you ever been in America, Mademoiselle?"

"No. I very nearly went once. I was to go with an invalid lady, but the plan was cancelled at the last moment. I much regretted this. They are very good, the Americans. They give much money to found schools and hospitals. And they are very practical."

"Do you remember hearing of the Armstrong kidnapping case?"

"No, what was that?"

Poirot explained.

Greta Ohlsson was indignant. Her yellow bun of hair quivered with her emotion.

"That there are in the world such evil men! It tries one's faith. The poor mother—my heart aches for her."

The amiable Swede departed, her kindly face flushed, her eyes suffused with tears.

Poirot was writing busily on a sheet of paper.

"What is it you write there, my friend?" asked M. Bouc.

"*Mon cher*, it is my habit to be neat and orderly. I make here a little chronological table of events."

He finished writing and passed the paper to M. Bouc.

9.15   Train leaves Belgrade.

about 9.40   Valet leaves Ratchett with sleeping draught beside him.

about 10.00   MacQueen leaves Ratchett.

about 10.40   Greta Ohlsson sees Ratchett (last seen alive). N.B. He was awake reading a book.

0.10   Train leaves Vincovci (late).

0.30   Train runs into a snowdrift.

0.37   Ratchett's bell rings. Conductor answers it. Ratchett says: *"Ce n'est rien.*
   Je me suis trompé."
about 1.17   Mrs. Hubbard thinks man is in her carriage. Rings for conductor.

M. Bouc nodded approval.

"That is very clear," he said.

"There is nothing there that strikes you as at all odd?"

"No, it seems all quite clear and aboveboard. It seems quite plain that the crime was committed at 1.15. The evidence of the watch shows us that, and Mrs. Hubbard's story fits in. For my mind, I will make a guess at the identity of the murderer. I say, my friend, that it is the big Italian. He comes from America—from Chicago—and remember an Italian's weapon is the knife, and he stabs not once but several times."

"That is true."

"Without a doubt, that is the solution of the mystery. Doubtless he and this Ratchett were in this kidnapping business together. Cassetti is an Italian name. In some way Ratchett did on him what they call the double-cross. The Italian tracks him down, sends him warning letters first, and finally revenges himself upon him in a brutal way. It was all quite simple."

Poirot shook his head doubtfully.

"It is hardly so simple as that, I fear," he murmured.

"Me, I am convinced it is the truth," said M. Bouc, becoming more and more enamoured of his theory.

"And what about the valet with the toothache who swears that the Italian never left the compartment?"

"That is the difficulty."

Poirot twinkled.

"Yes, it is annoying, that. Unlucky for your theory, and extremely lucky for our Italian friend that M. Ratchett's valet should have had the toothache."

"It will be explained," said M. Bouc with magnificent certainty.

Poirot shook his head again.

"No, it is hardly so simple as that," he murmured again.

Chapter 6

The Evidence of the Russian Princess

"Let us hear what Pierre Michel has to say about this button," he said.

The Wagon Lit conductor was recalled. He looked at them inquiringly.

M. Bouc cleared his throat.

"Michel," he said, "here is a button from your tunic. It was found in the American lady's compartment. What have you to say for yourself about it?"

The conductor's hand went automatically to his tunic.

"I have lost no button, Monsieur," he said. "There must be some mistake."

"That is very odd."

"I cannot account for it, Monsieur." The man seemed astonished, but not in any way guilty or confused.

M. Bouc said meaningly: "Owing to the circumstances in which it was found, it seems fairly certain that this button was dropped by the man who was in Mrs. Hubbard's compartment last night when she rang the bell."

"But, Monsieur, there was no one there. The lady must have imagined it."

"She did not imagine it, Michel. The assassin of M. Ratchett passed that way—*and dropped that button.*"

As the significance of M. Bouc's words became plain to him, Pierre Michel flew into a violent state of agitation.

"It is not true, Monsieur; it is not true!" he cried. "You are accusing me of the crime. Me, I am innocent. I am absolutely innocent! Why should I want to kill a Monsieur whom I have never seen before?"

"Where were you when Mrs. Hubbard's bell rang?"

"I told you, Monsieur, in the next coach talking to my colleague."

"We will send for him."

"Do so, Monsieur, I implore you, do so."

The conductor of the next coach was summoned. He immediately confirmed Pierre Michel's statement. He added that the conductor from the Bucharest coach had also been there. The three of them had been discussing the situation caused by the snow. They had been talking some ten minutes when Michel fancied he heard a bell. As he opened the doors connecting the two coaches, they had all heard it plainly—a bell ringing repeatedly. Michel had run post-haste to answer it.

"So you see, Monsieur, I am not guilty," cried Michel anxiously.

"And this button from a Wagon Lit tunic, how do you explain it?"

"I cannot, Monsieur. It is a mystery to me. All my buttons are intact."

Both of the other conductors also declared that they had not lost a button; also that they had not been inside Mrs. Hubbard's compartment at any time.

"Calm yourself, Michel," said M. Bouc, "and cast your mind back to the moment when you ran to answer Mrs. Hubbard's bell. Did you meet anyone at all in the corridor?"

"No, Monsieur."

"Did you see anyone going away from you down the corridor in the other direction?"

"Again, no, Monsieur."

"Odd," said M. Bouc.

"Not so very," said Poirot. "It is a question of time. Mrs. Hubbard wakes to find someone in her compartment. For a minute or two she lies paralysed, her eyes shut. Probably it was then that the man slipped out into the corridor. Then she starts ringing the bell. But the conductor does not come at once. It is only the third or fourth peal that he hears. I should say myself that there was ample time—"

"For what? For what, *mon cher*? Remember, there are thick drifts of snow all round the train."

"There are two courses open to our mysterious assassin," said Poirot slowly. "He could retreat into either of the toilets or—he could disappear into one of the compartments."

"But they were all occupied."

"Yes."

"You mean that he could retreat into his own compartment?"

Poirot nodded.

"It fits—it fits," murmured M. Bouc. "During that ten minutes' absence of the conductor, the murderer comes from his own compartment, goes into Ratchett's, kills him, locks and chains the door on the inside, goes out through Mrs. Hubbard's compartment, and is back safely in his own compartment by the time the conductor arrives."

Poirot murmured: "It is not quite so simple as that, my friend. Our friend the doctor here will tell you so."

With a gesture M. Bouc signified that the three conductors might depart.

"We have still to see eight passengers," said Poirot. "Five first-class passengers—Princess Dragomiroff, Count and Countess Andrenyi, Colonel Arbuthnot, and Mr. Hardman. Three second-class passengers—Miss Debenham, Antonio Foscarelli, and the lady's-maid, Fräulein Schmidt."

"Whom will you see first—the Italian?"

"How you harp on your Italian! No, we will start at the top of the tree. Perhaps Madame la Princesse will be so good as to spare us a few moments of her time. Convey that message to her, Michel."

"*Oui, Monsieur,*" said the conductor, who was just leaving the car.

"Tell her we can wait on her in her compartment if she does not wish to put herself to the trouble of coming here," called M. Bouc.

But Princess Dragomiroff declined to take this course. She appeared in the dining-car, inclined her head slightly and sat down opposite Poirot.

Her small toad-like face looked even yellower than the day before. She was certainly ugly, and yet, like the toad, she had eyes like jewels, dark and imperious, revealing latent energy and an intellectual force that could be felt at once.

Her voice was deep, very distinct, with a slight grating quality in it.

She cut short a flowery phrase of apology from M. Bouc.

"You need not offer apologies, Messieurs. I understand a murder has taken place. Naturally you must interview all the passengers. I shall be glad to give you all the assistance in my power."

"You are most amiable, Madame," said Poirot.

"Not at all. It is a duty. What do you wish to know?"

"Your full Christian names and address, Madame. Perhaps you would prefer to write them yourself?"

Poirot proffered a sheet of paper and pencil, but the Princess waved them aside.

"You can write it," she said. "There is nothing difficult. Natalia Dragomiroff, 17 Avenue Kléber, Paris."

"You are travelling home from Constantinople, Madame?"

"Yes. I have been staying at the Austrian Embassy. My maid is with me."

"Would you be so good as to give me a brief account of your movements last night from dinner onwards?"

"Willingly. I directed the conductor to make up my bed whilst I was in the dining-car. I retired to bed immediately after dinner. I read until the hour of eleven, when I turned out my light. I was unable to sleep owing to certain rheumatic pains from which I suffer. At about a quarter to one I rang for my maid. She massaged me and then read aloud till I felt sleepy. I cannot say exactly when she left me. It may have been half an hour afterward, it may have been later."

"The train had stopped then?"

"The train had stopped."

"You heard nothing—nothing unusual during the time, Madame?"

"I heard nothing unusual."

"What is your maid's name?"

"Hildegarde Schmidt."

"She has been with you long?"

"Fifteen years."

"You consider her trustworthy?"

"Absolutely. Her people come from an estate of my late husband's in Germany."

"You have been in America, I presume, Madame?"

The abrupt change of subject made the old lady raise her eyebrows. "Many times."

"Were you at any time acquainted with a family of the name of Armstrong—a family in which a tragedy occurred?"

With some emotion in her voice the old lady said: "You speak of friends of mine, Monsieur."

"You knew Colonel Armstrong well, then?"

"I knew him slightly, but his wife, Sonia Armstrong, was my goddaughter. I was on terms of friendship with her mother, the actress Linda Arden. Linda Arden was a great genius, one of the greatest tragic actresses in the world. As Lady Macbeth, as Magda, there was no one to touch her. I was not only an admirer of her art, I was a personal friend."

"She is dead?"

"No, no, she is alive, but she lives in complete retirement. Her health is very delicate, and she has to lie on a sofa most of the time."

"There was, I think, a second daughter?"

"Yes, much younger than Mrs. Armstrong."

"And she is alive?"

"Certainly."

"Where is she?"

The old woman bent an acute glance at him.

"I must ask you the reason for these questions. What have they to do with the matter in hand—the murder on this train?"

"They are connected in this way, Madame: the man who was murdered was the man responsible for the kidnapping and murder of Mrs. Armstrong's child."

"Ah!"

The straight brows came together. Princess Dragomiroff drew herself a little more erect.

"In my view, then, this murder is an entirely admirable happening! You will pardon my slightly biased point of view."

"It is most natural, Madame. And now to return to the question you did not answer. Where is the younger daughter of Linda Arden, the sister of Mrs. Armstrong?"

"I honestly cannot tell you, Monsieur. I have lost touch with the younger generation. I believe she married an Englishman some years ago and went to England, but at the moment I cannot recollect the name."

She paused a minute and then said:

"Is there anything further you want to ask me, gentlemen?"

"Only one thing, Madame, a somewhat personal question. The colour of your dressing gown."

She raised her eyebrows slightly. "I must suppose you have a reason for such a question. My dressing gown is of black satin."

"There is nothing more, Madame. I am much obliged to you for answering my questions so promptly."

She made a slight gesture with her heavily beringed hand. Then as she rose, and the others rose with her, she stopped.

"You will excuse me, Monsieur," she said, "but may I ask your name? Your face is somehow familiar to me."

"My name, Madame, is Hercule Poirot—at your service."

She was silent a minute, then: "Hercule Poirot," she said. "Yes. I remember now. This is Destiny."

She walked away, very erect, a little stiff in her movements.

"Voilà une grande dame," said M. Bouc. "What do you think of her, my friend?"

But Hercule Poirot merely shook his head.

"I am wondering," he said, "what she meant by Destiny."

Chapter 7

The Evidence of Count and Countess Andrenyi

Count and Countess Andrenyi were next summoned. The Count, however, entered the dining-car alone.

There was no doubt that he was a fine-looking man seen face-to-face. He was at least six feet in height, with broad shoulders and slender hips. He was dressed in very well-cut English tweeds and might have been taken for an Englishman had it not been for the length of his moustache and something in the line of the cheekbone.

"Well, Messieurs," he said, "what can I do for you?"

"You understand, Monsieur," said Poirot, "that in view of what has occurred I am obliged to put certain questions to all the passengers."

"Perfectly, perfectly," said the Count easily. "I quite understand your position. Not, I fear, that my wife and I can do much to assist you. We were asleep and heard nothing at all."

"Are you aware of the identity of the deceased, Monsieur?"

"I understood it was the big American—a man with a decidedly unpleasant face. He sat at that table at meal times." He indicated with a nod of his head the table at which Ratchett and MacQueen had sat.

"Yes, yes, Monsieur, you are perfectly correct. I meant—did you know the name of the man?"

"No." The Count looked thoroughly puzzled by Poirot's queries.

"If you want to know his name," he said, "surely it is on his passport?"

"The name on his passport is Ratchett," said Poirot. "But that, Monsieur, is not his real name. He is the man Cassetti, who was responsible for a celebrated kidnapping outrage in America."

He watched the Count closely as he spoke, but the latter seemed quite unaffected by this piece of news. He merely opened his eyes a little.

"Ah!" he said. "That certainly should throw light upon the matter. An extraordinary country, America."

"You have been there, perhaps, Monsieur le Comte?"

"I was in Washington for a year."

"You knew, perhaps, the Armstrong family?"

"Armstrong—Armstrong—it is difficult to recall. One met so many." He smiled, shrugged his shoulders. "But to come back to the matter in hand, gentlemen," he said. "What more can I do to assist you?"

"You retired to rest—when, Monsieur le Comte?"

Hercule Poirot's eyes stole to his plan. Count and Countess Andrenyi occupied compartment Nos. 12 and 13 adjoining.

"We had one compartment made up for the night whilst we were in the dining-car. On returning we sat in the other for a while—"

"Which number would that be?"

"No. 13. We played piquet together. At about eleven o'clock my wife retired for the night. The conductor made up my compartment and I also went to bed. I slept soundly until morning."

"Did you notice the stopping of the train?"

"I was not aware of it till this morning."

"And your wife?"

The Count smiled. "My wife always takes a sleeping draught when travelling by train. She took her usual dose of trional."

He paused. "I am sorry I am not able to assist you in any way."

Poirot passed him a sheet of paper and a pen.

"Thank you, Monsieur le Comte. It is a formality, but will you just let me have your name and address?"

The Count wrote slowly and carefully.

"It is just as well that I should write this for you," he said pleasantly. "The spelling of my country estate is a little difficult for those unacquainted with the language."

He passed the paper across to Poirot and rose.

"It will be quite unnecessary for my wife to come here," he said. "She can tell you nothing more than I have."

A little gleam came into Poirot's eye.

"Doubtless, doubtless," he said. "But all the same I think I should like to have just one little word with Madame la Comtesse."

"I assure you it is quite unnecessary." The Count's voice rang out authoritatively.

Poirot blinked gently at him.

"It will be a mere formality," he said. "But, you understand, it is necessary for my report."

"As you please."

The Count gave way grudgingly. He made a short foreign bow and left the dining-car.

Poirot reached out a hand to a passport. It set out the Count's names and titles. He passed on to the further information. "*Accompanied by*, wife; *Christian name*, Elena Maria; *maiden name*, Goldenberg; *age*, twenty." A spot of grease had been dropped on it at some time by a careless official.

"A diplomatic passport," said M. Bouc. "We must be careful, my friend, to give no offence. These people can have nothing to do with the murder."

"Be easy, *mon vieux*, I will be most tactful. A mere formality."

His voice dropped as the Countess Andrenyi entered the dining-car. She looked timid and extremely charming.

"You wish to see me, Messieurs?"

"A mere formality, Madame la Comtesse." Poirot rose gallantly, bowed her into the seat opposite him. "It is only to ask you if you saw or heard anything last night that may throw light upon this matter."

"Nothing at all, Monsieur. I was asleep."

"You did not hear, for instance, a commotion going on in the compartment next to yours? The American lady who occupies it had quite an attack of hysterics and rang for the conductor."

"I heard nothing, Monsieur. You see, I had taken a sleeping draught."

"Ah! I comprehend. Well, I need not detain you further." Then, as she rose swiftly—"Just one little minute. These particulars—your maiden name, age and so on—they are correct?"

"Quite correct, Monsieur."

"Perhaps you will sign this memorandum to that effect, then."

She signed quickly, in a graceful slanting handwriting—*Elena Andrenyi*.

"Did you accompany your husband to America, Madame?"

"No, Monsieur." She smiled, flushed a little. "We were not married then; we have been married only a year."

"Ah, yes, thank you, Madame. By the way, does your husband smoke?"

She stared at him as she stood poised for departure.

"Yes."

"A pipe?"

"No. Cigarettes and cigars."

"Ah! Thank you."

She lingered, her eyes watching him curiously. Lovely eyes they were, dark and almond—shaped with very long black lashes that swept the exquisite pallor of her cheeks. Her lips, very scarlet in the foreign fashion, were parted just a little. She looked exotic and beautiful.

"Why did you ask me that?"

"Madame," Poirot waved an airy hand, "detectives have to ask all sorts of questions. For instance, perhaps you will tell me the colour of your dressing gown?"

She stared at him. Then she laughed. "It is corn-coloured chiffon. Is that really important?"

"Very important, Madame."

She asked curiously: "Are you really a detective, then?"

"At your service, Madame."

"I thought there were no detectives on the train when it passed through Jugo-Slavia—not until one got to Italy."

"I am not a Jugo-Slavian detective, Madame. I am an international detective."

"You belong to the League of Nations?"

"I belong to the world, Madame," said Poirot dramatically. He went on: "I work mainly in London. You speak English?" he added in that language.

"I speak a leetle, yes." Her accent was charming. Poirot bowed once more.

"We will not detain you further, Madame. You see, it was not so very terrible."

She smiled, inclined her head and departed.

"Elle est jolie femme," said M. Bouc appreciatively. He sighed. "Well, that did not advance us much."

"No," said Poirot. "Two people who saw nothing and heard nothing."

"Shall we now see the Italian?"

Poirot did not reply for a moment. He was studying a grease spot on a Hungarian diplomatic passport.

Chapter 8

The Evidence of Colonel Arbuthnot

Poirot roused himself with a slight start. His eyes twinkled a little as they met the eager ones of M. Bouc.

"Ah! my dear old friend," he said, "you see I have become what they call the snob! The first class, I feel it should be attended to before the second class. Next, I think, we will interview the good-looking Colonel Arbuthnot."

Finding the Colonel's French to be of a severely limited description, Poirot conducted his interrogatory in English.

Arbuthnot's name, age, home address and exact military standing were all ascertained. Poirot proceeded:

"It is that you come home from India on what is called the leave—what we can call *en permission*?"

Colonel Arbuthnot, uninterested in what a pack of foreigners called anything, replied with true British brevity, "Yes."

"But you do not come home on the P. & O. boat?"

"No."

"Why not?"

"I chose to come by the overland route for reasons of my own."

("And that," his manner seemed to say, "is one for you, you interfering little jackanapes.")

"You came straight through from India?"

The Colonel replied drily: "I stopped for one night to see Ur of the Chaldees, and for three days in Baghdad with the A.O.C., who happens to be an old friend of mine."

"You stopped three days in Baghdad. I understand that the young English lady, Miss Debenham, also comes from Baghdad. Perhaps you met her there?"

"No, I did not. I first met Miss Debenham when she and I shared the railway convoy car from Kirkuk to Nissibin."

Poirot leaned forward. He became persuasive and a little more foreign than he need have been.

"Monsieur, I am about to appeal to you. You and Miss Debenham are the only two English people on the train. It is necessary that I should ask you each your opinion of the other."

"Highly irregular," said Colonel Arbuthnot coldly.

"Not so. You see, this crime, it was most probably committed by a woman. The man was stabbed no fewer than twelve times. Even the *chef de train* said at once, 'It is a woman.' Well, then, what is my first task? To give all the women travelling on the Istanbul-Calais coach what Americans call the 'once-over.' But to judge an Englishwoman is difficult. They are very reserved, the English. So I appeal to you, Monsieur, in the interest of justice. What sort of person is this Miss Debenham? What do you know about her?"

"Miss Debenham," said the Colonel with some warmth, "is a lady."

"Ah!" said Poirot with every appearance of being much gratified. "So you do not think that she is likely to be implicated in this crime?"

"The idea is absurd," said Arbuthnot. "The man was a perfect stranger — she had never seen him before."

"Did she tell you so?"

"She did. She commented at once upon his somewhat unpleasant appearance. If a woman *is* concerned, as you seem to think (to my mind without any evidence but on a mere assumption), I can assure you that Miss Debenham could not possibly be implicated."

"You feel warmly in the matter," said Poirot with a smile.

Colonel Arbuthnot gave him a cold stare. "I really don't know what you mean," he said.

The stare seemed to abash Poirot. He dropped his eyes and began fiddling with the papers in front of him.

"All this is by the way," he said. "Let us be practical and come to facts. This crime, we have reason to believe, took place at a quarter past one last night. It is part of the necessary routine to ask everyone on the train what he or she was doing at that time."

"Quite so. At a quarter past one, to the best of my belief, I was talking to the young American fellow — secretary to the dead man."

"Ah! were you in his compartment, or was he in yours?"

"I was in his."

"That is the young man of the name of MacQueen?"

"Yes."

"He was a friend or acquaintance of yours?"

"No, I never saw him before this journey. We fell into casual conversation yesterday and both became interested. I don't as a rule like Americans—haven't any use for 'em—"

Poirot smiled, remembering MacQueen's strictures on "Britishers."

"—but I liked this young fellow. He'd got hold of some tomfool idiotic ideas about the situation in India. That's the worst of Americans—they're so sentimental and idealistic. Well, he was interested in what I had to tell him. I've had nearly thirty years' experience of the country. And I was interested in what he had to tell me about the working of Prohibition in America. Then we got down to world politics in general. I was quite surprised to look at my watch and find it was a quarter to two."

"That is the time you broke up this conversation?"

"Yes."

"What did you do then?"

"Walked along to my own compartment and turned in."

"Your bed was made up ready?"

"Yes."

"That is the compartment—let me see—No. 15—the one next but one to the end away from the dining-car?"

"Yes."

"Where was the conductor when you went to your compartment?"

"Sitting at the end at a little table. As a matter of fact MacQueen called him just as I went in to my own compartment."

"Why did he call him?"

"To make up his bed, I suppose. The compartment hadn't been made up for the night."

"Now, Colonel Arbuthnot, I want you to think carefully. During the time you were talking to Mr. MacQueen, did anyone pass along the corridor outside the door?"

"A good many people, I should think. I wasn't paying attention."

"Ah! but I am referring to—let us say, the last hour and a half of your conversation. You got out at Vincovci, didn't you?"

"Yes, but only for about a minute. There was a blizzard on. The cold was something frightful. Made one quite thankful to get back to the fug, though as a rule I think the way these trains are overheated is something scandalous."

M. Bouc sighed. "It is very difficult to please everybody," he said. "The English they open everything—then others they come along and shut everything. It is very difficult."

Neither Poirot nor Colonel Arbuthnot paid any attention to him.

"Now, Monsieur, cast your mind back," said Poirot encouragingly. "It was cold outside. You have returned to the train. You sit down again, you smoke—perhaps a cigarette—perhaps a pipe—"

He paused for the fraction of a second.

"A pipe for me. MacQueen smoked cigarettes."

"The train starts again. You smoke your pipe. You discuss the state of Europe—of the world. It is late now. Most people have retired for the night. Does anyone pass the door? Think."

Arbuthnot frowned in the effort of remembrance.

"Difficult to say," he said. "You see I wasn't paying any attention."

"But you have the soldier's observation for detail. You notice without noticing, so to speak."

The Colonel thought again, but shook his head.

"I couldn't say. I don't remember anyone passing except the conductor. Wait a minute—and there was a woman, I think."

"You saw her? Was she old—young?"

"Didn't see her. Wasn't looking that way. Just a rustle and a sort of smell of scent."

"Scent? A *good* scent?"

"Well, rather fruity, if you know what I mean. I mean you'd smell it a hundred yards away. But mind you," the Colonel went on hastily, "this may have been earlier in the evening. You see, as you said just now, it was just one of those things you notice without noticing, so to speak. Some time that evening I said to myself—'Woman—scent—got it on pretty thick.' But *when* it was I can't be sure, except that—why, yes, it must have been after Vincovci."

"Why?"

"Because I remember—sniffing, you know—just when I was talking about the utter washout Stalin's Five Year Plan was turning out. I know the idea *woman* brought the idea of the position of women in Russia into my mind. And I know we hadn't got on to Russia until pretty near the end of our talk."

"You can't pin it down more definitely than that?"

"N-no. It must have been roughly within the last half-hour."

"It was after the train had stopped?"

The other nodded. "Yes, I'm almost sure it was."

"Well, we will pass from that. Have you ever been in America, Colonel Arbuthnot?"

"Never. Don't want to go."

"Did you ever know a Colonel Armstrong?"

"Armstrong—Armstrong—I've known two or three Armstrongs.

There was Tommy Armstrong in the 60th—you don't mean him? And Selby Armstrong—he was killed on the Somme."

"I mean the Colonel Armstrong who married an American wife and whose only child was kidnapped and killed."

"Ah, yes, I remember reading about that—shocking affair. I don't think I actually ever came across the fellow, though of course I knew of him. Toby Armstrong. Nice fellow. Everybody liked him. He had a very distinguished career. Got the V.C."

"The man who was killed last night was the man responsible for the murder of Colonel Armstrong's child."

Arbuthnot's face grew rather grim. "Then in my opinion the swine deserved what he got. Though I would have preferred to see him properly hanged—or electrocuted, I suppose, over there."

"In fact, Colonel Arbuthnot, you prefer law and order to private vengeance?"

"Well, you can't go about having blood feuds and stabbing each other like Corsicans or the Mafia," said the Colonel. "Say what you like, trial by jury is a sound system."

Poirot looked at him thoughtfully for a minute or two.

"Yes," he said. "I am sure that would be your view. Well, Colonel Arbuthnot, I do not think there is anything more I have to ask you. There is nothing you yourself can recall last night that in any way struck you—or shall we say strikes you now, looking back—as suspicious?"

Arbuthnot considered for a moment or two.

"No," he said. "Nothing at all. Unless—" he hesitated.

"But yes, continue, I pray of you."

"Well, it's nothing really," said the Colonel slowly. "But you said *any-thing*."

"Yes, yes. Go on."

"Oh! it's nothing. A mere detail. But as I got back to my compartment I noticed that the door of the one beyond mine—the end one, you know—"

"Yes, No. 16."

"Well, the door of it was not quite closed. And the fellow inside peered out in a furtive sort of way. Then he pulled the door to quickly. Of course I know there's nothing in that—but it just struck me as a bit odd. I mean, it's quite usual to open a door and stick your head out if you want to see anything. But it was the furtive way he did it that caught my attention."

"Ye-es," said Poirot doubtfully.

"I told you there was nothing to it," said Arbuthnot, apologetically. "But you know what it is—early hours of the morning—everything very still. The thing had a sinister look—like a detective story. All nonsense really."

He rose. "Well, if you don't want me any more—"

"Thank you, Colonel Arbuthnot, there is nothing else."

The soldier hesitated for a minute. His first natural distaste for being questioned by "foreigners" had evaporated.

"About Miss Debenham," he said rather awkwardly. "You can take it from me that she's all right. She's a *pukka sahib*."

Flushing a little, he withdrew.

"What," asked Dr. Constantine with interest, "does a *pukka sahib* mean?"

"It means," said Poirot, "that Miss Debenham's father and brothers were at the same kind of school as Colonel Arbuthnot was."

"Oh!" said Dr. Constantine, disappointed. "Then it has nothing to do with the crime at all."

"Exactly," said Poirot.

He fell into a reverie, beating a light tattoo on the table. Then he looked up.

"Colonel Arbuthnot smokes a pipe," he said. "In the compartment of Mr. Ratchett I found a pipe-cleaner. Mr. Ratchett smoked only cigars."

"You think—?"

"He is the only man so far who admits to smoking a pipe. And he knew of Colonel Armstrong—perhaps actually did know him, though he won't admit it."

"So you think it possible—?"

Poirot shook his head violently.

"That is just it—it is *im*possible—quite impossible—that an honourable, slightly stupid, upright Englishman should stab an enemy twelve times with a knife! Do you not feel, my friends, how impossible it is?"

"That is the psychology," said M. Bouc.

"And one must respect the psychology. This crime has a signature, and it is certainly not the signature of Colonel Arbuthnot. But now to our next interview."

This time M. Bouc did not mention the Italian. But he thought of him.

Chapter 9

The Evidence of Mr. Hardman

The last of the first-class passengers to be interviewed, Mr. Hardman, was the big flamboyant American who had shared a table with the Italian and the valet.

He wore a somewhat loud check suit, a pink shirt, and a flashy tie-pin, and was rolling something round his tongue as he entered the dining-car. He had a big, fleshy, coarse-featured face, with a good-humoured expression.

"Morning, gentlemen," he said. "What can I do for you?"

"You have heard of this murder, Mr.—er—Hardman?"

"Sure." He shifted the chewing gum deftly.

"We are of necessity interviewing all the passengers on the train."

"That's all right by me. Guess that's the only way to tackle the job."

Poirot consulted the passport lying in front of him.

"You are Cyrus Bethman Hardman, United States subject, forty-one years of age, travelling salesman for typewriting ribbons?"

"O.K. That's me."

"You are travelling from Stamboul to Paris?"

"That's so."

"Reason?"

"Business."

"Do you always travel first-class, Mr. Hardman?"

"Yes, sir. The firm pays my travelling expenses." He winked.

"Now, Mr. Hardman, we come to the events of last night."

The American nodded.

"What can you tell us about the matter?"

"Exactly nothing at all."

"Ah, that is a pity. Perhaps, Mr. Hardman, you will tell us exactly what you did last night from dinner onwards?"

For the first time the American did not seem ready with his reply. At last he said: "Excuse me, gentlemen, but just who are you? Put me wise."

"This is M. Bouc, a director of the Compagnie des Wagons Lits. This gentleman is the doctor who examined the body."

"And you yourself?"

"I am Hercule Poirot. I am engaged by the company to investigate this matter."

"I've heard of you," said Mr. Hardman. He reflected a minute or two longer. "Guess I'd better come clean."

"It will certainly be advisable for you to tell us all you know," said Poirot drily.

"You'd have said a mouthful if there was anything I *did* know. But I don't. I know nothing at all—just as I said. But I *ought* to know something. That's what makes me sore. I *ought* to."

"Please explain, Mr. Hardman."

Mr. Hardman sighed, removed the chewing gum, and dived into a pocket. At the same time his whole personality seemed to undergo a change. He became less of a stage character and more of a real person. The resonant nasal tones of his voice became modified.

"That passport's a bit of bluff," he said. "That's who I really am."

Poirot scrutinised the card flipped across to him. M. Bouc peered over his shoulder.

MR. CYRUS B. HARDMAN
MCNEIL'S DETECTIVE AGENCY
NEW YORK CITY

Poirot knew the name as that of one of the best-known and most reputable private detective agencies in New York.

"Now, Mr. Hardman," he said, "let us hear the meaning of this."

"Sure. Things came about this way. I'd come over to Europe trailing a couple of crooks—nothing to do with this business. The chase ended in Stamboul. I wired the Chief and got his instructions to return, and I would have been making my tracks back to little old New York when I got this."

He pushed across a letter.

THE TOKATLIAN HOTEL

Dear Sir: You have been pointed out to me as an operative of the McNeil Detective Agency. Kindly report at my suite at four o'clock this afternoon. S. E. Ratchett

"Eh bien?"

"I reported at the time stated, and Mr. Ratchett put me wise to the situation. He showed me a couple of letters he'd got."

"He was alarmed?"

"Pretended not to be, but he was rattled, all right. He put up a proposition to me. I was to travel by the same train as he did to Parrus and see that nobody got him. Well, gentlemen, I *did* travel by the same train, and in spite of me, somebody *did* get him. I certainly feel sore about it. It doesn't look any too good for me."

"Did he give you any indication of the line you were to take?"

"Sure. He had it all taped out. It was his idea that I should travel in the compartment alongside his. Well, that blew up right at the start. The only place I could get was berth No. 16, and I had a job getting that. I guess the conductor likes to keep that compartment up his sleeve. But that's neither here nor there. When I looked all round the situation, it seemed to me that No. 16 was a pretty good strategic position. There was only the dining-car in front of the Stamboul sleeping-car, and the door onto the platform at the front end was barred at night. The only way a thug could come was through the rear-end door to the platform, or along the train from the rear, and in either case he'd have to pass right by my compartment."

"You had no idea, I suppose, of the identity of the possible assailant?"

"Well, I knew what he looked like. Mr. Ratchett described him to me."

"What?"

All three men leaned forward eagerly.

Hardman went on.

"A small man—dark—with a womanish kind of voice. That's what the old man said. Said, too, that he didn't think it would be the first night out. More likely the second or third."

"He knew something," said M. Bouc.

"He certainly knew more than he told his secretary," commented Poirot thoughtfully. "Did he tell you anything about this enemy of his? Did he, for instance, say *why* his life was threatened?"

"No, he was kinda reticent about that part of it. Just said the fellow was out for his blood and meant to get it."

"A small man—dark—with a womanish voice," repeated Poirot thoughtfully. Then, fixing a sharp glance on Hardman, he asked: "You knew who he really was, of course?"

"Which, Mister?"

"Ratchett. You recognised him?"

"I don't get you."

"Ratchett was Cassetti, the Armstrong murderer."

Mr. Hardman gave vent to a prolonged whistle.

"That certainly is some surprise!" he said. "Yes, *sir!* No, I didn't recognise him. I was away out West when that case came on. I suppose I saw photos of him in the papers, but I wouldn't recognise my own mother when a newspaper photographer got through with her. Well, I don't doubt that a few people had it in for Cassetti all right."

"Do you know of anyone connected with the Armstrong case who answers to that description: small—dark—womanish voice?"

Hardman reflected a minute or two. "It's hard to say. Pretty nearly everyone connected with that case is dead."

"There was the girl who threw herself out of the window, remember."

"Sure. That's a good point, that. She was a foreigner of some kind. Maybe she had some Wop relations. But you've got to remember that there were other cases besides the Armstrong one. Cassetti had been running this kidnapping stunt for some time. You can't concentrate on that only."

"Ah, but we have reason to believe that this crime is connected with the Armstrong case."

Mr. Hardman cocked an inquiring eye. Poirot did not respond. The American shook his head.

"I can't call to mind anybody answering that description in the Armstrong case," he said slowly. "But of course I wasn't in it and didn't know much about it."

"Well, continue your narrative, Mr. Hardman."

"There's very little to tell. I got my sleep in the daytime and stayed awake on the watch at night. Nothing suspicious happened the first night. Last night was the same, as far as I was concerned. I had my door a little ajar and watched. No stranger passed."

"You are sure of that, Mr. Hardman?"

"I'm plumb certain. Nobody got on that train from outside, and nobody came along the train from the rear carriages. I'll take my oath on that."

"Could you see the conductor from your position?"

"Sure. He sits on that little seat almost flush with my door."

"Did he leave that seat at all after the train stopped at Vincovci?"

"That was the last station? Why, yes, he answered a couple of bells—

that would be just after the train came to a halt for good. Then, after that, he went past me into the rear coach—was there about a quarter of an hour. There was a bell ringing like mad and he came back running. I stepped out into the corridor to see what it was all about—felt a mite nervous, you understand—but it was only the American dame. She was raising hell about something or other. I grinned. Then he went on to another compartment and came back and got a bottle of mineral water for someone. After that he settled down in his seat till he went up to the far end to make somebody's bed up. I don't think he stirred after that until about five o'clock this morning."

"Did he doze off at all?"

"That I can't say. He may have."

Poirot nodded. Automatically his hands straightened the papers on the table. He picked up the official card once more.

"Be so good as just to initial this," he said.

The other complied.

"There is no one, I suppose, who can confirm your story of your identity, Mr. Hardman?"

"On this train? Well, not exactly. Unless it might be young MacQueen. I know him well enough—I've seen him in his father's office in New York. But that's not to say he'll remember me from a crowd of other operatives. No, Mr. Poirot, you'll have to wait and cable New York when the snow lets up. But it's O.K. I'm not telling the tale. Well, so long, gentlemen. Pleased to have met you, Mr. Poirot."

Poirot proffered his cigarette case. "But perhaps you prefer a pipe?"

"Not me." He helped himself, then strode briskly off.

The three men looked at each other.

"You think he is genuine?" asked Dr. Constantine.

"Yes, yes. I know the type. Besides, it is a story that would be very easy to disprove."

"He has given us a piece of very interesting evidence," said M. Bouc.

"Yes, indeed."

"A small man—dark—with a high-pitched voice," said M. Bouc thoughtfully.

"A description which applies to no one on the train," said Poirot.

Chapter 10

The Evidence of the Italian

"And now," said Poirot with a twinkle in his eye, "we will delight the heart of M. Bouc and see the Italian."

Antonio Foscarelli came into the dining-car with a swift, cat-like tread. His face beamed. It was a typical Italian face, sunny-looking and swarthy.

He spoke French well and fluently with only a slight accent.

"Your name is Antonio Foscarelli?"

"Yes, Monsieur."

"You are, I see, a naturalised American subject?"

The American grinned. "Yes, Monsieur. It is better for my business."

"You are an agent for Ford motor cars?"

"Yes, you see—"

A voluble exposition followed. At the end of it anything that the three men did not know about Foscarelli's business methods, his journeys, his income, and his opinion of the United States and most European countries seemed a negligible factor. This was not a man who had to have information dragged from him. It gushed out.

His good-natured, childish face beamed with satisfaction as, with a last eloquent gesture, he paused and wiped his forehead with a handkerchief.

"So you see," he said. "I do big business. I am up to date. I understand salesmanship!"

"You have been in the United States, then, for the last ten years on and off."

"Yes, Monsieur. Ah! well do I remember the day I first took the boat—to go to America, so far away! My mother, my little sister—"

Poirot cut short the flood of reminiscence.

"During your sojourn in the United States, did you ever come across the deceased?"

"Never. But I know the type. Oh! yes." He snapped his fingers expressively. "It is very respectable, very well-dressed, but underneath it is all wrong. Out of my experience I should say he was the big crook. I give you my opinion for what it is worth."

"Your opinion is quite right," said Poirot drily. "Ratchett was Cassetti, the kidnapper."

"What did I tell you? I have learned to be very acute—to read the face. It is necessary. Only in America do they teach you the proper way to sell. I—"

"You remember the Armstrong case?"

"I do not quite remember. The name, yes? It was a little girl, a baby, was it not?"

"Yes, a very tragic affair."

The Italian seemed the first person to demur to this view.

"Ah! well, these things they happen," he said philosophically, "in a great civilisation such as America—"

Poirot cut him short. "Did you ever come across any members of the Armstrong family?"

"No, I do not think so. It is difficult to say. I will give you some figures. Last year alone, I sold—"

"Monsieur, pray confine yourself to the point."

The Italian's hands flung themselves out in a gesture of apology. "A thousand pardons."

"Tell me, if you please, your exact movements last night from dinner onwards."

"With pleasure. I stay here as long as I can. It is more amusing. I talk to the American gentleman at my table. He sells typewriter ribbons. Then I go back to my compartment. It is empty. The miserable John Bull who shares it with me is away attending to his master. At last he comes back—very long face as usual. He will not talk—says yes and no. A miserable race, the English—not sympathetic. He sits in the corner, very stiff, reading a book. Then the conductor comes and makes our beds."

"Nos. 4 and 5," murmured Poirot.

"Exactly—the end compartment. Mine is the upper berth. I get up there. I smoke and read. The little Englishman has, I think, the toothache. He gets out a little bottle of stuff that smells very strong. He lies in bed and groans. Presently I sleep. Whenever I wake I hear him groaning."

"Do you know if he left the carriage at all during the night?"

"I do not think so. That, I should hear. The light from the corridor—one wakes up automatically thinking it is the customs examination at some frontier."

"Did he ever speak of his master? Ever express any animus against him?"

"I tell you he did not speak. He was not sympathetic. A fish."

"You smoke, you say—a pipe, cigarettes, cigar?"

"Cigarettes only."

Poirot proffered one, which he accepted.

"Have you ever been in Chicago?" inquired M. Bouc.

"Oh! yes—a fine city—but I know best New York, Cleveland, Detroit. You have been to the States? No? You should go. It—"

Poirot pushed a sheet of paper across to him.

"If you will sign this, and put your permanent address, please."

The Italian wrote with a flourish. Then he rose, his smile as engaging as ever.

"That is all? You do not require me further? Good day to you, Messieurs. I wish we could get out of the snow. I have an appointment in Milan." He shook his head sadly. "I shall lose the business." He departed.

Poirot looked at his friend.

"He has been a long time in America," said M. Bouc, "and he is an Italian, and Italians use the knife! And they are great liars! I do not like Italians."

"*Ça se voit*," said Poirot with a smile. "Well, it may be that you are right, but I will point out to you, my friend, that there is absolutely no evidence against the man."

"And what about the psychology? Do not Italians stab?"

"Assuredly," said Poirot. "Especially in the heat of a quarrel. But this—this is a different kind of crime. I have the little idea, my friend, that this is a crime very carefully planned and staged. It is a far-sighted, long-headed crime. It is not—how shall I express it?—a *Latin* crime. It is a crime that shows traces of a cool, resourceful, deliberate brain—I think an Anglo-Saxon brain."

He picked up the last two passports.

"Let us now," he said, "see Miss Mary Debenham."

Chapter 11

The Evidence of Miss Debenham

When Mary Debenham entered the dining-car she confirmed Poirot's previous estimate of her. She was very neatly dressed in a little black suit with a French grey shirt, and the smooth waves of her dark head were neat and unruffled. Her manner was as calm and unruffled as her hair.

She sat down opposite Poirot and M. Bouc and looked at them inquiringly.

"Your name is Mary Hermione Debenham and you are twenty-six years of age?" began Poirot.

"Yes."

"English?"

"Yes."

"Will you be so kind, Mademoiselle, as to write down your permanent address on this piece of paper?"

She complied. Her writing was clear and legible.

"And now, Mademoiselle, what have you to tell us of the affair last night?"

"I am afraid I have nothing to tell you. I went to bed and slept."

"Does it distress you very much, Mademoiselle, that a crime has been committed on this train?"

The question was clearly unexpected. Her grey eyes widened a little.

"I don't quite understand you?"

"It was a perfectly simple question that I asked you, Mademoiselle. I will repeat it. Are you very much distressed that a crime should have been committed on this train?"

"I have not really thought about it from that point of view. No, I cannot say that I am at all distressed."

"A crime—it is all in the day's work to you, eh?"

"It is naturally an unpleasant thing to have happen," said Mary Debenham quietly.

"You are very Anglo-Saxon, Mademoiselle. *Vous n'éprouvez pas d'émotion.*"

She smiled a little. "I am afraid I cannot have hysterics to prove my sensibility. After all, people die every day."

"They die, yes. But murder is a little more rare."

"Oh! certainly."

"You were not acquainted with the dead man?"

"I saw him for the first time when lunching here yesterday."

"And how did he strike you?"

"I hardly noticed him."

"He did not impress you as an evil personality?"

She shrugged her shoulders slightly. "Really, I cannot say I thought about it."

Poirot looked at her keenly.

"You are, I think, a little bit contemptuous of the way I prosecute my inquiries," he said with a twinkle. "Not so, you think, would an English inquiry be conducted. There everything would be cut and dried—it would be all kept to the facts—a well-ordered business. But I, Mademoiselle, have my little originalities. I look first at my witness, I sum up his or her character, and I frame my questions accordingly. Just a little minute ago I am asking questions of a gentleman who wants to tell me all his ideas on every subject. Well, him I keep strictly to the point. I want him to answer yes or no. This or that. And then you come. I see at once that you will be orderly and methodical. You will confine yourself to the matter in hand. Your answers will be brief and to the point. And because, Mademoiselle, human nature is perverse, I ask of you quite different questions. I ask what you feel, what you think. It does not please you, this method?"

"If you will forgive my saying so, it seems somewhat of a waste of time. Whether or not I liked Mr. Ratchett's face does not seem likely to be helpful in finding out who killed him."

"Do you know who the man Ratchett really was, Mademoiselle?"

She nodded. "Mrs. Hubbard has been telling everyone."

"And what do you think of the Armstrong affair?"

"It was quite abominable," said the girl crisply.

Poirot looked at her thoughtfully.

"You are travelling from Baghdad, I believe, Miss Debenham?"

"Yes."

"To London?"

"Yes."

"What have you been doing in Baghdad?"

"I have been acting as governess to two children."

"Are you returning to your post after your holiday?"

"I am not sure."

"Why is that?"

"Baghdad is rather out of things. I think I should prefer a post in London if I can hear of a suitable one."

"I see. I thought, perhaps, you might be going to be married."

Miss Debenham did not reply. She raised her eyes and looked Poirot full in the face. The glance said plainly: "You are impertinent."

"What is your opinion of the lady who shares your compartment— Miss Ohlsson?"

"She seems a pleasant, simple creature."

"What colour is her dressing gown?"

Mary Debenham stared. "A kind of brownish colour—natural wool."

"Ah! I may mention without indiscretion, I hope, that I noticed the colour of your dressing gown on the way from Aleppo to Stamboul. A pale mauve, I believe."

"Yes, that is right."

"Have you any other dressing gown, Mademoiselle? A scarlet dressing gown, for example?"

"No, that is not mine."

Poirot leant forward. He was like a cat pouncing on a mouse.

"Whose, then?"

The girl drew back a little, startled. "I don't know. What do you mean?"

"You do not say, 'No, I have no such thing.' You say, 'That is not mine.' Meaning that such a thing *does* belong to someone else."

She nodded.

"Somebody else on this train?"

"Yes."

"Whose is it?"

"I told you just now: I don't know. I woke up this morning about five o'clock with the feeling that the train had been standing still for a long time. I opened the door and looked out into the corridor, thinking we might be at a station. I saw someone in a scarlet kimono some way down the corridor."

"And you don't know who it was? Was she fair, or dark, or grey-haired?"

"I can't say. She had on a shingle cap and I only saw the back of her head."

"And in build?"

"Tallish and slim, I should judge, but it's difficult to say. The kimono was embroidered with dragons."

"Yes, yes, that is right—dragons." He was silent a minute. He murmured to himself: "I cannot understand. I cannot understand. None of this makes sense."

Then, looking up, he said: "I need not keep you further, Mademoiselle."

"Oh!" She seemed rather taken aback but rose promptly.

In the doorway, however, she hesitated a minute and then came back.

"The Swedish lady—Miss Ohlsson, is it?—seems rather worried. She says you told her she was the last person to see this man alive. She thinks, I believe, that you suspect her on that account. Can't I tell her that she has made a mistake? Really, you know, she is the kind of creature who wouldn't hurt a fly." She smiled a little as she spoke.

"What time was it that she went to fetch the aspirin from Mrs. Hubbard?"

"Just after half-past ten."

"She was away—how long?"

"About five minutes."

"Did she leave the compartment again during the night?"

"No."

Poirot turned to the doctor. "Could Ratchett have been killed as early as that?"

The doctor shook his head.

"Then I think you can reassure your friend, Mademoiselle."

"Thank you." She smiled suddenly at him, a smile that invited sympathy. "She's like a sheep, you know. She gets anxious and bleats."

She turned and went out.

Chapter 12

The Evidence of the German Lady's-maid

M. Bouc was looking at his friend curiously.

"I do not quite understand you, *mon vieux*. You were trying to do—what?"

"I was searching for a flaw, my friend."

"A flaw?"

"Yes—in the armour of a young lady's self-possession. I wished to shake her *sang-froid*. Did I succeed? I do not know. But I know this: she did not expect me to tackle the matter as I did."

"You suspect her," said M. Bouc slowly. "But why? She seems a very charming young lady—the last person in the world to be mixed up in a crime of this kind."

"I agree," said Constantine. "She is cold. She has not emotions. She would not stab a man—she would sue him in the law courts."

Poirot sighed.

"You must, both of you, get rid of your obsession that this is an unpremeditated and sudden crime. As for the reasons why I suspect Miss Debenham, there are two. One is because of something that I overheard, and that you do not as yet know."

He retailed to them the curious interchange of phrases he had overheard on the journey from Aleppo.

"That is curious, certainly," said M. Bouc when he had finished. "It needs explaining. If it means what you suspect it means, then they are both of them in it together—she and the stiff Englishman."

Poirot nodded.

"And that is just what is not borne out by the facts," he said. "See you, if they were both in this together, what should we expect to find? That each of them would provide an alibi for the other. Is not that so? But no—that does not happen. Miss Debenham's alibi is provided by a Swedish woman whom she has never seen before, and Colonel Arbuthnot's alibi is vouched for by MacQueen, the dead man's secretary. No, that solution of the puzzle is too easy."

"You said there was another reason for your suspicions of her," M. Bouc reminded him.

Poirot smiled.

"Ah! but that is only psychological. I ask myself, is it possible for Miss Debenham to have planned this crime? Behind this business, I am convinced, there is a cool, intelligent, resourceful brain. Miss Debenham answers to that description."

M. Bouc shook his head. "I think you are wrong, my friend. I do not see that young English girl as a criminal."

"Ah! Well," said Poirot, picking up the last passport. "To the final name on our list. Hildegarde Schmidt, lady's-maid."

Summoned by the attendant, Hildegarde Schmidt came into the restaurant car and stood waiting respectfully.

Poirot motioned her to sit down.

She did so, folding her hands and waiting placidly till he questioned her. She seemed a placid creature altogether—eminently respectable, perhaps not overintelligent.

Poirot's methods with Hildegarde Schmidt were a complete contrast to his handling of Mary Debenham.

He was at his kindest and most genial, setting the woman at her ease. Then, having got her to write down her name and address, he slid gently into his questions.

The interview took place in German.

"We want to know as much as possible about what happened last night," he said. "We know that you cannot give us much information bearing on the crime itself, but you may have seen or heard something that, while conveying nothing to you, may be valuable to us. You understand?"

She did not seem to. Her broad, kindly face remained set in its expression of placid stupidity as she answered:

"I do not know anything, Monsieur."

"Well, for instance you know that your mistress sent for you last night."

"That, yes."

"Do you remember the time?"

"I do not, Monsieur. I was asleep, you see, when the attendant came and told me."

"Yes, yes. Was it usual for you to be sent for in this way?"

"It was not unusual, Monsieur. The gracious lady often required attention at night. She did not sleep well."

"*Eh bien*, then, you received the summons and you got up. Did you put on a dressing gown?"

"No, Monsieur, I put on a few clothes. I would not like to go in to her Excellency in my dressing gown."

"And yet it is a very nice dressing gown—scarlet, is it not?"

She stared at him. "It is a dark blue flannel dressing gown, Monsieur."

"Ah! continue. A little pleasantry on my part, that is all. So you went along to Madame la Princesse. And what did you do when you got there?"

"I gave her massage, Monsieur, and then I read aloud. I do not read aloud very well, but her Excellency says that is all the better—so it sends her better to sleep. When she became sleepy, Monsieur, she told me to go, so I closed the book and I returned to my own compartment."

"Do you know what time that was?"

"No, Monsieur."

"Well, how long had you been with Madame la Princesse?"

"About half an hour, Monsieur."

"Good, continue."

"First, I fetched her Excellency an extra rug from my compartment. It was very cold in spite of the heating. I arranged the rug over her, and she wished me good night. I poured her out some mineral water. Then I turned out the light and left her."

"And then?"

"There is nothing more, Monsieur. I returned to my carriage and went to sleep."

"And you met no one in the corridor?"

"No, Monsieur."

"You did not, for instance, see a lady in a scarlet kimono with dragons on it?"

Her mild eyes bulged at him. "No, indeed, Monsieur. There was nobody about except the attendant. Everyone was asleep."

"But you did see the conductor?"

"Yes, Monsieur."

"What was he doing?"

"He came out of one of the compartments, Monsieur."

"What?" M. Bouc leaned forward. "Which one?"

Hildegarde Schmidt looked frightened again, and Poirot cast a reproachful glance at his friend.

"Naturally," he said. "The conductor often has to answer bells at night. Do you remember which compartment it was?"

"It was about the middle of the coach, Monsieur. Two or three doors from Madame la Princesse."

"Ah! tell us, if you please, exactly where this was and what happened?"

"He nearly ran into me, Monsieur. It was when I was returning from my compartment to that of the Princess with the rug."

"And he came out of a compartment and almost collided with you. In which direction was he going?"

"Towards me, Monsieur. He apologised and passed on down the corridor towards the dining-car. A bell began ringing, but I do not think he answered it." She paused and then said: "I do not understand. How is it—?"

Poirot spoke reassuringly.

"It is just a question of time," he said. "All a matter of routine. This poor conductor, he seems to have had a busy night—first waking you and then answering bells."

"It was not the same conductor who woke me, Monsieur. It was another one."

"Ah! another one! Had you seen him before?"

"No, Monsieur."

"Ah!—do you think you would recognise him if you saw him?"

"I think so, Monsieur."

Poirot murmured something in M. Bouc's ear. The latter got up and went to the door to give an order.

Poirot was continuing his questions in an easy, friendly manner.

"Have you ever been to America, Fräulein Schmidt?"

"Never, Monsieur. It must be a fine country."

"You have heard, perhaps, who this man who was killed really was—that he was responsible for the death of a little child?"

"Yes, I have heard, Monsieur. It was abominable—wicked. The good God should not allow such things. We are not so wicked as that in Germany."

Tears had come into the woman's eyes. Her strong, motherly soul was moved.

"It was an abominable crime," said Poirot gravely.

He drew a scrap of cambric from his pocket and handed it to her.

"Is this your handkerchief, Fräulein Schmidt?"

There was a moment's silence as the woman examined it. She looked up after a minute. The colour had mounted a little in her face.

"Ah! no, indeed. It is not mine, Monsieur."

"It has the initial H, you see. That is why I thought it was yours."

"Ah! Monsieur, it is a lady's handkerchief, that. A very expensive handkerchief. Embroidered by hand. It comes from Paris, I should say."

"It is not yours and you do not know whose it is?"

"I? Oh! no, Monsieur."

Of the three listening, only Poirot caught the nuance of hesitation in the reply.

M. Bouc whispered in his ear. Poirot nodded and said to the woman:

"The three sleeping-car attendants are coming in. Will you be so kind as to tell me which is the one you met last night as you were going with the rug to the Princess?"

The three men entered. Pierre Michel, the big blond conductor of the Athens-Paris coach, and the stout burly conductor of the Bucharest one.

Hildegarde Schmidt looked at them and immediately shook her head.

"No, Monsieur," she said. "None of these is the man I saw last night."

"But these are the only conductors on the train. You must be mistaken."

"I am quite sure, Monsieur. These are all tall, big men. The one I saw was small and dark. He had a little moustache. His voice when he said *'Pardon'* was weak, like a woman's. Indeed, I remember him very well, Monsieur."

Chapter 13

Summary of the Passengers' Evidence

"A small dark man with a womanish voice," said M. Bouc.

The three conductors and Hildegarde Schmidt had been dismissed.

M. Bouc made a despairing gesture. "But I understand nothing—but nothing of all this! The enemy that this Ratchett spoke of, he was then on the train after all? But where is he now? How can he have vanished into thin air? My head, it whirls. Say something, then, my friend, I implore you. Show me how the impossible can be possible!"

"It is a good phrase that," said Poirot. "The impossible cannot have happened, therefore the impossible must be possible in spite of appearances."

"Explain to me, then, quickly, what actually happened on the train last night."

"I am not a magician, *mon cher*. I am, like you, a very puzzled man. This affair advances in a very strange manner."

"It does not advance at all. It stays where it was."

Poirot shook his head. "No, that is not true. We are more advanced. We know certain things. We have heard the evidence of the passengers."

"And what has that told us? Nothing at all."

"I would not say that, my friend."

"I exaggerate, perhaps. The American Hardman, and the German maid—yes, they have added something to our knowledge. That is to say, they have made the whole business more unintelligible than it was."

"No, no, no," said Poirot soothingly.

M. Bouc turned upon him. "Speak, then, let us hear the wisdom of Hercule Poirot."

"Did I not tell you that I was, like you, a very puzzled man? But at least we can face our problem. We can arrange such facts as we have with order and method."

"Pray continue, Monsieur," said Dr. Constantine.

Poirot cleared his throat and straightened a piece of blotting paper.

"Let us review the case as it stands at this moment. First, there are certain indisputable facts. This man, Ratchett or Cassetti, was stabbed in twelve places and died last night. That is fact one."

"I grant it you—I grant it, *mon vieux*," said M. Bouc with a gesture of irony.

Hercule Poirot was not at all put out. He continued calmly.

"I will pass over for the moment certain rather peculiar appearances which Dr. Constantine and I have already discussed together. I will come to them presently. The next fact of importance, to my mind, is the *time* of the crime."

"That, again, is one of the few things we do know," said M. Bouc. "The crime was committed at a quarter past one this morning. Everything goes to show that that was so."

"Not *everything*. You exaggerate. There is, certainly, a fair amount of evidence to support that view."

"I am glad you admit that at least."

Poirot went on calmly, unperturbed by the interruption.

"We have before us three possibilities.

"(1)—that the crime was committed, as you say, at a quarter past one. This is supported by the evidence of the watch, by the evidence of Mrs. Hubbard, and by the evidence of the German woman, Hildegarde Schmidt. It agrees with the evidence of Dr. Constantine.

"(2)—that the crime was committed *later*, and that the evidence of the watch was deliberately faked in order to mislead.

"(3)—that the crime was committed *earlier*, and the evidence faked for the same reason as above.

"Now if we accept possibility (1) as the most likely to have occurred, and the one supported by most evidence, we must also accept certain facts arising from it. If the crime was committed at a quarter past one, the murderer cannot have left the train, and the questions arise: Where is he? And *who* is he?

"To begin with, let us examine the evidence carefully. We first hear of the existence of this man—the small dark man with a womanish voice— from the man Hardman. He says that Ratchett told him of this person and employed him to watch out for the man. There is no *evidence* to support this; we have only Hardman's word for it. Let us next examine the question: Is Hardman the person he pretends to be—an operative of a New York detective agency?

"What to my mind is so interesting in this case is that we have none of the facilities afforded to the police. We cannot investigate the *bona fides* of any of these people. We have to rely solely on deduction. That, to me, makes the matter very much more interesting. There is no routine work. It is all a matter of the intellect. I ask myself: Can we accept Hardman's account of himself? I make my decision and I answer 'Yes.' I am of the opinion that we *can* accept Hardman's account of himself."

"You rely on the intuition? What the Americans call 'the hunch'?" asked Dr. Constantine.

"Not at all. I regard the probabilities. Hardman is travelling with a false passport—that will at once make him an object of suspicion. The first thing that the police will do when they do arrive upon the scene is to detain Hardman and cable as to whether his account of himself is true. In the case of many of the passengers, to establish their *bona fides* will be difficult; in most cases it will probably not be attempted, especially since there seems nothing in the way of suspicion attaching to them. But in Hardman's case it is simple. Either he is the person he represents himself to be, or he is not. Therefore I say that all will prove to be in order."

"You acquit him of suspicion?"

"Not at all. You misunderstand me. For all I know, any American detective might have his own private reasons for wishing to murder Ratchett. No, what I am saying is that I think we *can* accept Hardman's own account of *himself.* This story, then, that he tells of Ratchett's seeking him out and employing him is not unlikely, and is most probably— though not of course certainly—true. If we are going to accept it as true, we must see if there is any confirmation of it. We find it in rather an unlikely place—in the evidence of Hildegarde Schmidt. Her description of the man she saw in Wagon Lit uniform tallies exactly. Is there any further confirmation of these two stories? There is. There is the button that Mrs. Hubbard found in her compartment. And there is also another corroborating statement which you may not have noticed."

"What is that?"

"The fact that both Colonel Arbuthnot and Hector MacQueen mention that the conductor passed their carriage. They attached no importance to the fact, but, Messieurs, *Pierre Michel has declared that he did not leave his seat except on certain specified occasions*—none of which would take him down to the far end of the coach past the compartment in which Arbuthnot and MacQueen were sitting.

"Therefore this story, the story of a small dark man with a womanish voice dressed in Wagon Lit uniform, rests on the testimony, direct or indirect, of four witnesses."

"One small point," said Dr. Constantine. "If Hildegarde Schmidt's story is true, how is it that the real conductor did not mention having seen her when he came to answer Mrs. Hubbard's bell?"

"That is explained, I think. When he arrived to answer Mrs. Hubbard, the maid was in with her mistress. When she finally returned to her own compartment, the conductor was in with Mrs. Hubbard."

M. Bouc had been waiting with difficulty until they had finished.

"Yes, yes, my friend," he said impatiently to Poirot. "But whilst I admire your caution, your method of advancing a step at a time, I submit that you have not yet touched the point at issue. We are all agreed that this person exists. The point is, *where did he go?*"

Poirot shook his head reprovingly.

"You are in error. You are inclined to put the cart before the horse. Before I ask myself, *'Where did this man vanish to?'* I ask myself, *'Did such a man really exist?'* Because, you see, if the man were an invention—a fabrication—how much easier to make him disappear! So I try to establish first that there really *is* such a flesh-and-blood person."

"And having arrived at the fact that there is—*eh bien*, where is he now?"

"There are only two answers to that, *mon cher*. Either he is still hidden on the train in a place of such extraordinary ingenuity that we cannot even think of it; or else he is, as one might say, *two persons*. That is, he is both himself—the man feared by M. Ratchett—and a passenger on the train so well disguised that M. Ratchett did not recognise him."

"It is an idea, that," said M. Bouc, his face lighting up. Then it clouded over again. "But there is one objection—"

Poirot took the words out of his mouth.

"The height of the man. It is that you would say? With the exception of Mr. Ratchett's valet, all the passengers are big men—the Italian, Colonel Arbuthnot, Hector MacQueen, Count Andrenyi. Well, that leaves us the valet—not a very likely supposition. But there is another possibility. Remember the 'womanish' voice. That gives us a choice of alternatives. The man may be disguised as a woman, or, alternatively, he may actually *be* a woman. A tall woman dressed in men's clothes would look small."

"But surely Ratchett would have known—"

"Perhaps he *did* know. Perhaps, already, this woman had attempted his life, wearing a man's clothes the better to accomplish her purpose. Ratchett may have guessed that she would use the same trick again, so he tells

Hardman to look for a man. But he mentions, however, a womanish voice."

"It is a possibility," said M. Bouc. "But—"

"Listen, my friend, I think that I should now tell you of certain inconsistencies noticed by Dr. Constantine."

He retailed at length the conclusions that he and the doctor had arrived at together from the nature of the dead man's wounds. M. Bouc groaned and held his head again.

"I know," said Poirot sympathetically. "I know exactly how you feel. The head spins, does it not?"

"The whole thing is a fantasy!" cried M. Bouc.

"Exactly. It is absurd—improbable—it cannot be. So I myself have said. And yet, my friend, *there it is*! One cannot escape from the facts."

"It is madness!"

"Is it not? It is so mad, my friend, that sometimes I am haunted by the sensation that really it must be very simple. . . . But that is only one of my 'little ideas'!"

"Two murderers," groaned M. Bouc. "And on the Orient Express—"

The thought almost made him weep.

"And now let us make the fantasy more fantastic," said Poirot cheerfully. "Last night on the train, there are two mysterious strangers. There is the Wagon Lit attendant answering to the description given us by M. Hardman, and seen by Hildegarde Schmidt, Colonel Arbuthnot and M. MacQueen. There is also a woman in a red kimono—a tall slim woman, seen by Pierre Michel, Miss Debenham, M. MacQueen and myself (and smelt, I may say, by Colonel Arbuthnot!). Who was she? No one on the train admits to having a scarlet kimono. She, too, has vanished. Was she one and the same with the spurious Wagon Lit attendant? Or was she some quite distinct personality? Where are they, these two? And incidentally, where are the Wagon Lit uniform and the scarlet kimono?"

"Ah! that is something definite." M. Bouc sprang up eagerly. "We must search all the passengers' luggage. Yes, that will be something."

Poirot rose also. "I will make a prophecy," he said.

"You know where they are?"

"I have a little idea."

"Where, then?"

"You will find the scarlet kimono in the baggage of one of the men, and you will find the uniform of the Wagon Lit conductor in the baggage of Hildegarde Schmidt."

"Hildegarde Schmidt? You think—"

"Not what you are thinking. I will put it like this. If Hildegarde

Schmidt is guilty, the uniform may be found in her baggage. But if she is innocent, it *certainly* will be."

"But how—" began M. Bouc and stopped. "What is this noise that approaches?" he cried. "It resembles a locomotive in motion."

The noise drew nearer. It consisted of shrill cries and protests in a woman's voice. The door at the end of the dining-car burst open. Mrs. Hubbard burst in.

"It's too horrible!" she cried. "It's just too horrible. In my sponge-bag. My sponge-bag! A great knife—all over blood!"

And suddenly toppling forward, she fainted heavily on M. Bouc's shoulder.

Chapter 14

The Evidence of the Weapon

With more vigour than chivalry, M. Bouc deposited the fainting lady with her head on the table. Dr. Constantine yelled for one of the restaurant attendants, who came at a run.

"Keep her head so," said the doctor. "If she revives give her a little cognac. You understand?"

Then he hurried off after the other two. His interest lay wholly in the crime—swooning middle-aged ladies did not interest him at all.

It is possible that Mrs. Hubbard revived rather more quickly by these methods than she might otherwise have done. A few minutes later she was sitting up, sipping cognac from a glass proffered by the attendant, and talking once more.

"I just can't tell you how terrible it was! I don't suppose anybody on this train can understand my feelings. I've always been very, very sensitive ever since I was a child. The mere sight of blood—*ugh*! Why, even now I get faint when I think about it!"

The attendant proffered the glass again. *"Encore un peu, Madame?"*

"D'you think I'd better? I'm a lifelong teetotaller. I never touch spirits or wine at any time. All my family are abstainers. Still, perhaps as this is only medicinal—"

She sipped once more.

In the meantime Poirot and M. Bouc, closely followed by Dr. Constantine, had hurried out of the restaurant car and along the corridor of the Stamboul coach towards Mrs. Hubbard's compartment.

Every traveller on the train seemed to be congregated outside the door. The conductor, a harassed look on his face, was keeping them back.

"Mais il n'y a rien à voir," he said, and repeated the sentiment in several other languages.

"Let me pass if you please," said M. Bouc.

Squeezing his rotundity past the obstructing passengers he entered the compartment, Poirot close behind him.

"I am glad you have come, Monsieur," said the conductor with a sigh of relief. "Everyone has been trying to enter. The American lady—such screams as she gave—*ma foi*, I thought she too had been murdered! I came at a run, and there she was screaming like a mad woman; and she cried out that she must fetch you, and she departed screeching at the top of her voice and telling everybody whose carriage she passed what had occurred."

He added, with a gesture of the hand: "*It* is in there, Monsieur. I have not touched it."

Hanging on the handle of the door that gave access to the next compartment was a large-checked rubber sponge-bag. Below it on the floor, just where it had fallen from Mrs. Hubbard's hand, was a straight-bladed dagger—a cheap affair, sham Oriental with an embossed hilt and a tapering blade. The blade was stained with patches of what looked like rust.

Poirot picked it up delicately.

"Yes," he murmured. "There is no mistake. Here is our missing weapon all right—eh, doctor?"

The doctor examined it.

"You need not be so careful," said Poirot. "There will be no finger-prints on it save those of Mrs. Hubbard."

Constantine's examination did not take long.

"It is the weapon all right," he said. "It would account for any of the wounds."

"I implore you, my friend, do not say that!"

The doctor looked astonished.

"Already we are heavily overburdened by coincidence. Two people decided to stab M. Ratchett last night. It is too much of a good thing that both of them should select the same weapon."

"As to that, the coincidence is not perhaps so great as it seems," said the doctor. "Thousands of these sham Eastern daggers are made and shipped to the bazaars of Constantinople."

"You console me a little, but only a little," said Poirot.

He looked thoughtfully at the door in front of him, then, lifting off the sponge-bag, he tried the handle. The door did not budge. About a foot above the handle was the door bolt. Poirot drew it back and tried again, but still the door remained fast.

"We locked it from the other side, you remember," said the doctor.

"That is true," said Poirot absently. He seemed to be thinking about something else. His brow was furrowed as though in perplexity.

"It agrees, does it not?" said M. Bouc. "The man passes through this carriage. As he shuts the communicating door behind him he feels the sponge-bag. A thought comes to him and he quickly slips the blood-stained knife inside. Then, all unwitting that he has awakened Mrs. Hubbard, he slips out through the other door into the corridor."

"As you say," murmured Poirot. "That is how it must have happened." But the puzzled look did not leave his face.

"But what is it?" demanded M. Bouc. "There is something, is there not, that does not satisfy you?"

Poirot darted a quick look at him.

"The same point does not strike you? No, evidently not. Well, it is a small matter."

The conductor looked into the carriage. "The American lady is coming back."

Dr. Constantine looked rather guilty. He had, he felt, treated Mrs. Hubbard rather cavalierly. But she had no reproaches for him. Her energies were concentrated on another matter.

"I'm going to say one thing right out," she said breathlessly as she arrived in the doorway. "I'm not going on any longer in this compartment! Why, I wouldn't sleep in it to-night if you paid me a million dollars."

"But, Madame—"

"I know what you are going to say, and I'm telling you right now that I won't do any such thing! Why, I'd rather sit up all night in the corridor." She began to cry. "Oh, if my daughter could only know—if she could see me now, why—"

Poirot interrupted firmly.

"You misunderstand, Madame. Your demand is most reasonable. Your baggage shall be changed at once to another compartment."

Mrs. Hubbard lowered her handkerchief. "Is that so? Oh! I feel better right away. But surely it's all full, unless one of the gentlemen—"

M. Bouc spoke.

"Your baggage, Madame, shall be moved out of this coach altogether. You shall have a compartment in the next coach, which was put on at Belgrade."

"Why, that's splendid. I'm not an extra nervous woman, but to sleep in that compartment next door to a dead man!" She shivered. "It would drive me plumb crazy."

"Michel," called M. Bouc. "Move this baggage into a vacant compartment in the Athens-Paris coach."

"Yes, Monsieur. The same one as this—the No. 3?"

"No," said Poirot before his friend could reply. "I think it would be better for Madame to have a different number altogether. The No. 12, for instance."

"*Bien, Monsieur.*"

The conductor seized the luggage. Mrs. Hubbard turned gratefully to Poirot.

"That's very kind and delicate of you. I appreciate it, I assure you."

"Do not mention it, Madame. We will come with you and see you comfortably installed."

Mrs. Hubbard was escorted by the three men to her new home. She looked round her happily. "This is fine."

"It suits you, Madame? It is, you see, exactly like the compartment you have left."

"That's so—only it faces the other way. But that doesn't matter, for these trains go first one way and then the other. I said to my daughter, 'I want a carriage facing the engine,' and she said, 'Why, Mamma, that'll be no good to you, for if you go to sleep one way, when you wake up, the train's going the other!' And it was quite true what she said. Why, last evening we went into Belgrade one way and out the other."

"At any rate, Madame, you are quite happy and contented now?"

"Well, no, I wouldn't say that. Here we are stuck in a snowdrift and nobody doing anything about it, and my boat sailing the day after to-morrow."

"Madame," said M. Bouc, "we are all in the same case—every one of us."

"Well, that's true," admitted Mrs. Hubbard. "But nobody else has had a murderer walking right through her compartment in the middle of the night."

"What still puzzles me, Madame," said Poirot, "is how the man got into your compartment if the communicating door was bolted as you say. You are sure that it *was* bolted?"

"Why, the Swedish lady tried it before my eyes."

"Let us just reconstruct that little scene. You were lying in your bunk—so—and you could not see for yourself, you say?"

"No, because of the sponge-bag. Oh! my, I shall have to get a new sponge-bag. It makes me feel sick at my stomach to look at this one."

Poirot picked up the sponge-bag and hung it on the handle of the communicating door into the next carriage.

"*Précisément.* I see," he said. "The bolt is just underneath the handle—the sponge-bag masks it. You could not see from where you were lying whether the bolt was turned or not."

"Why, that's just what I've been telling you!"

"And the Swedish lady, Miss Ohlsson, stood so, between you and the door. She tried it and told you it was bolted."

"That's so."

"All the same, Madame, she may have made an error. You see what I mean." Poirot seemed anxious to explain. "The bolt is just a projection of metal—so. When it is turned to the right, the door is locked. When it is left straight, the door is unlocked. Possibly she merely tried the door, and as it was locked on the other side she may have assumed that it was locked on your side."

"Well, I guess that would be rather stupid of her."

"Madame, the most kind, the most amiable, are not always the cleverest."

"That's so, of course."

"By the way, Madame, did you travel out to Smyrna this way?"

"No. I sailed right to Stamboul, and a friend of my daughter's, Mr. Johnson (a perfectly lovely man, I'd like to have you know him), met me and showed me all round Stamboul. But it was a very disappointing city—all tumbling down; and as for those mosques, and putting on those great shuffling things over your shoes—where was I?"

"You were saying that Mr. Johnson met you."

"That's so, and he saw me on board a French Messageries boat for Smyrna, and my daughter's husband was waiting right on the quay. What he'll say when he hears about all this! My daughter said this would be just the safest, easiest way imaginable. 'You just sit in your carriage,' she said, 'and you land right in Parrus, and there the American Express will meet you.' And, oh, dear, what am I to do about cancelling my steamship passage? I ought to let them know. I can't possibly make it now. This is just too terrible—"

Mrs. Hubbard showed signs of tears once more.

Poirot, who had been fidgeting slightly, seized his opportunity.

"You have had a shock, Madame. The restaurant attendant shall be instructed to bring you along some tea and some biscuits."

"I don't know that I'm so set on tea," said Mrs. Hubbard tearfully. "That's more an English habit."

"Coffee, then, Madame. You need some stimulant."

"That cognac's made my head feel mighty funny. I think I would like some coffee."

"Excellent. You must revive your forces."

"My, what a funny expression!"

"But first, Madame, a little matter of routine. You permit that I make a search of your baggage?"

"What for?"

"We are about to commence a search of all the passengers' luggage. I do not want to remind you of an unpleasant experience, but your sponge-bag—remember."

"Mercy! Perhaps you'd better! I just couldn't bear to get any more surprises of that kind."

The examination was quickly over. Mrs. Hubbard was travelling with the minimum of luggage—a hatbox, a cheap suitcase, and a well-burdened travelling bag. The contents of all three were simple and straightforward, and the examination would not have taken more than a couple of minutes had not Mrs. Hubbard delayed matters by insisting on due attention being paid to photographs of "my daughter" and of two rather ugly children— "my daughter's children. Aren't they cunning?"

Chapter 15

The Evidence of the Passengers' Luggage

Having delivered himself of various polite insincerities, and having told Mrs. Hubbard that he would order coffee to be brought to her, Poirot was able to take his leave accompanied by his two friends.

"Well, we have made a start and drawn a blank," observed M. Bouc. "Whom shall we tackle next?"

"It would be simplest, I think, just to proceed along the train, carriage by carriage. That means that we start with No. 16—the amiable Mr. Hardman."

Mr. Hardman, who was smoking a cigar, welcomed them affably.

"Come right in, gentlemen. That is, if it's humanly possible. It's just a mite cramped in here for a party."

M. Bouc explained the object of their visit, and the big detective nodded comprehendingly.

"That's O.K. To tell the truth I've been wondering you didn't get down to it sooner. Here are my keys, gentlemen, and if you like to search my pockets too, why, you're welcome. Shall I reach the grips down for you?"

"The conductor will do that. Michel!"

The contents of Mr. Hardman's two "grips" were soon examined and passed. They contained, perhaps, an undue proportion of spirituous liquor. Mr. Hardman winked.

"It's not often they search your grips at the frontiers—not if you fix the conductor. I handed out a wad of Turkish notes right away, and there's been no trouble so far."

"And at Paris?"

Mr. Hardman winked again. "By the time I get to Paris," he said, "what's left over of this little lot will go into a bottle labelled hairwash."

"You are not a believer in Prohibition, Monsieur Hardman," said M. Bouc with a smile.

"Well," said Hardman, "I can't say Prohibition has ever worried me any."

"Ah!" said M. Bouc. "The speakeasy." He pronounced the word with care, savouring it. "Your American terms are so quaint, so expressive," he said.

"Me, I would much like to go to America," said Poirot.

"You'd learn a few go-ahead methods over there," said Hardman. "Europe needs waking up. She's half asleep."

"It is true that America is the country of progress," agreed Poirot. "There is much that I admire about Americans. Only—I am perhaps old-fashioned—but me, I find the American women less charming than my own country-women. The French or the Belgian girl, coquettish, charming—I think there is no one to touch her."

Hardman turned away to peer out at the snow for a minute.

"Perhaps you're right, M. Poirot," he said. "But I guess every nation likes its own girls best." He blinked as though the snow hurt his eyes.

"Kind of dazzling, isn't it?" he remarked. "Say, gentlemen, this business is getting on my nerves. Murder and the snow and all. And nothing *doing*. Just hanging about and killing time. I'd like to get busy after someone or something."

"The true Western spirit of hustle," said Poirot with a smile.

The conductor replaced the bags and they moved on to the next compartment. Colonel Arbuthnot was sitting in a corner smoking a pipe and reading a magazine.

Poirot explained their errand. The Colonel made no demur. He had two heavy leather suitcases.

"The rest of my kit has gone by long sea," he explained.

Like most Army men the Colonel was a neat packer. The examination of his baggage took only a few minutes. Poirot noted a packet of pipe cleaners.

"You always use the same kind?" he asked.

"Usually. If I can get 'em."

"Ah!" Poirot nodded. These pipe cleaners corresponded exactly with the one he had found on the floor of the dead man's compartment.

Dr. Constantine remarked as much when they were out in the corridor again.

"Tout de même," murmured Poirot, "I can hardly believe it. It is not

dans son caractére, and when you have said that, you have said everything."

The door of the next compartment was closed. It was that occupied by
Princess Dragomiroff. They knocked on the door and the Princess's deep
voice called *"Entrez!"*

M. Bouc was spokesman. He was very deferential and polite as he explained their errand.

The Princess listened to him in silence, her small toadlike face quite
impassive.

"If it is necessary, Messieurs," she said quietly when he had finished,
"that is all there is to it. My maid has the keys. She will attend to it with
you."

"Does your maid always carry your keys, Madame?" asked Poirot.

"Certainly, Monsieur."

"And if, during the night at one of the frontiers, the customs officials
should require a piece of luggage to be opened?"

The old lady shrugged her shoulders. "It is very unlikely. But in such a
case, the conductor would fetch her."

"You trust her, then, implicitly, Madame?"

"I have told you so already," said the Princess quietly. "I do not employ people whom I do not trust."

"Yes," said Poirot thoughtfully. "Trust is indeed something in these
days. It is perhaps better to have a homely woman whom one can trust
than a more *chic* maid—for example, some smart Parisienne."

He saw the dark intelligent eyes come slowly round and fasten themselves upon his face. "What exactly are you implying, M. Poirot?"

"Nothing, Madame. I? Nothing."

"But yes. You think, do you not, that I should have a smart Frenchwoman to attend to my toilet?"

"It would be perhaps more usual, Madame." She shook her head.
"Schmidt is devoted to me." Her voice dwelt lingeringly on the words.
"Devotion—*c'est impayable.*"

The German woman had arrived with the keys. The Princess spoke to
her in her own language, telling her to open the valises and help the gentlemen in their search. She herself remained in the corridor looking out at
the snow, and Poirot remained with her, leaving M. Bouc to the task of
searching the luggage.

She regarded him with a grim smile.

"Well, Monsieur, do you not wish to see what my valises contain?"

He shook his head. "Madame, it is a formality, that is all."

"Are you so sure?"

"In your case, yes."

"And yet I knew and loved Sonia Armstrong. What do you think, then? That I would not soil my hands with killing such *canaille* as that man Cassetti? Well, perhaps you are right."

She was silent a minute or two. Then she said:

"With such a man as that, do you know what I should have liked to do? I should have liked to call to my servants: 'Flog this man to death and fling him out on the rubbish heap!' That is the way things were done when I was young, Monsieur."

Still he did not speak, just listened attentively.

She looked at him with a sudden impetuosity. "You do not say anything, M. Poirot. What is it that you are thinking, I wonder?"

He looked at her with a very direct glance. "I think, Madame, that your strength is in your will—not in your arm."

She glanced down at her thin, black-clad arms ending in those claw-like yellow hands with the rings on the fingers.

"It is true," she said. "I have no strength in these—none. I do not know whether I am sorry or glad."

Then she turned abruptly back towards her carriage where the maid was busily packing up the cases.

The Princess cut short M. Bouc's apologies.

"There is no need for you to apologise, Monsieur," she said. "A murder has been committed. Certain actions have to be performed. That is all there is to it."

"Vous êtes bien aimable, Madame."

She inclined her head slightly as they departed.

The doors of the next two carriages were shut. M. Bouc paused and scratched his head.

"Diable!" he said. "This may be awkward. These are diplomatic passports. Their luggage is exempt."

"From customs examination, yes. But a murder is different."

"I know. All the same—we do not want to have complications."

"Do not distress yourself, my friend. The Count and Countess will be reasonable. See how amiable Princess Dragomiroff was about it."

"She is truly *grande dame*. These two are also of the same position, but the Count impressed me as a man of somewhat truculent disposition. He was not pleased when you insisted on questioning his wife. And this will annoy him still further. Suppose—eh?—we omit them. After all, they can have nothing to do with the matter. Why should I stir up needless trouble for myself?"

"I do not agree with you," said Poirot. "I feel sure that Count Andrenyi will be reasonable. At any rate let us make the attempt."

And before M. Bouc could reply, he rapped sharply on the door of No. 13.

A voice from within cried, *"Entrez!"*

The Count was sitting in the corner near the door reading a newspaper. The Countess was curled up in the opposite corner near the window. There was a pillow behind her head and she seemed to have been asleep.

"Pardon, Monsieur le Comte," began Poirot. "Pray forgive this intrusion. It is that we are making a search of all the baggage on the train. In most cases a mere formality. But it has to be done. M. Bouc suggests that, as you have a diplomatic passport, you might reasonably claim to be exempt from such a search."

The Count considered for a moment.

"Thank you," he said. "But I do not think that I care to have an exception made in my case. I should prefer that our baggage should be examined like that of the other passengers."

He turned to his wife. "You do not object, I hope, Elena?"

"Not at all," said the Countess without hesitation.

A rapid and somewhat perfunctory search followed. Poirot seemed to be trying to mask an embarrassment by making various small pointless remarks, such as:

"Here is a label all wet on your suitcase, Madame," as he lifted down a blue morocco case with initials on it and a coronet.

The Countess did not reply to this observation. She seemed, indeed, rather bored by the whole proceeding, remaining curled up in her corner and staring dreamily out through the window whilst the men searched her luggage in the compartment next door.

Poirot finished his search by opening the little cupboard above the washbasin and taking a rapid glance at its contents—a sponge, face cream, powder and a small bottle labelled TRIONAL.

Then with polite remarks on either side, the search party withdrew.

Mrs. Hubbard's compartment, that of the dead man, and Poirot's own came next.

They now came to the second-class carriages. The first one, Nos. 10 and 11, was occupied by Mary Debenham, who was reading a book, and Greta Ohlsson, who was fast asleep but woke with a start at their entrance.

Poirot repeated his formula. The Swedish lady seemed agitated, Mary Debenham calmly indifferent. He addressed himself to the Swedish lady.

"If you permit, Mademoiselle, we will examine your baggage first, and then perhaps you would be so good as to see how the American lady is getting on. We have moved her into one of the carriages in the next coach, but she is still very much upset as the result of her discovery. I have ordered coffee to be sent to her, but I think she is of those to whom someone to talk to is a necessity of the first order."

The good lady was instantly sympathetic. She would go immediately. It must have been indeed a terrible shock to the nerves, and already the poor lady was upset by the journey and leaving her daughter. Ah, yes, certainly she would go at once—her case was not locked—and she would take with her some sal ammoniac.

She bustled off. Her possessions were soon examined. They were meagre in the extreme. She had evidently not yet noticed the missing wires from the hatbox.

Miss Debenham had put her book down. She was watching Poirot. When he asked her, she handed over her keys. Then, as he lifted down a case and opened it, she said:

"Why did you send her away, M. Poirot?"

"I, Mademoiselle? Why, to minister to the American lady."

"An excellent pretext—but a pretext all the same."

"I don't understand you, Mademoiselle."

"I think you understand me very well." She smiled. "You wanted to get me alone. Wasn't that it?"

"You are putting words into my mouth, Mademoiselle."

"And ideas into your head? No, I don't think so. The ideas are already there. That is right, isn't it?"

"Mademoiselle, we have a proverb—"

"*Qui s'excuse s'accuse*—is that what you were going to say? You must give me the credit for a certain amount of observation and common sense. For some reason or other you have got it into your head that I know something about this sordid business—this murder of a man I never saw before."

"You are imagining things, Mademoiselle."

"No, I am not imagining things at all. But it seems to me that a lot of time is wasted by not speaking the truth—by beating about the bush instead of coming straight out with things."

"And you do not like the waste of time. No, you like to come straight to the point. You like the direct method. *Eh bien*, I will give it to you, the direct method. I will ask you the meaning of certain words that I overheard on the journey from Syria. I had got out of the train to do what the English call 'stretch the legs' at the station of Konya. Your voice and the Colonel's, Mademoiselle, they came to me out of the night. You said to him, *'Not now. Not now. When it's all over. When it's behind us.'* What did you mean by those words, Mademoiselle?"

She asked very quietly, "Do you think I meant—murder?"

"It is I who am asking you, Mademoiselle."

She sighed—was lost a minute in thought. Then, as though rousing herself, she said:

"Those words had a meaning, Monsieur, but not one that I can tell you. I can only give you my solemn word of honour that I had never set eyes on this man Ratchett in my life until I saw him on this train."

"And—you refuse to explain those words?"

"Yes, if you like to put it that way—I refuse. They had to do with—with a task I had undertaken."

"A task that is now ended?"

"What do you mean?"

"It is ended, is it not?"

"Why should you think so?"

"Listen, Mademoiselle, I will recall to you another incident. There was a delay to the train on the day we were to reach Stamboul. You were very agitated, Mademoiselle. You, so calm, so self-controlled. You lost that calm."

"I did not want to miss my connection."

"So you said. But, Mademoiselle, the Orient Express leaves Stamboul every day of the week. Even if you had missed the connection it would only have been a matter of twenty-four hours' delay."

Miss Debenham for the first time showed signs of losing her temper.

"You do not seem to realise that one may have friends awaiting one's arrival in London, and that a day's delay upsets arrangements and causes a lot of annoyance."

"Ah, it is like that? There are friends awaiting your arrival? You do not want to cause them inconvenience?"

"Naturally."

"And yet—it is curious—"

"What is curious?"

"On this train—again we have a delay. And this time a more serious delay, since there is no possibility of sending a telegram to your friends or of getting them on the long—the long—"

"Long distance? The telephone, you mean."

"Ah, yes, the portmanteau call, as you say in England."

Mary Debenham smiled a little in spite of herself. "Trunk call," she corrected. "Yes, as you say, it is extremely annoying not to be able to get any word through, either by telephone or by telegraph."

"And yet, Mademoiselle, *this* time your manner is quite different. You no longer betray the impatience. You are calm and philosophical."

Mary Debenham flushed and bit her lip. She no longer felt inclined to smile.

"You do not answer, Mademoiselle?"

"I am sorry. I did not know that there was anything to answer."

"Your change of attitude, Mademoiselle."

"Don't you think that you are making rather a fuss about nothing, M. Poirot?"

Poirot spread out his hands in an apologetic gesture.

"It is perhaps a fault with us detectives. We expect the behaviour to be always consistent. We do not allow for changes of mood."

Mary Debenham made no reply.

"You know Colonel Arbuthnot well, Mademoiselle?"

He fancied that she was relieved by the change of subject.

"I met him for the first time on this journey."

"Have you any reason to suspect that he may have known this man Ratchett?"

She shook her head decisively. "I am quite sure he didn't."

"Why are you sure?"

"By the way he spoke."

"And yet, Mademoiselle, we found a pipe-cleaner on the floor of the dead man's compartment. And Colonel Arbuthnot is the only man on the train who smokes a pipe."

He watched her narrowly, but she displayed neither surprise nor emotion, merely said:

"Nonsense. It's absurd. Colonel Arbuthnot is the last man in the world to be mixed up in a crime—especially a theatrical kind of crime like this."

It was so much what Poirot himself thought that he found himself on the point of agreeing with her. He said instead:

"I must remind you that you do not know him very well, Mademoiselle."

She shrugged her shoulders. "I know the type well enough."

He said very gently:

"You still refuse to tell me the meaning of those words: 'When it's behind us'?"

She replied coldly, "I have nothing more to say."

"It does not matter," said Hercule Poirot. "I shall find out."

He bowed and left the compartment, closing the door after him.

"Was that wise, my friend?" asked M. Bouc. "You have put her on her guard—and through her you have put the Colonel on his guard also."

"*Mon ami*, if you wish to catch a rabbit you put a ferret into the hole, and if the rabbit is there—he runs. That is all I have done."

They entered the compartment of Hildegarde Schmidt.

The woman was standing in readiness, her face respectful but unemotional.

Poirot took a quick glance through the contents of the small case on the seat. Then he motioned to the attendant to get down the bigger suitcase from the rack.

"The keys?" he said.

"It is not locked, Monsieur."

Poirot undid the hasps and lifted the lid.

"Aha!" he said, and turning to M. Bouc, "You remember what I said? Look here a little moment!"

On the top of the suitcase was a hastily rolled-up brown Wagon Lit uniform.

The stolidity of the German woman underwent a sudden change.

"*Ach!*" she cried. "That is not mine. I did not put it there. I have never looked in that case since we left Stamboul. Indeed, indeed, it is true!" She looked from one to another of the men pleadingly.

Poirot took her gently by the arm and soothed her.

"No, no, all is well. We believe you. Do not be agitated. I am sure you did not hide the uniform there as I am sure that you are a good cook. See. You *are* a good cook, are you not?"

Bewildered, the woman smiled in spite of herself. "Yes, indeed, all my ladies have said so. I—"

She stopped, her mouth open, looking frightened again.

"No, no," said Poirot. "I assure you all is well. See, I will tell you how this happened. This man, the man you saw in Wagon Lit uniform, comes out of the dead man's compartment. He collides with you. That is bad luck for him. He has hoped that no one will see him. What to do next? He must get rid of his uniform. It is now not a safeguard, but a danger."

His glance went to M. Bouc and Dr. Constantine, who were listening attentively.

"There is the snow, you see. The snow which confuses all his plans. Where can he hide these clothes? All the compartments are full. No, he passes one whose door is open, showing it to be unoccupied. It must be the one belonging to the woman with whom he has just collided. He slips in, removes the uniform and jams it hurriedly into a suitcase on the rack. It may be some time before it is discovered."

"And then?" said M. Bouc.

"That we must discuss," said Poirot with a warning glance.

He held up the tunic. A button, the third down, was missing. Poirot slipped his hand into the pocket and took out a conductor's pass-key, used to unlock the doors of the compartments.

"Here is the explanation of how one man was able to pass through locked doors," said M. Bouc. "Your questions to Mrs. Hubbard were unnecessary. Locked or not locked, the man could easily get through the communicating door. After all, if a Wagon Lit uniform, why not a Wagon Lit key?"

"Why not indeed?" returned Poirot.

"We might have known it, really. You remember that Michel said that the door into the corridor of Mrs. Hubbard's compartment was locked when he came in answer to her bell."

"That is so, Monsieur," said the conductor. "That is why I thought the lady must have been dreaming."

"But now it is easy," continued M. Bouc. "Doubtless he meant to re-lock the communicating door also, but perhaps he heard some movement from the bed and it startled him."

"We have now," said Poirot, "only to find the scarlet kimono."

"True. And these last two compartments are occupied by men."

"We will search all the same."

"Oh! assuredly. Besides, I remember what you said."

Hector MacQueen acquiesced willingly in the search.

"I'd just as soon you did," he said with a rueful smile. "I feel I'm definitely the most suspicious character on the train. You've only got to find a will in which the old man left me all his money, and that'll just about fix things."

M. Bouc bent a suspicious glance upon him.

"That's only my fun," added MacQueen hastily. "He'd never have left me a cent, really. I was just useful to him—languages and so on. You're likely to be out of luck, you know, if you don't speak anything but good American. I'm no linguist myself, but I know what I call Shopping and Hotel—snappy bits in French and German and Italian."

His voice was a little louder than usual. It was as though he were slightly uneasy over the search in spite of his expressed willingness.

Poirot emerged. "Nothing," he said. "Not even a compromising bequest!"

MacQueen sighed. "Well, that's a load off my mind," he said humorously.

They moved on to the last compartment. The examination of the luggage of the big Italian and of the valet yielded no result.

The three men stood at the end of the coach looking at each other.

"What next?" said M. Bouc.

"We will go back to the dining-car," said Poirot. "We know now all that we can know. We have the evidence of the passengers, the evidence of their baggage, the evidence of our eyes. . . . We can expect no further help. It must be our part now to use our brains."

He felt in his pocket for his cigarette case. It was empty.

"I will join you in a moment," he said. "I shall need the cigarettes.

This is a very difficult, a very curious, affair. Who wore that scarlet kimono? Where is it now? I wish I knew. There is something in this case—some factor—that escapes me! It is difficult because it has been *made* difficult. But we will discuss it. Pardon me a moment."

He went hurriedly along the corridor to his own compartment. He had, he knew, a further supply of cigarettes in one of his valises.

He got it down and snapped back the lock.

Then he sat back on his heels and stared.

Neatly folded on the top of the case was a thin scarlet silk kimono embroidered with dragons.

"So," he murmured. "It is like that. A defiance. Very well, I take it up."

Part 3

Hercule Poirot Sits Back and Thinks

Chapter 1

Which of Them?

M. Bouc and Dr. Constantine were talking together when Poirot entered the dining-car. M. Bouc was looking depressed.

"Le voilà," said the latter when he saw Poirot. Then he added, as his friend sat down, "If you solve this case, *mon cher*, I shall indeed believe in miracles!"

"It worries you, this case?"

"Naturally it worries me. I cannot make head or tail of it."

"I agree," said the doctor. He looked at Poirot with interest. "To be frank," he said, "I cannot see what you are going to do next."

"No?" said Poirot thoughtfully.

He took out his cigarette case and lit one of his tiny cigarettes. His eyes were dreamy.

"That, to me, is the interest of this case," he said. "We are cut off from all the normal routes of procedure. Are these people whose evidence we have taken speaking the truth, or lying? We have no means of finding out—except such means as we can devise ourselves. It is an exercise, this, of the brain."

"That is all very fine," said M. Bouc. "But what have you to go upon?"

"I told you just now. We have the evidence of the passengers and the evidence of our own eyes."

"Pretty evidence—that of the passengers! It told us just nothing at all."

Poirot shook his head.

"I do not agree, my friend. The evidence of the passengers gave us several points of interest."

"Indeed," said M. Bouc sceptically. "I did not observe it."

"That is because you did not listen."

"Well, tell me, what did I miss?"

"I will just take one instance—the first evidence we heard, that of the young MacQueen. He uttered, to my mind, one very significant phrase."

"About the letters?"

"No, not about the letters. As far as I can remember, his words were: *'We travelled about. Mr. Ratchett wanted to see the world. He was hampered by knowing no languages. I acted more as a courier than a secretary.'*"

He looked from the doctor's face to that of M. Bouc.

"What? You still do not see? That is inexcusable—for you had a second chance again just now when he said, *'You're likely to be out of luck if you don't speak anything but good American.'*"

"You mean—?" M. Bouc still looked puzzled.

"Ah, it is that you want it given to you in words of one syllable. Well, here it is! *M. Ratchett spoke no French.* Yet, when the conductor came in answer to his bell last night, it was a voice speaking in *French* that told him that it was a mistake and that he was not wanted. It was, moreover, a perfectly idiomatic phrase that was used, not one that a man knowing only a few words of French would have selected. *'Ce n'est rien. Je me suis trompé.'*"

"It is true," cried Constantine excitedly. "We should have seen that! I remember your laying stress on the words when you repeated them to us. Now I understand your reluctance to rely upon the evidence of the dented watch. Already, at twenty-three minutes to one, Ratchett was dead—"

"And it was his murderer speaking!" finished M. Bouc impressively.

Poirot raised a deprecating hand.

"Let us not go too fast. And do not let us assume more than we actually know. It is safe, I think, to say that at that time—twenty-three minutes to one—*some other person* was in Ratchett's compartment, and that that person either was French or could speak the French language fluently."

"You are very cautious, *mon vieux.*"

"One should advance only a step at a time. We have no actual *evidence* that Ratchett was dead at that time."

"There is the cry that awakened you."

"Yes, that is true."

"In one way," said M. Bouc thoughtfully, "this discovery does not affect things very much. You heard someone moving about next door. That someone was not Ratchett, but the other man. Doubtless he is washing blood from his hands, clearing up after the crime, burning the incriminating letter. Then he waits till all is still, and, when he thinks it is safe and the coast is clear, he locks and chains Ratchett's door on the inside, unlocks the communicating door through into Mrs. Hubbard's compartment and slips out that way. In fact, it is exactly as we thought, *with the difference that Ratchett was killed about half an hour earlier* and the watch put on to a quarter past one to create an alibi."

"Not such a famous alibi," said Poirot. "The hands of the watch pointed to 1.15—the exact time when the intruder actually left the scene of the crime."

"True," said M. Bouc, a little confused. "What then does the watch convey to you?"

"If the hands were altered—I say *if*—then the time at which they were set *must* have a significance. The natural reaction would be to suspect anyone who had a reliable alibi for the time indicated—in this case, 1.15."

"Yes, yes," said the doctor. "That reasoning is good."

"We must also pay a little attention to the time the intruder *entered* the compartment. When had he an opportunity of doing so? Unless we are to assume the complicity of the real conductor, there was only one time when he could have done so—during the time the train stopped at Vincovci. After the train left Vincovci the conductor was sitting facing the corridor, and whereas any one of the passengers would pay little attention to a Wagon Lit attendant, the *one* person who *would* notice an impostor is the real conductor. But during the halt at Vincovci the conductor is out on the platform. The coast is clear."

"And by our former reasoning, it *must* be one of the passengers," said M. Bouc. "We come back to where we were. Which of them?"

Poirot smiled.

"I have made a list," he said. "If you like to see it, it will perhaps refresh your memory."

The doctor and M. Bouc pored over the list together. It was written out neatly in a methodical manner in the order in which the passengers had been interviewed.

Hector MacQueen—American subject, Berth No. 6, Second Class.
> *Motive:* Possibly arising out of association with dead man?
> *Alibi:* From midnight to A.M. (Midnight to 1.30 vouched for by Col. Arbuthnot, and 1.15 to 2 vouched for by conductor.)
> *Evidence against him:* None.
> *Suspicious circumstances:* None.

Conductor Pierre Michel—French subject.
> *Motive:* None.
> *Alibi:* From midnight to 2 A.M. (Seen by H. P. in corridor at same time as voice spoke from Ratchett's compartment at 12.37. From 1 A.M. to 1.16 vouched for by other two conductors.)

Evidence against him: None.
Suspicious circumstances: The Wagon Lit uniform found is a point in his favour since it seems to have been intended to throw suspicion on him.

Edward Masterman—English subject, Berth No. 4, Second Class.
Motive: Possibly arising out of connection with deceased, whose valet he was.
Alibi: From midnight to 2 A.M. (Vouched for by Antonio Foscarelli.)
Evidence against him or suspicious circumstances: None, except that he is the only man of the right height or size to have worn the Wagon Lit uniform. On the other hand, it is unlikely that he speaks French well.

Mrs. Hubbard—American subject, Berth No. 3, First Class.
Motive: None.
Alibi: From midnight to 2 A.M.—None.
Evidence against her or suspicious circumstances: Story of man in her compartment is substantiated by the evidence of Hardman and that of the woman Schmidt.

Greta Ohlsson—Swedish subject, Berth No. 10, Second Class.
Motive: None.
Alibi: From midnight to 2 A.M. (Vouched for by Mary Debenham.)
NOTE: Was last to see Ratchett alive.

Princess Dragomiroff—Naturalised French subject, Berth No. 14, First Class.
Motive: Was intimately acquainted with Armstrong family, and godmother to Sonia Armstrong.
Alibi: From midnight to 2 A.M. (Vouched for by conductor and maid.)
Evidence against her or suspicious circumstances: None.

Count Andrenyi—Hungarian subject, Diplomatic passport, Berth No. 13, First Class.
Motive: None.
Alibi: Midnight to 2 A.M. (Vouched for by conductor—this does not cover period from 1 to 1.15.)

Countess Andrenyi—As above, Berth 12.
Motive: None.
Alibi: Midnight to 2 A.M. Took trional and slept. (Vouched for by husband. Trional bottle in her cupboard.)

Colonel Arbuthnot—British subject, Berth No. 15, First Class.
Motive: None.
Alibi: Midnight to 2 A.M. Talked with MacQueen till 1.30. Went to own compartment and did not leave it. (Substantiated by MacQueen and conductor.)
Evidence against him or suspicious circumstances: Pipe cleaner.

Cyrus Hardman—American subject, Berth No. 16.
Motive: None known.
Alibi: Midnight to 2 A.M. Did not leave compartment. (Substantiated by conductor except for period 1 to 1.15.)
Evidence against him or suspicious circumstances: None.

Antonio Foscarelli—American subject (Italian by birth), Berth No. 5, Second Class.
Motive: None known.
Alibi: Midnight to 2 A.M. (Vouched for by Edward Masterman.)
Evidence against him or suspicious circumstances: None, except that weapon used might be said to suit his temperament (Vide M. Bouc.)

Mary Debenham—British subject, Berth No. 11, Second Class.
Motive: None.
Alibi: Midnight to 2 A.M. (Vouched for by Greta Ohlsson.)
Evidence against her or suspicious circumstances: Conversation overhead by H. P., and her refusal to explain it.

Hildegarde Schmidt—German subject, Berth No. 8, Second Class.
Motive: None.
Alibi: Midnight to 2 A.M. (Vouched for by conductor and her mistress.) Went to bed. Was aroused by conductor at 12.38 approx. and went to mistress.

NOTE:—The evidence of the passengers is supported by the statement of the conductor that no one entered or left Mr. Ratchett's compartment from midnight to 1 o'clock (when he himself went into the next coach) and from 1.15 to 2 o'clock.

"That document, you understand," said Poirot, "is a mere *précis* of the evidence we heard, arranged in that way for convenience."

With a grimace, M. Bouc handed it back. "It is not illuminating," he said.

"Perhaps you may find this more to your taste," said Poirot, with a slight smile as he handed him a second sheet of paper.

Chapter 2

Ten Questions

On the paper was written:

Things Needing Explanation
1. The handkerchief marked with the initial H. Whose is it?
2. The pipe-cleaner. Was it dropped by Colonel Arbuthnot? Or by someone else?
3. Who wore the scarlet kimono?
4. Who was the man or woman masquerading in Wagon Lit uniform?
5. Why do the hands of the watch point to 1.15?
6. Was the murder committed at that time?
7. Was it earlier?
8. Was it later?
9. Can we be sure that Ratchett was stabbed by more than one person?
10. What other explanation of his wounds can there be?

"Well, let us see what we can do," said M. Bouc, brightening a little at this challenge to his wits. "The handkerchief, to begin with. Let us by all means be orderly and methodical."

"Assuredly," said Poirot, nodding his head in a satisfied fashion.

M. Bouc continued somewhat didactically.

"The initial H is connected with three people—Mrs. Hubbard, Miss Debenham, whose second name is Hermione, and the maid, Hildegarde Schmidt."

"Ah! And of those three?"

"It is difficult to say. But I *think* I should vote for Miss Debenham. For all one knows she may be called by her second name and not her first.

Also there is already some suspicion attaching to her. That conversation you overheard, *mon cher*, was certainly a little curious, and so is her refusal to explain it."

"As for me, I plump for the American," said Dr. Constantine. "It is a very expensive handkerchief, that; and Americans, as all the world knows, do not care what they pay."

"So you both eliminate the maid?" asked Poirot.

"Yes. As she herself said, it is the handkerchief of a member of the upper classes."

"And the second question—the pipe-cleaner. Did Colonel Arbuthnot drop it, or somebody else?"

"That is more difficult. The English, they do not stab. You are right there. I incline to the view that someone else dropped the pipe-cleaner—and did so to incriminate the long-legged Englishman."

"As you said, M. Poirot," put in the doctor, "*two* clues is too much carelessness. I agree with M. Bouc. The handkerchief was a genuine oversight—hence none of the women will admit that it is hers. The pipe-cleaner is a faked clue. In support of that theory, you notice that Colonel Arbuthnot shows no embarrassment and admits freely to smoking a pipe and using that type of cleaner."

"You reason well," said Poirot.

"Question No. 3—Who wore the scarlet kimono?" went on M. Bouc. "As to that, I will confess I have not the slightest idea. Have you any views on the subject, Dr. Constantine?"

"None."

"Then we confess ourselves beaten there. The next question has, at any rate, possibilities. Who was the man or the woman masquerading in Wagon Lit uniform? Well, one can list with certainty a number of people that it could not have been. Hardman, Colonel Arbuthnot, Foscarelli, Count Andrenyi and Hector MacQueen are all too tall. Mrs. Hubbard, Hildegarde Schmidt and Greta Ohlsson are too broad. That leaves the valet, Miss Debenham, Princess Dragomiroff and Countess Andrenyi—and none of them sounds likely! Greta Ohlsson in one case, and Antonio Foscarelli in the other, both swear that Miss Debenham and the valet never left their compartments. Hildegarde Schmidt swears that the Princess was in hers, and Count Andrenyi has told us that his wife took a sleeping draught. Therefore it seems impossible that it can be anybody—which is absurd!"

"As our old friend Euclid says," murmured Poirot.

"It must be one of those four," said Dr. Constantine. "Unless it is someone from outside who has found a hiding-place—and that we agreed was impossible."

M. Bouc had passed on to the next question on the list.

"No. 5—Why do the hands of the broken watch point to 1.15? I can see two explanations of that. Either it was done by the murderer to establish an alibi, and afterwards, when he meant to leave the compartment, he was prevented by hearing people moving about; or else—wait—I have an idea coming—"

The other two waited respectfully while M. Bouc struggled in mental agony.

"I have it," he said at last. "It was *not* the Wagon Lit murderer who tampered with the watch! It was the person we have called the Second Murderer—the left-handed person—in other words the woman in the scarlet kimono. She arrives later and moves back the hands of the watch in order to make an alibi for herself."

"Bravo," said Dr. Constantine. "It is well imagined, that."

"In fact," said Poirot, "she stabbed him in the dark, not realizing that he was dead already, but somehow deduced that he had a watch in his pyjama pocket, took it out, put back the hands blindly, and gave it the requisite dent."

M. Bouc looked at him coldly. "Have you anything better to suggest, yourself?" he asked.

"At the moment—no," admitted Poirot. "All the same," he went on, "I do not think you have either of you appreciated the most interesting point about that watch."

"Does question No. 6 deal with it?" asked the doctor. "To that question—Was the murder committed at that time, 1.15?—I answer *No*."

"I agree," said M. Bouc. " 'Was it earlier?' is the next question. I say—Yes! You, too, doctor?"

The doctor nodded. "Yes, but the question 'Was it later?' can also be answered in the affirmative. I agree with your theory, M. Bouc, and so, I think, does M. Poirot, although he does not wish to commit himself. The First Murderer came earlier than 1.15, but the Second Murderer came *after* 1.15. And as regards the question of left-handedness, ought we not to take steps to ascertain which of the passengers is left-handed?"

"I have not completely neglected that point," said Poirot. "You may have noticed that I made each passenger write either a signature or an address. That is not conclusive, because some people do certain actions with the right hand and others with the left. Some write right-handed, but play golf left-handed. Still, it is something. Every person questioned took the pen in his or her right hand—with the exception of Princess Dragomiroff, who refused to write."

"Princess Dragomiroff—impossible," said M. Bouc.

"I doubt if she would have had the strength to inflict that left-handed blow," said Dr. Constantine dubiously. "That particular wound had been inflicted with considerable force."

"More force than a woman could use?"

"No, I would not say that. But I think more force than an elderly woman could display, and Princess Dragomiroff's physique is particularly frail."

"It might be a question of the influence of mind over body," said Poirot. "Princess Dragomiroff has great personality and immense will-power. But let us pass from that for the moment."

"To questions Nos. 9 and 10? Can we be sure that Ratchett was stabbed by more than one person, and what other explanation of the wounds can there be? In my opinion, medically speaking, there can be *no other* explanation of those wounds. To suggest that one man struck first feebly and then with violence, first with the right hand and then with the left, and after an interval of perhaps half an hour inflicted fresh wounds on a dead body—well, it does not make sense."

"No," said Poirot. "It does not make sense. And you think that two murderers do make sense?"

"As you yourself have said, what other explanation can there be?"

Poirot stared straight ahead of him. "That is what I ask myself," he said. "That is what I never cease to ask myself."

He leaned back in his seat.

"From now on, it is all here." He tapped himself on the forehead. "We have thrashed it all out. The facts are all in front of us—neatly arranged with order and method. The passengers have sat here, one by one, giving their evidence. We know all that can be known—*from outside.* . . ."

He gave M. Bouc an affectionate smile.

"It has been a little joke between us, has it not—this business of sitting back and *thinking* out the truth? Well, I am about to put my theory into practice—here before your eyes. You two must do the same. Let us all three close our eyes and *think.* . . .

"One or more of those passengers killed Ratchett. *Which of them?*"

Chapter 3

Certain Suggestive Points

It was quite a quarter of an hour before anyone spoke. M. Bouc and Dr. Constantine had started by trying to obey Poirot's instructions. They had endeavored to see through a maze of conflicting particulars to a clear and outstanding solution.

M. Bouc's thoughts had run something as follows:

"Assuredly I must think. But as far as that goes I have already thought. . . . Poirot obviously thinks that this English girl is mixed up in the matter. I cannot help feeling that that is most unlikely. . . . The English are extremely cold. Probably it is because they have no figures. . . . But that is not the point. It seems that the Italian could not have done it— a pity. I suppose the English valet is not lying when he said the other never left the compartment? But why should he? It is not easy to bribe the English; they are so unapproachable. The whole thing is most unfortunate. I wonder when we shall get out of this. There must be *some* rescue work in progress. They are so slow in these countries . . . it is hours before anyone thinks of doing anything. And the police of these countries, they will be most trying to deal with—puffed up with importance, touchy, on their dignity. They will make a grand affair of all this. It is not often that such a chance comes their way. It will be in all the newspapers. . . ."

And from there on, M. Bouc's thoughts went along a well-worn course which they had already traversed some hundred times.

Dr. Constantine's thoughts ran thus:

"He is queer, this little man. A genius? Or a crank? Will he solve this mystery? Impossible—I can see no way out of it. It is all too confusing. . . . Everyone is lying, perhaps. . . . But even then, that does not help one. If they are all lying, it is just as confusing as if they were speaking the truth. Odd about those wounds. I cannot understand it. . . . It would be easier to understand if he had been shot—after all, the term 'gunman' must mean that they shoot with a gun. A curious country, America. I should like to go there. It is so progressive. When I get home I must get hold of Demetrius Zagone—he has been to America, he has all the modern ideas. . . . I wonder what Zia is doing at this moment. If my wife ever finds out—"

His thoughts went on to entirely private matters. . . .

Hercule Poirot sat very still.

One might have thought he was asleep.

And then, suddenly, after a quarter of an hour's complete immobility his eyebrows began to move slowly up his forehead. A little sigh escaped him. He murmured beneath his breath.

"But after all, why not? And if so—why, if so, that would explain everything."

His eyes opened. They were green like a cat's. He said softly: "*Eh bien*. I have thought. And you?"

Lost in their reflections, both men started violently.

"I have thought also," said M. Bouc, just a shade guiltily. "But I have arrived at no conclusion. The elucidation of crime is your *métier*, not mine, my friend."

"I, too, have reflected with great earnestness," said the doctor, unblushingly recalling his thoughts from certain pornographic details. "I have thought of many possible theories, but not one that really satisfies me."

Poirot nodded amiably. His nod seemed to say:

"Quite right. That is the proper thing to say. You have given me the cue I expected."

He sat very upright, threw out his chest, caressed his moustaches and spoke in the manner of a practised speaker addressing a public meeting.

"My friends, I have reviewed the facts in my mind, and have also gone over to myself the evidence of the passengers—with this result: I see, nebulously as yet, a certain explanation that would cover the facts as we know them. It is a very curious explanation, and I cannot be sure as yet that it is the true one. To find out definitely I shall have to make certain experiments.

"I would like first to mention certain points which appear to me suggestive. Let us start with a remark made to me by M. Bouc in this very place on the occasion of our first lunch together on the train. He commented on the fact that we were surrounded by people of all classes, of all ages, of all nationalities. That is a fact somewhat rare at this time of year. The Athens-Paris and the Bucharest-Paris coaches, for instance, are almost empty. Remember also, the passenger who failed to turn up. He is, I think, significant. Then there are some minor points that strike me as suggestive—for instance, the position of Mrs. Hubbard's sponge-bag, the name of Mrs. Armstrong's mother, the detective methods of M. Hardman, the suggestion of M. MacQueen that Ratchett himself destroyed the charred note we found, Princess Dragomiroff's Christian name, and a grease spot on a Hungarian passport."

The two men stared at him.

"Do they suggest anything to you, those points?" asked Poirot.

"Not a thing," said M. Bouc frankly.

"And M. *le docteur?*"

"I do not understand in the least what you are talking of."

M. Bouc, meanwhile, seizing upon the one tangible thing his friend had mentioned, was sorting through the passports. With a grunt he picked up that of Count and Countess Andrenyi and opened it.

"Is this what you mean? This dirty mark?"

"Yes. It is a fairly fresh grease spot. You notice where it occurs?"

"At the beginning of the description of the Count's wife—her Christian name, to be exact. But I confess that I still do not see the point."

"I am going to approach it from another angle. Let us go back to the handkerchief found at the scene of the crime. As we stated not long ago, three people are associated with the letter H: Mrs. Hubbard, Miss Debenham and the maid, Hildegarde Schmidt. Now let us regard that handkerchief from another point of view. It is, my friends, an extremely expensive handkerchief—an *objet de luxe*, handmade, embroidered in Paris. Which of the passengers, apart from the initial, was likely to own such a handkerchief? Not Mrs. Hubbard, a worthy woman with no pretensions to reckless extravagance in dress. Not Miss Debenham—that class of Englishwoman has a dainty linen handkerchief, not an expensive wisp of cambric costing perhaps two hundred francs. And certainly not the maid. But there *are* two women on the train who would be likely to own such a handkerchief. Let us see if we can connect them in any way with the letter H. The two women I refer to are Princess Dragomiroff—"

"Whose Christian name is Natalia," put in M. Bouc ironically.

"Exactly. And her Christian name, as I said just now, is decidedly suggestive. The other woman is Countess Andrenyi. And at once something strikes us—"

"*You!*"

"*Me*, then. Her Christian name on her passport is disfigured by a blob of grease. Just an accident, anyone would say. But consider that Christian name. Elena. Suppose that, instead of Elena, it were *Helena*. That capital

H could be turned into a capital E and then run over the small e next to it quite easily—and then a spot of grease dropped to cover up the alteration."

"Helena!" cried M. Bouc. "It is an idea, that."

"Certainly it is an idea! I look about for any confirmation, however slight, of my idea—and I find it. One of the luggage labels on the Countess's baggage is slightly damp. It is one that happens to run over the first initial on top of the case. That label has been soaked off and put on again in a different place."

"You begin to convince me," said M. Bouc. "But the Countess Andrenyi—surely—"

"Ah, now, *mon vieux*, you must turn yourself round and approach an entirely different angle of the case. How was this murder intended to appear to everybody? Do not forget that the snow has upset all the murderer's original plans. Let us imagine, for a little minute, that there is no snow, that the train proceeded on its normal course. What, then, would have happened?

"The murder, let us say, would still have been discovered in all probability at the Italian frontier early this morning. Much of the same evidence would have been given to the Italian police. The threatening letters would have been produced by M. MacQueen; M. Hardman would have told his story; Mrs. Hubbard would have been eager to tell how a man passed through her compartment; the button would have been found. I imagine that two things only would have been different. The man would have passed through Mrs. Hubbard's compartment just before one o'clock—and the Wagon Lit uniform would have been found cast off in one of the toilets."

"You mean?"

"I mean that the murder was *planned to look like an outside job*. It would have been presumed that the assassin had left the train at Brod where it is timed to arrive at 0.58. Somebody would probably have passed a strange Wagon Lit conductor in the corridor. The uniform would be left in a conspicuous place so as to show clearly just how the trick had been played. No suspicion would have attached to the passengers. That, my friends, was how the affair was intended to appear to the outside world.

"But the accident to the train changes everything. Doubtless we have here the reason why the man remained in the compartment with his victim so long. He was waiting for the train to go on. But at last he realised that *the train was not going on*. Different plans would have to be made. The murderer would now be *known* to be still on the train."

"Yes, yes," said M. Bouc impatiently. "I see all that. But where does the handkerchief come in?"

"I am returning to it by a somewhat circuitous route. To begin with, you must realise that the threatening letters were in the nature of a blind. They might have been lifted bodily out of an indifferently written American crime novel. They are not *real*. They are, in fact, simply intended for the police. What we have to ask ourselves is: 'Did they deceive Ratchett?' On the face of it, the answer seems to be No. His instructions to Hardman seem to point to a definite 'private' enemy, of whose identity he was well aware. That is, if we accept Hardman's story as true. But Ratchett certainly received *one* letter of a very different character—the one containing a reference to the Armstrong baby, a fragment of which we found in his compartment. In case Ratchett had not realised it sooner, this was to make sure that he understood the reason of the threats against his life. That letter, as I have said all along, was *not* intended to be found. The murderer's first care was to destroy it. This, then, was the second hitch in his plans. The first was the snow, the second was our reconstruction of that fragment.

"That the note was destroyed so carefully can mean only one thing. *There must be on the train someone so intimately connected with the Armstrong family that the finding of that note would immediately direct suspicion upon that person.*

"Now we come to the other two clues that we found. I pass over the pipe-cleaner. We have already said a good deal about that. Let us pass on to the handkerchief. Taken at its simplest it is a clue which directly incriminates someone whose initial is H, and it was dropped there unwittingly by that person."

"Exactly," said Dr. Constantine. "She finds out that she has dropped the handkerchief and immediately takes steps to conceal her Christian name."

"How fast you go! You arrive at a conclusion much sooner than I would permit myself to do."

"Is there any other alternative?"

"Certainly there is. Suppose, for instance, that you have committed a crime and wish to cast the blame for it on someone else. Well, there is on the train a certain person connected intimately with the Armstrong family—a woman. Suppose, then, that you leave there a handkerchief belonging to that woman. She will be questioned, her connection with the Armstrong family will be brought out—*et voilà*: motive—*and* an incriminating article of evidence."

"But in such a case," objected the doctor, "the person indicated, being innocent, would not take steps to conceal her identity."

"Ah, really? That is what you think? That is, truly, the opinion of the police court. But I know human nature, my friend, and I tell you that, suddenly confronted with the possibility of being tried for murder, the most innocent person will lose his head and do the most absurd things. No, no, the grease spot and the changed label do not prove guilty—they only prove that the Countess Andrenyi is anxious for some reason to conceal her identity."

"What do you think her connection with the Armstrong family can be? She has never been in America, she says."

"Exactly, and she speaks English with a foreign accent, and she has a very foreign appearance which she exaggerates. But it should not be difficult to guess who she is. I mentioned just now the name of Mrs. Armstrong's mother. It was 'Linda Arden,' and she was a very celebrated actress—among other things a Shakespearean actress. Think of *As You Like It*, with the Forest of Arden and Rosalind. It was there she got the inspiration for her acting name. 'Linda Arden,' the name by which she was known all over the world, was not her real name. It may have been Goldenberg; it is quite likely that she had Central European blood in her veins—a strain of Jewish, perhaps. Many nationalities drift to America. I suggest to you, gentlemen, that that young sister of Mrs. Armstrong's, little more than a child at the time of the tragedy, was Helena Goldenberg, the younger daughter of Linda Arden, and that she married Count Andrenyi when he was an attaché in Washington."

"But Princess Dragomiroff says that the girl married an Englishman."

"Whose name she cannot remember! I ask you, my friends, is that really likely? Princess Dragomiroff loved Linda Arden as great ladies do love great artists. She was godmother to one of the actress's daughters. Would she forget so quickly the married name of the other daughter? It is not likely. No, I think we can safely say that Princess Dragomiroff was lying. She knew Helena was on the train, she had seen her. She realised at once, as soon as she heard who Ratchett really was, that Helena would be suspected. And so, when we question her as to the sister, she promptly lies—is vague, cannot remember, but 'thinks Helena married an Englishman'—a suggestion as far away from the truth as possible."

One of the restaurant attendants came through the door at the end and approached them. He addressed M. Bouc.

"The dinner, Monsieur, shall I serve it? It is ready some little time."

M. Bouc looked at Poirot. The latter nodded. "By all means, let dinner be served."

The attendant vanished through the doors at the other end. His bell could be heard ringing and his voice upraised:

"*Premier service. Le dîner est servi. Premier dîner*—First service."

Chapter 4

The Grease Spot on
a Hungarian Passport

Poirot shared a table with M. Bouc and the doctor.

The company assembled in the restaurant car was a very subdued one. They spoke little. Even the loquacious Mrs. Hubbard was unnaturally quiet. She murmured as she sat:

"I don't feel as though I had the heart to eat anything," and then partook of everything offered her, encouraged by the Swedish lady who seemed to regard her as a special charge.

Before the meal was served, Poirot had caught the chief attendant by the sleeve and murmured something to him. Constantine made a pretty good guess as to what the instructions had been when he noticed that the Count and Countess Andrenyi were always served last and that at the end of the meal there was a delay in making out their bill. It therefore came about that the Count and Countess were the last left in the restaurant car.

When they rose at length and moved in the direction of the door, Poirot sprang up and followed them.

"Pardon, Madame, you have dropped your handkerchief."

He was holding out to her the tiny monogrammed square.

She took it, glanced at it, then handed it back to him.

"You are mistaken, Monsieur, that is not my handkerchief."

"Not your handkerchief? Are you sure?"

"Perfectly sure, Monsieur."

"And yet, Madame, it has your initial—the initial H."

The Count made a sudden movement. Poirot ignored him. His eyes were fixed on the Countess's face.

Looking steadily at him she replied:

"I do not understand, Monsieur. My initials are E. A."

"I think not. Your name is Helena—not Elena. Helena Goldenberg, the younger daughter of Linda Arden—Helena Goldenberg, the sister of Mrs. Armstrong."

There was a dead silence for a minute or two. Both the Count and the Countess had gone deadly white.

Poirot said in a gentler tone: "It is of no use denying. That is the truth, is it not?"

The Count burst out furiously, "I demand, Monsieur, by what right you—"

She interrupted him, putting up a small hand towards his mouth.

"No, Rudolph. Let me speak. It is useless to deny what this gentleman says. We had better sit down and talk the matter out."

Her voice had changed. It still had the southern richness of tone, but it had become suddenly more clear cut and incisive. It was, for the first time, a definitely American voice.

The Count was silenced. He obeyed the gesture of her hand and they both sat down opposite Poirot.

"Your statement, Monsieur, is quite true," said the Countess. "I am Helena Goldenberg, the younger sister of Mrs. Armstrong."

"You did not acquaint me with that fact this morning, Madame la Comtesse."

"No."

"In fact, all that your husband and you told me was a tissue of lies."

"Monsieur!" cried the Count angrily.

"Do not be angry, Rudolph. M. Poirot puts the fact rather brutally, but what he says is undeniable."

"I am glad you admit the fact so freely, Madame. Will you now tell me your reasons for that, and also for altering your Christian name on your passport?"

"That was my doing entirely," put in the Count.

Helena said quietly: "Surely, M. Poirot, you can guess my reason— our reason. This man who was killed is the man who murdered my baby niece, who killed my sister, who broke my brother-in-law's heart. Three of the people I loved best and who made up my home—my world!"

Her voice rang out passionately. She was a true daughter of that mother the emotional force of whose acting had moved huge audiences to tears.

She went on more quietly.

"Of all the people on the train I alone had probably the best motive for killing him."

"And you did not kill him, Madame?"

"I swear to you, M. Poirot—and my husband knows and will swear also—that much as I may have been tempted to do so, I never lifted a hand against that man."

"I, too, gentlemen," said the Count. "I give you my word of honour that last night Helena never left her compartment. She took a sleeping draught exactly as I said. She is utterly and entirely innocent."

Poirot looked from one to the other of them.

"On my word of honour," repeated the Count.

Poirot shook his head slightly.

"And yet you took it upon yourself to alter the name in the passport?"

"Monsieur Poirot," the Count said earnestly and passionately, "consider my position. Do you think I could stand the thought of my wife dragged through a sordid police case? She was innocent, I knew it, but what she said was true—because of her connection with the Armstrong family she would have been immediately suspected. She would have been questioned—arrested, perhaps. Since some evil chance had taken us on the same train as this man Ratchett, there was, I felt sure, but one thing for it. I admit, Monsieur, that I lied to you—all, that is, save in one thing. My wife never left her compartment last night."

He spoke with an earnestness that it was hard to gainsay.

"I do not say that I disbelieve you, Monsieur," said Poirot slowly. "Your family is, I know, a proud and ancient one. It would be bitter indeed for you to have your wife dragged into an unpleasant police case. With that I can sympathise. But how then do you explain the presence of your wife's handkerchief actually in the dead man's compartment?"

"That handkerchief is not mine, Monsieur," said the Countess.

"In spite of the initial H?"

"In spite of the initial. I have handkerchiefs not unlike that, but not one that is exactly of that pattern. I know, of course, that I cannot hope to make you believe me, but I assure you that it is so. That handkerchief is not mine."

"It may have been placed there by someone in order to incriminate you?"

She smiled a little. "You are enticing me to admit that, after all, it is mine? But indeed, M. Poirot, it isn't." She spoke with great earnestness.

"Then why, if the handkerchief was not yours, did you alter the name in the passport?"

The Count answered this.

"Because we heard that a handkerchief had been found with the initial H on it. We talked the matter over together before we came to be interviewed. I pointed out to Helena that if it were seen that her Christian name began with an H she would immediately be subjected to much more rigorous questioning. And the thing was so simple—to alter Helena to Elena was easily done."

"You have, M. le Comte, the makings of a very fine criminal," remarked Poirot dryly. "A great natural ingenuity, and an apparently remorseless determination to mislead justice."

"Oh, no, no." The girl leaned forward. "M. Poirot, he's explained to you how it was." She broke from French into English. "I was scared—absolutely dead scared, you understand. It had been so awful—that time—and to have it all raked up again. And to be suspected and perhaps thrown into prison. I was just scared stiff, M. Poirot. Can't you understand at all?"

Her voice was lovely—deep—rich—pleading, the voice of the daughter of Linda Arden the actress.

Poirot looked gravely at her.

"If I am to believe you, Madame—and I do not say that I will *not* believe you—then you must help me."

"Help you?"

"Yes. The reason for the murder lies in the past—in that tragedy which broke up your home and saddened your young life. Take me back into the past, Mademoiselle, that I may find there the link that explains the whole thing."

"What can there be to tell you? They are all dead." She repeated mournfully: "All dead—all dead—Robert, Sonia—darling, darling Daisy. She was so sweet—so happy—she had such lovely curls. We were all just crazy about her."

"There was another victim, Madame. An indirect victim, you might say."

"Poor Susanne? Yes, I had forgotten about her. The police questioned her. They were convinced that she had something to do with it. Perhaps she had—but if so only innocently. She had, I believe, chatted idly with someone, giving information as to the time of Daisy's outings. The poor thing got terribly wrought up—she thought she was being held responsible." She shuddered. "She threw herself out of the window. Oh! it was horrible."

She buried her face in her hands.

"What nationality was she, Madame?"

"She was French."

"What was her last name?"

"It's absurd, but I can't remember—we all called her Susanne. A pretty, laughing girl. She was devoted to Daisy."

"She was the nursery-maid, was she not?"

"Yes."

"Who was the nurse?"

"She was a trained hospital nurse. Stengelberg her name was. She too was devoted to Daisy—and to my sister."

"Now, Madame, I want you to think carefully before you answer this question. Have you, since you were on this train, seen anyone that you recognised?"

She stared at him. "I? No, no one at all."

"What about Princess Dragomiroff?"

"Oh! her. I know her, of course. I thought you meant anyone—anyone from—from that time."

"So I did, Madame. Now think carefully. Some years have passed, remember. The person might have altered his or her appearance."

Helena pondered deeply. Then she said: "No—I am sure—there is no one."

"You yourself—you were a young girl at the time—did you have no one to superintend your studies or to look after you?"

"Oh! yes, I had a dragon—a sort of governess to me and secretary to Sonia combined. She was English—or rather Scotch; a big red-haired woman."

"What was her name?"

"Miss Freebody."

"Young or old?"

"She seemed frightfully old to me. I suppose she couldn't have been more than forty. Susanne, of course, used to look after my clothes and maid me."

"And there were no other inmates of the house?"

"Only servants."

"And you are certain, quite certain, Madame, that you have recognised no one on the train?"

She replied earnestly: "No one, Monsieur. No one at all."

Chapter 5

The Christian Name of Princess Dragomiroff

When the Count and Countess had departed, Poirot looked across at the other two.

"You see," he said, "we make progress."

"Excellent work," said M. Bouc cordially. "On my part, I should never have dreamed of suspecting Count and Countess Andrenyi. I will admit I thought them quite *hors de combat*. I suppose there is no doubt that she committed the crime? It is rather sad. Still, they will not guillotine her. There are extenuating circumstances. A few years' imprisonment—that will be all."

"In fact you are quite certain of her guilt."

"My dear friend—surely there is no doubt of it? I thought your reassuring manner was only to smooth things over till we are dug out of the snow and the police take charge."

"You do not believe the Count's positive assertion—on his word of honor—that his wife is innocent?"

"*Mon cher*—naturally—what else *could* he say? He adores his wife. He wants to save her! He tells his lie very well—quite in the grand *seigneur* manner. But what else than a lie could it be?"

"Well, you know, I had the preposterous idea that it might be the truth."

"No, no. The handkerchief, remember. The handkerchief clinches the matter."

"Oh, I am not so sure about the handkerchief. You remember, I always told you that there were two possibilities as to the ownership of the handkerchief."

"All the same—"

M. Bouc broke off. The door at the end had opened, and Princess Dragomiroff entered the dining-car. She came straight to them and all three men rose to their feet.

She spoke to Poirot, ignoring the others.

"I believe, Monsieur," she said, "that you have a handkerchief of mine."

Poirot shot a glance of triumph at the other two.

"Is this it, Madame?"

He produced the little square of fine cambric.

"That is it. It has my initial in the corner."

"But, Madame la Princesse, that is the letter H," said M. Bouc. "Your Christian name—pardon me—is Natalia."

She gave him a cold stare.

"That is correct, Monsieur. My handkerchiefs are always initialed in the Russian characters. H is N in Russian."

M. Bouc was somewhat taken aback. There was something about this indomitable old lady which made him feel flustered and uncomfortable.

"You did not tell us that this handkerchief was yours at the inquiry this morning."

"You did not ask me," said the Princess dryly.

"Pray be seated, Madame," said Poirot.

She sighed. "I may as well, I suppose." She sat down.

"You need not make a long business of this, Messieurs.

"Your next question will be—How did my handkerchief come to be lying by a murdered man's body? My reply to that is that I have no idea."

"You have really no idea?"

"None whatever."

"You will excuse me, Madame, but how much can we rely upon the truthfulness of your replies?"

Poirot said the words very softly.

Princess Dragomiroff answered contemptuously. "I suppose you mean because I did not tell you that Helena Andrenyi was Mrs. Armstrong's sister?"

"In fact you deliberately lied to us in the matter."

"Certainly. I would do the same again. Her mother was my friend. I believe, Messieurs, in loyalty—to one's friends and one's family and one's caste."

"You do not believe in doing your utmost to further the ends of justice?"

"In this case I consider that justice—strict justice—has been done."

Poirot leaned forward.

"You see my difficulty, Madame. In this matter of the handkerchief, even, am I to believe you? Or are you shielding your friend's daughter?"

"Oh! I see what you mean." Her face broke into a grim smile. "Well, Messieurs, this statement of mine can be easily proved. I will give you the address of the people in Paris who make my handkerchiefs. You have only to show them the one in question and they will inform you that it was made to my order over a year ago. The handkerchief is mine, Messieurs."

She rose.

"Have you anything further you wish to ask me?"

"Your maid, Madame, did she recognise this handkerchief when we showed it to her this morning?"

"She must have done so. She saw it and said nothing? Ah, well, that shows that she too can be loyal."

With a slight inclination of her head she passed out of the dining-car.

"So that was it," murmured Poirot softly. "I noticed just a trifling hesitation when I asked the maid if she knew to whom the handkerchief belonged. She was uncertain whether or not to admit that it was her mistress's. But how does that fit in with that strange central idea of mine? Yes, it might well be."

"Ah!" said M. Bouc with a characteristic gesture. "She is a terrible old lady, that!"

"Could she have murdered Ratchett?" asked Poirot of the doctor.

He shook his head.

"Those blows—the ones delivered with great force penetrating the muscle—never, never could anyone with so frail a physique inflict them."

"But the feebler ones?"

"The feebler ones, yes."

"I am thinking," said Poirot, "of the incident this morning when I said to her that the strength was in her will rather than in her arm. It was in the nature of a trap, that remark. I wanted to see if she would look down at her right or her left arm. She did neither. She looked at them both. But she made a strange reply. She said, 'No, I have no strength in these. I do not know whether to be sorry or glad.' A curious remark that. It confirms me in my belief about the crime."

"It did not settle the point about the left-handedness."

"No. By the way, did you notice that Count Andrenyi keeps his handkerchief in his right-hand breast pocket?"

M. Bouc shook his head. His mind reverted to the astonishing revelations of the last half-hour. He murmured:

"Lies—and again lies. It amazes me, the number of lies we had told to us this morning."

"There are more still to discover," said Poirot cheerfully.

"You think so?"

"I shall be very much disappointed if it is not so."

"Such duplicity is terrible," said M. Bouc. "But it seems to please you," he added reproachfully.

"It has this advantage," said Poirot. "If you confront anyone who has lied with the truth, he will usually admit it—often out of sheer surprise. It is only necessary to guess *right* to produce your effect.

"That is the only way to conduct this case. I select each passenger in turn, consider his or her evidence, and say to myself, '*If* so and so is lying, on what *point* is he lying, and what is the *reason* for the lie?' And I answer, 'If he is lying—if, you mark—it could only be for such a reason and on such a point.' We have done that once very successfully with Countess Andrenyi. We shall now proceed to try the same method on several other persons."

"And supposing, my friend, that your guess happens to be wrong?"

"Then one person, at any rate, will be completely freed from suspicion."

"Ah!—a process of elimination."

"Exactly."

"And whom do we tackle next?"

"We are going to tackle that *pukka sahib*, Colonel Arbuthnot."

Chapter 6

A Second Interview with Colonel Arbuthnot

Colonel Arbuthnot was clearly annoyed at being summoned to the dining-car for a second interview. His face wore a most forbidding expression as he sat down and said:

"Well?"

"All my apologies for troubling you a second time," said Poirot. "But there is still some information that I think you might be able to give us."

"Indeed? I hardly think so."

"To begin with, you see this pipe cleaner?"

"Yes."

"Is it one of yours?"

"Don't know. I don't put a private mark on them, you know."

"Are you aware, Colonel Arbuthnot, that you are the only man amongst the passengers in the Stamboul-Calais carriage who smokes a pipe?"

"In that case it probably is one of mine."

"Do you know where it was found?"

"Not the least idea."

"It was found by the body of the murdered man."

Colonel Arbuthnot raised his eyebrows.

"Can you tell us, Colonel Arbuthnot, how it is likely to have got there?"

"If you mean, did I drop it there myself, no, I didn't."

"Did you go into Mr. Ratchett's compartment at any time?"

"I never even spoke to the man."

"You never spoke to him and you did not murder him?"

The Colonel's eyebrows went up again sardonically.

"If I had, I should hardly be likely to acquaint you with the fact. As a matter of fact I *didn't* murder the fellow."

"Ah, well," murmured Poirot. "It is of no consequence."

"I beg your pardon?"

"I said that it was of no consequence."

"Oh!" Arbuthnot looked taken aback. He eyed Poirot uneasily.

"Because, you see," continued the little man, "the pipe cleaner, it is of no importance. I can myself think of eleven other excellent explanations of its presence."

Arbuthnot stared at him.

"What I really wished to see you about was quite another matter," went on Poirot. "Miss Debenham may have told you, perhaps, that I overheard some words spoken to you at the station of Konya?"

Arbuthnot did not reply.

"She said, *'Not now. When it's all over. When it's behind us!'* Do you know to what those words referred?"

"I am sorry, M. Poirot, but I must refuse to answer that question."

"Pourquoi?"

The Colonel said stiffly, "I suggest that you ask Miss Debenham herself for the meaning of those words."

"I have done so."

"And she refused to tell you?"

"Yes."

"Then I should think it would have been perfectly plain—even to you—that my lips are sealed."

"You will not give away a lady's secret?"

"You can put it that way, if you like."

"Miss Debenham told me that they referred to a private matter of her own."

"Then why not accept her word for it?"

"Because, Colonel Arbuthnot, Miss Debenham is what one might call a highly suspicious character."

"Nonsense," said the Colonel with warmth.

"It is not nonsense."

"You have nothing whatever against her."

"Not the fact that Miss Debenham was companion governess in the Armstrong household at the time of the kidnapping of little Daisy Armstrong?"

There was a minute's dead silence.

Poirot nodded his head gently.

"You see," he said. "We know more than you think. If Miss Debenham is innocent, why did she conceal that fact? Why did she tell me that she had never been in America?"

The Colonel cleared his throat. "Aren't you possibly making a mistake?"

"I am making no mistake. Why did Miss Debenham lie to me?"

Colonel Arbuthnot shrugged his shoulders. "You had better ask her. I still think that you are wrong."

Poirot raised his voice and called. One of the restaurant attendants came from the far end of the car.

"Go and ask the English lady in No. 11 if she will be good enough to come here."

"Bien, Monsieur."

The man departed. The four men sat in silence. Colonel Arbuthnot's face looked as though it were carved out of wood, rigid and impassive.

The man returned.

"The lady is just coming, Monsieur."

"Thank you."

A minute or two later Mary Debenham entered the dining-car.

Chapter 7

The Identity of Mary Debenham

She wore no hat. Her head was thrown back as though in defiance. The sweep of her hair back from her face, the curve of her nostril suggested the figurehead of a ship plunging gallantly into a rough sea. In that moment she was beautiful.

Her eyes went to Arbuthnot for a minute—just a minute.

She said to Poirot, "You wished to see me?"

"I wished to ask you, Mademoiselle, why you lied to us this morning?"

"Lied to you? I don't know what you mean."

"You concealed the fact that at the time of the Armstrong tragedy you were actually living in the house. You told me that you had never been in America."

He saw her flinch for a moment and then recover herself.

"Yes," she said. "That is true."

"No, Mademoiselle, it was false."

"You misunderstood me. I mean that it is true that I lied to you."

"Ah, you admit it?"

Her lips curved into a smile. "Certainly, since you have found me out."

"You are at least frank, Mademoiselle."

"There does not seem anything else for me to be."

"Well, of course, that is true. And now, Mademoiselle, may I ask you the reason for these evasions?"

"I should have thought the reason leapt to the eye, M. Poirot?"

"It does not leap to mine, Mademoiselle."

She said in a quiet even voice with a trace of hardness in it, "I have my living to get."

"You mean—?"

She raised her eyes and looked him full in the face.

"How much do you know, M. Poirot, of the fight to get and keep decent employment? Do you think that a girl who had been detained in connection with a murder case, whose name and perhaps photograph were reproduced in the English papers—do you think that any nice ordinary middle-class Englishwoman would want to engage that girl as governess to her daughters?"

"I do not see why not—if no blame attached to you."

"Oh, blame—it is not *blame*—it is the publicity! So far, M. Poirot, I have succeeded in life. I have had well-paid, pleasant posts. I was not going to risk the position I had attained when no good end could have been served."

"I will venture to suggest, Mademoiselle, that I would have been the best judge of that, not you."

She shrugged her shoulders.

"For instance, you could have helped me in the matter of identification."

"What do you mean?"

"Is it possible, Mademoiselle, that you did not recognise in the Countess Andrenyi Mrs. Armstrong's young sister whom you taught in New York?"

"Countess Andrenyi? No." She shook her head. "It may seem extraordinary to you—but I did not recognise her. She was not grown up, you see, when I knew her. That was over three years ago. It is true that the Countess reminded me of someone; it puzzled me. But she looks so foreign—I never connected her with the little American schoolgirl. I only glanced at her casually when coming into the restaurant car, and I noticed her clothes more than her face." She smiled faintly. "Women do! And then—well—I had my own preoccupations."

"You will not tell me your secret, Mademoiselle?"

Poirot's voice was very gentle and persuasive.

She said in a low voice, "I can't—I can't."

And suddenly, without warning, she broke down, dropping her face down upon her outstretched arms and crying as though her heart would break.

The Colonel sprang up and stood awkwardly beside her.

"I—look here—"

He stopped and turning round scowled fiercely at Poirot.

"I'll break every bone in your damned body, you dirty little whippersnapper," he said.

"Monsieur," protested M. Bouc.

Arbuthnot had turned back to the girl. "Mary—for God's sake—"

She sprang up. "It's nothing. I'm all right. You don't need me any more, do you, M. Poirot? If you do, you must come and find me. Oh, what an idiot—what an idiot I'm making of myself!" She hurried out of the car.

Arbuthnot, before following her, turned once more on Poirot.

"Miss Debenham's got nothing to do with this business—nothing, do you hear? And if she's worried and interfered with, you'll have me to deal with." He strode out.

"I like to see an angry Englishman," said Poirot. "They are very amusing. The more emotional they feel, the less command they have of language."

But M. Bouc was not interested in the emotional reactions of Englishmen. He was overcome by admiration of his friend.

"Mon cher, vous être épatant!" he cried. "Another miraculous guess."

"It is incredible how you think of these things," said Dr. Constantine admiringly.

"Oh, I claim no credit this time. It was not a guess. Countess Andrenyi practically told me."

"Comment? Surely not?"

"You remember, I asked her about her governess or companion? I had already decided in my mind that *if* Mary Debenham were mixed up in the matter, she must have figured in the household in some such capacity."

"Yes, but the Countess Andrenyi described a totally different person."

"Exactly. A tall middle-aged woman with red hair—in fact, the exact opposite in every respect of Miss Debenham, so much so as to be quite remarkable. But then she had to invent a name quickly, and there it was that the unconscious association of ideas gave her away. She said Miss Freebody, you remember."

"Yes?"

"Eh bien, you may not know it, but there is a shop in London that was called until recently Debenham & Freebody. With the name Debenham running in her head, the Countess clutches at another name quickly, and the first that comes is Freebody. Naturally I understood immediately."

"That is yet another lie. Why did she do it?"

"Possibly more loyalty. It makes things a little difficult."

"Ma foi!" said M. Bouc with violence. "But does everybody on this train tell lies?"

"That," said Poirot, "is what we are about to find out."

Chapter 8

Further Surprising Revelations

"Nothing would surprise me now," said M. Bouc. "Nothing! Even if everybody in the train proved to have been in the Armstrong household, I should not express surprise."

"That is a very profound remark," said Poirot. "Would you like to see what your favorite suspect, the Italian, has to say for himself?"

"You are going to make another of these famous guesses of yours?"

"Precisely."

"It is really a *most* extraordinary case," said Constantine.

"No, it is most natural."

M. Bouc flung up his arms in comic despair. "If this is what you call natural, *mon ami*—" Words failed him.

Poirot had by this time requested the dining-car attendant to fetch Antonio Foscarelli.

The big Italian had a wary look in his eye as he came in. He shot nervous glances from side to side like a trapped animal.

"What do you want?" he said. "I have nothing more to tell you—nothing, do you hear? *Per Dio*—" He struck his hand on the table.

"Yes, you have something more to tell us," said Poirot firmly. "The truth!"

"The truth?" He shot an uneasy glance at Poirot. All the assurance and geniality had gone out of his manner.

"*Mais oui.* It may be that I know it already. But it will be a point in your favour if it comes from you spontaneously."

"You talk like the American police. 'Come clean'—that is what they say—'come clean.' "

"Ah! so you have had experience of the New York police?"

"No, no, never. They could not prove a thing against me—but it was not for want of trying."

Poirot said quietly: "That was in the Armstrong case, was it not? You were the chauffeur?"

His eyes met those of the Italian. The bluster went out of the big man. He was like a pricked balloon.

"Since you know—why ask me?"

"Why did you lie this morning?"

"Business reasons. Besides, I do not trust the Jugo-Slav police. They hate the Italians. They would not have given me justice."

"Perhaps it is exactly justice that they *would* have given you!"

"No, no, I had nothing to do with this business last night. I never left my carriage. The long-faced Englishman, he can tell you so. It was not I who killed this pig—this Ratchett. You cannot prove anything against me."

Poirot was writing something on a sheet of paper. He looked up and said quietly: "Very good. You can go."

Foscarelli lingered uneasily. "You realise that it was not I? That I could have had nothing to do with it?"

"I said that you could go."

"It is a conspiracy. You are going to frame me? All for a pig of a man who should have gone to the chair! It was an infamy that he did not. If it had been me—if I had been arrested—"

"But it was not you. You had nothing to do with the kidnapping of the child."

"What is that you are saying? Why, that little one—she was the delight of the house. Tonio, she called me. And she would sit in the car and pretend to hold the wheel. All the household worshipped her! Even the police came to understand that. Ah, the beautiful little one!"

His voice had softened. The tears came into his eyes. Then he wheeled round abruptly on his heel and strode out of the dining-car.

"Pietro," called Poirot.

The dining-car attendant came at a run.

"The No. 10—the Swedish lady."

"Bien, Monsieur."

"Another?" cried M. Bouc. "Ah, no—it is not possible. I tell you it is not possible."

"Mon cher—we have to *know.* Even if in the end everybody on the train proves to have had a motive for killing Ratchett, we have to know. Once we know, we can settle once for all where the guilt lies."

"My head is spinning," groaned M. Bouc.

Greta Ohlsson was ushered in sympathetically by the attendant. She was weeping bitterly.

She collapsed on the seat facing Poirot and wept steadily into a large handkerchief.

"Now do not distress yourself, Mademoiselle. Do not distress yourself." Poirot patted her on the shoulder. "Just a few little words of truth, that is all. You were the nurse who was in charge of little Daisy Armstrong?"

"It is true—it is true," wept the wretched woman. "Ah, she was an angel—a little sweet trustful angel. She knew nothing but kindness and love—and she was taken away by that wicked man—cruelly treated—and her poor mother—and the other little one who never lived at all. You cannot understand—you cannot know—if you had been there as I was—if you had seen the whole terrible tragedy! I ought to have told you the truth about myself this morning. But I was afraid—afraid. I did so rejoice that that evil man was dead—that he could not any more kill or torture little children. Ah! I cannot speak—I have no words. . . ."

She wept with more vehemence than ever.

Poirot continued to pat her gently on the shoulder. "There—there—I comprehend—I comprehend everything—everything, I tell you. I will ask you no more questions. It is enough that you have admitted what I know to be the truth. I understand, I tell you."

By now inarticulate with sobs, Greta Ohlsson rose and groped her way blindly towards the door. As she reached it she collided with a man coming in.

It was the valet—Masterman.

He came straight up to Poirot and spoke in his usual quiet, unemotional voice.

"I hope I'm not intruding, sir. I thought it best to come along at once, sir, and tell you the truth. I was Colonel Armstrong's batman in the War, sir, and afterwards I was his valet in New York. I'm afraid I concealed that fact this morning. It was very wrong of me, sir, and I thought I'd better come and make a clean breast of it. But I hope, sir, that you're not suspecting Tonio in any way. Old Tonio, sir, wouldn't hurt a fly. And I can swear positively that he never left the carriage all last night. So, you see, sir, he couldn't have done it. Tonio may be a foreigner, sir, but he's a very gentle creature. Not like those nasty murdering Italians one reads about."

He stopped.

Poirot looked steadily at him. "Is that all you have to say?"

"That is all, sir."

He paused; then, as Poirot did not speak, he made an apologetic little bow and after a momentary hesitation left the dining-car in the same quiet unobtrusive fashion as he had come.

"This," said Dr. Constantine, "is more wildly improbable than any *roman policier* I have ever read."

"I agree," said M. Bouc. "Of the twelve passengers in that coach, nine have been proved to have had a connection with the Armstrong case. What next, I ask you? Or should I say, who next?"

"I can almost give you the answer to your question," said Poirot. "Here comes our American sleuth, Mr. Hardman."

"Is he, too, coming to confess?"

Before Poirot could reply the American had reached their table. He cocked an alert eye at them and sitting down he drawled out: "Just exactly what's up on this train? It seems bughouse to me."

Poirot twinkled at him.

"Are you quite sure, Mr. Hardman, that you yourself were not the gardener at the Armstrong home?"

"They didn't have a garden," replied Mr. Hardman literally.

"Or the butler?"

"Haven't got the fancy manners for a place like that. No, I never had any connection with the Armstrong house—but I'm beginning to believe I'm about the only one on this train who hadn't! Can you beat it? That's what I say—can you beat it?"

"It is certainly a little surprising," said Poirot mildly.

"*C'est rigolo*," burst from M. Bouc.

"Have you any ideas of your own about the crime, Mr. Hardman?" inquired Poirot.

"No, sir. It's got me beat. I don't know how to figure it out. They can't *all* be in it—but which one is the guilty party is beyond me. How did you get wise to all this? That's what I want to know."

"I just guessed."

"Then, believe me, you're a pretty slick guesser. Yes, I'll tell the world you're a slick guesser."

Mr. Hardman leaned back and looked at Poirot admiringly.

"You'll excuse me," he said, "but no one would believe it to look at you. I take off my hat to you. I do indeed."

"You are too kind, M. Hardman."

"Not at all. I've got to hand it to you."

"All the same," said Poirot, "the problem is not yet quite solved. Can we say with authority that we know who killed M. Ratchett?"

"Count me out," said Mr. Hardman. "I'm not saying anything at all. I'm just full of natural admiration. What about the other two you haven't had a guess at yet? The old American dame, and the lady's-maid? I suppose we can take it that they're the only innocent parties on the train?"

"Unless," said Poirot, smiling, "we can fit them into our little collection as—shall we say—housekeeper and cook in the Armstrong household?"

"Well, nothing in the world would surprise me now," said Mr. Hardman with quiet resignation. "Bughouse—that's what this business is—bughouse!"

"Ah! *mon cher*, that would be indeed stretching coincidence a little too far," said M. Bouc. "They cannot all be in it."

Poirot looked at him. "You do not understand," he said. "You do not understand at all. Tell me, do you know who killed Ratchett?"

"Do you?" countered M. Bouc.

Poirot nodded. "Oh, yes," he said. "I have known for some time. It is so clear that I wonder you have not seen it also." He looked at Hardman and asked: "And you?"

The detective shook his head. He stared at Poirot curiously. "I don't know," he said. "I don't know at all. Which of them was it?"

Poirot was silent a minute. Then he said:

"If you will be so good, M. Hardman, assemble everyone here. There are two possible solutions of this case. I want to lay them both before you all."

Chapter 9

Poirot Propounds Two Solutions

The passengers came crowding into the restaurant car and took their seats round the tables. They all bore more or less the same expression, one of expectancy mingled with apprehension. The Swedish lady was still weeping, and Mrs. Hubbard was comforting her.

"Now you must just take a hold on yourself, my dear. Everything's going to be perfectly all right. You mustn't lose your grip on yourself. If one of us is a nasty murderer, we know quite well it isn't you. Why, anyone would be crazy even to think of such a thing. You sit here, and I'll stay right by you—and don't you worry any." Her voice died away as Poirot stood up.

The Wagon Lit conductor was hovering in the doorway. "You permit that I stay, Monsieur?"

"Certainly, Michel."

Poirot cleared his throat.

"*Messieurs et mesdames*, I will speak in English since I think all of you know a little of that language. We are here to investigate the death of Samuel Edward Ratchett—*alias* Cassetti. There are two possible solutions of the crime. I shall put them both before you, and I shall ask M. Bouc and Dr. Constantine here to judge which solution is the right one.

"Now you all know the facts of the case. Mr. Ratchett was found stabbed this morning. He was last known to be alive at 12.37 last night when he spoke to the Wagon Lit conductor through the door. A watch in his pyjama pocket was found to be badly dented, and it had stopped at a quarter past one. Dr. Constantine, who examined the body when found, puts the time of death as having been between midnight and two in the morning. At half an hour after midnight, as you all know, the train ran into a snowdrift. After that time *it was impossible for anyone to leave the train.*

"The evidence of Mr. Hardman, who is a member of a New York detective agency"—(Several heads turned to look at Mr. Hardman.)— "shows that no one could have passed his compartment (No. 16 at the extreme end) without being seen by him. We are therefore forced to the conclusion that the murderer is to be found among the occupants of one particular coach—the Stamboul-Calais coach.

"That, I will say, *was* our theory."

"*Comment?*" ejaculated M. Bouc, startled.

"But I will put before you an alternative theory. It is very simple. Mr. Ratchett had a certain enemy whom he feared. He gave Mr. Hardman a description of this enemy and told him that the attempt, if made at all, would most probably be made on the second night out from Stamboul.

"Now I put it to you, ladies and gentlemen, that Mr. Ratchett knew a good deal more than he told. The enemy, as Mr. Ratchett expected, joined the train *at Belgrade or else at Vincovci* by the door left open by Colonel Arbuthnot and Mr. MacQueen, who had just descended to the platform. He was provided with a suit of Wagon Lit uniform, which he wore over his ordinary clothes, and a pass-key which enabled him to gain access to Mr. Ratchett's compartment in spite of the door's being locked. Mr. Ratchett was under the influence of a sleeping draught. This man stabbed him with great ferocity and left the compartment through the communicating door leading to Mrs. Hubbard's compartment—"

"That's so," said Mrs. Hubbard, nodding her head.

"He thrust the dagger he had used into Mrs. Hubbard's sponge-bag in passing. Without knowing it, he lost a button of his uniform. Then he slipped out of the compartment and along the corridor. He hastily thrust the uniform into a suitcase in an empty compartment, and a few minutes later, dressed in ordinary clothes, he left the train just before it started off, using the same means for egress—the door near the dining-car."

Everybody gasped.

"What about that watch?" demanded Mr. Hardman.

"There you have the explanation of the whole thing. *Mr. Ratchett had omitted to put his watch back an hour as he should have done at Tzari-brod.* His watch still registered Eastern European time, which is one hour *ahead* of Central European time. It was a quarter past *twelve* when Mr. Ratchett was stabbed—not a quarter past one."

"But it is absurd, that explanation!" cried M. Bouc. "What of the voice that spoke from the compartment at twenty-three minutes to one? It was either the voice of Ratchett—or else that of his murderer."

"Not necessarily. It might have been—well—a third person. One who had gone in to speak to Ratchett and found him dead. He rang the bell to summon the conductor; then, as you express it, the wind rose in him—he was afraid of being accused of the crime, and he spoke pretending to be Ratchett."

"C'est possible," admitted M. Bouc grudgingly.

Poirot looked at Mrs. Hubbard. "Yes, Madame, you were going to say—"

"Well, I don't quite know what I was going to say. Do you think I forgot to put my watch back too?"

"No, Madame. I think you heard the man pass through—but unconsciously. Later you had a nightmare of a man being in your compartment and woke up with a start and rang for the conductor."

"Well, I suppose that's possible," admitted Mrs. Hubbard.

Princess Dragomiroff was looking at Poirot with a very direct glance. "How do you explain the evidence of my maid, Monsieur?"

"Very simply, Madame. Your maid recognised the handkerchief I showed her as yours. She somewhat clumsily tried to shield you. She did encounter the man, but earlier—while the train was at Vincovci station. She pretended to have seen him at a later hour, with a confused idea of giving you a water-tight alibi."

The Princess bowed her head. "You have thought of everything, Monsieur. I—I admire you."

There was a silence.

Then everyone jumped as Dr. Constantine suddenly hit the table a blow with his fist.

"But no," he said. "No, no, and again no! That is an explanation that will not hold water. It is deficient in a dozen minor points. The crime was not committed so—M. Poirot must know that perfectly well."

Poirot turned a curious glance on him. "I see," he said, "that I shall have to give you my second solution. But do not abandon this one too abruptly. You may agree with it later."

He turned back again to face the others.

"There is another possible solution of the crime. This is how I arrived at it.

"When I had heard all the evidence, I leaned back and shut my eyes, and began to *think*. Certain points presented themselves to me as worthy of attention. I enumerated these points to my two colleagues. Some I have already elucidated—such as a grease spot on a passport, and so on. I will run over the points that remain. The first and most important is a remark made to me by M. Bouc in the restaurant car at lunch on the first day after leaving Stamboul—to the effect that the company assembled was interesting because it was so varied—representing as it did all classes and nationalities.

"I agreed with him, but when this particular point came into my mind, I tried to imagine whether such an assembly was ever likely to be collected under any other conditions. And the answer I made to myself was—only in America. In America there might be a household composed of just such varied nationalities—an Italian chauffeur, an English governess, a Swedish nurse, a German lady's-maid, and so on. That led me to my scheme of 'guessing'—that is, casting each person for a certain part in the Armstrong drama much as a producer casts a play. Well, that gave me an extremely interesting and satisfactory result.

"I had also examined in my own mind each separate person's evidence, with some curious results. Take first the evidence of Mr. MacQueen. My first interview with him was entirely satisfactory. But in my second he made rather a curious remark. I had described to him the finding of a note mentioning the Armstrong case. He said, 'But surely—' and then paused and went on, 'I mean—that was rather careless of the old man.'

"Now I could feel that that was not what he had started out to say. *Supposing what he had meant to say was 'But surely that was burnt!'* In which case, *MacQueen knew of the note and of its destruction*—in other words, he was either the murderer or an accomplice of the murderer. Very good.

"Then the valet. He said his master was in the habit of taking a sleeping draught when travelling by train. That might be true, but *would Ratchett have taken one last night?* The automatic under his pillow gave the lie to that statement. Ratchett intended to be on the alert last night. Whatever narcotic was administered to him must have been given without his knowledge. By whom? Obviously by MacQueen or the valet.

"Now we come to the evidence of Mr. Hardman. I believed all that he told me about his own identity, but when it came to the actual methods he had employed to guard Mr. Ratchett, his story was neither more nor less than absurd. The only way to have protected Ratchett effectively was to pass the night actually in his compartment or in some spot where he could watch the door. The one thing that his evidence *did* show plainly was that *no one in any other part of the train could possibly have murdered Ratchett*. It drew a clear circle round the Stamboul-Calais carriage. That seemed to me a rather curious and inexplicable fact, and I put it aside to think over.

"You probably all know by now of the few words I overheard between Miss Debenham and Colonel Arbuthnot. The interesting thing to my mind was the fact that Colonel Arbuthnot called her *Mary* and was clearly on terms of intimacy with her. But the Colonel was supposed to have met her only a few days previously. And I know Englishmen of the Colonel's type—even if he had fallen in love with the young lady at first sight, he would have advanced slowly and with decorum, not rushing things. Therefore I concluded that Colonel Arbuthnot and Miss Debenham were in reality well acquainted and were for some reason pretending to be strangers. Another small point was Miss Debenham's easy familiarity with the term 'long distance' for a telephone call. Yet Miss Debenham had told me that she had never been in the States.

"To pass to another witness. Mrs. Hubbard had told us that lying in bed she had been unable to see whether the communicating door was bolted or not, and so had asked Miss Ohlsson to see for her. Now—though her statement would have been perfectly true if she had been occupying compartment No. 2, 4, 12 or any *even* number, in which the bolt is directly under the handle of the door—in the *uneven* numbers such as compartment No. 3 the bolt is well *above* the handle and could not therefore be masked by the sponge-bag in the least. I was forced to the conclusion that Mrs. Hubbard was inventing an incident that had never occurred.

"And here let me say just a word or two about *times*. To my mind the really interesting point about the dented watch is the place where it was found—in Ratchett's pyjama pocket, a singularly uncomfortable and unlikely place to keep one's watch, especially as there is a watch 'hook' provided just by the head of the bed. I felt sure, therefore, that the watch had been deliberately placed in the pocket—faked. The crime, then, was not committed at a quarter past one.

"Was it then committed earlier? To be exact, at twenty-three minutes to one? My friend M. Bouc advanced as an argument in favour of it the loud cry which awoke me from sleep. But if Ratchett had been heavily drugged, *he could not have cried out.* If he had been capable of crying out, he would have been capable of making some kind of struggle to defend himself, and there were no signs of any such struggle.

"I remembered that MacQueen had called attention, not once but twice (and the second time in a very blatant manner), to the fact that Ratchett could speak no French. I came to the conclusion that the whole business at twenty-three minutes to one was a comedy played for my benefit! Anyone might see through the watch business—it is a common enough device in detective stories. They assumed that I *should* see through it and that, pluming myself on my own cleverness, I would go on to assume that since Ratchett spoke no French, the voice I heard at twenty-three minutes to one could not have been his, and that Ratchett must have been already dead. But I am convinced that at twenty-three minutes to one Ratchett was still lying in his drugged sleep.

"But the device has succeeded! I have opened my door and looked out. I have actually heard the French phrase used. If I am so unbelievably dense as not to realise the significance of that phrase, it must be brought to my attention. If necessary, MacQueen can come right out in the open. He can say, 'Excuse me, M. Poirot, *that can't have been Mr. Ratchett speaking*. He couldn't speak French.'

"Now, what was the real time of the crime? And who killed him?

"In my opinion—and this is only an opinion—Ratchett was killed at some time very close upon two o'clock, the latest hour the doctor gives us as possible.

"As to who killed him—"

He paused, looking at his audience. He could not complain of any lack of attention. Every eye was fixed upon him. In the stillness you could have heard a pin drop.

He went on slowly:

"I was particularly struck by the extraordinary difficulty of proving a case against any one person on the train, and by the rather curious coincidence that in each case the testimony giving an alibi came from what I might describe as an 'unlikely' person. Thus, Mr. MacQueen and Colonel Arbuthnot provided alibis for each other—two persons between whom it seemed most unlikely there should have been any prior acquaintanceship. The same thing happened with the English valet and the Italian, and with the Swedish lady and the English girl. I said to myself: This is extraordinary—they cannot *all* be in it!

"And then, Messieurs, I saw light. They *were* all in it. For so many people connected with the Armstrong case to be travelling by the same train through coincidence was not only unlikely: it was *impossible*. It must be not chance, but *design*. I remembered a remark of Colonel Arbuthnot's about trial by jury. A jury is composed of twelve people—there were twelve passengers—Ratchett was stabbed twelve times. And the thing that had worried me all along—the extraordinary crowd travelling in the Stamboul-Calais coach at a slack time of year—this was explained.

"Ratchett had escaped justice in America. There was no question as to his guilt. I visualised a self-appointed jury of twelve people who had condemned him to death and who by the exigencies of the case had themselves been forced to be his executioners. And immediately, on that assumption, the whole case fell into beautiful shining order.

"I saw it as a perfect mosaic, each person playing his or her allotted part. It was so arranged that, if suspicion should fall on any one person, the evidence of one or more of the others would clear the accused person and confuse the issue. Hardman's evidence was necessary in case some outsider should be suspected of the crime and be unable to prove an alibi. The passengers in the Stamboul carriage were in no danger. Every minute detail of their evidence was worked out beforehand. The whole thing was a very cleverly planned jigsaw puzzle, so arranged that every fresh piece of knowledge that came to light made the solution of the whole more difficult. As my friend M. Bouc remarked, the case seemed fantastically impossible! That was exactly the impression intended to be conveyed.

"Did this solution explain everything? Yes, it did. The nature of the wounds—each inflicted by a different person. The artificial threatening letters—artificial since they were unreal, written only to be produced as evidence. (Doubtless there *were* real letters, warning Ratchett of his fate, which MacQueen destroyed, substituting for them these others.) Then Hardman's story of being called in by Ratchett—a lie, of course, from beginning to end. The description of the mythical 'small dark man with a womanish voice'—a convenient description since it had the merit of not incriminating any of the actual Wagon Lit conductors and would apply equally well to a man or a woman.

"The idea of stabbing is at first sight a curious one, but on reflection nothing else would fit the circumstances so well. A dagger was a weapon that could be used by everyone—strong or weak—and it made no noise. I fancy, though I may be wrong, that each person in turn entered Ratchett's darkened compartment through that of Mrs. Hubbard—and struck! They themselves would never know which blow actually killed him.

"The final letter which Ratchett had probably found on his pillow was carefully burnt. With no clue pointing to the Armstrong case there would be absolutely no reason for suspecting any of the passengers on the train. It would be put down as an outside job, and the 'small dark man with the womanish voice' would actually have been seen by one or more of the passengers leaving the train at Brod!

"I do not know exactly what happened when the conspirators discovered that this part of their plan was impossible owing to the accident to the train. There was, I imagine, a hasty consultation, and then they decided to go through with it. It was true that now one and all of the passengers were bound to come under suspicion, but that possibility had already been foreseen and provided for. The only additional thing to be done was to confuse the issue even further. Two so-called 'clues' were dropped in the dead man's compartment—one incriminating Colonel Arbuthnot (who had the strongest alibi and whose connection with the Armstrong family was probably the hardest to prove); and the second clue, the handkerchief, incriminating Princess Dragomiroff who, by virtue of her social position, her particularly frail physique and the alibi given her by her maid and the conductor, was practically in an unassailable position.

"Further to confuse the issue, a red herring was drawn across the trail—the mythical woman in the red kimono. Again I am to bear witness to this woman's existence. There is a heavy bang at my door. I get up and look out—and see the scarlet kimono disappearing in the distance. A judicious selection of people—the conductor, Miss Debenham and MacQueen—will also have seen her. It was, I think, someone with a sense of humour who thoughtfully placed the scarlet kimono on the top of my suitcase whilst I was interviewing people in the dining-car. Where the garment came from in the first place, I do not know. I suspect it is the property of Countess Andrenyi, since her luggage contained only a chiffon negligee so elaborate as to be rather a teagown than a dressing gown.

"When MacQueen first learned that the letter which had been so carefully burnt had in part escaped destruction, and that the word Armstrong was exactly the word remaining, he must at once have communicated his news to the others. It was at this minute that the position of Countess Andrenyi became acute, and her husband immediately took steps to alter the passport. It was their second piece of bad luck!

"They one and all agreed to deny utterly any connection with the Armstrong family. They knew I had no immediate means of finding out the truth, and they did not believe that I should go into the matter unless my suspicions were aroused against one particular person.

"Now there was one further point to consider. Allowing that my theory of the crime was the correct one, and I believed that it *must* be the correct one, then obviously the Wagon Lit conductor himself must be privy to the plot. But if so, that gave us thirteen persons, not twelve. Instead of the usual formula 'Of so many people one is guilty,' I was faced with the problem that of thirteen persons one and one only was innocent. Which was that person?

"I came to a very odd conclusion. I came to the conclusion that the person who had taken no part in the crime was the person who would be considered the most likely to do so. I refer to Countess Andrenyi. I was impressed by the earnestness of her husband when he swore to me solemnly on his honour that his wife never left her compartment that night. I decided that Count Andrenyi took, so to speak, his wife's place.

"If so, then Pierre Michel was definitely one of the twelve. But how could one explain his complicity? He was a decent man who had been many years in the employ of the company—not the kind of man who could be bribed to assist in a crime. Then Pierre Michel must be involved in the Armstrong case. But that seemed very improbable. Then I remembered that the dead nursery-maid had been French. Supposing that that unfortunate girl had been Pierre Michel's daughter. That would explain everything—it would also explain the place chosen for the staging of the crime. Were there any others whose part in the drama was not clear?

Colonel Arbuthnot I put down as a friend of the Armstrongs. They had probably been through the War together. The maid, Hildegarde Schmidt— I could guess her place in the Armstrong household. I am, perhaps, over greedy, but I sense a good cook instinctively. I laid a trap for her—she fell into it. I said I knew she was a good cook. She answered: 'Yes, indeed, all my ladies have said so.' But if you are employed as a *lady's-maid* your employers seldom have a chance of learning whether or not you are a good cook.

"Then there was Hardman. He seemed quite definitely not to belong to the Armstrong household. I could only imagine that he had been in love with the French girl. I spoke to him of the charm of foreign women—and again I obtained the reaction I was looking for. Sudden tears came into his eyes, which he pretended were dazzled by the snow.

"There remains Mrs. Hubbard. Now Mrs. Hubbard, let me say, played the most important part in the drama. By occupying the compartment communicating with that of Ratchett she was more open to suspicion than anyone else. In the nature of things she could not have an alibi to fall back upon. To play the part she played—the perfectly natural, slightly ridiculous American fond mother—an artist was needed. But there *was* an artist connected with the Armstrong family: Mrs. Armstrong's mother—Linda Arden, the actress. . . ."

He stopped.

Then in a soft rich dreamy voice, quite unlike the one she had used throughout the journey, Mrs. Hubbard said:

"I always fancied myself in comedy parts."

She went on, still dreamily:

"That slip about the sponge-bag was silly. It shows that you should always rehearse properly. We tried it on the way out—I was in an even-number compartment then, I suppose. I never thought of the bolts being in different places."

She shifted her position a little and looked straight at Poirot.

"You know all about it, M. Poirot. You're a very wonderful man. But even you can't quite imagine what it was like—that awful day in New York. I was just crazy with grief; so were the servants. And Colonel Arbuthnot was there too. He was John Armstrong's best friend."

"He saved my life in the War," said Arbuthnot.

"We decided then and there (perhaps we were mad—I don't know) that the sentence of death that Cassetti had escaped had got to be carried out. There were twelve of us—or rather eleven; Susanne's father was over in France, of course. First we thought we'd draw lots as to who should do it, but in the end we decided on this way. It was the chauffeur, Antonio, who suggested it. Mary worked out all the details later with Hector MacQueen.

He'd always adored Sonia—my daughter—and it was he who explained to us exactly how Cassetti's money had managed to get him off.

"It took a long time to perfect our plan. We had first to track Ratchett down. Hardman managed that in the end. Then we had to try and get Masterman and Hector into his employment—or at any rate one of them. Well, we managed that. Then we had a consultation with Susanne's father. Colonel Arbuthnot was very keen on having twelve of us. He seemed to think it made it more in order. He didn't like the stabbing idea much, but he agreed that it did solve most of our difficulties. Well, Susanne's father was willing. Susanne had been his only child. We knew from Hector that Ratchett would be coming back from the East sooner or later by the Orient Express. With Pierre Michel actually working on that train, the chance was too good to be missed. Besides, it would be a good way of not incriminating any outsiders.

"My daughter's husband had to know, of course, and he insisted on coming on the train with her. Hector wangled it so that Ratchett selected the right day for travelling, when Michel would be on duty. We meant to engage every carriage in the Stamboul-Calais coach, but unfortunately there was one carriage we couldn't get. It had been reserved long beforehand for a director of the company. 'Mr. Harris,' of course, was a myth. But it would have been awkward to have any stranger in Hector's compartment. And then, at the last minute, *you* came. . . ."

She stopped.

"Well," she said, "you know everything now, M. Poirot. What are you going to do about it? If it must all come out, can't you lay the blame upon me and me only? I would have stabbed that man twelve times willingly. It wasn't only that he was responsible for my daughter's death and her child's and that of the other child who might have been alive and happy now. It was more than that: there had been other children kidnapped before Daisy, and there might be others in the future. Society had condemned him—we were only carrying out the sentence. But it's unnecessary to bring all these others into it. All these good faithful souls—and poor Michel—and Mary and Colonel Arbuthnot—they love each other. . . ."

Her voice was wonderful, echoing through the crowded space—that deep, emotional, heart-stirring voice that had thrilled many a New York audience.

Poirot looked at his friend.

"You are a director of the company, M. Bouc," he said. "What do you say?"

M. Bouc cleared his throat.

"In my opinion, M. Poirot," he said, "the first theory you put forward was the correct one—decidedly so. I suggest that that is the solution we offer to the Jugo-Slavian police when they arrive. You agree, Doctor?"

"Certainly I agree," said Dr. Constantine. "As regards the medical evidence, I think—er—that I made one or two fantastic suggestions."

"Then," said Poirot, "having placed my solution before you, I have the honour to retire from the case. . . ."

MURDER IN MESOPOTAMIA

Dedicated to
MY MANY ARCHÆOLOGICAL FRIENDS
IN IRAQ AND SYRIA

Contents

FOREWORD
By Giles Reilly, M.D.

The events chronicled in this narrative took place some four years ago. Circumstances have rendered it necessary, in my opinion, that a straightforward account of them should be given to the public. There have been the wildest and most ridiculous rumours suggesting that important evidence was suppressed and other nonsense of that kind. Those misconstructions have appeared more especially in the American press.

For obvious reasons it was desirable that the account should not come from the pen of one of the expedition staff, who might reasonably be supposed to be prejudiced.

I therefore suggested to Miss Amy Leatheran that she should undertake the task. She is obviously the person to do it. She has a professional character of the highest, she is not biased by having any previous connection with the University of Pittstown Expedition to Iraq and she was an observant and intelligent eye-witness.

It was not very easy to persuade Miss Leatheran to undertake this task—in fact, persuading her was one of the hardest jobs of my professional career—and even after it was completed she displayed a curious reluctance to let me see the manuscript. I discovered that this was partly due to some critical remarks she had made concerning my daughter Sheila. I soon disposed of that, assuring her that as children criticize their parents freely in print nowadays, parents are only too delighted when their offspring come in for their share of abuse! Her other objection was extreme modesty about her literary style. She hoped I would "put the grammar right and all that." I have, on the contrary, refused to alter so much as a single word. Miss Leatheran's style in my opinion is vigorous, individual and entirely apposite. If she calls Hercule Poirot "Poirot" in one paragraph and "Mr. Poirot" in the next, such a variation is both interesting and suggestive. At one moment she is, so to speak, "remembering her manners" (and hospital nurses are great sticklers for etiquette) and at the next her interest in what she is telling is that of a pure human being— cap and cuffs forgotten!

The only thing I have done is to take the liberty of writing a first chapter—aided by a letter kindly supplied by one of Miss Leatheran's friends. It is intended to be in the nature of a frontispiece—that is, it gives a rough sketch of the narrator.

Chapter 1

Foreword

In the hall of the Tigris Palace Hotel in Baghdad a hospital nurse was finishing a letter. Her fountain-pen drove briskly over the paper.

". . . Well, dear, I think that's really all my news. I must say it's been nice to see a bit of the world—though England for me every time, thank you! The dirt and the mess in Baghdad you wouldn't believe—and not romantic at all like you'd think from the Arabian Nights! Of course, it's pretty just on the river, but the town itself is just awful—and no proper shops at all. Major Kelsey took me through the bazaars, and of course there's no denying they're quaint—but just a lot of rubbish and hammering away at copper pans till they make your head ache—and not what I'd like to use myself unless I was sure about the cleaning. You've got to be so careful of verdigris with copper pans.

"I'll write and let you know if anything comes of the job that Dr. Reilly spoke about. He said this American gentleman was in Baghdad now and might come and see me this afternoon. It's for his wife—she has 'fancies,' so Dr., Reilly said. He didn't say any more than that, and of course, dear, one knows what that usually means (but I hope not actually D.T.'s!). Of course, Dr. Reilly didn't say anything—but he had a look—if you know what I mean. This Dr. Leidner is an archaeologist and is digging up a mound out in the desert somewhere for some American museum.

"Well, dear, I will close now. I thought what you told me about little Stubbins was simply killing! Whatever did Matron say?

"No more now.

"Yours ever,
"Amy Leatheran."

Enclosing the letter in an envelope, she addressed it to Sister Curshaw, St. Christopher's Hospital, London.

As she put the cap on her fountain pen, one of the native boys approached her.

"A gentleman come see you. Dr. Leidner."

Nurse Leatheran turned. She saw a man of middle height with slightly stooping shoulders, a brown beard and gentle tired eyes.

Dr. Leidner saw a woman of thirty-five of erect, confident bearing. He saw a good-humoured face with slightly prominent blue eyes and glossy brown hair. She looked, he thought, just what a hospital nurse for a nervous case ought to look. Cheerful, robust, shrewd and matter of fact.

Nurse Leatheran, he thought, would do.

Chapter 2

Introducing Amy Leatheran

I don't pretend to be an author or to know anything about writing. I'm doing this simply because Dr. Reilly asked me to, and somehow when Dr. Reilly asks you to do a thing you don't like to refuse.

"Oh, but, doctor," I said, "I'm not literary—not literary at all."

"Nonsense!" he said. "Treat it as case notes, if you like."

Well, of course, you *can* look at it that way.

Dr. Reilly went on. He said that an unvarnished plain account of the Tell Yarimjah business was badly needed.

"If one of the interested parties writes it, it won't carry conviction. They'll say it's biased one way or another."

And of course that was true, too. I was in it all and yet an outsider, so to speak.

"Why don't you write it yourself, doctor?" I asked.

"I wasn't on the spot—you were. Besides," he added with a sigh, "my daughter won't let me."

The way he knuckles under to that chit of a girl of his is downright disgraceful. I had half a mind to say so, when I saw that his eyes were twinkling. That was the worst of Dr. Reilly. You never knew whether he was joking or not. He always said things in the same slow melancholy way—but half the time there was a twinkle underneath it.

"Well," I said doubtfully. "I suppose I *could*."

"Of course you could."

"Only I don't quite know how to set about it."

"There's a good precedent for that. Begin at the beginning, go on to the end and then leave off."

"I don't even know quite where and what the beginning was," I said doubtfully.

"Believe me, nurse, the difficulty of beginning will be nothing to the difficulty of knowing how to stop. At least that's the way it is with me when I have to make a speech. Some one's got to catch hold of my coat-tails and pull me down by main force."

"Oh, you're joking, doctor."

"It's profoundly serious I am. Now what about it?"

Another thing was worrying me. After hesitating a moment or two I said:

"You know, doctor, I'm afraid I might tend to be—well, a little *personal* sometimes."

"God bless my soul, woman, the more personal you are the better! This is a story of human beings—not dummies! Be personal—be prejudiced—be catty—be anything you please! Write the thing your own way. We can always prune out the bits that are libellous afterwards! You go ahead. You're a sensible woman, and you'll give a sensible common-sense account of the business."

So that was that, and I promised to do my best.

And here I am beginning, but as I said to the doctor, it's difficult to know just where to start.

I suppose I ought to say a word or two about myself. I'm thirty-two and my name is Amy Leatheran. I took my training at St. Christopher's and after that did two years' maternity. I did a certain amount of private work and I was for four years at Miss Bendix's Nursing Home in Devonshire Place. I came out to Iraq with a Mrs. Kelsey. I'd attended her when her baby was born. She was coming out to Baghdad with her husband and had already got a children's nurse booked who had been for some years with friends of hers out there. Their children were coming home and going to school, and the nurse had agreed to go to Mrs. Kelsey when they left. Mrs. Kelsey was delicate and nervous about the journey out with so young a child, so Major Kelsey arranged that I should come out with her and look after her and the baby. They would pay my passage home unless we found some one needing a nurse for the return journey.

Well, there is no need to describe the Kelseys—the baby was a little love and Mrs. Kelsey quite nice, though rather the fretting kind. I enjoyed the voyage very much. I'd never been on a long trip on the sea before.

Dr. Reilly was on board the boat. He was a black-haired, long-faced man who said all sorts of funny things in a low, sad voice. I think he enjoyed pulling my leg and used to make the most extraordinary statements to see if I would swallow them. He was the civil surgeon at a place called Hassanieh—a day and a half's journey from Baghdad.

I had been about a week in Baghdad when I ran across him and he asked when I was leaving the Kelseys. I said that it was funny his asking that because as a matter of fact the Wrights (the other people I mentioned) were going home earlier than they had meant to and their nurse was free to come straightaway.

He said that he had heard about the Wrights and that that was why he had asked me.

"As a matter of fact, nurse, I've got a possible job for you."

"A case?"

He screwed his face up as though considering.

"You could hardly call it a case. It's just a lady who has—shall we say—fancies?"

"Oh!" I said.

(One usually knows what *that* means—drink or drugs!)

Dr. Reilly didn't explain further. He was very discreet.

"Yes," he said. "A Mrs. Leidner. Husband's an American—an American Swede to be exact. He's the head of a large American dig."

And he explained how this expedition was excavating the site of a big Assyrian city something like Ninevch. The expedition house was not actually very far from Hassanieh, but it was a lonely spot and Dr. Leidner had been worried for some time about his wife's health.

"He's not been very explicit about it, but it seems she has these fits of recurring nervous terrors."

"Is she left alone all day amongst natives?" I asked.

"Oh, no, there's quite a crowd—seven or eight. I don't fancy she's ever alone in the house. But there seems to be no doubt that she's worked herself up into a queer state. Leidner has any amount of work on his shoulders, but he's crazy about his wife and it worries him to know she's in this state. He felt he'd be happier if he knew that some responsible person with expert knowledge was keeping an eye on her."

"And what does Mrs. Leidner herself think about it?"

Dr. Reilly answered gravely.

"Mrs. Leidner is a very lovely lady. She's seldom of the same mind about anything two days on end. But on the whole she favours the idea." He added, "She's an odd woman. A mass of affectation and, I should fancy, a champion liar—but Leidner seems honestly to believe that she is scared out of her life by something or other."

"What did she herself say to you, doctor?"

"Oh, she hasn't consulted me! She doesn't like me anyway—for several reasons. It was Leidner who came to me and propounded this plan. Well, nurse, what do you think of the idea? You'd see something of the country before you go home—they'll be digging for another two months. And excavation is quite interesting work."

After a moment's hesitation while I turned the matter over in my mind:

"Well," I said. "I really think I might try it."

"Splendid," said Dr. Reilly, rising. "Leidner's in Baghdad now. I'll tell him to come round and see if he can fix things up with you."

Dr. Leidner came to the hotel that afternoon. He was a middle-aged man with a rather nervous, hesitating manner. There was something gentle and kindly and rather helpless about him.

He sounded very devoted to his wife, but he was very vague about what was the matter with her.

"You see," he said, tugging at his beard in a rather perplexed manner that I later came to know to be characteristic of him, "my wife is really in a very nervous state. I—I'm quite worried about her."

"She is in good physical health?" I asked.

"Yes—oh, yes, I think so. No, I should not think there was anything the matter with her physically. But she—well—imagines things, you know."

"What kind of things?" I asked.

But he shied off from the point, merely murmuring perplexedly:

"She works herself up over nothing at all. . . . I really can see no foundations for these fears."

"Fears of what, Dr. Leidner?"

He said vaguely, "Oh, just—nervous terrors, you know."

Ten to one, I thought to myself, it's drugs. And he doesn't realize it! Lots of men don't. Just wonder why their wives are so jumpy and have such extraordinary changes of mood.

I asked whether Mrs. Leidner herself approved of the idea of my coming.

His face lighted up.

"Yes. I was surprised. Most pleasurably surprised. She said it was a very good idea. She said she would feel very much safer."

The word struck me oddly. *Safer*. A very queer word to use. I began to surmise that Mrs. Leidner might be a mental case.

He went on with a kind of boyish eagerness.

"I'm sure you'll get on very well with her. She's really a very charming woman." He smiled disarmingly. "She feels you'll be the greatest comfort to her. I felt the same as soon as I saw you. You look, if you will allow me to say so, so splendidly healthy and full of common sense. I'm sure you're just the person for Louise."

"Well, we can but try, Dr. Leidner," I said cheerfully. "I'm sure I hope I can be of use to your wife. Perhaps she's nervous of natives."

"Oh, dear me, no." He shook his head, amused at the idea. "My wife likes Arabs very much—she appreciates their simplicity and their sense of humour. This is only her second season—we have been married less than two years—but she already speaks quite a fair amount of Arabic."

I was silent for a moment or two, then I had one more try.

"Can't you tell me at all what it is your wife is afraid of, Dr. Leidner?" I asked.

He hesitated. Then he said slowly, "I hope—I believe—that she will tell you that herself."

And that's all I could get out of him.

Chapter 3

Gossip

It was arranged that I should go to Tell Yarimjah the following week.

Mrs. Kelsey was settling into her house at Alwiyah, and I was glad to be able to take a few things off her shoulders.

During that time I heard one or two allusions to the Leidner expedition. A friend of Mrs. Kelsey's, a young squadron-leader, pursed his lips in surprise as he exclaimed:

"Lovely Louise. So that's her latest!" He turned to me. "That's our nickname for her, nurse. She's always known as Lovely Louise."

"Is she so very handsome then?" I asked.

"It's taking her at her own valuation. *She* thinks she is!"

"Now don't be spiteful, John," said Mrs. Kelsey. "You know it's not only she who thinks so! Lots of people have been very smitten by her."

"Perhaps you're right. She's a bit long in the tooth, but she has a certain attraction."

"You were completely bowled over yourself," said Mrs. Kelsey, laughing.

The squadron-leader blushed and admitted rather shamefacedly:

"Well, she has a way with her. As for Leidner himself, he worships the ground she walks on—and all the rest of the expedition has to worship too! It's expected of them!"

"How many are there altogether?" I asked.

"All sorts and nationalities, nurse," said the squadron-leader cheerfully. "An English architect, a French Father from Carthage—he does the inscriptions—tablets and things, you know. And then there's Miss Johnson. She's English too—sort of general bottle-washer. And a little plump man who does the photography—he's an American. And the Mercados. Heaven knows what nationality they are. She's quite young—a snaky-looking creature—and oh! doesn't she hate Lovely Louise! And there are a couple of youngsters, and that's the lot. A few odd fish, but nice on the whole—don't you agree, Pennyman?"

He was appealing to an elderly man who was sitting thoughtfully twirling a pair of pince-nez.

The latter started and looked up.

"Yes—yes—very nice indeed. Taken individually, that is. Of course, Mercado is rather a queer fish—"

"He has such a very *odd* beard," put in Mrs. Kelsey. "A queer limp kind."

Major Pennyman went on without noticing her interruption.

"The young 'uns are both nice. The American's rather silent, and the English boy talks a bit too much. Funny, it's usually the other way round. Leidner himself is a delightful fellow—so modest and unassuming. Yes, individually they are all pleasant people. But somehow or other, I may have been fanciful, but the last time I went to see them I got a queer impression of something being wrong. I don't know what it was exactly. . . . Nobody seemed quite natural. There was a queer atmosphere of tension. I can explain best what I mean by saying that they all passed the butter to each other too politely."

Blushing a little, because I don't like airing my own opinions too much, I said:

"If people are too much cooped up together it's got a way of getting on their nerves. I know that myself from experience in hospital."

"That's true," said Major Kelsey, "but it's early in the season, hardly time for that particular irritation to have set in."

"An expedition is probably like our life here in miniature," said Major Pennyman. "It has its cliques and rivalries and jealousies."

"It sounds as though they'd got a good many newcomers this year," said Major Kelsey.

"Let me see." The squadron-leader counted them off on his fingers. "Young Coleman is new, so is Reiter. Emmott was out last year and so were the Mercados. Father Lavigny is a new-comer. He's come in place of Dr. Byrd, who was ill this year and couldn't come out. Carey, of course, is an old hand. He's been out ever since the beginning, five years ago. Miss Johnson's been out nearly as many years as Carey."

"I always thought they got on so well together at Tell Yarimjah," remarked Major Kelsey. "They seemed like a happy family—which is really surprising when one considers what human nature is! I'm sure Nurse Leatheran agrees with me."

"Well," I said. "I don't know that you're not right! The rows I've known in hospital and starting often from nothing more than a dispute about a pot of tea."

"Yes, one tends to get petty in close communities," said Major Penny-man. "All the same I feel there must be something more to it in this case. Leidner is such a gentle, unassuming man, with really a remarkable amount of tact. He's always managed to keep his expedition happy and on good terms with each other. And yet I *did* notice that feeling of tension the other day."

Mrs. Kelsey laughed.

"And you don't see the explanation? Why, it leaps to the eye!"

"What do you mean?"

"*Mrs*. Leidner, of course."

"Oh, come, Mary," said her husband, "she's a charming woman—not at all the quarrelsome kind."

"I didn't say she was quarrelsome. She *causes* quarrels!"

"In what way? And why should she?"

"Why? Why? Because she's bored. She's not an archaeologist, only the wife of one. She's bored shut away from any excitements and so she provides her own drama. She amuses herself by setting other people by the ears."

"Mary, you don't know in the least. You're merely imagining."

"Of course I'm imagining! But you'll find I'm right. Lovely Louise doesn't look like the Mona Lisa for nothing! She mayn't mean any harm, but she likes to see what will happen."

"She's devoted to Leidner."

"Oh! I dare say. I'm not suggesting vulgar intrigues. But she's an *allumeuse*, that woman."

"Women are so sweet to each other," said Major Kelsey.

"I know. Cat, cat, cat, that's what you men say. But we're usually right about our own sex."

"All the same," said Major Pennyman thoughtfully, "assuming all Mrs. Kelsey's uncharitable surmises to be true, I don't think it would quite account for that curious sense of tension—rather like the feeling there is before a thunderstorm. I had the impression very strongly that the storm might break any minute."

"Now don't frighten nurse," said Mrs. Kelsey. "She's going there in three days' time and you'll put her right off."

"Oh, you won't frighten me," I said, laughing.

All the same I thought a good deal about what had been said. Dr. Leidner's curious use of the word "safer" recurred to me. Was it his wife's secret fear, unacknowledged or expressed perhaps, that was reacting on the rest of the party? Or was it the actual tension (or perhaps the unknown cause of it) that was reacting on *her* nerves?

I looked up the word "allumeuse" that Mrs. Kelsey had used in a dictionary, but couldn't get any sense out of it.

"Well," I thought to myself, "I must wait and see."

Chapter 4

I Arrive in Hassanieh

Three days later I left Baghdad.

I was sorry to leave Mrs. Kelsey and the baby, who was a little love and was thriving splendidly, gaining her proper number of ounces every week. Major Kelsey took me to the station and saw me off. I should arrive at Kirkuk the following morning, and there some one was to meet me.

I slept badly. I never sleep very well in a train and I was troubled by dreams.

The next morning, however, when I looked out of the window it was a lovely day and I felt interested and curious about the people I was going to see.

As I stood on the platform hesitating and looking about me I saw a young man coming towards me. He had a round pink face, and really, in all my life, I have never seen any one who seemed so exactly like a young man out of one of Mr. P. G. Wodehouse's books.

"Hallo, 'allo, 'allo," he said. "Are you Nurse Leatheran? Well, I mean you must be—I can see that. Ha ha! My name's Coleman. Dr. Leidner sent me along. How are you feeling? Beastly journey and all that? Don't I know these trains! Well, here we are—had any breakfast? This your kit? I say, awfully modest, aren't you? Mrs. Leidner has four suitcases and a trunk—to say nothing of a hat-box and a patent pillow, and this, that and the other. Am I talking too much? Come along to the old bus."

There was what I heard called later a station wagon waiting outside. It was a little like a wagonette, a little like a lorry and a little like a car. Mr.

Coleman helped me in, explaining that I had better sit next to the driver so as to get less jolting.

Jolting! I wonder the whole contraption didn't fall to pieces! And nothing like a road—just a sort of track all ruts and holes. Glorious East indeed! When I thought of our splendid arterial roads in England it made me quite homesick.

Mr. Coleman leaned forward from his seat behind me and yelled in my ear a good deal.

"Track's in pretty good condition," he shouted just after we had all been thrown up in our seats till we nearly touched the roof.

And apparently he was speaking quite seriously.

"Very good for you—jogs the liver," he said. "You ought to know that, nurse."

"A stimulated liver won't be much good to me if my head's split open," I observed tartly.

"You should come along here after it's rained! The skids are glorious. Most of the time one's going sideways."

To this I did not respond.

Presently we had to cross the river, which we did on the craziest ferry-boat you can imagine. To my mind it was a mercy we ever got across, but every one seemed to think it was quite usual.

It took us about four hours to get to Hassanieh, which, to my surprise, was quite a big place. Very pretty it looked, too, before we got there from the other side of the river—standing up quite white and fairy-like with minarets. It was a bit different, though, when one had crossed the bridge and come right into it. Such a smell, and everything ramshackle and tumble-down, and mud and mess everywhere.

Mr. Coleman took me to Dr. Reilly's house, where, he said, the doctor was expecting me to lunch.

Dr. Reilly was just as nice as ever, and his house was nice too, with a bathroom and everything spick and span. I had a nice bath, and by the time I got back into my uniform and came down I was feeling fine.

Lunch was just ready and we went in, the doctor apologizing for his daughter, whom he said was always late.

We'd just had a very good dish of eggs in sauce when she came in and Dr. Reilly said, "Nurse, this is my daughter Sheila."

She shook hands, hoped I'd had a good journey, tossed off her hat, gave a cool nod to Mr. Coleman and sat down.

"Well, Bill," she said. "How's everything?"

He began to talk to her about some party or other that was to come off at the club, and I took stock of her.

I can't say I took to her much. A thought too cool for my liking. An off-hand sort of girl, though good-looking. Black hair and blue eyes—a pale sort of face and the usual lip-sticked mouth. She'd a cool, sarcastic way of talking that rather annoyed me. I had a probationer like her under me once—a girl who worked well, I'll admit, but whose manner always riled me.

It looked to me rather as though Mr. Coleman was gone on her. He stammered a bit, and his conversation became slightly more idiotic than it was before, if that was possible! He reminded me of a large stupid dog wagging its tail and trying to please.

After lunch Dr. Reilly went off to the hospital, and Mr. Coleman had some things to get in the town, and Miss Reilly asked me whether I'd like to see round the town a bit or whether I'd rather stop in the house. Mr. Coleman, she said, would be back to fetch me in about an hour.

"Is there anything to see?" I asked.

"There are some picturesque corners," said Miss Reilly. "But I don't know that you'd care for them. They're extremely dirty."

The way she said it rather nettled me. I've never been able to see that picturesqueness excuses dirt.

In the end she took me to the club, which was pleasant enough, over-looking the river, and there were English papers and magazines there.

When we got back to the house Mr. Coleman wasn't there yet, so we sat down and talked a bit. It wasn't easy somehow.

She asked me if I'd met Mrs. Leidner yet.

"No," I said. "Only her husband."

"Oh," she said. "I wonder what you'll think of her?"

I didn't say anything to that. And she went on:

"I like Dr. Leidner very much. Everybody likes him."

That's as good as saying, I thought, that you don't like his wife.

I still didn't say anything and presently she asked abruptly:

"What's the matter with her? Did Dr. Leidner tell you?"

I wasn't going to start gossiping about a patient before I got there even, so I said evasively:

"I understand she's a bit run down and wants looking after."

She laughed—a nasty sort of laugh—hard and abrupt.

"Good God," she said. "Aren't nine people looking after her already enough?"

"I suppose they've all got their work to do," I said.

"Work to do? Of course they've got work to do. But Louise comes first—she sees to that all right."

"No," I said to myself. "You *don't* like her."

"All the same," went on Miss Reilly, "I don't see what she wants with a professional hospital nurse. I should have thought amateur assistance was more in her line; not some one who'll jam a thermometer in her mouth, and count her pulse and bring everything down to hard facts."

Well, I must admit it, I was curious.

"You think there's nothing the matter with her?" I asked.

"Of course there's nothing the matter with her! The woman's as strong as an ox. 'Dear Louise hasn't slept.' 'She's got black circles under her eyes.' Yes—put there with a blue pencil! Anything to get attention, to have everybody hovering round her, making a fuss of her!"

There was something in that, of course. I had (what nurse hasn't?) come across many cases of hypochondriacs whose delight it is to keep a whole household dancing attendance. And if a doctor or a nurse were to say to them, "There's nothing on earth the matter with you!" well, to begin with they wouldn't believe it, and their indignation would be as genuine as indignation can be.

Of course it was quite possible that Mrs. Leidner might be a case of this kind. The husband, naturally, would be the first to be deceived. Husbands, I've found, arc a credulous lot where illness is concerned. But all the same, it didn't quite square with what I'd heard. It didn't, for instance, fit in with that word "safer."

Funny how that word had got kind of stuck in my mind.

Reflecting on it, I asked:

"Is Mrs. Leidner a nervous woman? Is she nervous, for instance, of living out far from anywhere?"

"What is there to be nervous of? Good heavens, there are ten of them! And they've got guards too—because of the antiquities. Oh, no, she's not nervous—at least—"

She seemed struck by some thought and stopped—going on slowly after a minute or two.

"It's odd your saying that."

"Why?"

"Flight-Lieutenant Jervis and I rode over the other day. It was in the morning. Most of them were up on the dig. She was sitting writing a letter and I suppose she didn't hear us coming. The boy who brings you in wasn't about for once, and we came straight up on to the verandah. Apparently she saw Flight-Lieutenant Jervis's shadow thrown on the wall— and she fairly screamed! Apologized, of course. Said she thought it was a strange man. A bit odd, that. I mean, even if it was a strange man, why get the wind up?"

I nodded thoughtfully.

Miss Reilly was silent, then burst out suddenly.

"I don't know what's the matter with them there this year. They've all got the jumps. Johnson goes about so glum she can't open her mouth. David never speaks if he can help it. Bill, of course, never stops, and somehow his chatter seems to make the others worse. Carey goes about looking as though something would snap any minute. And they all watch each other as though—as though—Oh, I don't know, but it's *queer*."

It was odd, I thought, that two such dissimilar people as Miss Reilly and Major Pennyman should have been struck in the same manner.

Just then Mr. Coleman came bustling in. Bustling was just the word for it. If his tongue had hung out and he had suddenly produced a tail to wag you wouldn't have been surprised.

"Hallo-allo," he said. "Absolutely the world's best shopper—that's me. Have you shown nurse all the beauties of the town?"

"She wasn't impressed," said Miss Reilly dryly.

"I don't blame her," said Mr. Coleman heartily. "Of all the one-horse tumble-down places!"

"Not a lover of the picturesque or the antique, are you, Bill? I can't think why you are an archaeologist."

"Don't blame me for that. Blame my guardian. He's a learned bird— fellow of his college—browses among books in bedroom slippers—that kind of man. Bit of a shock for him to have a ward like me."

"I think it's frightfully stupid of you to be forced into a profession you don't care for," said the girl sharply.

"Not forced, Sheila, old girl, not forced. The old man asked if I had any special profession in mind, and I said I hadn't, and so he wangled a season out here for me."

"But haven't you any idea really what you'd *like* to do? You *must* have!"

"Of course I have. My idea would be to give work a miss altogether. What I'd like to do is to have plenty of money and go in for motor-racing."

"You're absurd!" said Miss Reilly.

She sounded quite angry.

"Oh, I realize that it's quite out of the question," said Mr. Coleman cheerfully. "So, if I've got to do something, I don't much care what it is so long as it isn't mugging in an office all day long. I was quite agreeable to seeing a bit of the world. Here goes, I said, and along I came."

"And a fat lot of use you must be, I expect!"

"There you're wrong. I can stand up on the dig and shout '*Y' Allah'* with anybody! And as a matter of fact I'm not so dusty at drawing. Imitating handwriting used to be my speciality at school. I'd have made a first-class forger. Oh, well, I may come to that yet. If my Rolls-Royce splashes you with mud as you're waiting for a bus, you'll know that I've taken to crime."

Miss Reilly said coldly:

"Don't you think it's about time you started instead of talking so much?"

"Hospitable, aren't we, nurse?"

"I'm sure Nurse Leatheran is anxious to get settled in."

"You're always sure of everything," retorted Mr. Coleman with a grin.

That was true enough, I thought. Cock-sure little minx.

I said dryly:

"Perhaps we'd better start, Mr. Coleman."

"Right you are, nurse."

I shook hands with Miss Reilly and thanked her, and we set off.

"Damned attractive girl, Sheila," said Mr. Coleman. "But always ticking a fellow off."

We drove out of the town and presently took a kind of track between green crops. It was very bumpy and full of ruts.

After about half an hour Mr. Coleman pointed to a big mound by the riverbank ahead of us and said:

"Tell Yarimjah."

I could see little black figures moving about it like ants.

As I was looking they suddenly began to run all together down the side of the mound.

"Fidos," said Mr. Coleman. "Knocking off time. We knock off an hour before sunset."

The expedition house lay a little way back from the river.

The driver rounded a corner, bumped through an extremely narrow arch and there we were.

The house was built round a courtyard. Originally it had occupied only the south side of the courtyard with a few unimportant out-buildings on the east. The expedition had continued the building on the other two sides. As the plan of the house was to prove of special interest later, I append a rough sketch of it.

All the rooms opened on to the courtyard, and most of the windows—the exception being in the original south building where there were windows giving on the outside country as well. These windows, however, were barred on the outside. In the south-west corner a staircase ran up to a long flat roof with a parapet running the length of the south side of the building which was higher than the other three sides.

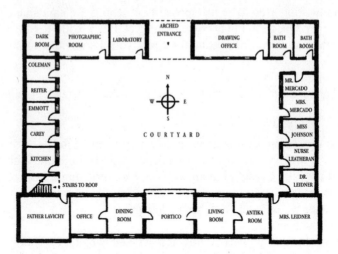

Mr. Coleman led me along the east side of the courtyard and round to where a big open verandah occupied the centre of the south side. He pushed open a door at one side of it and we entered a room where several people were sitting round a tea table.

"Toodle-oodle-oo!" said Mr. Coleman. "Here's Sairey Gamp."

The lady who was sitting at the head of the table rose and came to greet me.

I had my first glimpse of Louise Leidner.

Chapter 5

Tell Yarimjah

I don't mind admitting that my first impression on seeing Mrs. Leidner was one of downright surprise. One gets into the way of imagining a person when one hears them talked about. I'd got it firmly into my head that Mrs. Leidner was a dark, discontented kind of woman. The nervy kind, all on edge. And then, too, I'd expected her to be—well, to put it frankly—a bit vulgar.

She wasn't a bit like what I'd imagined her! To begin with, she was very fair. She wasn't a Swede, like her husband, but she might have been as far as looks went. She had that blonde Scandinavian fairness that you don't very often see. She wasn't a young woman. Midway between thirty and forty, I should say. Her face was rather haggard, and there was some grey hair mingled with the fairness. Her eyes, though, were lovely. They were the only eyes I've ever come across that you might truly describe as violet. They were very large, and there were faint shadows underneath them. She was very thin and fragile-looking, and if I say that she had an air of intense weariness and was at the same time very much alive, it sounds like nonsense—but that's the feeling I got. I felt, too, that she was a lady through and through. And that means something—even nowadays.

She put out her hand and smiled. Her voice was low and soft with an American drawl in it.

"I'm so glad you've come, nurse. Will you have some tea? Or would you like to go to your room first?"

I said I'd have tea, and she introduced me to the people sitting round the table.

"This is Miss Johnson—and Mr. Reiter. Mrs. Mercado. Mr. Emmott.

Father Lavigny. My husband will be in presently. Sit down here between Father Lavigny and Miss Johnson."

I did as I was bid and Miss Johnson began talking to me, asking about my journey and so on.

I liked her. She reminded me of a matron I'd had in my probationer days whom we had all admired and worked hard for.

She was getting on for fifty, I should judge, and rather mannish in appearance, with iron-grey hair cropped short. She had an abrupt, pleasant voice, rather deep in tone. She had an ugly rugged face with an almost laughably turned-up nose which she was in the habit of rubbing irritably when anything troubled or perplexed her. She wore a tweed coat and skirt made rather like a man's. She told me presently that she was a native of Yorkshire.

Father Lavigny I found just a bit alarming. He was a tall man with a great black beard and pince-nez. I had heard Mrs. Kelsey say that there was a French monk there, and I now saw that Father Lavigny was wearing a monk's robe of some white woollen material. It surprised me rather, because I always understood that monks went into monasteries and didn't come out again.

Mrs. Leidner talked to him mostly in French, but he spoke to me in quite fair English. I noticed that he had shrewd, observant eyes which darted about from face to face.

Opposite me were the other three. Mr. Reiter was a stout, fair young man with glasses. His hair was rather long and curly, and he had very round blue eyes. I should think he must have been a lovely baby, but he wasn't much to look at now! In fact he was just a little like a pig. The other young man had very short hair cropped close to his head. He had a long, rather humorous face and very good teeth, and he looked very attractive when he smiled. He said very little, though, just nodded if spoken to or answered in monosyllables. He, like Mr. Reiter, was an American. The last person was Mrs. Mercado, and I couldn't have a good look at her because whenever I glanced in her direction I always found her staring at me with a kind of hungry stare that was a bit disconcerting to say the least of it. You might have thought a hospital nurse was a strange animal the way she was looking at me. No manners at all!

She was quite young—not more than about twenty-five—and sort of dark and slinky-looking, if you know what I mean. Quite nice-looking in a kind of way, but rather as though she might have what my mother used to call "a touch of the tar-brush." She had on a very vivid pullover and her nails matched it in colour. She had a thin bird-like eager face with big eyes and rather a tight, suspicious mouth.

The tea was very good—a nice strong blend—not like the weak China stuff that Mrs. Kelsey always had and that had been a sore trial to me.

There was toast and jam and a plate of rock buns and a cutting cake. Mr. Emmott was very polite passing me things. Quiet as he was he always seemed to notice when my plate was empty.

Presently Mr. Coleman bustled in and took the place beyond Miss Johnson. There didn't seem to be anything the matter with *his* nerves. He talked away nineteen to the dozen.

Mrs. Leidner sighed once and cast a wearied look in his direction but it didn't have any effect. Nor did the fact that Mrs. Mercado, to whom he was addressing most of his conversation, was far too busy watching me to do more than make perfunctory replies.

Just as we were finishing, Dr. Leidner and Mr. Mercado came in from the dig.

Dr. Leidner greeted me in his nice kind manner. I saw his eyes go quickly and anxiously to his wife's face and he seemed to be relieved by what he saw there. Then he sat down at the other end of the table and Mr. Mercado sat down in the vacant place by Mrs. Leidner. He was a tall, thin, melancholy man, a good deal older than his wife, with a sallow complexion and a queer, soft, shapeless-looking beard. I was glad when he came in, for his wife stopped staring at me and transferred her attention to him, watching him with a kind of anxious impatience that I found rather odd. He himself stirred his tea dreamily and said nothing at all. A piece of cake lay untasted on his plate.

There was still one vacant place, and presently the door opened and a man came in.

The moment I saw Richard Carey I felt he was one of the handsomest men I'd seen for a long time—and yet I doubt if that were really so. To say a man is handsome and at the same time to say he looks like a death's head sounds a rank contradiction, and yet it was true. His head gave the effect of having the skin stretched unusually tightly over the bones—but they were beautiful bones. The lean line of jaw and temple and forehead was so sharply outlined that he reminded me of a bronze statue. Out of this lean brown face looked two of the brightest and most intensely blue eyes I have ever seen. He stood about six foot and was, I should imagine, a little under forty years of age.

Dr. Leidner said:

"This is Mr. Carey, our architect, nurse."

He murmured something in a pleasant, inaudible English voice and sat down by Mrs. Mercado.

Mrs. Leidner said:

"I'm afraid the tea is a little cold, Mr. Carey."

He said: "Oh, that's quite all right Mrs. Leidner. My fault for being late. I wanted to finish plotting those walls."

Mrs. Mercado said, "Jam, Mr. Carey?"

Mr. Reiter pushed forward the toast.

And I remember Major Pennyman saying:

"I can explain best what I mean by saying that they all passed the butter to each other a shade too politely."

Yes, there was something a little too odd about it. . . .

A shade formal. . . .

You'd have said it was a party of strangers—not people who had known each other—some of them—for quite a number of years.

Chapter 6

First Evening

After tea Mrs. Leidner took me to show me my room.

Perhaps here I had better give a short description of the arrangement of the rooms. This was very simple and can easily be understood by a reference to the plan.

On either side of the big open porch were doors leading into the two principal rooms. That on the right led into the dining-room, where we had had tea. The one on the other side led into an exactly similar room (I have called it the living-room) which was used as a sitting-room and kind of informal workroom—that is, a certain amount of drawing (other than the strictly architectural) was done there, and the more delicate pieces of pottery were brought there to be pieced together. Through the living-room one passed into the antiquities-room where all the finds from the dig were brought in and stored on shelves and in pigeon-holes, and also laid out on big benches and tables. From the antika-room there was no exit save through the living-room.

Beyond the antika-room, but reached through a door which gave on the courtyard, was Mrs. Leidner's bedroom. This, like the other rooms on that side of the house, had a couple of barred windows looking out over the ploughed countryside. Round the corner next to Mrs. Leidner's room, but with no actual communicating door, was Dr. Leidner's room. This was the first of the rooms on the east side of the building. Next to it was the room that was to be mine. Next to me was Miss Johnson's, with Mr. and Mrs. Mercado's beyond. After that came two so-called bathrooms.

(When I once used that last term in the hearing of Dr. Reilly he laughed at me and said a bathroom was either a bathroom or not a bathroom! All the same, when you've got used to taps and proper plumbing, it seems strange to call a couple of mud-rooms with a tin hip-bath in each of them, and muddy water brought in kerosene tins, *bathrooms!*)

All this side of the building had been added by Dr. Leidner to the original Arab house. The bedrooms were all the same, each with a window and a door giving on to the courtyard.

Along the north side were the drawing office, the laboratory and the photographic rooms.

To return to the verandah, the arrangement of rooms was much the same on the other side. There was the dining-room leading into the office where the files were kept and the cataloguing and typing was done. Corresponding to Mrs. Leidner's room was that of Father Lavigny, who was given the largest bedroom; he used it also for the decoding—or whatever you call it—of tablets.

In the south-west corner was the staircase running up to the roof. On the west side were first the kitchen quarters and then four small bedrooms used by the young men—Carey, Emmott, Reiter and Coleman.

At the north-west corner was the photographic-room with the dark-room leading out of it. Next to that the laboratory. Then came the only entrance—the big arched doorway through which we had entered. Outside were sleeping quarters for the native servants, the guard-house for the soldiers, and stables, etc., for the water horses. The drawing-office was to the right of the archway occupying the rest of the north side.

I have gone into the arrangements of the house rather fully here because I don't want to have to go over them again later.

As I say, Mrs. Leidner herself took me round the building and finally established me in my bedroom, hoping that I should be comfortable and have everything I wanted.

The room was nicely though plainly furnished—a bed, a chest of drawers, a wash-stand and a chair.

"The boys will bring you hot water before lunch and dinner—and in the morning, of course. If you want it any other time, go outside and clap your hands, and when the boy comes say, *jib mai' har*. Do you think you can remember that?"

I said I thought so and repeated it a little haltingly.

"That's right. And be sure and shout it. Arabs don't understand anything said in an ordinary 'English' voice."

"Languages are funny things," I said. "It seems odd there should be such a lot of different ones."

Mrs. Leidner smiled.

"There is a church in Palestine in which the Lord's Prayer is written up in—ninety, I think it is—different languages."

"Well!" I said, "I must write and tell my old aunt that. She *will* be interested."

Mrs. Leidner fingered the jug and basin absently and shifted the soap-dish an inch or two.

"I do hope you'll be happy here," she said. "And not get too bored."

"I'm not often bored," I assured her. "Life's not long enough for that."

She did not answer. She continued to toy with the wash-stand as though abstractedly.

Suddenly she fixed her dark violet eyes on my face.

"What exactly did my husband tell you, nurse?"

Well, one usually says the same thing to a question of that kind.

"I gathered you were a bit run-down and all that, Mrs. Leidner," I said glibly. "And that you just wanted some one to look after you and take any worries off your hands."

She bent her head slowly and thoughtfully.

"Yes," she said. "Yes—that will do very well."

That was just a little bit enigmatic, but I wasn't going to question it. Instead I said:

"I hope you'll let me help you with anything there is to do in the house. You mustn't let me be idle."

She smiled a little.

"Thank you, nurse."

Then she sat down on the bed and, rather to my surprise, began to cross-question me rather closely. I say rather to my surprise because, from the moment I set eyes on her, I felt sure that Mrs. Leidner was a lady. And a lady, in my experience, very seldom displays curiosity about one's private affairs.

But Mrs. Leidner seemed anxious to know everything there was to know about me. Where I'd trained and how long ago. What had brought me out to the East. How it had come about that Dr. Reilly had recommended me. She even asked me if I had ever been in America or had any relations in America. One or two other questions she asked me that seemed quite purposeless at the time, but of which I saw the significance later.

Then, suddenly, her manner changed. She smiled—a warm sunny smile—and she said, very sweetly, that she was very glad I had come and that she was sure I was going to be a comfort to her.

She got up from the bed and said:

"Would you like to come up to the roof and see the sunset? It's usually very lovely about this time."

I agreed willingly.

As we went out of the room she asked:

"Were there many other people on the train from Baghdad? Any men?"

I said that I hadn't noticed anybody in particular. There had been two Frenchmen in the restaurant-car the night before. And a party of three men whom I gathered from their conversation had to do with the Pipe line.

She nodded and a faint sound escaped her. It sounded like a small sigh of relief.

We went up to the roof together.

Mrs. Mercado was there, sitting on the parapet, and Dr. Leidner was bending over looking at a lot of stones and broken pottery that were laid out in rows. There were big things he called querns, and pestles and celts and stone axes, and more broken bits of pottery with queer patterns on them than I've ever seen all at once.

"Come over here," called out Mrs. Mercado. "Isn't it *too*, too beautiful?"

It certainly was a beautiful sunset. Hassanieh in the distance looked quite fairy-like with the setting sun behind it, and the River Tigris flowing between its wide banks looked like a dream river rather than a real one.

"Isn't it lovely, Eric?" said Mrs. Leidner.

The doctor looked up with abstracted eyes, murmured, "Lovely, lovely," perfunctorily and went on sorting potsherds.

Mrs. Leidner smiled and said:

"Archaeologists only look at what lies beneath their feet. The sky and the heavens don't exist for them."

Mrs. Mercado giggled.

"Oh, they're very queer people—you'll soon find *that* out, nurse," she said.

She paused and then added:

"We are all *so* glad you've come. We've been so very worried about our dear Mrs. Leidner, haven't we, Louise?"

"Have you?"

Her voice was not encouraging.

"Oh, yes. She really has been *very* bad, nurse. All sorts of alarms and excursions. You know when anybody says to me of some one, 'It's just nerves,' I always say: But what could be *worse?* Nerves are the core and centre of one's being, aren't they?"

"Puss, puss," I thought to myself.

Mrs. Leidner said dryly:

"Well, you needn't be worried about me any more, Marie. Nurse is going to look after me."

"Certainly I am," I said cheerfully.

"I'm sure that will make all the difference," said Mrs. Mercado. "We've all felt that she ought to see a doctor or do *something*. Her nerves have really been all to pieces, haven't they, Louise dear?"

"So much so that I seem to have got on *your* nerves with them," said Mrs. Leidner. "Shall we talk about something more interesting than my wretched ailments?"

I understood then that Mrs. Leidner was the sort of woman who could easily make enemies. There was a cool rudeness in her tone (not that I blamed her for it) which brought a flush to Mrs. Mercado's rather sallow cheeks. She stammered out something, but Mrs. Leidner had risen and had joined her husband at the other end of the roof. I doubt if he heard her coming till she laid her hand on his shoulder, then he looked up quickly. There was affection and a kind of eager questioning in his face.

Mrs. Leidner nodded her head gently. Presently, her arm through his, they wandered to the far parapet and finally down the steps together.

"He's devoted to her, isn't he?" said Mrs. Mercado.

"Yes," I said. "It's very nice to see."

She was looking at me with a queer, rather eager sidelong glance.

"What do you think is really the matter with her, nurse?" she asked, lowering her voice a little.

"Oh, I don't suppose it's much," I said cheerfully. "Just a bit run down, I expect."

Her eyes still bored into me as they had done at tea. She said abruptly: "Are you a mental nurse?"

"Oh, dear no!" I said. "What made you think that?"

She was silent for a moment, then she said:

"Do you know how queer she's been? Did Dr. Leidner tell you?"

I don't hold with gossiping about my cases. On the other hand, it's my experience that it's often very hard to get the truth out of the relatives, and until you know the truth you're often working in the dark and doing no good. Of course, when there's a doctor in charge, it's different. He tells you what it's necessary for you to know. But in this case there wasn't a doctor in charge. Dr. Reilly had never been called in professionally. And in my own mind I wasn't at all sure that Dr. Leidner had told me all he could have done. It's often the husband's instinct to be reticent—and more honour to him, I say. But all the same, the more I knew the better I could tell which line to take. Mrs. Mercado (whom I put down in my own mind as a thoroughly spiteful little cat) was clearly dying to talk. And frankly, on the human side as well as the professional, I wanted to hear what she had to say. You can put it that I was just every-day curious if you like.

I said, "I gather Mrs. Leidner's not been quite her normal self lately?"

Mrs. Mercado laughed disagreeably.

"Normal? I should say not. Frightening us to death. One night it was fingers tapping on her window. And then it was a hand without an arm attached. But when it came to a yellow face pressed against the window — and when she rushed to the window there was nothing there — well, I ask you, it *is* a bit creepy for all of us."

"Perhaps somebody was playing a trick on her," I suggested.

"Oh, no, she fancied it all. And only three days ago at dinner they were firing off shots in the village — nearly a mile away — and she jumped up and screamed out — it scared us all to death. As for Dr. Leidner, he rushed to her and behaved in the most ridiculous way. 'It's nothing, darling, it's nothing at all,' he kept saying. I think, you know, nurse, men sometimes *encourage* women in these hysterical fancies. It's a pity because it's a bad thing. Delusions shouldn't be encouraged."

"Not if they *are* delusions," I said dryly.

"What else could they be?"

I didn't answer because I didn't know what to say. It was a funny business. The shots and the screaming were natural enough — for any one in a nervous condition, that is. But this queer story of a spectral face and hand was different. It looked to me like one of two things — either Mrs. Leidner had made the story up (exactly as a child shows off by telling lies about something that never happened in order to make herself the centre of attraction) or else it was, as I had suggested, a deliberate practical joke. It was the sort of thing, I reflected, that an unimaginative hearty sort of young fellow like Mr. Coleman might think very funny. I decided to keep a close watch on him. Nervous patients can be scared nearly out of their minds by a silly joke.

Mrs. Mercado said with a sideways glance at me:

"She's very romantic-looking, nurse, don't you think so? The sort of woman things *happen* to."

"Have many things happened to her?" I asked.

"Well, her first husband was killed in the war when she was only twenty. I think that's very pathetic and romantic, don't you?"

"It's one way of calling a goose a swan," I said dryly.

"Oh! nurse. What an extraordinary remark!"

It was really a very true one. The amount of women you hear say, "If Donald — or Arthur — or whatever his name was — had *only* lived." And I sometimes think but if he had, he'd have been a stout, unromantic, short-tempered, middle-aged husband as likely as not.

It was getting dark and I suggested that we should go down. Mrs. Mercado agreed and asked if I would like to see the laboratory. "My husband will be there — working."

I said I would like to very much and we made our way there. The place was lighted by a lamp but it was empty. Mrs. Mercado showed me some of the apparatus and some copper ornaments that were being treated, and also some bones coated with wax.

"Where can Joseph be?" said Mrs. Mercado.

She looked into the drawing-office, where Carey was at work. He hardly looked up as we entered, and I was struck by the extraordinary look of strain on his face. It came to me suddenly: "This man is at the end of his tether. Very soon, something will snap." And I remembered somebody else had noticed that same tenseness about him.

As we went out again I turned my head for one last look at him. He was bent over his paper, his lips pressed very closely together, and that "death's head" suggestion of his bones very strongly marked. Perhaps it was fanciful, but I thought that he looked like a knight of old who was going into battle and knew he was going to be killed.

And again I felt what an extraordinary and quite unconscious power of attraction he had.

We found Mr. Mercado in the living-room. He was explaining the idea of some new process to Mrs. Leidner. She was sitting on a straight wooden chair, embroidering flowers in fine silks, and I was struck anew by her strange, fragile, unearthly appearance. She looked a fairy creature more than flesh and blood.

Mrs. Mercado said, her voice high and shrill:

"Oh, *there* you are, Joseph. We thought we'd find you in the lab."

He jumped up looking startled and confused, as though her entrance had broken a spell. He said stammeringly:

"I—I must go now. I'm in the middle of—middle of—"

He didn't complete the sentence but turned towards the door.

Mrs. Leidner said in her soft, drawling voice:

"You must finish telling me some other time. It was very interesting."

She looked up at us, smiled rather sweetly but in a faraway manner, and bent over her embroidery again.

In a minute or two, she said:

"There are some books over there, nurse. We've got quite a good selection. Choose one and sit down."

I went over to the bookshelf. Mrs. Mercado stayed for a minute or two, then, turning abruptly, she went out. As she passed me I saw her face and I didn't like the look of it. She looked wild with fury.

In spite of myself I remembered some of the things Mrs. Kelsey had said and hinted about Mrs. Leidner. I didn't like to think they were true because I liked Mrs. Leidner, but I wondered, nevertheless, if there mightn't perhaps be a grain of truth behind them.

I didn't think it was all her fault, but the fact remained that dear ugly Miss Johnson, and that common little spitfire Mrs. Mercado, couldn't hold a candle to her in looks or in attraction. And after all, men are men all over the world. You soon see a lot of that in my profession.

Mercado was a poor fish, and I don't suppose Mrs. Leidner really cared two hoots for his admiration—but his wife cared. If I wasn't mistaken, she minded badly and would be quite willing to do Mrs. Leidner a bad turn if she could.

I looked at Mrs. Leidner sitting there and sewing at her pretty flowers, so remote and far away and aloof. I felt somehow I ought to warn her. I felt that perhaps she didn't know how stupid and unreasoning and violent jealousy and hate can be—and how little it takes to set them smouldering.

And then I said to myself, "Amy Leatheran, you're a fool. Mrs. Leidner's no chicken. She's close on forty if she's a day, and she must know all about life there is to know."

But I felt that all the same perhaps she didn't.

She had such a queer untouched look.

I began to wonder what her life had been. I knew she'd only married Dr. Leidner two years ago. And according to Mrs. Mercado her first husband had died nearly twenty years ago.

I came and sat down near her with a book, and presently I went and washed my hands for supper. It was a good meal—some really excellent curry. They all went to bed early and I was glad for I was tired.

Dr. Leidner came with me to my room to see I had all I wanted.

He gave me a warm handclasp and said eagerly:

"She likes you, nurse. She's taken to you at once. I'm so glad. I feel everything's going to be all right now."

His eagerness was almost boyish.

I felt, too, that Mrs. Leidner had taken a liking to me, and I was pleased it should be so.

But I didn't quite share his confidence. I felt, somehow, that there was more to it all than he himself might know.

There was *something*—something I couldn't get at. But I felt it in the air.

My bed was comfortable, but I didn't sleep well for all that. I dreamt too much.

The words of a poem by Keats, that I'd had to learn as a child, kept running through my head. I kept getting them wrong and it worried me. It was a poem I'd always hated—I suppose because I'd had to learn it whether I wanted to or not. But somehow when I woke up in the dark I saw a sort of beauty in it for the first time.

"Oh, say what ails thee, knight at arms, alone—and (what was it?)—

palely loitering . . . ?" I saw the knight's face in my mind for the first time—and it was Mr. Carey's face—a grim, tense, bronzed face like some of those poor young men I remembered as a girl during the war . . . and I felt sorry for him—and then I fell off to sleep again and I saw that the Belle Dame sans Merci was Mrs. Leidner and she was leaning sideways on a horse with an embroidery of flowers in her hands—and then the horse stumbled and everywhere there were bones coated in wax, and I woke up all goose-flesh and shivering, and told myself that curry never *had* agreed with me at night.

Chapter 7

The Man at the Window

I think I'd better make it clear right away that there isn't going to be any local colour in this story. I don't know anything about archaeology and I don't know that I very much want to. Messing about with people and places that are buried and done with doesn't make sense to me. Mr. Carey used to tell me that I hadn't got the archaeological temperament and I've no doubt he was quite right.

The very first morning after my arrival Mr. Carey asked if I'd like to come and see the palace he was—*planning* I think he called it. Though how you can plan for a thing that's happened long ago I'm sure I don't know! Well, I said I'd like to, and to tell the truth, I was a bit excited about it. Nearly three thousand years old that palace was, it appeared. I wondered what sort of palaces they had in those days, and if it would be like the pictures I'd seen of Tutankhamen's tomb furniture. But would you believe it, there was nothing to see but *mud!* Dirty mud walls about two feet high—and that's all there was to it. Mr. Carey took me here and there telling me things—how this was the great court, and there were some chambers here and an upper storey and various other rooms that opened off the central court. And all I thought was, "But how does he *know?*" though, of course, I was too polite to say so. I can tell you it *was* a disappointment! The whole excavation looked like nothing but mud to me—no marble or gold or anything handsome—my aunt's house in Cricklewood would have made a much more imposing ruin! And those old Assyrians or whatever they were called themselves *kings*. When Mr. Carey had shown me his old "palace," he handed me over to Father Lavigny, who showed me the rest of the mound. I was a little afraid of Father Lavigny, being a monk and a foreigner and having such a deep voice and all, but he was very kind—though rather vague. Sometimes I felt it wasn't much more real to him than it was to me.

Mrs. Leidner explained that later. She said that Father Lavigny was only interested in "written documents"—as she called them. They wrote everything on clay, these people, queer heathenish-looking marks too, but quite sensible. There were even school tablets—the teacher's lesson on one side and the pupil's effort on the back of it. I confess that that did interest me rather—it seemed so human, if you know what I mean.

Father Lavigny walked round the work with me and showed me what were temples or palaces and what were private houses, and also a place which he said was an early Akkadian cemetery. He spoke in a funny jerky way, just throwing in a scrap of information and then reverting to other subjects.

He said:

"It is strange that you have come here. Is Mrs. Leidner really ill, then?"

"Not exactly ill," I said cautiously.

He said:

"She is an odd woman. A dangerous woman, I think."

"Now what do you mean by that?" I said. "Dangerous? How dangerous?"

He shook his head thoughtfully.

"I think she is ruthless," he said. "Yes, I think she could be absolutely ruthless."

"If you'll excuse me," I said, "I think you're talking nonsense."

He shook his head.

"You do not know women as I do," he said.

And that was a funny thing, I thought, for a monk to say. But of course I suppose he might have heard a lot of things in confession. But that rather puzzled me, because I wasn't sure if monks heard confessions or if it was only priests. I supposed he *was* a monk with that long woollen robe—all sweeping up the dirt—and the rosary and all!

"Yes, she could be ruthless," he said musingly. "I am quite sure of that. And yet—though she is so hard—like stone, like marble—yet she is afraid. What is she afraid of?"

That, I thought, is what we should all like to know!

At least it was possible that her husband did know, but I didn't think any one else did.

He fixed me with a sudden bright, dark eye.

"It is odd here? You find it odd? Or quite natural?"

"Not quite natural," I said, considering. "It's comfortable enough as far as the arrangements go—but there isn't quite a comfortable feeling."

"It makes *me* uncomfortable. I have the idea"—he became suddenly a little more foreign—"that something prepares itself. Dr. Leidner, too, he is not quite himself. Something is worrying him also."

"His wife's health?"

"That perhaps. But there is more. There is—how shall I say it—an uneasiness."

And that was just it, there was an uneasiness.

We didn't say any more just then, for Dr. Leidner came towards us. He showed me a child's grave that had just been uncovered. Rather pathetic it was—the little bones—and a pot or two and some little specks that Dr. Leidner told me were a bead necklace.

It was the workmen that made me laugh. You never saw such a lot of scarecrows—all in long petticoats and rags, and their heads tied up as though they had toothache. And every now and then, as they went to and fro carrying away baskets of earth, they began to sing—at least I suppose it was meant to be singing—a queer sort of monotonous chant that went on and on over and over again. I noticed that most of their eyes were terrible—all covered with discharge, and one or two looked half blind. I was just thinking what a miserable lot they were when Dr. Leidner said, "Rather a fine-looking lot of men, aren't they?" and I thought what a queer world it was and how two different people could see the same thing each of them the other way round. I haven't put that very well, but you can guess what I mean.

After a bit Dr. Leidner said he was going back to the house for a midmorning cup of tea. So he and I walked back together and he told me things. When *he* explained, it was all quite different. I sort of *saw* it all—how it used to be—the streets and the houses, and he showed me ovens where they baked bread and said the Arabs used much the same kind of ovens nowadays.

We got back to the house and found Mrs. Leidner had got up. She was looking better to-day, not so thin and worn. Tea came in almost at once and Dr. Leidner told her what had turned up during the morning on the dig. Then he went back to work and Mrs. Leidner asked me if I would like to see some of the finds they had made up to date. Of course I said "Yes," so she took me through into the antika-room. There was a lot of stuff lying about—mostly broken pots it seemed to me—or else ones that were all mended and stuck together. The whole lot might have been thrown away, I thought.

"Dear, dear," I said, "it's a pity they're all so broken, isn't it? Are they really worth keeping?"

Mrs. Leidner smiled a little and she said:

"You mustn't let Eric hear you. Pots interest him more than anything else, and some of these are the oldest things we have—perhaps as much as seven thousand years old." And she explained how some of them came from a very deep cut on the mound down towards the bottom, and how, thousands of years ago, they had been broken and mended with bitumen, showing people prized their things just as much then as they do nowadays.

"And now," she said, "we'll show you something more exciting."

And she took down a box from the shelf and showed me a beautiful gold dagger with dark-blue stones in the handle.

I exclaimed with pleasure.

Mrs. Leidner laughed.

"Yes, everybody likes gold! Except my husband."

"Why doesn't Dr. Leidner like it?"

"Well, for one thing it comes expensive. You have to pay the workmen who find it the weight of the object in gold."

"Good gracious!" I exclaimed. "But why?"

"Oh, it's a custom. For one thing it prevents them from stealing. You see, if they *did* steal it wouldn't be for the archaeological value but for the intrinsic value. They could melt it down. So we make it easy for them to be honest."

She took down another tray and showed me a really beautiful gold drinking-cup with a design of rams' heads on it.

Again I exclaimed.

"Yes, it is beautiful, isn't it? These came from a prince's grave. We found other royal graves but most of them had been plundered. This cup is our best find. It is one of the most lovely ever found anywhere. Early Akkadian. Unique."

Suddenly, with a frown, Mrs. Leidner brought the cup up close to her eyes and scratched at it delicately with her nail.

"How extraordinary! There's actually wax on it. Some one must have been in here with a candle."

She detached the little flake and replaced the cup in its place.

After that she showed me some queer little terra-cotta figurines—but most of them were just rude. Nasty minds those old people had, I say.

When we went back to the porch Mrs. Mercado was sitting polishing her nails. She was holding them out in front of her admiring the effect. I thought myself that anything more hideous than that orange red could hardly have been imagined.

Mrs. Leidner had brought with her from the antika-room a very delicate little saucer broken in several pieces, and this she now proceeded to join together. I watched her for a minute or two and then asked if I could help.

"Oh, yes, there are plenty more." She fetched quite a supply of broken pottery and we set to work. I soon got into the hang of it and she praised my ability. I suppose most nurses are handy with their fingers.

"How busy everybody is," said Mrs. Mercado. "It makes me feel dreadfully idle. Of course I *am* idle."

"Why shouldn't you be if you like?" said Mrs. Leidner.

Her voice was quite uninterested.

At twelve we had lunch. Afterwards Dr. Leidner and Mr. Mercado cleaned some pottery, pouring a solution of hydrochloric acid over it. One pot went a lovely plum colour and a pattern of bulls' horns came out on another one. It was really quite magical. All the dried mud that no washing would remove sort of foamed and boiled away.

Mr. Carey and Mr. Coleman went out on the dig and Mr. Reiter went off to the photographic room.

"What will you do, Louise?" Dr. Leidner asked his wife. "I suppose you'll rest for a bit?"

I gathered that Mrs. Leidner usually lay down every afternoon.

"I'll rest for about an hour. Then perhaps I'll go out for a short stroll."

"Good. Nurse will go with you, won't you?"

"Of course," I said.

"No, no," said Mrs. Leidner. "I like going alone. Nurse isn't to feel so much on duty that I'm not allowed out of her sight."

"Oh, but I'd like to come," I said.

"No, really, I'd rather you didn't." She was quite firm—almost peremptory. "I must be by myself every now and then. It's necessary to me."

I didn't insist, of course. But as I went off for a short sleep myself it struck me as odd that Mrs. Leidner, with her nervous terrors, should be quite content to walk by herself without any kind of protection.

When I came out of my room at half-past three the courtyard was deserted save for a little boy with a large copper bath who was washing pottery, and Mr. Emmott, who was sorting and arranging it. As I went towards them Mrs. Leidner came in through the archway. She looked more alive than I had seen her yet. Her eyes shone and she looked uplifted and almost gay.

Dr. Leidner came out from the laboratory and joined her. He was showing her a big dish with bulls' horns on it.

"The prehistoric levels are being extraordinarily productive," he said. "It's been a good season so far. Finding that tomb right at the beginning was a real piece of luck. The only person who might complain is Father Lavigny. We've had hardly any tablets so far."

"He doesn't seem to have done very much with the few we have had," said Mrs. Leidner dryly. "He may be a very fine epigraphist but he's a remarkably lazy one. He spends all his afternoons sleeping."

"We miss Byrd," said Dr. Leidner. "This man strikes me as slightly unorthodox—though, of course, I'm not competent to judge. But one or two of his translations have been surprising to say the least of it. I can hardly believe, for instance, that he's right about that inscribed brick, and yet he must know."

After tea Mrs. Leidner asked me if I would like to stroll down to the river. I thought that perhaps she feared that her refusal to let me accompany her earlier in the afternoon might have hurt my feelings.

I wanted her to know that I wasn't the touchy kind, so I accepted at once.

It was a lovely evening. A path led between barley fields and then through some flowering fruit trees. Finally we came to the edge of the Tigris. Immediately on our left was the Tell with the workmen singing in their queer monotonous chant. A little to our right was a big water-wheel which made a queer groaning noise. It used to set my teeth on edge at first. But in the end I got fond of it and it had a queer soothing cffcct on me. Beyond the water-wheel was the village from which most of the workmen came.

"It's rather beautiful, isn't it?" said Mrs. Leidner.

"It's very peaceful," I said. "It seems funny to me to be so far away from everywhere."

"Far from everywhere," repeated Mrs. Leidner. "Yes. Here at least one might expect to be safe."

I glanced at her sharply, but I think she was speaking more to herself than to me, and I don't think she realized that her words had been revealing.

We began to walk back to the house.

Suddenly Mrs. Leidner clutched my arm so violently that I nearly cried out.

"Who's that, nurse? What's he doing?"

Some little distance ahead of us, just where the path ran near the expedition house, a man was standing. He wore European clothes and he seemed to be standing on tiptoe and trying to look in at one of the windows.

As we watched he glanced round, caught sight of us, and immediately continued on the path towards us. I felt Mrs. Leidner's clutch tighten.

"Nurse," she whispered. "Nurse . . ."

"It's all right, my dear, it's all right," I said reassuringly.

The man came along and passed us. He was an Iraqi, and as soon as she saw him near to, Mrs. Leidner relaxed with a sigh.

"He's only an Iraqi after all," she said.

We went on our way. I glanced up at the windows as I passed. Not only were they barred, but they were too high from the ground to permit of any one seeing in, for the level of the ground was lower here than on the inside of the courtyard.

"It must have been just curiosity," I said.

Mrs. Leidner nodded.

"That's all. But just for a minute I thought—"

She broke off.

I thought to myself, "You thought *what?* That's what I'd like to know. *What* did you think?"

But I knew one thing now—that Mrs. Leidner was afraid of a definite flesh and blood person.

Chapter 8

Night Alarm

It's a little difficult to know exactly what to note in the week that followed my arrival at Tell Yarimjah.

Looking back as I do from my present standpoint of knowledge I can see a good many little signs and indications that I was quite blind to at the time.

To tell the story properly, however, I think I ought to try and recapture the point of view that I actually held—puzzled, uneasy, and increasingly conscious of *something* wrong.

For one thing *was* certain, that curious sense of strain and constraint was *not* imagined. It was genuine. Even Bill Coleman the insensitive commented upon it.

"This place gets under my skin," I heard him say. "Are they always such a glum lot?"

It was David Emmott to whom he spoke, the other assistant. I had taken rather a fancy to Mr. Emmott; his taciturnity was not, I felt sure, unfriendly. There was something about him that seemed very steadfast and reassuring in an atmosphere where one was uncertain what any one was feeling or thinking.

"No," he said in answer to Mr. Coleman. "It wasn't like this last year."

But he didn't enlarge on the theme, or say any more.

"What I can't make out is what it's all about," said Mr. Coleman in an aggrieved voice.

Emmott shrugged his shoulders but didn't answer.

I had a rather enlightening conversation with Miss Johnson. I liked her very much. She was capable, practical and intelligent. She had, it was quite obvious, a distinct hero worship for Dr. Leidner.

On this occasion she told me the story of his life since his young days. She knew every site he had dug, and the results of the dig. I would almost dare swear she could quote from every lecture he had ever delivered. She considered him, she told me, quite the finest field archaeologist living.

"And he's so simple. So completely unworldly. He doesn't know the meaning of the word conceit. Only a really great man could be so simple."

"That's true enough," I said. "Big people don't need to throw their weight about."

"And he's so light-hearted too. I can't tell you what fun we used to have—he and Richard Carey and I—the first years we were out here. We were such a happy party. Richard Carey worked with him in Palestine, of course. Theirs is a friendship of ten years or so. Oh, well, I've known him for seven."

"What a handsome man Mr. Carey is," I said.

"Yes—I suppose he is."

She said it rather curtly.

"But he's just a little bit quiet, don't you think?"

"He usedn't to be like that," said Miss Johnson quickly. "It's only since—"

She stopped abruptly.

"Only since—?" I prompted.

"Oh, well." Miss Johnson gave a characteristic motion of her shoulders. "A good many things are changed nowadays."

I didn't answer. I hoped she would go on—and she did—prefacing her remarks with a little laugh as though to detract from their importance.

"I'm afraid I'm rather a conservative old fogy. I sometimes think that if an archaeologist's wife isn't really interested, it would be wiser for her not to accompany the expedition. It often leads to friction."

"Mrs. Mercado—" I suggested.

"Oh, her!" Miss Johnson brushed the suggestion aside. "I was really thinking of Mrs. Leidner. She's a very charming woman—and one can quite understand why Dr. Leidner 'fell for her'—to use a slang term. But I can't help feeling she's out of place here. She—it unsettles things."

So Miss Johnson agreed with Mrs. Kelsey that it was Mrs. Leidner who was responsible for the strained atmosphere. But then where did Mrs. Leidner's own nervous fears come in?

"It unsettles *him*," said Miss Johnson earnestly. "Of course, I'm—well, I'm like a faithful but jealous old dog. I don't like to see him so worn out and worried. His whole mind ought to be on the work—not taken up with his wife and her silly fears! If she's nervous of coming to out-of-the-way places, she ought to have stayed in America. I've no patience with people who come to a place and then do nothing but grouse about it!"

And then, a little fearful of having said more than she meant to say, she went on:

"Of course I admire her very much. She's a lovely woman and she's got great charm of manner when she chooses."

And there the subject dropped.

I thought to myself that it was always the same way—wherever women are cooped up together, there's bound to be jealousy. Miss Johnson clearly didn't like her chief's wife (that was perhaps natural) and unless I was much mistaken Mrs. Mercado fairly hated her.

Another person who didn't like Mrs. Leidner was Sheila Reilly. She came out once or twice to the dig, once in a car and twice with some young man on a horse—on two horses I mean, of course. It was at the back of my mind that she had a weakness for the silent young American, Emmott. When he was on duty at the dig she used to stay talking to him, and I thought, too, that *he* admired *her*.

One day, rather injudiciously, I thought, Mrs. Leidner commented upon it at lunch.

"The Reilly girl is still hunting David down," she said with a little laugh. "Poor David, she chases you up on the dig even! How foolish girls are!"

Mr. Emmott didn't answer, but under his tan his face got rather red. He raised his eyes and looked right into hers with a very curious expression—a straight, steady glance with something of a challenge in it.

She smiled very faintly and looked away.

I heard Father Lavigny murmur something, but when I said "Pardon?" he merely shook his head and did not repeat his remark.

That afternoon Mr. Coleman said to me:

"Matter of fact I didn't like Mrs. L. any too much at first. She used to jump down my throat every time I opened my mouth. But I've begun to understand her better now. She's one of the kindest women I've ever met. You find yourself telling her all the foolish scrapes you ever got into before you know where you are. She's got her knife into Sheila Reilly, I know, but then Sheila's been damned rude to her once or twice. That's the worst of Sheila—she's got no manners. And a temper like the devil!"

That I could well believe. Dr. Reilly spoilt her.

"Of course she's bound to get a bit full of herself, being the only young woman in the place. But that doesn't excuse her talking to Mrs. Leidner as though Mrs. Leidner were her great-aunt. Mrs. L's not exactly a chicken, but she's a damned good-looking woman. Rather like those fairy women who come out of marshes with lights and lure you away." He added bitterly, "You wouldn't find Sheila luring any one. All she does is to tick a fellow off."

I only remember two other incidents of any kind of significance.

One was when I went to the laboratory to fetch some acetone to get the stickiness off my fingers from mending the pottery. Mr. Mercado was sitting in a corner, his head was laid down on his arms and I fancied he was asleep. I took the bottle I wanted and went off with it.

That evening, to my great surprise, Mrs. Mercado tackled me.

"Did you take a bottle of acetone from the lab?"

"Yes," I said. "I did."

"You know perfectly well that there's a small bottle always kept in the antika-room."

She spoke quite angrily.

"Is there? I didn't know."

"I think you did! You just wanted to come spying round. I know what hospital nurses are."

I stared at her.

"I don't know what you're talking about, Mrs. Mercado," I said with dignity. "I'm sure I don't want to spy on any one."

"Oh, no! Of course not. Do you think I don't know what you're here for?"

Really, for a minute or two I thought she must have been drinking. I went away without saying any more. But I thought it was very odd.

The other thing was nothing very much. I was trying to entice a pi dog pup with a piece of bread. It was very timid, however, like all Arab dogs—and was convinced I meant no good. It slunk away and I followed it—out through the archway and round the corner of the house. I came round so sharply that before I knew I had cannoned into Father Lavigny and another man who were standing together—and in a minute I realized that the second man was the same one Mrs. Leidner and I had noticed that day trying to peer through the window.

I apologized and Father Lavigny smiled, and with a word of farewell greeting to the other man he returned to the house with me.

"You know," he said, "I am very ashamed. I am a student of Oriental languages and none of the men on the men work can understand me! It is humiliating, do you not think? I was trying my Arabic on that man, who is a townsman, to see if I got on better—but it still wasn't very success-ful. Leidner says my Arabic is too pure."

That was all. But it just passed through my head that it was odd the same man should still be hanging round the house.

That night we had a scare.

It must have been about two in the morning. I'm a light sleeper, as most nurses have to be. I was awake and sitting up in bed by the time that my door opened.

"Nurse, nurse!"

It was Mrs. Leidner's voice low and urgent.

I struck a match and lighted the candle.

She was standing by the door in a long blue dressing-gown. She was looking petrified with terror.

"There's some one—some one—in the room next to mine. . . . I heard him—scratching on the wall."

I jumped out of bed and came to her.

"It's all right," I said. "I'm here. Don't be afraid, my dear."

She whispered:

"Get Eric."

I nodded and ran out and knocked on his door. In a minute he was with us. Mrs. Leidner was sitting on my bed, her breath coming in great gasps.

"I heard him," she said. "I heard him—scratching on the wall."

"Some one in the antika-room?" cried Dr. Leidner.

He ran out quickly—and it just flashed across my mind how differently these two had reacted. Mrs. Leidner's fear was entirely personal, but Dr. Leidner's mind leaped at once to his precious treasures.

"The antika-room!" breathed Mrs. Leidner. "Of course! How stupid of me."

And rising and pulling her gown round her, she bade me come with her. All traces of her panic-stricken fear had vanished.

We arrived in the antika-room to find Dr. Leidner and Father Lavigny. The latter had also heard a noise, had risen to investigate, and had fancied he saw a light in the antika-room. He had delayed to put on slippers and snatch up a torch and had found no one by the time he got there. The door, moreover, was duly locked, as it was supposed to be at night.

Whilst he was assuring himself that nothing had been taken, Dr. Leidner had joined him.

Nothing more was to be learned. The outside archway door was locked. The guard swore nobody could have got in from outside, but as they had probably been fast asleep this was not conclusive. There were no marks or traces of an intruder and nothing had been taken.

It was possible that what had alarmed Mrs. Leidner was the noise made by Father Lavigny taking down boxes from the shelves to assure himself that all was in order.

On the other hand, Father Lavigny himself was positive that he had *(a)* heard footsteps passing his window and *(b)* seen the flicker of a light, possibly a torch, in the antika-room.

Nobody else had heard or seen anything.

The incident is of value in my narrative because it led to Mrs. Leidner's unburdening herself to me on the following day.

Chapter 9

Mrs. Leidner's Story

We had just finished lunch. Mrs. Leidner went to her room to rest as usual. I settled her on her bed with plenty of pillows and her book, and was leaving the room when she called me back.

"Don't go, nurse, there's something I want to say to you."

I came back into the room.

"Shut the door."

I obeyed.

She got up from the bed and began to walk up and down the room. I could see that she was making up her mind to something and I didn't like to interrupt her. She was clearly in great indecision of mind.

At last she seemed to have nerved herself to the required point. She turned to me and said abruptly:

"Sit down."

I sat down by the table very quietly. She began nervously:

"You must have wondered what all this is about?"

I just nodded without saying anything.

"I've made up my mind to tell you—everything! I must tell some one or I shall go mad."

"Well," I said. "I think really it would be just as well. It's not easy to know the best thing to do when one's kept in the dark."

She stopped in her uneasy walk and faced me.

"Do you know what I'm frightened of?"

"Some man," I said.

"Yes—but I didn't say whom—I said what."

I waited.

She said:

"I'm afraid of being killed!"

Well, it was out now. I wasn't going to show any particular concern. She was near enough hysterics as it was.

"Dear me," I said. "So that's it, is it?"

Then she began to laugh. She laughed and she laughed—and the tears ran down her face.

"The way you said that!" she gasped. "The way you said it . . ."

"Now, now," I said. "This won't do." I spoke sharply. I pushed her into a chair, went over to the wash-stand and got a cold sponge and bathed her forehead and wrists.

"No more nonsense," I said. "Tell me calmly and sensibly all about it."

That stopped her. She sat up and spoke in her natural voice.

"You're a treasure, nurse," she said. "You make me feel as though I'm six. I'm going to tell you."

"That's right," I said. "Take your time and don't hurry."

She began to speak, slowly and deliberately.

"When I was a girl of twenty I married. A young man in one of our state departments. It was in 1918."

"I know," I said. "Mrs. Mercado told me. He was killed in the war."

But Mrs. Leidner shook her head.

"That's what she thinks. That's what everybody thinks. The truth is something quite different. I was a queer patriotic, enthusiastic girl, nurse, full of idealism. When I'd been married a few months I discovered—by a quite unforeseeable accident—that my husband was a spy in German pay. I learned that the information supplied by him had led directly to the sinking of an American transport and the loss of hundreds of lives. I don't know what most people would have done. . . . But I'll tell you what I did. I went straight to my father, who was in the War Department, and told him the truth. Frederick *was* killed in the war—but he was killed in America—shot as a spy."

"Oh, dear, dear!" I ejaculated. "How terrible!"

"Yes," she said. "It was terrible. He was so kind, too—so gentle. . . . And all the time . . . But I never hesitated. Perhaps I was wrong."

"It's difficult to say," I said. "I'm sure I don't know what one would do."

"What I'm telling you was never generally known outside the state departments. Ostensibly my husband had gone to the front and had been killed. I had a lot of sympathy and kindness shown me as a war widow."

Her voice was bitter and I nodded comprehendingly.

"Lots of people wanted to marry me, but I always refused. I'd had too bad a shock. I didn't feel I could ever *trust* any one again."

"Yes, I can imagine feeling like that."

"And then I became very fond of a certain young man. I wavered. An amazing thing happened! I got an anonymous letter—from Frederick—saying that if I ever married another man, he'd kill me!"

"From Frederick? From your dead husband?"

"Yes. Of course, I thought at first I was mad or dreaming. . . . At last I went to my father. He told me the truth. My husband hadn't been shot after all. He'd escaped—but his escape did him no good. He was involved in a train wreck a few weeks later and his dead body was found amongst others. My father had kept the fact of his escape from me, and since the man had died anyway he had seen no reason to tell me anything until now.

"But the letter I received opened up entirely new possibilities. Was it perhaps a fact that my husband was still alive?

"My father went into the matter as carefully as possible. And he declared that as far as one could humanly be sure the body that was buried as Frederick's *was* Frederick's. There had been a certain amount of disfiguration, so that he could not speak with absolute cast-iron certainty, but he reiterated his solemn belief that Frederick was dead and that this letter was a cruel and malicious hoax.

"The same thing happened more than once. If I seemed to be on intimate terms with any man, I would receive a threatening letter."

"In your husband's handwriting?"

She said slowly:

"That is difficult to say. I had no letters of his. I had only my memory to go by."

"There was no allusion or special form of words used that could make you sure?"

"No. There *were* certain terms—nicknames, for instance—private between us—if one of those had been used or quoted, then I should have been quite sure."

"Yes," I said thoughtfully. "That is odd. It looks as though it *wasn't* your husband. But is there any one else it could be?"

"There is a possibility. Frederick had a younger brother—a boy of ten or twelve at the time of our marriage. He worshipped Frederick and Frederick was devoted to him. What happened to this boy, William his name was, I don't know. It seems to me possible that, adoring his brother as fanatically as he did, he may have grown up regarding me as directly responsible for his death. He had always been jealous of me and may have invented this scheme by way of punishment."

"It's possible," I said. "It's amazing the way children do remember if they've had a shock."

"I know. This boy may have dedicated his life to revenge."

"Please go on."

"There isn't very much more to tell. I met Eric three years ago. I meant never to marry. Eric made me change my mind. Right up to our wedding day I waited for another threatening letter. None came. I decided that whoever the writer might be, he was either dead, or tired of his cruel sport. *Two days after our marriage I got this.*"

Drawing a small attaché-case which was on the table towards her, she unlocked it, took out a letter and handed it to me.

The ink was slightly faded. It was written in a rather womanish hand with a forward slant.

You have disobeyed. Now you cannot escape. You must be Frederick Bosner's wife only! You have got to die.

"I was frightened—but not so much as I might have been to begin with. Being with Eric made me feel safe. Then, a month later, I got a second letter."

I have not forgotten. I am making my plans. You have got to die. Why did you disobey?

"Does your husband know about this?"

Mrs. Leidner answered slowly.

"He knows that I am threatened. I showed him both letters when the second one came. He was inclined to think the whole thing a hoax. He thought also that it might be some one who wanted to blackmail me by pretending my first husband was alive."

She paused and then went on.

"A few days after I received the second letter we had a narrow escape from death by gas poisoning. Somebody entered our apartment after we were asleep and turned on the gas. Luckily I woke and smelled the gas in time. Then I lost my nerve. I told Eric how I had been persecuted for years, and I told him that I was sure this madman, whoever he might be, did really mean to kill me. I think that for the first time I really did think it *was* Frederick. There was always something a little ruthless behind his gentleness.

"Eric was still, I think, less alarmed than I was. He wanted to go to the police. Naturally I wouldn't hear of that. In the end we agreed that I should accompany him here, and that it might be wise if I didn't return to America in the summer but stayed in London and Paris.

"We carried out our plan and all went well. I felt sure that now everything would be all right. After all, we had put half the globe between ourselves and my enemy.

"And then—a little over three weeks ago—I received a letter—with an Iraq stamp on it."

She handed me a third letter.

You thought you could escape. You were wrong. You shall not be false to me and live. I have always told you so. Death is coming very soon.

"And a week ago—*this!* Just lying on the table here. It had not even gone through the post."

I took the sheet of paper from her. There was just one phrase scrawled across it.

I have arrived.

She stared at me.

"You see? You understand? He's going to kill me. It may be Frederick—it may be little William—*but he's going to kill me.*"

Her voice rose shudderingly. I caught her wrist.

"Now—now," I said warningly. "Don't give way. We'll look after you. Have you got any sal volatile?"

She nodded towards the wash-stand and I gave her a good dose.

"That's better," I said, as the colour returned to her cheeks.

"Yes, I'm better now. But oh, nurse, do you see why I'm in this state? When I saw that man looking in through my window, I thought: *He's come.* . . . Even when *you* arrived I was suspicious. I thought you might be a man in disguise—"

"The idea!"

"Oh, I know it sounds absurd. But you might have been in league with him perhaps—not a hospital nurse at all."

"But that's nonsense!"

"Yes, perhaps. But I've got beyond sense."

Struck by a sudden idea, I said:

"You'd *recognize* your husband, I suppose?"

She answered slowly.

"I don't even know that. It's over fifteen years ago. I mightn't recognize his face."

Then she shivered.

"I saw it one night—but it was a *dead* face. There was a tap, tap, tap on the window. And then I saw a face, a dead face, ghastly and grinning against the pane. I screamed and screamed. . . . And they said there wasn't anything there!"

I remembered Mrs. Mercado's story.

"You don't think," I said hesitatingly, "that you *dreamt* that?"

"I'm sure I didn't!"

I wasn't so sure. It was the kind of nightmare that was quite likely under the circumstances and that easily might be taken for a waking occurrence. However, I never contradict a patient. I soothed Mrs. Leidner as best I could and pointed out that if any stranger arrived in the neighbourhood it was pretty sure to be known.

I left her, I think, a little comforted, and I went in search of Dr. Leidner and told him of our conversation.

"I'm glad she's told you," he said simply. "It has worried me dreadfully. I feel sure that all those faces and tappings on the window-pane have been sheer imagination on her part. I haven't known what to do for the best. What do you think of the whole thing?"

I didn't quite understand the tone in his voice, but I answered promptly enough.

"It's possible," I said, "that these letters may be just a cruel and malicious hoax."

"Yes, that is quite likely. But what are we to *do?* They are driving her mad. I don't know what to think."

I didn't either. It had occurred to me that possibly a woman might be concerned. Those letters had a feminine note about them. Mrs. Mercado was at the back of my mind.

Supposing that by some chance she had learnt the facts of Mrs. Leidner's first marriage. She might be indulging her spite by terrorizing the other woman.

I didn't quite like to suggest such a thing to Dr. Leidner. It's so difficult to know how people are going to take things.

"Oh, well," I said cheerfully, "we must hope for the best. I think Mrs. Leidner seems happier already from just talking about it. That's always a help, you know. It's bottling things up that makes them get on your nerves."

"I'm very glad she has told you," he repeated. "It's a good sign. It shows she likes and trusts you. I've been at my wits' end to know what to do for the best."

It was on the tip of my tongue to ask him whether he'd thought of giving a discreet hint to the local police, but afterwards I was glad I hadn't done so.

What happened was this. On the following day Mr. Coleman was going in to Hassanieh to get the workmen's pay. He was also taking in all our letters to catch the air mail.

The letters, as written, were dropped into a wooden box on the dining-room window-sill. Last thing that night Mr. Coleman took them out and was sorting them out into bundles and putting rubber-bands round them.

Suddenly he gave a shout.

"What is it?" I asked.

He held out a letter with a grin.

"It's our Lovely Louise—she really *is* going balmy. She's addressed a letter to some one at 42nd Street, Paris, France. I don't think that can be right, do you? Do you mind taking it to her and asking what she *does* mean? She's just gone off to bed."

I took it from him and ran off to Mrs. Leidner with it and she amended the address.

It was the first time I had seen Mrs. Leidner's handwriting, and I wondered idly where I had seen it before, for it was certainly quite familiar to me.

It wasn't till the middle of the night that it suddenly came to me.

Except that it was bigger and rather more straggling, *it was extraordinarily like the writing on the anonymous letters.*

New ideas flashed through my head.

Had Mrs. Leidner conceivably written those letters *herself?*

And did Dr. Leidner half suspect the fact?

Chapter 10

Saturday Afternoon

Mrs. Leidner told me her story on a Friday.

On Saturday morning there was a feeling of slight anti-climax in the air.

Mrs. Leidner, in particular, was inclined to be very off-hand with me and rather pointedly avoided any possibility of a *tête-à-tête*. Well, *that* didn't surprise me! I've had the same thing happen to me again and again. Ladies tell their nurses things in a sudden burst of confidence, and then, afterwards, they feel uncomfortable about it and wish they hadn't! It's only human nature.

I was very careful not to hint or remind her in any way of what she had told me. I purposely kept my conversation as matter-of-fact as possible.

Mr. Coleman had started in to Hassanieh in the morning, driving himself in the lorry with the letters in a knapsack. He also had one or two commissions to do for the members of the expedition. It was pay-day for the men, and he would have to go to the bank and bring out the money in coins of small denominations. All this was a long business and he did not expect to be back until the afternoon. I rather suspected he might be lunching with Sheila Reilly.

Work on the dig was usually not very busy on the afternoon of pay-day as at three-thirty the paying-out began.

The little boy, Abdullah, whose business it was to wash pots, was established as usual in the centre of the courtyard, and again as usual, kept up his queer nasal chant. Dr. Leidner and Mr. Emmott were going to put in some work on the pottery until Mr. Coleman returned, and Mr. Carey went up to the dig.

Mrs. Leidner went to her room to rest. I settled her as usual and then went to my own room, taking a book with me as I did not feel sleepy. It was then about a quarter to one, and a couple of hours passed quite pleasantly. I was reading *Death in a Nursing Home*—really a most exciting story—though I don't think the author knew much about the way nursing homes are run! At any rate I've never known a nursing home like that! I really felt inclined to write to the author and put him right about a few points.

When I put the book down at last (it was the red-haired parlourmaid and I'd never suspected her once!) and looked at my watch I was quite surprised to find it was twenty minutes to three!

I got up, straightened my uniform, and came out into the courtyard.

Abdullah was still scrubbing and still singing his depressing chant, and David Emmott was standing by him sorting the scubbed pots, and putting the ones that were broken into boxes to await mending. I strolled over towards them just as Dr. Leidner came down the staircase from the roof.

"Not a bad afternoon," he said cheerfully. "I've made a bit of a clearance up there. Louise will be pleased. She's complained lately that there's not room to walk about. I'll go and tell her the good news."

He went over to his wife's door, tapped on it and went in.

It must, I suppose, have been about a minute and a half later that he came out again. I happened to be looking at the door when he did so. It was like a nightmare. He had gone in a brisk, cheerful man. He came out like a drunken one—reeling a little on his feet, and with a queer dazed expression on his face.

"Nurse—" he called in a queer, hoarse voice. "Nurse—"

I saw at once something was wrong, and I ran across to him. He looked awful—his face was all grey and twitching, and I saw he might collapse any minute.

"My wife . . ." he said. "My wife . . . Oh, my God . . ."

I pushed past him into the room. Then I caught my breath.

Mrs. Leidner was lying in a dreadful huddled heap by the bed.

I bent over her. She was quite dead—must have been dead an hour at least. The cause of death was perfectly plain—a terrific blow on the front of the head just over the right temple. She must have got up from the bed and been struck down where she stood.

I didn't handle her more than I could help.

I glanced round the room to see if there was anything that might give a clue, but nothing seemed out of place or disturbed. The windows were closed and fastened, and there was no place where the murderer could have hidden. Obviously he had been and gone long ago.

I went out, closing the door behind me.

Dr. Leidner had collapsed completely now. David Emmott was with him and turned a white, inquiring face to me.

In a few low words I told him what had happened.

As I always suspected, he was a first-class person to rely on in trouble. He was perfectly calm and self-possessed. Those blue eyes of his opened very wide, but otherwise he gave no sign at all.

He considered for a moment and then said:

"I suppose we must notify the police as soon as possible. Bill ought to be back any minute. What shall we do with Leidner?"

"Help me to get him into his room."

He nodded.

"Better lock this door first, I suppose," he said.

He turned the key in the lock of Mrs. Leidner's door, then drew it out and handed it to me.

"I guess you'd better keep this, nurse. Now then."

Together we lifted Dr. Leidner and carried him into his own room and laid him on his bed. Mr. Emmott went off in search of brandy. He returned, accompanied by Miss Johnson.

Her face was drawn and anxious, but she was calm and capable, and I felt satisfied to leave Dr. Leidner in her charge.

I hurried out into the courtyard. The station wagon was just coming in through the archway. I think it gave us all a shock to see Bill's pink, cheerful face as he jumped out with his familiar "Hallo, 'allo, 'allo! Here's the oof!" He went on gaily, "No highway robberies—"

He came to a halt suddenly. "I say, is anything up? What's the matter with you all? You look as though the cat had killed your canary."

Mr. Emmott said shortly:

"Mrs. Leidner's dead—killed."

"*What?*" Bill's jolly face changed ludicrously. He stared, his eyes goggling. "Mother Leidner dead! You're pulling my leg."

"Dead?" It was a sharp cry. I turned to see Mrs. Mercado behind me. "Did you say Mrs. Leidner had been *killed?*"

"Yes," I said. "Murdered."

"No!" she gasped. "Oh, no! I won't believe it. Perhaps she's committed suicide."

"Suicides don't hit themselves on the head," I said dryly. "It's murder all right, Mrs. Mercado."

She sat down suddenly on an upturned packing-case.

She said, "Oh, but this is horrible—*horrible* . . ."

Naturally it was horrible. We didn't need *her* to tell us so! I wondered if perhaps she was feeling a bit remorseful for the harsh feelings she had harboured against the dead woman, and all the spiteful things she had said.

After a minute or two she asked rather breathlessly:

"What are you going to do?"

Mr. Emmott took charge in his quiet way.

"Bill, you'd better get in again to Hassanieh as quick as you can. I don't know much about the proper procedure. Better get hold of Captain Maitland, he's in charge of the police here, I think. Get Dr. Reilly first. He'll know what to do."

Mr. Coleman nodded. All the facetiousness was knocked out of him. He just looked young and frightened. Without a word he jumped into the station wagon and drove off.

Mr. Emmott said rather uncertainly, "I suppose we ought to have a hunt round." He raised his voice and called:

"Ibrahim!"

"Na'am."

The house-boy came running. Mr. Emmott spoke to him in Arabic. A vigorous colloquy passed between them. The boy seemed to be emphatically denying something.

At last Mr. Emmott said in a perplexed voice:

"He says there's not been a soul here this afternoon. No stranger of any kind. I suppose the fellow must have slipped in without their seeing him."

"Of course he did," said Mrs. Mercado. "He slunk in when the boys weren't looking."

"Yes," said Mr. Emmott.

The slight uncertainty in his voice made me look at him inquiringly.

He turned and spoke to the little pot-boy, Abdullah, asking him a question.

The boy replied vehemently at length.

The puzzled frown on Mr. Emmott's brow increased.

"I don't understand it," he murmured under his breath. "I don't understand it at all."

But he didn't tell me what he didn't understand.

Chapter 11

An Odd Business

I'm adhering as far as possible to telling only my personal part in the business. I pass over the events of the next two hours, the arrival of Captain Maitland and the police and Dr. Reilly. There was a good deal of general confusion, questioning, all the routine business, I suppose.

In my opinion we began to get down to brass tacks about five o'clock when Dr. Reilly asked me to come with him into the office.

He shut the door, sat down in Dr. Leidner's chair, motioned me to sit down opposite him, and said briskly:

"Now, then, nurse, let's get down to it. There's something damned odd here."

I settled my cuffs and looked at him inquiringly.

He drew out a notebook.

"This is for my own satisfaction. Now, what time was it exactly when Dr. Leidner found his wife's body?"

"I should say it was almost exactly a quarter to three," I said.

"And how do you know that?"

"Well, I looked at my watch when I got up. It was twenty to three then."

"Let's have a look at this watch of yours."

I slipped it off my wrist and held it out to him.

"Right to the minute. Excellent woman. Good, that's *that* fixed. Now did you form any opinion as to how long she'd been dead?"

"Oh, really, doctor," I said, "I shouldn't like to say."

"Don't be so professional. I want to see if your estimate agrees with mine."

"Well, I should say she'd been dead at least an hour."

"Quite so. I examined the body at half-past four and I'm inclined to put the time of death between 1.15 and 1.45. We'll say half-past one at a guess. That's near enough."

He stopped and drummed thoughtfully with his fingers on the table.

"Damned odd, this business," he said. "Can you tell me about it—you were resting, you say? Did you hear anything?"

"At half-past one? No, doctor. I didn't hear anything at half-past one or at any other time. I lay on my bed from a quarter to one until twenty to three and I didn't hear anything except that droning noise the Arab boy makes, and occasionally Mr. Emmott shouting up to Dr. Leidner on the roof."

"The Arab boy—yes."

He frowned.

At that moment the door opened and Dr. Leidner and Captain Maitland came in. Captain Maitland was a fussy little man with a pair of shrewd grey eyes.

Dr. Reilly rose and pushed Dr. Leidner into his chair.

"Sit down, man. I'm glad you've come. We shall want you. There's something very queer about this business."

Dr. Leidner bowed his head. "I know." He looked at me. "My wife confided the truth to Nurse Leatheran. We mustn't keep anything back at this juncture, nurse, so please tell Captain Maitland and Dr. Reilly just what passed between you and my wife yesterday."

As nearly as possible I gave our conversation verbatim.

Captain Maitland uttered an occasional ejaculation. When I had finished he turned to Dr. Leidner.

"And this is all true, Leidner—eh?"

"Every word Nurse Leatheran has told you is correct."

"What an extraordinary story," said Dr. Reilly. "You can produce these letters?"

"I have no doubt they will be found amongst my wife's belongings."

"She took them out of the attaché-case on her table," I said.

"Then they are probably still there."

He turned to Captain Maitland and his usually gentle face grew hard and stern.

"There must be no question of hushing this story up, Captain Maitland. The one thing necessary is for this man to be caught and punished."

"You believe it actually is Mrs. Leidner's former husband?" I asked.

"Don't you think so, nurse?" asked Captain Maitland.

"Well, I think it is open to doubt," I said hesitatingly.

"In any case," said Dr. Leidner, "the man is a murderer—and I should say a dangerous lunatic also. He *must* be found, Captain Maitland. He must. It should not be difficult."

Dr. Reilly said slowly:

"It may be more difficult than you think . . . eh, Maitland?"

Captain Maitland tugged at his moustache without replying.

Suddenly I gave a start.

"Excuse me," I said, "but there's something perhaps I ought to mention."

I told my story of the Iraqi we had seen trying to peer through the window, and of how I had seen him hanging about the place two days ago trying to pump Father Lavigny.

"Good," said Captain Maitland, "we'll make a note of that. It will be something for the police to go on. The man may have some connection with the case."

"Probably paid to act as a spy," I suggested. "To find out when the coast was clear."

Dr. Reilly rubbed his nose with a harassed gesture.

"That's the devil of it," he said. "Supposing the coast wasn't clear—eh?"

I stared at him in a puzzled fashion.

Captain Maitland turned to Dr. Leidner.

"I want you to listen to me very carefully, Leidner. This is a review of the evidence we've got up to date. After lunch, which was served at twelve o'clock and was over by five and twenty to one, your wife went to her room accompanied by Nurse Leatheran, who settled her comfortably. You yourself went up to the roof, where you spent the next two hours, is that right?"

"Yes."

"Did you come down from the roof at all during that time?"

"No."

"Did any one come up to you?"

"Yes, Emmott did pretty frequently. He went to and fro between me and the boy, who was washing pottery down below."

"Did you yourself look over into the courtyard at all?"

"Once or twice—usually to call to Emmott about something."

"On each occasion the boy was sitting in the middle of the courtyard washing pots?"

"Yes."

"What was the longest period of time when Emmott was with you and absent from the courtyard?"

Dr. Leidner considered.

"It's difficult to say—perhaps ten minutes. Personally I should say two or three minutes, but I know by experience that my sense of time is not very good when I am absorbed and interested in what I am doing."

Captain Maitland looked at Dr. Reilly. The latter nodded. "We'd better get down to it," he said.

Captain Maitland took out a small notebook and opened it.

"Look here, Leidner, I'm going to read to you exactly what every member of your expedition was doing between one and two this afternoon."

"But surely—"

"Wait. You'll see what I'm driving at in a minute. First Mr. and Mrs. Mercado. Mr. Mercado says he was working in his laboratory. Mrs. Mercado says she was in her bedroom shampooing her hair. Miss Johnson says she was in the living-room taking impressions of cylinder seals. Mr. Reiter says he was in the dark-room developing plates. Father Lavigny says he was working in his bedroom. As to the two remaining members of the expedition, Carey and Coleman, the former was up on the dig and Coleman was in Hassanieh. So much for the members of the expedition. Now for the servants. The cook—your Indian chap—was sitting immediately outside the archway chatting to the guard and plucking a couple of fowls. Ibrahim and Mansur, the house-boys, joined him there at about 1.15. They both remained there laughing and talking until 2.30—*by which time your wife was already dead.*"

Dr. Leidner leaned forward.

"I don't understand—you puzzle me. What are you hinting at?"

"Is there any means of access to your wife's room except by the door into the courtyard?"

"No. There are two windows, but they are heavily barred—and besides, I think they were shut."

He looked at me questioningly.

"They were closed and latched on the inside," I said promptly.

"In any case," said Captain Maitland, "even if they had been open, no one could have entered or left the room that way. My fellows and I have assured ourselves of that. It is the same with all the other windows giving on the open country. They all have iron bars and all the bars are in good condition. To have got into your wife's room, a stranger *must* have come through the arched doorway into the courtyard. But we have the united assurances of the guard, the cook and the house-boy that *nobody did so.*"

Dr. Leidner sprang up.

"What do you mean? What do you mean?"

"Pull yourself together, man," said Dr. Reilly quietly. "I know it's a shock, but it's got to be faced. *The murderer didn't come from outside—*so he must have come from *inside.* It looks as though Mrs. Leidner must have been murdered *by a member of your own expedition.*"

Chapter 12

"I Didn't Believe . . ."

"No. No!"

Dr. Leidner sprang up and walked up and down in an agitated manner.

"It's impossible what you say, Reilly. Absolutely impossible. One of *us*? Why, every single member of the expedition was devoted to Louise!"

A queer little expression pulled down the corners of Dr. Reilly's mouth. Under the circumstances it was difficult for him to say anything, but if ever a man's silence was eloquent his was at that minute.

"Quite impossible," reiterated Dr. Leidner. "They were all devoted to her. Louise had such wonderful charm. Every one felt it."

Dr. Reilly coughed.

"Excuse me, Leidner, but after all that's only your opinion. If any member of the expedition had disliked your wife they would naturally not advertise the fact to you."

Dr. Leidner looked distressed.

"True — quite true. But all the same, Reilly, I think you are wrong. I'm sure every one was fond of Louise."

He was silent for a moment or two and then burst out.

"This idea of yours is infamous. It's — it's frankly incredible."

"You can't get away from — er — the facts," said Captain Maitland.

"Facts? Facts? Lies told by an Indian cook and a couple of Arab house-boys. You know these fellows as well as I do, Reilly; so do you, Maitland. Truth as truth means nothing to them. They say what you want them to say as a mere matter of politeness."

"In this case," said Dr. Reilly dryly, "they are saying what we *don't* want them to say. Besides, I know the habits of your household fairly well. Just outside the gate is a kind of social club. Whenever I've been over here in the afternoon I've always found most of your staff there. It's the natural place for them to be."

"All the same I think you are assuming too much. Why shouldn't this man—this devil—have got in earlier and concealed himself somewhere?"

"I agree that that is not actually impossible," said Dr. Reilly coolly. "Let us assume that a stranger *did* somehow gain admission unseen. He would have to remain concealed until the right moment (and he certainly couldn't have done so in Mrs. Leidner's room, there is no cover there) and take the risk of being seen entering the room and leaving it—with Emmott and the boy in the courtyard most of the time."

"The boy. I'd forgotten the boy," said Dr. Leidner. "A sharp little chap. But surely, Maitland, the boy *must* have seen the murderer go into my wife's room?"

"We've elucidated that. The boy was washing pots the whole afternoon with one exception. Somewhere around half-past one—Emmott can't put it closer than that—he went up to the roof and was with you for ten minutes—that's right, isn't it?"

"Yes. I couldn't have told you the exact time but it must have been about that."

"Very good. Well, during that ten minutes, the boy, seizing his chance to be idle, strolled out and joined the others outside the gate for a chat. When Emmott came down he found the boy absent and called him angrily, asking him what he meant by leaving his work. As far as I can see, *your wife must have been murdered during that ten minutes.*"

With a groan, Dr. Leidner sat down and hid his face in his hands.

Dr. Reilly took up the tale, his voice quiet and matter-of-fact.

"The time fits in with my evidence," he said. "She'd been dead about three hours when I examined her. The only question is—who did it?"

There was a silence. Dr. Leidner sat up in his chair and passed a hand over his forehead.

"I admit the force of your reasoning, Reilly," he said quietly. "It certainly *seems* as though it were what people call 'an inside job.' But I feel convinced that somewhere or other there is a mistake. It's plausible but there must be a flaw in it. To begin with, you are assuming that an amazing coincidence has occurred."

"Odd that you should use that word," said Dr. Reilly.

Without paying any attention Dr. Leidner went on:

"My wife receives threatening letters. She has reason to fear a certain person. Then she is—killed. And you ask me to believe that she is killed—

not by that person—but by some one entirely different! I say that that is ridiculous."

"It seems so—yes," said Dr. Reilly meditatively.

He looked at Captain Maitland. "Coincidence—eh? What do you say, Maitland? Are you in favour of the idea? Shall we put it up to Leidner?"

Captain Maitland gave a nod.

"Go ahead," he said shortly.

"Have you ever heard of a man called Hercule Poirot, Leidner?"

Dr. Leidner stared at him, puzzled.

"I think I have heard the name, yes," he said vaguely. "I once heard a Mr. Van Aldin speak of him in very high terms. He is a private detective, is he not?"

"That's the man."

"But surely he lives in London, so how will that help us?"

"He lives in London, true," said Dr. Reilly, "but this is where the coincidence comes in. He is now, not in London, but in Syria, and *he will actually pass through Hassanieh on his way to Baghdad to-morrow!*"

"Who told you this?"

"Jean Berat, the French consul. He dined with us last night and was talking about him. It seems he has been disentangling some military scandal in Syria. He's coming through here to visit Baghdad, and afterwards returning through Syria to London. How's that for a coincidence?"

Dr. Leidner hesitated a moment and looked apologetically at Captain Maitland.

"What do you think, Captain Maitland?"

"Should welcome co-operation," said Captain Maitland promptly. "My fellows are good scouts at scouring the countryside and investigating Arab blood feuds, but frankly, Leidner, this business of your wife's seems to me rather out of my class. The whole thing looks confoundedly fishy. I'm more than willing to have the fellow take a look at the case."

"You suggest that I should appeal to this man Poirot to help us?" said Dr. Leidner. "And suppose he refuses?"

"He won't refuse," said Dr. Reilly.

"How do you know?"

"Because I'm a professional man myself. If a really intricate case of say—cerebrospinal meningitis comes my way and I'm invited to take a hand, I shouldn't be able to refuse. This isn't an ordinary crime, Leidner."

"No," said Dr. Leidner. His lips twitched with sudden pain.

"Will you then, Reilly, approach this Hercule Poirot on my behalf?"

"I will."

Dr. Leidner made a gesture of thanks.

"Even now," he said slowly, "I can't realize it—that Louise is really dead."

I could bear it no longer.

"Oh! Dr. Leidner," I burst out. "I—I can't tell you how badly I feel about this. I've failed so badly in my duty. It was my job to watch over Mrs. Leidner—to keep her from harm."

Dr. Leidner shook his head gravely.

"No, no, nurse, you've nothing to reproach yourself with," he said slowly. "It's *I*, God forgive me, who am to blame. . . . *I didn't believe*—all along I didn't believe . . . I didn't dream for one moment that there was any *real* danger . . ."

He got up. His face twitched.

"*I let her go to her death.* . . . Yes, I let her go to her death—*not believing*—"

He staggered out of the room.

Dr. Reilly looked at me.

"I feel pretty culpable too," he said. "I thought the good lady was playing on his nerves."

"I didn't take it really seriously either," I confessed.

"We were all three wrong," said Dr. Reilly gravely.

"So it seems," said Captain Maitland.

Chapter 13

Hercule Poirot Arrives

I don't think I shall ever forget my first sight of Hercule Poirot. Of course, I got used to him later on, but to begin with it was shock, and I think every one else must have felt the same!

I don't know what I'd imagined—something rather like Sherlock Holmes—long and lean with a keen, clever face. Of course, I knew he was a foreigner, but I hadn't expected him to be *quite* as foreign as he was, if you know what I mean.

When you saw him you just wanted to laugh! He was like something on the stage or at the pictures. To begin with, he wasn't above five foot five, I should think—an odd plump little man, quite old, with an enormous moustache, and a head like an egg. He looked like a hairdresser in a comic play!

And this was the man who was going to find out who killed Mrs. Leidner!

I suppose something of my disgust must have shown in my face, for almost straightaway he said to me with a queer kind of twinkle:

"You disapprove of me, *ma sœur?* Remember, the pudding proves itself only when you eat it."

The proof of the pudding's in the eating, I *suppose* he meant.

Well, that's a true enough saying, but I couldn't say I felt much confidence myself!

Dr. Reilly brought him out in his car soon after lunch on Sunday, and his first procedure was to ask us all to assemble together.

We did so in the dining-room, all sitting round the table. Mr. Poirot sat at the head of it with Dr. Leidner one side and Dr. Reilly the other.

When we were all assembled, Dr. Leidner cleared his throat and spoke in his gentle, hesitating voice.

"I dare say you have all heard of M. Hercule Poirot. He was passing through Hassanieh to-day, and has very kindly agreed to break his journey to help us. The Iraq police and Captain Maitland are, I am sure, doing their very best, but—but there are circumstances in the case"—he floundered and shot an appealing glance at Dr. Reilly—"there may, it seems, be difficulties. . . ."

"It is not all the square and overboard—no?" said the little man at the top of the table. Why, he couldn't even speak English properly!

"Oh, he *must* be caught!" cried Mrs. Mercado. "It would be unbearable if he got away!"

I noticed the little foreigner's eyes rest on her appraisingly.

"He? Who is *he*, madame?" he asked.

"Why, the murderer, of course."

"Ah! the murderer," said Hercule Poirot.

He spoke as though the murderer was of no consequence at all!

We all stared at him. He looked from one face to another.

"It is likely, I think," he said, "that you have none of you been brought in contact with a case of murder before?"

There was a general murmur of assent.

Hercule Poirot smiled.

"It is clear, therefore, that you do not understand the A.B.C. of the position. There are unpleasantnesses! Yes, there are a lot of unpleasantnesses. To begin with, there is *suspicion*."

"Suspicion?"

It was Miss Johnson who spoke. Mr. Poirot looked at her thoughtfully. I had an idea that he regarded her with approval. He looked as though he were thinking, "Here is a sensible, intelligent person!"

"Yes, mademoiselle," he said. "Suspicion! Let us not make the bones about it. *You are all under suspicion here in this house.* The cook, the house-boy, the scullion, the pot-boy—yes, and all the members of the expedition too."

Mrs. Mercado started up, her face working.

"How *dare* you? How dare you say such a thing! This is odious—unbearable! Dr. Leidner—you can't sit here and let this man—and let this man—"

Dr. Leidner said wearily:

"Please try and be calm, Marie."

Mr. Mercado stood up too. His hands were shaking and his eyes were bloodshot.

"I agree. It is an outrage—an insult—"

"No, no," said Mr. Poirot. "I do not insult you. I merely ask you all to face facts. *In a house where murder has been committed, every inmate comes in for a certain share of suspicion.* I ask you what evidence is there that the murderer came from outside at all?"

Mrs. Mercado cried:

"But of course he did! It stands to reason! Why—" She stopped and said more slowly, "Anything else would be incredible!"

"You are doubtless correct, madame," said Poirot with a bow. "I explain to you only how the matter must be approached. First I assure myself of the fact that every one in this room is innocent. After that I seek the murderer elsewhere."

"Is it not possible that that may be a little late in the day?" asked Father Lavigny suavely.

"The tortoise, *mon père*, overtook the hare."

Father Lavigny shrugged his shoulders.

"We are in your hands," he said resignedly. "Convince yourself as soon as may be of our innocence in this terrible business."

"As rapidly as possible. It was my duty to make the position clear to you, so that you may not resent the impertinence of any questions I may have to ask. Perhaps, *mon père*, the Church will set an example?"

"Ask any questions you please of me," said Father Lavigny gravely.

"This is your first season, out here?"

"Yes."

"And you arrived—when?"

"Three weeks ago almost to a day. That is, on the 27th of February."

"Coming from?"

"The Order of the *Pères Blancs* at Carthage."

"Thank you, *mon père*. Were you at any time acquainted with Mrs. Leidner before coming here?"

"No, I had never seen the lady until I met her here."

"Will you tell me what you were doing at the time of the tragedy?"

"I was working on some cuneiform tablets in my own room."

I noticed that Poirot had at his elbow a rough plan of the building.

"That is the room at the south-west corner corresponding to that of Mrs. Leidner on the opposite side?"

"Yes."

"At what time did you go to your room?"

"Immediately after lunch. I should say at about twenty minutes to one."

"And you remained there until—when?"

"Just before three o'clock. I had heard the station wagon come back—and then I heard it drive off again. I wondered why, and came out to see."

"During the time that you were there did you leave the room, at all?"

"No, not once."

"And you heard or saw nothing that might have any bearing on the tragedy?"

"No."

"You have no window giving on the courtyard in your room?"

"No, both the windows give on the countryside."

"Could you hear at all what was happening in the courtyard?"

"Not very much. I heard Mr. Emmott passing my room and going up to the roof. He did so once or twice."

"Can you remember at what time?"

"No, I'm afraid I can't. I was engrossed in my work, you see."

There was a pause and then Poirot said:

"Can you say or suggest anything at all that might throw light on this business. Did you, for instance, notice anything in the days preceding the murder?"

Father Lavigny looked slightly uncomfortable.

He shot a half-questioning look at Dr. Leidner.

"That is rather a difficult question, monsieur," he said gravely. "If you ask me, I must reply frankly that in my opinion Mrs. Leidner was clearly in dread of some one or something. She was definitely nervous about strangers. I imagine she had a reason for this nervousness of hers—but I *know* nothing. She did not confide in me."

Poirot cleared his throat and consulted some notes that he held in his hand.

"Two nights ago I understand there was a scare of burglary."

Father Lavigny replied in the affirmative and retailed his story of the light seen in the antika-room and the subsequent futile search.

"You believe, do you not, that some unauthorized person was on the premises at that time?"

"I don't know what to think," said Father Lavigny frankly. "Nothing was taken or disturbed in any way. It might have been one of the house-boys—"

"Or a member of the expedition?"

"Or a member of the expedition. But in that case there would be no reason for the person not admitting the fact."

"But it *might* equally have been a stranger from outside?"

"I suppose so."

"Supposing a stranger *had* been on the premises, could he have concealed himself successfully during the following day and until the afternoon of the day following that?"

He asked the question half of Father Lavigny and half of Dr. Leidner. Both men considered the question carefully.

"I hardly think it would be possible," said Dr. Leidner at last with some reluctance. "I don't see where he could possibly conceal himself, do you, Father Lavigny?"

"No—no—I don't."

Both men seemed reluctant to put the suggestion aside.

Poirot turned to Miss Johnson.

"And you, mademoiselle? Do you consider such a hypothesis feasible?"

After a moment's thought Miss Johnson shook her head.

"No," she said. "I don't. Where could any one hide? The bedrooms are all in use and, in any case, are sparsely furnished. The dark-room, the drawing-office and the laboratory were all in use the next day—so were all these rooms. There are no cupboards or corners. Perhaps, if the servants were in collusion—"

"That is possible, but unlikely," said Poirot.

He turned once more to Father Lavigny.

"There is another point. The other day Nurse Leatheran here noticed you talking to a man outside. She had previously noticed that same man trying to peer in at one of the windows on the outside. It rather looks as though the man were hanging round the place deliberately."

"That is possible, of course," said Father Lavigny thoughtfully.

"Did you speak to this man first, or did he speak to you?"

Father Lavigny considered for a moment or two.

"I believe—yes, I am sure, that he spoke to me."

"What did he say?"

Father Lavigny made an effort of memory.

"He said, I think, something to the effect was this the American expedition house? And then something else about the Americans employing a lot of men on the work. I did not really understand him very well, but I endeavoured to keep up a conversation so as to improve my Arabic. I thought, perhaps, that being a townee he would understand me better than the men on the dig do."

"Did you converse about anything else?"

"As far as I remember, I said Hassanieh was a big town—and we then agreed that Baghdad was bigger—and I think he asked whether I was an Armenian or a Syrian Catholic—something of that kind."

Poirot nodded.

"Can you describe him?"

Again Father Lavigny frowned in thought.

"He was rather a short man," he said at last, "and squarely built. He had a very noticeable squint and was of fair complexion."

Mr. Poirot turned to me.

"Does that agree with the way you would describe him?" he asked.

"Not exactly," I said hesitatingly. "I should have said he was tall rather than short, and very dark complexioned. He seemed to me of a rather slender build. I didn't notice any squint."

Mr. Poirot gave a despairing shrug of the shoulders.

"It is always so! If you were of the police how well you would know it! The description of the same man by two different people—never does it agree. Every detail is contradicted."

"I'm fairly sure about the squint," said Father Lavigny. "Nurse Leatheran may be right about the other points. By the way, when I said *fair*, I only meant fair for an *Iraqi*. I expect nurse would call that dark."

"Very dark," I said obstinately. "A dirty dark-yellow colour."

I saw Dr. Reilly bite his lip and smile.

Poirot threw up his hands.

"*Passons!*" he said. "This stranger hanging about, he may be important—he may not. At any rate he must be found. Let us continue our inquiry."

He hesitated for a minute, studying the faces turned towards him round the table, then, with a quick nod, he singled out Mr. Reiter.

"Come, my friend," he said. "Let us have your account of yesterday afternoon."

Mr. Reiter's pink, plumb face flushed scarlet.

"Me?" he said.

"Yes, you. To begin with, your name and your age?"

"Carl Reiter, twenty-eight."

"American—yes?"

"Yes, I come from Chicago."

"This is your first season?"

"Yes. I'm in charge of the photography."

"Ah, yes. And yesterday afternoon, how did you employ yourself?"

"Well—I was in the dark-room most of the time."

"*Most* of the time—eh?"

"Yes. I developed some plates first. Afterwards I was fixing up some objects to photograph."

"Outside?"

"Oh, no, in the photographic room."

"The dark-room opens out of the photographic room?"

"Yes."

"And so you never came outside the photographic room?"

"No."

"Did you notice anything that went on in the courtyard?"

The young man shook his head.

"I wasn't noticing anything," he explained. "I was busy. I heard the car come back, and as soon as I could leave what I was doing I came out to see if there was any mail. It was then that I—heard."

"And you began your work in the photographic room—when?"

"At ten minutes to one."

"Were you acquainted with Mrs. Leidner before you joined this expedition?"

The young man shook his head.

"No, sir. I never saw her till I actually got here."

"Can you think of *anything*—any incident—however small—that might help us?"

Carl Reiter shook his head.

He said helplessly:

"I guess I don't know anything at all, sir."

"Mr. Emmott?"

David Emmott spoke clearly and concisely in his pleasant soft American voice.

"I was working with the pottery from a quarter to one till a quarter to three—overseeing the boy Abdullah, sorting it, and occasionally going up to the roof to help Dr. Leidner."

"How often did you go up to the roof?"

"Four times, I think."

"For how long?"

"Usually a couple of minutes—not more. But on one occasion after I'd been working a little over half an hour I stayed as long as ten minutes—discussing what to keep and what to fling away."

"And I understand that when you came down you found the boy had left his place?"

"Yes. I called him angrily and he reappeared from outside the archway. He had gone out to gossip with the others."

"That was the only time he left his work?"

"Well, I sent him up once or twice to the roof with pottery."

Poirot said gravely:

"It is hardly necessary to ask you, Mr. Emmott, whether you saw any one enter or leave Mrs. Leidner's room during that time?"

Mr. Emmott replied promptly.

"I saw no one at all. Nobody even came out into the courtyard during the two hours I was working."

"And to the best of your belief it was half-past one when both you and the boy were absent and the courtyard was empty?"

"It couldn't have been far off that time. Of course, I can't say *exactly*."

Poirot turned to Dr. Reilly.

"That agrees with your estimate of the time of death, doctor?"

"It does," said Dr. Reilly.

Mr. Poirot stroked his great curled moustaches.

"I think we can take it," he said gravely, "that Mrs. Leidner met her death during that ten minutes."

Chapter 14

One of Us?

There was a little pause—and in it a wave of horror seemed to float round the room.

I think it was at that moment that I first believed Dr. Reilly's theory to be right.

I *felt* that the murderer was in the room. Sitting with us—listening. *One of us* . . .

Perhaps Mrs. Mercado felt it too. For she suddenly gave a short sharp cry.

"I can't help it," she sobbed. "I—it's *so terrible!*"

"Courage, Marie," said her husband.

He looked at us apologetically.

"She is so sensitive. She feels things so much."

"I—I was so fond of Louise," sobbed Mrs. Mercado.

I don't know whether something of what I felt showed in my face, but I suddenly found that Mr. Poirot was looking at me, and that a slight smile hovered on his lips.

I gave him a cold glance, and at once he resumed his inquiry.

"Tell me, madame," he said, "of the way you spent yesterday afternoon?"

"I was washing my hair," sobbed Mrs. Mercado. "It seems awful not to have known anything about it. I was quite happy and busy."

"You were in your room?"

"Yes."

"And you did not leave it?"

"No. Not till I heard the car. Then I came out and I heard what had happened. Oh, it was *awful!*"

"Did it surprise you?"

Mrs. Mercado stopped crying. Her eyes opened resentfully.

"What do you mean, M. Poirot? Are you suggesting—"

"What should I mean, madame? You have just told us how fond you were of Mrs. Leidner. She might, perhaps, have confided in you."

"Oh, I see. . . . No—no, dear Louise never told me anything—anything *definite*, that is. Of course, I could see she was terribly worried and nervous. And there were those strange occurrences—hands tapping on the window and all that."

"Fancies, I remember you said," I put in, unable to keep silent.

I was glad to see that she looked momentarily disconcerted.

Once again I was conscious of Mr. Poirot's amused eye glancing in my direction.

He summed up in a business-like way.

"It comes to this, madame, you were washing your hair—you heard nothing and you saw nothing. Is there anything at all you can think of that would be a help to us in any way?"

Mrs. Mercado took no time to think.

"No, indeed there isn't. It's the deepest mystery! But I should say there is no doubt—no doubt *at all* that the murderer came from outside. Why, it stands to reason."

Poirot turned to her husband.

"And you, monsieur, what have you to say?"

Mr. Mercado stared nervously. He pulled at his beard in an aimless fashion.

"Must have been. Must have been," he said. "Yet how could any one wish to harm her? She was so gentle—so kind—" He shook his head. "Whoever killed her must have been a fiend—yes, a fiend!"

"And you yourself, monsieur, how did you pass yesterday afternoon?"

"I?" he stared vaguely.

"You were in the laboratory, Joseph," his wife prompted him.

"Ah, yes, so I was—so I was. My usual tasks."

"At what time did you go there?"

Again he looked helplessly and inquiringly at Mrs. Mercado.

"At ten minutes to one, Joseph."

"Ah, yes, at ten minutes to one."

"Did you come out in the courtyard at all?"

"No—I don't think so." He considered. "No, I am sure I didn't."

"When did you hear of the tragedy?"

"My wife came and told me. It was terrible—shocking. I could hardly believe it. Even now, I can hardly believe it is true."

Suddenly he began to tremble.

"It is horrible—horrible . . ."

Mrs. Mercado came quickly to his side.

"Yes, yes, Joseph, we all feel that. But we mustn't give way. It makes it so much more difficult for poor Dr. Leidner."

I saw a spasm of pain pass across Dr. Leidner's face, and I guessed that this emotional atmosphere was not easy for him. He gave a half glance at Poirot as though in appeal. Poirot responded quickly.

"Miss Johnson?" he said.

"I'm afraid I can tell you very little," said Miss Johnson. Her cultured well-bred voice was soothing after Mrs. Mercado's shrill treble. She went on:

"I was working in the living-room—taking impressions of some cylinder seals on plasticine."

"And you saw or noticed nothing?"

"No."

Poirot gave her a quick glance. His ear had caught what mine had—a faint note of indecision.

"Are you quite sure, mademoiselle? Is there something that comes back to you vaguely?"

"No—not really—"

"Something you saw, shall we say, out of the corner of your eye hardly knowing you saw it."

"No, certainly not," she replied positively.

"Something you *heard* then. Ah, yes, something you are not quite sure whether you heard or not?"

Miss Johnson gave a short vexed laugh.

"You press me very closely, M. Poirot. I'm afraid you are encouraging me to tell you what I am, perhaps, only imagining."

"Then there *was* something you—shall we say—imagined?"

Miss Johnson said slowly, weighing her words in a detached way:

"I have imagined—since—that at some time during the afternoon I heard a very faint cry. . . . What I mean is that I dare say I did hear a cry. All the windows in the living-room were open and one hears all sorts of sounds from people working in the barley fields. But you see—since—I've got the idea into my head that it was—that it was Mrs. Leidner I heard. And that's made me rather unhappy. Because if I'd jumped up and run along to her room—well, who knows? I might have been in time . . ."

Dr. Reilly interposed authoritatively.

"Now, don't start getting that into your head," he said. "I've no doubt but that Mrs. Leidner (forgive me, Leidner) was struck down almost as soon as the man entered the room, and it was that blow that killed her. No second blow was struck. Otherwise she would have had time to call for help and make a real outcry."

"Still, I might have caught the murderer," said Miss Johnson.

"What time was this, mademoiselle?" asked Poirot. "In the neighbourhood of half-past one?"

"It must have been about that time—yes." She reflected a minute.

"That would fit in," said Poirot thoughtfully. "You heard nothing else—the opening or shutting of a door, for instance."

Miss Johnson shook her head.

"No, I do not remember anything of that kind."

"You were sitting at a table, I presume. Which way were you facing? The courtyard? The antika-room? The verandah? Or the open countryside?"

"I was facing the courtyard."

"Could you see the boy Abdullah washing pots from where you were?"

"Oh, yes, if I looked up, but of course, I was very intent on what I was doing. All my attention was on that."

"If any one had passed the courtyard window, though, you would have noticed it?"

"Oh, yes, I am almost sure of that."

"And nobody did so?"

"No."

"But if any one had walked, say, across the middle of the courtyard, would you have noticed that?"

"I think—probably not—unless, as I said before, I had happened to look up and out of the window."

"You did not notice the boy Abdullah leave his work and go out to join the other servants?"

"No."

"Ten minutes," mused Poirot. "That fatal ten minutes."

There was a momentary silence.

Miss Johnson lifted her head suddenly and said:

"You know, M. Poirot, I think I have unintentionally misled you. On thinking it over, I do not believe that I could possibly have heard any cry uttered in Mrs. Leidner's room from where I was. The antika-room lay between me and her—and I understand her windows were found closed."

"In any case, do not distress yourself, mademoiselle," said Poirot kindly. "It is not really of much importance."

"No, of course not. I understand that. But you see, it *is* of importance to me, because I feel I might have done something."

"Don't distress yourself, dear Anne," said Dr. Leidner with affection. "You must be sensible. What you heard was probably one Arab bawling to another some distance away in the fields."

Miss Johnson flushed a little at the kindliness of his tone. I even saw tears spring to her eyes. She turned her head away and spoke even more gruffly than usual.

"Probably was. Usual thing after a tragedy—start imagining things that aren't so at all."

Poirot was once more consulting his notebook.

"I do not suppose there is much more to be said. Mr. Carey?"

Richard Carey spoke slowly—in a wooden, mechanical manner.

"I'm afraid I can add nothing helpful. I was on duty at the dig. The news was brought to me there."

"And you know or can think of nothing helpful that occurred in the days immediately preceding the murder?"

"Nothing at all."

"Mr. Coleman?"

"I was right out of the whole thing," said Mr. Coleman with—was it just a shade of regret—in his tone. "I went into Hassanieh yesterday morning to get the money for the men's wages. When I came back Emmott told me what had happened and I went back in the bus to get the police and Dr. Reilly."

"And beforehand?"

"Well, sir, things were a bit jumpy—but you know that already. There was the antika-room scare and one or two before that—hands and faces at the window—you remember, sir," he appealed to Dr. Leidner, who bent his head in assent. "I think, you know, that you'll find some Johnny *did* get in from outside. Must have been an artful sort of beggar."

Poirot considered him for a minute or two in silence.

"You are an Englishman, Mr. Coleman?" he asked at last.

"That's right, sir. All British. See the trademark. Guaranteed genuine."

"This is your first season?"

"Quite right."

"And you are passionately keen on archaeology?"

This description of himself seemed to cause Mr. Coleman some embarrassment. He got rather pink and shot the side look of a guilty schoolboy at Dr. Leidner.

"Of course—it's all very interesting," he stammered. "I mean—I'm not exactly a brainy chap . . ."

He broke off rather lamely. Poirot did not insist.

He tapped thoughtfully on the table with the end of his pencil and carefully straightened an inkpot that stood in front of him.

"It seems then," he said, "that that is as near as we can get for the moment. If any one of you thinks of something that has for the time being slipped his or her memory do not hesitate to come to me with it. It will be well now, I think, for me to have a few words alone with Dr. Leidner and Dr. Reilly."

It was the signal for a breaking up of the party. We all rose and filed out of the door. When I was half-way out, however, a voice recalled me.

"Perhaps," said Mr. Poirot, "Nurse Leatheran will be so kind as to remain. I think her assistance will be valuable to us."

I came back and resumed my seat at the table.

Chapter 15

Poirot Makes a Suggestion

Dr. Reilly had risen from his seat. When every one had gone out he carefully closed the door. Then, with an inquiring glance at Poirot, he proceeded to shut the window giving on the courtyard. The others were already shut. Then he, too, resumed his seat at the table.

"*Bien!*" said Poirot. "We are now private and undisturbed. We can speak freely. We have heard what the members of the expedition have to tell us and— But yes, *ma, sœur*, what is it you think?"

I got rather red. There was no denying that the queer little man had sharp eyes. He'd seen the thought passing through my mind—I suppose my face *had* shown a bit too clearly what I was thinking!

"Oh, it's nothing—" I said, hesitating.

"Come on, nurse," said Dr. Reilly. "Don't keep the specialist waiting."

"It's nothing really," I said hurriedly. "It only just passed through my mind, so to speak, that perhaps even if any one did know or suspect something it wouldn't be easy to bring it out in front of everybody else—or even, perhaps, in front of Dr. Leidner."

Rather to my astonishment, M. Poirot nodded his head in vigorous agreement.

"Precisely. Precisely. It is very just what you say there. But I will explain. That little reunion we have just had—it served a purpose. In England before the races you have a parade of the horses, do you not? They go in front of the grandstand so that every one may have an opportunity of seeing and judging them. That is the purpose of my little assembly. In the sporting phrase, I run my eye over the possible starters."

Dr. Leidner cried out violently, "I do not believe for one minute that *any* member of my expedition is implicated in this crime!"

Then, turning to me, he said authoritatively:

"Nurse, I should be much obliged if you would tell M. Poirot here and now exactly what passed between my wife and you two days ago."

Thus urged, I plunged straightaway into my story, trying as far as possible to recall the exact words and phrases Mrs. Leidner had used.

When I had finished, M. Poirot said:

"Very good. Very good. You have the mind neat and orderly. You will be of great service to me here."

He turned to Dr. Leidner.

"You have these letters?"

"I have them here. I thought that you would want to see them first thing."

Poirot took them from him, read them, and scrutinized them carefully as he did so. I was rather disappointed that he didn't dust powder over them or examine them with a microscope or anything like that—but I realized that he wasn't a very young man and that his methods were probably not very up to date. He just read them in the way that any one might read a letter.

Having read them he put them down and cleared his throat.

"Now," he said, "let us proceed to get our facts clear and in order. The first of these letters was received by your wife shortly after her marriage to you in America. There had been others but these she destroyed. The first letter was followed by a second. A very short time after the second arrived you both had a near escape from coal gas poisoning. You then came abroad and for nearly two years no further letters were received. They started again at the beginning of your season this year—that is to say, within the last three weeks. That is correct?"

"Absolutely."

"Your wife displayed every sign of panic and, after consulting Dr. Reilly, you engaged Nurse Leatheran here to keep your wife company and allay her fears?"

"Yes."

"Certain incidents occurred—hands tapping at the window—a spectral face—noises in the antika-room. You did not witness any of these phenomena yourself?"

"No."

"In fact nobody did except Mrs. Leidner?"

"Father Lavigny saw a light in the antika-room."

"Yes, I have not forgotten that."

He was silent for a minute or two, then he said:

"Had your wife made a will?"

"I do not think so."

"Why was that?"

"It did not seem worth it from her point of view."

"Is she not a wealthy woman?"

"Yes, during her lifetime. Her father left her a considerable sum of money in trust. She could not touch the principal. At her death it was to pass to any children she might have—and failing children to the Pittstown Museum."

Poirot drummed thoughtfully on the table.

"Then we can, I think," he said, "eliminate one motive from the case. It is, you comprehend, what I look for first. *Who benefits by the deceased's death?* In this case it is a museum. Had it been otherwise, had Mrs. Leidner died intestate but possessed of a considerable fortune, I should imagine that it would prove an interesting question as to who inherited the money—you—or a former husband. But there would have been this difficulty, the former husband would have had to resurrect himself in order to claim it, and I should imagine that he would then be in danger of arrest, though I hardly fancy that the death penalty would be exacted so long after the war. However, these speculations need not arise. As I say, I settle first the question of money. For the next step I proceed always to suspect the husband or wife of the deceased! In this case, in the first place, you are proved never to have gone near your wife's room yesterday afternoon, in the second place, you lose instead of gain by your wife's death, and in the third place—"

He paused.

"Yes?" said Dr. Leidner.

"In the third place," said Poirot slowly. "I can, I think, appreciate devotion when I see it. I believe Dr. Leidner, that your love for your wife was the ruling passion of your life. It is so, is it not?"

Dr. Leidner answered quite simply:

"Yes."

Poirot nodded.

"Therefore," he said, "we can proceed."

"Hear, hear, let's get down to it," said Dr. Reilly with some impatience.

Poirot gave him a reproving glance.

"My friend, do not be impatient. In a case like this everything must be approached with order and method. In fact, that is my rule in every case. Having disposed of certain possibilities, we now approach a very important point. It is vital that, as you say—all the cards should be on the table—there must be nothing kept back."

"Quite so," said Dr. Reilly.

"That is why I demand the whole truth," went on Poirot.

Dr. Leidner looked at him in surprise.

"I assure you, M. Poirot, that I have kept nothing back. I have told you everything that I know. There have been no reserves."

"Tout de même, you have not told me *everything."*

"Yes, indeed. I cannot think of any detail that has escaped me."

He looked quite distressed.

Poirot shook his head gently.

"No," he said. *"You have not told me, for instance, why you installed Nurse Leatheran in the house."*

Dr. Leidner looked completely bewildered.

"But I have explained that. It is obvious. My wife's nervousness—her fears . . ."

Poirot leaned forward. Slowly and emphatically he wagged a finger up and down.

"No, no, no. There is something there that is not clear. Your wife is in danger, yes—she is threatened with death, yes. You send—*not for the police*—not for a private detective even—but for a *nurse!* It does not make the sense, that!"

"I—I—" Dr. Leidner stopped. The colour rose in his cheeks. "I thought—" He came to a dead stop.

"Now we are coming to it," Poirot encouraged him. "You thought—what?"

Dr. Leidner remained silent. He looked harassed and unwilling.

"See you," Poirot's tone became winning and appealing, "it all rings true what you have told me, except for that. Why a *nurse?* There is an answer—yes. In fact, there can be only one answer. *You did not believe yourself in your wife's danger."*

And then with a cry Dr. Leidner broke down.

"God help me," he groaned. "I didn't. I didn't."

Poirot watched him with the kind of attention a cat gives a mouse-hole—ready to pounce when the mouse shows itself.

"What *did* you think then?" he asked.

"I don't know. I don't know . . ."

"But you do know. You know perfectly. Perhaps I can help you—with a guess. *Did you, Dr. Leidner, suspect that these letters were all written by your wife herself?"*

There wasn't any need for him to answer. The truth of Poirot's guess was only too apparent. The horrified hand he held up, as though begging for mercy, told its own tale.

I drew a deep breath. So I *had* been right in my half-formed guess! I recalled the curious tone in which Dr. Leidner had asked me what I thought of it all. I nodded my head slowly and thoughtfully, and suddenly awoke to the fact that M. Poirot's eyes were on me.

"Did you think the same, nurse?"

"The idea did cross my mind," I said truthfully.

"For what reason?"

I explained the similarity of the handwriting on the letter that Mr. Coleman had shown me.

Poirot turned to Dr. Leidner.

"Had you, too noticed that similarity?"

Dr. Leidner bowed his head.

"Yes, I did. The writing was small and cramped—not big and generous like Louise's, but several of the letters were formed the same way. I will show you."

From an inner breast pocket he took out some letters and finally selected a sheet from one which he handed to Poirot. It was part of a letter written to him by his wife. Poirot compared it carefully with the anonymous letters.

"Yes," he murmured. "Yes. There are several similarities—a curious way of forming the letter *s*, a distinctive *e*. I am not a handwriting expert—I cannot pronounce definitely (and for that matter, I have never found two handwriting experts who agree on any point whatsoever)—but one can at least say this—the similarity between the two handwritings is very marked. It seems highly probable that they were all written by the same person. But it is not *certain*. We must take all contingencies into mind."

He leaned back in his chair and said thoughtfully:

"There are three possibilities. First, the similarity of the handwriting is pure coincidence. Second, that these threatening letters were written by Mrs. Leidner herself for some obscure reason. Third, that they were written by some one *who deliberately copies her handwriting*. Why? There seems no sense in it. One of these three possibilities must be the correct one."

He reflected for a minute or two and then, turning to Dr. Leidner, he asked, with a resumal of his brisk manner.

"When the possibility that Mrs. Leidner herself was the author of these letters first struck you, what theory did you form?"

Dr. Leidner shook his head.

"I put the idea out of my head as quickly as possible. I felt it was monstrous."

"Did you search for no explanation?"

"Well," he hesitated, "I wondered if worrying and brooding over the past had perhaps affected my wife's brain slightly. I thought she might possibly have written those letters to herself without being conscious of having done so. That is possible, isn't it?" he added, turning to Dr. Reilly.

Dr. Reilly pursed up his lips.

"The human brain is capable of almost anything," he replied vaguely.

But he shot a lightning glance at Poirot, and as if in obedience to it, the latter abandoned the subject.

"The letters are an interesting point," he said. "But we must concentrate on the case as a whole. There are, as I see it, three possible solutions."

"Three?"

"Yes. Solution one: the simplest. Your wife's first husband is still alive. He first threatens her and then proceeds to carry out his threats. If we accept this solution, our problem is to discover how he got in or out without being seen.

"Solution two: Mrs. Leidner, for reasons of her own (reasons probably more easily understood by a medical man than a layman), writes herself threatening letters. The gas business is staged by her (remember, it was she who roused you by telling you she smelt gas). But, *if Mrs. Leidner wrote herself the letters, she cannot be in danger from the supposed writer*. We must, therefore, look elsewhere for the murderer. We must look, in fact, amongst the members of your staff. Yes," in answer to a murmur of protest from Dr. Leidner, "that is the only logical conclusion. To satisfy a private grudge one of them killed her. That person, I may say, was probably aware of the letters—or was at any rate aware that Mrs. Leidner feared or was pretending to fear some one. That fact, in the murderer's opinion, rendered the murder quite safe for him. He felt sure it would be put down to a mysterious outsider—the writer of the threatening letters.

"A variant of this solution is that the murderer actually wrote the letters himself, being aware of Mrs. Leidner's past history. But in that case it is not quite clear *why* the criminal should have copied Mrs. Leidner's own handwriting since, as far as we can see, it would be more to his or her advantage that they should appear to be written by an outsider.

"The third solution is the most interesting to my mind. I suggest that the letters are genuine. They are written by Mrs. Leidner's first husband (or his younger brother), *who is actually one of the expedition staff*."

Chapter 16

The Suspects

Dr. Leidner sprang to his feet.

"Impossible! Absolutely impossible! The idea is absurd!"

Mr. Poirot looked at him quite calmly but said nothing.

"You mean to suggest that my wife's former husband is one of the expedition *and that she didn't recognize him?*"

"Exactly. Reflect a little on the facts. Nearly twenty years ago your wife lived with this man for a few months. Would she know him if she came across him after that lapse of time? I think not. His face will have changed, his build will have changed—his voice may not have changed so much, but that is a detail he can attend to himself. And remember, *she is not looking for him amongst her own household.* She visualizes him as somewhere outside—a stranger. No, I do not think she would recognize him. And there is a second possibility. The young brother—the child of those days who was so passionately devoted to his elder brother. He is now a man. Will she recognize a child of ten or twelve years old in a man nearing thirty? Yes, there is young William Bosner to be reckoned with. Remember, his brother in his eyes may not loom as a traitor but as a patriot, a martyr for his own country—Germany. In his eyes *Mrs. Leidner* is the traitor—the monster who sent his beloved brother to death! A susceptible child is capable of great hero worship, and a young mind can easily be obsessed by an idea which persists into adult life."

"Quite true," said Dr. Reilly. "The popular view that a child forgets easily is not an accurate one. Many people go right through life in the grip of an idea which has been impressed on them in very tender years."

"*Bien.* You have these two possibilities. Frederick Bosner, a man by now of fifty odd, and William Bosner, whose age would be something short of thirty. Let us examine the members of your staff from these two points of view."

"This is fantastic," murmured Dr. Leidner. "*My* staff! The members of my own expedition."

"And consequently considered above suspicion," said Poirot dryly. "A very useful point of view. *Commençons!* Who could emphatically *not* be Frederick or William?"

"The women."

"Naturally. Miss Johnson and Mrs. Mercado are crossed off. Who else?"

"Carey. He and I have worked together for years before I even met Louise—"

"And also he is the wrong age. He is, I should judge, thirty-eight or nine, two young for Frederick, too old for William. Now for the rest. There is Father Lavigny and Mr. Mercado. Either of them might be Frederick Bosner."

"But, my dear sir," cried Dr. Leidner in a voice of mingled irritation and amusement, "Father Lavigny is known all over the world as an epigraphist and Mercado has worked for years in a well-known museum in New York. It is *impossible* that either of them should be the man you think!"

Poirot waved an airy hand.

"Impossible—impossible—I take no account of the word! The impossible, always I examine it very closely! But we will pass on for the moment. Who else have you? Carl Reiter, a young man with a German name, David Emmott—"

"He has been with me two seasons, remember."

"He is a young man with the gift of patience. *If* he committed a crime, it would not be in a hurry. All would be very well prepared."

Dr. Leidner made a gesture of despair.

"And lastly, William Coleman," continued Poirot.

"He is an Englishman."

"*Pourquoi pas?* Did not Mrs. Leidner say that the boy left America and could not be traced? He might easily have been brought up in England."

"You have an answer to everything," said Dr. Leidner.

I was thinking hard. Right from the beginning I had thought Mr. Coleman's manner rather more like a P. G. Wodehouse book than like a real live young man. Had he really been playing a part all the time?

Poirot was writing in a little book.

"Let us proceed with order and method," he said. "On the first count we have two names. Father Lavigny and Mr. Mercado. On the second we have Coleman, Emmott and Reiter.

"Now let us pass to the opposite aspect of the matter—means and opportunity. *Who amongst the expedition had the means and the opportunity of committing the crime?* Carey was on the dig, Coleman was in Hassanieh, you yourself were on the roof. That leaves us Father Lavigny, Mr. Mercado, Mrs. Mercado, David Emmott, Carl Reiter, Miss Johnson and Nurse Leatheran."

"Oh!" I exclaimed, and I bounded in my chair.

Mr. Poirot looked at me with twinkling eyes.

"Yes, I'm afraid, *ma sœur*, that you have got to be included. It would have been quite easy for you to have gone along and killed Mrs. Leidner while the courtyard was empty. You have plenty of muscle and strength, and she would have been quite unsuspicious until the moment the blow was struck."

I was so upset that I couldn't get a word out. Dr. Reilly, I noticed, was looking highly amused.

"Interesting case of a nurse who murdered her patients one by one," he murmured.

Such a look as I gave him!

Dr. Leidner's mind had been running on a different tack.

"Not Emmott, M. Poirot," he objected. "You can't include him. He was on the roof with me, remember, during that ten minutes."

"Nevertheless we cannot exclude him. He could have come down, gone straight to Mrs. Leidner's room, killed her, and *then* called the boy back. Or he might have killed her on one of the occasions when he had *sent the boy up to you.*"

Dr. Leidner shook his head, murmuring:

"What a nightmare! It's all so—fantastic."

To my surprise Poirot agreed.

"Yes, that is true. *This is a fantastic crime.* One does not often come across them. Usually murder is very sordid—very simple. But this is unusual murder . . . I suspect, Dr. Leidner, that your wife was an unusual woman."

He had hit the nail on the head with such accuracy that I jumped.

"Is that true, nurse?" he asked.

Dr. Leidner said quietly:

"Tell him what Louise was like, nurse. You are unprejudiced."

I spoke quite frankly.

"She was very lovely," I said. "You couldn't help admiring her and wanting to do things for her. I've never met any one like her before."

"Thank you," said Dr. Leidner and smiled at me.

"That is valuable testimony coming from an outsider," said Poirot politely. "Well, let us proceed. Under the heading of *means and opportunity* we have seven names. Nurse Leatheran, Miss Johnson, Mrs. Mercado, Mr. Mercado, Mr. Reiter, Mr. Emmott and Father Lavigny."

Once more he cleared his throat. I've always noticed that foreigners can make the oddest noises.

"Let us for the moment assume that our third theory is correct. That is, that the murderer is Frederick or William Bosner, and that Frederick or William Bosner is a member of the expedition staff. By comparing both lists we can narrow down our suspects on this count to four. Father Lavigny, Mr. Mercado, Carl Reiter and David Emmott."

"Father Lavigny is out of the question," said Dr. Leidner with decision. "He is one of the *Pères Blancs* in Carthage."

"And his beard's quite real," I put in.

"*Ma sœur,*" said Poirot, "a murderer of the first class *never* wears a false beard!"

"How do you know the murderer is of the first class?" I asked rebelliously.

"Because if he were not, the whole truth would be plain to me at this instant—and it is not."

That's pure conceit, I thought to myself.

"Anyway," I said, reverting to the beard, "it must have taken quite a time to grow."

"That is a practical observation," said Poirot. Dr. Leidner said irritably:

"But it's ridiculous—quite ridiculous. Both he and Mercado are well-known men. They've been known for years."

Poirot turned to him.

"You have not the true vision. You do not appreciate an important point. *If Frederick Bosner is not dead—what has he been doing all these years?* He must have taken a different name. He must have built himself up a career."

"As a *Père Blanc?*" asked Dr. Reilly sceptically.

"It is a little fantastic that, yes," confessed Poirot. "But we cannot put it right out of court. Besides, there are other possibilities."

"The young 'uns?" said Reilly. "If you want my opinion, on the face of it there's only one of your suspects that's even plausible."

"And that is?"

"Young Carl Reiter. There's nothing actually against him, but come down to it and you've got to admit a few things—he's the right age, he's got a German name, he's new this year and he had the opportunity all right. He'd only got to pop out of his photographic place, cross the courtyard to do his dirty work and hare back again while the coast was clear. If any one were to have dropped into the photographic room while he was out of it, he can always say later that he was in the dark-room. I don't say he's your man but if you are going to suspect some one I say he's by far and away the most likely."

M. Poirot didn't seem very receptive. He nodded gravely but doubtfully.

"Yes," he said. "He is the most plausible, but it may not be so simple as all that."

Then he said:

"Let us say no more at present. I would like now if I may to examine the room where the crime took place."

"Certainly." Dr. Leidner fumbled in his pockets then looked at Dr. Reilly.

"Captain Maitland took it," he said.

"Maitland gave it to me," said Reilly. "He had to go off on that Kurdish business."

He produced the key.

Dr. Leidner said hesitatingly:

"Do you mind—if I don't— Perhaps, nurse—"

"Of course. Of course," said Poirot. "I quite understand. Never do I wish to cause you unnecessary pain. If you will be good enough to accompany me, *ma sœur*."

"Certainly," I said.

Chapter 17

The Stain by the Wash-stand

Mrs. Leidner's body had been taken to Hassanieh for the post-mortem, but otherwise her room had been left exactly as it was. There was so little in it that it had not taken the police long to go over it.

To the right of the door as you entered was the bed. Opposite the door were the two barred windows giving on the countryside. Between them was a plain oak table with two drawers that served Mrs. Leidner as a dressing-table. On the east wall there was a line of hooks with dresses hung up protected by cotton bags and a deal chest of drawers. Immediately to the left of the door was the wash-stand. In the middle of the room was a good-sized plain oak table with a blotter and inkstand and a small attaché-case. It was in the latter that Mrs. Leidner had kept the anonymous letters. The curtains were short strips of native material—white striped with orange. The floor was of stone with some goatskin rugs on it, three narrow ones of brown striped with white in front of the two windows and the wash-stand, and a larger better quality one of white with brown stripes lying between the bed and the writing-table.

There were no cupboards or alcoves or long curtains—nowhere, in fact, where any one could have hidden. The bed was a plain iron one with a printed cotton quilt. The only trace of luxury in the room were three pillows all made of the best soft and billowy down. Nobody but Mrs. Leidner had pillows like these.

In a few brief dry words Dr. Reilly explained where Mrs. Leidner's body had been found—in a heap on the rug beside the bed.

To illustrate his account, he beckoned me to come forward.

"If you don't mind, nurse?" he said.

I'm not squeamish. I got down on the floor and arranged myself as far as possible in the attitude in which Mrs. Leidner's body had been found.

"Leidner lifted her head when he found her," said the doctor. "But I questioned him closely and it's obvious that he didn't actually change her position."

"It seems quite straightforward," said Poirot. "She was lying on the bed, asleep or resting—some one opens the door, she looks up, rises to her feet—"

"And he struck her down," finished the doctor. "The blow would produce unconsciousness and death would follow very shortly. You see—"

He explained the injury in technical language.

"Not much blood, then?" said Poirot.

"No, the blood escaped internally into the brain."

"*Eh bien,*" said Poirot, "that seems straightforward enough—except for one thing. *If* the man who entered was a stranger, why did not Mrs. Leidner cry out at once for help? If she had screamed she would have been heard. Nurse Leatheran here would have heard her, and Emmott and the boy."

"That's easily answered," said Dr. Reilly dryly. *"Because it wasn't a stranger."*

Poirot nodded.

"Yes," he said meditatively. "She may have been *surprised* to see the person—but she was not *afraid.* Then, as he struck, she *may* have uttered a half cry—too late."

"The cry Miss Johnson heard?"

"Yes, if she *did* hear it. But on the whole I doubt it. These mud walls are thick and the windows were closed."

He stepped up to the bed.

"You left her actually lying down?" he asked me. I explained exactly what I had done.

"Did she mean to sleep or was she going to read?"

"I gave her two books—a light one and a volume of memoirs. She usually read for a while and then sometimes dropped off for a short sleep."

"And she was—what shall I say—quite as usual?"

I considered.

"Yes. She seemed quite normal and in good spirits," I said. "Just a shade off-hand, perhaps, but I put that down to her having confided in me the day before. It makes people a little uncomfortable sometimes."

Poirot's eyes twinkled.

"Ah, yes, indeed, me, I know that well."

He looked round the room.

"And when you came in here after the murder, was everything as you had seen it before?"

I looked round also.

"Yes, I think so. I don't remember anything being different."

"There was no sign of the weapon with which she was struck?"

"No."

Poirot looked at Dr. Reilly.

"What was it in your opinion?"

The doctor replied promptly.

"Something pretty powerful of a fair size and without any sharp corners or edges. The rounded base of a statue, say—something like that. Mind you, I'm not suggesting that that *was* it. But that type of thing. The blow was delivered with great force."

"Struck by a strong arm? A man's arm?"

"Yes—unless—"

"Unless—what?"

Dr. Reilly said slowly:

"It is just possible that Mrs. Leidner might have been on her knees—in which case, the blow being delivered from above with a heavy implement, the force needed would not have been so great."

"On her knees," mused Poirot. "It is an idea—that."

"It's only an idea, mind," the doctor hastened to point out. "There's absolutely nothing to indicate it."

"But it's possible."

"Yes. And after all, in view of the circumstances, it's not fantastic. Her fear might have led her to kneel in supplication rather than to scream when her instinct would tell her it was too late—that nobody could get there in time."

"Yes," said Poirot thoughtfully. "It is an idea. . . ."

It was a very poor one, I thought. I couldn't for one moment imagine Mrs. Leidner on her knees to any one.

Poirot made his way slowly round the room. He opened the windows, tested the bars, passed his head through and satisfied himself that by no means could his shoulders be made to follow his head.

"The windows were shut when you found her," he said. "Were they also shut when you left her at a quarter to one?"

"Yes, they were always shut in the afternoon. There is no gauze over these windows as there is in the living-room and dining-room. They are kept shut to keep out the flies."

"And in any case no one could get in that way," mused Poirot. "And the walls are of the most solid—mud-brick—and there are no trap-doors and no sky-lights. No, there is only one way into this room—*through the door*. And there is only one way to the door—through the courtyard. And there is only one entrance to the courtyard—*through the archway*. And outside the archway there were five people and they all tell the same story, and I do not think, me, that they are lying. . . . No, they are not lying. They are not bribed to silence. The murderer was *here*. . . ."

I didn't say anything. Hadn't I felt the same thing just now when we were all cooped up round that table?

Slowly Poirot prowled round the room. He took up a photograph from the chest of drawers. It was of an elderly man with a white goatee beard. He looked inquiringly at me.

"Mrs. Leidner's father," I said. "She told me so."

He put it down again and glanced over the articles on the dressing-table—all of plain tortoiseshell—simple but good. He looked up at a row of books on a shelf, repeating the titles aloud.

"*Who Were the Greeks? Introduction to Relativity. Life of Lady Hester Stanhope. Crewe Train. Back to Methuselah. Linda Condon.* Yes, they tell us something, perhaps.

"She was not a fool, your Mrs. Leidner. She had a mind."

"Oh! she was a *very* clever woman," I said eagerly. "Very well read and up in everything. She wasn't a bit ordinary."

He smiled as he looked over at me.

"No," he said. "I've already realized that."

He passed on. He stood for some moments at the wash-stand where there was a big array of bottles and toilet creams.

Then, suddenly, he dropped on his knees and examined the rug.

Dr. Reilly and I came quickly to join him. He was examining a small dark brown stain, almost invisible on the brown of the rug. In fact it was only just noticeable where it impinged on one of the white stripes.

"What do you say, doctor?" he said. "Is that blood?"

Dr. Reilly knelt down.

"Might be," he said. "I'll make sure if you like?"

"If you would be so amiable."

Mr. Poirot examined the jug and basin. The jug was standing on the side of the wash-stand. The basin was empty, but beside the wash-stand there was an old kerosene tin containing slop water.

He turned to me.

"Do you remember, nurse? Was this jug *out* of the basin or *in* it when you left Mrs. Leidner at a quarter to one?"

"I can't be sure," I said after a minute or two. "I rather think it was standing in the basin."

"Ah?"

"But you see," I said hastily, "I only think so because it usually was.

The boys leave it like that after lunch. I just feel that if it hadn't been in I should have noticed it."

He nodded quite appreciatively.

"Yes, I understand that. It is your hospital training. If everything had not been just so in the room, you would quite unconsciously have set it to rights hardly noticing what you were doing. And after the murder? Was it like it is now?"

I shook my head.

"I didn't notice then," I said. "All I looked for was whether there was any place any one could be hidden or if there were anything the murderer had left behind him."

"It's blood all right," said Dr. Reilly, rising from his knees. "Is it important?"

Poirot was frowning perplexedly. He flung out his hands with petulance.

"I cannot tell. How can I tell? It may mean nothing at all. I can say, if I like, that the murderer touched her—that there was blood on his hands—very little blood, but still blood—and so he came over here and washed them. Yes, it may have been like that. But I cannot jump to conclusions and say that it *was* so. That stain may be of no importance at all."

"There would have been very little blood," said Dr. Reilly dubiously. "None would have spurted out or anything like that. It would have just oozed a little from the wound. Of course, if he'd probed it at all . . ."

I gave a shiver. A nasty sort of picture came up in my mind. The vision of somebody—perhaps that nice pig-faced photographic boy, striking down that lovely woman and then bending over her probing the wound with his finger in an awful gloating fashion and his face, perhaps, quite different . . . all fierce and mad. . . .

Dr. Reilly noticed my shiver.

"What's the matter, nurse?" he said.

"Nothing—just goose-flesh," I said. "A goose walking over my grave."

Mr. Poirot turned round and looked at me.

"I know what you need," he said. "Presently when we have finished here and I go back with the doctor to Hassanieh we will take you with us. You will give Nurse Leatheran tea, will you not, doctor?"

"Delighted."

"Oh, no, doctor," I protested. "I couldn't think of such a thing."

M. Poirot gave me a little friendly tap on the shoulder. Quite an English tap, not a foreign one.

"You, *ma sœur*, will do as you are told," he said. "Besides, it will be of advantage to me. There is a good deal more that I want to discuss, and I cannot do it here where one must preserve the decencies. The good Dr.

Leidner, he worshipped his wife and he is sure—oh, so sure—that every-body else felt the same about her! But that, in my opinion, would not be human nature! No, we want to discuss Mrs. Leidner with—how do you say—the gloves removed? That is settled then. When we have finished here, we take you with us to Hassanieh."

"I suppose," I said doubtfully, "that I ought to be leaving anyway. It's rather awkward."

"Do nothing for a day or two," said Dr. Reilly. "You can't very well go until after the funeral."

"That's all very well," I said. "And supposing I get murdered too, doctor?"

I said it half jokingly and Dr. Reilly took it in the same fashion and would, I think, have made some jocular response.

But M. Poirot, to my astonishment stood stock-still in the middle of the floor and clasped his hands to his head.

"Ah! if that were possible," he murmured. "It is a danger—yes—a great danger—and what can one do? How can one guard against it?"

"Why, M. Poirot," I said, "I was only joking! Who'd want to murder me, I should like to know?"

"You—or another," he said, and I didn't like the way he said it at all. Positively creepy.

"But why?" I persisted.

He looked at me very straight then.

"I joke, mademoiselle," he said, "and I laugh. *But there are some things that are no joke*. There are things that my profession has taught me. And one of these things, the most terrible thing, is this:

"Murder is a habit . . ."

Chapter 18

Tea at Dr. Reilly's

Before leaving, Poirot made a round of the expedition house and the out-buildings. He also asked a few questions of the servants at second hand—that is to say, Dr. Reilly translated the questions and answers from English into Arabic and vice versa.

These questions dealt mainly with the appearance of the stranger Mrs. Leidner and I had seen looking through the window and to whom Father Lavigny had been talking on the following day.

"Do you really think that fellow had anything to do with it?" asked Dr. Reilly when we were bumping along in his car on our way to Hassanieh.

"I like all the information there is," was Poirot's reply.

And really, that described his methods very well. I found later that there wasn't anything—no small scrap of insignificant gossip—in which he wasn't interested. Men aren't usually so gossipy.

I must confess I was glad of my cup of tea when we got to Dr. Reilly's house. M. Poirot, I noticed, put five lumps of sugar in his.

Stirring it carefully with his teaspoon he said:

"And now we can talk, can we not? We can make up our minds who is likely to have committed the crime."

"Lavigny, Mercado, Emmott or Reiter?" asked Dr. Reilly.

"No, no—that was theory number three. I wish to concentrate now on theory number two—leaving aside all question of a mysterious husband or brother-in-law turning up from the past. Let us discuss now quite simply which member of the expedition had the means and opportunity to kill Mrs. Leidner, and who is likely to have done so."

"I thought you didn't think much of that theory."

"Not at all. But I have some natural delicacy," said Poirot reproachfully. "Can I discuss in the presence of Dr. Leidner the motives likely to lead to the murder of his wife by a member of the expedition? That would not have been delicate at all. I had to sustain the fiction that his wife was adorable and that every one adored her!

"But naturally it was not like that at all. Now we can be brutal and impersonal and say what we think. We have no longer to consider people's feelings. And that is where Nurse Leatheran is going to help us. She is, I am sure, a very good observer."

"Oh, I don't know about that," I said.

Dr. Reilly handed me a plate of hot scones—"to fortify yourself," he said. They were very good scones.

"Come now," said M. Poirot in a friendly, chatty way. "You shall tell me, *ma sœur*, exactly what each member of the expedition felt towards Mrs. Leidner."

"I was only there a week, M. Poirot," I said.

"Quite long enough for one of your intelligence. A nurse sums up quickly. She makes her judgments and abides by them. Come, let us make a beginning. Father Lavigny, for instance?"

"Well, there now, I really couldn't say. He and Mrs. Leidner seemed to like talking together. But they usually spoke French and I'm not very good at French myself though I learnt it as a girl at school. I've an idea they talked mainly about books."

"They were, as you might say, companionable together—yes?"

"Well, yes, you might put it that way. But, all the same, I think Father Lavigny was puzzled by her and—well—almost annoyed by being puzzled, if you know what I mean."

And I told him of the conversation I had had with him out on the dig that first day when he had called Mrs. Leidner a "dangerous woman."

"Now that is very interesting," M. Poirot said. "And she—what do you think she thought of him?"

"That's rather difficult to say, too. It wasn't easy to know what Mrs. Leidner thought of people. Sometimes, I fancy, *he* puzzled *her*. I remember her saying to Dr. Leidner that he was unlike any priest she had ever known."

"A length of hemp to be ordered for Father Lavigny," said Dr. Reilly facetiously.

"My dear friend," said Poirot. "Have you not, perhaps, some patients to attend? I would not for the world detain you from your professional duties."

"I've got a whole hospital of them," said Dr. Reilly.

And he got up and said a wink was as good as a nod to a blind horse, and went out laughing.

"That is better," said Poirot. "We will have now an interesting conversation *tête-à-tête*. But you must not forget to eat your tea."

He passed me a plate of sandwiches and suggested my having a second cup of tea. He really had very pleasant, attentive manners.

"And now," he said, "let us continue with your impressions. Who was there who in your opinion did *not* like Mrs. Leidner?"

"Well," I said, "it's only my opinion and I don't want it repeated as coming from me."

"Naturally not."

"But in my opinion little Mrs. Mercado fairly hated her!"

"Ah! And Mr. Mercado?"

"He was a bit soft on her," I said. "I shouldn't think women apart from his wife had ever taken much notice of him. And Mrs. Leidner had a nice kind way of being interested in people and the things they told her. It rather went to the poor man's head, I fancy."

"And Mrs. Mercado—she was not pleased?"

"She was just plain jealous—that's the truth of it. You've got to be very careful when there's a husband and wife about, and that's a fact. I could tell you some surprising things. You've no idea the extraordinary things women get into their heads when it's a question of their husbands."

"I do not doubt the truth of what you say. So Mrs. Mercado was jealous? And she hated Mrs. Leidner?"

"I've seen her look at her as though she'd have liked to kill her—oh, gracious!" I pulled myself up. "Indeed, M. Poirot, I didn't mean to say—I mean that is, not for one moment—"

"No, no. I quite understand. The phrase slipped out. A very convenient one. And Mrs. Leidner, was she worried by this animosity of Mrs. Mercado's?"

"Well," I said, reflecting, "I don't really think she was worried at all. In fact, I don't even know whether she noticed it. I thought once of just giving her a hint—but I didn't like to. Least said soonest mended. That's what I say."

"You are doubtless wise. Can you give me any instances of how Mrs. Mercado showed her feelings?"

I told him about our conversation on the roof.

"So she mentioned Mrs. Leidner's first marriage," said Poirot thoughtfully. "Can you remember—in mentioning it—did she look at you as though she wondered whether you had heard a different version?"

"You think she may have known the truth about it?"

"It is a possibility. She may have written those letters—and engineered a tapping hand and all the rest of it."

"I wondered something of the same kind myself. It seemed the kind of petty revengeful thing she might do."

"Yes. A cruel streak, I should say. But hardly the temperament for cold-blooded brutal murder unless, of course—"

He paused and then said:

"It is odd, that curious thing she said to you. *'I know why you are here.'* What did she mean by it?"

"I can't imagine," I said frankly.

"She thought you were there for some ulterior reason apart from the declared one. What reason? And why should she be so concerned in the matter? Odd, too, the way you tell me she stared at you all through tea the day you arrived."

"Well, she's not a lady, M. Poirot," I said primly.

"That, *ma sœur*, is an excuse but not an explanation."

I wasn't quite sure for the minute what he meant. But he went on quickly.

"And the other members of the staff?"

I considered.

"I don't think Miss Johnson liked Mrs. Leidner either very much. But she was quite open and above-board about it. She as good as admitted she was prejudiced. You see, she's very devoted to Dr. Leidner and had worked with him for years. And of course, marriage does change things—there's no denying it."

"Yes," said Poirot. "And from Miss Johnson's point of view it would be an unsuitable marriage. It would really have been much more suitable if Dr. Leidner had married *her*."

"It would really," I agreed. "But there, that's a man all over. Not one in a hundred considers suitability. And one can't really blame Dr. Leidner. Miss Johnson, poor soul, isn't so much to look at. Now Mrs. Leidner was really beautiful—not young, of course—but oh! I wish you'd known her. There was something about her. . . . I remember Mr. Coleman saying she was like a thingummyjig that came to lure people into marshes. That wasn't a very good way of putting it but—oh, well—you'll laugh at me but there *was* something about her that was—well—unearthly."

"She could cast a spell—yes, I understand," said Poirot.

"Then I don't think she and Mr. Carey got on very well either," I went on. "I've an idea *he* was jealous just like Miss Johnson. He was always very stiff with her and so was she with him. You know—she passed him things and was very polite and called him Mr. Carey rather formally. He was an old friend of her husband's, of course, and some women can't stand their husband's old friends. They don't like to think that any one knew them before they did—at least that's rather a muddled way of putting it—"

"I quite understand. And the three young men? Coleman, you say, was inclined to be poetic about her."

I couldn't help laughing.

"It was funny, M. Poirot," I said. "He's much a matter-of-fact young man."

"And the other two?"

"I don't really know about Mr. Emmott. He's always so quiet and never says much. She was very nice to him always. You know—friendly—called him David and used to tease him about Miss Reilly and things like that."

"Ah, really? And did he enjoy that?"

"I don't quite know," I said doubtfully. "He'd just look at her. Rather funnily. You couldn't tell what he was thinking."

"And Mr. Reiter?"

"She wasn't always very kind to him," I said slowly. "I think he got on her nerves. She used to say quite sarcastic things to him."

"And did he mind?"

"He used to get very pink, poor boy. Of course, she didn't *mean* to be unkind."

And then suddenly, from feeling a little sorry for the boy, it came over me that he was very likely a cold-blooded murderer and had been playing a part all the time.

"Oh, M. Poirot," I exclaimed. "What do you think *really* happened?"

He shook his head slowly and thoughtfully.

"Tell me," he said. "You are not afraid to go back there to-night?"

"Oh, *no*," I said. "Of course, I remember what you said, but who would want to murder *me?*"

"I do not think that any one could," he said slowly. "That is partly why I have been so anxious to hear all you could tell me. No, I think—I am sure—you are quite safe."

"If any one had told me in Baghdad—" I began and stopped.

"Did you hear any gossip about the Leidners and the expedition before you came here?" he asked.

I told him about Mrs. Leidner's nickname and just a little of what Mrs. Kelsey had said about her.

In the middle of it the door opened and Miss Reilly came in. She had been playing tennis and had her racquet in her hand.

I gathered Poirot had already met her when he arrived in Hassanieh.

She said how do you do to me in her usual off-hand manner and picked up a sandwich.

"Well, M. Poirot," she said. "How are you getting on with our local mystery?"

"Not very fast, mademoiselle."

"I see you've rescued nurse from the wreck."

"Nurse Leatheran has been giving me valuable information about the various members of the expedition. Incidentally I have learnt a good deal—about the victim. And the victim, mademoiselle, is very often the clue to the mystery."

Miss Reilly said:

"That's rather clever of you, M. Poirot. It's certainly true that if ever a woman deserved to be murdered Mrs. Leidner was that woman!"

"Miss Reilly!" I cried, scandalized.

She laughed, a short, nasty laugh.

"Ah!" she said. "I thought you hadn't been hearing quite the truth. Nurse Leatheran, I'm afraid, was quite taken in, like many other people. Do you know, M. Poirot, I rather hope that this case isn't going to be one of your successes. I'd quite like the murderer of Louise Leidner to get away with it. In fact, I wouldn't much have objected to putting her out of the way myself."

I was simply disgusted with the girl. M. Poirot, I must say, didn't turn a hair. He just bowed and said quite pleasantly:

"I hope, then, that you have an alibi for yesterday afternoon?"

There was a moment's silence and Miss Reilly's racquet went clattering down to the floor. She didn't bother to pick it up. Slack and untidy like all her sort! She said in a rather breathless voice:

"Oh, yes, I was playing tennis at the club. But, seriously, M. Poirot, I wonder if you know anything at all about Mrs. Leidner and the kind of woman she was?"

Again he made a funny little bow and said:

"You shall inform me, mademoiselle."

She hesitated a minute and then spoke with a callousness and lack of decency that really sickened me.

"There's a convention that one doesn't speak ill of the dead. That's stupid, I think. The truth's always the truth. On the whole it's better to keep your mouth shut about living people. You might conceivably injure them. The dead are past that. But the harm they've done lives after them sometimes. Not quite a quotation from Shakespeare but very nearly! Has nurse told you of the queer atmosphere there was at Tell Yarimjah? Has she told you how jumpy they all were? And how they all used to glare at each other like enemies? That was Louise Leidner's doing. When I was a kid out here three years ago they were the happiest, jolliest lot imaginable. Even last year they were pretty well all right. But this year there was a blight over them—and it was *her* doing. She was the kind of woman who won't let anybody else be happy! There *are* women like that and she was one of them! She wanted to break up things always. Just for fun—or for the sense of power—or perhaps just because she was made that way. And she was the kind of woman who had to get hold of every male creature within reach!"

"Miss Reilly," I cried, "I don't think that's true. In fact I *know* it isn't."

She went on without taking the least notice of me.

"It wasn't enough for her to have her husband adore her. She had to make a fool of that long-legged shambling idiot of a Mercado. Then she got hold of Bill. Bill's a sensible cove, but she was getting him all mazed and bewildered. Carl Reiter she just amused herself by tormenting. It was easy. He's a sensitive boy. And she had a jolly good go at David.

"David was better sport to her because he put up a fight. He felt her charm—but he wasn't having any. I think because he'd got sense enough to know that she didn't really care a damn. And that's why I hate her so. She's not sensual. She doesn't *want* affairs. It's just cold-blooded experiment on her part and the fun of stirring people up and setting them against each other. She dabbled in that too. She's the sort of woman who's never had a row with any one in her life—but rows always happen where she is! She *makes* them happen. She's a kind of female Iago. She *must* have drama. But she doesn't want to be involved *herself*. She's always outside pulling strings—looking on—enjoying it. Oh, do you see *at all* what I mean?"

"I see, perhaps, more than you know, mademoiselle," said Poirot.

I couldn't make his voice out. He didn't sound indignant. He sounded—oh, well, I can't explain it.

Sheila Reilly seemed to understand for she flushed all over her face.

"You can think what you choose," she said. "But I'm right about her. She was a clever woman and she was bored and she experimented—with people—like other people experiment with chemicals. She enjoyed working on poor old Johnson's feelings and seeing her bite on the bullet and control herself like the old sport she is. She liked goading little Mercado into a white-hot frenzy. She liked flicking *me* on the raw—and she could do it too, every time! She liked finding out things about people and holding it over them. Oh, I don't mean crude blackmail—I mean just letting them know that she *knew*—and leaving them uncertain what she meant to do about it. My God, though, that woman was an artist! There was nothing crude about *her* methods!"

"And her husband?" asked Poirot.

"She never wanted to hurt him," said Miss Reilly slowly. "I've never known her anything but sweet to him. I suppose she was fond of him. He's a dear—wrapped up in his own world—his digging and his theories. And he worshipped her and thought her perfection. That might have annoyed some women. It didn't annoy her. In a sense he lived in a fool's paradise—

and yet it wasn't a fool's paradise because to him she was what he thought her. Though it's hard to reconcile that with—"

She stopped.

"Go on, mademoiselle," said Poirot.

She turned suddenly on me.

"What have you said about Richard Carey?"

"About Mr. Carey?" I asked, astonished.

"About her and Carey?"

"Well," I said, "I've mentioned that they didn't hit it off very well—"

To my surprise she broke into a fit of laughter.

"Didn't hit it off very well! You fool! He's head over ears in love with her. And it's tearing him to pieces—because he worships Leidner too. He's been his friend for years. That would be enough for her, of course. She's made it her business to come between them. But all the same I've fancied—"

"Eh bien?"

She was frowning, absorbed in thought.

"I've fancied that she'd gone too far for once—that she was not only biter but bit! Carey's attractive. He's as attractive as hell. . . . She was a cold devil—but I believe she could have lost her coldness with him. . . ."

"I think it's just scandalous what you're saying," I cried. "Why, they hardly spoke to each other!"

"Oh, didn't they?" She turned on me. "A hell of a lot you know about it. It was 'Mr. Carey' and 'Mrs. Leidner' in the house, but they used to meet outside. She'd walk down the path to the river. And he'd leave the dig for an hour at a time. They used to meet among the fruit trees.

"I saw him once just leaving her, striding back to the dig, and she was standing, looking after him. I was a female cad, I suppose. I had some glasses with me and I took them out and had a good look at her face. If you ask me I believed she cared like hell for Richard Carey. . . ."

She broke off and looked at Poirot.

"Excuse my butting in on your case," she said with a sudden rather twisted grin, "but I thought you'd like to have the local colour correct."

And she marched out of the room.

"M. Poirot," I cried. "I don't believe one word of it all!"

He looked at me and he smiled, and he said (very queerly I thought):

"You can't deny, nurse, that Miss Reilly has shed a certain—illumination on the case."

Chapter 19

A New Suspicion

We couldn't say any more just then because Dr. Reilly came in, saying jokingly that he'd killed off the most tiresome of his patients.

He and M. Poirot settled down to a more or less medical discussion of the psychology and mental state of an anonymous letter-writer. The doctor cited cases that he had known professionally, and M. Poirot told various stories from his own experience.

"It is not so simple as it seems," he ended. "There is the desire for power and very often a strong inferiority complex."

Dr. Reilly nodded.

"That's why you often find that the author of anonymous letters is the last person in the place to be suspected. Some quiet inoffensive little soul who apparently can't say Boo to a goose—all sweetness and Christian meekness on the outside—and seething with all the fury of hell underneath!"

Poirot said thoughtfully:

"Should you say Mrs. Leidner had any tendency to an inferiority complex?"

Dr. Reilly scraped out his pipe with a chuckle.

"Last woman on earth I'd describe that way. No repressions about her. Life, life and more life—that's what she wanted—and got, too!"

"Do you consider it a possibility, psychologically speaking, that she wrote those letters?"

"Yes, I do. But if she did, the reason arose out of her instinct to dramatize herself. Mrs. Leidner was a bit of a film star in private life! She *had* to be the centre of things—in the limelight. By the law of opposites she married Leidner who's about the most retiring and modest man I know. He adored her—but adoration by the fireside wasn't enough for her. She had to be the persecuted heroine as well."

"In fact," said Poirot, smiling, "you don't subscribe to his theory that she wrote them and retained no memory of her act?"

"No, I don't. I didn't turn down the idea in front of him. You can't very well say to a man who's just lost a dearly loved wife that that same wife was a shameless exhibitionist, and that she drove him nearly crazy with anxiety to satisfy her sense of the dramatic. As a matter of fact it wouldn't be safe to tell any man the truth about his wife! Funnily enough, I'd trust most women with the truth about their husbands. Women can accept the fact that a man is a rotter, a swindler, a drug-taker, a confirmed liar, and a general swine without batting an eyelash and without its impairing their affection for the brute in the least! Women are wonderful realists."

"Frankly, Dr. Reilly, what *was* your exact opinion of Mrs. Leidner?"

Dr. Reilly lay back in his chair and puffed slowly at his pipe.

"Frankly—it's hard to say! I didn't know her well enough. She'd got charm—any amount of it. Brains, sympathy. . . . What else? She hadn't any of the ordinary unpleasant vices. She wasn't sensual or lazy or even particularly vain. She was, I've always thought (but I've no proofs of it), a most accomplished liar. What I don't know (and what I'd like to know) is whether she lied to herself or only to other people. I'm rather partial to liars myself. A woman who doesn't lie is a woman without imagination and without sympathy. I don't think she was really a man-hunter—she just liked the sport of bringing them down 'with my bow and arrow.' If you get my daughter on the subject—"

"We have had that pleasure," said Poirot with a slight smile.

"H'm," said Dr. Reilly. "She hasn't wasted much time! Shoved her knife into her pretty thoroughly, I should imagine! The younger generation has no sentiment towards the dead. It's a pity all young people are prigs! They condemn the 'old morality' and then proceed to set up a much more hard and fast code of their own. If Mrs. Leidner had had half a dozen affairs Sheila would probably have approved of her as 'living her life fully'—or 'obeying her blood instincts.' What she doesn't see is that Mrs. Leidner was acting true to type—*her* type. The cat *is* obeying its blood instinct when it plays with the mouse! It's made that way. Men aren't little boys to be shielded and protected. They've got to meet cat women—and faithful spaniel, yours-till-death adoring women, and hen-pecking nagging bird women—and all the rest of it! Life's a battlefield—not a picnic! I'd like to see Sheila honest enough to come off her high horse and admit that she hated Mrs. Leidner for good old thoroughgoing personal reasons. Sheila's about the only young girl in this place and she naturally assumes that she ought to have it all her own way with the young things in trousers. Naturally it annoys her when a woman, who in her view is middle-aged and who has already two husbands to her credit, comes along and licks her on her own ground. Sheila's a nice child, healthy and reasonably good-looking and attractive to the other sex as she should be. But Mrs. Leidner was something out of the ordinary in that line. She'd got just that sort of calamitous magic that plays the deuce with things — a kind of Belle Dame sans Merci."

I jumped in my chair. What a coincidence his saying that!

"Your daughter — I am not indiscreet — she has perhaps a *tendresse* for one of the young men out there?"

"Oh, I don't suppose so. She's had Emmott and Coleman dancing attendance on her as a matter of course. I don't know that she cares for one more than the other. There are a couple of young Air Force chaps too. I fancy all's fish that comes to her net at present. No, I think it's age daring to defeat youth that annoys her so much! She doesn't know as much of the world as I do. It's when you get to my age that you really appreciate a schoolgirl complexion and a clear eye and a firmly knit young body. But a woman over thirty can listen with rapt attention and throw in a word here and there to show the talker what a fine fellow he is — and few young men can resist that! Sheila's a pretty girl — but Louise Leidner was beautiful. Glorious eyes and that amazing golden fairness. Yes, she was a beautiful woman."

Yes, I thought to myself, he's right. Beauty's a wonderful thing. She *had* been beautiful. It wasn't the kind of looks you were jealous of — you just sat back and admired. I felt that first day I met her that I'd do *anything* for Mrs. Leidner!

All the same, that night as I was being driven back to the Tell Yarimjah (Dr. Reilly made me stay for an early dinner) one or two things came back to my mind and made me rather uncomfortable. At the time I hadn't believed a word of all Sheila Reilly's outpouring. I'd taken it for sheer spite and malice.

But now I suddenly remembered the way Mrs. Leidner had insisted on going for a stroll by herself that afternoon and wouldn't hear of me coming with her. I couldn't help wondering if perhaps, after all, *she had* been going to meet Mr. Carey. . . . And of course, it *was* a little odd, really, the way he and she spoke to each other so formally. Most of the others she called by their Christian names.

He never seemed to look at her, I remembered. That might be because he disliked her — or it might be just the opposite. . . .

I gave myself a little shake. Here I was fancying and imagining all sorts of things—all because of a girl's spiteful outbursts! It just showed how unkind and dangerous it was to go about saying that kind of thing.

Mrs. Leidner *hadn't* been like that at all. . . .

Of course, *she* hadn't liked Sheila Reilly. She'd really been—almost catty about her that day at lunch to Mr. Emmott.

Funny, the way he'd looked at her. The sort of way that you couldn't possibly tell what he was thinking. You never could tell what Mr. Emmott was thinking. He was so quiet. But very nice. A nice dependable person.

Now Mr. Coleman was a foolish young man if there ever was one!

I'd got to that point in my meditations when we arrived. It was just on nine o'clock and the big door was closed and barred.

Ibrahim came running with his great key to let me in.

We all went to bed early at Tell Yarimjah. There weren't any lights showing in the living-room. There was a light in the drawing-office and one in Dr. Leidner's office, but nearly all the other windows were dark. Every one must have gone to bed even earlier than usual.

As I passed the drawing-office to go to my room I looked in. Mr. Carey was in his shirtsleeves working over his big plan.

Terribly ill, he looked, I thought. So strained and worn. It gave me quite a pang. I don't know what there was about Mr. Carey—it wasn't what he *said* because he hardly said anything—and that of the most ordinary nature, and it wasn't what he *did*, for that didn't amount to much either—and yet you just couldn't help noticing him, and everything about him seemed to matter more than it would have about any one else. He just *counted*, if you know what I mean.

He turned his head and saw me. He removed his pipe from his mouth and said:

"Well, nurse, back from Hassanieh?"

"Yes, Mr. Carey. You're up working late. Everybody else seems to have gone to bed."

"I thought I might as well get on with things," he said. "I was a bit behind-hand. And I shall be out on the dig all to-morrow. We're starting digging again."

"Already?" I asked, shocked.

He looked at me rather queerly.

"It's the best thing, I think. I put it up to Leidner. He'll be in Hassanieh most of to-morrow seeing to things. But the rest of us will carry on here. You know it's not too easy all sitting around and looking at each other as things are."

He was right there, of course. Especially in the nervy, jumpy state every one was in.

"Well, of course you're right in a way," I said. "It takes one's mind off if one's got something to do."

The funeral, I knew, was to be the day after tomorrow.

He had bent over his plan again. I don't know why, but my heart just ached for him. I felt certain that he wasn't going to get any sleep.

"If you'd like a sleeping draught, Mr. Carey?" I said hesitatingly.

He shook his head with a smile.

"I'll carry on, nurse. Bad habit, sleeping draughts."

"Well, good-night, Mr. Carey," I said. "If there's anything I can do—"

"Don't think so, thank you, nurse. Good-night."

"I'm terribly sorry," I said, rather too impulsively I suppose.

"Sorry?" He looked surprised.

"For—for everybody. It's all so dreadful. But especially for you."

"For me? Why for me?"

"Well, you're such an old friend of them both."

"I'm an old friend of Leidner's. I wasn't a friend of hers particularly."

He spoke as though he had actually disliked her. Really, I wished Miss Reilly could have heard him!

"Well, good-night," I said and hurried along to my room.

I fussed around a bit in my room before undressing. Washed out some handkerchiefs and a pair of wash-leather gloves and wrote up my diary. I just looked out of my door again before I really started to get ready for bed. The lights were still on in the drawing-office and in the south building.

I supposed Dr. Leidner was still up and working in his office. I wondered whether I ought to go and say goodnight to him. I hesitated about it—I didn't want to seem officious. He might be busy and not want to be disturbed. In the end, however, a sort ot uneasiness drove me on. After all, it couldn't do any harm. I'd just say good-night, ask if there was anything I could do and come away.

But Dr. Leidner wasn't there. The office itself was lit up but there was no one in it except Miss Johnson. She had her head down on the table and was crying as though her heart would break.

It gave me quite a turn. She was such a quiet, self-controlled woman. It was pitiful to see her.

"Whatever is it, my dear?" I cried. I put my arm round her and patted her. "Now, now, this won't do at all. . . . You mustn't sit here crying all by yourself."

She didn't answer and I felt the dreadful shuddering sobs that were racking her.

"Don't, my dear, don't," I said. "Take a hold on yourself. I'll go and make you a cup of nice hot tea."

She raised her head and said:

"No, no, it's all right, nurse. I'm being a fool."

"What's upset you, my dear?" I asked.

She didn't answer at once, then she said:

"It's all too awful. . . ."

"Now don't start thinking of it," I told her. "What's happened has happened and can't be mended. It's no use fretting."

She sat up straight and began to pat her hair.

"I'm making rather a fool of myself," she said in her gruff voice. "I've been clearing up and tidying the office. Thought it was best to *do* something. And then—it all came over me suddenly—"

"Yes, yes," I said hastily. "I know. A nice strong cup of tea and a hot-water bottle in your bed is what you want," I said.

And she had them too. I didn't listen to any protests.

"Thank you, nurse," she said when I'd settled her in bed, and she was sipping her tea and the hot-water bottle was in. "You're a nice kind sensible woman. It's not often I make such a fool of myself."

"Oh, anybody's liable to do that at a time like this," I said, "what with one thing and another. The strain and the shock and the police here, there and everywhere. Why, I'm quite jumpy myself."

She said slowly in rather a queer voice:

"What you said in there is true. What's happened has happened and can't be mended. . . ."

She was silent for a minute or two and then said—rather oddly, I thought:

"She was never a nice woman!"

Well, I didn't argue the point. I'd always felt it was quite natural for Miss Johnson and Mrs. Leidner not to hit it off.

I wondered if, perhaps, Miss Johnson had secretly had a feeling that she was pleased Mrs. Leidner was dead, and had then been ashamed of herself for the thought.

I said:

"Now you go to sleep and don't worry about anything."

I just picked up a few things and set the room to rights. Stockings over the back of the chair and coat and skirt on a hanger. There was a little ball of crumpled paper on the floor where it must have fallen out of a pocket.

I was just smoothing it out to see whether I could safely throw it away when she quite startled me.

"Give that to me!"

I did so—rather taken aback. She'd called out so peremptorily. She snatched it from me—fairly snatched it—and then held it in the candle flame till it was burnt to ashes.

As I say, I was startled—and I just stared at her.

I hadn't had time to see what the paper was—she'd snatched it so quick. But funnily enough, as it burned it curled over towards me and I just saw that there were words written in ink on the paper.

It wasn't till I was getting into bed that I realized why they'd looked sort of familiar to me.

It was the same handwriting as that of the anonymous letters.

Was *that* why Miss Johnson had given way to a fit of remorse? Had it been her all along who had written those anonymous letters?

Chapter 20

Miss Johnson, Mrs. Mercado, Mr. Reiter

I don't mind confessing that the idea came as a complete shock to me. I'd never thought of associating *Miss Johnson* with the letters. Mrs. Mercado, perhaps. But Miss Johnson was a real lady, and so self-controlled and sensible.

But I reflected, remembering the conversation I had listened to that evening between M. Poirot and Dr. Reilly, and that might be just *why*.

If it were Miss Johnson who had written the letters it explained a lot. Mind you, I didn't think for a minute Miss Johnson had had anything to do with the murder. But I *did* see that her dislike of Mrs. Leidner might have made her succumb to the temptation of well—putting the wind up her—to put it vulgarly.

She might have hoped to frighten away Mrs. Leidner from the dig.

But then Mrs. Leidner had been murdered and Miss Johnson had felt terrible pangs of remorse—first for her cruel trick and also, perhaps, because she realized that those letters were acting as a very good shield to the actual murderer. No wonder she had broken down so utterly. She was, I was sure, a decent soul at heart. And it explained, too, why she had caught so eagerly at my consolation of "what's happened's happened and can't be amended."

And then her cryptic remark—her vindication of herself—"She was never a nice woman!"

The question was, what was *I* to do about it?

I tossed and turned for a good while and in the end decided I'd let M. Poirot know about it at the first opportunity.

He came out next day but I didn't get a chance of speaking to him what you might call privately.

We had just a minute alone together and before I could collect myself to know how to begin, he had come close to me and was whispering instructions in my ear.

"Me, I shall talk to Miss Johnson—and others, perhaps, in the living-room. You have the key of Mrs. Leidner's room still?"

"Yes," I said.

"*Très bien*. Go there, shut the door behind you and give a cry—not a scream—a cry. You understand what I mean—it is alarm—surprise that I want you to express—not mad terror. As for the excuse if you are heard— I leave that to you—the stepped toe or what you will."

At that moment Miss Johnson came out into the courtyard and there was no time for more.

I understood well enough what M. Poirot was after. As soon as he and Miss Johnson had gone into the living-room I went across to Mrs. Leidner's room and, unlocking the door, went in and pulled the door to behind me.

I can't say I didn't feel a bit of a fool standing up in an empty room and giving a yelp all for nothing at all. Besides, it wasn't so easy to know just how loud to do it. I gave a pretty loud "Oh" and then tried it a bit higher and a bit lower.

Then I came out again and prepared my excuse of a stepped (stubbed I *suppose* he meant!) toe.

But it soon appeared that no excuse would be needed. Poirot and Miss Johnson were talking together earnestly and there had clearly been no interruption.

"Well," I thought, "that settles that. Either Miss Johnson imagined that cry she heard or else it was something quite different."

I didn't like to go in and interrupt them. There was a deck-chair on the porch so I sat down there. Their voices floated out to me.

"The position is delicate, you understand," Poirot was saying. "Dr. Leidner—obviously he adored his wife—"

"He worshipped her," said Miss Johnson.

"He tells me, naturally, how fond all his staff was of her! As for them, what can they say! Naturally they say the same thing. It is politeness. It is decency. It *may* also be the truth! But also it may *not!* And I am convinced, mademoiselle, that the key to this enigma lies in a complete understanding of Mrs. Leidner's character. If I could get the opinion—the honest opinion—of every member of the staff, I might, from the whole, build up a picture. Frankly, that is why I am here to-day. I knew Dr. Leidner would be in Hassanieh. That makes it easy for me to have a interview with each of you here in turn, and beg your help."

"That's all very well," began Miss Johnson and stopped.

"Do not make me the British *clichès*," Poirot begged. "Do not say it is not the cricket or the football, that to speak anything but well of the dead is not done—that—*enfin*—there is loyalty! Loyalty, it is a pestilential thing in crime. Again and again it obscures the truth."

"I've no particular loyalty to Mrs. Leidner," said Miss Johnson dryly. There was indeed a sharp and acid tone in her voice. "Dr. Leidner's a different matter. And, after all, she was his wife."

"Precisely—precisely. I understand that you would not wish to speak against your chief's wife. But this is not a question of a testimonial. It is a question of sudden and mysterious death. If I am to believe that it is a martyred angel who has been killed it does not add to the easiness of my task."

"I certainly shouldn't call her an angel," said Miss Johnson and the acid tone was even more in evidence.

"Tell me your opinion, frankly, of Mrs. Leidner—as a woman."

"H'm! To begin with, M. Poirot, I'll give you this warning. I'm prejudiced. I am—we all were—devoted to Dr. Leidner. And, I suppose, when Mrs. Leidner came along, we were jealous. We resented the demands she made on his time and attention. The devotion he showed her irritated us. I'm being truthful, M. Poirot, and it isn't very pleasant for me. I resented her presence here—yes, I did, though, of course, I tried never to show it. It made a difference to us, you see."

"Us? You say us?"

"I mean Mr. Carey and myself. We're the two old-timers, you see. And we didn't much care for the new order of things. I suppose that's natural, though perhaps it was rather petty of us. But it *did* make a difference."

"What kind of a difference?"

"Oh! to everything. We used to have such a happy time. A good deal of fun, you know, and rather silly jokes, like people do who work together. Dr. Leidner was quite light-hearted—just like a boy."

"And when Mrs. Leidner came she changed all that?"

"Well, I suppose it wasn't her *fault*. It wasn't so bad last year. And please believe, M. Poirot, that it wasn't anything she *did*. She's always been charming to me—quite charming. That's why I've felt ashamed sometimes. It wasn't her fault that little things she said and did seemed to rub me up the wrong way. Really nobody could be nicer than she was."

"But nevertheless things were changed this season? There was a different atmosphere."

"Oh, entirely. Really, I don't know what it was. Everything seemed to go wrong—not with the work—I mean with us—our tempers and our nerves. All on edge. Almost the sort of feeling you get when there is a thunderstorm coming."

"And you put that down to Mrs. Leidner's influence?"

"Well, it was never like that before she came," said Miss Johnson dryly. "Oh! I'm a cross-grained, complaining old dog. Conservative—liking things always the same. You really mustn't take any notice of me, M. Poirot."

"How would you describe to me Mrs. Leidner's character and temperament?"

Miss Johnson hesitated for a moment. Then she said slowly:

"Well, of course, she was temperamental. A lot of ups and downs. Nice to people one day and perhaps wouldn't speak to them the next. She was very kind, I think. And very thoughtful for others. All the same you could see she had been thoroughly spoilt all her life. She took Dr. Leidner's waiting on her hand and foot as perfectly natural. And I don't think she ever really appreciated what a very remarkable—what a really great—man she had married. That used to annoy me sometimes. And of course she was terribly highly strung and nervous. The things she used to imagine and the states she used to get into! I was thankful when Dr. Leidner brought Nurse Leatheran here. It was too much for him having to cope both with his work and with his wife's fears."

"What is your own opinion of these anonymous letters she received?"

I had to do it. I leaned forward in my chair till I could just catch sight of Miss Johnson's profile turned to Poirot in answer to his question.

She was looking perfectly cool and collected.

"I think some one in America had a spite against her and was trying to frighten or annoy her."

"Pas plus serieux que ça?"

"That's my opinion. She was a very handsome woman, you know, and might easily have had enemies. I think those letters were written by some spiteful woman. Mrs. Leidner being of a nervous temperament took them seriously."

"She certainly did that," said Poirot. "But remember—the last of them arrived by hand."

"Well, I suppose that *could* have been managed if any one had given their minds to it. Women will take a lot of trouble to gratify their spite, M. Poirot."

They will indeed, I thought to myself!

"Perhaps you are right, mademoiselle. As you say, Mrs. Leidner was handsome. By the way, you know Miss Reilly, the doctor's daughter?"

"Sheila Reilly? Yes, of course."

Poirot adopted a very confidential, gossipy tone.

"I have heard a rumour (naturally I do not like to ask the doctor) that there was a *tendresse* between her and one of the members of Dr. Leidner's staff. Is that so, do you know?"

Miss Johnson appeared rather amused.

"Oh, young Coleman and David Emmott were both inclined to dance attendance. I believe there was some rivalry as to who was to be her partner in some event at the club. Both the boys went in on Saturday evenings to the club as a general rule. But I don't know that there was anything in it on her side. She's the only young creature in the place, you know, and so she's by way of being the belle of it. She's got the Air Force dancing attendance on her as well."

"So you think there is nothing in it?"

"Well—I don't know." Miss Johnson became thoughtful. "It is true that she comes out this way fairly often. Up to the dig and all that. In fact, Mrs. Leidner was chaffing David Emmott about it the other day—saying the girl was running after him. Which was rather a catty thing to say, I thought, and I don't think he liked it. . . . Yes, she was here a good deal. I saw her riding towards the dig on that awful afternoon." She nodded her head towards the open window. "But neither David Emmott nor Coleman were on duty that afternoon. Richard Carey was in charge. Yes, perhaps she is attracted to one of the boys—but she's such a modern unsentimental young woman that one doesn't know quite how seriously to take her. I'm sure I don't know which of them it is. Bill's a nice boy, and not nearly such a fool as he pretends to be. David Emmott is a dear—and there's a lot to him. He is the deep, quiet kind."

Then she looked quizzically at Poirot and said:

"But has this any bearing on the crime, M. Poirot?"

M. Poirot threw up his hands in a very French fashion.

"You made me blush, mademoiselle," he said. "You expose me as a mere gossip. But what will you, I am interested always in the love affairs of young people."

"Yes," said Miss Johnson with a little sigh. "It's nice when the course of true love runs smooth."

Poirot gave an answering sigh. I wondered if Miss Johnson was thinking of some love affair of her own when she was a girl. And I wondered if M. Poirot had a wife, and if he went on in the way you always hear foreigners do, with mistresses and things like that. He looks so comic I couldn't imagine it.

"Sheila Reilly has a lot of character," said Miss Johnson. "She's young and she's crude, but she's the right sort."

"I take your word for it, mademoiselle," said Poirot.

He got up and said, "Are there any other members of the staff in the house?"

"Marie Mercado is somewhere about. All the men are up on the dig today. I think they wanted to get out of the house. I don't blame them. If you'd like to go up to the dig—"

She came out on the verandah and said, smiling to me:

"Nurse Leatheran won't mind taking you, I dare say."

"Oh, certainly, Miss Johnson," I said.

"And you'll come back to lunch, won't you, M. Poirot?"

"Enchanted, mademoiselle."

Miss Johnson went back into the living-room where she was engaged in cataloguing.

"Mrs. Mercado's on the roof," I said. "Do you want to see her first?"

"It would be as well, I think. Let us go up."

As we went up the stairs I said:

"I did what you told me. Did you hear anything?"

"Not a sound."

"That will be a weight off Miss Johnson's mind at any rate," I said. "She's been worrying that she might have done something about it."

Mrs. Mercado was sitting on the parapet, her head bent down, and she was so deep in thought that she never heard us till Poirot halted opposite her and bade her good-morning.

Then she looked up with a start.

She looked ill this morning, I thought, her small face pinched and wizened and great dark circles under her eyes.

"Encore moi," said Poirot. "I come to-day with a special object."

And he went on much in the same way as he had done to Miss Johnson, explaining how necessary it was that he should get a true picture of Mrs. Leidner.

Mrs. Mercado, however, wasn't as honest as Miss Johnson had been. She burst into fulsome praise which, I was pretty sure, was quite far removed from her real feelings.

"Dear, *dear* Louise! It's so hard to explain her to some one who didn't know her. She was such an *exotic* creature. Quite different from any one else. You felt that, I'm sure, nurse? A martyr to nerves, of course, and full of fancies, but one put up with things in her one wouldn't from any one else. And she was so *sweet* to us all, wasn't she, nurse? And so *humble* about herself—I mean she didn't know anything about archæology, and she was so eager to learn. Always asking my husband about the chemical processes for treating the metal objects and helping Miss Johnson to mend pottery. Oh, we were all *devoted* to her."

"Then it is not true, madame, what I have heard, that there was a certain tenseness—an uncomfortable atmosphere—here?"

Mrs. Mercado opened her opaque black eyes very wide.

"Oh! who *can* have been telling you that? Nurse? Dr. Leidner? I'm sure *he* would never notice anything, poor man."

And she shot a thoroughly unfriendly glance at me.

Poirot smiled easily.

"I have my spies, madame," he declared gaily. And just for a minute I saw her eyelids quiver and blink.

"Don't you think," asked Mrs. Mercado with an air of great sweetness, "that after an event of this kind, every one always pretends a lot of things that never were? You know—tension, atmosphere, a 'feeling that something was going to happen'? I think people just *make up* these things afterwards."

"There is a lot in what you say, madame," said Poirot.

"And it really *wasn't* true! We were a thoroughly happy family here."

"That woman is one of the most utter liars I've ever known," I said indignantly, when M. Poirot and I were clear of the house and walking along the path to the dig. "I'm sure she simply hated Mrs. Leidner really!"

"She is hardly the type to whom one would go for the truth," Poirot agreed.

"Waste of time talking to her," I snapped.

"Hardly that—hardly that. If a person tells you lies with her lips she is sometimes telling you truth with her eyes. What is she afraid of, little Madame Mercado? I saw fear in her eyes. Yes—decidedly she is afraid of something. It is very interesting."

"I've got something to tell you, M. Poirot," I said.

Then I told him all about my return the night before and my strong belief that Miss Johnson was the writer of the anonymous letters.

"So *she's* a liar too!" I said. "The cool way she answered you this morning about these same letters!"

"Yes," said Poirot. "It was interesting that. *For she let out the fact that she knew all about those letters.* So far they have not been spoken of in the presence of the staff. Of course, it is quite possible that Dr. Leidner told her about them yesterday. They are old friends, he and she. But if he did not—well—then it is curious and interesting, is it not?"

My respect for him went up. It was clever the way he had tricked her into mentioning the letters.

"Are you going to tackle her about them?" I asked.

Mr. Poirot seemed quite shocked by the idea.

"No, no, indeed. Always it is unwise to parade one's knowledge. Until the last minute I keep everything here." He tapped his forehead. "At the right moment—I make the spring—like the panther—and, *mon Dieu!* the consternation!"

I couldn't help laughing to myself at little M. Poirot in the rôle of a panther.

We had just reached the dig. The first person we saw was Mr. Reiter, who was busy photographing some walling.

It's my opinion that the men who were digging just hacked out walls wherever they wanted them. That's what it looked like anyway. Mr. Carey explained to me that you could feel the difference at once with a pick, and he tried to show me—but I never saw. When the man said *"Libn"*—mud-brick—it was just ordinary dirt and mud as far as I could see.

Mr. Reiter finished his photographs and handed over the camera and the plates to his boy and told him to take them back to the house.

Poirot asked him one or two questions about exposures and film packs and so on which he answered very readily. He seemed pleased to be asked about his work.

He was just tendering his excuses for leaving us when Poirot plunged once more into his set speech. As a matter of fact it wasn't quite a set speech because he varied it a little each time to suit the person he was talking to. But I'm not going to write it all down every time. With sensible people like Miss Johnson he went straight to the point, and with some of the others he had to beat about the bush a bit more. But it came to the same in the end.

"Yes, yes, I see what you mean," said Mr. Reiter. "But indeed, I do not see that I can be much help to you. I am new here this season and I did not speak much with Mrs. Leidner. I regret, but indeed I can tell you nothing."

There was something a little stiff and foreign in the way he spoke, though, of course, he hadn't got any accent—except an American one, I mean.

"You can at least tell me whether you liked or disliked her?" said Poirot with a smile.

Mr. Reiter got quite red and stammered:

"She was a charming person—most charming. And intellectual. She had a very fine brain—yes."

"*Bien!* You liked her. And she liked you?"

Mr. Reiter got redder still.

"Oh, I—I don't know that she noticed me much. And I was unfortunate once or twice. I was always unlucky when I tried to do anything for her. I'm afraid I annoyed her by my clumsiness. It was quite unintentional . . . I would have done *anything*—"

Poirot took pity on his flounderings.

"Perfectly—perfectly. Let us pass to another matter. Was it a happy atmosphere in the house?"

"Please."

"Were you all happy together? Did you laugh and talk?"

"No—no, not exactly that. There was a little—stiffness."

He paused, struggling with himself, and then said:

"You see, I am not very good in company. I am clumsy. I am shy. Dr. Leidner always he has been most kind to me. But—it is stupid—I cannot overcome my shyness. I say always the wrong thing. I upset water jugs. I am unlucky."

He really looked like a large awkward child.

"We all do these things when we are young," said Poirot, smiling. "The poise, the *savoir faire*, it comes later."

Then with a word of farewell we walked on.

He said:

"That, *ma sœur*, is either an extremely simple young man or a very remarkable actor."

I didn't answer. I was caught up once more by the fantastic notion that one of these people was a dangerous and cold-blooded murderer. Somehow, on this beautiful still sunny morning, it seemed impossible.

Chapter 21

Mr. Mercado, Richard Carey

"They work in two separate places, I see," said Poirot, halting.

Mr. Reiter had been doing his photography on an outlying portion of the main excavation. A little distance away from us a second swarm of men were coming and going with baskets.

"That's what they call the deep cut," I explained. "They don't find much there, nothing but rubbishy broken pottery, but Dr. Leidner always says it's very interesting, so I suppose it must be."

"Let us go there."

We walked together slowly for the sun was hot.

Mr. Mercado was in command. We saw him below us talking to the foreman, an old man like a tortoise who wore a tweed coat over his long striped cotton gown.

It was a little difficult to get down to them as there was only a narrow path or stair and basket boys were going up and down it constantly, and they always seemed to be as blind as bats and never to think of getting out of the way.

As I followed Poirot down he said suddenly over his shoulder:

"Is Mr. Mercado right-handed or left-handed?"

Now that was an extraordinary question if you like!

I thought a minute, then:

"Right-handed," I said decisively.

Poirot didn't condescend to explain. He just went on and I followed him.

Mr. Mercado seemed rather pleased to see us.

His long melancholy face lit up.

M. Poirot pretended to an interest in archæology that I'm sure he couldn't have really felt, but Mr. Mercado responded at once.

He explained that they had already cut down through twelve levels of house occupation.

"We are now definitely in the fourth millennium," he said with enthusiasm.

I always thought a millennium was in the future—the time when everything comes right.

Mr. Mercado pointed out belts of ashes (how his hand did shake! I wondered if he might possibly have malaria) and he explained how the pottery changed in character, and about burials—and how they had had one level almost entirely composed of infant burials—poor little things—and about flexed position and orientation which seemed to mean the way the bones were lying.

And then suddenly, just as he was stooping down to pick up a kind of flint knife that was lying with some pots in a corner, he leapt into the air with a wild yell.

He spun round to find me and Poirot staring at him in astonishment.

He clapped his hand to his left arm.

"Something stung me—like a red-hot needle."

Immediately Poirot was galvanized into energy.

"Quick, *mon cher*, let us see. Nurse Leatheran!" I came forward.

He seized Mr. Mercado's arm and deftly rolled back the sleeve of his khaki shirt to the shoulder.

"There," said Mr. Mercado, pointing.

About three inches below the shoulder there was a minute prick from which the blood was oozing.

"Curious," said Poirot. He peered into the rolled-up sleeve. "I can see nothing. It was an ant, perhaps?"

"Better put on a little iodine," I said.

I always carry an iodine pencil with me, and I whipped it out and applied it. But I was a little absent-minded as I did so, for my attention had been caught by something quite different. Mr. Mercado's arm, all the way up the forearm to the elbow, was marked all over by tiny punctures. I knew well enough what *they* were—*the marks of a hypodermic needle.*

Mr. Mercado rolled down his sleeve again and recommenced his explanations. M. Poirot listened, but didn't try to bring the conversation round to the Leidners. In fact he didn't ask Mr. Mercado anything at all.

Presently we said good-by to Mr. Mercado and climbed up the path again.

"It was neat that, did you not think so?" my companion asked.

"Neat?" I asked.

M. Poirot took something from behind the lapel of his coat and surveyed it affectionately. To my surprise I saw that it was a long sharp darning needle with a blob of sealing wax making it into a pin.

"M. Poirot," I cried, "did *you* do that?"

"I was the stinging insect—yes. And very neatly I did it, too, do you not think so? You did not see me."

That was true enough. I never saw him do it. And I'm sure Mr. Mercado hadn't suspected. He must have been quick as lightning.

"But, M. Poirot, why?" I asked.

He answered me by another question.

"Did you notice anything, sister?" he asked.

I nodded my head slowly.

"Hypodermic marks," I said.

"So now we know something about Mr. Mercado," said Poirot. "I suspected—but I did not *know*. It is always necessary to *know*."

"And you don't care how you set about it!" I thought, but didn't say.

Poirot suddenly clapped his hand to his pocket.

"Alas, I have dropped my handkerchief down there. I concealed the pin in it."

"I'll get it for you," I said and hurried back.

I'd got the feeling, you see, by this time, that M. Poirot and I were the doctor and nurse in charge of a case. At least, it was more like an operation and he was the surgeon. Perhaps I oughtn't to say so, but in a queer way I was beginning to enjoy myself.

I remember just after I'd finished my training, I went to a case in a private house and the need for an immediate operation arose, and the patient's husband was cranky about nursing homes. He just wouldn't hear of his wife being taken to one. Said it had to be done in the house.

Well, of course it was just splendid for me! Nobody else to have a look in! I was in charge of everything. Of course, I was terribly nervous—I thought of everything conceivable that doctor could want, but even then I was afraid I might have forgotten something. You never know with doctors. They ask for absolutely anything sometimes! But everything went spendidly! I had each thing ready as he asked for it, and he actually told me I'd done first rate after it was over—and that's a thing most doctors wouldn't bother to do! The G.P. was very nice too. And I ran the whole thing myself!

The patient recovered, too, so everybody was happy.

Well, I felt rather the same now. In a way M. Poirot reminded me of that surgeon. *He* was a little man, too. Ugly little man with a face like a monkey, but a wonderful surgeon. He knew instinctively just where to go. I've seen a lot of surgeons and I know what a lot of difference there is.

Gradually I'd been growing a kind of confidence in M. Poirot. I felt that he, too, knew exactly what he was doing. And I was getting to feel that it was my job to help him—as you might say—to have the forceps and the swabs and all handy just when he wanted them. That's why it seemed just as natural for me to run off and look for his handkerchief as it would have been to pick up a towel that a doctor had thrown on the floor.

When I'd found it and got back I couldn't see him at first. But at last I caught sight of him. He was sitting a little way from the mound talking to Mr. Carey. Mr. Carey's boy was standing near with that great big rod thing with metres marked on it, but just at that moment he said something to the boy and the boy took it away. It seemed he had finished with it for the time being.

I'd like to get this next bit quite clear. You see, I wasn't quite sure what M. Piorot did or didn't want me to do. He might, I mean, have sent me back for that handkerchief *on purpose*. To get me out of the way.

It was just like an operation over again. You've got to be careful to hand the doctor just what he wants and not what he *doesn't* want. I mean, suppose you gave him the artery forceps at the wrong moment, and were late with them at the right moment! Thank goodness I know my work in the theatre well enough. I'm not likely to make mistakes there. But in this business I was really the rawest of raw little probationers. And so I had to be particularly careful not to make any silly mistakes.

Of course, I didn't for one moment imagine that M. Poirot didn't want me to hear what he and Mr. Carey were saying. But he might have thought he'd get Mr. Carey to talk better if I wasn't there.

Now I don't want anybody to get it into their heads that I'm the kind of woman who goes about eavesdropping on private conversations. I wouldn't do such a thing. Not for a moment. Not however much I wanted to.

And what I mean is if it *had* been a private conversation I wouldn't for a moment have done what, as a matter of fact, I actually did do.

As I looked at it I was in a privileged position. After all, you hear many a thing when a patient's coming round after an anæsthetic. The patient wouldn't want you to hear it—and usually has no idea you *have* heard it—but the fact remains you *do* hear it. I just took it that Mr. Carey was the patient. He'd be none the worse for what he didn't know about. And if you think that I was just curious, well, I'll admit that I *was* curious. I didn't want to miss anything I could help.

All this is just leading up to the fact that I turned aside and went by a round-about way up behind the big dump until I was a foot from where they were, but concealed from them by the corner of the dump. And if any one says it was dishonourable I just beg to disagree. *Nothing* ought to be hidden from the nurse in charge of the case, though, of course, it's the doctor to say what shall be *done*.

I don't know, of course, what M. Poirot's line of approach had been, but by the time I'd got there he was aiming straight for the bull's eye, so to speak.

"Nobody appreciates Dr. Leidner's devotion to his wife more than I do," he was saying. "But it is often the case that one learns more about a person from their enemies than from their friends."

"You suggest that their faults are more important than their virtues?" said Mr. Carey. His tone was dry and ironic.

"Undoubtedly—when it comes to murder. It seems odd that as far as I know nobody has yet been murdered for having too perfect a character! And yet perfection is undoubtedly an irritating thing."

"I'm afraid I'm hardly the right person to help you," said Mr. Carey. "To be perfectly honest, Mrs. Leidner and I didn't hit it off particularly well. I don't mean that we were in any sense of the word enemies, but we were not exactly friends. Mrs. Leidner was, perhaps, a shade jealous of my old friendship with her husband. I, for my part, although I admired her very much and thought she was an extremely attractive woman, was just a shade resentful of her influence over Leidner. As a result we were quite polite to each other, but not intimate."

"Admirably explained," said Poirot.

I could just see their heads, and I saw Mr. Carey's turn sharply as though something in M. Poirot's detached tone struck him disagreeably.

M. Poirot went on:

"Was not Dr. Leidner distressed that you and his wife did not get on together better?"

Carey hesitated a minute before saying:

"Really—I'm not sure. He never said anything. I always hoped he didn't notice it. He was very wrapped up in his work, you know."

"So the truth, according to you, is that you did not really like Mrs. Leidner?"

Carey shrugged his shoulders.

"I should probably have liked her very much if she hadn't been Leidner's wife."

He laughed as though amused by his own statement.

Poirot was arranging a little heap of broken potsherds. He said in a dreamy, far-away voice:

"I talked to Miss Johnson this morning. She admitted that she was prejudiced against Mrs. Leidner and did not like her very much, although she hastened to add that Mrs. Leidner had always been charming to her."

"All quite true, I should say," said Carey.

"So I believed. Then I had a conversation with Mrs. Mercado. She told me at great length how devoted she had been to Mrs. Leidner and how much she had admired her."

Carey made no answer to this, and after waiting a minute or two Poirot went on:

"That—I did not believe! Then I come to you and that which you tell me—well, again—*I do not believe . . .*"

Carey stiffened. I could hear the anger—repressed anger—in his voice.

"I really cannot help your beliefs—or your disbeliefs, M. Poirot. You've heard the truth and you can take it or leave it as far as I am concerned."

Poirot did not grow angry. Instead he sounded particularly meek and depressed.

"Is it my fault what I do—or do not believe? I have a sensitive ear, you know. And then—there are always plenty of stories going about—rumours floating in the air. One listens—and perhaps—one learns something! Yes, there *are* stories. . . ."

Carey sprang to his feet. I could see clearly a little pulse that beat in his temple. He looked simply splendid! So lean and so brown—and that wonderful jaw, hard and square. I don't wonder women fell for that man.

"What stories?" he asked savagely.

Poirot looked sideways at him.

"Perhaps you can guess. The usual sort of story—about you and Mrs. Leidner."

"What foul minds people have!"

"*N'est ce pas?* They are like dogs. However deep you bury an unpleasantness a dog will always root it up again."

"And you believe these stories?"

"I am willing to be convinced—of the truth," said Poirot gravely.

"I doubt if you'd know the truth if you heard it," Carey laughed rudely.

"Try me and see," said Poirot, watching him.

"I will then! You shall have the truth! I hated Louise Leidner—there's the truth for you! I hated her like hell!"

Chapter 22

David Emmott, Father Lavigny
and a Discovery

Turning abruptly away, Carey strode off with long angry strides.

Poirot sat looking after him and presently he murmured:

"Yes—I see. . . ."

Without turning his head he said in a slightly louder voice:

"Do not come round the corner for a minute, nurse. In case he turns his head. Now it is all right. You have my handkerchief? Many thanks. You are most amiable."

He didn't say anything at all about my having been listening—and how he knew I *was* listening I can't think. He'd never once looked in that direction. I was rather relieved he didn't say anything. I mean, I felt all right with *myself* about it, but it might have been a little awkward explaining to him. So it was a good thing he didn't seem to want explanations.

"Do you think he did hate her, M. Poirot?" I asked.

Nodding his head slowly with a curious expression on his face, Poirot answered.

"Yes—I think he did."

Then he got up briskly and began to walk to where the men were working on the top of the mound. I followed him. We couldn't see any one but Arabs at first but we finally found Mr. Emmott lying face downwards blowing dust off a skeleton that had just been uncovered.

He gave his pleasant grave smile when he saw us.

"Have you come to see round?" he asked. "I'll be free in a minute."

He sat up, took his knife and began daintily cutting the earth away from round the bones, stopping every now and then to use either a bellows or his own breath. A very insanitary proceeding the latter, I thought.

"You'll get all sorts of nasty germs in your mouth, Mr. Emmott," I protested.

"Nasty germs are my daily diet, nurse," he said gravely. "Germs can't do anything to an archæologist—they just get naturally discouraged trying."

He scraped a little more away round the thigh bone. Then he spoke to the foreman at his side directing him exactly what he wanted done.

"There," he said, rising to his feet. "That's ready for Reiter to photograph after lunch. Rather nice stuff she had in with her."

He showed us a little verdigrisy copper bowl and some pins. And a lot of gold and blue things that had been her necklace of beads.

The bones and all the objects were brushed and cleaned with a knife and kept in position ready to be photographed.

"Who is she?" asked Poirot.

"First millennium. A lady of some consequence perhaps. Skull looks rather odd—I must get Mercado to look at it. It suggests death by foul play."

"A Mrs. Leidner of two thousand odd years ago?" said Poirot.

"Perhaps," said Mr. Emmott.

Bill Coleman was doing something with a pick to a wall face.

David Emmott called something to him which I didn't catch and then started showing M. Poirot round.

When the short explanatory tour was over Emmott looked at his watch.

"We knock off in ten minutes," he said. "Shall we walk back to the house?"

"That will suit me excellently," said Poirot.

We walked slowly along the well-worn path.

"I expect you are all glad to get back to work again," said Poirot.

Emmott replied gravely:

"Yes, it's much the best thing. It's not been any too easy loafing about the house and making conversation."

"Knowing all the time *that one of you was a murderer.*"

Emmott did not answer. He made no gesture of dissent. I knew now that he had had a suspicion of the truth from the very first when he had questioned the house-boys.

After a few minutes he asked quietly:

"Are you getting anywhere, M. Poirot?"

Poirot said gravely:

"Will you help me to get somewhere?"

"Why, naturally."

Watching him closely, Poirot said:

"The hub of the case is Mrs. Leidner. I want to know about Mrs. Leidner."

David Emmott said slowly:

"What do you mean by knowing about her?"

"I do not mean where she came from and what her maiden name was. I do not mean the shape of her face and the colour of her eyes. I mean her—herself."

"You think that counts in the case?"

"I am quite sure of it."

Emmott was silent for a moment or two, then he said:

"Maybe you're right."

"And that is where you can help me. You can tell me what sort of a woman she was."

"Can I? I've often wondered about it myself."

"Didn't you make up your mind on the subject?"

"I think I did in the end."

"Eh bien?"

But Mr. Emmott was silent for some minutes, then he said:

"What did nurse think of her? Women are said to sum up other women quickly enough, and a nurse has a wide experience of types."

Poirot didn't give me any chance of speaking even if I had wanted to. He said quickly:

"What I want to know is what a *man* thought of her?"

Emmott smiled a little.

"I expect they'd all be much the same." He paused and said, "She wasn't young, but I think she was about the most beautiful woman I've ever come across."

"That's hardly an answer, Mr. Emmott."

"It's not so far off one, M. Poirot."

He was silent a minute or two and then he went on:

"There used to be a fairy story I read when I was a kid. A northern fairy story about the Snow Queen and Little Kay. I guess Mrs. Leidner was rather like that—always taking Little Kay for a ride."

"Ah, yes, a tale of Hans Andersen, is it not? And there was a girl in it. Little Gerda, was that her name?"

"Maybe. I don't remember much of it."

"Can't you go a little further, Mr. Emmott?"

David Emmott shook his head.

"I don't even know if I've summed her up correctly. She wasn't easy to read. She'd do a devilish thing one day, and a really fine one the next.

But I think you're about right when you say that she's the hub of the case. That's what she always wanted to be—*at the centre of things*. And she liked to get *at* other people—I mean, she wasn't just satisfied with being passed the toast and the peanut butter, she wanted you to turn your mind and soul inside out for her to look at it."

"And if one did not give her that satisfaction?" asked Poirot.

"Then she could turn ugly!"

I saw his lips close resolutely and his jaws set.

"I suppose, Mr. Emmott, you would not care to express a plain unofficial opinion as to who murdered her?"

"I don't know," said Emmott. "I really haven't the slightest idea. I rather think that, if I'd been Carl—Carl Reiter, I mean—I would have had a shot at murdering her. She was a pretty fair devil to him. But, of course, he asks for it by being so darned sensitive. Just invites you to give him a kick in the pants."

"And did Mrs. Leidner give him—a kick in the pants?" inquired Poirot.

Emmott gave a sudden grin.

"No. Pretty little jabs with an embroidery needle—that was her method. He *was* irritating, of course. Just like some blubbering, poor-spirited kid. But a needle's a painful weapon."

I stole a glance at Poirot and thought I detected a slight quiver of his lips.

"But you don't really believe that Carl Reiter killed her?" he asked.

"No. I don't believe you'd kill a woman because she persistently made you look a fool at every meal."

Poirot shook his head thoughtfully.

Of course, Mr. Emmott made Mrs. Leidner sound quite inhuman. There was something to be said on the other side too.

There had been something terribly irritating about Mr. Reiter's attitude. He jumped when she spoke to him, and did idiotic things like passing her the marmalade again and again when he knew she never ate it. I'd have felt inclined to snap at him a bit myself.

Men don't understand how their mannerisms can get on women's nerves so that you feel you just have to snap.

I thought I'd just mention that to Mr. Poirot some time.

We had arrived back by now and Mr. Emmott offered Poirot a wash and took him into his room.

I hurried across the courtyard to mine.

I came out again about the same time they did and we were all making for the dining-room when Father Lavigny appeared in the doorway of his room and invited Poirot in.

Mr. Emmott came on round and he and I went into the dining-room together.

Miss Johnson and Mrs. Mercado were there already, and after a few minutes Mr. Mercado, Mr. Reiter and Bill Coleman joined us.

We were just sitting down and Mercado had told the Arab boy to tell Father Lavigny lunch was ready when we were all startled by a faint, muffled cry.

I suppose our nerves weren't very good yet, for we all jumped, and Miss Johnson got quite pale and said:

"*What was that?* What's happened?"

Mrs. Mercado stared at her and said:

"My dear, what *is* the matter with you? It's some noise outside in the fields."

But at that minute Poirot and Father Lavigny came in.

"We thought some one was hurt," Miss Johnson said.

"A thousand pardons, mademoiselle," cried Poirot.

"The fault is mine. Father Lavigny, he explains to me some tablets, and I take one to the window to see better—and, *ma foi*, not looking where I was going, I steb the toe, and the pain is sharp for the moment and I cry out."

"We thought it was another murder," said Mrs. Mercado, laughing.

"Marie!" said her husband.

His tone was reproachful and she flushed and bit her lip.

Miss Johnson hastily turned the conversation to the dig and what objects of interest had turned up that morning. Conversation all through lunch was sternly archæological.

I think we all felt it was the safest thing.

After we had had coffee we adjourned to the living-room. Then the men, with the exception of Father Lavigny, went off to the dig again.

Father Lavigny took Poirot through into the antika-room and I went with them. I was getting to know the things pretty well by now and I felt a thrill of pride—almost as though it were my own property—when Father Lavigny took down the gold cup and I heard Poirot's exclamation of admiration and pleasure.

"How beautiful! What a work of art!"

Father Lavigny agreed eagerly and began to point out its beauties with real enthusiasm and knowledge.

"No wax on it to-day," I said.

"Wax?" Poirot stared at me.

"Wax?" So did Father Lavigny.

I explained my remark.

"Ah, *je comprends,*" said Father Lavigny. "Yes, yes, candle grease."

That led direct to the subject of the midnight visitor. Forgetting my presence they both dropped into French and I left them together and went back into the living-room.

Mrs. Mercado was darning her husband's socks and Miss Johnson was reading a book. Rather an unusual thing for her. She usually seemed to have something to work at.

After a while Father Lavigny and Poirot came out, and the former excused himself on the score of work. Poirot sat down with us.

"A most interesting man," he said, and asked how much work there had been for Father Lavigny to do so far.

Miss Johnson explained that tablets had been scarce and that there had been very few inscribed bricks or cylinder seals. Father Lavigny, however, had done his share of work on the dig and was picking up colloquial Arabic very fast.

That led the talk to cylinder seals, and presently Miss Johnson fetched from a cupboard a sheet of impressions made by rolling them out on plasticine.

I realized as we bent over them, admiring the spirited designs, that these must be what she had been working at on that fatal afternoon.

As we talked I noticed that Poirot was rolling and kneading a little ball of plasticine between his fingers.

"You use a lot of plasticine, mademoiselle?" he asked.

"A fair amount. We seem to have got through a lot already this year—though I can't imagine how. But half our supply seems to have gone."

"Where is it kept, mademoiselle?"

"Here—in this cupboard."

As she replaced the sheet of impressions she showed him the shelf with rolls of plasticine. Durofix, photographic paste and other stationery supplies.

Poirot stooped down.

"And this—what is this, mademoiselle?"

He had slipped his hand right to the back and had brought out a curious crumpled object.

As he straightened it out we could see that it was a kind of mask, with eyes and mouth crudely painted on in Indian ink and the whole thing roughly smeared with plasticine.

"How perfectly extraordinary," cried Miss Johnson. "I've never seen it before. How did it get there? And what is it?"

"As to how it got there, well, one hiding-place is as good as another, and I presume that this cupboard would not have been turned out till the end of the season. As to what it *is*—that, too, I think, is not difficult to say. *We have here the face that Mrs. Leidner described.* The ghostly face seen in the semi-dusk outside her window—without body attached."

Mrs. Mercado gave a little shriek.

Miss Johnson was white to the lips. She murmured:

"Then it was *not* fancy. It was a trick—a wicked trick! But who played it?"

"Yes," cried Mrs. Mercado. "Who could have done such a wicked, wicked thing?"

Poirot did not attempt a reply. His face was very grim as he went into the next room, returned with an empty cardboard box in his hand and put the crumpled mask into it.

"The police must see this," he explained.

"It's horrible," said Miss Johnson in a low voice. "Horrible!"

"Do you think everything's hidden here somewhere?" cried Mrs. Mercado shrilly. "Do you think perhaps the weapon—the club she was killed with—all covered with blood still, perhaps . . . Oh! I'm frightened—I'm frightened . . ."

Miss Johnson gripped her by the shoulder.

"Be quiet," she said fiercely. "Here's Dr. Leidner. We mustn't upset him."

Indeed, at that very moment the car had driven into the courtyard. Dr. Leidner got out of it and came straight across and in at the living-room door. His face was set in lines of fatigue and he looked twice the age he had three days ago.

He said in a quiet voice:

"The funeral will be at eleven o'clock to-morrow. Major Deane will read the service."

Mrs. Mercado faltered something, then slipped out of the room.

Dr. Leidner said to Miss Johnson:

"You'll come, Anne?"

And she answered:

"Of course, my dear, we'll all come. Naturally."

She didn't say anything else, but her face must have expressed what her tongue was powerless to do, for his face lightened up with affection and a momentary ease.

"Dear Anne," he said. "You are such a wonderful comfort and help to me. My dear old friend."

He laid his hand on her arm and I saw the red colour creep up in her face as she muttered, gruff as ever:

"That's all right."

But I just caught a glimpse of her expression and knew that, for one short moment, Anne Johnson was a perfectly happy woman.

And another idea flashed across my mind. Perhaps soon, in the natural course of things, turning to his old friend for sympathy, a new and happy state of things might come about.

Not that I'm really a matchmaker, and of course it was indecent to think of such a thing before the funeral even. But after all, it *would* be a happy solution. He was very fond of her, and there was no doubt she was absolutely devoted to him and would be perfectly happy devoting the rest of her life to him. That is, if she could bear to hear Louise's perfections sung all the time. But women can put up with a lot when they've got what they want.

Dr. Leidner then greeted Poirot, asking him if he had made any progress.

Miss Johnson was standing behind Dr. Leidner and she looked hard at the box in Poirot's hand and shook her head, and I realized that she was pleading with Poirot not to tell him about the mask. She felt, I was sure, that he had enough to bear for one day.

Poirot fell in with her wish.

"These things march slowly, monsieur," he said.

Then, after a few desultory words, he took his leave.

I accompanied him out to his car.

There were half a dozen things I wanted to ask him, but somehow, when he turned and looked at me, I didn't ask anything after all. I'd as soon have asked a surgeon if he thought he'd made a good job of an operation. I just stood meekly waiting for instructions.

Rather to my surprise he said:

"Take care of yourself, my child."

And then he added:

"I wonder if it is well for you to remain here?"

"I must speak to Dr. Leidner about leaving," I said. "But I thought I'd wait until after the funeral."

He nodded in approval.

"In the meantime," he said, "do not try and find out too much. You understand, I do not want you to be clever!" And he added with a smile, "It is for you to hold the swabs and for me to do the operation."

Wasn't it funny, his actually saying that?

Then he said quite irrelevantly:

"An interesting man, that Father Lavigny."

"A monk being an archæologist seems odd to me," I said.

"Ah, yes, you are a Protestant. Me, I am a good Catholic. I know something of priests and monks."

He frowned, seemed to hesitate, then said:

"Remember, he is quite clever enough to turn you inside out if he likes."

If he was warning me against gossiping I felt that I didn't need any such warning!

It annoyed me and though I didn't like to ask him any of the things I really wanted to know, I didn't see why I shouldn't at any rate say one thing.

"You'll excuse me, M. Poirot," I said. "But it's 'stubbed your toe,' not *stepped* or *stebbed*."

"Ah? Thank you, *ma sœur*."

"Don't mention it. But it's just as well to get a phrase right."

"I will remember," he said—quite meekly for him.

And he got in the car and was driven away, and I went slowly back across the courtyard wondering about a lot of things.

About the hypodermic marks on Mr. Mercado's arm, and what drug it was he took. And about that horrid yellow smeared mask. And how odd it was that Poirot and Miss Johnson hadn't heard my cry in the living-room that morning, whereas we had all heard Poirot perfectly well in the dining-room at lunch time—and yet Father Lavigny's room and Mrs. Leidner's were just the same distance from the living-room and the dining-room respectively.

And then I felt rather pleased that I'd taught *Doctor* Poirot one English phrase correctly!

Even if he *was* a great detective he'd realize he *didn't* know *everything!*

Chapter 23

I Go Psychic

The funeral was, I thought, a very affecting affair.

As well as ourselves, all the English people in Hassanieh attended it. Even Sheila Reilly was there looking quiet and subdued in a dark coat and skirt. I hoped that she was feeling a little remorseful for all the unkind things she had said.

When we got back to the house I followed Dr. Leidner into the office and broached the subject of my departure. He was very nice about it, thanked me for what I had done (Done! I had been worse than useless) and insisted on my accepting an extra week's salary.

I protested because really I felt I'd done nothing to earn it.

"Indeed, Dr. Leidner, I'd rather not have any salary at all. If you'd just refund me my travelling expenses that's all I want."

But he wouldn't hear of that.

"You see," I said, "I don't feel I deserve it, Dr. Leidner. I mean, I've— well, I've failed. She—my coming didn't save her."

"Now don't get that idea into your head, nurse," he said earnestly. "After all, I didn't engage you as a female detective. I never dreamt my wife's life was in danger. I was convinced it was all nerves and that she'd worked herself up into a rather curious mental state. You did all any one could do. She liked and trusted you. And I think in her last days she felt happier and safer because of your being here. There's nothing for you to reproach yourself with."

His voice quivered a little and I knew what he was thinking. *He* was the only one to blame for not having taken Mrs. Leidner's fears seriously.

"Dr. Leidner," I said curiously. "Have you ever come to any conclusion about those anonymous letters?"

He said with a sigh:

"I don't know what to believe. Has M. Poirot come to any definite conclusion?"

"He hadn't yesterday," I said, steering rather neatly, I thought, between truth and fiction. After all, he hadn't until I told him about Miss Johnson.

It was on my mind that I'd like to give Dr. Leidner a hint and see if he reacted. In the pleasure of seeing him and Miss Johnson together the day before, and his affection and reliance on her, I'd forgotten all about the letters. Even now I felt it was perhaps rather mean of me to bring it up. Even if she had written them, she had had a bad time after Mrs. Leidner's death. Yet I did want to see whether that particular possibility had ever entered Dr. Leidner's head.

"Anonymous letters are usually the work of a woman," I said. I wanted to see how he'd take it.

"I suppose they are," he said with a sigh. "But you seem to forget, nurse, that these may be genuine. They may actually be written by Frederick Bosner."

"No, I haven't forgotten," I said. "But I can't believe somehow that that's the real explanation."

"I do," he said. "It's all nonsense his being one of the expedition staff. That is just an ingenious theory of M. Poirot's. I believe that the truth is much simpler. The man is a madman, of course. He's been hanging round the place—perhaps in disguise of some kind. And somehow or other he got in on that fatal afternoon. The servants may be lying—they may have been bribed."

"I suppose it's possible," I said doubtfully.

Dr. Leidner went on with a trace of irritability.

"It is all very well for M. Poirot to suspect the members of my expedition. I am perfectly certain *none* of them have anything to do with it! I have worked with them. I *know* them!"

He stopped suddenly, then he said:

"Is that your experience, nurse? That anonymous letters are usually written by women?"

"It isn't always the case," I said. "But there's a certain type of feminine spitefulness that finds relief that way."

"I suppose you are thinking of Mrs. Mercado?" he said.

Then he shook his head.

"Even if she were malicious enough to wish to hurt Louise she would hardly have the necessary knowledge," he said.

I remembered the earlier letters in the attaché-case.

If Mrs. Leidner had left that unlocked and Mrs. Mercado had been alone in the house one day pottering about, she might easily have found them and read them. Men never seem to think of the simplest possibilities!

"And apart from her there is only Miss Johnson," I said, watching him.

"That would be quite ridiculous!"

The little smile with which he said it was quite conclusive. The idea of Miss Johnson being the author of the letters had never entered his head! I hesitated just for a minute—but I didn't say anything. One doesn't like giving away a fellow woman, and besides, I had been a witness of Miss Johnson's genuine and moving remorse. What was done was done. Why expose Dr. Leidner to a fresh disillusion on top of all his other troubles?

It was arranged that I should leave on the following day, and I had arranged through Dr. Reilly to stay for a day or two with the matron of the hospital whilst I made arrangements for returning to England either via Baghdad or direct via Nissibin by car and train.

Dr. Leidner was kind enough to say that he would like me to choose a memento from amongst his wife's things.

"Oh, no, really, Dr. Leidner," I said. "I couldn't. It's much too kind of you."

He insisted.

"But I should like you to have something. And Louise, I am sure, would have wished it."

Then he went on to suggest that I should have her tortoiseshell toilet set!

"Oh, no, Dr. Leidner! Why, that's a most *expensive* set. I couldn't really."

"She had no sisters, you know—no one who wants these things. There is no one else to have them."

I could quite imagine that he wouldn't want them to fall into Mrs. Mercado's greedy little hands. And I didn't think he'd want to offer them to Miss Johnson.

He went on kindly:

"You just think it over. By the way, here is the key of Louise's jewel case. Perhaps you will find something there you would rather have. And I should be very grateful if you would pack up—all—all her clothes. I dare say Reilly can find a use for them amongst some of the poor Christian families in Hassanieh."

I was very glad to be able to do that for him, and I expressed my willingness.

I set about it at once.

Mrs. Leidner had only had a very simple wardrobe with her and it was

soon sorted and packed up into a couple of suitcases. All her papers had
been in the small attaché-case. The jewel case contained a few simple trin-
kets—a pearl ring, a diamond brooch, a small string of pearls and one or
two plain gold bar brooches of the safety-pin type, and a string of large
amber beads.

Naturally I wasn't going to take the pearls or the diamonds, but I hesitated a bit between the amber beads and the toilet set. In the end, however, I didn't see why I shouldn't take the latter. It was a kindly thought
on Dr. Leidner's part, and I was sure there wasn't any patronage about it.
I'd take it in the spirit it had been offered without any false pride. After
all, I *had* been fond of her.

Well, that was all done and finished with. The suitcases packed, the
jewel case locked up again and put separate to give to Dr. Leidner with
the photograph of Mrs. Leidner's father and one or two other personal little odds and ends.

The room looked bare and forlorn emptied of all its accoutrements,
when I'd finished. There was nothing more for me to do—and yet somehow or other I shrank from leaving the room. It seemed as though there
were something still to do there—something I ought to *see*—or something I ought to have *known*.

I'm not superstitious but the idea *did* pop into my head that perhaps
Mrs. Leidner's spirit was hanging about the room and trying to get in
touch with me.

I remember once at the hospital some of us girls got a planchette and
really it wrote some very remarkable things.

Perhaps, although I'd never thought of such a thing, I might be medi-
umistic.

As I say, one gets all worked up to imagine all sorts of foolishness
sometimes.

I prowled round the room uneasily, touching this and that. But, of
course, there wasn't anything in the room but bare furniture. There was
nothing slipped behind drawers or tucked away. I couldn't hope for anything of that kind.

In the end (it sounds rather batty, but as I say, one gets worked up) I
did rather a queer thing.

I went and lay down on the bed and closed my eyes.

I deliberately tried to forget who and what I was. I tried to think myself back to that fatal afternoon. I was Mrs. Leidner lying here resting,
peaceful and unsuspicious.

It's extraordinary how you can work yourself up.

I'm a perfectly normal matter-of-fact individual—not the least little bit spooky, but I tell you that after I'd lain there about five minutes I began to *feel* spooky.

I didn't try to resist. I deliberately encouraged the feeling. I said to myself:

"I'm Mrs. Leidner. I'm Mrs. Leidner. I'm lying here—half asleep. Presently—very soon now—the door's going to open."

I kept on saying that—as though I were hypnotizing myself.

It's just about half-past one . . . it's just about the time. . . . The door is going to open . . . *the door is going to open.* . . . I shall see who comes in. . . ."

I kept my eyes glued on that door. Presently it was going to open. I should *see* it open. And I should see *the person who opened it.*

I must have been a little over-wrought that afternoon to imagine I could solve the mystery that way.

But I did believe it. A sort of chill passed down my back and settled in my legs. They felt numb—paralyzed.

"You're going into a trance," I said. "And in that trance you'll see . . ."

And once again I repeated monotonously again and again:

"The door is going to open—the door is going to open. . . ."

The cold numbed feeling grew more intense.

And then, slowly, *I saw the door just beginning to open.*

It was horrible.

I've never known anything so horrible before or since.

I was paralyzed—chilled through and through. I couldn't move. For the life of me I couldn't have moved.

And I was terrified. Sick and blind and dumb with terror.

That slowly opening door.

So noiseless.

In a minute I should see . . .

Slowly—slowly—wider and wider.

Bill Coleman came quietly in.

He must have had the shock of his life!

I bounded off the bed with a scream of terror and hurled myself across the room.

He stood stock-still, his blunt pink face pinker and his mouth opened wide with surprise.

"Hallo-allo-allo," he said. "What's up, nurse?"

I came back to reality with a crash.

"Goodness, Mr. Coleman," I said. "How you startled me!"

"Sorry," he said with a momentary grin.

I saw then that he was holding a little bunch of scarlet ranunculus in his hand. They were pretty little flowers and they grew wild on the sides of the Tell. Mrs. Leidner had been very fond of them.

He blushed and got rather red as he said:

"One can't get any flowers or things in Hassanieh. Seemed rather rotten not to have any flowers for the grave. I thought I'd just nip in here and put a little posy in that little pot thing she always had flowers in on her table. Sort of show she wasn't forgotten—eh? A bit asinine, I know, but—well—I mean to say—"

I thought it was very nice of him. He was all pink with embarrassment like Englishmen are when they've done anything sentimental. I thought it was a very sweet thought.

"Why, I think that's a very nice idea, Mr. Coleman," I said.

And I picked up the little pot and went and got some water in it and we put the flowers in.

I really thought much more of Mr. Coleman for this idea of his. It showed he had a heart and nice feelings about things.

He didn't ask me again what made me let out such a squeal and I'm thankful he didn't. I should have felt a fool explaining.

"Stick to common sense in future, woman," I said to myself as I settled my cuffs and smoothed my apron. "You're not cut out for this psychic stuff."

I bustled about doing my own packing and kept myself busy for the rest of the day.

Father Lavigny was kind enough to express great distress at my leaving. He said my cheerfulness and common sense had been such a help to everybody. Common sense! I'm glad he didn't know about my idiotic behaviour in Mrs. Leidner's room.

"We have not seen M. Poirot to-day," he remarked.

I told him that Poirot had said he was going to be busy all day sending off telegrams.

Father Lavigny raised his eyebrows.

"Telegrams? To America?"

"I suppose so. He said 'All over the world!' but I think that was rather a foreign exaggeration."

And then I got rather red, remembering that Father Lavingny was a foreigner himself.

He didn't seem offended though, just laughed quite pleasantly and asked me if there were any news of the man with the squint.

I said I didn't know but I hadn't heard of any.

Father Lavigny asked me again about the time Mrs. Leidner and I had noticed the man and how he had seemed to be standing on tiptoe and peering through the window.

"It seems clear the man had some overwhelming interest in Mrs. Leidner," he said thoughtfully. "I have wondered since whether the man could possibly have been a European got up to look like an Iraqi?"

That was a new idea to me and I considered it carefully. I had taken it for granted that the man was a native, but of course, when I came to think of it, I was really going by the cut of his clothes and the yellowness of his skin.

Father Lavigny declared his intention of going round outside the house to the place where Mrs. Leidner and I had seen the man standing.

"You never know, he might have dropped something. In the detective stories the criminal always does."

"I expect in real life criminals are more careful," I said.

I fetched some socks I had just finished darning and put them on the table in the living-room for the men to sort out when they came in, and then, as there was nothing much more to do, I went up on the roof.

Miss Johnson was standing there but she didn't hear me. I got right up to her before she noticed me.

But long before that I'd seen that there was something very wrong.

She was standing in the middle of the roof staring straight in front of her, and there was the most awful look on her face. As though she'd seen something she couldn't possibly believe.

It gave me quite a shock.

Mind you, I'd seen her upset the other evening, but this was quite different.

"My dear," I said, hurrying to her, "whatever's the matter?"

She turned her head at that and stood looking at me—almost as if she didn't see me.

"What is it?" I persisted.

She made a queer sort of grimace—as though she were trying to swallow but her throat were too dry. She said hoarsely:

"I've just seen something."

"What have you seen? Tell me. Whatever can it be? You look all in."

She gave an effort to pull herself together, but she still looked pretty dreadful.

She said, still in that same dreadful choked voice.

"I've seen how some one could come in from outside—and no one would ever guess."

I followed the direction of her eyes but I couldn't see anything.

Mr. Reiter was standing in the door of the photographic room and Father Lavigny was just crossing the courtyard—but there was nothing else.

I turned back puzzled and found her eyes fixed on mine with the strangest expression in them.

"Really," I said, "I don't see what you mean. Won't you explain?"

But she shook her head.

"Not now. Later. We *ought* to have seen. Oh, we ought to have seen!"

"If you'd only tell me—"

But she shook her head.

"I've got to think it out first."

And pushing past me, she went stumbling down the stairs.

I didn't follow her as she obviously didn't want me with her. Instead I sat down on the parapet and tried to puzzle things out. But I didn't get anywhere. There was only the one way into the courtyard—through the big arch. Just outside it I could see the water-boy and his horse and the Indian cook talking to him. Nobody could have passed them and come in without their seeing him.

I shook my head in perplexity and went downstairs again.

Chapter 24

Murder Is a Habit

We all went to bed early that night. Miss Johnson had appeared at dinner and had behaved more or less as usual. She had, however, a sort of dazed look, and once or twice quite failed to take in what other people said to her.

It wasn't somehow a very comfortable sort of meal. You'd say, I suppose, that that was natural enough in a house where there'd been a funeral that day. But I know what I mean.

Lately our meals had been hushed and subdued, but for all that there had been a feeling of comradeship. There had been sympathy with Dr. Leidner in his grief and a fellow feeling of being all in the same boat amongst the others.

But to-night I was reminded of my first meal there — when Mrs. Mercado had watched me and there had been that curious feeling as though something might snap any minute.

I'd felt the same thing — only very much intensified — when we'd sat round the dining-room table with Poirot at the head of it.

To-night it was particularly strong. Every one was on edge — jumpy — on tenterhooks. If any one had dropped something I'm sure somebody would have screamed.

As I say, we all separated early afterwards. I went to bed almost at once. The last thing I heard as I was dropping off to sleep was Mrs. Mercado's voice saying goodnight to Miss Johnson just outside my door.

I dropped off to sleep at once — tired by my exertions and even more by my silly experience in Mrs. Leidner's room. I slept heavily and dreamlessly for several hours.

I awoke when I did awake with a start and a feeling of impending ca-
tastrophe. Some sound had woken me, and as I sat up in bed listening I
heard it again.

An awful sort of agonized choking groan.

I had lit my candle and was out of bed in a twinkling. I snatched up a
torch, too, in case the candle should blow out. I came out of my door and
stood listening. I knew the sound wasn't far away. It came again—from
the room immediately next to mine—Miss Johnson's room.

I hurried in. Miss Johnson was lying in bed, her whole body contorted
in agony. As I set down the candle and bent over her, her lips moved and
she tried to speak—but only an awful hoarse whisper came. I saw that
the corners of her mouth and the skin of her chin were burnt a kind of
greyish white.

Her eyes went from me to a glass that lay on the floor evidently where
it had dropped from her hand. The light rug was stained a bright red
where it had fallen. I picked it up and ran a finger over the inside, drawing back my hand with a sharp exclamation. Then I examined the inside
of the poor woman's mouth.

There wasn't the least doubt what was the matter. Somehow or other,
intentionally or otherwise, she'd swallowed a quantity of corrosive acid—
oxalic or hydrochloric, I suspected.

I ran out and called to Dr. Leidner and he woke the others, and we
worked over her for all we were worth, but all the time I had an awful
feeling it was no good. We tried a strong solution of carbonate of soda—
and followed it with olive oil. To ease the pain I gave her a hypodermic
of morphine sulphate.

David Emmott had gone off to Hassanieh to fetch Dr. Reilly, but before he came it was over.

I won't dwell on the details. Poisoning by a strong solution of hydrochloric acid (which is what it proved to be) is one of the most painful
deaths possible.

It was when I was bending over her to give her the morphia that she
made one ghastly effort to speak. It was only a horrible strangled whisper
when it came.

"The window . . ." she said. *"Nurse . . . the window . . ."*

But that was all—she couldn't go on. She collapsed completely.

I shall never forget that night. The arrival of Dr. Reilly. The arrival of
Captain Maitland. And finally with the dawn, Hercule Poirot.

He it was who took me gently by the arm and steered me into the dining-
room where he made me sit down and have a cup of good strong tea.

"There, *mon enfant*," he said, "that is better. You are worn out."

Upon that, I burst into tears.

"It's too awful," I sobbed. "It's been like a nightmare. Such awful suffering. And her eyes . . . Oh, M. Poirot—her eyes . . ."

He patted me on the shoulder. A woman couldn't have been kinder.

"Yes, yes—do not think of it. You did all you could."

"It was one of the corrosive acids."

"It was a strong solution of hydrochloric acid."

"The stuff they use on the pots?"

"Yes. Miss Johnson probably drank it off before she was fully awake. That is—unless she took it on purpose."

"Oh, M. Poirot, what an awful idea!"

"It is a possibility, after all. What do you think?"

I considered for a moment and then shook my head decisively.

"I don't believe it. No, I don't believe it for a moment." I hesitated and then said, "I think she found out something yesterday afternoon."

"What is that you say? She found out something?"

I repeated to him the curious conversation we had had together.

Poirot gave a low soft whistle.

"La pauvre femme!" he said. "She said she wanted to think it over—eh? That is what signed her death warrant. If she had only spoken out—then—at once."

He said:

"Tell me again her exact words?"

I repeated them.

"She saw how some one could have come in from outside without any of you knowing? Come, *ma sœur*, let us go up to the roof and you shall show me just where she was standing."

We went up to the roof together and I showed Poirot the exact spot where Miss Johnson had stood.

"Like this?" said Poirot. "Now what do I see? I see half the courtyard—and the archway—and the doors of the drawing-office and the photographic room and the laboratory. Was there any one in the courtyard?"

"Father Lavigny was just going towards the archway and Mr. Reiter was standing in the door of the photographic room."

"And still I do not see in the least how any one could come in from outside and none of you know about it. . . . But *she* saw . . ."

He gave it up at last, shaking his head.

"Sacré nom d'un chien—va! What *did* she see?"

The sun was just rising. The whole eastern sky was a riot of rose and orange and pale, pearly grey.

"What a beautiful sunrise," said Poirot gently.

The river wound away to our left and the Tell stood up outlined in gold colour. To the south were the blossoming trees and the peaceful cultivation. The water-wheel groaned in the distance—a faint unearthly sound. In the north were the slender minarets and the clustering fairy whiteness of Hassanieh.

It was all incredibly beautiful.

And then, close at my elbow, I heard Poirot give a long deep sigh.

"Fool that I have been," he murmured. "When the truth is so clear—so clear."

Chapter 25

Suicide or Murder?

I hadn't time to ask Poirot what he meant, for Captain Maitland was calling up to us and asking us to come down.

We hurried down the stairs.

"Look here, Poirot," he said. "Here's another complication. The monk fellow is missing."

"Father Lavigny?"

"Yes. Nobody noticed it till just now. Then it dawned on somebody that he was the only one of the party not around, and we went to his room. His bed's not been slept in and there's no sign of him."

The whole thing was like a bad dream. First Miss Johnson's death and then the disappearance of Father Lavigny.

The servants were called and questioned, but they couldn't throw any light on the mystery. He had last been seen at about eight o'clock the night before. Then he had said he was going out for a stroll before going to bed.

Nobody had seen him come back from that stroll.

The big doors had been closed and barred at nine o'clock as usual. Nobody, however, remembered unbarring them in the morning. The two house-boys each thought the other one must have done the unfastening.

Had Father Lavigny ever returned the night before? Had he, in the course of his earlier walk, discovered anything of a suspicious nature, gone out to investigate it later, and perhaps fallen a third victim?

Captain Maitland swung round as Dr. Reilly came up with Mr. Mercado behind him.

"Hallo, Reilly. Got anything?"

"Yes. The stuff came from the laboratory here. I've just been checking up the quantities with Mercado. It's HCI from the lab."

"The laboratory—eh? Was it locked up?"

Mr. Mercado shook his head. His hands were shaking and his face was twitching. He looked a wreck of a man.

"It's never been the custom," he stammered. "You see—just now— we're using it all the time. I—nobody ever dreamt—"

"Is the place locked up at night?"

"Yes—all the rooms are locked. The keys are hung up just inside the living-room."

"So if any one had a key to that they could get the lot."

"Yes."

"And it's a perfectly ordinary key, I suppose?"

"Oh, yes."

"Nothing to show whether she took it herself from the laboratory?" asked Captain Maitland.

"She didn't," I said loudly and positively.

I felt a warning touch on my arm. Poirot was standing close behind me.

And then something rather ghastly happened.

Not ghastly in itself—in fact it was just the incongruousness that made it seem worse than anything else.

A car drove into the courtyard and a little man jumped out. He was wearing a sun helmet and a short thick trench coat.

He came straight to Dr. Leidner, who was standing by Dr. Reilly, and shook him warmly by the hand.

"*Vous voilà, mon cher,*" he cried. "Delighted to see you. I passed this way on Saturday afternoon—en route to the Italians at Fugima. I went to the dig but there wasn't a single European about and alas! I cannot speak Arabic. I had not time to come to the house. This morning I leave Fugima at five—two hours here with you—and then I catch the convoy on. *Eh bien*, and how is the season going?"

It was ghastly.

The cheery voice, the matter-of-fact manner, all the pleasant sanity of an everyday world now left far behind. He just bustled in, knowing nothing and noticing nothing—full of cheerful bonhomie.

No wonder Dr. Leidner gave an inarticulate gasp and looked in mute appeal at Dr. Reilly.

The doctor rose to the occasion.

He took the little man (he was a French archaeologist called Verrier who dug in the Greek islands, I heard later) aside and explained to him what had occurred.

Verrier was horrified. He himself had been staying at an Italian dig right away from civilization for the last few days and had heard nothing.

He was profuse in condolences and apologies, finally striding over to Dr. Leidner and clasping him warmly by both hands.

"What a tragedy! My God, what a tragedy! I have no words. *Mon pauvre collègue.*"

And shaking his head in one last ineffectual effort to express his feelings, the little man climbed into his car and left us.

As I say, that momentary introduction of comic relief into tragedy seemed really more gruesome than anything else that had happened.

"The next thing," said Dr. Reilly firmly, "is breakfast. Yes, I insist. Come, Leidner, you must eat."

Poor Dr. Leidner was almost a complete wreck. He came with us to the dining-room and there a funereal meal was served. I think the hot coffee and fried eggs did us all good, though no one actually felt they wanted to eat. Dr. Leidner drank some coffee and sat twiddling his beard. His face was grey, drawn with pain and bewilderment.

After breakfast, Captain Maitland got down to things.

I explained how I had woken up, heard a queer sound and had gone into Miss Johnson's room.

"You say there was a glass on the floor?"

"Yes. She must have dropped it after drinking."

"Was it broken?"

"No, it had fallen on the rug. (I'm afraid the acid's ruined the rug, by the way.) I picked the glass up and put it back on the table."

"I'm glad you've told us that. There are only two sets of fingerprints on it, and one set is certainly Miss Johnson's own. The other must be yours."

He was silent for a moment, then he said:

"Please go on."

I described carefully what I'd done and the methods I had tried, looking rather anxiously at Dr. Reilly for approval. He gave it with a nod.

"You tried everything that could possibly have done any good," he said. And though I was pretty sure I had done so, it was a relief to have my belief confirmed.

"Did you know exactly what she had taken?" Captain Maitland asked.

"No—but I could see, of course, that it was a corrosive acid."

Captain Maitland asked gravely:

"Is it your opinion, nurse, that Miss Johnson deliberately administered this stuff to herself?"

"Oh, no," I exclaimed. "I never thought of such a thing!"

I don't know why I was so sure. Partly, I think, because of M. Poirot's hints. His "murder is a habit" had impressed itself on my mind. And then one doesn't readily believe that any one's going to commit suicide in such a terribly painful way.

I said as much and Captain Maitland nodded thoughtfully.

"I agree that it isn't what one would choose," he said. "But if any one were in great distress of mind and this stuff were easily available it might be taken for that reason."

"*Was* she in great distress of mind?" I asked doubtfully.

"Mrs. Mercado says so. She says that Miss Johnson was quite unlike herself at dinner last night—that she hardly replied to anything that was said to her. Mrs. Mercado is quite sure that Miss Johnson was in terrible distress over something and that the idea of making away with herself had already occurred to her."

"Well, I don't believe it for a moment," I said bluntly.

Mrs. Mercado indeed! Nasty slinking little cat!

"Then what *do* you think?"

"I think she was murdered," I said bluntly.

He rapped out his next question sharply. I felt rather that I was in the orderly room.

"Any reasons?"

"It seems to me by far and away the most possible solution."

"That's just your private opinion. There was no reason why the lady should be murdered?"

"Excuse me," I said, "there was. She found out something."

"Found out something? What did she find out?"

I repeated our conversation on the roof word for word.

"She refused to tell you what her discovery was?"

"Yes. She said she must have time to think it over."

"But she was very excited by it?"

"Yes."

"*A way of getting in from outside.*" Captain Maitland puzzled over it, his brows knit. "Had you no idea at all of what she was driving at?"

"Not in the least. I puzzled and puzzled over it but I couldn't even get a glimmering."

Captain Maitland said:

"What do you think, M. Poirot?"

Poirot said:

"I think you have there a possible motive."

"For murder?"

"For murder."

Captain Maitland frowned.

"She wasn't able to speak before she died?"

"Yes, she just managed to get out two words."

"What were they?"

"The window . . ."

"The window?" repeated Captain Maitland. "Did you understand to what she was referring?"

I shook my head.

"How many windows were there in her bedroom?"

"Just the one."

"Giving on the courtyard?"

"Yes."

"Was it open or shut? Open, I seem to remember. But perhaps one of you opened it?"

"No, it was open all the time. I wondered—"

I stopped.

"Go on, nurse."

"I examined the window, of course, but I couldn't see anything unusual about it. I wondered whether, perhaps, somebody changed the glasses that way."

"Changed the glasses?"

"Yes. You see, Miss Johnson always takes a glass of water to bed with her. I think that glass must have been tampered with and a glass of acid put there in its place."

"What do you say, Reilly?"

"If it's murder, that was probably the way it was done," said Dr. Reilly promptly. "No ordinary moderately observant human being would drink a glass of acid in mistake for one of water—if they were in full possession of their waking faculties. But if any one's accustomed to drinking off a glass of water in the middle of the night, that person might easily stretch out an arm, find the glass in the accustomed place, and still half asleep, toss off enough of the stuff to be fatal before realizing what had happened."

Captain Maitland reflected a minute.

"I'll have to go back and look at that window. How far is it from the head of the bed?"

I thought.

"With a very long stretch you could just reach the little table that stands by the head of the bed."

"The table on which the glass of water was?"

"Yes."

"Was the door locked?"

"No."

"So whoever it was could have come in that way and made the substitution?"

"Oh, yes."

"There would be more risk that way," said Dr. Reilly. "A person who is sleeping quite soundly will often wake up at the sound of a footfall. If the table could be reached from the window it would be the safer way."

"I'm not only thinking of the glass," said Captain Maitland absent-mindedly.

Rousing himself, he addressed me once again.

"It's your opinion that when the poor lady felt she was dying she was anxious to let you know that somebody had substituted acid for water through the open window? Surely the person's *name* would have been more to the point?"

"She mayn't have known the name," I pointed out.

"Or it would have been more to the point if she'd managed to hint what it was that she had discovered the day before?"

Dr. Reilly said:

"When you're dying, Maitland, you haven't always got a sense of proportion. One particular fact very likely obsesses your mind. That a murderous hand had come through the window may have been the principal fact obsessing her at the minute. It may have seemed to her important that she should let people know that. In my opinion she wasn't far wrong either. It *was* important! She probably jumped to the fact that you'd think it was suicide. If she could have used her tongue freely, she'd probably have said 'It wasn't suicide. I didn't take it myself. Somebody else must have put it near my bed *through the window*.' "

Captain Maitland drummed with his fingers for a minute or two without replying. Then he said:

"There are certainly two ways of looking at it. It's either suicide or murder. Which do you think, Dr. Leidner?"

Dr. Leidner was silent for a minute or two, then he said quietly and decisively:

"Murder. Anne Johnson wasn't the sort of woman to kill herself."

"No," allowed Captain Maitland. "Not in the normal run of things. But there might be circumstances in which it would be quite a natural thing to do."

"Such as?"

Captain Maitland stooped to a bundle which I had previously noticed him place by the side of his chair. He swung it on to the table with something of an effort.

"There's something here that none of you know about," he said. "We found it under the bed."

He fumbled with the knot of the covering, then threw it back revealing a heavy great quern or grinder.

That was nothing in itself—there were a dozen or so already found in the course of the excavations.

What riveted our attention on this particular specimen was a dull, dark stain and a fragment of something that looked like hair.

"That'll be your job, Reilly," said Captain Maitland. "But I shouldn't say that there's much doubt about this being the instrument with which Mrs. Leidner was killed!"

Chapter 26

Next It Will Be Me!

It was rather horrible. Dr. Leidner looked as though he were going to faint and I felt a bit sick myself.

Dr. Reilly examined it with professional gusto.

"No fingerprints, I presume?" he threw out.

"No fingerprints."

Dr. Reilly took out a pair of forceps and investigated delicately.

"H'm—a fragment of human tissue—and hair—fair blonde hair. That's the unofficial verdict. Of course, I'll have to make a proper test, blood group, etc., but there's not much doubt. Found under Miss Johnson's bed? Well, well—so *that's* the big idea. She did the murder, and then, God rest her, remorse came to her and she finished herself off. It's a theory—a pretty theory."

Dr. Leidner could only shake his head helplessly.

"Not Anne—not Anne," he murmured.

"I don't know where she hid this to begin with," said Captain Maitland. "Every room was searched after the first crime."

Something jumped into my mind and I thought, "In the stationery cupboard," but I didn't say anything.

"Wherever it was, she became dissatisfied with its hiding-place and took it into her own room, which had been searched with all the rest. Or perhaps she did that after making up her mind to commit suicide."

"I don't believe it," I said aloud.

And I couldn't somehow believe that kind nice Miss Johnson had battered out Mrs. Leidner's brains. I just couldn't *see* it happening! And yet it *did* fit in with some things—her fit of weeping that night, for instance.

After all, I'd said "remorse" myself—only I'd never thought it was re-morse for anything but the smaller more insignificant crime.

"I don't know what to believe," said Captain Maitland. "There's the French Father's disappearance to be cleared up too. My men are out hunting around in case he's been knocked on the head and his body rolled into a convenient irrigation ditch."

"Oh! I remember now—" I began.

Every one looked towards me inquiringly.

"It was yesterday afternoon," I said. "He'd been cross-questioning me about the man with a squint who was looking in at the window that day. He asked me just where he'd stood on the path and then he said he was going out to have a look round. He said in detective stories the criminal always dropped a convenient clue."

"Damned if any of my criminals ever do," said Captain Maitland. "So that's what he was after, was it? By jove, I wonder if he *did* find any-thing. A bit of a coincidence if both he and Miss Johnson discovered a clue to the identity of the murderer at practically the same time."

He added irritably, "Man with a squint? Man with a squint? There's more in this tale of that fellow with a squint than meets the eye. I don't know why the devil my fellows can't lay hold of him?"

"Probably because he hasn't got a squint," said Poirot quietly.

"Do you mean he faked it? Didn't know you could fake an actual squint."

Poirot merely said:

"A squint can be a very useful thing."

"The devil it can! I'd give a lot to know where that fellow is now, squint or no squint!"

"At a guess," said Poirot, "he has already passed the Syrian frontier."

"We've warned Tell Kotchek and Abu Kemal—all the frontier posts, in fact."

"I should imagine that he took the route through the hills. The route lorries sometimes take when running contraband."

Captain Maitland grunted.

"Then we'd better telegraph Deir ez Zor?"

"I did so yesterday—warning them to look out for a car with two men in it whose passports will be in the most impeccable order."

Captain Maitland favoured him with a stare.

"*You* did, did you? Two men—eh?"

Poirot nodded.

"There are two men in this."

"It strikes me, M. Poirot, that you've been keeping quite a lot of things up your sleeve."

Poirot shook his head.

"No," he said. "Not really. The truth came to me only this morning when I was watching the sun rise. A very beautiful sunrise."

I don't think that any of us had noticed that Mrs. Mercado was in the room. She must have crept in when we were all taken aback by the production of that horrible great blood-stained stone.

But now, without the least warning, she set up a noise like a pig having its throat cut.

"Oh, my God!" she cried. "I see it all. I see it all now. *It was Father Lavigny*. He's mad—religious mania. He thinks women are sinful. *He's killing them all*. First Mrs. Leidner—then Miss Johnson. And next it will be *me*. . . ."

With a scream of frenzy she flung herself across the room and clutched at Dr. Reilly's coat.

"I won't stay here, I tell you! I won't stay here a day longer. There's danger. There's danger all round. He's hiding somewhere—waiting his time. He'll spring out on me!"

Her mouth opened and she began screaming again.

I hurried over to Dr. Reilly, who had caught her by the wrists. I gave her a sharp slap on each cheek and with Dr. Reilly's help, I sat her down in a chair.

"Nobody's going to kill you," I said. "We'll see to that. Sit down and behave yourself."

She didn't scream any more. Her mouth closed and she sat looking at me with startled, stupid eyes.

Then there was another interruption. The door opened and Sheila Reilly came in.

Her face was pale and serious. She came straight to Poirot.

"I was at the post office early, M. Poirot," she said, "and there was a telegram there for you—so I brought it along."

"Thank you, mademoiselle."

He took it from her and tore it open while she watched his face.

It did not change, that face. He read the telegram, smoothed it out, folded it up neatly and put it in his pocket.

Mrs. Mercado was watching him. She said in a choked voice:

"Is that—from America?"

He shook his head.

"No, madame," he said. "It is from Tunis."

She stared at him for a moment as though she did not understand, then with a long sigh, she leant back in her seat.

"Father Lavigny," she said. "I *was* right. I've always thought there was something queer about him. He said things to me once . . . I suppose he's mad. . . ." She paused and then said, "I'll be quiet. But I *must* leave this place. Joseph and I can go in and sleep at the Rest House."

"Patience, madame," said Poirot. "I will explain everything."

Captain Maitland was looking at him curiously.

"Do you consider you've definitely got the hang of this business?" he demanded.

Poirot bowed.

It was a most theatrical bow. I think it rather annoyed Captain Maitland.

"Well," he barked. "Out with it, man."

But that wasn't the way Hercule Poirot did things. I saw perfectly well that he meant to make a song and dance of it. I wondered if he really *did* know the truth, or if he was just showing off.

He turned to Dr. Reilly.

"Will you be so good, Dr. Reilly, as to summon the others?"

Dr. Reilly jumped up and went off obligingly. In a minute or two the other members of the expedition began to file into the room. First Reiter and Emmott. Then Bill Coleman. Then Richard Carey and finally Mr. Mercado.

Poor man, he really looked like death. I suppose he was mortally afraid that he'd get hauled over the coals for carelessness in leaving dangerous chemicals about.

Every one seated themselves round the table very much as we had done on the day M. Poirot arrived. Both Bill Coleman and David Emmott hesitated before they sat down, glancing towards Sheila Reilly. She had her back to them and was standing looking out of the window.

"Chair, Sheila?" said Bill.

David Emmott said in his low pleasant drawl, "Won't you sit down?"

She turned then and stood for a minute looking at them. Each was indicating a chair, pushing it forward. I wondered whose chair she would accept.

In the end she accepted neither.

"I'll sit here," she said brusquely. And she sat down on the edge of a table quite close to the window.

"That is," she added, "if Captain Maitland doesn't mind my staying?"

I'm not quite sure what Captain Maitland would have said. Poirot forestalled him.

"Stay by all means, mademoiselle," he said. "It is, indeed, necessary that you should."

She raised her eyebrows.

"Necessary?"

"That is the word I used, mademoiselle. There are some questions I shall have to ask you."

Again her eyebrows went up but she said nothing further. She turned her face to the window as though determined to ignore what went on in the room behind her.

"And now," said Captain Maitland, "perhaps we shall get at the truth!"

He spoke rather impatiently. He was essentially a man of action. At this very moment I feel sure that he was fretting to be out and doing things—directing the search for Father Lavigny's body, or alternatively sending out parties for his capture and arrest.

He looked at Poirot with something akin to dislike.

"If the beggar's got anything to say, why doesn't he say it?"

I could see the words on the tip of his tongue.

Poirot gave a slow appraising glance at us all, then rose to his feet.

I don't know what I expected him to say—something dramatic certainly. He was that kind of person.

But I certainly didn't expect him to start off with a phrase in Arabic.

Yet that is what happened. He said the words slowly and solemnly— and really quite religiously, if you know what I mean.

"Bismillahi ar rahman ar rahim."

And then he gave the translation in English.

"In the name of Allah, the Merciful, the Compassionate."

Chapter 27

Beginning of a Journey

"Bismillahi ar rahman ar rahim. That is the Arab phrase used before starting out on a journey. *Eh bien*, we too, start on a journey. A journey into the past. A journey into the strange places of the human soul."

I don't think that up till that moment I'd ever felt any of the so-called "glamour of the East." Frankly, what had struck me was the *mess* everywhere. But suddenly, with M. Poirot's words, a queer sort of vision seemed to grow up before my eyes. I thought of words like Samarkand and Ispahan—and of merchants with long beards—and kneeling camels—and staggering porters carrying great bales on their backs held by a rope round the forehead—and women with henna-stained hair and tattooed faces kneeling by the Tigris and washing clothes, and I heard their queer, wailing chants and the far-off groaning of the water-wheel. . . .

They were mostly things I'd seen and heard and thought nothing much of. But now, somehow they seemed *different*—like a piece of fusty old stuff you take into the light and suddenly see the rich colours of an old embroidery. . . .

Then I looked round the room we were sitting in and I got a queer feeling that what M. Poirot said was true—we *were* all starting on a journey. We were here together now, but we were all going our different ways.

And I looked at every one as though, in a sort of way, I were seeing them for the first time—*and* for the last time—which sounds stupid, but it was what I felt all the same.

Mr. Mercado was twisting his fingers nervously—his queer light eyes

with their dilated pupils were staring at Poirot. Mrs. Mercado was looking at her husband. She had a strange watchful look like a tigress waiting
to spring. Dr. Leidner seemed to have shrunk in some curious fashion.
This last blow had just crumpled him up. You might almost say he wasn't
in the room at all. He was somewhere far away in a place of his own. Mr.
Coleman was looking straight at Poirot. His mouth was slightly open and
his eyes protruded. He looked almost idiotic. Mr. Emmott was looking
down at his feet and I couldn't see his face properly. Mr. Reiter looked
bewildered. His mouth was pushed out in a pout and that made him look
more like a nice clean pig then ever. Miss Reilly was looking steadily out
of the window. I don't know what she was thinking or feeling. Then I
looked at Mr. Carey, and somehow his face hurt me and I looked away.
There we were, all of us. And somehow I felt that when M. Poirot had
finished we'd all be somewhere quite different. . . .

It was a queer feeling. . . .

Poirot's voice went quietly on. It was like a river running evenly between its banks . . . running to the sea. . . .

"From the very beginning, I have felt that to understand this case one
must seek not for external signs or clues, but for the trucr clues of the
clash of personalities and the secrets of the heart.

"And I may say that though I have now arrived at what I believe to be
the true solution of the case. *I have no material proof of it.* I *know* it is so,
because it *must* be so, because *in no other way* can every single fact fit
into its ordered and recognized place.

"And that, to my mind, is the most satisfying solution there can be."

He paused and then went on:

"I will start my journey at the moment when I myself was brought into
the case—when I had it presented to me as an accomplished happening.
Now, every case, in my opinion, has a definite *shape* and *form*. The pattern of this case, to my mind, all revolved round the personality of
Mrs. Leidner. Until I knew *exactly what kind of a woman Mrs. Leidner
was* I should not be able to know why she was murdered and who murdered her.

"That, then, was my starting point—the personality of Mrs. Leidner.

"There was also one other psychological point of interest—the curious
state of tension described as existing amongst the members of the expedition. This was attested to by several different witnesses—some of them
outsiders—and I made a note that although hardly a starting point, it
should nevertheless be borne in mind during my investigations.

"The accepted idea seemed to be that it was directly the result of Mrs.
Leidner's influence on the members of the expedition, but for reasons

which I will outline to you later this did not seem to me entirely accept-
able.

"To start with, as I say, I concentrated solely and entirely on the personality of Mrs. Leidner. I had various means of assessing that personality. There were the reactions she produced in a number of people, all
varying widely in character and temperament, and there was what I could
glean by my own observation. The scope of the latter was naturally limited. But I *did* learn certain facts.

"Mrs. Leidner's tastes were simple and even on the austere side. She
was clearly not a luxurious woman. On the other hand, some embroidery
she had been doing was of an extreme fineness and beauty. That indicated a woman of fastidious and artistic taste. From the observation of
the books in her bedroom I formed a further estimate. She had brains,
and I also fancied that she was, essentially, an egoist.

"It had been suggested to me that Mrs. Leidner was a woman whose
main preoccupation was to attract the opposite sex—that she was, in fact,
a sensual woman. This I did not believe to be the case.

"In her bedroom I noticed the following books on a shelf: *Who Were
the Greeks? Introduction to Relativity, Life of Lady Hester Stanhope,
Back to Methuselah, Linda Condon, Crewe Train.*

"She had, to begin with, an interest in culture and in modern science—
that is, a distinct intellectual side. Of the novels *Linda Condon*, and in a
lesser degree *Crewe Train*, seemed to show that Mrs. Leidner had a sympathy and interest in the independent woman—unencumbered or en-
trapped by man. She was also obviously interested by the personality of
Lady Hester Stanhope. *Linda Condon* is an exquisite study of the worship of her own beauty by a woman. *Crewe Train* is a study of a passion-
ate individualist. *Back to Methuselah* is in sympathy with the intellectual
rather than the emotional attitude to life. I felt that I was beginning to understand the dead woman.

"I next studied the reactions of those who had formed Mrs. Leidner's
immediate circle—and my picture of the dead woman grew more and
more complete.

"It was quite clear to me from the accounts of Dr. Reilly and others
that Mrs. Leidner was one of those women who are endowed by Nature
not only with beauty but with the kind of calamitous magic which sometimes accompanies beauty and can, indeed, exist independently of it.
Such women usually leave a trail of violent happenings behind them.
They bring disaster—sometimes on others—sometimes on themselves.

"I was convinced that Mrs. Leidner was a woman who essentially
worshipped *herself* and who enjoyed more than anything else the sense
of *power*. Wherever she was, she *must* be the centre of the universe. And

every one round her, man or woman, had got to acknowledge her sway. With some people that was easy. Nurse Leatheran, for instance, a generous-natured woman with a romantic imagination, was captured instantly and gave in ungrudging manner full appreciation. But there was a second way in which Mrs. Leidner exercised her sway—the way of fear. Where conquest was too easy she indulged a more cruel side to her nature—but I wish to reiterate emphatically that it was not what you might call *conscious* cruelty. It was as natural and unthinking as is the conduct of a cat with a mouse. Where consciousness came in, she was essentially kind and would often go out of her way to do kind and thoughtful actions for other people.

"Now of course the first and most important problem to solve was the problem of the anonymous letters. Who had written them and why? I asked myself: Had Mrs. Leidner written them *herself?*

"To answer this problem it was necessary to go back a long way—to go back, in fact, to the date of Mrs. Leidner's first marriage. It is here we start on our journey proper. The journey of Mrs. Leidner's life.

"First of all we must realize that the Louise Leidner of all those years ago is essentially the same Louise Leidner of the present time.

"She was young then, of remarkable beauty—that same haunting beauty that affects a man's spirit and senses as no mere material beauty can—and she was already essentially an egoist.

"Such women naturally revolt from the idea of marriage. They may be attracted by men, but they prefer to belong to themselves. They are truly *La Belle Dame sans Merci* of the legend. Nevertheless Mrs. Leidner *did* marry—and we can assume, I think, that her husband must have been a man of a certain force of character.

"Then the revelation of his traitorous activities occurs and Mrs. Leidner acts in the way she told Nurse Leatheran. She gave information to the Government.

"Now I submit that there was a psychological significance in her action. She told Nurse Leatheran that she was a very patriotic idealistic girl and that that feeling was the cause of her action. But it is a well-known fact that we all tend to deceive ourselves as to the motives for our own actions. Instinctively we select the best-sounding motive! Mrs. Leidner may have believed herself that it was patriotism that inspired her action, but I believe myself that it was really the outcome of an unacknowledged desire to get rid of her husband! She disliked domination—she disliked the feeling of belonging to some one else—in fact she disliked playing second fiddle. She took a patriotic way of regaining her freedom.

"But underneath her consciousness was a gnawing sense of guilt which was to play its part in her future destiny.

"We now come directly to the question of the letters. Mrs. Leidner was highly attractive to the male sex. On several occasions she was attracted by them—but in each case a threatening letter played its part and the affair came to nothing.

"Who wrote those letters? Frederick Bosner or his brother William or *Mrs. Leidner herself?*

"There is a perfectly good case for either theory. It seems clear to me that Mrs. Leidner was one of those women who do inspire devouring devotions in men, the type of devotion which can become an obsession. I find it quite possible to believe in a Frederick Bosner to whom Louise, his wife, mattered more than anything in the world! She had betrayed him once and he dared not approach her openly, but he was determined at least that she should be his or no one's. He preferred her death to her belonging to another man.

"On the other hand, if Mrs. Leidner had, deep down, a dislike of entering into the marriage bond, it is possible that she took this way of extricating herself from difficult positions. She was a huntress who, the prey once attained, had no further use for it! Craving drama in her life, she invented a highly satisfactory drama—a resurrected husband forbidding the banns! It satisfied her deepest instincts. It made her a romantic figure, a tragic heroine, and it enabled her not to marry again.

"This state of affairs continued over a number of years. Every time there was any likelihood of marriage—a threatening letter arrived.

"*But now we come to a really interesting point.* Dr. Leidner came upon the scene—and no forbidding letter arrived! Nothing stood in the way of her becoming Mrs. Leidner. Not until *after* her marriage did a letter arrive.

"At once we ask ourselves—why?

"Let us take each theory in turn.

"*If* Mrs. Leidner wrote the letters herself the problem is easily explained. Mrs. Leidner really *wanted* to marry Dr. Leidner. And so she *did* marry him. But in that case, *why did she write herself a letter afterwards?* Was her craving for drama too strong to be suppressed? And why only those two letters? After that no other letter was received until a year and a half later.

"Now take the other theory, that the letters were written by her first husband, Frederick Bosner (or his brother). Why did the threatening letter arrive *after* the marriage? Presumably Frederick could not have *wanted* her to marry Leidner. Why, then, did he not stop the marriage? He had done so successfully on former occasions. And why, *having waited till the marriage had taken place*, did he then resume his threats?

"The answer, an unsatisfactory one, is that he was somehow or other unable to protest sooner. He may have been in prison or he may have been abroad.

"There is next the attempted gas poisoning to consider. It seems extremely unlikely that it was brought about by an outside agency. The likely persons to have staged it were Dr. and Mrs. Leidner themselves. There seems no conceivable reason why *Dr.* Leidner should do such a thing, so we are brought to the conclusion that *Mrs.* Leidner planned and carried it out herself.

"Why? More drama?

"After that Dr. and Mrs. Leidner go abroad and for eighteen months they lead a happy, peaceful life with no threats of death to disturb it. They put that down to having successfully covered their traces, but such an explanation is quite absurd. In these days going abroad is quite inadequate for that purpose. And especially was that so in the case of the Leidners. He was the director of a museum expedition. By inquiry at the museum, Frederick Bosner could at once have obtained his correct address. Even granting that he was in too reduced circumstances to pursue the couple himself, there would be no bar to his continuing his threatening letters. And it seems to me that a man with his obsession would certainly have done so.

"Instead nothing is heard of him until nearly two years later when the letters are resumed.

"*Why* were the letters resumed?

"A very difficult question—most easily answered by saying that Mrs. Leidner was bored and wanted more drama. But I was not quite satisfied with that. This particular form of drama seemed to me a shade too vulgar and too crude to accord well with her fastidious personality.

"The only thing to do was to keep an open mind on the question.

"There were three definite possibilities: (1) the letters were written by Mrs. Leidner herself; (2) they were written by Frederick Bosner (or young William Bosner); (3) they might have been written *originally* by either Mrs. Leidner or her first husband, but they were now *forgeries*—that is, they were being written by a *third* person who was aware of the earlier letters.

"I now come to direct consideration of Mrs. Leidner's entourage.

"I examined first the actual opportunities that each member of the staff had had for committing the murder.

"Roughly, on the face of it, *any one* might have committed it (as far as opportunity went), with the exception of three persons.

"Dr. Leidner, by overwhelming testimony, had never left the roof. Mr. Carey was on duty at the mound. Mr. Coleman was in Hassanieh.

"But those alibis, my friends, were not *quite* as good as they looked. I except Dr. Leidner's. There is absolutely no doubt that he was on the roof all the time and did not come down until quite an hour and a quarter after the murder had happened.

"But was it *quite* certain that Mr. Carey was on the mound all the time?

"And had Mr. Coleman *actually been in Hassanieh* at the time the murder took place?"

Bill Coleman reddened, opened his mouth, shut it and looked round uneasily.

Mr. Carey's expression did not change.

Poirot went on smoothly.

"I also considered one other person who, I satisfied myself, would be perfectly capable of committing murder *if she felt strongly enough*. Miss Reilly has courage and brains and a certain quality of ruthlessness. When Miss Reilly was speaking to me on the subject of the dead woman, I said to her, jokingly, that I hoped she had an alibi. I think Miss Reilly was conscious then that she had had in her heart the desire, at least, to kill. At any rate she immediately uttered a very silly and purposeless lie. She said she had been playing tennis on that afternoon. The next day I learned from a casual conversation with Miss Johnson that far from playing tennis, Miss Reilly *had actually been near this house at the time of the murder*. It occurred to me that Miss Reilly, if not guilty of the crime, might be able to tell me something useful."

He stopped and then said quietly:

"Will you tell us, Miss Reilly, what you *did* see that afternoon?"

The girl did not answer at once. She still looked out of the window without turning her head, and when she spoke it was in a detached and measured voice.

"I rode out to the dig after lunch. It must have been about a quarter to two when I got there."

"Did you find any of your friends on the dig?"

"No, there seemed to be no one there but the Arab foreman."

"You did not see Mr. Carey?"

"No."

"Curious," said Poirot. "No more did M. Verrier when he went there that same afternoon."

He looked invitingly at Carey, but the latter neither moved nor spoke.

"Have you any explanation, Mr. Carey?"

"I went for a walk. There was nothing of interest turning up."

"In which direction did you go for a walk?"

"Down by the river."

"Not back towards the house?"

"No."

"I suppose," said Miss Reilly, "that you were waiting for some one who didn't come."

He looked at her but didn't answer.

Poirot did not press the point. He spoke once more to the girl.

"Did you see anything else, mademoiselle?"

"Yes. I was not far from the expedition house when I noticed the expedition lorry drawn up in a wadi. I thought it was rather queer. Then I saw Mr. Coleman. He was walking along with his head down as though he were searching for something."

"Look here," burst out Mr. Coleman. "I—"

Poirot stopped him with an authoritative gesture.

"Wait. Did you speak to him, Miss Reilly?"

"No, I didn't."

"Why?"

The girl said slowly:

"Because, from time to time, he started and looked round with an extraordinary furtive look. It—gave me an unpleasant feeling. I turned my horse's head and rode away. I don't think he saw me. I was not very near and he was absorbed in what he was doing."

"Look here," Mr. Coleman was not to be hushed any longer. "I've got a perfectly good explanation for what—I admit—looks a bit fishy. As a matter of fact, the day before I had slipped a jolly fine cylinder seal into my coat pocket instead of putting it in the antika-room—forgot all about it. And then I discovered I'd been and lost it out of my pocket—dropped it somewhere. I didn't want to get into a row about it so I decided I'd have a jolly good search on the quiet. I was pretty sure I'd dropped it on the way to or from the dig. I rushed over my business in Hassanieh. Sent a walad to do some of the shopping and got back early. I stuck the bus where it wouldn't show and had a jolly good hunt for over an hour. And didn't find the damn thing at that! Then I got into the bus and drove on to the house. Naturally, everyone thought I'd just got back."

"And you did not undeceive them?" asked Poirot sweetly.

"Well, that was pretty natural under the circumstances, don't you think?"

"I hardly agree," said Poirot.

"Oh, come now—don't go looking for trouble—that's *my motto!* But you can't fasten anything on me. I never went into the courtyard, and you can't find any one who'll say I did."

"That, of course, has been the difficulty," said Poirot. "The evidence of the servants that *no one entered the courtyard from outside.* But it occurred to me, upon reflection, that that was really *not* what they had said.

They had sworn that *no stranger* had entered the premises. They had not been asked *if a member of the expedition* had done so."

"Well, you ask them," said Coleman. "I'll eat my hat if they saw me or Carey either."

"Ah! but that raises rather an interesting question. They would notice *a stranger* undoubtedly—but would they have even *noticed* a member of the expedition? The members of the staff are passing in and out all day. The servants would hardly notice their going and coming. It is possible, I think, that either Mr. Carey or Mr. Coleman *might* have entered and the servants' minds would have no remembrance of such an event."

"Bunkum!" said Mr. Coleman.

Poirot went on calmly:

"Of the two, I think Mr. Carey was the least likely to be noticed going or coming. Mr. Coleman had started to Hassanieh in the car that morning and he would be expected to return in it. His arrival on foot would there-fore be noticeable."

"Of course it would!" said Coleman.

Richard Carey raised his head. His deep-blue eyes looked straight at Poirot.

"Are you accusing me of murder, M. Poirot?" he asked.

His manner was quite quiet but his voice had a dangerous undertone.

Poirot bowed to him.

"As yet I am only taking you all on a journey—my journey towards the truth. I had now established one fact—that all the members of the ex-pedition staff, and also Nurse Leatheran, could in actual *fact* have com-mitted the murder. That there was very little likelihood of some of them having committed it was a secondary matter.

"I had examined *means* and *opportunity*. I next passed to *motive*. I dis-covered that *one and all of you could be credited with a motive!*"

"Oh! M. Poirot," I cried. "Not *me!* Why, I was a stranger. I'd only just come."

"*Eh bien, ma sœur*, and was not that *just what Mrs. Leidner had been fearing? A stranger* from *outside?*"

"But—but—Why, Dr. Reilly knew all about me! He suggested my coming!"

"How much did he really know about you? *Mostly what you yourself had told him.* Impostors have passed themselves off as hospital nurses before now."

"You can write to St. Christopher's," I began.

"For the moment will you silence yourself. Impossible to proceed while you conduct this argument. I do not say I suspect you *now*. All I say is that, keeping the open mind, you might quite easily be some one other than you pretended to be. There are many successful female impersonators, you know. Young William Bosner might be something of that kind."

I was about to give him a further piece of my mind. Female impersonator indeed! But he raised his voice and hurried on with such an air of determination that I thought better of it.

"I am going now to be frank—brutally so. It is necessary. I am going to lay bare the underlying structure of this place.

"I examined and considered every single soul here. To begin with Dr. Leidner, I soon convinced myself that his love for his wife was the mainspring of his existence. He was a man torn and ravaged with grief. Nurse Leatheran I have already mentioned. If she were a female impersonator she was a most amazingly successful one, and I inclined to the belief that she was exactly what she said she was—a thoroughly competent hospital nurse."

"Thank you for nothing," I interposed.

"My attention was immediately attracted towards Mr. and Mrs. Mercado, who were both of them clearly in a state of great agitation and unrest. I considered first Mrs. Mercado. Was she capable of murder and if so for what reasons?

"Mrs. Mercado's physique was frail. At first sight it did not seem possible that she could have had the physical strength to strike down a woman like Mrs. Leidner with a heavy stone implement. If, however, Mrs. Leidner had been on her knees at the time, the thing would at least be *physically possible*. There are ways in which one woman can induce another to go down on her knees. Oh! not emotional ways! For instance, a woman might be turning up the hem of a skirt and ask another woman to put in the pins for her. The second woman would kneel on the ground quite unsuspectingly.

"But the motive? Nurse Leatheran had told me of the angry glances she had seen Mrs. Mercado direct at Mrs. Leidner. Mr. Mercado had evidently succumbed easily to Mrs. Leidner's spell. But I did not think the solution was to be found in mere jealousy. I was sure Mrs. Leidner was not in the least interested really in Mr. Mercado—and doubtless Mrs. Mercado was aware of the fact. She might be furious with her for the moment, but for *murder* there would have to be greater provocation. But Mrs. Mercado was essentially a fiercely maternal type. From the way she looked at her husband I realized, not only that she loved him, but that she would fight for him tooth and nail—and more than that—*that she envisaged the possibility of having to do so*. She was constantly on her guard and uneasy. The uneasiness was for him—not for herself. And when I studied Mr. Mercado I could make a fairly easy guess at what the trouble was. I took means to assure myself of the truth of my guess. Mr. Mercado was a drug addict—in an advanced stage of the craving.

"Now I need probably not tell you all that the taking of drugs over a long period has the result of considerably blunting the moral sense.

"Under the influence of drugs a man commits actions that he would not have dreamed of committing a few years earlier before he began the practice. In some cases a man has committed murder—and it has been difficult to say whether he was wholly responsible for his actions or not. The law of different countries varies slightly on that point. The chief characteristic of the drug-fiend criminal is overweening confidence in his own cleverness.

"I thought it possible that there was some discreditable incident, perhaps a criminal incident, in Mr. Mercado's past which his wife had somehow or other succeeded in hushing up. Nevertheless his career hung on a thread. If anything of this past incident were bruited about, Mr. Mercado would be ruined. His wife was always on the watch. But there was Mrs. Leidner to be reckoned with. She had a sharp intelligence and a love of power. She might even induce the wretched man to confide in her. It would just have suited her peculiar temperament to feel she knew a secret which she could reveal at any minute with disastrous effects.

"Here, then, was a possible motive for murder on the part of the Mercados. To protect her mate, Mrs. Mercado, I felt sure, would stick at nothing! Both she and her husband had had the opportunity—during that ten minutes when the courtyard was empty."

Mrs. Mercado cried out, "It's not *true!*"

Poirot paid no attention.

"I next considered Miss Johnson. Was *she* capable of murder?

"I thought she was. She was a person of strong will and iron self-control. Such people are constantly repressing themselves—and one day the dam bursts! But if Miss Johnson had committed the crime it could only be for some reason connected with Dr. Leidner. If in any way she felt convinced that Mrs. Leidner was spoiling her husband's life, then the deep unacknowledged jealousy far down in her would leap at the chance of a plausible motive and give itself rein.

"Yes, Miss Johnson was distinctly a possibility.

"Then there were the three young men.

"First Carl Reiter. If, by any chance, one of the expedition staff was William Bosner, then Reiter was by far the most likely person. But if he *was* William Bosner, then he was certainly a most accomplished actor! If he were merely *himself*, had he any reason for murder?

"Regarded from Mrs. Leidner's point of view, Carl Reiter was far too easy a victim for good sport. He was prepared to fall on his face and wor-

ship immediately. Mrs. Leidner despised undiscriminating adoration—
and the door-mat attitude nearly always brings out the worst side of a
woman. In her treatment of Carl Reiter Mrs. Leidner displayed really deliberate cruelty. She inserted a gibe here—a prick there. She made the
poor young man's life a hell to him."

Poirot broke off suddenly and addressed the young man in a personal,
highly confidential manner.

"*Mon ami*, let this be a lesson to you. You are a *man*. Behave, then,
like a *man!* It is against Nature for a man to grovel. Women and Nature
have almost exactly the same reactions! Remember it is better to take the
largest plate within reach and fling it at a woman's head than it is to wrig-
gle like a worm whenever she looks at you!"

He dropped his private manner and reverted to his lecture style.

"Could Carl Reiter have been goaded to such a pitch of torment that
he turned on his tormentor and killed her? Suffering does queer things to
a man. I could not be *sure* that it was *not so!*

"Next, William Coleman. His behaviour, as reported by Miss Reilly, is
certainly suspicious. If he was the criminal it could only be because his
cheerful personality concealed the hidden one of William Bosner. I do
not think William Coleman, as William Coleman, has the temperament
of a murderer. His faults might lie in another direction. Ah! perhaps
Nurse Leatheran can guess what they would be?"

How *did* the man do it? I'm sure I didn't look as though I was thinking
anything at all.

"It's nothing really," I said, hesitating. "Only if it's to be all truth, Mr.
Coleman *did* say once himself that he would have made a good forger."

"A good point," said Poirot. "Therefore if he had come across some of
the old threatening letters, he could have copied them without difficulty."

"Oy, oy, oy!" called out Mr. Coleman. "This is what they call a frame-up."

Poirot swept on.

"As to his being or not being William Bosner such a matter is difficult
of verification. But Mr. Coleman has spoken of a *guardian*—not of a
father—and there is nothing definitely to veto the idea."

"Tommyrot," said Mr. Coleman. "Why all of you listen to this chap
beats me."

"Of the three young men there remains Mr. Emmott," went on Poirot.
"He again might be a possible shield for the identity of William Bosner.
Whatever *personal* reasons he might have for the removal of Mrs. Leidner I soon realized that I should have no means of learning them from
him. He could keep his own counsel remarkably well, and there was not
the least chance of provoking him nor of tricking him into betraying himself on any point. Of all the expedition he seemed to be the best and most

dispassionate judge of Mrs. Leidner's personality. I think that he always knew her for exactly what she was—but what impression her personality made on him I was unable to discover. I fancy that Mrs. Leidner herself must have been provoked and angered by his attitude.

"I may say that of all the expedition, *as far as character and capability were concerned*, Mr. Emmott seemed to me the most fitted to bring a clever and well-timed crime off satisfactorily."

For the first time Mr. Emmott raised his eyes from the toes of his boots.

"Thank you," he said.

There seemed to be just a trace of amusement in his voice.

"The last two people on my list were Richard Carey and Father Lavigny.

"According to the testimony of Nurse Leatheran and others, Mr. Carey and Mrs. Leidner disliked each other. They were both civil with an effort. Another person, Miss Reilly, propounded a totally different theory to account for their attitude of frigid politeness.

"I soon had very little doubt that Miss Reilly's explanation was the correct one. I acquired my certitude by the simple expedient of provoking Mr. Carey into reckless and unguarded speech. It was not difficult. As I soon saw, he was in a state of high nervous tension. In fact he was—and is—very near a complete nervous breakdown. A man who is suffering up to the limit of his capacity can seldom put up much of a fight.

"Mr. Carey's barriers came down almost immediately. He told me, with a sincerity that I did not for a moment doubt, that he hated Mrs. Leidner.

"And he was undoubtedly speaking the truth. He *did* hate Mrs. Leidner. But *why* did he hate her?

"I have spoken of women who have calamitous magic. But men have that magic too. There are men who are able without the least effort to attract women. What they call in these days *le sex appeal!* Mr. Carey had this quality very strongly. He was to begin with devoted to his friend and employer, and indifferent to his employer's wife. That did not suit Mrs. Leidner. She *must* dominate—and she set herself out to capture Richard Carey. But here, I believe, something entirely unforeseen took place. She herself, for perhaps the first time in her life, fell a victim to an overmastering passion. She fell in love—really in love—with Richard Carey.

"And he—was unable to resist her. Here is the truth of the terrible state of nervous tension that he has been enduring. He has been a man torn by two opposing passions. He loved Louise Leidner—yes, but he also hated her. He hated her for undermining his loyalty to his friend.

There is no hatred so great as that of a man who has been made to love a woman against his will.

"I had here all the motive that I needed. I was convinced that *at certain moments* the most natural thing for Richard Carey to do would have been to strike with all the force of his arm at the beautiful face that had cast a spell over him.

"All along I had felt sure that the murder of Louise Leidner was a *crime passionnel*. In Mr. Carey I had found an ideal murderer for that type of crime.

"There remains one other candidate for the title of murderer—Father Lavigny. My attention was attracted to the good Father straightaway by a certain discrepancy between his description of the strange man who had been seen peering in at the window and the one given by Nurse Leatheran. In all accounts given by different witnesses there is usually *some* discrepancy, but this was absolutely glaring. Moreover, Father Lavigny insisted on a certain characteristic—a squint—which ought to make identification much easier.

"But very soon it became apparent that *while Nurse Leatheran's description was substantially accurate*, Father Lavigny's was *nothing of the kind*. It looked almost as though Father Lavigny was deliberately misleading us—as though he did *not want the man caught*.

"But in that case *he must know something about this curious person*. He had been seen talking to the man but we had only his word for what they had been talking about.

"What had the Iraqi been doing when Nurse Leatheran and Mrs. Leidner saw him? Trying to peer through the window—Mrs. Leidner's window, so they thought, but I realized when I went and stood where they had been, that it might equally have been *the antika-room window*.

"The night after that an alarm was given. Some one was in the antika-room. Nothing proved to have been taken, however. The interesting point to me is that when Dr. Leidner got there he found *Father Lavigny there before him*. Father Lavigny tells his story of seeing a light. *But again we have only his word for it*.

"I begin to get curious about Father Lavigny. The other day when I make the suggestion that Father Lavigny may be Frederick Bosner Dr. Leidner pooh-poohs the suggestion. He says Father Lavigny is a well-known man. I advance the supposition that Frederick Bosner, who has had nearly twenty years to make a career for himself, under a new name, may very possibly *be* a well-known man by this time! All the same, I do not think that he has spent the intervening time in a religious community. A very much simpler solution presents itself.

"Did any one at the expedition know Father Lavigny by sight before

he came? Apparently not. Why then should not it be *some one impersonating the good Father?* I found out that a telegram had been sent to
Carthage on the sudden illness of Dr. Byrd, who was to have accompanied the expedition. To intercept a telegram, what could be easier? As to
the work, there was no other epigraphist attached to the expedition. With
a smattering of knowledge a clever man *might* bluff his way through.
There had been very few tablets and inscriptions so far, and already I
gathered that Father Lavigny's pronouncements had been felt to be
somewhat unusual.

"It looked very much as though Father Lavigny were an *impostor*.

"But was he Frederick Bosner?

"Somehow affairs did not seem to be shaping themselves that way.
The truth seemed likely to lie in quite a different direction.

"I had a lengthy conversation with Father Lavigny. I am a practising
Catholic and I know many priests and members of religious communities. Father Lavigny struck me as not ringing quite true to his rôle. But he
struck me, on the other hand, as familiar in quite a different capacity. I
had met men of his type quite frequently—but they were not members of
a religious community. Far from it!

"I began to send off telegrams.

"And then, unwittingly, Nurse Leatheran gave me a valuable clue. We
were examining the gold ornaments in the antika-room and she mentioned a trace of wax having been found adhering to a gold cup. Me, I
say, 'Wax?' and Father Lavigny, he said 'Wax?' and his tone was enough!
I knew in a flash what he was doing here."

Poirot paused and addressed himself directly to Dr. Leidner.

"I regret to tell you, monsieur, that the gold cup in the antika-room,
the gold dagger, the hair ornaments and several other things *are not the
genuine articles found by you.* They are very clever electrotypes. Father
Lavigny, I have just learned by this last answer to my telegrams, is none
other than Raoul Menier, one of the cleverest thieves known to the
French police. He specializes in thefts from museums of *objets d'art* and
such like. Associated with him is Ali Yusuf, a semi-Turk, who is a first-
class working jeweller. Our first knowledge of Menier was when certain
objects in the Louvre were found not to be genuine—in every case it was
discovered that a distinguished archæologist *not known previously by
sight to the director* had recently had the handling of the spurious articles
when paying a visit to the Louvre. On inquiry all these distinguished
gentlemen denied having paid a visit to the Louvre at the times stated!

"I have learned that Menier was in Tunis preparing the way for a theft
from the Holy Fathers when your telegram arrived. Father Lavigny, who
was in ill-health, was forced to refuse, but Menier managed to get hold of

the telegram and substitute one of acceptance. He was quite safe in doing so. Even if the monks should read in some paper (in itself an unlikely thing) that Father Lavigny was in Iraq they would only think that the newspapers had got hold of a half truth as so often happens.

"Menier and his accomplice arrived. The latter is seen when he is re-connoitering the antika-room from outside. The plan is for Father Lavi-gny to take wax impressions. Ali then makes clever duplicates. There are always certain collectors who are willing to pay a good price for genuine antiques and will ask no embarrassing questions. Father Lavigny will ef-fect the substitution of the fake for the genuine article—preferably at night.

"And that is doubtless what he was doing when Mrs. Leidner heard him and gave the alarm. What can he do? He hurriedly makes up a story of having seen a light in the antika-room.

"That 'went down,' as you say, very well. But Mrs. Leidner was no fool. She may have remembered the trace of wax she had noticed and then put two and two together. And if she did, what will she do then? Would it not be *dans son caractère* to do nothing at once, but to enjoy herself by letting hints slip to the discomfiture of Father Lavigny. She will let him see that she suspects—but not that she *knows*. It is, perhaps, a dangerous game, but she enjoys a dangerous game.

"And perhaps she plays that game too long. Father Lavigny sees the truth, and strikes before she realizes what he means to do.

"Father Lavigny is Raoul Menier—a thief. Is he also—a *murderer?*"

Poirot paced the room. He took out a handkerchief, wiped his fore-head and went on:

"That was my position this morning. There were eight distinct possi-bilities and I did not know which of these possibilities was the right one. I still did not know *who was the murderer*.

"But murder is a habit. The man or woman who kills once will kill again.

"And by the second murder, the murderer was delivered into my hands.

"All along it was ever present in the back of my mind that some one of these people might have knowledge that they had kept back—knowledge incriminating the murderer.

"If so, that person would be in danger.

"My solicitude was mainly on account of Nurse Leatheran. She had an energetic personality and a brisk inquisitive mind. I was terrified of her finding out more than it was safe for her to know.

"As you all know, a second murder did take place. But the victim was not Nurse Leatheran—it was Miss Johnson.

"I like to think that I should have reached the correct solution anyway by pure reasoning, but it is certain that Miss Johnson's murder helped me to it much quicker.

"To begin with, one suspect was eliminated—Miss Johnson herself—for I did not for a moment entertain the theory of suicide.

"Let us examine now the facts of this second murder.

"Fact one: On Sunday evening Nurse Leatheran finds Miss Johnson in tears, and that same evening Miss Johnson burns a fragment of a letter which nurse believes to be in the same handwriting as that of the anonymous letters.

"Fact two: The evening before her death Miss Johnson is found by Nurse Leatheran standing on the roof in a state that Nurse describes as one of incredulous horror. When nurse questions her she says, 'I've seen how some one could come in from outside—and no one would ever guess.' She won't say any more. Father Lavigny is crossing the courtyard and Mr. Reiter is at the door of the photographic room.

"Fact three: Miss Johnson is found dying. The only words she can manage to articulate are 'the window—the window—'

"Those are the facts, and these are the problems with which we are faced:

"What is the truth of the letters?

"What did Miss Johnson see from the roof?

"What did she mean by 'the window—the window'?

"*Eh bien*, let us take the second problem first as the easiest of solution. I went up with Nurse Leatheran and I stood where Miss Johnson had stood. From there she could see the courtyard and the archway and the north side of the building and two members of the staff. Had her words anything to do with either Mr. Reiter or Father Lavigny?

"Almost at once a possible explanation leaped to my brain. If a stranger came in from *outside* he could only do so in *disguise*. And there was only *one* person whose general appearance lent itself to such an impersonation. Father Lavigny! With a sun helmet, sun glasses, black beard and a monk's long woollen robe, a stranger could pass in without the servants *realizing* that a stranger had entered.

"Was *that* Miss Johnson's meaning? Or had she gone further? Did she realize that Father Lavigny's whole *personality* was a disguise. That he was some one other than he pretended to be?

"Knowing what I did know about Father Lavigny I was inclined to call the mystery solved. Raoul Menier was the murderer. He had killed Mrs. Leidner to silence her before she could give him away. Now *another person lets him see that she has penetrated his secret*. She, too, must be removed.

"And so everything is explained! The second murder. Father Lavigny's flight—minus robe and beard. (He and his friend are doubtless careering through Syria with excellent passports as two commercial travellers.) His action in placing the blood-stained quern under Miss Johnson's bed.

"As I say, I was almost satisfied—but not quite. For the perfect solution must explain *everything*—and this does not do so.

"It does not explain, for instance, why Miss Johnson should say 'the window—the window,' as she was dying. It does not explain her fit of weeping over the letter. It does not explain her mental attitude on the roof—her incredulous horror and her refusal to tell Nurse Leatheran what it was that *she now suspected or knew*.

"It was a solution that fitted the *outer* facts, but it did not satisfy the *psychological* requirements.

"And then, as I stood on the roof, going over in my mind those three points: the letters, the roof, the window, I *saw*—just as Miss Johnson had seen!

"And this time what I saw explained everything!"

Chapter 28

Journey's End

Poirot looked round. Every eye was now fixed upon him. There had been a certain relaxation—a slackening of tension. Now the tension suddenly returned.

There was something coming . . . something . . .

Poirot's voice, quiet and unimpassioned, went on:

"The letters, the roof, 'the window' . . . Yes, everything was explained—everything fell into place.

"I said just now that three men had alibis for the time of the crime. Two of those alibis I have shown to be worthless. I saw now my great—my amazing mistake. The third alibi was worthless too. Not only *could* Dr. Leidner have committed the murder—but I was convinced that he *had* committed it."

There was a silence, a bewildered uncomprehending silence. Dr. Leidner said nothing. He seemed lost in his faraway world still. David Emmott, however, stirred uneasily and spoke.

"I don't know what you mean to imply, M. Poirot. I told you that Dr. Leidner never left the roof until at least a quarter to three. That is the absolute truth. I swear it solemnly. I am not lying. And it would have been quite impossible for him to have done so without my seeing him."

Poirot nodded.

"Oh, I believe you. *Dr. Leidner did not leave the roof.* That is an undisputed fact. But what I saw—and what Miss Johnson had seen—was that *Dr. Leidner could murder his wife from the roof without leaving it.*"

We all stared.

"The *window*," cried Poirot. "Her window! That is what I realized—

just as Miss Johnson realized it. Her window was directly underneath, on the side away from the courtyard. And Dr. Leidner was alone up there with no one to witness his actions. And those heavy stone querns and grinders were up there all ready to his hand. So simple, so very simple, granted one thing—*that the murderer had the opportunity to move the body before any one else saw it.* . . . Oh, it is beautiful—of an unbelievable simplicity!

"Listen—it went like this:

"Dr. Leidner is on the roof working with the pottery. He calls you up, Mr. Emmott, and while he holds you in talk he notices that, as usually happens, the small boy takes advantage of your absence to leave his work and go outside the courtyard. He keeps you with him ten minutes, then he lets you go and as soon as you are down below shouting to the boy he sets his plan in operation.

"He takes from his pocket the plasticine-smeared mask with which he has already scared his wife on a former occasion and dangles it over the edge of the parapet till it taps on his wife's window.

"That, remember, is the window giving on the countryside facing the opposite direction to the courtyard.

"Mrs. Leidner is lying on her bed half asleep. She is peaceful and happy. Suddenly the mask begins tapping on the window and attracts her attention. But it is not dusk now—it is broad daylight—there is nothing terrifying about it. She recognizes it for what it is—a crude form of trickery! She is not frightened but indignant. She does what any other woman would do in her place. Jumps off the bed, opens the window, passes her head through the bars and turns her face upwards to see who is playing the trick on her.

"Dr. Leidner is waiting. He has in his hands, poised and ready, a heavy quern. At the psychological moment *he drops it.* . . .

"With a faint cry (heard by Miss Johnson) Mrs. Leidner collapses on the rug underneath the window.

"Now there is a hole in this quern, and through that Dr. Leidner had previously passed a cord. He has now only to haul in the cord and bring up the quern. He replaces the latter neatly, blood-stained side down, amongst the other objects of that kind on the roof.

"Then he continues his work for an hour or more till he judges the moment has come for the second act. He descends the stairs, speaks to Mr. Emmott and Nurse Leatheran, crosses the courtyard and enters his wife's room. This is the explanation he himself gives of his movements there.

" *'I saw my wife's body in a heap by the bed. For a moment or two I felt paralyzed as though I couldn't move. Then at last I went and knelt down by her and lifted up her head. I saw she was dead. . . . At last I got* up. I felt dazed and as though I were drunk. I managed to get to the door and call out.'

"A perfectly possible account of the actions of a grief-dazed man. Now listen to what I believe to be the truth. Dr. Leidner enters the room, hurries to the window, and having pulled on a pair of gloves, closes and fastens it, then picks up his wife's body and transports it to a position between the bed and the door. Then he notices a slight stain on the window-side rug. He cannot change it with the other rug, they are a different size, but he does the next best thing. He puts the stained rug in front of the wash-stand and the rug from the wash-stand under the window. *If* the stain is noticed, it will be connected with the *wash-stand—not with the window*—a very important point. There must be no suggestion that the window played any part in the business. Then he comes to the door and acts the part of the overcome husband, and that, I imagine, is not difficult. For he *did* love his wife."

"My good man," cried Dr. Reilly impatiently, "if he loved her, why did he kill her? Where's the motive? Can't you speak, Leidner? Tell him he's mad."

Dr. Leidner neither spoke nor moved.

Poirot said:

"Did I not tell you all along that this was a *crime passionnel*? Why did her first husband, Frederick Bosner, threaten to kill her? Because he loved her. . . . And in the end, you see, he made his boast good. . . .

"Mais oui—mais oui—once I realized that it is Dr. Leidner who did the killing everything falls into place. . . .

"For the second time I recommence my journey from the beginning— Mrs. Leidner's first marriage—the threatening letters—her second marriage. The letters prevented her marrying any other man—but they did not prevent her marrying Dr. Leidner. How simple that is—*if Dr. Leidner is actually Frederick Bosner.*

"Once more let us start our journey—from the point of view this time of young Frederick Bosner.

"To begin with he loves his wife Louise with an overpowering passion, such as only a woman of her kind can evoke. She betrays him. He is sentenced to death. He escapes. He is involved in a railway accident but he manages to emerge with a second personality—*that of a young Swedish archæologist, Eric Leidner*, whose body is badly disfigured and who will be conveniently buried as Frederick Bosner.

"What is the new Eric Leidner's attitude to the woman who was willing to send him to his death? First and most important, *he still loves her*. He sets to work to build up his new life. He is a man of great ability, his profession is congenial to him and he makes a success of it. *But he never forgets the ruling passion of his life.* He keeps himself informed of his wife's movements. Of one thing he is cold-bloodedly determined (remember Mrs. Leidner's own description of him to Nurse Leatheran— gentle and kind but ruthless), *she shall belong to no other man.* Whenever he judges it necessary he despatches a letter. He imitates some of the peculiarities of her handwriting in case she should think of taking his letters to the police. Women who write sensational anonymous letters to themselves are such a common phenomenon that the police will be sure to jump to that solution given the likeness of the handwriting. At the same time he leaves her in doubt as to whether he is really alive or not.

"At last, after many years, he judges that the time has arrived; he re-enters her life. All goes well. His wife never dreams of his real identity. He is a well-known man. The upstanding, good-looking young fellow is now a middle-aged man with a beard and stooping shoulders. And so we see history repeating itself. As before, Frederick is able to dominate Louise. For the second time she consents to marry him. *And no letter comes to forbid the banns.*

"But *afterwards* a letter *does* come. Why?

"I think that Dr. Leidner was taking no chances. The intimacy of marriage *might* awaken a memory. He wishes to impress on his wife, once and for all, *that Eric Leidner and Frederick Bosner are two* different people. So much so that a threatening letter comes from the former on account of the latter. The rather puerile gas poisoning business follows— arranged by Dr. Leidner, of course. Still with the same object in view.

"After that he is satisfied. No more letters need come. They can settle down to happy married life together.

"And then, after nearly two years, *the letters recommence.*

"*Why? Eh bien*, I think I know. *Because the threat underlying the letters was always a genuine threat.* (That is why Mrs. Leidner has always been frightened. She *knew* her Frederick's gentle but ruthless nature.) *If she belongs to any other man but him he would kill her. And she has given herself to Richard Carey.*

"And so, having discovered this, cold-bloodedly, calmly, Dr. Leidner prepares the scene for murder.

"You see now the important part played by Nurse Leatheran? Dr. Leidner's rather curious conduct (it puzzled me at the very first) in securing her services for his wife is explained. It was vital that a reliable professional witness should be able to state incontrovertibly that Mrs. Leidner had been dead *over an hour* when her body was found—that is, that she had been killed at a time when *everybody could swear her husband was on the roof.* A suspicion *might* have arisen that he had killed her when he entered the room and found the body—but that was out of the question when a trained hospital nurse would assert positively that she had already been dead an hour.

"Another thing that is explained is the curious state of tension and strain that had come over the expedition this year. I never from the first thought that that could be attributed solely to *Mrs.* Leidner's influence. For several years this particular expedition had had a reputation for happy good-fellowship. In my opinion the state of mind of a community is always directly due to the influence of the man at the top. Dr. Leidner, quiet though he was, was a man of great personality. It was due to his tact, to his judgment, to his sympathetic manipulation of human beings that the atmosphere had always been such a happy one.

"If there was a change, therefore, the change must be due to the man at the top—in other words, to *Dr.* Leidner. It was Dr. Leidner, not Mrs. Leidner, who was responsible for the tension and uneasiness. No wonder the staff felt the change without understanding it. The kindly genial Dr. Leidner, outwardly the same, was only playing the part of himself. The real man was an obsessed fanatic plotting to kill.

"And now we will pass on to the second murder—that of Miss Johnson. In tidying up Dr. Leidner's papers in the office (a job she took on herself unasked, craving for something to do) she must have come on some unfinished draft of one of the anonymous letters.

"It must have been both incomprehensible and extremely upsetting to her! Dr. Leidner has been deliberately terrorizing his wife! She cannot understand it—but it upsets her badly. It is in this mood that Nurse Leatheran discovers her crying.

"I do not think at the moment that she suspects Dr. Leidner of being the murderer, but my experiments with sounds in Mrs. Leidner's and Father Lavigny's rooms are not lost upon her. She realizes that if it *was* Mrs. Leidner's cry she heard, *the window in her room must have been open, not shut.* At the moment that conveys nothing vital to her, *but she remembers it.*

"Her mind goes on working—ferreting its way towards the truth. Perhaps she makes some reference to the letters which Dr. Leidner understands and his manner changes. She may see that he is, suddenly, afraid.

"But Dr. Leidner *cannot* have killed his wife! He was on the *roof* all the time.

"And then, one evening, as she herself is on the roof puzzling about it, the truth comes to her in a flash. Mrs. Leidner has been killed from up *here*, through the open window.

"It was at that minute that Nurse Leatheran found her.

"And immediately, her old affection reasserting itself, she puts up a quick camouflage. Nurse Leatheran must not guess the horrifying discovery she has just made.

"She looks deliberately in the opposite direction (towards the courtyard) and makes a remark suggested to her by Father Lavigny's appearance as he crosses the courtyard.

"She refuses to say more. She has got to 'think things out.'

"And Dr. Leidner, who has been watching her anxiously, *realizes that she knows the truth*. She is not the kind of woman to conceal her horror and distress from him.

"It is true that as yet she has not given him away—but how long can he depend upon her?

"Murder is a habit. That night he substitutes a glass of acid for her glass of water. There is just a chance she may be believed to have deliberately poisoned herself. There is even a chance she may be considered to have done the first murder and has now been overcome with remorse. To strengthen the latter idea he takes the quern from the roof and puts it under her bed.

"No wonder that poor Miss Johnson, in her death agony, could only try desperately to impart her hard-won information. Through 'the window,' *that* is how Mrs. Leidner was killed, *not* through the door—through the *window*. . . .

"And so thus, everything is explained, everything falls into place. . . . Psychologically perfect.

"But there is no proof. No proof at all. . . ."

None of us spoke. We were lost in a sea of horror. . . . Yes, and not only horror. Pity, too.

Dr. Leidner had neither moved nor spoken. He sat just as he had done all along. A tired, worn, elderly man.

At last he stirred slightly and looked at Poirot with gentle tired eyes.

"No," he said, "there is no proof. But that does not matter. You knew that I would not deny truth. . . . I have never denied truth . . . I think— really—I am rather glad . . . I'm so tired . . ."

Then he said simply:

"I'm sorry about Anne. That was bad—senseless—it wasn't *me!* And she suffered, too, poor soul. Yes, that wasn't me. It was fear. . . ."

A little smile just hovered on his pain-twisted lips.

"You would have made a good archæologist, M. Poirot. You have the gift of re-creating the past.

"It was all very much as you said.

"I loved Louise and I killed her . . . If you'd known Louise you'd have understood. . . . No, I think you understand anyway. . . ."

Chapter 29

L'Envoi

There isn't really any more to say about things.

They got "Father" Lavigny and the other man just as they were going on board a steamer at Beyrouth.

Sheila Reilly married young Emmott. I think that will be good for her. He's no door-mat—he'll keep her in her place. She'd have ridden roughshod over poor Bill Coleman.

I nursed him, by the way, when he had appendicitis a year ago. I got quite fond of him. His people were sending him out to farm in South Africa.

I've never been out East again. It's funny—sometimes I wish I could. I think of the noise the water-wheel made and the women washing, and that queer haughty look that camels give you—and I get quite a home-sick feeling. After all, perhaps dirt isn't really so unhealthy as one is brought up to believe!

Dr. Reilly usually looks me up when he's in England, and as I said, it's he who's got me into this. "Take it or leave it," I said to him. "I know the grammar's all wrong and it's not properly written or anything like that—but there it is."

And he took it. Made no bones about it. It will give me a queer feeling if it's ever printed.

M. Poirot went back to Syria and about a week later he went home on the Orient Express and got himself mixed up in another murder. He was clever, I don't deny it, but I shan't forgive him in a hurry for pulling my leg the way he did. Pretending to think I might be mixed up in the crime and not a real hospital nurse at all!

Doctors are like that sometimes. Will have their joke, some of them will, and never think of *your* feelings!

I've thought and thought about Mrs. Leidner and what she was really like. . . . Sometimes it seems to me she was just a terrible woman—and other times I remember how nice she was to me and how soft her voice was—and her lovely fair hair and everything—and I feel that perhaps, after all, she was more to be pitied than blamed. . . .

And I can't help but pity Dr. Leidner. I know he was a murderer twice over, but it doesn't seem to make any difference. He was so dreadfully fond of her. It's awful to be fond of any one like that.

Somehow, the more I get older, and the more I see of people and sadness and illness and everything, the sorrier I get for every one. Sometimes, I declare, I don't know what's become of the good strict principles my aunt brought me up with. A very religious woman she was, and most particular. There wasn't one of our neighbours whose faults she didn't know backwards and forwards. . . .

Oh, dear, it's quite true what Dr. Reilly said. How does one stop writing? If I could find a really good telling phrase.

I must ask Dr. Reilly for some Arab one.

Like the one M. Poirot used.

In the name of Allah, the Merciful, the Compassionate . . .

Something like that.

THEY CAME TO BAGHDAD

Chapter 1

Captain Crosbie came out of the bank with the pleased air of one who has cashed a cheque and has discovered that there is just a little more in his account than he thought there was.

Captain Crosbie often looked pleased with himself. He was that kind of man. In figure he was short and stocky, with rather a red face and a bristling military moustache. He strutted a little when he walked. His clothes were, perhaps, just a trifle loud, and he was fond of a good story. He was popular among other men. A cheerful man, commonplace but kindly, unmarried. Nothing remarkable about him. There are heaps of Crosbies in the East.

The street into which Captain Crosbie emerged was called Bank Street for the excellent reason that most of the banks in the city were situated in it. Inside the bank it was cool and dark and rather musty. The predominant sound was of large quantities of typewriters clicking in the background.

Outside in Bank Street it was sunny and full of swirling dust, and the noises were terrific and varied. There were the persistent honking of motor horns, the cries of vendors of various wares. There were hot disputes between small groups of people who seemed ready to murder each other but were really fast friends; men, boys and children were selling every type of tree, sweetmeats, oranges and bananas, bath towels, combs, razor blades and other assorted merchandise carried rapidly through the streets on trays. There was also a perpetual and ever renewed sound of throat clearing and spitting, and above it the thin melancholy wail of men conducting donkeys and horses among the stream of motors and pedestrians shouting *"Balek-Balek!"*

It was eleven o'clock in the morning in the city of Baghdad.

Captain Crosbie stopped a rapidly running boy with an armful of newspapers and bought one. He turned the corner of Bank Street and came into Rashid Street which is the main street of Baghdad, running through it for about four miles, parallel with the river Tigris.

Captain Crosbie glanced at the headlines in the paper, tucked it under his arm, walked for about two hundred yards and then turned down a small alleyway and into a large Khan or Court. At the further side of this he pushed open a door with a brass plate and found himself in an office.

A neat young Iraqi clerk left his typewriter and came forward smiling a welcome.

"Good morning, Captain Crosbie. What can I do for you?"

"Mr. Dakin in his room? Good, I'll go through."

He passed through a door, up some very steep stairs and along a rather dirty passage. He knocked at the end door and a voice said "Come in."

It was a high rather bare room. There were an oil stove with a saucer of water on top of it, a long low cushioned seat with a little coffee table in front of it and a large rather shabby desk. The electric light was on and the daylight was carefully excluded. Behind the shabby desk was a rather shabby man, with a tired and indecisive face—the face of one who has not got on in the world and knows it and has ceased to care.

The two men, the cheerful self-confident Crosbie, and the melancholy fatigued Dakin, looked at each other.

Dakin said, "Hullo, Crosbie. Just in from Kirkuk?"

The other nodded. He shut the door carefully behind him. It was a shabby looking door, badly painted, but it had one rather unexpected quality; it fitted well, with no crevices and no space at the bottom.

It was, in fact, soundproof.

With the closing of the door, the personalities of both men changed ever so slightly. Captain Crosbie became less aggressive and cocksure. Mr. Dakin's shoulders drooped less, his manner was less hesitating. If anyone had been in the room listening they would have been surprised to find that Dakin was the man in authority.

"Any news, sir?" asked Crosbie.

"Yes." Dakin sighed. He had before him a paper which he had just been busy decoding. He dotted down two more letters and said:

"It's to be held in Baghdad."

Then he struck a match, set light to the paper and watched it burn. When it had smouldered to ashes, he blew gently. The ashes flew up and scattered.

"Yes," he said. "They've settled on Baghdad. Twentieth of next month. We're to 'preserve all secrecy.' "

"They've been talking about it in the Suq—for three days," said Crosbie drily.

The tall man smiled his weary smile.

"Top secret! No top secrets in the East, are there, Crosbie?"

"No, sir. If you ask me, there aren't any top secrets anywhere. During the war I often noticed a barber in London knew more than the High Command."

"It doesn't matter much in this case. If the meeting is arranged for Baghdad it will soon have to be made public. And then the fun—our particular fun—starts."

"Do you think it ever will take place, sir?" asked Crosbie sceptically. "Does the great Dictator" (thus disrespectfully did Captain Crosbie refer to the head of a Great European Power) "really mean to come?"

"I think he does this time, Crosbie," said Dakin thoughtfully. "Yes, I think so. And if the meeting comes off—comes off without a hitch—well, it might be the saving of—everything. If some kind of understanding could only be reached—" he broke off.

Crosbie still looked slightly sceptical. "Is—forgive me, sir—is understanding of any kind possible?"

"In the sense you mean, Crosbie, probably not! If it were just a bringing together of two men representing totally different ideologies, probably the whole thing would end as usual—in increased suspicion and misunderstanding. But there's the third element. If that fantastic story of Carmichael's is true—"

He broke off.

"But surely, sir, it can't be true. It's too fantastic!"

The other was silent for a few moments. He was seeing, very vividly, an earnest troubled face, hearing a quiet nondescript voice saying fantastic and unbelievable things. He was saying to himself, as he had said then, "Either my best, my most reliable man has gone mad; or else—this thing is true. . . ."

He said in the same thin melancholy voice:

"Carmichael believed it. Everything he could find out confirmed his hypothesis. He wanted to go there to find out more—to get proof . . . Whether I was wise to let him or not, I don't know. If he doesn't get back, it's only my story of what Carmichael told me, which again is a story of what someone told him. Is that enough? I don't think so. It is, as you say, such a fantastic story . . . But if the man himself is here, in Baghdad, on the twentieth, to tell his own story, the story of an eyewitness and to produce proof—"

"Proof?" said Crosbie sharply.

The other nodded.

"Yes, he's got proof."

"How do you know?"

"The agreed formula. The message came through Salah Hassan." He quoted carefully: *"A white camel with a load of oats is coming over the Pass."*

He paused and then went on:

"So Carmichael has got what he went to get, but he didn't get away unsuspected. They're on his trail. Whatever route he takes will be watched, and what is far more dangerous, they'll be waiting for him— here. First on the frontier. And if he succeeds in passing the frontier, there will be a cordon drawn round the Embassies and the Consulates. Look at this."

He shuffled amongst the papers on his desk and read out:

"An Englishman travelling in his car from Persia to Iraq shot dead— Supposedly by bandits. A Kurdish merchant travelling down from the hills ambushed and killed. Another Kurd, Abdul Hassan, suspected of being a cigarette smuggler, shot by the police. Body of a man, afterwards identified as an Armenian lorry driver, found on the Rowanduz road. All of them, mark you, of roughly the same description. Height, weight, hair, build, it corresponds with a description of Carmichael. They're taking no chances. They're out to get him. Once he's in Iraq the danger will be greater still. A gardener at the Embassy, a servant at the Consulate, an official at the Airport, in the Customs, at the Railway Stations . . . all hotels watched . . . A cordon, stretched tight."

Crosbie raised his eyebrows.

"You think it's as widespread as all that, sir?"

"I've no doubt of it. Even in our show there have been leakages. That's the worst of all. How am I to be sure that the measures we're adopting to get Carmichael safely into Baghdad aren't known already to the other side? It's one of the elementary moves of the game, as you know, to have someone in the pay of the other camp."

"Is there anyone you—suspect?"

Slowly Dakin shook his head.

Crosbie sighed.

"In the meantime," he said, "we carry on?"

"Yes."

"What about Crofton Lee?"

"He's agreed to come to Baghdad."

"Everyone's coming to Baghdad," said Crosbie. "Even the great Dictator, according to you, sir. But if anything should happen to the President—while he's here—the balloon will go up with a vengeance."

"Nothing must happen," said Dakin. "That's our business. To see it doesn't."

When Crosbie had gone Dakin sat bent over his desk. He murmured under his breath.

"They came to Baghdad. . . ."

On the blotting pad he drew a circle and wrote under it *Baghdad*—Then, dotted round it, he sketched a camel, an aeroplane, a steamer, a small puffing train—all converging on the circle. Then on the corner of the pad he drew a spider's web. In the middle of the spider's web he wrote a name: *Anna Scheele*. Underneath that he put a big query mark.

Then he took his hat, and left the office. As he walked along Rashid Street some man asked another who that was.

"That? Oh, that's Dakin. In one of the oil companies. Nice fellow, but never gets on. Too lethargic. They say he drinks. He'll never get anywhere. You've got to have drive to get on in this part of the world."

II

"Have you got the reports on the Krugenhorf property, Miss Scheele?"

"Yes, Mr. Morganthal."

Miss Scheele, cool and efficient, slipped the papers in front of her employer.

He grunted as he read.

"Satisfactory, I think."

"I certainly think so, Mr. Morganthal."

"Is Schwartz here?"

"He's waiting in the outer office."

"Have him sent right in now."

Miss Scheele pressed a buzzer—one of six.

"Will you require me, Mr. Morganthal?"

"No, I don't think so, Miss Scheele."

Anna Scheele glided noiselessly from the room.

She was a platinum blonde—but not a glamorous blonde. Her pale flaxen hair was pulled straight back from her forehead into a neat roll at the neck. Her pale blue intelligent eyes looked out on the world from behind strong glasses. Her face had neat small features, but was quite expressionless. She had made her way in the world not by her charm but by sheer efficiency. She could memorize anything, however complicated, and produce names, dates and times without having to refer to notes. She could organize the staff of a big office in such a way that it ran as by well oiled machinery. She was discretion itself and her energy, though controlled and disciplined, never flagged.

Otto Morganthal, head of the New York firm of Morganthal, Brown and Shipperke, international bankers, was well aware that to Anna Scheele he owed more than mere money could repay. He trusted her completely. Her memory, her experience, her judgment, her cool level head were invaluable. He paid her a large salary and would have made it a larger one, had she asked for it.

She knew not only the details of his business but the details of his private life. When he had consulted her in the matter of the second Mrs. Morganthal, she had advised divorce and suggested the exact amount of alimony. She had not expressed sympathy or curiosity. She was not, he would have said, that kind of woman. He didn't think she had any feelings, and it had never occurred to him to wonder what she thought about. He would indeed have been astonished if he had been told that she had any thoughts—other that is, than thoughts connected with Morganthal, Brown and Shipperke, and with the problems of Otto Morganthal.

So it was with complete surprise that he heard her say as she prepared to leave his office,

"I should like three weeks' absence from New York if I might have it, Mr. Morganthal. Starting from Tuesday next."

Staring at her, he said uneasily: "It will be awkward—very awkward."

"I don't think it will be too difficult, Mr. Morganthal. Miss Wygate is fully competent to deal with things. I shall leave her my notes and full instructions. Mr. Cornwall can attend to the Ascher Merger."

Still uneasily he asked:

"You're not ill, or anything?"

He couldn't imagine Miss Scheele being ill. Even germs respected Anna Scheele and kept out of her way.

"Oh no, Mr. Morganthal. I want to go to London to see my sister there."

"Your sister?" He didn't know she had a sister. He had never conceived of Miss Scheele as having any family or relations. She had never mentioned having any. And here she was, casually referring to a sister in London. She had been over in London with him last fall but she had never mentioned having a sister then.

With a sense of injury he said,

"I never knew you had a sister in England?"

Miss Scheele smiled very faintly.

"Oh yes, Mr. Morganthal. She is married to an Englishman connected with the British Museum. It is necessary for her to undergo a very serious operation. She wants me to be with her. I should like to go."

In other words, Otto Morganthal saw, she had made up her mind to go.

He said grumblingly, "All right, all right . . . Get back as soon as you can. I've never seen the market so jumpy. All this damned communism. War may break out at any moment. It's the only solution, I sometimes think. The whole country's riddled with it—riddled with it. And now the President's determined to go to this fool conference at Baghdad. It's a put-up job in my opinion. They're out to get him. Baghdad! Of all the outlandish places!"

"Oh I'm sure he'll be very well guarded," Miss Scheele said soothingly.

"They got the Shah of Persia last year, didn't they? They got Bernadotte in Palestine. It's madness—that's what it is—madness.

"But then," added Mr. Morganthal heavily, "all the world is mad."

Chapter 2

Victoria Jones was sitting moodily on a seat in FitzJames Gardens. She was wholly given up to reflections—or one might almost say moralizations—on the disadvantages inherent in employing one's particular talents at the wrong moment.

Victoria was, like most of us, a girl with both qualities and defects. On the credit side she was generous, warm hearted and courageous. Her natural leaning towards adventure may be regarded as either meritorious or the reverse in this modern age which places the value of security high. Her principal defect was a tendency to tell lies at both opportune and inopportune moments. The superior fascination of fiction to fact was always irresistible to Victoria. She lied with fluency, ease and artistic fervour. If Victoria was late for an appointment (which was often the case) it was not sufficient for her to murmur an excuse of her watch having stopped (which actually was quite often the case) or of an unaccountably delayed bus. It would appear preferable to Victoria to tender the mendacious explanation that she had been hindered by an escaped elephant lying across a main bus route, or by a thrilling smash and grab raid in which she herself had played a part to aid the police. To Victoria an agreeable world would be one where tigers lurked in the Strand and dangerous bandits infested Tooting.

A slender girl, with an agreeable figure and first class legs, Victoria's features might actually have been described as plain. They were small and neat. But there was a piquancy about her, for "little indiarubber face," as one of her admirers had named her, could twist those immobile features into a startling mimicry of almost anybody.

It was this last named talent that had led to her present predicament. Employed as a typist by Mr. Greenholtz of Greenholtz, Simmon and Lederbetter, of Graysholme Street, London, W.C.2, Victoria had been whiling away a dull morning by entertaining the three other typists and the office boy with a vivid performance of Mrs. Greenholtz paying a visit to her husband's office. Secure in the knowledge that Mr. Greenholtz had gone round to his solicitors, Victoria let herself go.

"Why do you say we not have that Knole settee, daddee?" she demanded in a high whining voice. "Mrs. Dievtakis she have one in electric blue satin. You say it is money that is tight? But then why you take that blonde girl out dining and dancing—Ah! you think I do not know—and if you take that girl—then I have a settee and all done plum coloured and gold cushions. And when you say it is a business dinner you are a damn fool—yes—and come back with lipstick on your shirt. So I have the Knole settee and I order a fur cape—very nice—all like mink but not really and I get him very cheap and it is good business—"

The sudden failure of her audience—at first entranced, but now suddenly resuming work with spontaneous agreement caused Victoria to break off and swing round to where Mr. Greenholtz was standing in the doorway, observing her.

Victoria, unable to think of anything relevant to say, merely said "Oh!"

Mr. Greenholtz grunted.

Flinging off his overcoat Mr. Greenholtz proceeded to his private office and banged the door. Almost immediately his buzzer sounded, two shorts and a long. That was a summons for Victoria.

"It's for you, Jonesey," a colleague remarked unnecessarily, her eyes alight with the pleasure occasioned by the misfortunes of others. The other typists collaborated in this sentiment by ejaculating: "You're for it, Jones" and "On the mat, Jonesey." The office boy, an unpleasant child, contented himself with drawing a forefinger across his throat and uttering a sinister noise.

Victoria picked up her notebook and pencil and sailed into Mr. Greenholtz's office with such assurance as she could muster.

"You want me, Mr. Greenholtz?" she murmured, fixing a limpid gaze on him.

Mr. Greenholtz was rustling three pound notes and searching his pockets for coin of the realm.

"So there you are," he observed. "I've had about enough of you, young lady. Do you see any particular reason why I shouldn't pay you a week's salary in lieu of notice and pack you off here and now?"

Victoria (an orphan) had just opened her mouth to explain how the plight of a mother at this moment suffering a major operation had so demoralized her that she had become completely light headed, and how her small salary was all the aforesaid mother had to depend upon, when, taking an opening glance at Mr. Greenholtz's unwholesome face, she shut her mouth and changed her mind.

"I couldn't agree with you more," she said heartily and pleasantly. "I think you're absolutely right, if you know what I mean."

Mr. Greenholtz appeared slightly taken aback. He was not used to having his dismissals treated in this approving and congratulatory spirit. To conceal a slight discomfiture he sorted through the pile of coins on the desk in front of him. He then sought once more in his pockets.

"Ninepence short," he murmured gloomily.

"Never mind," said Victoria kindly. "Take yourself to the pictures or spend it on sweets."

"Don't seem to have any stamps, either."

"It doesn't matter. I never write letters."

"I could send it after you," said Mr. Greenholtz but without much conviction.

"Don't bother. What about a reference?" said Victoria.

Mr. Greenholtz's choler returned.

"Why the Hell should I give you a reference?" he demanded wrathfully.

"It's usual," said Victoria.

Mr. Greenholtz drew a piece of paper towards him and scrawled a few lines. He shoved it towards her.

"That do for you?"

Miss Jones has been with me two months as a shorthand typist. Her shorthand is inaccurate and she cannot spell. She is leaving owing to wasting time in office hours.

Victoria made a grimace.

"Hardly a recommendation," she observed.

"It wasn't meant to be," said Mr. Greenholtz.

"I think," said Victoria, "that you ought at least to say I'm honest, sober and respectable. I am, you know. And perhaps you might add that I'm discreet."

"Discreet?" barked Mr. Greenholtz.

Victoria met his gaze with an innocent stare.

"Discreet," she said gently.

Remembering sundry letters taken down and typed by Victoria, Mr. Greenholtz decided that prudence was the better part of rancour.

He snatched back the paper, tore it up and indited a fresh one.

"Miss Jones has been with me for two months as a shorthand typist. She is leaving owing to redundancy of office staff."

"How about that?"

"It could be better," said Victoria, "but it will do."

So it was that with a week's salary (less ninepence) in her bag Victoria was sitting in meditation upon a bench in FitzJames Gardens which are a triangular plantation of rather sad shrubs flanking a church and overlooked by a tall warehouse.

It was Victoria's habit on any day when it was not actually raining to purchase one cheese, and one lettuce and tomato sandwich at a Milk Bar and eat this simple lunch in these pseudo rural surroundings.

Today, as she munched meditatively, she was telling herself, not for the first time, that there was a time and place for everything—and that the office was definitely not the place for imitations of the boss's wife. She must, in future, curb the natural exuberance that led her to brighten up the performance of a dull job. In the meantime, she was free of Greenholtz, Simmon and Lederbetter, and the prospect of obtaining a situation elsewhere filled her with pleasurable anticipation. Victoria was always delighted when she was about to take up a new job. One never knew, she always felt, what might happen.

She had just distributed the last crumb of bread to three attentive sparrows who immediately fought each other with fury for it, when she became aware of a young man sitting at the other end of the seat. Victoria had noticed him vaguely already, but her mind full of good resolutions for the future, she had not observed him closely until now. What she now saw (out of the corner of her eye) she liked very much. He was a good looking young man, cherubically fair, but with a firm chin and extremely blue eyes which had been, she rather imagined, examining her with covert admiration for some time.

Victoria had no inhibitions about making friends with strange young men in public places. She considered herself an excellent judge of character and well able to check any manifestations of freshness on the part of unattached males.

She proceeded to smile frankly at him and the young man responded like a marionette when you pull the string.

"Hullo," said the young man. "Nice place, this. Do you often come here?"

"Nearly every day."

"Just my luck that I never came here before. Was that your lunch you were eating?"

"Yes."

"I don't think you eat enough. I'd be starving if I only had two sandwiches. What about coming along and having a sausage at the S.P.O. in Tottenham Court Road?"

"No, thanks. I'm quite all right. I couldn't eat any more now."

She rather expected that he would say: "Another day" but he did not. He merely sighed—then he said:

"My name's Edward. What's yours?"

"Victoria."

"Why did your people want to call you after a railway station?"

"Victoria isn't only a railway station," Miss Jones pointed out. "There's Queen Victoria as well."

"Mm, yes. What's your other name?"

"Jones."

"Victoria Jones," said Edward trying it over on his tongue. He shook his head. "They don't go together."

"You're quite right," said Victoria with feeling. "If I were Jenny it would be rather nice—Jenny Jones. But Victoria needs something with a bit more class to it. Victoria Sackville-West for instance. That's the kind of thing one needs. Something to roll round the mouth."

"You could tack something on to the Jones," said Edward with sympathetic interest.

"Bedford Jones."

"Carisbrooke Jones."

"St. Clair Jones."

"Lonsdale Jones."

This agreeable game was interrupted by Edward's glancing at his watch and uttering a horrified ejaculation.

"I must tear back to my blinking boss—er—what about you?"

"I'm out of a job. I was sacked this morning."

"Oh I say, I am sorry," said Edward with real concern.

"Well, don't waste sympathy, because I'm not sorry at all. For one thing, I'll easily get another job, and besides that, it was really rather fun."

And delaying Edward's return to duty still further, she gave him a spirited rendering of this morning's scene, reenacting her impersonation of Mrs. Greenholtz to Edward's immense enjoyment.

"You really are marvellous, Victoria," he said. "You ought to be on the stage."

Victoria accepted this tribute with a gratified smile and remarked that Edward had better be running along if he didn't want to get the sack himself.

"Yes—and I shouldn't get another job as easily as you will. It must be wonderful to be a good shorthand typist," said Edward with envy in his voice.

"Well actually I'm not a good shorthand typist," Victoria admitted frankly, "but fortunately even the lousiest of shorthand typists can get some sort of a job nowadays—at any rate an educational or charitable one—they can't afford to pay much and so they get people like me. I prefer the learned type of job best. These scientific names and places and terms are so frightful anyway that if you can't spell them properly it doesn't really shame you because nobody could. What's your job? I suppose you're out of one of the services. R.A.F.?"

"Good guess."

"Fighter pilot?"

"Right again. They're awfully decent about getting us jobs and all that, but you see, the trouble is, that we're not particularly brainy. I mean one didn't need to be brainy in the R.A.F. They put me in an office with a lot of files and figures and some thinking to do and I just folded up. The whole thing seemed utterly purposeless anyway. But there it is. It gets you down a bit to know that you're absolutely no good."

Victoria nodded sympathetically—Edward went on bitterly:

"Out of touch. Not in the picture any more. It was all right during the war—one could keep one's end up all right—I got the D.F.C. for instance—but now—well, I might as well write myself off the map."

"But there ought to be—"

Victoria broke off. She felt unable to put into words her conviction that those qualities that brought a D.F.C. to their owner should somewhere have their appointed place in the world of 1950.

"It's got me down, rather," said Edward. "Being no good at anything, I mean. Well—I'd better be pushing off—I say—would you mind—would it be most awful cheek—if I only could—"

As Victoria opened surprised eyes, stammering and blushing, Edward produced a small camera.

"I would like so awfully to have a snapshot of you. You see, I'm going to Baghdad tomorrow."

"To Baghdad?" exclaimed Victoria with lively disappointment.

"Yes. I mean I wish I wasn't—now. Earlier this morning I was quite bucked about it—it's why I took this job really—to get out of this country."

"What sort of job is it?"

"Pretty awful. Culture—poetry, all that sort of thing. A Dr. Rathbone's my boss. Strings of letters after his name, peers at you soulfully through pince-nez. He's terrifically keen on uplift and spreading it far and wide. He opens bookshops in remote places—he's starting one in Baghdad. He gets Shakespeare's and Milton's works translated into Arabic and Kurdish and Persian and Armenian and has them all on tap. Silly, I think, be-

cause you've got the British Council doing much the same thing all over
the place. Still, there it is. It gives me a job so I oughtn't to complain."

"What do you actually do?" asked Victoria.

"Well, really it boils down to being the old boy's personal Yes-man
and Dogsbody. Buy the tickets, make the reservations, fill up the passport
forms, check the packing of all the horrid little poetic manuals, run round
here, there, and everywhere. Then, when we get out there I'm supposed
to fraternise—kind of glorified youth movement—all nations together in
a united drive for uplift." Edward's tone became more and more melancholy. "Frankly, it's pretty ghastly, isn't it?"

Victoria was unable to administer much comfort.

"So you see," said Edward, "if you wouldn't mind awfully—one sideways and one looking right at me—oh I say, that's wonderful—"

The camera clicked twice and Victoria showed that purring compla-
cence displayed by young women who know they have made an impression on an attractive member of the opposite sex.

"But it's pretty foul really, having to go off just when I've met you,"
said Edward. "I've half a mind to chuck it—but I suppose I couldn't do
that at the last moment—not after all those ghastly forms and visas and
everything. Wouldn't be a very good show, what?"

"It mayn't turn out as bad as you think," said Victoria consolingly.

"N-no," said Edward doubtfully. "The funny thing is," he added, "that
I've got a feeling there's something fishy somewhere."

"Fishy?"

"Yes. Bogus. Don't ask me why. I haven't any reason. Sort of feeling
one gets sometimes. Had it once about my port oil. Began fussing about
the damned thing and sure enough there was a washer wedged in the
spur-gear pump."

The technical terms in which this was couched made it quite unintelligible to Victoria, but she got the main idea.

"You think he's bogus—Rathbone?"

"Don't see how he can be. I mean he's frightfully respectable and
learned and belongs to all these societies—and sort of hobnobs with
Archbishops and Principals of Colleges. No, it's just a feeling—Well,
time will show. So long. I wish you were coming, too."

"So do I," said Victoria.

"What are you going to do?"

"Go round to St. Guildric's Agency in Gower Street and look for another job," said Victoria gloomily.

"Goodbye, Victoria. Partir, say mourir un peu," added Edward with a
very British accent. "These French johnnies know their stuff. Our En-

glish chaps just maunder on about parting being a sweet sorrow—silly asses."

"Goodbye, Edward, good luck."

"I don't suppose you'll ever think about me again."

"Yes, I shall."

"You're absolutely different from any girl I've ever seen before—I only wish—" The clock chimed a quarter, and Edward said, "Oh Hell—I must fly—"

Retreating rapidly, he was swallowed up by the great maw of London. Victoria, remaining behind on her seat absorbed in meditation, was conscious of two distinct streams of thought.

One dealt with the theme of Romeo and Juliet. She and Edward, she felt, were somewhat in the position of that unhappy couple, although perhaps Romeo and Juliet had expressed their feelings in rather more high class language. But the position, Victoria thought, was the same. Meeting, instant attraction—frustration—two fond hearts thrust asunder. A remembrance of a rhyme once frequently recited by her old nurse came to mind.

> *Jumbo said to Alice, "I love you."*
> *Alice said to Jumbo, "I don't believe you do;*
> *If you really loved me, as you say you do,*
> *You wouldn't go to America and leave me in the Zoo."*

Substitute Baghdad for America and there you were!

Victoria rose at last, dusting crumbs from her lap, and walked briskly out of FitzJames Gardens in the direction of Gower Street. Victoria had come to two decisions: the first was that (like Juliet) she loved this young man, and meant to have him.

The second decision that Victoria had come to was that as Edward would shortly be in Baghdad, the only thing to do was for her to go to Baghdad also. What was now occupying her mind was how this could be accomplished. That it could be accomplished somehow or other, Victoria did not doubt. She was a young woman of optimism and force of character.

Parting is such sweet sorrow appealed to her as a sentiment no more than it did to Edward.

"Somehow," said Victoria to herself, "I've got to get to Baghdad!"

Chapter 3

The Savoy Hotel welcomed Miss Anna Scheele with the empressment due to an old and valued client—they inquired after the health of Mr. Morganthal—and assured her that if her suite was not to her liking she had only to say so—for Anna Scheele represented *Dollars*.

Miss Scheele bathed, dressed, made a telephone call to a Kensington number and then went down in the lift. She passed through the revolving doors and asked for a taxi. It drew up and she got in and directed it to Cartier's in Bond Street.

As the taxi turned out of the Savoy approach into the Strand a little dark man who had been standing looking into a shop window suddenly glanced at his watch and hailed a taxi that was conveniently cruising past and which had been singularly blind to the hails of an agitated woman with parcels a moment or two previously.

The taxi followed along the Strand keeping the first taxi in sight. As they were both held up by the lights in going round Trafalgar Square, the man in the second taxi looked out of the left hand window and made a slight gesture with his hand. A private car, which had been standing in the side street by the Admiralty Arch started its engine and swung into the stream of traffic behind the second taxi.

The traffic had started on again. As Anna Scheele's taxi followed the stream of traffic going to the left into Pall Mall, the taxi containing the little dark man swung away to the right continuing round Trafalgar Square. The private car, a grey Standard, was now close behind Anna Scheele. It contained two passengers, a fair, rather vacant-looking young man at the wheel and a smartly dressed young woman beside him. The

Standard followed Anna Scheele's taxi along Piccadilly and up Bond Street. Here for a moment it paused by the curb and the young woman got out.

She called brightly and conventionally,

"Thanks so much."

The car went on. The young woman walked along glancing every now and again into a window. A block held up the traffic. The young woman passed both the Standard and Anna Scheele's taxi. She arrived at Cartier's and went inside.

Anna Scheele paid off her taxi and went into the jeweller's. She spent some time looking at various pieces of jewellery. In the end she selected a sapphire and diamond ring. She wrote a cheque for it on a London bank. At the sight of the name on it, a little extra empressment came into the assistant's manner.

"Glad to see you in London again, Miss Scheele. Is Mr. Morganthal over?"

"No."

"I wondered. We have a very fine star sapphire here—I know he is interested in star sapphires. If you would care to see it?"

Miss Scheele expressed her willingness to see it, duly admired it, and promised to mention it to Mr. Morganthal.

She went out again into Bond Street, and the young woman who had been looking at clip earrings expressed herself as unable to make up her mind and emerged also.

The grey Standard car, having turned to the left in Grafton Street and gone down to Piccadilly, was just coming up Bond Street again. The young woman showed no signs of recognition.

Anna Scheele had turned into the Arcade. She entered a florist's. She ordered three dozen long stemmed roses, a bowl full of sweet big purple violets, a dozen sprays of white lilac, and a jar full of mimosa. She gave an address for them to be sent.

"That will be twelve pounds, eighteen shillings, madam."

Anna Scheele paid and went out. The young woman who had just come in asked the price of a bunch of primroses but did not buy them.

Anna Scheele crossed Bond Street and went along Burlington Street and turned into Savile Row. Here she entered the establishment of one of those tailors who, while catering essentially for men, occasionally condescend to cut a suit for certain favoured members of the feminine sex.

Mr. Bolford received Miss Scheele with the greeting accorded to a valued client, and the materials for a suit were considered.

"Fortunately, I can give you our export quality. When will you be returning to New York, Miss Scheele?"

"On the twenty-third."

"We can manage that nicely. By the clipper, I presume?"

"Yes."

"And how are things in America? They are very sadly here—very sadly indeed." Mr. Bolford shook his head like a doctor describing a patient. "No heart in things, if you know what I mean. And no one coming along who takes any pride in a good job of work. D'you know who will cut your suit, Miss Scheele? Mr. Lantwick—seventy-two years of age he is, and he's the only man I've got I can really trust to cut for our best people. All the others—"

Mr. Bolford's plump hands waved them away.

"Quality," he said. "That's what this country used to be renowned for. Quality! Nothing cheap, nothing flashy. When we try mass production we're no good at it, and that's a fact. That's your country's specialty, Miss Scheele. What we ought to stand for, and I say it again, is quality. Take time over things, and trouble, and turn out an article that no one in the world can beat. Now what day shall we say for the first fitting? This day week? At 11.30? Thank you very much."

Making her way through the archaic gloom round bales of material, Anna Scheele emerged into daylight again. She hailed a taxi and returned to the Savoy. A taxi that was drawn up on the opposite side of the street and which contained a little dark man, took the same route but did not turn into the Savoy. It drove round to the Embankment and there picked up a short plump woman who had recently emerged from the service entrance of the Savoy.

"What about it, Louisa? Been through her room?"

"Yes. Nothing."

Anna Scheele had lunch in the restaurant. A table had been kept for her by the window. The Maitre d'Hôtel inquired affectionately after the health of Otto Morganthal.

After lunch Anna Scheele took her key and went up to her suite. The bed had been made, fresh towels were in the bathroom and everything was spick and span. Anna crossed to the two light air cases that constituted her luggage, one was open, the other locked. She cast an eye over the contents of the unlocked one, then taking her keys from her purse she unlocked the other. All was neat, folded, as she had folded things, nothing had apparently been touched or disturbed. A brief case of leather lay on top. A small Leica camera and two rolls of films were in one corner. The films were still sealed and unopened. Anna ran her nail across the flap and pulled it up. Then she smiled, very gently. The single almost invisible blond hair that had been there was there no longer. Deftly she scattered a little powder over the shiny leather of the brief case and blew it off. The brief case remained clear and shiny. There were no finger-prints. But that morning after patting a little brilliantine onto the smooth flaxen cap of her hair, she had handled the brief case. There should have been fingerprints on it, her own.

She smiled again.

"Good work," she said to herself. "But not quite good enough. . . ."

Deftly, she packed a small overnight case and went downstairs again. A taxi was called and she directed the driver to 17 Elmsleigh Gardens.

Elmsleigh Gardens was a quiet, rather dingy Kensington Square. Anna paid off the taxi and ran up the steps to the peeling front door. She pressed the bell. After a few minutes an elderly woman opened the door with a suspicious face which immediately changed to a beam of wel-come.

"Won't Miss Elsie be pleased to see you! She's in the study at the back. It's only the thought of your coming that's been keeping her spirits up."

Anna went quickly along the dark hallway and opened the door at the far end. It was a small shabby, comfortable room with large worn leather armchairs. The woman sitting in one of them, jumped up.

"Anna, darling."

"Elsie."

The two women kissed each other affectionately.

"It's all arranged," said Elsie. "I go in tonight. I do hope—"

"Cheer up," said Anna. "Everything is going to be quite all right."

II

The small dark man in the raincoat entered a public call box at High Street Kensington Station, and dialled a number.

"Valhalla Gramophone Company?"

"Yes."

"Sanders here."

"Sanders of the River? What river?"

"River Tigris. Reporting on A.S. arrived this morning from New York. Went to Cartier's. Bought sapphire and diamond ring costing one hun-dred and twenty pounds. Went to florist's, Jane Kent—twelve pounds eighteen shillings' worth of flowers to be delivered at a nursing home in Portland Place. Ordered coat and skirt at Bolford and Avory's. None of these firms known to have any suspicious contacts, but particular atten-tion will be paid to them in future. A.S.'s room at Savoy gone through. Nothing suspicious found. Brief case in suitcase containing papers relat-ing to Paper Merger with Wolfensteins. All aboveboard. Camera and two rolls of apparently unexposed films. Possibility of films being photostatic records, substituted other films for them, but original films reported upon as being straightforward unexposed films. A.S. took small overnight case and went to sister at 17 Elmsleigh Gardens. Sister entering nursing home in Portland Place this evening for internal operation. This confirmed from nursing home and also appointment book of surgeon. Visit of A.S. seems perfectly aboveboard. Showed no uneasiness or consciousness of being followed. Understand she is spending tonight at nursing home. Has kept on her room at the Savoy. Return passage to New York by clipper booked for twenty-third."

The man who called himself Sanders of the River paused and added a postscript off the record as it were.

"And if you ask what I think, it's all a mare's nest! Throwing money about, that's all she's doing. Twelve pounds eighteen on flowers! I ask you!"

Chapter 4

It says a good deal for the buoyancy of Victoria's temperament that the possibility of failing to attain her objective did not for a moment occur to her. Not for her the lines about ships that pass in the night. It was certainly unfortunate, when she had—well—frankly—fallen for an attractive young man, that that young man should prove to be just on the verge of departure to a place distant some three thousand miles. He might so easily have been going to Aberdeen or Brussels or even Birmingham.

That it should be Baghdad, thought Victoria, was just her luck! Never the less, difficult though it might be, she intended to get to Baghdad somehow or other. Victoria walked purposefully along Tottenham Court Road, revolving ways and means. Baghdad. What went on in Baghdad? According to Edward: "Culture." Could she, in some way, play up culture? Unesco? Unesco was always sending people here, there and everywhere, sometimes to the most delectable places. But these were usually, Victoria reflected, superior young women with university degrees who had got into the racket early on.

Victoria, deciding that first things came first, finally bent her steps to a travel agency, and there made her inquiries. There was no difficulty, it seemed, in travelling to Baghdad. You could go by air, by long sea to Basrah, by train to Marseilles and by boat to Beirut and across the desert by car. You could go via Egypt. You could go all the way by train if you were determined to do so, but visas were at present difficult and uncertain and were apt to have actually expired by the time you received them. Baghdad was in the sterling area and money therefore presented no difficulties. Not, that is to say, in the clerk's meaning of the word. What it all boiled down to was that there was no difficulty whatsoever in getting to Baghdad, so long as you had between sixty and a hundred pounds in cash.

As Victoria had at this moment three pounds ten (less ninepence), an extra twelve shillings, and five pounds in the P.O. Savings Bank, the simple and straightforward way was out of the question.

She made tentative queries as to a job as Air Hostess or stewardess, but these, she gathered, were highly coveted posts for which there was a waiting list.

Victoria next visited St. Guildric's Agency where Miss Spenser, sitting behind her efficient desk, welcomed her as one of those who were destined to pass through the office with reasonable frequency.

"Dear me, Miss Jones, not out of a post again. I really hoped this last one—"

"Quite impossible," said Victoria firmly. "I really couldn't begin to tell you what I had to put up with."

A pleasurable flush rose in Miss Spenser's pallid cheek.

"Not—" she began—"I do hope not—He didn't seem to me really that sort of a man—but of course he is a trifle gross—I do hope—"

"It's quite all right," said Victoria. She conjured up a pale brave smile. "I can take care of myself."

"Oh, of course, but it's the unpleasantness."

"Yes," said Victoria. "It is unpleasant. However—" she smiled bravely again.

Miss Spenser consulted her books.

"The St. Leonard's Assistance to Unmarried Mothers want a typist," said Miss Spenser. "Of course, they don't pay very much—"

"Is there any chance," asked Victoria brusquely, "of a post in Baghdad?"

"In Baghdad?" said Miss Spenser in lively astonishment.

Victoria saw she might as well have said in Kamskatka or at the South Pole.

"I should very much like to get to Baghdad," said Victoria.

"I hardly think—in a secretary's post you mean?"

"Anyhow," said Victoria. "As a nurse or a cook, or looking after a lunatic. Anyway at all."

Miss Spenser shook her head.

"I'm afraid I can't hold out much hope. There was a lady in yesterday with two little girls who was offering a passage to Australia."

Victoria waved away Australia.

She rose. "If you did hear of anything. Just the fare out—that's all I need." She met the curiosity in the other woman's eye by explaining— "I've got—er—relations out there. And I understand there are plenty of well paid jobs. But of course, one has to get there first."

"Yes," repeated Victoria to herself as she walked away from St. Guildric's Bureau. "One has to get there."

It was an added annoyance to Victoria that, as is customary, when one has had one's attention suddenly focussed on a particular name or subject, everything seemed to have suddenly conspired to force the thought of Baghdad on to her attention.

A brief paragraph in the evening paper she bought stated that Dr. Pauncefoot Jones, the well known archaeologist, had started excavation on the ancient city of Murik, situated a hundred and twenty miles from Baghdad. An advertisement mentioned Shipping Lines to Basrah (and thence by train to Baghdad, Mosul etc.). In the newspaper that lined her stocking drawer, a few lines of print about students in Baghdad leapt to her eyes. *The Thief of Baghdad* was on at the local cinema, and in the high class highbrow bookshop into whose window she always gazed, a New Biography of Haroun al Rashid, Caliph of Baghdad, was prominently displayed.

The whole world, it seemed to her, had suddenly become Baghdad conscious. And until that afternoon at approximately 1.45 she had, for all intents and purposes, never heard of Baghdad, and certainly never thought about it.

The prospects of getting there were unsatisfactory, but Victoria had no idea of giving up. She had a fertile brain and the optimistic outlook that if you want to do a thing there is always some way of doing it.

She employed the evening in drawing up a list of possible approaches. It ran:

Insert advertisement?
Try Foreign Office?
Try Iraq Legation?
What about Date firms?
Ditto Shipping firms?
British Council?
Selfridge's Information Bureau?
Citizen's Advice Bureau?

None of them, she was forced to admit, seemed very promising. She added to the list:

Somehow or other, get hold of a hundred pounds?

II

The intense mental efforts of concentration that Victoria had made overnight, and possibly the subconscious satisfaction at no longer having to be punctually in the office at nine a.m., made Victoria oversleep herself.

She awoke at five minutes past ten, and immediately jumped out of bed and began to dress. She was just passing a final comb through her rebellious dark hair when the telephone rang.

Victoria reached for the receiver.

A positively agitated Miss Spenser was at the other end.

"So glad to have caught you, my dear. Really the most amazing coincidence."

"Yes?" cried Victoria.

"As I say, really a startling coincidence. A Mrs. Hamilton Clipp—travelling to Baghdad in three days' time—has broken her arm—needs someone to assist her on journey—I rang you up at once. Of course I don't know if she has also applied to any other agencies—"

"I'm on my way," said Victoria. "Where is she?"

"The Savoy."

"And what's her silly name? Tripp?"

"Clipp, dear. Like a paper clip, but with two P's—I can't think why, but she's an American," ended Miss Spenser as if that explained everything.

"Mrs. Clipp at the Savoy."

"Mr. and Mrs. Hamilton Clipp. It was actually the husband who rang up."

"You're an angel," said Victoria. "Goodbye."

She hurriedly brushed her suit and wished it were slightly less shabby, recombed her hair so as to make it seem less exuberant and more in keeping with the role of ministering angel and experienced traveller. Then she took out Mr. Greenholtz's recommendation and shook her head over it.

We must do better than that, said Victoria.

From a 19 bus, Victoria alighted at Green Park, and entered the Ritz Hotel. A quick glance over the shoulder of a woman reading in the bus had proved rewarding. Entering the writing room Victoria wrote herself some generous lines of praise from Lady Cynthia Bradbury who had been announced as having just left England for East Africa . . . *"excellent in illness,"* wrote Victoria, *"and most capable in every way. . . ."*

Leaving the Ritz she crossed the road and walked a short way up Albemarle Street until she came to Balderton's Hotel, renowned as the haunt of the higher clergy and of old fashioned dowagers up from the country.

In less dashing handwriting, and making neat small Greek e's she wrote a recommendation from the Bishop of Llangow.

Thus equipped, Victoria caught a No. 9 bus and proceeded to the Savoy.

At the reception desk she asked for Mrs. Hamilton Clipp and gave her name as coming from St. Guildric's Agency. The clerk was just about to pull the telephone towards him when he paused, looked across, and said,

"That is Mr. Hamilton Clipp now."

Mr. Hamilton Clipp was an immensely tall and very thin grey haired American of kindly aspect and slow deliberate speech.

Victoria told him her name and mentioned the Agency.

"Why now, Miss Jones, you'd better come right up and see Mrs. Clipp. She's still in our suite. I fancy she's interviewing some other young lady, but she may have gone by now."

Cold panic clutched at Victoria's heart.

Was it to be so near and yet so far?

They went up in the lift to the third floor.

As they walked along the deep carpeted corridor, a young woman came out of a door at the far end and came towards them. Victoria had a kind of hallucination that it was herself who was approaching. Possibly, she thought, because the young woman's tailor made suit was so exactly what she would have liked to be wearing herself. "And it would fit me too. I'm just her size. How I'd like to tear it off her," thought Victoria with a reversion to primitive female savagery.

The young woman passed them. A small velvet hat perched on the side of her fair hair partially hid her face, but Mr. Hamilton Clipp turned to look after her with an air of surprise.

"Well now," he said to himself. "Who'd have thought of that? Anna Scheele."

He added in an explanatory way,

"Excuse me, Miss Jones. I was surprised to recognise a young lady whom I saw in New York only a week ago, secretary to one of our big International bankers—"

He stopped as he spoke at a door in the corridor. The key was hanging in the lock and with a brief tap, Mr. Hamilton Clipp opened the door and stood aside for Victoria to precede him into the room.

Mrs. Hamilton Clipp was sitting on a high backed chair near the window and jumped up as they came in. She was a short bird-like sharp-eyed woman. Her right arm was encased in plaster.

Her husband introduced Victoria.

"Why, it's all been most unfortunate," exclaimed Mrs. Clipp breathlessly. "Here we were, with a full itinerary, and enjoying London and all our plans made and my passage booked. I'm going out to pay a visit to my married daughter in Iraq, Miss Jones. I've not seen her for nearly two years. And then what do I do but take a crash—as a matter of fact, it was actually in Westminster Abbey—down some stone steps—and there I was. They rushed me to Hospital and they've set it, and all things considered it's not too uncomfortable—but there it is, I'm kind of helpless, and however I'd manage travelling, I don't know. And George here, is just tied up with business, and simply can't get away for at least another three weeks. He suggested that I should take a nurse along with me—but after all, once I'm out there I don't need a nurse hanging around, Sadie can do all that's necessary—and it means paying her fare back as well, and so I thought I'd ring up the Agencies and see if I couldn't find someone who'd be willing to come along just for the fare out."

"I'm not exactly a nurse," said Victoria managing to imply that that was practically what she was. "But I've had a good deal of experience of nursing." She produced the first testimonial. "I was with Lady Cynthia Bradbury for over a year. And if you should want any correspondence or secretarial work done, I acted as my uncle's secretary for some months. My uncle," said Victoria modestly, "is the Bishop of Llangow."

"So your uncle's a Bishop. Dear me, how interesting."

Both the Hamilton Clipps were, Victoria thought, decidedly impressed. And so they should be after the trouble she had taken!

Mrs. Hamilton Clipp handed the two testimonials to her husband.

"It really seems quite wonderful," she said reverently. "Quite Providential. It's an answer to prayer."

Which, indeed, was exactly what it was, thought Victoria.

"You're taking up a position of some kind out there? Or joining a relative?" asked Mrs. Hamilton Clipp.

In the flurry of manufacturing testimonials, Victoria had quite forgotten that she might have to account for her reasons for travelling to Baghdad. Caught unprepared, she had to improvise rapidly. The paragraph she had read yesterday came to her mind.

"I'm joining my uncle out there. Dr. Pauncefoot Jones," she explained.

"Indeed? The archaeologist?"

"Yes." For one moment Victoria wondered whether she were perhaps endowing herself with too many distinguished uncles. "I'm terribly interested in his work, but of course I've no special qualifications so it was out of the question for the Expedition to pay my fare out. They're not too well off for funds. But if I can get out on my own, I can join them and make myself useful."

"It must be very very interesting work," said Mr. Hamilton Clipp, "and Mesopotamia is certainly a great field for archaeology."

"I'm afraid," said Victoria turning to Mrs. Clipp, "that my uncle the

Bishop is up in Scotland this moment. But I can give you his secretary's telephone number. She is staying in London at the moment. Pimlico 87693—one of the Fulham Palace extensions. She'll be there any time from (Victoria's eyes slid to the clock on the mantelpiece) 11.30 onwards if you would like to ring her up and ask about me."

"Why, I'm sure—" Mrs. Clipp began, but her husband interrupted.

"Time's very short, you know. This plane leaves day after tomorrow. Now have you got a passport, Miss Jones?"

"Yes." Victoria felt thankful that owing to a short holiday trip to France last year, her passport was up to date. "I brought it with me in case," she added.

"Now that's what I call businesslike," said Mr. Clipp approvingly. If any other candidate had been in the running, she had obviously dropped out now. Victoria with her good recommendations, and her uncles, and her passport on the spot had successfully made the grade.

"You'll want the necessary visas," said Mr. Clipp, taking the passport. "I'll run round to our friend Mr. Burgeon in American Express, and he'll get everything fixed up. Perhaps you'd better call round this afternoon, so you can sign whatever's necessary."

This Victoria agreed to do.

As the door of the apartment closed behind her, she heard Mrs. Hamilton Clipp say to Mr. Hamilton Clipp—

"Such a nice straightforward girl. We really are in luck."

Victoria had the grace to blush.

She hurried back to her flat and sat glued to the telephone prepared to assume the gracious refined accents of a Bishop's secretary in case Mrs. Clipp should seek confirmation of her capability. But Mrs. Clipp had obviously been so impressed by Victoria's straightforward personality that she was not going to bother with these technicalities. After all, the engagement was only for a few days as a travelling companion.

In due course, papers were filled up and signed, the necessary visas were obtained and Victoria was bidden to spend the final night at the Savoy so as to be on hand to help Mrs. Clipp get off at 7 a.m. on the following morning for Airways House and Heathrow Aerodrome.

Chapter 5

The boat that had left the marshes two days before paddled gently along the Shatt el Arab. The stream was swift and the old man who was propelling the boat needed to do very little. His movements were gentle and rhythmic. His eyes were half closed. Almost under his breath he sang very softly, a sad unending Arab chant

ASRI BI LEL YA YAMALI
HADHI ALEK YA IBN ALI

Thus, on innumerable other occasions, had Abdul Suleiman of the Marsh Arabs come down the river to Basrah. There was another man in the boat, a figure often seen nowadays, with a pathetic mingling of West and East in his clothing. Over his long robe of striped cotton he wore a discarded khaki tunic, old and stained and torn. A faded red knitted scarf was tucked into the ragged coat. His head showed again the dignity of the Arab dress, the inevitable keffiyah of black and white held in place by the black silk *agal*. His eyes, unfocussed in a wide stare, looked out blearily over the river bund. Presently he, too, began to hum in the same key and tone. He was a figure like thousands of other figures in the Mesopotamia landscape. There was nothing to show that he was an Englishman, and that he carried with him a secret that influential men in almost every country in the world were striving to intercept and to destroy, along with the man who carried it.

His mind went hazily back over the last weeks. The ambush in the mountains. The ice cold of the snow coming over the Pass. The caravan of camels. The four days spent trudging on foot over bare desert in company with two men carrying a portable "cinema." The days in the black tent and the journeying with the Aneizeh tribe, old friends of his. All difficult, all fraught with danger—slipping again and again through the cordon spread out to look for him and intercept him.

"Henry Carmichael. British agent. Age about thirty. Brown hair, dark eyes, five foot ten. Speaks Arabic, Kurdish, Persian, Armenian, Hindustani, Turkish and many mountain dialects. Befriended by the tribesmen. Dangerous."

Carmichael had been born in Kashgar where his father was a Government official. His childish tongue had lisped various dialects and patois—his nurses, and later his bearers, had been natives of many different races. In nearly all the wild places of the Middle East he had friends.

Only in the cities and the towns did his contacts fail him. Now, approaching Basrah, he knew that the critical moment of his mission had come. Sooner or later, he had got to reenter the civilised zone. Though Baghdad was his ultimate destination, he had judged it wise not to approach it direct. In every town in Iraq facilities were awaiting him, carefully discussed and arranged many months beforehand. It had had to be left to his own judgement where he should, so to speak, make his landing ground. He had sent no word to his superiors, even through the indirect channels where he could have done so. It was safer thus. The easy plan, the aeroplane waiting at the appointed rendezvous—had failed, as he had suspected it would fail. That rendezvous had been known to his enemies. Leakage! Always that deadly, that incomprehensible, leakage.

And so it was that his apprehensions of danger were heightened. Here in Basrah, in sight of safety, he felt instinctively sure that the danger would be greater than during the wild hazards of his journey. And to fail at the last lap—that would hardly bear thinking about.

Rhythmically pulling at his oars, the old Arab murmured without turning his head.

"The moment approaches, my son. May Allah prosper you."

"Do you tarry long in the city, my father. Return to the marshes. I would not have harm befall you."

"That is as Allah decrees. It is in his hands."

"In shâ Allâh," the other repeated.

For a moment he longed intensely to be a man of Eastern and not of Western blood. Not to worry over the chances of success or failure, not to calculate again and again the hazards, repeatedly asking himself if he had planned wisely and with forethought. To throw responsibility on the All Merciful, the All Wise. In shâ Allâh, I shall succeed!

Even saying the words over to himself he felt the calmness and the fatalism of the country overwhelming him and he welcomed it. Now, in a few moments, he must step from the haven of the boat, walk the streets of the city, run the gauntlet of keen eyes. Only by feeling as well as looking like an Arab could he succeed.

The boat turned gently into the water-way that ran at right angles to the river. Here all kinds of river craft were tied up, and other boats were coming in before and after them. It was a lovely, almost Venetian scene; the boats with their high scrolled prows and the soft faded colours of their paintwork. There were hundreds of them tied up close alongside each other.

The old man asked softly,

"The moment has come. There are preparations made for you?"

"Yes, indeed, my plans are set. The hour has come for me to leave."

"May God make your path straight, and may He lengthen the years of your life."

Carmichael gathered his striped skirts about him and went up the slippery stone steps to the wharf above.

All about him were the usual waterside figures. Small boys, orange sellers squatting down by their trays of merchandise. Sticky squares of cakes and sweetmeats, trays of bootlaces and cheap combs and pieces of elastic. Contemplative strollers, spitting raucously from time to time, wandering along with their beads clicking in their hands. On the opposite side of the street where the shops were and the banks, busy young *effendis* walked briskly in European suits of a slightly purplish tinge. There were Europeans, too, English and foreigners. And nowhere was there interest shown, or curiosity, because one amongst fifty or so Arabs had just climbed onto the wharf from a boat.

Carmichael strolled along very quietly, his eyes taking in the scene with just the right touch of childlike pleasure in his surroundings. Every now and then he hawked and spat, not too violently, just to be in the picture. Twice he blew his nose with his fingers.

And so, the stranger come to town, he reached the bridge at the top of the canal, and turned over it and passed into the Suq.

Here all was noise and movement. Energetic tribesmen strode along, pushing others out of their way—laden donkeys made their way along, their drivers calling out raucously. *Balek-balek* . . . Children quarrelled and squealed and ran after Europeans calling hopefully, Baksheesh, madame. Baksheesh. Meskin-meskin . . .

Here the produce of the West and the East were equally for sale, side by side. Aluminum saucepans, cups and saucers and teapots, hammered copper ware, silverwork from Amara, cheap watches, enamel mugs, embroideries and gay patterned rugs from Persia. Brass bound chests from

Kuwait, secondhand coats and trousers and children's woolly cardigans. Local quilted bedcovers, painted glass lamps, stacks of clay water jars and pots. All the cheap merchandise of civilisation together with the native products.

All as normal and as usual. After his long sojourn in the wilder spaces, the bustle and confusion seemed strange to Carmichael, but it was all as it should be, he could detect no jarring note, no sign of interest in his presence. And yet, with the instinct of one who has for long years known what it is to be a hunted man, he felt a growing uneasiness—a vague sense of menace. He could detect nothing amiss. No one had looked at him. No one, he was almost sure, was following him or keeping him under observation. Yet he had that indefinable certainty of danger.

He moved up a narrow dark turning, again to the right, then to the left. Here, among the small booths, he came to the opening of a khan, and stepped through the doorway into the court. Various shops were all round it. Carmichael went to one where *ferwahs* were hanging—the sheepskin coats of the North. He stood there handling them tentatively. The owner of the store was offering coffee to a customer, a tall bearded man of fine presence, who wore green round his fez, showing him to be a Hajji who had been to Mecca.

Carmichael stood there fingering the *ferwah*.

"Besh hadha?" he asked.

"Seven dinars."

"Too much."

The Hajji said, "You will deliver the carpets at my Khan?"

"Without fail," said the merchant. "You start tomorrow?"

"At dawn for Kerbela."

"It is my city, Kerbela," said Carmichael. "It is fifteen years now since I have seen the Tomb of the Hussein."

"It is a holy city," said the Hajji.

The shopkeeper said over his shoulder to Carmichael,

"There are cheaper *ferwahs* in the inner room."

"A white *ferwah* from the north is what I need."

"I have such a one in the farther room."

The merchant indicated the door set back in the inner wall.

The ritual had gone according to pattern—a conversation such as might be heard any day in any Suq—but the sequence was exact—the keywords all there—Kerbela—white *ferwah*.

Only, as Carmichael passed to cross the room and enter the inner enclosure, he raised his eyes to the merchant's face—and knew instantly that the face was not the one he expected to see. Though he had seen this particular man only once before, his keen memory was not at fault. There was a resemblance, a very close resemblance, but it was not the same man.

He stopped. He said, his tone one of mild surprise,

"Where, then, is Salah Hassan?"

"He was my brother. He died three days ago. His affairs are in my hands."

Yes, this was probably a brother. The resemblance was very close. And it was possible that the brother was also employed by the department. Certainly the responses had been correct. Yet it was with an increased awareness that Carmichael passed through into the dim inner chamber. Here again was merchandise piled on shelves, coffee pots and sugar hammers of brass and copper, old Persian silver, heaps of embroideries, folded abas, enamelled Damascus trays and coffee sets.

A white *ferwah* lay carefully folded by itself on a small coffee table. Carmichael went to it and picked it up. Underneath it was a set of European clothes, a worn, slightly flashy business suit. The pocket book with money and credentials was already in the breast pocket. An unknown Arab had entered the store; Mr. Walter Williams of Messrs. Cross and Co. Importers and Shipping agents would emerge and would keep certain appointments made for him in advance. There was, of course, a real Mr. Walter Williams—it was as careful as that—a man with a respectable open business past. All according to plan. With a sigh of relief Carmichael started to unbutton his ragged Army jacket. All was well.

If a revolver had been chosen as the weapon, Carmichael's mission would have failed then and there. But there are advantages in a knife—noticeably noiselessness.

On the shelf in front of Carmichael was a big copper coffee pot and that coffee pot had been recently polished to the order of an American tourist who was coming in to collect it. The gleam of the knife was reflected in that shining rounded surface—a whole picture, distorted but apparent, was reflected there. The man slipping through the hangings behind Carmichael, the long curved knife he had just pulled from beneath his garments. In another moment that knife would have been buried in Carmichael's back.

Like a flash Carmichael wheeled round. With a low flying tackle he brought the other to the ground. The knife flew across the room. Carmichael disentangled himself quickly, leaped over the other's body, rushed through the outer room where he caught a glimpse of the merchant's startled malevolent face and the placid surprise of the fat Hajji. Then he was out, across the Khan, back into the crowded Suq, turning first one way, then another, strolling again now, showing no signs of haste in a country where to hurry is to appear unusual.

And walking thus, almost aimlessly, stopping to examine a piece of stuff, to feel a texture, his brain was working with furious activity. The machinery had broken down! Once more, he was on his own, in hostile country. And he was disagreeably aware of the significance of what had just happened.

It was not only the enemies on his trail he had to fear. Nor was it the enemies guarding the approaches to civilisation. There were enemies to fear within the system. For the passwords had been known, the responses had come pat and correct. The attack had been timed for exactly the moment when he had been lulled into security. Not surprising, perhaps, that there was treachery from within. It must have always been the aim of the enemy to introduce one or more of their own number into the system. Or, perhaps, to buy the man that they needed. Buying a man was easier than one might think—one could buy with other things than money.

Well, no matter how it had come about, there it was. He was on the run—back on his own resources. Without money, without the help of a new personality, and his appearance known. Perhaps at this very moment he was being quietly followed.

He did not turn his head. Of what use would that be? Those who followed were not novices at the game.

Quietly, aimlessly, he continued to stroll. Behind his listless manner he was reviewing various possibilities. He came out of the Suq at last and crossed the little bridge over the canal. He walked on until he saw the big painted hatchment over the doorway and the legend: British Consulate.

He looked up the street and down. No one seemed to be paying the least attention to him. Nothing, it appeared, was easier than just to step into the British Consulate.

He thought, for a moment, of a mousetrap, an open mousetrap with its enticing piece of cheese. That, too, was easy and simple for the mouse . . .

Well, the risk had to be taken. He didn't see what else he could do.

He went throught the doorway.

Chapter 6

Richard Baker sat in the outer office of the British Consulate waiting until the Consul was disengaged.

He had come ashore from the *Indian Queen* that morning and seen his baggage through the customs. It consisted almost entirely of books. Pyjamas and shirts were strewed among them, rather as an afterthought.

The *Indian Queen* had arrived on time and Richard, who had allowed a margin of two days, since small cargo boats such as the *Indian Queen* were frequently delayed, had now two days in hand before he need proceed, via Baghdad, to his ultimate destination, Tell Aswad, the site of the ancient city of Murik.

His plans were already made as to what to do with these two days. A certain reputed mound containing ancient remains at a spot near the sea shore in Kuwait had long excited his curiosity. This was a heaven sent opportunity to investigate same.

He drove to the Airport Hotel and inquired as to the methods of getting to Kuwait. A plane left at ten o'clock the following morning, he was told, and he could return the next day. Everything therefore was plain sailing. There were, of course, the inevitable formalities, exit visa and visa for Kuwait. For these he would have to repair to the British Consulate. The Consul General at Basrah, Mr. Clayton, Richard had met some years previously in Persia. It would be pleasant, Richard thought, to meet him again.

The Consulate had several entrances. A main gate for cars. Another small gate leading out from the garden to the road that lay alongside the Shatt el Arab. The business entrance to the Consulate was in the main street. Richard went in, gave his card to the man on duty, was told the Consul General was engaged at the moment but would soon be free, and was shown into a small waiting room to the left of the passage which ran straight through from the entrance to the garden beyond.

There were several people already in the waiting room. Richard hardly glanced at them. He was, in any case, seldom interested by members of the human race. A fragment of antique pottery was always more exciting to him than a mere human being born somewhere in the twentieth century A.D.

He allowed his thoughts to dwell pleasantly on some aspects of the Mari letters and the movements of the Benjaminite tribes in 1750 B.C.

It would be hard to say exactly what awoke him to a vivid sense of the present and of his fellow human beings. It was, first, an uneasiness, a sense of tension. It came to him, he thought, though he could not be sure, through his nose. Nothing you could diagnose in concrete terms—but it was there, unmistakable, taking him back to days in the late war. One occasion in particular when he, and two others, had been parachuted from a plane, and had waited in the small cold hours of dawn for the moment to do their stuff. A moment when morale was low, when the full hazards of the undertaking were clearly perceived, a moment of dread lest one might not be adequate, a shrinking of the flesh. The same acrid, almost imperceptible tang in the air.

The small of fear . . .

For some moments, this registered only subconsciously. Half of his mind still obstinately strove to focus itself B.C. But the pull of the present was too strong.

Someone in this small room was in deadly fear . . .

He looked round. An Arab in a ragged khaki tunic, his fingers idly slipping over the amber beads he held. A stoutish Englishman with a grey moustache—the commercial traveller type—who was jotting down figures in a small notebook and looking absorbed and important. A tired looking man, very dark skinned, who was leaning back in a reposeful attitude, his face placid and uninterested. A man who looked like an Iraqi clerk. An elderly Persian in flowing snowy robes. They all seemed quite unconcerned.

The clicking of the amber beads fell into a definite rhythm. It seemed, in an odd way, familiar. Richard jerked himself to attention. He had been nearly asleep. Short long—long—short—that was Morse—definite Morse signalling. He was familiar with Morse; part of his job during the war had dealt with signalling. He could read it easily enough. *OWL.* F.L.O.R.E.A.T.E.T.O.N.A. What the devil! Yes, that was it. It was being repeated *Floreat Etona*. Tapped out (or rather clicked out) by a ragged Arab. Hullo, what was this? "Owl. Eton. Owl."

His own nickname at Eton—where he had been sent with an unusually large and solid pair of spectacles.

He looked across the room at the Arab, noting every detail of his appearance—the striped robe—the old khaki tunic—the ragged hand-knitted red scarf full of dropped stitches. A figure such as you saw hundreds of on the waterfront. The eyes met his vacantly with no sign of recognition. But the beads continued to click.

Fakir here. Stand by. Trouble.

Fakir? *Fakir?* Of course! Fakir Carmichael! A boy who had been born or who had lived in some outlandish part of the world—Turkestan, Afghanistan?—

Richard took out his pipe. He took an exploratory pull at it—peered into the bowl and then tapped it on an adjacent ashtray: *Message received.*

After that, things happened very fast. Later, Richard was at pains to sort them out.

The Arab in the torn army jacket got up and crossed towards the door. He stumbled as he was passing Richard, his hand went out and clutched Richard to steady himself. Then he righted himself, apologised and moved towards the door.

It was so surprising and happened so quickly that it seemed to Richard like a cinema scene rather than real life. The stout commercial traveller dropped his notebook and tugged at something in his coat pocket. Because of his plumpness and the tight fit of the coat, he was a second or two in getting it out and in that second or two Richard acted. As the man brought the revolver up, Richard struck it out of his hand. It went off and a bullet buried itself in the floor.

The Arab had passed through the doorway and had turned towards the Consul's office, but he paused suddenly, and turning he ran swiftly the other way to the door by which he had entered and into the busy street.

The kavass ran to Richard's side where he stood holding the stout man's arm. Of the other occupants of the room, the Iraqi clerk was dancing excitedly on his feet, the dark thin man was staring and the elderly Persian gazed into space unmoved.

Richard said:

"What the devil are you doing, brandishing a revolver like that?"

There was just a moment's pause, and then the stout man said in a plaintive cockney voice,

"Sorry, old man. Absolute accident. Just clumsy."

"Nonsense. You were going to shoot at that Arab fellow who's just run out."

"No, no, old man, not shoot him. Just give him a fright. Recognised him suddenly as a fellow who swindled me over some antikas. Just a bit of fun."

Richard Baker was a fastidious soul who disliked publicity of any kind. His instincts were to accept the explanation at its face value. After all, what could he prove? And would old Fakir Carmichael thank him for making a song and dance about the matter? Presumably if he were on some hush-hush, cloak and dagger business he would not.

Richard relaxed his grasp on the man's arm. The fellow was sweating, he noticed.

The kavass was talking excitedly. It was very wrong, he was saying, to bring firearms into the British Consulate. It was not allowed. The Consul would be very angry.

"I apologise," said the fat man. "Little accident—that's all." He thrust some money into the kavass's hand who pushed it back again indignantly.

"I'd better get out of this," said the stout man. "I won't wait to see the Consul." He thrust a card suddenly on Richard. "That's me and I'm at the Airport Hotel if there's any fuss, but actually it was a pure accident. Just a joke if you know what I mean."

Reluctantly, Richard watched him walk with an uneasy swagger out of the room and turn towards the street.

He hoped he had done right, but it was a difficult thing to know what to do when one was as much in the dark as he was.

"Mr. Clayton, he is disengaged now," said the kavass.

Richard followed the man along the corridor. The open circle of sunlight at the end grew larger. The Consul's room was on the right at the extreme end of the passage.

Mr. Clayton was sitting behind his desk. He was a quiet grey haired man with a thoughtful face.

"I don't know whether you remember me?" said Richard. "I met you in Teheran two years ago."

"Of course. You were with Dr. Pauncefoot Jones, weren't you? Are you joining him again this year?"

"Yes. I'm on my way there now, but I've got a few days to spare, and I rather wanted to run down to Kuwait. There's no difficulty, I suppose?"

"Oh no. There's a plane tomorrow morning. It's only about an hour and a half. I'll wire to Archie Gaunt—he's the President there. He'll put you up. And we can put you up here for the night."

Richard protested slightly.

"Really—I don't want to bother you and Mrs. Clayton. I can go to the hotel."

"The Airport Hotel's very full. We'd be delighted to have you here. I know my wife would like to meet you again. At the moment—let me see—we've got Crosbie of the Oil Company and some young sprig of Dr. Rathbone's who's down here clearing some cases of books through the customs. Come upstairs and see Rosa—"

He got up and escorted Richard out through the door and into the sunlit garden. A light of steps led up to the living quarters of the Consulate.

Gerald Clayton pushed open the wire door at the top of the steps and ushered his guest into a long dim hallway with attractive rugs on the floor and choice examples of furniture on either side. It was pleasant coming into the cold dimness after the glare outside.

Clayton called, "Rosa, Rosa," and Mrs. Clayton whom Richard remembered as a buoyant personality with abounding vitality came out of an end room.

"You remember Richard Baker, dear? He came to see us with Dr. Pauncefoot Jones in Teheran."

"Of course," said Mrs. Clayton shaking hands. "We went to the bazaars together and you bought some lovely rugs."

It was Mrs. Clayton's delight when not buying things herself to urge on her friends and acquaintances to seek for bargains in the local Suqs. She always had a wonderful knowledge of values and was an excellent bargainer.

"One of the best purchases I've ever made," said Richard. "And entirely owing to your good offices."

"Baker wants to fly to Kuwait tomorrow," said Gerald Clayton. "I've said that we can put him up here for tonight."

"But if it's any trouble," began Richard.

"Of course, it's no trouble," said Mrs. Clayton. "You can't have the best spare room, because Captain Crosbie has got it, but we can make you quite comfortable. You don't want to buy a nice Kuwait chest, do you? Because they've got some lovely ones in the Suq just now. Gerald won't let me buy another one for here, though it would be quite useful to keep extra blankets in."

"You've got three already, dear," said Clayton mildly. "Now, if you'll excuse me, Baker. I must get back to the office. There seems to have been a spot of trouble in the outer office. Somebody let off a revolver, I understand."

"One of the local sheikhs, I suppose," said Mrs. Clayton. "They are so excitable and they do so love firearms."

"On the contrary," said Richard. "It was an Englishman. His intention seemed to be to take a pot shot at an Arab." He added gently, "I knocked his arm up."

"So you were in it all," said Clayton. "I didn't realise that." He fished a card out of his pocket. "Robert Hall. Achilles Works, Enfield seems to be his name. I don't know what he wanted to see me about. He wasn't drunk, was he?"

"He said it was a joke," said Richard drily, "and that the gun went off by accident."

Clayton raised his eyebrows.

"Commercial travellers don't usually carry loaded guns in their pockets," he said.

Clayton, Richard thought, was no fool.

"Perhaps I ought to have stopped him going away."

"It's difficult to know what one should do when these things happen. The man he fired at wasn't hurt."

"No."

"Probably was better to let the thing slide, then."

"I wonder what was behind it?"

"Yes, yes . . . I wonder too."

Clayton looked a little distrait.

"Well, I must be getting back," he said and hurried away.

Mrs. Clayton took Richard into the drawing room, a large inside room, with green cushions and curtains, and offered him a choice of coffee or beer. He chose beer and it came deliciously iced.

She asked him why he was going to Kuwait and he told her.

She asked him why he hadn't got married yet, and Richard said he didn't think he was the marrying kind, to which Mrs. Clayton said briskly: "Nonsense." Archaeologists, she said, made splendid husbands,—and were there any young women coming out to the Dig this season? One or two, Richard said, and Mrs. Pauncefoot Jones of course.

Mrs. Clayton asked hopefully if they were nice girls who were coming out, and Richard said he didn't know because he hadn't met them yet. They were very inexperienced, he said.

For some reason this made Mrs. Clayton laugh.

Then a short stocky man with an abrupt manner came in and was introduced as Captain Crosbie. Mr. Baker, said Mrs. Clayton, was an archaeologist and dug up the most wildly interesting things thousands of years old. Captain Crosbie said he never could understand how archaeologists were able to say so definitely how old these things were. Always used to think they must be the most awful liars, ha ha, said Captain Crosbie. Richard looked at him in a rather tired kind of way. No, said Captain Crosbie, but how did an archaeologist know how old a thing was?

Richard said that that would take a long time to explain, and Mrs. Clayton quickly took him away to see his room.

"He's very nice," said Mrs. Clayton, "but not quite quite, you know. Hasn't got any idea of culture."

Richard found his room exceedingly comfortable, and his appreciation of Mrs. Clayton as a hostess rose still higher.

Feeling in the pocket of his coat, he drew out a folded up piece of dirty paper. He looked at it with surprise, for he knew quite well that it had not been there earlier in the morning.

He remembered how the Arab had clutched him when he stumbled. A man with deft fingers might have slipped this into his pocket without his being aware of it.

He unfolded the paper. It was dirty and seemed to have been folded and refolded many times.

In six lines of rather crabbed handwriting Major John Wilberforce recommended one Ahmed Mohammed as an industrious and willing worker, able to drive a lorry and do minor repairs and strictly honest—It was, in fact, the usual type of "chit" or recommendation given in the East. It was dated eighteen months back, which again is not unusual, as these chits are hoarded carefully by their possessors.

Frowning to himself, Richard went over the events of the morning in his precise orderly fashion.

Fakir Carmichael, he was now well assured, had been in fear of his life. He was a hunted man and he had bolted into the Consulate. Why? To find security? But instead of that he had found a more instant menace. The enemy, or a representative of the enemy, had been waiting for him. This commercial traveller chap must have had very definite orders—to be willing to risk shooting Carmichael in the Consulate in the presence of witnesses. It must, therefore, have been very urgent. And Carmichael had appealed to his old school friend for help, and had managed to pass this seemingly innocent document into his possession. It must, therefore, be very important, and if Carmichael's enemies caught up with him, and found that he no longer possessed this document, they would doubtless put two and two together and look for any person or persons to whom Carmichael might conceivably have passed it on.

What then was Richard Baker to do with it?

He could pass it on to Clayton, as His Britannic Majesty's representative.

Or he could keep it in his own possession until such time as Carmichael claimed it?

After a few minutes' reflection he decided to do the latter.

But first he took certain precautions.

Tearing a blank half sheet of paper off an old letter, he sat down to compose a reference for a lorry driver in much the same terms, but using different wording—if this message was a code that took care of that— though it was possible, of course, that there was a message written in some kind of invisible ink.

Then he smeared his own composition with dust from his shoes— rubbed it in his hands, folded and refolded it—until it gave a reasonable appearance of age and dirt.

Then he crumpled it up and put it into his pocket. The original he stared at for some time whilst he considered and rejected various possibilities.

Finally, with a slight smile, he folded and refolded it until he had a small oblong. Taking a stick of plasticine (without which he never travelled) out of his bag, he first wrapped his packet in oilsilk cut from his spongebag, then encased it in plasticine. This done he rolled and patted out the plasticine till he had a smooth surface. On this he rolled out an impression from a cylinder seal that he had with him.

He studied the result with grim appreciation.

It showed a beautifully carved design of the Sun God Shamash, armed with the Sword of Justice.

"Let's hope that's a good omen," he said to himself.

That evening, when he looked in the pocket of the coat he had worn in the morning, the screwed up paper had gone.

Chapter 7

Life, thought Victoria, life at last! Sitting in her seat at Airways Terminal there had come the magic moment when the words "Passengers for Cairo, Baghdad and Teheran, take your places in the bus, please," had been uttered.

Magic names, magic words. Devoid of glamour to Mrs. Hamilton Clipp who, as far as Victoria could make out, had spent a large portion of her life jumping from boats into aeroplanes and from aeroplanes into trains, with brief intervals at expensive hotels in between. But to Victoria they were a marvellous change from the oft repeated phrases "Take this down, please, Miss Jones." "The kettle's boiling, ducks, just make the tea, will you." "I know where you can get the most marvellous perm." Trivial boring everyday happenings! And now: Cairo, Baghdad, Teheran—all the romance of the glorious East (and Edward at the end of it).

Victoria returned to earth to hear her employer whom she had already diagnosed as a non-stop talker, concluding a series of remarks by saying:

"—and nothing really clean if you know what I mean. I'm always very very careful what I eat. The filth of the streets and the bazaars you wouldn't believe. And the unhygienic rags the people wear. And some of the toilets—why, you just couldn't call them toilets at all!"

Victoria listened dutifully to these depressing remarks, but her own sense of glamour remained undimmed. Dirt and germs meant nothing in her young life. They arrived at Heathrow and she assisted Mrs. Clipp to alight from the bus. She was already in charge of passports, tickets, money, etc.

"My," said that lady, "it certainly is a comfort to have you with me,

Miss Jones. I just don't know what I'd have done if I'd had to travel alone."

Travelling by air, Victoria thought, was rather like being taken on a school treat. Brisk teachers, kind but firm, were at hand to shepherd you at every turn. Air hostesses, in trim uniform with the authority of nursery governesses dealing with feeble minded children, explained kindly just what you were to do. Victoria almost expected them to preface their remarks with: "Now, children."

Tired looking young gentlemen behind desks extended weary hands to check passports, to enquire intimately of money and jewellery. They managed to induce a sense of guilt in those questioned. Victoria, suggestible by nature, knew a sudden longing to describe her one meagre brooch as a diamond tiara value ten thousand pounds, just to see the expression on the bored young man's face. Thoughts of Edward restrained her.

The various barriers passed, they sat down to wait once more in a large room giving directly on the aerodrome. Outside the roar of a plane being revved up gave the proper background. Mrs. Hamilton Clipp was now happily engaged in making a running commentary on their fellow travellers.

"Aren't those two little children just too cute for words? But what an ordeal to travel alone with a couple of children. British, I guess they are. That's a well-cut suit the mother has on. She looks kind of tired, though. That's a good looking man—rather Latin looking, I'd say. What a loud check that man has on—I'd call it very bad taste. Business, I guess. That man over there's a Dutchman; he was just ahead of us at the controls. That family over there is either Turkish or Persian, I should say. There don't seem to be any Americans. I guess they go mostly Pan American. I'd say those three men talking together are Oil, wouldn't you? I just love looking at people and wondering about them. Mr. Clipp says to me I've got a real yen for human nature. It seems to me just natural to take an interest in your fellow creatures. Wouldn't you say that mink coat over there cost every bit of three thousand dollars?"

Mrs. Clipp sighed. Having duly appraised her fellow travellers, she became restless.

"I'd like to know what we are waiting for like this. That plane's revved up four times. We're all here. Why can't they get on with things? They're certainly not keeping to schedule."

"Would you like a cup of coffee, Mrs. Clipp? I see there is a buffet at the end of the room?"

"Why, no, thank you, Miss Jones. I had coffee before I started, and my stomach feels too unsettled right now to take anything more. What are we waiting for, I'd like to know?"

Her question seemed to be answered almost before the words were out of her mouth.

The door leading from the corridor out of the Customs and Passport department swung open with a rush and a tall man came through with the effect of a gust of wind. Air officials of the line hovered around him. Two large canvas sacks sealed were carried by an officer of B.O.A.C.

Mrs. Clipp sat up with alacrity.

"He's certainly some big noise," she remarked.

"And knows it," thought Victoria.

There was something of calculated sensationalism about the late traveller. He wore a kind of dark grey travelling cloak with a capacious hood at the back. On his head was what was in essence a wide sombrero, but in light grey. He had silver grey curling hair, worn rather long, and a beautiful silver grey moustache curling up at the ends. The effect was that of a handsome stage bandit. Victoria, who disliked theatrical men who posed, looked at him with disapproval.

The Air Officials were, she noted with displeasure, all over him.

"Yes, Sir Rupert." "Of course, Sir Rupert." "The plane is leaving immediately, Sir Rupert."

With a swirl of his voluminous cloak, Sir Rupert passed out through the door leading to the aerodrome. The door swung to behind him with vehemence.

"Sir Rupert," murmured Mrs. Clipp. "Now who would he be, I wonder?"

Victoria shook her head, though she had a vague feeling that the face and general appearance were not unknown to her.

"Somebody important in your Government," suggested Mrs. Clipp.

"I shouldn't think so," said Victoria.

The few members of the Government she had ever seen had impressed her as men anxious to apologise for being alive. Only on platforms did they spring into pompous and didactic life.

"Now then, please," said the smart Nursery Governess Air Hostess. "Take your seats in the plane. This way. As quickly as you can, please."

Her attitude implied that a lot of dawdling children had been keeping the patient grown-ups waiting.

Everybody filed out onto the aerodrome.

The great plane was waiting, its engine ticking over like the satisfied purring of a gigantic lion.

Victoria and a steward helped Mrs. Clipp on board and settled her in her seat. Victoria sat next to her on the aisle. Not until Mrs. Clipp was comfortably ensconced, and Victoria had fastened her safety belt, did the girl have leisure to observe that in front of them was sitting the great man.

The doors closed. A few seconds later, the plane began to move slowly along the ground.

"We're really going," thought Victoria in ecstasy. "Oh, isn't it frightening. Suppose it never gets up off the ground? Really I don't see how it can!"

During what seemed an age the plane taxied along the aerodrome, then it turned slowly round and stopped. The engines rose to a ferocious roar. Chewing gum, barley sugar and cotton wool were handed round.

Louder and louder, fiercer and fiercer. Then, once more, the aeroplane moved forward. Mincingly at first, then faster—faster still—they were rushing along the ground.

"It will never go up," thought Victoria, "we'll be killed."

Faster—more smoothly—no jars—no bumps—they were off the ground skimming along, up, round, back over the car park and the main road, up, higher—a silly little train puffing below—dolls' houses—toy cars on roads . . . Higher still—and suddenly the earth below lost interest, was no longer human or alive—just a large flat map with lines and circles and dots.

Inside the plane people undid their safety belts, lit cigarettes, opened magazines. Victoria was in a new world—a world so many feet long and a very few feet wide, inhabited by twenty to thirty people. Nothing else existed.

She peered out of the small window again. Below her were clouds, a fluffy pavement of clouds. The plane was in the sun. Below the clouds somewhere was the world she had known heretofore.

Victoria pulled herself together. Mrs. Hamilton Clipp was talking. Victoria removed cotton wool from her ear and bent attentively towards her.

In the seat in front of her, Sir Rupert rose, tossed his wide brimmed grey felt hat to the rack, drew up his hood over his head and relaxed into his seat.

"Pompous ass," thought Victoria, unreasonably prejudiced.

Mrs. Clipp was established with a magazine open in front of her. At intervals, she nudged Victoria when on trying to turn the page with one hand, the magazine slipped.

Victoria looked round her. She decided that air travel was really rather boring. She opened a magazine, found herself faced with an advertisement that said "Do you want to increase your efficiency as a shorthand typist?" shuddered, shut the magazine, leant back, and began to think of Edward.

They came down at Castel Benito Aerodrome in a storm of rain. Victoria was by now feeling slightly sick, and it took all her energies to accomplish her duties vis-à-vis with her employer. They were driven through scurrying rain to the rest house. The magnificent Sir Rupert, Victoria noted, had been met by an officer in uniform with red tabs, and hurried off in a staff car to some dwelling of the mighty in Tripolitania.

They were allotted rooms; Victoria helped Mrs. Clipp with her toilet and left her to rest on her bed in a dressing gown until it was time for the evening meal. Victoria retired to her own room, lay down and closed her eyes, grateful to be spared the sight of the heaving and sinking floor.

She awakened an hour later in good health and spirits and went to help Mrs. Clipp. Presently a rather more peremptory Air Hostess instructed them that cars were ready to convey them to the evening meal. After dinner, Mrs. Clipp got into conversation with some of her fellow travellers. The man in the loud check coat seemed to have taken a fancy to Victoria and told her at some length all about the manufacture of lead pencils.

Later, they were conveyed back to their sleeping quarters and told curtly that they must be ready to depart at 5.30 a.m. the following morning.

"We haven't seen much of Tripolitania, have we," said Victoria rather sadly. "Is Air Travel always like this?"

"Why, yes, I'd say so. It's just positively sadistic the way they get you up in the mornings. After that, often they keep you hanging round the aerodrome for an hour or two. Why, in Rome, I remember they called us at 3.30. Breakfast in the restaurant at 4 o'clock. And then actually at the Airport we didn't leave until eight. Still the great thing is they get you to your destination right away with no fooling about on the way."

Victoria sighed. She could have done with a good deal of fooling about. She wanted to see the world.

"And what do you, know, my dear," continued Mrs. Clipp excitedly, "you know that interesting looking man? The Britisher? The one that there's all the fuss about. I've found out who he is. That's Sir Rupert Crofton Lee, the great traveller. You've heard of him, of course."

Yes, Victoria remembered now. She had seen several pictures in the press about six months ago. Sir Rupert was a great authority upon the interior of China. He was one of the few people who had been to Tibet and visited Lhasa. He had travelled through the unknown parts of Kurdistan and Asia Minor. His books had had a wide sale, for they had been racily and wittily written. If Sir Rupert was just noticeably a self advertiser, it was with good reason. He made no claims that were not fully justified. The cloak with the hood and the wide brimmed hat were, Victoria remembered now, a deliberate fashion of his own choosing.

"Isn't that thrilling, now?" demanded Mrs. Clipp with all a lion hunter's enthusiasm as Victoria adjusted the bedclothes over her recumbent form.

Victoria agreed that it was very thrilling, but she said to herself that she preferred Sir Rupert's books to his personality. He was, she considered, what children call "a show off!"

A start was made in good order the next morning. The weather had cleared and the sun was shining. Victoria still felt disappointed to have seen so little of Tripolitania. Still the plane was due to arrive at Cairo by lunch time and the departure to Baghdad did not take place until the following morning, so she would at least be able to see a little of Egypt in the afternoon.

They were flying over the sea, but clouds soon blocked out the blue water below them and Victoria settled back in her seat with a yawn. In front of her Sir Rupert was already asleep. The hood had fallen back from his head which was hanging forwards, nodding at intervals. Victoria observed with a faint malicious pleasure that he had a small boil starting on the back of his neck. Why she should have been pleased at this fact was hard to say—perhaps it made the great man seem more human and vulnerable. He was as other men, after all—prone to the small annoyances of the flesh. It may be said that Sir Rupert had kept up his Olympian manner and had taken no notice whatever of his fellow travellers.

"Who does he think he is, I wonder?" thought Victoria to herself. The answer was obvious. He was Sir Rupert Crofton Lee, a celebrity, and she was Victoria Jones, an indifferent shorthand typist, and of no account whatever.

On arrival at Cairo, Victoria and Mrs. Hamilton Clipp had lunch together. The latter then announced that she was going to nap until six o'clock, and suggested that Victoria might like to go and see the Pyramids.

"I've arranged for a car for you, Miss Jones, because I know that owing to your Treasury regulations, you won't be able to cash any money here."

Victoria who had in any case no money to cash, was duly grateful, and said so with some effusion.

"Why, that's nothing at all. You've been very very kind to me. And, travelling with dollars, everything is easy for us. Mrs. Kitchin—the lady with the two cute children—is very anxious to go, also, so I suggested you'd join up with her—if that suits you?"

So long as she saw the world, anything suited Victoria.

"That's fine. Then you'd better get off right now."

The afternoon at the Pyramids was duly enjoyed. Victoria, though reasonably fond of children, might have enjoyed it more without Mrs. Kitchin's offspring. Children when sight seeing is in progress are apt to be somewhat of a handicap. The youngest child became so fretful that the two women returned earlier from the expedition than they had meant to do.

Victoria threw herself on her bed with a yawn. She wished very much that she could stay a week in Cairo—perhaps go up the Nile. "And what would you use for money, my girl?" she asked herself witheringly. It was already a miracle that she was being transported to Baghdad free of charge.

And what, enquired a cold inward voice, are you going to do, once you are landed in Baghdad with only a few pounds in your pocket?

Victoria waved that query aside. Edward must find her a job. Or failing that, she would find herself a job. Why worry?

Her eyes, dazzled with strong sunlight, closed gently.

A knock on the door, as she thought, roused her. She called "Come in"; then as there was no response, she got off the bed, crossed to the door and opened it.

But the knock had not been at her door, but at the next door down the passage. Another of the inevitable Air Hostesses, dark haired and trim in her uniform, was knocking at Sir Rupert Crofton Lee's door. He opened it just as Victoria looked out.

"What's the matter now?"

He sounded annoyed and sleepy.

"I'm so sorry to disturb you, Sir Rupert," cooed the Air Hostess, "but would you mind coming to the B.O.A.C. office. It's just three doors down the passage here. Just a small detail about the flight to Baghdad tomorrow."

"Oh, very well."

Victoria withdrew into her room. She was less sleepy now. She glanced at her watch. Only half past four. An hour and a half until Mrs. Clipp would be requiring her. She decided to go out and walk about Heliopolis. Walking, at least, required no money.

She powdered her nose and resumed her shoes. They felt rather full of feet. The visit to the Pyramids had been hard on feet.

She came out of her room and walked along the corridor towards the main hall of the Hotel. Three doors down she passed the B.O.A.C. office. It had a card announcing the fact nailed to the door. Just as she passed it, the door opened and Sir Rupert came out. He was walking fast and he overtook her in a couple of strides. He went on ahead of her, his cloak swinging, and Victoria fancied that he was annoyed about something.

Mrs. Clipp was in a somewhat petulant mood when Victoria reported for duty at six o'clock.

"I'm worried about the excess on my baggage, Miss Jones. I took it that I'd paid for that right through, but it seems that it's only paid until

Cairo. We go on tomorrow by Iraqi Airways. My ticket is a through ticket, but not the excess baggage. Perhaps you'd go and find out if that is really so? Because maybe I ought to change another traveller's cheque."

Victoria agreed to make enquiries. She could not find the B.O.A.C. office at first, and finally located it in the far corridor—the other side of the hall—quite a big office. The other, she supposed, had been a small office only used during the afternoon siesta hours. Mrs. Clipp's fears about the excess baggage were found to be justified which annoyed that lady very much.

Chapter 8

On the fifth floor of a block of offices in the City of London are situated the offices of the Valhalla Gramophone Company. The man who sat behind the desk in that office was reading a book on economics. The telephone rang and he picked up the receiver. He said in a quiet unemotional voice:

"Valhalla Gramophone Company."

"Sanders here."

"Sanders of the River? What River?"

"River Tigris. Reporting as to A. S. We've lost her."

There was a moment's silence. Then the quiet voice spoke again, with a steely note in it.

"Did I hear what you said correctly?"

"We've lost Anna Scheele."

"No names. This is a very serious error on your part. How did it come about?"

"She went into that nursing home. I told you before. Her sister was having an operation."

"Well?"

"The operation went off all right. We expected A. S. to return to the Savoy. She had kept on her suite. She didn't return. Watch had been kept on the nursing home and we were quite sure she hadn't left it. We assumed she was still there."

"And she isn't?"

"We've just found out. She left there, in an ambulance, the day after the operation."

"She deliberately fooled you?"

"Looks like it. I'd swear she didn't know she was being followed. We took every precaution. There were three of us and—".

"Never mind the excuses. Where did the ambulance take her?"

"To University College Hospital."

"What have you learnt from the Hospital?"

"That a patient was brought in accompanied by a Hospital Nurse. The Hospital Nurse must have been Anna Scheele. They've no idea where she went after she brought the patient in."

"And the patient?"

"The patient knows nothing. She was under morphia."

"So Anna Scheele walked out of University College Hospital dressed as a nurse and may now be anywhere?"

"Yes. If she goes back to the Savoy—"

The other interrupted.

"She won't go back to the Savoy."

"Shall we check up on other hotels?"

"Yes, but I doubt if you'll get any result. That's what she'd expect you to do."

"What instructions otherwise?"

"Check on the ports—Dover, Folkestone, etc. Check with Air Lines. In particular check all bookings to Baghdad by plane for the next fortnight. The passage won't be booked in her own name. Check up on all passengers of suitable age."

"Her baggage is still at the Savoy. Perhaps she'll claim."

"She won't do anything of the sort. You may be a fool—she isn't! Does the sister know anything?"

"We're in contact with her special nurse at the Home. Apparently the sister thinks A. S. is in Paris doing business for Morganthal and staying at Ritz Hotel. She believes A. S. is flying home to States on 23rd."

"In other words A. S. has told her nothing. She wouldn't. Check up on those air passages. It's the only hope. She's got to get to Baghdad—and Air is the only way she can do it in time, and, Sanders—"

"Yes?"

"No more failures. This is your last chance."

Chapter 9

Young Mr. Shrivenham of the British Embassy shifted from one foot to the other and gazed upwards as the plane zoomed over Baghdad aerodrome. There was a considerable dust-storm in progress. Palm trees, houses, human beings were all shrouded in a thick brown haze. It had come on quite suddenly.

Lionel Shrivenham observed in a tone of deep distress:

"Ten to one they can't come down here."

"What will they do?" asked his friend Harold.

"Go on to Basrah, I imagine. It's clear there, I hear."

"You're meeting some kind of a V.I.P., aren't you?"

Young Mr. Shrivenham groaned again.

"Just my luck. The new Ambassador has been delayed coming out. Lansdowne, the Counsellor, is in England. Rice, the Oriental Counsellor, is ill in bed with gastric flu, dangerously high temperature. Best is in Teheran, and here am I, left with the whole bag of tricks. No end of a flap about this fellow. I don't know why. Even the hush hush boys are in a flap. He's one of these world travellers, always off somewhere inaccessible on a camel. Don't see why he's so important, but apparently he's absolutely the cat's whiskers, and I'm to conform to his slightest wish. If he gets carried on to Basrah he'll probably be wild. Don't know what arrangements I'd better lay on. Train up tonight? Or get the R.A.F. to fly him up tomorrow?"

Mr. Shrivenham sighed again, as his sense of injury and responsibility deepened. Since his arrival three months ago in Baghdad he had been consistently unlucky. One more raspberry, he felt, would finally blight what might have been a promising career.

The plane swooped overhead once more.

"Evidently thinks he can't make it," said Shrivenham, then added excitedly: "Hullo—I believe he's coming down."

A few moments later and the plane had taxied sedately to its place and Shrivenham stood ready to greet the V.I.P.

His unprofessional eye noted "rather a pretty girl . . ." before he sprang forward to greet the buccaneer-like figure in the swirling cloak.

"Practically fancy dress," he thought to himself disapprovingly as he said aloud:

"Sir Rupert Crofton Lee? I'm Shrivenham of the Embassy."

Sir Rupert, he thought, was slightly curt in manner—perhaps understandable after the strain of circling round the city uncertain whether a landing could be effected or not.

"Nasty day," continued Shrivenham. "Had a lot of this sort of thing this year. Ah, you've got the bags. Then, if you'll follow me, sir, it's all laid on . . ."

As they left the aerodrome in the car, Shrivenham said:

"I thought for a bit that you were going to be carried on to some other airport, sir. Didn't look as though the pilot could make a landing. Came up suddenly, this dust-storm."

Sir Rupert blew out his cheeks importantly as he remarked:

"That would have been disastrous—quite disastrous. Had my schedule been jeopardised, young man, I can tell you that the results would have been grave and far-reaching in the extreme."

"Lot of cock," thought Shrivenham disrespectfully. "These V.I.P.'s think their potty affairs are what makes the world go round."

Aloud he said respectfully:

"I expect that's so, sir."

"Have you any idea when the Ambassador will reach Baghdad?"

"Nothing definite as yet, sir."

"I shall be sorry to miss him. Haven't seen him since—let me see, yes, India in 1938."

Shrivenham preserved a respectful silence.

"Let me see, Rice is here, isn't he?"

"Yes, sir, he's Oriental Counsellor."

"Capable fellow. Knows a lot. I'll be glad to meet him again."

Shrivenham coughed.

"As a matter of fact, sir, Rice is on the sick list. They've taken him to hospital for observation. Violent type of gastro enteritis. Something a bit worse than the usual Baghdad tummy, apparently."

"What's that?" Sir Rupert turned his head sharply. "Bad gastro enteritis—hm. Came on suddenly, did it?"

"Day before yesterday, sir."

Sir Rupert was frowning. The rather affected grandiloquence of manner had dropped from him. He was a simpler man—and somewhat of a worried one.

"I wonder," he said. "Yes, I wonder."

Shrivenham looked politely enquiring.

"I'm wondering," said Sir Rupert, "if it might be a case of Scheele's Green. . . ."

Baffled, Shrivenham remained silent.

They were just approaching the Feisal Bridge, and the car swung off to the left towards the British Embassy.

Suddenly Sir Rupert leant forward.

"Just stop a minute, will you?" he said sharply. "Yes, right hand side. Where all those pots are."

The car glided in to the right hand curb and stopped. It was a small native shop piled high with crude white clay pots and water jars.

A short stocky European who had been standing talking to the proprietor moved away towards the bridge as the car drew up. Shrivenham thought it was Crosbie of the I and P whom he had met once or twice.

Sir Rupert sprang from the car and strode up to the small booth. Picking up one of the pots, he started a rapid conversation in Arabic with the proprietor. The flow of speech was too fast for Shrivenham whose Arabic was as yet slow and painstaking and distinctly limited in vocabulary.

The proprietor was beaming, his hands flew wide, he gesticulated, he explained at length. Sir Rupert handled different pots, apparently asking questions about them. Finally he selected a narrow mouthed water jar, tossed the man some coins and went back to the car.

"Interesting technique," said Sir Rupert. "Been making them like this for thousands of years, same shape as in one of the hill districts in Armenia."

His finger slipped down through the narrow aperture, twisting round and round.

"It's very crude stuff," said Shrivenham unimpressed.

"Oh, no artistic merit! But interesting historically. See these indications of lugs here? You pick up many a historical tip from observation of the simple things in daily use. I've got a collection of them."

The car turned in through the gates of the British Embassy.

Sir Rupert demanded to be taken straight to his room. Shrivenham was amused to note that, his lecture on the clay pot ended, Sir Rupert had left it nonchalantly in the car. Shrivenham made a point of carrying it up-stairs and placing it meticulously upon Sir Rupert's bedside table.

"Your pot, sir."

"Eh? Oh, thank you, my boy."

Sir Rupert appeared distrait. Shrivenham left him after repeating that luncheon would be ready shortly and drinks awaited his choice.

When the young man had left the room, Sir Rupert went to the win-dow and unfolded the small slip of paper that had been tucked into the mouth of the pot. He smoothed it out. There were two lines of writing on it. He read them over carefully, then set light to the paper with a match.

Then he summoned a servant.

"Yes, sir? I unpack for you, sir?"

"Not yet. I want to see Mr. Shrivenham—up here."

Shrivenham arrived with a slight apprehensive expression.

"Anything I can do, sir? Anything wrong?"

"Mr. Shrivenham, a drastic change has occurred in my plans. I can count upon your discretion, of course?"

"Oh absolutely, sir."

"It is some time since I was in Baghdad; actually I have not been here since the war. The hotels lie mainly on the other bank, do they not?"

"Yes, sir. In Rashid Street."

"Backing on the Tigris?"

"Yes. Babylonian Palace is the biggest of them. That's the more or less official hotel."

"What do you know about a hotel called the Tio?"

"Oh, a lot of people go there. Food's rather good and it's run by a ter-rific character called Marcus Tio. He's quite an institution in Baghdad."

"I want you to book me a room there, Mr. Shrivenham."

"You mean—you're not going to stay at the Embassy?" Shrivenham looked nervously apprehensive. "But—but—it's all laid on, sir."

"What is laid on can be laid off," barked Sir Rupert.

"Of, of course, sir. I didn't mean. . . ."

Shrivenham broke off. He had a feeling that in the future someone was going to blame him.

"I have certain somewhat delicate negotiations to carry out. I learn that they cannot be carried out from the Embassy. I want you to book me a room tonight at the Tio Hotel and I wish to leave the Embassy in a rea-sonably unobtrusive manner. That is to say I do not want to drive up to the Tio in an Embassy car. I also require a seat booked on the plane leav-ing for Cairo the day after tomorrow."

Shrivenham looked more dismayed still.

"But I understood you were staying five days—"

"That is no longer the case. It is imperative that I reach Cairo as soon as my business here is terminated. It would not be safe for me to remain longer."

"Safe?"

A sudden grim smile transformed Sir Rupert's face. The manner which Shrivenham had been likening to that of a Prussian drill sergeant was laid aside. The man's charm became suddenly apparent.

"Safety hasn't usually been one of my preoccupations, I agree," he said. "But in this case it isn't only my own safety I have to consider—my safety includes the safety of a lot of other people as well. So make those arrangements for me. If the air passage is difficult, apply for priority. Until I leave here tonight, I shall remain in my room." He added, as Shrivenham's mouth opened in surprise, "Officially, I'm sick. Touch of malaria." The other nodded. "So I shan't need food."

"But surely we can send you up—"

"Twenty-four hours' fast is nothing to me. I've gone hungrier longer than that on some of my journeys. You just do as I tell you."

Downstairs, Shrivenham was greeted by his colleagues and groaned in answer to their enquiries.

"Cloak and dagger stuff in a big way," he said. "Can't quite make his grandiloquence Sir Rupert Crofton Lee out. Whether it's genuine or play-acting. That swirling cloak and bandit's hat and all the rest of it. Fellow who'd read one of his books told me that although he's a bit of a self advertiser, he really has done all these things and been to these places—but I don't know . . . Wish Thomas Rice was up and about to cope. That reminds me, what's Scheele's Green?"

"Scheele's Green?" said his friend, frowning. "Something to do with wallpaper, isn't it? Poisonous. It's a form of arsenic, I think."

"Cripes!" said Shrivenham, staring, "I thought it was a disease. Something like amoebic dysentery."

"Oh no, it's something in the chemical line. What wives do their husbands in with, or vice versa."

Shrivenham had relapsed into startled silence. Certain disagreeable facts were becoming clear to him. Crofton Lee had suggested, in effect, that Thomas Rice, Oriental Counsellor to the Embassy was suffering, not from gastro enteritis, but from arsenical poisoning. Added to that Sir Rupert had suggested that his own life was in danger, and his decision not to eat food and drink prepared in the kitchens of the British Embassy shook Shrivenham's decorous British soul to the core. He couldn't imagine what to make of it all.

Chapter 10

Victoria, breathing in hot choking yellow dust, was unfavourably impressed by Baghdad. From the Airport to the Tio Hotel, her ears had been assailed by continuous and incessant noise. Horns of cars blaring with maddening persistence, voices shouting, whistles blowing, then more deafening senseless blaring of motor horns. Added to the loud incessant noises of the street was a small thin trickle of continuous sound which was Mrs. Hamilton Clipp talking.

Victoria arrived at the Tio Hotel in a dazed condition.

A small alleyway led back from the fanfare of Rashid Street towards the Tigris. A short flight of steps to go up and there at the entrance of the Hotel, they were greeted by a very stout young man with a beaming smile who, metaphorically at least, gathered them to his heart. This, Victoria gathered was Marcus—or more correctly Mr. Tio, the owner of the Tio Hotel.

His words of welcome were interrupted by shouted orders to various underlings regarding the disposal of their baggage.

"And here you are, once more, Mrs. Clipp—but your arm—why is it in that funny stuff?—(You fools, do not carry that with the strap! Imbeciles! Don't trail that coat!)—But, my dear—what a day to arrive—never, I thought, would the plane land. It went round and round and round. Marcus, I said to myself—it is not you that will travel by planes—all this hurry, what does it matter?—And you have brought a young lady with you—it is nice always to see a new young lady in Baghdad—why did not Mr. Harrison come down to meet you—I expected him yesterday—but my dear, you must have a drink at once—"

Now, somewhat dazed, Victoria, her head reeling slightly under the effect of a double whisky authoritatively pressed upon her by Marcus, was standing in a high whitewashed room containing a large brass bedstead, a very sophisticated dressing table of newest French design, an aged Victorian wardrobe, and two vivid plush chairs. Her modest baggage reposed at her feet and a very old man with a yellow face and white whiskers had grinned and nodded at her as he placed towels in the bathroom and asked her if she would like the water made hot for a bath.

"How long would it take?"

"Twenty minutes, half an hour. I go and do it now."

With a fatherly smile he withdrew. Victoria sat down on the bed and passed an experimental hand over her hair. It felt clogged with dust and her face was sore and gritty. She looked at herself in the glass. The dust had changed her hair from black to a strange reddish brown. She pulled aside a corner of the curtain and looked out onto a wide balcony which gave on the river. But there was nothing to be seen of the Tigris except a thick yellow haze. A prey to deep depression, Victoria said to herself: "What a hateful place."

Then rousing herself, she stepped across the landing and tapped on Mrs. Clipp's door. Prolonged and active ministrations would be required of her here before she could attend to her own cleansing and rehabilitation.

After a bath, lunch and a prolonged nap, Victoria stepped out from her bedroom onto the balcony and gazed with approval across the Tigris. The dust-storm had subsided. Instead of a yellow haze, a pale clear light was appearing. Across the river was a delicate silhouette of palm trees and irregularly placed houses.

Voices came up to Victoria from the garden below. She stepped to the edge of the balcony and looked over.

Mrs. Hamilton Clipp, that indefatigable talker and friendly soul, had struck up an acquaintanceship with an Englishwoman—one of those weatherbeaten Englishwomen of indeterminate age who can always be found in any foreign city.

"—and whatever I'd have done without her, I really don't know," Mrs. Clipp was saying. "She's just the sweetest girl you can imagine. And very well connected. A niece of the Bishop of Llangow."

"Bishop of who?"

"Why, Llangow, I think it was."

"Nonsense, there's no such person," said the other.

Victoria frowned. She recognized the type of County Englishwoman who is unlikely to be taken in by the mention of spurious Bishops.

"Why, then, perhaps I got the name wrong," Mrs. Clipp said doubtfully.

"But," she resumed, "she certainly is a very charming and competent girl."

The other said "Ha!" in a noncommittal manner.

Victoria resolved to give this lady as wide a berth as possible. Something told her that inventing stories to satisfy that kind of woman was no easy job.

Victoria went back into her room, sat on the bed, and gave herself up to speculation on her present position.

She was staying at the Tio Hotel which was, she was fairly sure, not at all inexpensive. She had four pounds seventeen shillings in her possession. She had eaten a hearty lunch for which she had not yet paid and for which Mrs. Hamilton Clipp was under no obligation to pay. Travelling expenses to Baghdad were what Mrs. Clipp had offered. The bargain was completed. Victoria had got to Baghdad. Mrs. Clipp had received the skilled attention of a Bishop's niece, an ex-hospital nurse and competent secretary. All that was over, to the mutual satisfaction of both parties. Mrs. Hamilton Clipp would depart on the evening train to Kirkuk—and that was that. Victoria toyed hopefully with the idea that Mrs. Clipp might press upon her a parting present in the form of hard cash, but abandoned it reluctantly as unlikely. Mrs. Clipp could have no idea that Victoria was in really dire financial straits.

What then must Victoria do? The answer came immediately. Find Edward, of course.

With a sense of annoyance she realised that she was quite unaware of Edward's last name. Edward—Baghdad. Very much, Victoria reflected, like the Saracen maid who arrived in England knowing only the name of her lover "Gilbert" and "England". A romantic story—but certainly inconvenient. True that in England at the time of the Crusades, nobody, Victoria thought, had had any surname at all. On the other hand England was larger than Baghdad. Still, England was sparsely populated then—

Victoria wrenched her thoughts away from these interesting speculations and returned to hard facts. She must find Edward immediately and Edward must find her a job. Also immediately.

She did not know Edward's last name, but he had come to Baghdad as the secretary of a Dr. Rathbone and presumably Dr. Rathbone was a man of importance.

Victoria powdered her nose, patted her hair and started down stairs in search of information.

The beaming Marcus, passing through the hall of his establishment, hailed her with delight.

"Ah, it is Miss Jones, you will come with me and have a drink, will you not, my dear? I like very much English ladies. All the English ladies in Baghdad, they are my friends. Everyone is very happy in my Hotel. Come, we will go into the bar."

Victoria, not at all averse to free hospitality, consented gladly.

Sitting on a stool and drinking gin, she began her search for information.

"Do you know a Dr. Rathbone who has just come to Baghdad?" she asked.

"I know everyone in Baghdad," said Marcus Tio joyfully. "And everybody knows Marcus. That is true, what I am telling you. Oh! I have many many friends."

"I'm sure you have," said Victoria. "Do you know Dr. Rathbone?"

"Last week I have the Air Marshal commanding all Middle East passing through. He says to me, 'Marcus, you villain, I haven't seen you since '46. You haven't grown any thinner.' Oh, he is very nice man. I like him very much."

"What about Dr. Rathbone? Is he a nice man?"

"I like, you know, people who can enjoy themselves. I do not like sour faces. I like people to be gay and young and charming—like you. He says to me, that Air Marshal, 'Marcus you like too much the women.' But I say to him: 'No, my trouble is I like too much Marcus . . .' " Marcus roared with laughter, breaking off to call out, "Jesus—Jesus!"

Victoria looked startled, but it appeared that Jesus was the barman's Christian name. Victoria felt again that the East was an odd place.

"Another gin and orange, and whisky," Marcus commanded.

"I don't think I—"

"Yes, yes, you will—they are very very weak."

"About Dr. Rathbone," persisted Victoria.

"That Mrs. Hamilton Clipp—what an odd name—with whom you arrive, she is American—is she not? I like also American people but I like English best. American peoples, they look always very worried. But sometimes, yes, they are good sports. Mr. Summers—you know him?— he drink so much when he come to Baghdad, he go to sleep for three days and not wake up. It is too much, that. It is not nice."

"Please, do help me," said Victoria.

Marcus looked surprised.

"But of course I help you. I always help my friends. You tell me what you want—and at once it shall be done. Special steak—or turkey cooked very nice with rice and raisins and herbs—or little baby chickens."

"I don't want baby chickens," said Victoria. "At least not now," she added prudently. "I want to find this Dr. Rathbone. Dr. Rathbone. He's just arrived in Baghdad. With a—with a—secretary."

"I do not know," said Marcus. "He does not stay at the Tio."

The implication was clearly that anyone who did not stay at the Tio did not exist for Marcus.

"But there are other hotels," persisted Victoria, "or perhaps he has a house?"

"Oh, yes, there are other hotels. Babylonian Palace, Senacherib, Zobeide Hotel. They are good hotels, yes, but they are not like the Tio."

"I'm sure they're not," Victoria assured him. "But you don't know if Dr. Rathbone is staying at one of them? There is some kind of society he runs—something to do with culture—and books."

Marcus became quite serious at the mention of culture.

"It is what we need," he said. "There must be much culture. Art and music, it is very nice, very nice indeed. I like violin sonatas myself if it is not very long."

While thoroughly agreeing with him, especially in regard to the end of the speech, Victoria realised that she was not getting any nearer to her objective. Conversation with Marcus was, she thought, most entertaining, and Marcus was a charming person in his childlike enthusiasm for life, but conversation with him reminded her of Alice in Wonderland's endeavours to find a path that led to the hill. Every topic found them returning to the point of departure—Marcus!

She refused another drink and rose sadly to her feet. She felt slightly giddy. The cocktails had been anything but weak. She went out from the bar onto the terrace outside and stood by the railing looking across the river, when somebody spoke from behind her.

"Excuse me, but you'd better go and put a coat on. Daresay it seems like summer to you coming out from England, but it gets very cold about sundown."

It was the Englishwoman who had been talking to Mrs. Clipp earlier. She had the hoarse voice of one who is in the habit of training and calling to sporting dogs. She wore a fur coat, had a rug over her knees and was sipping a whisky and soda.

"Oh, thank you," said Victoria and was about to escape hurriedly when her intentions were defeated.

"I must introduce myself. I'm Mrs. Cardew Trench." (The implication was clearly: one of the Cardew Trenches.) "I believe you arrived with Mrs.—what's her name—Hamilton Clipp."

"Yes," said Victoria, "I did."

"She told me you were the niece of the Bishop of Llangow."

Victoria rallied.

"Did she really?" she inquired with the correct trace of light amusement.

"Got it wrong, I suppose?"

Victoria smiled.

"Americans are bound to get some of our names wrong. It does sound a little like Llangow. My uncle," said Victoria improvising rapidly, "is the Bishop of Languao."

"Languao?"

"Yes—in the Pacific Archipelago. He's a Colonial bishop, of course."

"Oh, a Colonial bishop," said Mrs. Cardew Trench, her voice falling at least three semitones.

As Victoria had anticipated: Mrs. Cardew Trench was magnificently unaware of Colonial bishops.

"That explains it," she added.

Victoria thought with pride that it explained it very well for a spur of the moment plunge!

"And what are you doing out here?" asked Mrs. Cardew Trench with that inexorable geniality that conceals natural curiosity of disposition.

"Looking for a young man I talked to for a few moments in a public square in London," was hardly an answer that Victoria could give. She said, remembering the newspaper paragraph she had read, and her statement to Mrs. Clipp, "I'm joining my uncle, Dr. Pauncefoot Jones."

"Oh, so that's who you are." Mrs. Cardew Trench was clearly delighted at having "placed" Victoria. "He's a charming little man, though a bit absent-minded—still I suppose that's only to be expected. Heard him lecture last year in London—excellent delivery—couldn't understand a word of what it was all about, though. Yes, he passed through Baghdad about a fortnight ago. I think he mentioned some girls were coming out later in the season."

Hurriedly, having established her status, Victoria chipped in with a question.

"Do you know if Dr. Rathbone's out here?" she asked.

"Just come out," said Mrs. Cardew Trench. "I believe they've asked him to give a lecture at the Institute next Thursday. On World Relationships and Brotherhood—or something like that. All nonsense if you ask me. The more you try to get people together, the more suspicious they get of each other. All this poetry and music and translating Shakespeare and Wordsworth into Arabic and Chinese and Hindustani. 'A primrose by the river's brim, etc.' . . . what's the good of that to people who've never seen a primrose?"

"Where is he staying, do you know?"

"At the Babylonian Palace Hotel, I believe. But his headquarters are up near the Museum. The Olive Branch—ridiculous name. Full of young women in slacks with unwashed necks and spectacles."

"I know his secretary slightly," said Victoria.

"Oh yes, whatshisname Edward Thingummy—nice boy—too good for that long haired racket—did well in the war, I hear. Still a job's a job, I suppose. Nice looking boy—those earnest young women are quite fluttered by him, I fancy."

A pang of devastating jealousy pierced Victoria.

"The Olive Branch," she said. "Where did you say it was?"

"Up past the turning to the second bridge. One of the turnings off Rashid Street—tucked away rather. Not far from the copper bazaar.

"And how's Mrs. Pauncefoot Jones?" continued Mrs. Cardew Trench. "Coming out soon? I hear she's been in poor health?"

But having got the information she wanted, Victoria was taking no more risks in invention. She glanced at her wristwatch and uttered an exclamation.

"Oh dear—I promised to wake Mrs. Clipp at half past six and help her to prepare for the journey. I must fly."

The excuse was true enough, though Victoria had substituted half past six for seven o'clock. She hurried upstairs feeling quite exhilarated. Tomorrow she would get in touch with Edward at the Olive Branch. Earnest young women with unwashed necks, indeed! They sounded most unattractive . . . Still, Victoria reflected uneasily that men are less critical of dingy necks than middle-aged hygienic Englishwomen are—especially if the owners of the said necks are gazing with large eyes of admiration and adoration at the male subject in question.

The evening passed rapidly. Victoria had an early meal in the dining room with Mrs. Hamilton Clipp, the latter talking nineteen to the dozen on every subject under the sun. She urged Victoria to come and pay a visit later—and Victoria noted down the address carefully, because, after all, one never knew . . . She accompanied Mrs. Clipp to Baghdad North station, saw her safely ensconced in her compartment and was introduced to an acquaintance also travelling to Kirkuk who would assist Mrs. Clipp with her toilet on the following morning.

The engine uttered loud melancholy screams, like a soul in distress, Mrs. Clipp thrust a thick envelope into Victoria's hand, said: "Just a little remembrance, Miss Jones, of our very pleasant companionship which I hope you will accept with my most grateful thanks." Victoria said: "But it's really too kind of you, Mrs. Clipp," in a delighted voice, the engine gave forth a final supreme banshee wail of anguish, and the train pulled slowly out of the station.

Victoria took a taxi from the station back to the hotel since she had not the faintest idea how to get back to it any other way and there did not seem anyone about whom she could ask.

On her return to the Tio, she ran up to her room and eagerly opened the envelope. Inside were a couple of pairs of nylon stockings.

Victoria at any other moment would have been enchanted—nylon stockings having been usually beyond the reach of her purse. At the moment, however, hard cash was what she had been hoping for. Mrs. Clipp, however, had been far too delicate to think of giving her a five dinar note. Victoria wished heartily that she had not been quite so delicate.

However, tomorrow there would be Edward. Victoria undressed, got into bed and in five minutes was fast asleep, dreaming that she was waiting at an aerodrome for Edward, but that he was held back from joining her by a spectacled girl who clasped him firmly round the neck while the aeroplane began slowly to move away . . .

Chapter 11

Victoria awoke to a morning of vivid sunshine. Having dressed, she went out onto the wide balcony outside her window. Sitting in a chair a little way along with his back to her was a man with curling grey hair growing down onto a muscular red brown neck. When the man turned his head sideways Victoria recognised, with a distinct feeling of surprise, Sir Rupert Crofton Lee. Why she should be so surprised she could hardly have said. Perhaps because she had assumed as a matter of course that a V.I.P. such as Sir Rupert would have been staying at the Embassy and not at a hotel. Nevertheless, there he was, staring at the Tigris with a kind of concentrated intensity. She noticed, even, that he had a pair of field glasses slung over the side of his chair. Possibly, she thought, he studied birds.

A young man whom Victoria had at one time thought attractive, had been a bird enthusiast, and she had accompanied him on several week-end tramps, to be made to stand as though paralysed in wet weeds and icy winds, for what seemed like hours, to be at last told in tones of ecstasy to look through the glasses at some drab looking bird on a remote twig which in appearance, as far as Victoria could see, compared unfavourably in bird appeal with a common robin or chaffinch.

Victoria made her way downstairs, encountering Marcus Tio on the terrace between the two buildings of the hotel.

"I see you've got Sir Rupert Crofton Lee staying here," she said.

"Oh, yes," said Marcus, beaming, "he's a nice man—a very nice man."

"Do you know him well?"

"No, this is the first time I see him. Mr. Shrivenham of the British

Embassy bring him here last night. Mr. Shrivenham, he is very nice man, too. I know him very well."

Proceeding into breakfast, Victoria wondered if there was anyone whom Marcus would not consider a very nice man. He appeared to exercise a wide charity.

After breakfast, Victoria started forth in search of the Olive Branch.

A London bred Cockney, she had no idea of the difficulties involved in finding any particular place in a city such as Baghdad, until she had started on her quest.

Coming across Marcus again on her way out, she asked him to direct her to the Museum.

"It is a very nice Museum," said Marcus, beaming. "Yes. Full of interesting, very very old things. Not that I have been there myself. But I have friends, archaeological friends, who stay here always when they come through Baghdad. Mr. Baker—Mr. Richard Baker, you know him? And Professor Kalzman? And Dr. Pauncefoot Jones—and Mr. and Mrs. McIntyre—they all come to the Tio. They are my friends. And they tell me about what is in the Museum. Very very interesting."

"Where is it, and how do I get there?"

"You go straight along Rashid Street—a long way—past the turn to the Feisal Bridge and past Bank Street—you know Bank Street?"

"I don't know anything," said Victoria.

"And then there is another street—also going down to a bridge and it is along there on the right. You ask for Mr. Betoun Evans, he is English Adviser there—very nice man. And his wife, she is very nice, too, she came here as Transport Sergeant during the war. Oh, she is very very nice."

"I don't really want to go actually to the Museum," said Victoria. "I want to find a place—a Society—a kind of club called the Olive Branch."

"If you want olives," said Marcus, "I give you beautiful olives—very fine quality. They keep them especially for me—for the Tio Hotel. You see, I send you some to your table tonight."

"That's very kind of you," said Victoria and escaped towards Rashid Street.

"To the left," Marcus shouted after her, "not to the right. But it is a long way to the Museum. You had better take a taxi."

"Would a taxi know where the Olive Branch was?"

"No, they do not know where anything is! You say to the driver left, right, stop, straight on—just where you want to go."

"In that case, I might as well walk," said Victoria.

She reached Rashid Street and turned to the left.

Baghdad was entirely unlike her idea of it. A crowded main thorough-
fare thronged with people, cars hooting violently, people shouting, European goods for sale in the shop windows, hearty spitting all round her
with prodigious throat clearing as a preliminary. No mysterious Eastern
figures, most of the people wore tattered or shabby Western clothes, old
army and air force tunics, the occasional shuffling black robed and veiled
figures were almost inconspicuous amongst the hybrid European styles
of dress. Whining beggars came up to her—women with dirty babies in
their arms. The pavement under her feet was uneven with occasional
gaping holes.

She pursued her way, feeling suddenly strange and lost and far from
home. Here was no glamour of travel, only confusion.

She came at last to the Feisal Bridge, passed it and went on. In spite of
herself she was intrigued by the curious mixtures of things in the shop
windows. Here were babies' shoes and woollies, toothpaste and cosmet-
ics, electric torches and china cups and saucers—all shown together.
Slowly a kind of fascination came over her, the fascination of assorted
merchandise coming from all over the world to meet the strange assorted
and varied wants of a mixed population.

She found the Museum, but not the Olive Branch. To one accustomed
to finding her way about London it seemed incredible that here was no
one she could ask. She knew no Arabic. Those shopkeepers who spoke to
her in English as she passed, pressing their wares, presented blank faces
when she asked for direction to the Olive Branch.

If one could only "ask a policeman," but gazing at the policemen ac-
tively waving their arms, and blowing their whistles, she realised that
here that would be no solution.

She went into a bookshop with English books in the window, but a
mention of the Olive Branch drew only a courteous shrug and shake of
the head. Regrettably they had no idea at all.

And then, as she walked along the street, a prodigious hammering and
clanging came to her ears and peering down a long dim alley, she remembered that Mrs. Cardew Trench had said the Olive Branch was near the
Copper Bazaar. Here, at least, was the Copper Bazaar.

Victoria plunged in, and for the next three quarters of an hour she forgot the Olive Branch completely. The Copper Bazaar fascinated her. The
blowlamps, the melting metal, the whole business of craftsmanship came
like a revelation to the little Cockney used only to finished products
stacked up for sale. She wandered at random through the Suq, passed out
of the Copper Bazaar, came to the gay striped horse blankets, and the
cotton quilted bed covers. Here European merchandise took on a totally
different guise, in the arched cool darkness it had the exotic quality of

something from overseas, something strange and rare. Bales of cheap printed cottons in gay colours made a feast for the eyes.

Occasionally with a shout of *Balek, Balek*, a donkey or laden mule pushed past her, or men bearing great loads balanced on their backs. Little boys rushed up to her with trays slung round their necks.

"See, lady, elastic, good elastic, English elastic. Comb, English comb?"

The wares were thrust at her, close to her nose, with vehement urgings to buy. Victoria walked in a happy dream. This was really seeing the world. At every turn of the vast arched cool world of alleyways you came to something totally unexpected—an alley of tailors, sitting stitching, with smart pictures of European men's tailoring, a line of watches and cheap jewellery. Bales of velvets and rich metal embroidered brocades, then a chance turn and you were walking down an alley of cheap and shoddy second-hand European clothes, quaint pathetic little faded jumpers and long straggly vests.

Then every now and then there were glimpses into vast quiet courtyards open to the sky.

She came to a vast vista of men's trouserings, with crosslegged dignified merchants in turbans sitting in the middle of their little square recesses.

"Balek!"

A heavily-laden donkey coming up behind her made Victoria turn aside into a narrow alleyway open to the sky that twisted through tall houses. Walking along it she came, quite by chance, to the object of her search. Through an opening she looked into a small square courtyard and at the farther side of it an open doorway with THE OLIVE BRANCH on a huge sign and a rather impossible-looking plaster bird holding an unrecognisable twig in its beak.

Joyously Victoria sped across the courtyard and in at the open door. She found herself in a dimly lit room with tables covered with books and periodicals and more books ranged round on shelves. It looked a little like a book shop, except that there were little groups of chairs arranged together here and there.

Out of the dimness a young woman came up to Victoria and said in careful English,

"What can I do for you, yes, please?"

Victoria looked at her. She wore corduroy trousers and an orange flannel shirt and had black dank hair cut in a kind of depressed bob. So far she would have looked more suited to Bloomsbury, but her face was not Bloomsbury. It was a melancholy face with great sad dark eyes and a heavy nose.

"This is—is this—is—is Dr. Rathbone here?"

Maddening still not to know Edward's surname! Even Mrs. Cardew Trench had called him Edward Thingummy.

"Yes. Dr. Rathbone. The Olive Branch. You wish to join us? Yes? That will be very nice."

"Well, perhaps. I'd—can I see Dr. Rathbone, please?"

The young woman smiled in a tired way.

"We do not disturb. I have a form. I tell you all about everything. Then you sign your name. It is two dinars, please."

"I'm not sure yet that I want to join," said Victoria, alarmed at the mention of two dinars. "I'd like to see Dr. Rathbone—or his secretary. His secretary would do."

"I explain. I explain to you everything. We are all friends here, friends together, friends for the future—reading very fine educational books—reciting poems each to other."

"Dr. Rathbone's secretary," said Victoria loudly and clearly. "He particularly told me to ask for him."

A kind of mulish sullenness came into the young woman's face.

"Not today," she said. "I explain—"

"Why not today? Isn't he here? Isn't Dr. Rathbone here?"

"Yais, Dr. Rathbone is here. He is upstairs. We do not disturb."

A kind of Anglo-Saxon intolerance of foreigners swept over Victoria. Regrettably, instead of the Olive Branch creating friendly international feelings, it seemed to be having the opposite effect as far as she was concerned.

"I have just arrived from England," she said—and her accents were almost those of Mrs. Cardew Trench herself—"and I have a very important message for Dr. Rathbone which I must deliver to him personally. Please take me to him at once! I am sorry to disturb him, but I have got to see him.

"At once!" she added, to clinch matters.

Before an imperious Briton who means to get his or her own way, barriers nearly always fall. The young woman turned at once and led the way to the back of the room and up a staircase and along a gallery overlooking the courtyard. Here she stopped before a door and knocked. A man's voice said, Come in.

Victoria's guide opened the door and motioned to Victoria to pass in.

"It is a lady from England for you."

Victoria walked in.

From behind a large desk covered with papers, a man got up to greet her.

He was an imposing-looking elderly man of about sixty with a high domed forehead and white hair. Benevolence, kindliness and charm were the most apparent qualities of his personality. A producer of plays would have cast him without hesitation for the role of the great philanthropist.

He greeted Victoria with a warm smile and an outstretched hand.

"So you've just come out of England," he said. "First visit East, eh?"

"Yes."

"I wonder what you think of it all . . . You must tell me sometime. Now, let me see, have I met you before or not? I'm so short-sighted and you didn't give your name."

"You don't know me," said Victoria, "but I'm a friend of Edward's."

"A friend of Edward's," said Dr. Rathbone. "Why, that's splendid. Does Edward know you're in Baghdad?"

"Not yet," said Victoria.

"Well, that will be a pleasant surprise for him when he gets back."

"Back?" said Victoria, her voice falling.

"Yes, Edward's in Basrah at the moment. I had to send him down there to see about some crates of books that have come out for us. There have been most vexatious delays in the Customs—we simply have not been able to get them cleared. The personal touch is the only thing, and Edward's good at that sort of thing. He knows just when to charm and when to bully, and he won't rest till he's got the thing through. He's a sticker. A very fine quality in a young man. I think a lot of Edward."

His eyes twinkled.

"But I don't suppose I need to sing Edward's praises to you, young lady."

"When—when will Edward be back from Basrah?" asked Victoria faintly.

"Well—now that I couldn't say. He won't come back till he's finished the job—and you can't hurry things too much in this country. Tell me where you are staying and I'll make sure he gets in touch with you as soon as he gets back."

"I was wondering—" Victoria spoke desperately, aware of her financial plight. "I was wondering if—if I could do some work here?"

"Now that I do appreciate," said Dr. Rathbone warmly. "Yes, of course you can. We need all the workers, all the help we can get. And especially English girls. Our work is going splendidly—quite splendidly—but there's lots more to be done. Still people are keen. I've got thirty voluntary helpers already—thirty—all of 'em keen as mustard! If you're really in earnest, you can be most valuable."

The word voluntary struck unpleasantly on Victoria's ear.

"I really wanted a paid position," she said.

"Oh dear!" Dr. Rathbone's face fell. "That's rather more difficult. Our paid staff is very small—and for the moment, with the voluntary help, it's quite adequate."

"I can't afford not to take a job," explained Victoria. "I'm a competent shorthand typist," she added without a blush.

"I'm sure you're competent, my dear young lady, you radiate competence, if I may say so. But with us it's a question of L.S.D. But even if you take a job elsewhere, I hope you'll help us in your spare time. Most of our workers have their own regular jobs. I'm sure you'll find helping us really inspiring. There must be an end of all the savagery in the world, the wars, the misunderstandings, the suspicions. A common meeting ground, that's what we all need. Drama, art, poetry—the great things of the spirit—no room there for petty jealousies or hatreds."

"N-no," said Victoria doubtfully, recalling friends of hers who were actresses and artists and whose lives seemed to be obsessed by jealousy of the most trivial kind, and by hatreds of a peculiarly virulent intensity.

"I've had the 'Midsummer Night's Dream' translated into forty different languages," said Dr. Rathbone. "Forty different sets of young people all reacting to the same wonderful piece of literature. Young people—that's the secret. I've no use for anybody but the young. Once the mind and spirit are musclebound, it's too late. No, it's the young who must get together. Take that girl downstairs, Catherine, the one who showed you up here. She's a Syrian from Damascus. You and she are probably about the same age. Normally you'd never come together, you'd have nothing in common. But at the Olive Branch you and she and many many others, Russians, Jewesses, Iraqis, Turkish girls, Armenians, Egyptians, Persians, all meet and like each other and read the same books and discuss pictures and music (we have excellent lecturers who come out) all of you finding out and being excited by encountering a different point of view—why, that's what the world is meant to be."

Victoria could not help thinking that Dr. Rathbone was slightly overoptimistic in assuming that all those divergent elements who were coming together would necessarily like each other. She and Catherine, for instance, had not liked each other at all. And Victoria strongly suspected that the more they saw of each other the greater their dislike would grow.

"Edward's splendid," said Dr. Rathbone. "Gets on with everybody. Better, perhaps, with the girls than with the young men. The men students out here are apt to be difficult at first—suspicious—almost hostile. But the girls adore Edward, they'll do anything for him. He and Catherine get on particularly well."

"Indeed," said Victoria coldly. Her dislike of Catherine grew even more intense.

"Well," said Dr. Rathbone, smiling, "come and help us if you can."

It was a dismissal. He pressed her hand warmly. Victoria went out of the room and down the stairs. Catherine was standing near the door talking to a girl who had just come in with a small suitcase in her hand. She was a good-looking dark girl, and just for a moment Victoria fancied that she had seen her before somewhere. But the girl looked at her without any sign of recognition. The two young women had been talking eagerly together in some language Victoria did not know. They stopped when she appeared and remained silent, staring at her. She walked past them to the door, forcing herself to say "Goodbye" politely to Catherine as she went out.

She found her way out from the winding alley into Rashid Street and slowly back to the Hotel, her eyes unseeing of the throngs around her. She tried to keep her mind from dwelling on her own predicament (penniless in Baghdad) by fixing her mind on Dr. Rathbone and the general setup of the Olive Branch. Edward had had an idea in London that there was something "fishy" about his job. What was fishy? Dr. Rathbone? Or the Olive Branch itself?

Victoria could hardly believe that there was anything fishy about Dr. Rathbone. He appeared to her to be one of those misguided enthusiasts who insist on seeing the world in their own idealistic manner, regardless of realities.

What had Edward meant by fishy? He'd been very vague. Perhaps he didn't really know himself.

Could Dr. Rathbone be some kind of colossal fraud?

Victoria, fresh from the soothing charm of his manner, shook her head. His manner had certainly changed, ever so slightly, at the idea of paying her a salary. He clearly preferred people to work for nothing.

But that, thought Victoria, was a sign of common sense.

Mr. Greenholtz, for instance, would have felt just the same.

Chapter 12

Victoria arrived back at the Tio, rather footsore, to be hailed enthusiastically by Marcus who was sitting out on the grass terrace overlooking the river and talking to a thin rather shabby middleaged man.

"Come and have a drink with us, Miss Jones. Martini—sidecar? This is Mr. Dakin. Miss Jones from England. Now then, my dear, what will you have?"

Victoria said she would have a sidecar "and some of those lovely nuts?" she suggested hopefully, remembering that nuts were nutritious.

"You like nuts. Jesus!" He gave the order in rapid Arabic. Mr. Dakin said in a sad voice that he would have a lemonade.

"Ah," cried Marcus, "but that is ridiculous. Ah, here is Mrs. Cardew Trench. You know Mr. Dakin? What will you have?"

"Gin and lime," said Mrs. Cardew Trench, nodding to Dakin in an off-hand manner. "You look hot," she added to Victoria.

"I've been walking round seeing the sights."

When the drinks came, Victoria ate a large plateful of pistachio nuts and also some potato chips.

Presently, a short thickset man came up the steps and the hospitable Marcus hailed him in his turn. He was introduced to Victoria as Captain Crosbie; and by the way his slightly protuberant eyes goggled at her, Victoria gathered that he was susceptible to feminine charm.

"Just come out?" he asked her.

"Yesterday."

"Thought I hadn't seen you around."

"She is very nice and beautiful, is she not?" said Marcus joyfully.

"Oh, yes, it is very nice to have Miss Victoria. I will give a party for her—a very nice party."

"With baby chickens?" said Victoria hopefully.

"Yes, yes—and foie gras—Strasburg foie gras—and perhaps caviare—and then we have a dish with fish—very nice—a fish from the Tigris, but all with sauce and mushrooms. And then there is a turkey stuffed in the way we have it at my home—with rice and raisins and spice—and all cooked so! Oh, it is very good—but you must eat very much of it—not just a tiny spoonful. Or if you like it better you shall have a steak—a really big steak and tender—I see to it. We will have a long dinner that goes on for hours. It will be very nice. I do not eat myself—I only drink."

"That will be lovely," said Victoria in a faint voice. The description of these viands made her feel quite giddy with hunger. She wondered if Marcus really meant to give this party and if so, how soon it could possibly happen.

"Thought you'd gone to Basrah," said Mrs. Cardew Trench to Crosbie.

"Got back yesterday," said Crosbie.

He looked up at the balcony.

"Who's the bandit?" he asked. "Feller in fancy dress in the big hat."

"That, my dear, is Sir Rupert Crofton Lee," said Marcus. "Mr. Shrivenham brought him here from the Embassy last night. He is very nice man, very distinguished traveller. He rides on camels over the Sahara, and climbs up mountains. It is very uncomfortable and dangerous, that kind of life. I should not like it myself."

"Oh, he's that chap, is he?" said Crosbie. "I've read his book."

"I came over on the plane with him," said Victoria.

Both men, or so it seemed to her, looked at her with interest.

"He's frightfully stuck up and pleased with himself," said Victoria with disparagement.

"Knew his aunt in Simla," said Mrs. Cardew Trench. "The whole family is like that. Clever as they make them, but can't help boasting of it."

"He's been sitting out there doing nothing all the morning," said Victoria with slight disapproval.

"It is his stomach," explained Marcus. "Today he cannot eat anything. It is sad."

"I can't think," said Mrs. Cardew Trench, "why you're the size you are, Marcus, when you never eat anything."

"It is the drink," said Marcus. He sighed deeply. "I drink far too much. Tonight my sister and her husband come. I will drink and drink almost until morning." He sighed again, then uttered his usual sudden roar. "Jesus! Jesus! Bring the same again."

"Not for me," said Victoria hastily, and Mr. Dakin refused also, finishing up his lemonade, and ambling gently away while Crosbie went up to his room.

Mrs. Cardew Trench flicked Dakin's glass with her fingernail, "Lemonade as usual?" she said. "Bad sign, that."

Victoria asked why it was a bad sign.

"When a man only drinks when he's alone."

"Yes, my dear," said Marcus. "That is so."

"Does he really drink, then?" asked Victoria.

"That's why he's never got on," said Mrs. Cardew Trench. "Just manages to keep his job and that's all."

"But he is a very nice man," said the charitable Marcus.

"Pah," said Mrs. Cardew Trench. "He's a wet fish. Potters and dilly dallies about—no stamina—no grip on life. Just one more Englishman who's come out East and gone to seed."

Thanking Marcus for the drink and refusing a second, Victoria went up to her room, removed her shoes, and lay down on her bed to do some serious thinking. The three pounds odd to which her capital had dwindled was, she fancied, already due to Marcus for board and lodging. Owing to his generous disposition, and if she could sustain life mainly on alcoholic liquor assisted by nuts, olives and chip potatoes, she might solve the purely alimentary problem of the next few days. How long would it be before Marcus presented her with her bill, and how long would he allow it to run unpaid? She had no idea. He was not really, she thought, careless in business matters. She ought, of course, to find somewhere cheaper to live. But how would she find out where to go? She ought to find herself a job—quickly. But where did one apply for jobs? What kind of a job? Who could she ask about looking for one? How terribly handicapping to one's style it was to be dumped down practically penniless in a foreign city where one didn't know the ropes. With just a little knowledge of the terrain, Victoria felt confident (as always) that she could hold her own. When would Edward get back from Basrah? Perhaps (horror) Edward would have forgotten all about her. Why on earth had she come rushing out to Baghdad in this asinine way? Who and what was Edward after all? Just another young man with an engaging grin and an attractive way of saying things. And what—what—what was his surname? If she knew that, she might wire him—no good, she didn't even know where he was staying. She didn't know anything—that was the trouble—that was what was cramping her style.

And there was no one to whom she could go for advice. Not Marcus who was kind but never listened. Not Mrs. Cardew Trench (who had had suspicions from the first). Not Mrs. Hamilton Clipp who had vanished to Kirkuk. Not Dr. Rathbone—

She must get some money—or get a job—any job. Look after children, stick stamps on in an office, serve in a restaurant . . . Otherwise they would send her to a Consul and she would be repatriated to England and never see Edward again . . .

At this point, worn out with emotion, Victoria fell asleep.

She woke some hours later and deciding that she might as well be hanged for a sheep as a lamb, went down to the restaurant and worked her way solidly through the entire menu—a generous one. When she had finished, she felt slightly like a boa constrictor, but definitely heartened.

"It's no good worrying any more," thought Victoria. "I'll leave it all till tomorrow. Something may turn up, or I may think of something, or Edward may come back."

Before going to bed she strolled out onto the terrace by the river. Since in the feelings of those living in Baghdad it was arctic winter, nobody else was out there except one of the waiters who was leaning over a railing staring down into the water, and he sprang away guiltily when Victoria appeared and hurried back into the hotel by the service door.

Victoria to whom, coming from England, it appeared to be an ordinary summer night with a slight nip in the air, was enchanted by the Tigris seen in the moonlight with the further bank looking mysterious and Eastern with its fringes of palms.

"Well, anyway, I've got here," said Victoria, cheering up a good deal, "and I'll manage somehow. Something is bound to turn up."

With this Micawber-like pronouncement, she went up to bed, and the waiter slipped quietly out again and resumed his task of attaching a knotted rope so that it hung down to the river's edge.

Presently another figure came out of the shadows and joined him. Mr. Dakin said in a low voice,

"All in order?"

"Yes, sir, nothing suspicious to report."

Having completed the task to his satisfaction, Mr. Dakin retreated into the shadows, exchanged his waiter's white coat for his own nondescript blue pinstripe and ambled gently along the terrace until he stood outlined against the water's edge, just where the steps led up from the street below.

"Getting pretty chilly in the evenings now," said Crosbie strolling out from the bar and down to join him. "Suppose you don't feel it so much, coming from Teheran."

They stood there for a moment or two smoking. Unless they raised their voices, nobody could overhear them. Crosbie said quietly,

"Who's the girl?"

"Niece apparently of the archaeologist, Pauncefoot Jones."

"Oh well—that should be all right. But coming on the same plane as Crofton Lee—"

"It's certainly as well," said Dakin, "to take nothing for granted."

The men smoked in silence for a few moments.

Crosbie said: "You really think it's advisable to shift the thing from the Embassy to here?"

"I think so, yes."

"In spite of the whole thing being taped down to the smallest detail."

"It was taped down to the smallest detail in Basrah—and that went wrong."

"Oh, I know. Mohammed Salah Hassan was poisoned, by the way."

"Yes—he would be. Was there any signs of an approach to the Consulate?"

"I suspect there may have been. Bit of a shindy there. Chap drew a revolver." He paused and added, "Richard Baker grabbed him and disarmed him."

"Richard Baker," said Dakin thoughtfully.

"Know him? He's—"

"Yes, I know him."

There was a pause and then Dakin said,

"Improvisation. That's what I'm banking on. If we have, as you say, got everything taped—and our plans are known, then it's easy for the other side to have got us taped, too. I very much doubt if Carmichael would even so much as get near the Embassy—and even if he reached it—" He shook his head.

"Here, only you and I and Crofton Lee are wise to what's going on."

"They'll know Crofton Lee moved here from the Embassy."

"Oh, of course. That was inevitable. But don't you see, Crosbie, that whatever show they put up against our improvisation has got to be improvised, too. It's got to be hastily thought of and hastily arranged. It's got to come, so to speak, from the outside. There's no question here of someone established in the Tio six months ago waiting. The Tio's never been in the picture until now. There's never been any idea or suggestion of using the Tio as the rendezvous."

He looked at his watch. "I'll go up now and see Crofton Lee."

Dakin's raised hand had no need to tap on Sir Rupert's door. It opened silently to let him in.

The traveller had only one small reading lamp alight and had placed his chair beside it. As he sat down again, he gently slipped a small automatic pistol onto the table within reach of his hand.

He said: "What about it, Dakin? Do you think he'll come?"

"I think so, yes, Sir Rupert." Then he said, "You've never met him, have you?"

The other shook his head.

"No. I'm looking forward to meeting him tonight. That young man, Dakin, must have got guts."

"Oh yes," said Mr. Dakin in his flat voice. "He's got guts."

He sounded a little surprised at the fact needing to be stated.

"I don't mean only courage," said the other. "Lots of courage in the war—magnificent. I mean—"

"Imagination?" suggested Dakin.

"Yes. To have the guts to believe something that isn't in the least degree probable. To risk your life finding out that a ridiculous story isn't ridiculous at all. That takes something that the modern young man usually hasn't got. I hope he'll come."

"I think he'll come," said Mr. Dakin.

Sir Rupert glanced at him sharply.

"You've got it all sewn up?"

"Crosbie's on the balcony, and I shall be watching the stairs. When Carmichael reaches you, tap on the wall and I'll come in."

Crofton Lee nodded.

Dakin went softly out of the room. He went to the left and onto the balcony and walked to the extreme corner. Here, too, a knotted rope dropped over the edge and came to earth in the shade of a eucalyptus tree and some Judas bushes.

Mr. Dakin went back past Crofton Lee's door and into his own room beyond. His room had a second door in it, leading onto the passage behind the rooms, and it opened within a few feet of the head of the stairs. With this door unobtrusively ajar, Mr. Dakin settled down to his vigil.

It was about four hours later that a *gufa*, that primitive craft of the Tigris, dropped gently downstream and came to shore on the mud flat beneath the Tio Hotel. A few moments later a slim figure swarmed up the rope and crouched amongst the Judas trees.

Chapter 13

It had been Victoria's intention to go to bed and to sleep and to leave all problems until the morning; but having already slept most of the afternoon, she found herself devastatingly wide awake.

In the end she switched on the light, finished a magazine story she had been reading in the plane, darned her stockings, tried on her new nylons, wrote out several different advertisements requiring employment—(she could ask tomorrow where these should be inserted) wrote three or four tentative letters to Mrs. Hamilton Clipp, each setting out a different and more ingenious set of unforeseen circumstances which had resulted in her being "stranded" in Baghdad, sketched out one or two telegrams appealing for help to her sole surviving relative, a very old, crusty, and unpleasant gentleman in the North of England who had never helped anybody in his life, tried out a new style of hairdo, and finally with a sudden yawn decided that at last she really was desperately sleepy and ready for bed and repose.

It was at this moment that without any warning her bedroom door swung open, a man slipped in, turned the key in the lock behind him and said to her urgently,

"For God's sake hide me somewhere—quickly . . ."

Victoria's reactions were never slow. In the twinkling of an eye she had noted the laboured breathing, the fading voice, the way the man held an old red knitted scarf bunched on his breast with a desperate clutching hand. And she rose immediately in response to the adventure.

The room did not lend itself to many hiding places. There was the wardrobe, a chest of drawers, a table and the rather pretentious dressing table. The bed was a large one—almost a double bed and memories of childish hide-and-seek made Victoria's reaction prompt.

"Quick," she said. She swept off pillows, and raised sheet and blanket. The man lay across the top of the bed. Victoria pulled sheet and blanket over him, dumped the pillows on top and sat down herself on the side of the bed.

Almost immediately there came a low insistent knocking on the door.

Victoria called out, "Who is it?" in a faint alarmed voice.

"Please," said a man's voice outside. "Open, please. It is the police."

Victoria crossed the room, pulling her dressing gown round her. As she did so, she noticed the man's red knitted scarf was lying on the floor and she caught it up and swept it into a drawer, then she turned the key and opened the door of her room a small way, peering out with an expression of alarm.

A dark-haired young man in a mauve pinstripe suit was standing outside and behind him was a man in police officer's uniform.

"What's the matter?" Victoria asked, letting a quaver creep into her voice.

The young man smiled brilliantly and spoke in very passable English.

"I am so sorry, miss, to disturb you at this hour," he said, "but we have a criminal escaped. He has run into this hotel. We must look in every room. He is a very dangerous man."

"Oh dear!" Victoria fell back, opening the door wide. "Do come in, please, and look. How very frightening. Look in the bathroom, please. Oh! and the wardrobe—and, I wonder, would you mind looking under the bed? He might have been there all the evening."

The search was very rapid.

"No, he is not here."

"You're sure he's not under the bed? No, how silly of me. He couldn't be in here at all. I locked the door when I went to bed."

"Thank you, miss, and good evening."

The young man bowed and withdrew with his uniformed assistant.

Victoria, following him to the door, said,

"I'd better lock it again, hadn't I? To be safe."

"Yes, that will be best, certainly. Thank you."

Victoria relocked the door and stood by it for some few minutes. She heard the police officers knock in the same way on the door the other side of the passage, heard the door open, an exchange of remarks and the indignant hoarse voice of Mrs. Cardew Trench, and then the door closing. It reopened a few minutes later, and the sound of their footsteps moved down the passage. The next knock came from much further away.

Victoria turned and walked across the room to the bed. It was born in upon her that she had probably been excessively foolish. Led away by the romantic spirit, and by the sound of her own language, she had impulsively lent aid to what was probably an extremely dangerous criminal. A disposition to be on the side of the hunted against the hunter sometimes brings unpleasant consequences. Oh, well, thought Victoria, I'm in for it now, anyway!

Standing beside the bed she said curtly,

"Get up."

There was no movement, and Victoria said sharply, though without raising her voice,

"They've gone. You can get up now."

But still there was no sign of movement from under the slightly raised hump of pillows. Impatiently, Victoria threw them all off.

The young man lay just as she had left him. But now his face was a queer greyish colour and his eyes were closed.

Then, with a sharp catch in her breath, Victoria noticed something else—a bright red stain seeping through onto the blanket.

"Oh no," said Victoria, almost as though pleading with someone. "Oh, no—no!"

And as though in recognition of that plea the wounded man opened his eyes. He stared at her, stared as though from very far away at some object he was not quite certain of seeing.

His lips parted—the sound was so faint that Victoria scarcely heard.

She bent down.

"What?"

She heard this time. With difficulty, great difficulty, the young man said two words. Whether she heard them correctly or not Victoria did not know. They seemed to her quite nonsensical and without meaning. What he said was, "*Lucifer—Basrah . . .*"

The eyelids drooped and flickered over the wide anxious eyes. He said one word more—a name. Then his head jerked back a little and he lay still.

Victoria stood quite still, her heart beating violently. She was filled now with an intense pity and anger. What to do next she had no idea. She must call someone—get someone to come—She was alone here with a dead man and sooner or later the police would want an explanation.

While her brain worked rapidly on the situation, a small sound made her turn her head. The key had fallen out of her bedroom door, and as she stared at it, she heard the sound of the lock turning. The door opened and Mr. Dakin came in, carefully closing the door behind him.

He walked across to her, saying quietly,

"Nice work, my dear. You think quickly. How is he?"

With a catch in her voice Victoria said:

"I think he's—he's dead."

She saw the other's face alter, caught just a flash of intense anger, then his face was just as she had seen it the day before—only now it seemed to her that the indecision and flabbiness of the man had vanished, giving place to something quite different.

He bent down—and gently loosened the ragged tunic.

"Very neatly stabbed through the heart," said Dakin as he straightened up. "He was a brave lad—and a clever one."

Victoria found her voice.

"The police came. They said he was a criminal. Was he a criminal?"

"No. He wasn't a criminal."

"Were they—were they the police?"

"I don't know," said Dakin. "They may have been. It's all the same."

Then he asked her:

"Did he say anything—before he died?"

"Yes."

"What was it?"

"He said Lucifer—and then Basrah. And then after a pause he said a name—a French name it sounded like—but I mayn't have got it right."

"What did it sound like to you?"

"I think it was Lefarge."

"Lefarge," said Dakin thoughtfully.

"What does it all mean?" said Victoria, and added with some dismay, "And what am I to do?"

"We must get you out of it as far as we can," said Dakin. "As for what it's all about, I'll come back and talk to you later. The first thing to do is to get hold of Marcus. It's his hotel and Marcus has a great deal of sense, though one doesn't always realise it in talking to him. I'll get hold of him. He won't have gone to bed. It's only half past one. He seldom goes to bed before two o'clock. Just attend to your appearance before I bring him in. Marcus is very susceptible to beauty in distress."

He left the room. As though in a dream she moved over to the dressing table, combed back her hair, made up her face to a becoming pallor and collapsed onto a chair as she heard footsteps approaching. Dakin came in without knocking. Behind him loomed the bulk of Marcus Tio. This time Marcus was serious. There was not the usual smile on his face.

"Now, Marcus," said Mr. Dakin, "you must do what you can about this. It's been a terrible shock to this poor girl. The fellow burst in, collapsed—she's got a very kind heart and she hid him from the police. And now he's dead. She oughtn't to have done it, perhaps, but girls are softhearted."

"Of course she did not like the police," said Marcus. "Nobody likes the police. I do not like the police. But I have to stand well with them because of my hotel. You want me to square them with money?"

"We just want to get the body away quietly."

"That is very nice, my dear. And I, too, I do not want a body in my hotel. But it is, as you say, not so easy to do?"

"I think it could be managed," said Dakin. "You've got a doctor in your family, haven't you?"

"Yes, Paul, my sister's husband, is a doctor. He is a very nice boy. But I do not want him to get into trouble."

"He won't," said Dakin. "Listen, Marcus. We move the body from Miss Jones' room across into my room. That lets her out of it. Then I use your telephone. In ten minutes' time a young man reels into the hotel from the street. He is very drunk, he clutches his side. He demands me at the top of his voice. He staggers into my room and collapses. I come out and call you and ask for a doctor. You produce your brother-in-law. He sends for an ambulance and he goes in it with this drunken friend of mine. Before they get to the hospital my friend is dead. He has been stabbed. That is all right for you. He has been stabbed in the street before coming into your hotel."

"My brother-in-law takes away the body—and the young man who plays the part of the drunkard, he goes away quietly in the morning perhaps?"

"That's the idea."

"And there is no body found in my hotel? And Miss Jones she does not get any worry or annoyance? I think, my dear, that that is all a very good idea."

"Good, then if you'll make sure the coast is clear, I'll get the body across to my room. Those servants of yours potter round the corridors half the night. Go along to your room and raise a shindy. Get them all running to fetch you things."

Marcus nodded and left the room.

"You're a strong girl," said Dakin. "Can you manage to help me to carry him across the corridor to my room?"

Victoria nodded. Between them they lifted the limp body, carried it across the deserted corridor (in the distance Marcus' voice could be heard upraised in furious anger) and laid it on Dakin's bed.

Dakin said:

"Got a pair of scissors? Then cut off top of your under-blanket where it's stained. I don't think the stain's gone through to the mattress. The tunic soaked up most of it. I'll come along to you in about an hour. Here, wait a minute, take a pull from this flask of mine."

Victoria obeyed.

"Good girl," said Dakin. "Now go back to your room. Turn out the light. As I said, I'll be along in about an hour."

"And you'll tell me what it all means?"

He gave her a long rather peculiar stare but did not answer her question.

Chapter 14

Victoria lay in bed with her light out, listening through the darkness. She heard sounds of loud drunken altercation. Heard a voice declaring: "Felt I got to look you up, ole man. Had a row with a fellow outside." She heard bells ring. Heard other voices. Heard a good deal of commotion. Then came a stretch of comparative silence—except for the far off playing of Arab music on a gramophone in somebody's room. When it seemed to her as though hours had passed, she heard the gentle opening of her door, sat up in bed and switched on the bedside lamp.

"That's right," said Dakin approvingly.

He brought a chair up to the bedside and sat down in it. He sat there, staring at her in the considering manner of a physician making a diagnosis.

"Tell me what it's all about?" demanded Victoria.

"Suppose," said Dakin, "that you tell me all about yourself first. What are you doing here? Why did you come to Baghdad?"

Whether it was the events of the night, or whether it was something in Dakin's personality (Victoria thought afterwards that it was the latter) Victoria for once did not launch out on an inspired and meretricious account of her presence in Baghdad. Quite simply and straightforwardly she told him everything. Her meeting with Edward, her determination to get to Baghdad, the miracle of Mrs. Hamilton Clipp, and her own financial destitution.

"I see," said Dakin when she'd finished.

He was silent for a moment before he spoke.

"Perhaps I'd like to keep you out of this. I'm not sure. But the point is you can't be kept out of it! You're in it, whether I like it or not. And as you're in it, you might as well work for me."

"You've got a job for me?" Victoria sat up in bed, her cheeks bright with anticipation.

"Perhaps. But not the kind of job you're thinking of. This is a serious job, Victoria. And it's dangerous."

"Oh, that's all right," said Victoria cheerfully. She added doubtfully, "It's not dishonest, is it? Because though I know I tell an awful lot of lies, I wouldn't really like to do anything that was dishonest."

Dakin smiled a little.

"Strangely enough, your capacity to think up a convincing lie quickly is one of your qualifications for the job. No, it's not dishonest. On the contrary, you are enlisted in the cause of law and order. I'm going to put you in the picture—only in a general kind of way, but so that you can understand fully what it is you are doing and exactly what the dangers are. You seem to be a sensible young woman and I don't suppose you've thought much about world politics which is just as well, because as Hamlet very wisely remarked, 'There is nothing either good or bad, but thinking makes it so.' "

"I know everybody says there's going to be another war sooner or later," said Victoria.

"Exactly," said Mr. Dakin. "Why does everybody say so, Victoria?"

She frowned. "Why, because Russia—the Communists—America—" she stopped.

"You see," said Dakin. "Those aren't your own opinions or words. They're picked up from newspapers, and casual talk, and the wireless. There are two divergent points of view dominating different parts of the world; that is true enough. And they are represented loosely in the public mind as 'Russia and the Communists' and 'America'. Now the only hope for the future, Victoria, lies in peace, in production, in constructive activities and not destructive ones. Therefore, everything depends on those who hold those two divergent viewpoints, either agreeing to differ and each contenting themselves with their respective spheres of activity, or else finding a mutual basis for agreement or at least toleration. Instead of that, the opposite is happening, a wedge is being driven in the whole time to force two mutually suspicious groups further and further apart. Certain things led one or two people to believe that this activity comes from a third party or group working under cover and so far absolutely unsuspected by the world at large. Whenever there is a chance of agreement being reached or any sign of dispersal of suspicion, some incident occurs to plunge one side back in distrust, or the other side into definite hysterical fear. These things are not accidents, Victoria, they are deliberately produced for a calculated effect."

"But why do you think so and who's doing it?"

"One of the reasons we think so is because of money. The money, you see, is coming from the wrong sources. Money, Victoria, is always the great clue to what is happening in the world. As a physician feels your pulse, to get a clue to your state of health, so money is the life blood that feeds any great movement or cause. Without it, the movement can't make headway. Now here, there are very large sums of money involved and although very cleverly and artfully camouflaged, there is definitely something wrong about where the money comes from and where it is going. A great many unofficial strikes, various threats to Governments in Europe who show signs of recovery, are staged and brought into being by Communists, zealots for their cause—but the funds for these measures do not come from Communist sources, and traced back, they come from very strange and unlikely quarters. It is not Capitalist money, though it naturally passes through Capitalist hands. Another point, enormous sums of money seem to be going completely out of circulation. As much as though—to put it simply—you spent your salary every week on things—bracelets or tables or chairs—and those things then disappeared or passed out of ordinary circulation and sight. All over the world a great demand for diamonds and other precious stones has arisen. They change hands a dozen or more times until finally they disappear and cannot be traced.

"This, of course, is only a vague sketch. The upshot is that somewhere a third group of people whose aim is as yet obscure, are fomenting strife and misunderstanding and are engaging in cleverly camouflaged money and jewel transactions for their own ends. We have reason to believe that in every country there are agents of this group, some established there many years ago. Some are in very high and responsible positions, others are playing humble parts, but all are working with one unknown end in view. In substance, it is exactly like the Fifth Column activities at the beginning of the last war, only this time it is on a world wide scale."

"But who are these people?" Victoria demanded.

"They are not, we think, of any special nationality. What they want is, I fear, the betterment of the world! The delusion that by force you can impose the Millennium on the human race is one of the most dangerous delusions in existence. Those who are out only to line their own pockets can do little harm—mere greed defeats its own ends. But the belief in a superstratum of human beings—in Supermen to rule the rest of the decadent world—that, Victoria, is the most evil of all beliefs. For when you say, 'I am not as other men'—you have lost the two most valuable qualities we have ever tried to attain:—humility and brotherhood."

He coughed. "Well, I mustn't preach a sermon. Let me just explain to you what we do know. There are various centers of activity. One in the Argentine, one in Canada—certainly one or more in the United States of America, and I should imagine, though we can't tell, one in Russia. And now we come to a very interesting phenomenon.

"In the past two years, twenty-eight promising young scientists of various nationalities have quietly faded out of their background. The same thing has happened with constructional engineers, with aviators, with electricians and many other skilled trades. These disappearances have this in common: those concerned are all young, all ambitious, and all without close ties. Besides those we know of, there must be many many more, and we are beginning to guess at something of what they may be accomplishing."

Victoria listened, her brows drawn together.

"You might say it was impossible in these days for anything to go on in any country, unknown to the rest of the world. I do not, of course, mean undercover activities; those may go on anywhere. But anything on a large scale of up-to-date production. And yet there are still obscure parts of the world, remote from trade routes, cut off by mountains and deserts, in the midst of peoples who still have the power to bar out strangers and which are never known or visited except by a solitary and exceptional traveller. Things could go on there the news of which would never penetrate to the outside world, or only as a dim and ridiculous rumour.

"I won't particularize the spot. It can be reached from China—and nobody knows what goes on in the interior of China. It can be reached from the Himalayas, but the journey there, save to the initiated, is hard and long to travel. Machinery and personnel dispatched from all over the globe reaches it, after being diverted from its ostensible destination. The mechanics of it all need not be gone into.

"But one man got interested in following up a certain trail. He was an unusual man, a man who has friends and contacts throughout the East. He was born in Kashgar and he knows a score of local dialects and languages. He suspected and he followed up the trail. What he heard was so incredible that when he got back to civilization and reported it, he was not believed. He admitted that he had had fever and he was treated as a man who had had delirium.

"Only two people believed his story. One was myself. I never object to believing impossible things—they're so often true. The other—" he hesitated.

"Yes?" said Victoria.

"The other was Sir Rupert Crofton Lee, a great traveller, and a man who had himself travelled through these remote regions and who knew something about their possibilities.

"The upshot of it all was that Carmichael, that's my man, decided to go and find out for himself. It was a desperate and hazardous journey, but he was as well equipped as any man to carry it through. That was nine months back. We heard nothing until a few weeks ago and then news came through. He was alive and he'd got what he went to get. Definite proof.

"But the other side were on to him. It was vital to them that he should never get back with his proofs. And we've had ample evidence of how the whole system is penetrated and infiltrated with their agents. Even in my own department there are leaks. And some of those leaks, Heaven help us, are at a very high level.

"Every frontier has been watched for him. Innocent lives have been sacrificed in mistake for his—they don't set much store by human life. But somehow or other he got through unscathed—until tonight."

"Then that was who—he was?"

"Yes, my dear. A very brave and indomitable young man."

"But what about the proofs? Did they get those?"

A very slow smile showed on Dakin's tired face.

"I don't think they did. No, knowing Carmichael, I'm pretty sure they didn't. But he died without being able to tell us where those proofs are and how to get hold of them. I think he probably tried to say something when he was dying that should give us the clue." He repeated slowly, "Lucifer—Basrah—Lefarge. He'd been in Basrah—tried to report at the Consulate and narrowly missed being shot. It's possible that he left the proofs somewhere in Basrah. What I want you to do, Victoria, is to go there and try to find out."

"Me?"

"Yes. You've no experience. You don't know what you're looking for. But you heard Carmichael's last words and they may suggest something to you when you get there. Who knows—you may have beginner's luck?"

"I'd love to go to Basrah," said Victoria eagerly.

Dakin smiled.

"Suits you because your man is there, eh? That's all right. Good camouflage, too. Nothing like a genuine love affair for camouflage. You go to Basrah, keep your eyes and ears open and look about you. I can't give you any instructions on how to set about things—in fact, I'd much rather not. You seem a young woman with plenty of ingenuity of your own. What the words Lucifer and Lefarge mean—assuming that you heard correctly—I don't know. I'm inclined to agree with you that Lefarge must be a name. Look out for that name."

"How do I get to Basrah?" said Victoria in a business-like way. "And what do I use for money?"

Dakin took out his pocketbook and handed her a wad of paper money.

"That's what you use for money. As for how you get to Basrah, fall into conversation with that old trout Mrs. Cardew Trench tomorrow morning, say you're anxious to visit Basrah before you go off to this dig you're pretending to work at. Ask her about a hotel. She'll tell you at once you must stay at the Consulate and will send a telegram to Mrs. Clayton. You'll probably find your Edward there. The Claytons keep open house—everyone who passes through stays with them. Beyond that, I can't give you any tips except one. If—er—anything unpleasant happens, if you're asked what you know and who put you up to what you're doing—don't try and be heroic. Spill the beans at once."

"Thank you very much," said Victoria gratefully. "I'm an awful coward about pain, and if anyone were to torture me I'm afraid I shouldn't hold out."

"They won't bother to torture you," said Mr. Dakin. "Unless some sadistic element enters in. Torture's very old fashioned. A little prick with a needle and you answer every question truthfully without realising you're doing it. We live in a scientific age. That's why I didn't want you to get grand ideas of secrecy. You won't be telling them anything they don't know already. They'll be wise to me after this evening—bound to be. And to Rupert Crofton Lee."

"What about Edward? Do I tell him?"

"That I must leave to you. Theoretically, you're to hold your tongue about what you're doing to everybody. Practically!" His eyebrows went up quizzically. "You put him in danger, too. There's that aspect of it. Still, I gather he had a good record in the Air Force. I don't suppose danger will worry him. Two heads are often better than one. So he thinks there's something fishy about this 'Olive Branch' he's working for? That's interesting—very interesting."

"Why?"

"Because we think so, too," said Dakin.

Then he added:

"Just two parting tips. First, if you don't mind my saying so, don't tell too many different kinds of lies. It's harder to remember and live up to. I know you're a bit of a virtuoso, but keep it simple, is my advice."

"I'll remember," said Victoria with becoming humility. "And the other tip?"

"Just keep your ears strained for any mention of a young woman called Anna Scheele."

"Who is she?"

"We don't know much about her. We could do with knowing a little more."

Chapter 15

"Of course you must stay at the Consulate," said Mrs. Cardew Trench. "Nonsense, my dear—you can't stay at the Airport Hotel. The Claytons will be delighted. I've known them for years. We'll send a wire and you can go down on tonight's train. They know Dr. Pauncefoot Jones quite well."

Victoria had the grace to blush. The Bishop of Llangow, alias the Bishop of Languao was one thing; a real flesh and blood Dr. Pauncefoot Jones was quite another.

"I suppose," thought Victoria guiltily, "I could be sent to prison for that—false pretences or something."

Then she cheered herself up by reflecting that it was only if you attempted to obtain money by false statements that the rigours of the law were set in motion. Whether this was really so or not, Victoria did not know, being as ignorant of the law as most average people, but it had a cheering sound.

The train journey had all the fascination of novelty—to Victoria's idea the train was hardly an express—but she had begun to feel conscious of her Western impatience.

A Consular car met her at the station and she was driven to the Consulate. The car drove in through big gates into a delightful garden and drew up before a flight of steps leading up to a balcony surrounding the house. Mrs. Clayton, a smiling energetic woman, came through the swinging wire mesh door to meet her.

"We're so pleased to see you," she said. "Basrah's really delightful this time of year, and you oughtn't to leave Iraq without seeing it. Luckily there's no one much here just at the moment—sometimes we just don't know where to turn so as to fit people in, but there's no one here now except Dr. Rathbone's young man who's quite charming. You've just missed Richard Baker, by the way. He left before I got Mrs. Cardew Trench's telegram."

Victoria had no idea who Richard Baker was—but it seemed fortunate that he had left when he did.

"He had been down to Kuwait for a couple of days," continued Mrs. Clayton. "Now that's a place you ought to see—before it's spoilt. I daresay it soon will be. Every place gets ruined sooner or later. What would you like first—a bath or some coffee?"

"A bath, please," said Victoria gratefully.

"How's Mrs. Cardew Trench? This is your room and the bathroom's along here. Is she an old friend of yours?"

"Oh no," said Victoria truthfully. "I've only just met her."

"And I suppose she turned you inside out in the first quarter of an hour? She's a terrific gossip as I expect you've gathered. Got quite a mania for knowing all about everybody. But she's quite good company and a really first class bridge player. Now are you sure you wouldn't like some coffee or something first?"

"No, really."

"Good—then I'll see you later. Have you got everything you want?"

Mrs. Clayton buzzed away like a cheerful bee, and Victoria took a bath, and attended to her face and her hair with the meticulous care of a young woman who is shortly going to be reunited to a young man who has taken her fancy.

If possible, Victoria hoped to meet Edward alone. She did not think that he would make any tactless remarks—fortunately he knew her as Jones and the additional Pauncefoot would probably cause him no surprise. The surprise would be that she was in Iraq at all, and for that Victoria hoped that she could catch him alone even for a bare second or two.

With this end in view, when she had put on a summer frock (for to her the climate of Basrah recalled a June day in London) she slipped out quietly through the wire door and took up her position on the balcony where she could intercept Edward when he arrived back from whatever he was doing—wrestling with the Customs officials, she presumed.

The first arrival was a tall thin man with a thoughtful face, and as he came up the steps, Victoria slipped round the corner of the balcony. As she did so, she actually saw Edward entering through a garden door that gave on to the river bend.

Faithful to the tradition of Juliet, Victoria leaned over the balcony and gave a prolonged hiss.

Edward (who was looking, Victoria thought, more attractive than ever) turned his head sharply, looking about him.

"Hist! Up here," called Victoria in a low voice.

Edward raised his head, and an expression of utter astonishment appeared on his face.

"Good Lord," he exclaimed. "It's Charing Cross!"

"Hush. Wait for me. I'm coming down."

Victoria sped round the balcony, down the steps and along round the corner of the house to where Edward had remained obediently standing, the expression of bewilderment still on his face.

"I can't be drunk so early in the day," said Edward. "It is you?"

"Yes, it's me," said Victoria happily and ungrammatically.

"But what are you doing here? How did you get here? I thought I was never going to see you again."

"I thought so too."

"It's really just like a miracle. How did you get here?"

"I flew."

"Naturally you flew. You couldn't have got here in the time, otherwise. But I mean what blessed and wonderful chance brought you to Basrah?"

"The train," said Victoria.

"You're doing it on purpose, you little brute. God, I'm pleased to see you. But how did you get here—really?"

"I came out with a woman who'd broken her arm—a Mrs. Clipp. An American. I was offered the job the day after I met you, and you'd talked about Baghdad, and I was a bit fed up with London, so I thought, well, why not see the world?"

"You really are awfully sporting, Victoria. Where's this Clipp woman, here?"

"No, she's gone to a daughter near Kirkuk. It was only a journey out job."

"Then what are you doing now?"

"I'm still seeing the world," said Victoria. "But it has required a few subterfuges. That's why I wanted to get at you before we met in public, I mean, I don't want any tactless references to my being a shorthand typist out of a job when you last saw me."

"As far as I'm concerned, you're anything you say you are. I'm ready for briefing."

"The idea is," said Victoria, "that I am Miss Pauncefoot Jones. My uncle is an eminent archaeologist who is excavating in some more or less inaccessible place out here, and I am joining him there shortly."

"And none of that is true?"

"Naturally not. But it makes quite a good story."

"Oh, yes, excellent. But suppose you and old Pussyfoot Jones come face to face?"

"Pauncefoot. I don't think that is likely. As far as I can make out once archaeologists start to dig, they go on digging like mad, and don't stop."

"Rather like terriers. I say, there's a lot in what you say. Has he got a real niece?"

"How should I know?" said Victoria.

"Oh, then you're not impersonating anybody in particular. That makes it easier."

"Yes, after all, a man can have lots of nieces. Or, at a pinch, I could say I'm only a cousin but that I always call him uncle."

"You think of everything," said Edward admiringly. "You really are an amazing girl, Victoria. I've never met anyone like you. I thought I wouldn't see you again for years, and when I did see you, you'd have forgotten all about me. And now here you are."

The admiring and humble glance which Edward cast on her caused Victoria intense satisfaction. If she had been a cat she would have purred.

"But you'll want a job, won't you?" said Edward. "I mean, you haven't come into a fortune or anything?"

"Far from it! Yes," said Victoria slowly, "I shall want a job. I went into your Olive Branch place, as a matter of fact, and saw Dr. Rathbone and asked him for a job, but he wasn't very responsive—not to a salaried job, that is."

"The old beggar's fairly tight with his money," said Edward. "His idea is that everybody comes and works for the love of the thing."

"Do you think he's a phoney, Edward?"

"N—o. I don't know exactly what I do think. I don't see how he can be anything but on the square—he doesn't make any money out of the show. So far as I can see all that terrific enthusiasm must be genuine. And yet, you know, I don't really feel he's a fool."

"We'd better go in," said Victoria. "We can talk later."

"I'd no idea you and Edward knew each other," exclaimed Mrs. Clayton.

"Oh, we're old friends," laughed Victoria. "Only, as a matter of fact, we'd lost sight of each other. I'd no idea Edward was in this country."

Mr. Clayton, who was the quiet thoughtful-looking man Victoria had seen coming up the steps, asked:

"How did you get on this morning, Edward? Any progress?"

"It seems very uphill work, sir. The cases of books are there, all present and correct, but the formalities needed to clear them seem unending."

Clayton smiled.

"You're new to the delaying tactics of the East."

"The particular official who's wanted always seems to be away that day," complained Edward. "Everyone is very pleasant and willing—only nothing seems to happen."

Everyone laughed and Mrs. Clayton said consolingly:

"You'll get them through in the end. Very wise of Dr. Rathbone to send someone down personally. Otherwise they'd probably stay here for months."

"They are very suspicious about bombs. Also subversive literature. They suspect everything."

"Dr. Rathbone isn't shipping out bombs here disguised as books, I hope," said Mrs. Clayton laughing.

Victoria thought she caught a sudden flicker in Edward's eye, as though Mrs. Clayton's remark had opened up a new line of thought.

Clayton said, with a hint of reproof: "Dr. Rathbone's a very learned and well-known man, my dear. He's a Fellow of various important Societies and is known and respected all over Europe."

"That would make it all the easier for him to smuggle in bombs," Mrs. Clayton pointed out with irrepressible spirits.

Victoria could see that Gerald Clayton did not quite like this light-hearted suggestion.

He frowned at his wife.

Business being at a standstill during the midday hours, Edward and Victoria went out together after lunch to stroll about and see the sights. Victoria was delighted with the river, the Shatt el Arab, with its bordering of date palm groves. She adored the Venetian look of the high-powered Arab boats tied up in the canal in the town. Then they wandered into the Suq and looked at Kuwait bride chests studded with patterned brass and other attractive merchandise.

It was not until they turned towards the Consulate and Edward was preparing himself to assail the Customs department once more that Victoria said suddenly,

"Edward, what's your name?"

Edward stared at her.

"What on earth do you mean, Victoria?"

"Your last name. Don't you realise that I don't know it."

"Don't you? No, I suppose you don't. It's Goring."

"Edward Goring. You've no idea what a fool I felt going into that Olive Branch place and wanting to ask for you and not knowing anything but Edward."

"Was there a dark girl there? Rather long bobbed hair?"

"Yes."

"That's Catherine. She's awfully nice. If you'd said Edward she'd have known at once."

"I daresay she would," said Victoria with reserve.

"She's a frightfully nice girl. Didn't you think so?"

"Oh quite . . ."

"Not actually good looking—in fact nothing much to look at, but she's frightfully sympathetic."

"Is she?" Victoria's voice was now quite glacial—but Edward apparently noticed nothing.

"I don't really know what I should have done without her. She put me in the picture and helped me out when I might have made a fool of myself. I'm sure you and she will be great friends."

"I don't suppose we shall have the opportunity."

"Oh yes, you will. I'm going to get you a job in the show."

"How are you going to manage that?"

"I don't know but I shall manage it somehow. Tell old Rattlebones what a wonderful typist et cetera you are."

"He'll soon find out I'm not," said Victoria.

"Anyway, I shall get you into the Olive Branch somehow. I'm not going to have you beetling round on your own. Next thing I know, you'd be heading for Burma or darkest Africa. No, young Victoria, I'm going to have you right under my eye. I'm not going to take any chances on your running out on me. I don't trust you an inch. You're too fond of seeing the world."

"You sweet idiot," thought Victoria, "don't you know wild horses wouldn't drive me away from Baghdad!"

Aloud she said: "Well, it would be quite fun to have a job at the Olive Branch."

"I wouldn't describe it as fun. It's all terribly earnest. As well as being absolutely goofy."

"And you still think there's something wrong about it?"

"Oh, that was only a wild idea of mine."

"No," said Victoria thoughtfully. "I don't think it was only a wild idea. I think it's true."

Edward turned on her sharply.

"What makes you say that?"

"Something I heard—from a friend of mine."

"Who was it?"

"Just a friend."

"Girls like you have too many friends," grumbled Edward. "You are a devil, Victoria. I love you madly and you don't care a bit."

"Oh, yes, I do," said Victoria. "Just a little bit."

Then, concealing her delighted satisfaction, she asked:

"Edward, is there anyone called Lefarge connected with the Olive Branch or with anything else?"

"Lefarge?" Edward looked puzzled. "No, I don't think so. Who is he?"

Victoria pursued her inquiries.

"Or anyone called Anna Scheele?"

This time Edward's reaction was very different. He turned on her abruptly, caught her by the arm and said:

"What do you know about Anna Scheele?"

"Ow! Edward, let go! I don't know anything about her. I just wanted to know if you did."

"Where did you hear about her? Mrs. Clipp?"

"No—not Mrs. Clipp—at least I don't think so, but actually she talked so fast and so unendingly about everyone and everything that I probably wouldn't remember if she had mentioned her."

"But what made you think this Anna Scheele had anything to do with the Olive Branch?"

"Has she?"

Edward said slowly, "I don't know . . . It's all so—so vague."

They were standing outside the garden door to the Consulate. Edward glanced at his watch. "I must go and do my stuff," he said. "Wish I knew some Arabic. But we've got to get together, Victoria. There's a lot I want to know."

"There's a lot I want to tell you," said Victoria.

Some tender heroine of a more sentimental age might have sought to keep her man out of danger. Not so, Victoria. Men, in Victoria's opinion were born to danger as the sparks fly upwards. Edward wouldn't thank her for keeping him out of things. And, on reflection, she was quite certain that Mr. Dakin hadn't intended her to keep him out of things.

II

At sunset that evening Edward and Victoria walked together in the Consulate garden. In deference to Mrs. Clayton's insistence that the weather was wintry Victoria wore a woollen coat over her summer frock. The sunset was magnificent but neither of the young people noticed it. They were discussing more important things.

"It began quite simply," said Victoria, "with a man coming into my room at the Tio Hotel and getting stabbed."

It was not, perhaps, most people's idea of a simple beginning. Edward stared at her and said: "Getting what?"

"Stabbed," said Victoria. "At least I think it was stabbed, but it might have been shot, only I don't think so because then I would have heard the noise of the shot. Anyway," she added, "he was dead."

"How could he come into your room if he was dead?"

"Oh, Edward, don't be stupid."

Alternately baldly and vaguely, Victoria told her story. For some mysterious reason Victoria could never tell of truthful occurrences in a dramatic fashion. Her narrative was halting and incomplete and she told it with the air of one offering a palpable fabrication.

When she had come to the end, Edward looked at her doubtfully and said, "You do feel all right, Victoria, don't you? I mean you haven't had a touch of the sun or—a dream, or anything?"

"Of course not."

"Because, I mean, it seems such an absolutely impossible thing to have happened."

"Well, it did happen," said Victoria touchily.

"And all that melodramatic stuff about world forces and mysterious secret installations in the heart of Tibet or Baluchistan. I mean, all that simply couldn't be true. Things like that don't happen."

"That's what people always say before they've happened."

"Honest to God, Charing Cross—are you making all this up?"

"No!" cried Victoria exasperated.

"And you've come down here looking for someone called Lefarge and someone called Anna Scheele—"

"Whom you've heard of yourself," Victoria put in. "You had heard of her, hadn't you?"

"I'd heard the name—yes."

"How? Where? At the Olive Branch?"

Edward was silent for some moments, then he said:

"I don't know if it means anything. It was just—odd—"

"Go on. Tell me."

"You see, Victoria, I'm so different from you; I'm not as sharp as you are. I just feel, in a queer kind of way, that things are wrong somehow—I don't know why I think so. You spot things as they go along and deduce things from them. I'm not clever enough for that. I just feel vaguely that things are—well—wrong—but I don't know why."

"I feel like that sometimes, too," said Victoria. "Like Sir Rupert on the balcony of the Tio."

"Who's Sir Rupert?"

"Sir Rupert Crofton Lee. He was on the plane coming out. Very haughty and showing off. A V.I.P. You know. And when I saw him sitting out on the balcony at the Tio in the sun, I had that queer feeling you've just said of something being wrong, but not knowing what it was."

"Rathbone asked him to lecture to the Olive Branch, I believe, but he couldn't make it. Flew back to Cairo or Damascus or somewhere yesterday morning."

"Well, go on about Anna Scheele."

"Oh, Anna Scheele. It was nothing really. It was just one of the girls."

"Catherine?" said Victoria instantly.

"I believe it was Catherine now I think of it."

"Of course, it was Catherine. That's why you don't want to tell me about it."

"Nonsense, that's quite absurd."

"Well, what was it?"

"Catherine said to one of the other girls, 'When Anna Scheele comes, we can go forward. Then we take our orders from her—and from her alone'."

"That's frightfully important, Edward."

"Remember, I'm not even sure that that was the name," Edward warned her.

"Didn't you think it queer at the time?"

"No, of course I didn't. I thought it was just some female who was coming out to boss things. A kind of Queen Bee. Are you sure you're not imagining all this, Victoria?"

Immediately he quailed slightly before the glance his young friend gave him.

"All right, all right," he said hastily. "Only you'll admit the whole story does sound queer. So like a thriller—a young man coming in and gasping out one word that doesn't mean anything—and then dying—It just doesn't seem real."

"You didn't see the blood," said Victoria and shivered slightly.

"It must have given you a terrible shock," said Edward sympathetically.

"It did," said Victoria. "And then on top of it, you come along and ask me if I'm making it all up."

"I'm sorry. But you are rather good at making things up. The Bishop of Llangow and all that!"

"Oh, that was just girlish *joie de vivre*," said Victoria. "This is serious, Edward, really serious."

"This man, Dakin—is that his name?—impressed you as knowing what he was talking about?"

"Yes, he was very convincing. But, look here, Edward, how do you know—"

A hail from the balcony interrupted her.

"Come in—you two—drinks waiting."

"Coming," called Victoria.

Mrs. Clayton, watching them coming towards the steps, said to her husband:

"There's something in the wind here! Nice couple of children—probably haven't got a bean between them. Shall I tell you what I think, Gerald?"

"Certainly, dear. I'm always interested to hear your ideas."

"I think that girl has come out here to join her uncle on his Dig simply and solely because of that young man."

"I hardly think so, Rosa. They were quite astonished to see each other."

"Poosh!" said Mrs. Clayton. "That's nothing. He was astonished, I daresay."

Gerald Clayton shook his head at her and smiled.

"She's not an archaeological type," said Mrs. Clayton. "They're usually earnest girls with spectacles—and very often damp hands."

"My dear, you can't generalize in that way."

"—And intellectual and all that. This girl is an amiable nitwit with a lot of common sense. Quite different. He's a nice boy. A pity he's tied up with all this silly Olive Branch stuff—but I suppose jobs are hard to get. They should find jobs for these boys."

"It's not so easy, dear, they do try. But you see, they've no training, no experience and usually not much habit of concentration."

Victoria went to bed that night in a turmoil of mixed feelings.

The object of her quest was attained, Edward was found! She suffered from the inevitable reaction. Do what she might a feeling of anticlimax persisted.

It was partly Edward's disbelief that made everything that had happened seem stagey and unreal. She, Victoria Jones, a little London typist, had arrived in Baghdad, had seen a man murdered almost before her eyes, had become a secret agent or something equally melodramatic, and had finally met the man she loved in a tropical garden with palms waving overhead, and in all probability not far from the spot where the original Garden of Eden was said to be situated.

A fragment of a nursery rhyme floated through her head.

How many miles to Babylon?
Threescore and ten:
Can I get there by candlelight?
Yes, and back again.

But she wasn't back again—she was still in Babylon.

Perhaps she would never get back—she and Edward in Babylon.

Something she had meant to ask Edward—there in the garden. Garden of Eden—she and Edward—Ask Edward—but Mrs. Clayton had called—and it had gone out of her head—But she must remember—because it was important—It didn't make sense—Palms—garden—Edward—Saracen Maiden—Anna Scheele—Rupert Crofton Lee—All wrong somehow—And if only she could remember—

A woman coming towards her along a hotel corridor—a woman in a tailored suit—it was herself—but when the woman got near she saw the face was Catherine's. Edward and Catherine—absurd! "Come with me," she said to Edward, "we will find M. Lefarge—" And suddenly there he was, wearing lemon yellow kid gloves and a little pointed black beard.

Edward was gone now and she was alone. She must get back from Babylon before the candles went out.

And we are for the dark.

Who had said that? Violence, terror—evil—blood on a ragged khaki tunic. She was running—running—down a hotel corridor. And they were coming after her.

Victoria woke up with a gasp.

III

"Coffee?" said Mrs. Clayton. "How do you like your eggs? Scrambled?"

"Lovely."

"You look rather washed out. Not feeling ill?"

"No, I didn't sleep very well last night. I don't know why. It's a very comfortable bed."

"Turn the wireless on, will you, Gerald? It's time for the news."

Edward came in just as the pips were sounding.

"In the House of Commons last night, the Prime Minister gave fresh details of the cuts in dollar imports.

"A report from Cairo announces that the body of Sir Rupert Crofton Lee has been taken from the Nile. Victoria put down her coffee cup sharply and Mrs. Clayton uttered an ejaculation. *Sir Rupert left his Hotel yesterday afternoon, after arriving by plane from Baghdad, and did not return to it that night. He had been missing for twenty-four hours when his body was recovered. Death was due to a stab wound in the heart and not to drowning. Sir Rupert was a renowned traveller, was famous for his travels through China and Baluchistan and was the author of several books."*

"Murdered!" exclaimed Mrs. Clayton. "I think Cairo is worse than any place now. Did you know anything about all this, Gerry?"

"I knew he was missing," said Mr. Clayton. "It appears he got a note, brought by hand, and left the Hotel in a great hurry on foot without saying where he was going."

"You see," said Victoria to Edward after breakfast when they were alone together. "It is all true. First this man Carmichael and now Sir Rupert Crofton Lee. I feel sorry now I called him a show off. It seems unkind. All the people who know or guess about this queer business are being got out of the way. Edward, do you think it will be me next?"

"For Heaven's sake don't look so pleased by the idea, Victoria! Your sense of drama is much too strong. I don't see why anyone should eliminate you because you don't really know anything—but do, please, do, be awfully careful."

"We'll both be careful. I've dragged you into it."

"Ah. That's all right. Relieves the monotony."

"Yes, but take care of yourself."

She gave a sudden shiver.

"It's rather awful. He was so very much alive—Crofton Lee, I mean—and now he's dead too. It's frightening, really frightening."

Chapter 16

"Find your young man?" asked Mr. Dakin.

Victoria nodded.

"Find anything else?"

Rather mournfully, Victoria shook her head.

"Well, cheer up," said Mr. Dakin. "Remember in this game, results are few and far between. You might have picked up something there—one never knows, but I wasn't in any way counting on it."

"Can I still go on trying?" asked Victoria.

"Do you want to?"

"Yes, I do. Edward thinks he can get me a job at the Olive Branch. If I keep my ears and eyes open, I might find out something, mightn't I? They know something about Anna Scheele there."

"Now that's very interesting, Victoria. How did you learn that?"

Victoria repeated what Edward had told her—about Catherine's remarks that when "Anna Scheele came" they would take their orders from her.

"Very interesting," said Mr. Dakin.

"Who is Anna Scheele?" asked Victoria. "I mean, you must know something about her—or is she just a name?"

"She's more than a name. She's confidential secretary to an American banker—head of an international banking firm. She left New York and came to London about ten days ago. Since then she's disappeared."

"Disappeared? She's not dead?"

"If so, her dead body hasn't been found."

"But she may be dead?"

"Oh yes, she may be dead."

"Was she—coming to Baghdad?"

"I've no idea. It would seem from the remarks of this young woman Catherine, that she was. Or shall we say—is—since as yet there's no reason to believe she isn't still alive."

"Perhaps I can find out more at the Olive Branch."

"Perhaps you can—but I must warn you once more to be very careful, Victoria. The organization you are up against are quite ruthless. I would much rather not have your dead body found floating down the Tigris."

Victoria gave a little shiver and murmured:

"Like Sir Rupert Crofton Lee. You know that morning he was at the Hotel here there was something odd about him—something that surprised me. I wish I could remember what it was . . ."

"In what way—odd?"

"Well—different." Then in response to the inquiring look, she shook her head vexedly. "It will come back to me, perhaps. Anyway I don't suppose it really matters."

"Anything might matter."

"If Edward gets me a job, he thinks I ought to get a room like the other girls in a sort of boarding house or paying guest place, not stay on here."

"It would create less surmise. Baghdad hotels are very expensive. Your young man seems to have his head screwed on the right way."

"Do you want to see him?"

Dakin shook his head emphatically.

"No, tell him to keep right away from me. You, unfortunately, owing to the circumstances on the night of Carmichael's death, are bound to be suspect. But Edward is not linked with that occurrence or with me in any way—and that's valuable."

"I've been meaning to ask you," said Victoria. "Who actually did stab Carmichael? Was it someone who followed him here?"

"No," said Dakin slowly. "That couldn't have been so."

"Couldn't?"

"He came in a *gufa*—one of those native boats—and he wasn't followed. We know that because I had someone watching the river."

"Then it was someone—in the Hotel?"

"Yes, Victoria. And what is more someone in one particular wing of the Hotel—for I myself was watching the stairs and no one came up them."

He watched her rather puzzled face and said quietly:

"That doesn't really give us very many names. You and I and Mrs. Cardew Trench, and Marcus and his sisters. A couple of elderly servants who have been here for years. A man called Harrison from Kirkuk against whom nothing is known. A nurse who works at the Jewish Hospital . . . It might be any of them—yet all of them are unlikely for one very good reason."

"What is that?"

"Carmichael was on his guard. He knew that the peak moment of his mission was approaching. He was a man with a very keen instinct for danger. How did that instinct let him down?"

"Those police that came—" began Victoria.

"Ah, they came after—up from the street. They'd had a signal, I suppose. But they didn't do the stabbing. That must have been done by someone Carmichael knew well, whom he trusted . . . or alternately whom he judged negligible. If I only knew . . ."

II

Achievement brings with it its own anticlimax. To get to Baghdad, to find Edward, to penetrate the secrets of the Olive Branch: all this had appeared as an entrancing program. Now, her objective attained, Victoria, in a rare moment of self questioning, sometimes wondered what on earth she was doing! The rapture of reunion with Edward had come and gone. She loved Edward, Edward loved her. They were, on most days, working under the same roof—but thinking about it dispassionately, what on earth were they doing?

By some means or other, sheer force of determination, or ingenious persuasion, Edward had been instrumental in Victoria's being offered a meagrely paid job at the Olive Branch. She spent most of her time in a small dark room with the electric light on, typing on a very faulty machine various notices and letters and manifestos of the milk and water program of the Olive Branch activities. Edward had had a hunch there was something wrong about the Olive Branch. Mr. Dakin had seemed to agree with that view. She, Victoria, was here to find out what she could, but as far as she could see, there was nothing to find out! The Olive Branch activities dripped with the honey of international peace. Various gatherings were held with orangeade to drink and depressing edibles to go with it, and at these Victoria was supposed to act as quasi hostess; to mix, to introduce, to promote general good feeling among various foreign nationals, who were inclined to stare with animosity at one another, and wolf refreshments hungrily.

As far as Victoria could see, there were no undercurrents, no conspiracies, no inner rings. All was aboveboard, mild as milk and water, and desperately dull. Various dark-skinned young men made tentative love to her, others lent her books to read which she skimmed through and found tedious. She had, by now, left the Tio Hotel and had taken up her quarters with some other young women workers of various nationalities in a house on the West Bank of the river. Amongst these young women was Catherine, and it seemed to Victoria that Catherine watched her with a suspicious eye; but whether this was because Catherine suspected her of being a spy on the activities of the Olive Branch or whether it was the more delicate matter of Edward's affections, Victoria was unable to make up her mind. She rather fancied the latter. It was known that Edward had secured Victoria her job and several pairs of jealous dark eyes looked at her without undue affection.

The fact was, Victoria thought moodily, that Edward was far too attractive. All these girls had fallen for him, and Edward's engaging friendly manner to one and all did nothing to help. By agreement between them, Victoria and Edward were to show no signs of special intimacy. If they were to find out anything worth finding out, they must not be suspected of working together. Edward's manner to her was the same as to any of the other young women, with an added shade of coldness.

Though the Olive Branch itself seemed so innocuous, Victoria had a distinct feeling that its head and founder was in a different category. Once or twice she was aware of Dr. Rathbone's dark thoughtful gaze resting upon her, and though she countered it with her most innocent and kitten-like expression, she felt a sudden throb of something like fear.

Once, when she had been summoned to his presence (for explanation of a typing error), the matter went further than a glance.

"You are happy working with us, I hope?" he asked.

"Oh, yes, indeed, sir," said Victoria, and added: "I'm sorry I make so many mistakes."

"We don't mind mistakes. A soulless machine would be no use to us. We need youth, generosity of spirit, broadness of outlook."

Victoria endeavoured to look eager and generous.

"You must love the work . . . love the object for which you are working . . . look forward to the glorious future. Are you truly feeling all that, dear child?"

"It's all so new to me," said Victoria. "I really don't feel I have taken it all in yet."

"Get together—get together—young people everywhere must get together. That is the main thing. You enjoy our evenings of free discussion and comradeship?"

"Oh! yes," said Victoria who loathed them.

"Agreement, not dissension—brotherhood, not hatred. Slowly and surely it is growing—you do feel that, don't you?"

Victoria thought of the endless petty jealousies, the violent dislikes, the endless quarrels, hurt feelings, apologies demanded; and hardly knew what she was expected to say.

"Sometimes," she said cautiously, "people are difficult."

"I know . . . I know . . ." Dr. Rathbone sighed. His noble domed forehead furrowed itself in perplexity. "What is this I hear of Michael Rakounian striking Isaac Nahoum and cutting his lip open?"

"They were just having a little argument," said Victoria.

Dr. Rathbone brooded mournfully.

"Patience and faith," he murmured. "Patience and faith."

Victoria murmured a dutiful assent and turned to leave. Then, remembering she had left her typescript, she came back again. The glance she caught in Dr. Rathbone's eye startled her a little. It was a keen suspicious glance, and she wondered uneasily just how closely she was being watched, and what Dr. Rathbone really thought about her.

Her instructions from Mr. Dakin were very precise. She was to obey certain rules for communicating with him if she had anything to report. He had given her an old faded pink handkerchief. If she had anything to report she was to walk, as she often did when the sun was setting, along the river bank, near her hostel. There was a narrow path in front of the houses there for perhaps a quarter of a mile. In one place a big flight of steps led down to the water's edge and boats were constantly being tied up there. There was a rusty nail in one of the wooden posts at the top. Here she was to affix a small piece of the pink handkerchief if she wanted to get into communication with Dakin. So far, Victoria reflected bitterly, there had been no need for anything of the sort. She was merely doing an ill-paid job in a slovenly fashion. Edward she saw at rare intervals, since he was always being sent to far off places by Dr. Rathbone. At the moment, he had just come back from Persia. During his absence, she had had one short and somewhat unsatisfactory interview with Dakin. Her instructions had been to go to the Tio Hotel and ask if she had left a cardigan behind. The answer having been in the negative, Marcus appeared and immediately swept her out onto the river bank for a drink. During the process Dakin had shambled in from the street and had been hailed by Marcus to join them and presently, as Dakin supped lemonade, Marcus had been called away and the two of them sat there on opposite sides of the small painted table.

Rather apprehensively Victoria confessed her utter lack of success, but Dakin was indulgently reassuring.

"My dear child, you don't even know what you are looking for or even if there is anything to find. Taken by and large, what is your considered opinion of the Olive Branch?"

"It's a thoroughly dim show," said Victoria slowly.

"Dim, yes. But not bogus?"

"I don't know," said Victoria slowly. "People are so sold on the idea of culture if you know what I mean?"

"You mean that where anything cultured is concerned, nobody examines *bona fides* in the way they would if it were a charitable or a financial proposition? That's true. And you'll find genuine enthusiasts there, I've no doubt. But is the organization being used?"

"I think there's a lot of Communist activity going on," said Victoria doubtfully. "Edward thinks so, too—he's making me read Karl Marx and leave it about just to see what reactions there will be."

Dakin nodded.

"Interesting. Any response so far?"

"No, not yet."

"What about Rathbone? Is he genuine?"

"I think really that he is—" Victoria sounded doubtful.

"He's the one I worry about, you see," said Dakin. "Because he's a big noise. Suppose there is Communist plotting going on—students and young revolutionaries have very little chance of coming in contact with the President. Police measures will look after bombs thrown from the street. But Rathbone's different. He's one of the high ups, a distinguished man with a fine record of public beneficence. He could come in close contact with the distinguished visitors. He probably will. I'd like to know about Rathbone."

Yes, Victoria thought to herself, it all revolved around Rathbone. On that first meeting in London, weeks ago, Edward's vague remarks about the "fishiness" of the show had had their origin in his employer. And there must, Victoria decided suddenly, have been some incident, some word, that had awakened Edward's uneasiness. For that, in Victoria's belief, was how minds worked. Your vague doubt or distrust was never just a hunch—it was really always due to a cause. If Edward, now, could be made to think back, to remember; between them they might hit upon the fact or incident that had aroused his suspicions. In the same way, Victoria thought, she herself must try to think back to what it was that had so surprised her when she came out upon the balcony at the Tio and found Sir Rupert Croften Lee sitting there in the sun. It was true that she had expected him to be at the Embassy and not at the Tio Hotel but that was not enough to account for the strong feeling she had had that his sitting there was quite impossible! She would go over and over the events of that morning, and Edward must be urged to go over and over his early association with Dr. Rathbone. She would tell him so when next she got him alone. But to get Edward alone was not easy. To begin with, he had been away in Persia and now that he was back, private communications at the Olive Branch were out of the question where the slogan of the last war (*Les oreilles enemis nous écoutent*) might have been written up all over the walls. In the Armenian household where she was a paying guest, privacy was equally impossible. Really, thought Victoria to herself, for all I see of Edward, I might as well have stayed in England!

That this was not quite true, was proved very shortly afterwards.

Edward came to her with some sheets of manuscript and said:

"Dr. Rathbone would like this typed out at once, please, Victoria. Be especially careful of the second page, there are some rather tricky Arab names on it."

Victoria, with a sigh, inserted a sheet of paper in her typewriter and started off in her usual dashing style. Dr. Rathbone's handwriting was not particularly difficult to read and Victoria was just congratulating herself that she had made fewer mistakes than usual. She laid the top sheet aside and proceeded to the next—and at once realised the meaning of Edward's injunction to be careful of the second page. A tiny note in Edward's handwriting was pinned to the top of it.

Go for a walk along the Tigris bank past the Beit Melik Ali tomorrow morning about eleven.

The following day was Friday, the weekly holiday. Victoria's spirits rose mercurially. She would wear her jade green pullover. She ought really to get her hair shampooed. The amenities of the house where she lived made it difficult to wash it herself. "And it really needs it," she murmured aloud.

"What did you say?" Catherine, at work on a pile of circulars and envelopes, raised her head suspiciously from the next table.

Victoria quickly crumpled up Edward's note in her hand as she said lightly:

"My hair wants washing. Most of these hairdressing places look so frightfully dirty, I don't know where to go."

"Yes, they are dirty and expensive, too. But I know a girl who washes hair very well and the towels are clean. I will take you there."

"That's very kind of you, Catherine," said Victoria.

"We will go tomorrow. It is holiday."

"Not tomorrow," said Victoria.

"Why not tomorrow?"

A suspicious stare was bent upon her. Victoria felt her usual annoyance and dislike of Catherine rising.

"I'd rather go for a walk—get some air. One is so cooped up here."

"Where can you walk? There is nowhere to walk in Baghdad."

"I shall find somewhere," said Victoria.

"It would be better to go to the Cinema. Or there is an interesting lecture."

"No, I want to get out. In England we like going for walks."

"Because you are English, you are so proud and stuck up. What does it mean to be English? Next than nothing. Here we spit upon the English."

"If you start spitting on me you may get a surprise," said Victoria, wondering as usual at the ease with which angry passions seemed to rise at the Olive Branch.

"What would you do?"

"Try and see."

"Why do you read Karl Marx? You cannot understand it. You are much too stupid. Do you think they would ever accept you as a member of the Communist party? You are not well enough educated politically."

"Why shouldn't I read it? It was meant for people like me—workers."

"You are not a worker. You are a bourgeoise. You cannot even type properly. Look at the mistakes you make."

"Some of the cleverest people can't spell," said Victoria with dignity. "And how can I work when you keep talking to me?"

She rattled off a line at breakneck speed—and was then somewhat chagrined to find that as a result of unwittingly depressing the shift key, she had written a line of exclamation points, figures and brackets. Removing the sheet from the machine she replaced it with another and applied herself diligently until, her task finished, she took the result in to Dr. Rathbone.

Glancing over it and murmuring, "Shiraz is in Iran not Iraq—and anyway you don't spell Iraq with a K . . . Wasit—not Wuzle—er—thank you, Victoria."

Then, as she was leaving the room, he called her back.

"Victoria, are you happy here?"

"Oh yes, Dr. Rathbone."

The dark eyes under the massive brows were very searching. She felt uneasiness rising.

"I'm afraid we do not pay you very much."

"That doesn't matter," said Victoria. "I like the work."

"Do you really?"

"Oh, yes," said Victoria. "One feels," she added, "that this sort of thing is really worth while."

Her limpid gaze met the dark searching eyes and did not falter.

"And you manage—to live?"

"Oh yes—I've found quite a good cheap place—with some Armenians. I'm quite all right."

"There is a shortage at present of shorthand typists in Baghdad," said

Dr. Rathbone. "I think, you know, that I could get you a better position than the one you have here."

"But I don't want any other position."

"You might be wise to take one."

"Wise?" Victoria faltered a little.

"That is what I said. Just a word of warning—of advice."

There was something faintly menacing now in his tone.

Victoria opened her eyes still wider.

"I really don't understand, Dr. Rathbone," she said.

"Sometimes it is wiser not to mix oneself up in things one does not understand."

She felt quite sure of the menace this time, but she continued to stare in kitten-eyed innocence.

"Why did you come and work here, Victoria? Because of Edward?"

Victoria flushed angrily.

"Of course not," she said indignantly. She was much annoyed.

Dr. Rathbone nodded his head.

"Edward has his way to make. It will be many many years before he is in a position to be of any use to you. I should give up thinking of Edward if I were you. And, as I say, there are good positions to be obtained at present, with a good salary and prospects—and which will bring you among your own kind."

He was still watching her, Victoria thought, very closely. Was this a test? She said with an affectation of eagerness,

"But I really am very keen on the Olive Branch, Dr. Rathbone."

He shrugged his shoulders then and she left him, but she could feel his eyes in the centre of her spine as she left the room.

She was somewhat disturbed by the interview. Had something occurred to arouse his suspicions? Did he guess that she might be a spy placed in the Olive Branch to find out its secrets? His voice and manner had made her feel unpleasantly afraid. His suggestion that she had come there to be near Edward had made her angry at the time and she had vigorously denied it, but she realised now that it was infinitely safer that Dr. Rathbone should suppose her to have come to the Olive Branch for Edward's sake, than to have even an inkling that Mr. Dakin had been instrumental in the matter. Anyway, owing to her idiotic blush, Rathbone probably did think that it was Edward—so that all had really turned out for the best.

Nevertheless, she went to sleep that night with an unpleasant little clutch of fear at her heart.

Chapter 17

It proved fairly simple on the following morning for Victoria to go out by herself with few explanations. She had inquired about the Beit Melek Ali and had learnt it was a big house built right out on the river some way down the west bank.

So far, Victoria had had very little time to explore her surroundings and she was agreeably surprised when she came to the end of the narrow street and found herself actually on the river bank. She turned to her right and made her way slowly along the edge of the high bank. Sometimes the going was precarious—the bank had been eaten away and had not always been repaired or built up again. One house had steps in front of it which, if you took one more, would land you in the river on a dark night. Victoria looked down at the water below and edged her way round. Then, for a while, the way was wide and paved. The houses on her right hand had an agreeable air of secrecy. They offered no hint as to their occupancy. Occasionally the central door stood open, and peering inside Victoria was fascinated by the contrasts. On one such occasion she looked into a courtyard with a fountain playing and cushioned seats and deck chairs round it, with tall palms growing up and a garden beyond, that looked like the backcloth of a stage set. The next house, looking much the same outside, opened on a litter of confusion and dark passages, with five or six dirty children playing in rags. Then she came to palm gardens in thick groves. On her left she had passed uneven steps leading down to the river and an Arab boatman seated in a primitive rowing boat gesticulated and called, asking evidently if she wanted to be taken across to the other side. She must by now, Victoria judged, be just about opposite the

Tio Hotel, though it was hard to distinguish difference in the architecture viewed from this side, and the hotel buildings looked more or less alike. She came now to a road leading down through the palms and then to two tall houses with balconies. Beyond was a big house built right out onto the river with a garden and balustrade. The path on the bank passed on the inside of what must be the Beit Melek Ali or the House of King Ali.

In a few minutes more Victoria had passed its entrance and had come to a more squalid part; the river was hidden from her by palm plantations fenced off with rusty barbed wire. On the right were tumbledown houses inside rough mudbrick walls, and small shanties with children playing in the dirt and clouds of flies hanging over garbage heaps. A road led away from the river and a car was standing there—a somewhat battered and archaic car. By the car, Edward was standing.

"Good," said Edward, "you've got here. Get in."

"Where are we going?" asked Victoria, entering the battered automobile with delight. The driver, who appeared to be an animate bundle of rags, turned round and grinned happily at her.

"We're going to Babylon," said Edward. "It's about time we had a day out."

The car started with a terrific jerk and bumped madly over the rude paving stones.

"To Babylon?" cried Victoria. "How lovely it sounds. Really to Babylon?"

The car swerved to the left and they were bowling upon a well paved road of imposing width.

"Yes, but don't expect too much. Babylon—if you know what I mean—isn't quite what it was."

Victoria hummed:

"*How many miles to Babylon?*
Three score and ten:
Can I get there by candlelight?
Yes, and back again.

I used to sing that when I was a small child. It always fascinated me. And now we're really going there!"

"And we'll get back by candlelight. Or we should. Actually you never know in this country."

"This car looks very much as though it might break down."

"It probably will. There's sure to be simply everything wrong with it. But these Iraqis are frightfully good at tying it up with string and saying Inshallah, and then it goes again."

"It's always Inshallah, isn't it?"

"Yes, nothing like laying the responsibility upon the Almighty."

"The road isn't very good, is it?" gasped Victoria, bouncing in her seat. The deceptively well-paved and wide road had not lived up to its promise. The road was still wide but was now corrugated with ruts.

"It gets worse later on," shouted Edward.

They bounced and bumped happily. The dust rose in clouds round them. Large lorries covered with Arabs tore along in the middle of the track and were deaf to all intimations of the horn.

They passed walled-in gardens, and parties of women and children and donkeys, and to Victoria it was all new and part of the enchantment of going to Babylon with Edward beside her.

They reached Babylon bruised and shaken in a couple of hours. The meaningless pile of ruined mud and burnt brick was somewhat of a disappointment to Victoria who expected something in the way of columns and arches, looking like pictures she had seen on Baalbek.

But little by little her disappointment ebbed as they scrambled over mounds and lumps of burnt brick, led by the Guide. She listened with only half an ear to his profuse explanations, but as they went along the Processional Way to the Ishtar Gate, with the faint reliefs of unbelievable animals high on the walls, a sudden sense of the grandeur of the past came to her and a wish to know something about this vast proud city that now lay dead and abandoned. Presently their duty to Antiquity accomplished, they sat down by the Babylonian Lion to eat the picnic lunch that Edward had brought with him. The Guide moved away, smiling indulgently and telling them firmly that they must see the Museum later.

"Must we?" said Victoria dreamily. "Things all labelled and put into cases don't seem a bit real somehow. I went to the British Museum once. It was awful, and dreadfully tiring on the feet."

"The past is always boring," said Edward. "The future's much more important."

"This isn't boring," said Victoria waving a sandwich towards the panorama of tumbled brick. "There's a feeling of—of greatness here. What's the poem

When you were a King in Babylon
And I was a Christian Slave?

Perhaps we were. You and I, I mean."

"I don't think there were any Kings in Babylon by the time there were Christians," said Edward. "I think Babylon stopped functioning somewhere about five or six hundred B.C. Some archaeologist or other is always turning up to give lectures about these things—but I really never grasp any of the dates—I mean not until proper Greek and Roman ones."

"Would you have liked being a King in Babylon, Edward?"

Edward drew a deep breath.

"Yes, I should."

"Then we'll say you were. You're in a new incarnation now."

"They understood how to be Kings in those days!" said Edward. "That's why they could rule the world and bring it into shape."

"I don't know that I should have liked being a slave much," said Victoria meditatively, "Christian or otherwise."

"Milton was quite right," said Edward. "Better to reign in Hell than serve in Heaven. I always admired Milton's Satan."

"I never quite got around to Milton," said Victoria apologetically. "But I did go and see Comus at Sadler's Wells and it was lovely, and Margot Fonteyn danced like a kind of frozen angel."

"If you were a slave, Victoria," said Edward, "I should free you and take you into my harem—over there," he added gesticulating vaguely at a pile of debris.

A glint came into Victoria's eye.

"Talking of harems—" she began.

"How are you getting on with Catherine?" asked Edward hastily.

"How did you know I was thinking about Catherine?"

"Well, you were, weren't you? Honestly, Viccy, I do want you to become friends with Catherine."

"Don't call me Viccy."

"All right, Charing Cross. I want you to become friends with Catherine."

"How fatuous men are! Always wanting their girl friends to like each other."

Edward sat up energetically. He had been reclining with his hands behind his head.

"You've got it all wrong, Charing Cross. Anyway, your references to harems are simply silly—"

"No, they're not. The way all those girls glower intensely at you and yearn at you! It makes me mad."

"Splendid," said Edward. "I love you to be mad. But to return to Catherine. The reason I want you to be friends with Catherine is that I'm fairly sure she's the best way of approach to all the things we want to find out. She knows something."

"You really think so?"

"Remember what I heard her say about Anna Scheele."

"I'd forgotten that."

"How have you been getting on with Karl Marx? Any results?"

"Nobody's made a bee-line at me and invited me into the fold. In fact, Catherine told me yesterday the Party wouldn't accept me, because I'm not sufficiently politically educated. And to have to read all that dreary stuff—honestly, Edward, I haven't the brains for it."

"You're not politically aware, are you?" Edward laughed. "Poor Charing Cross. Well, well, Catherine may be frantic with brains and intensity and political awareness, my fancy is still a little cockney typist who can't spell any words of three syllables."

Victoria frowned suddenly. Edward's words brought back to her mind the curious interview she had had with Dr. Rathbone. She told Edward about it. He seemed much more upset than she would have expected him to be.

"This is serious, Victoria, really serious. Try and tell me exactly what he said."

Victoria tried her best to recall the exact words Rathbone had used.

"But I don't see," she said, "why it upsets you so."

"Eh?" Edward seemed abstracted. "You don't see—But my dear girl, don't you realise that this shows that they've got wise to you. They're warning you off. I don't like it, Victoria—I don't like it at all."

He paused and then said gravely,

"Communists, you know, are very ruthless. It's part of their creed to stick at nothing. I don't want you knocked on the head and thrown into the Tigris, darling."

How odd, thought Victoria, to be sitting amid the ruins of Babylon debating whether or not she was likely in the near future to be knocked on the head and thrown into the Tigris. Half closing her eyes, she thought dreamily, "I shall wake up soon and find I'm in London dreaming a wonderful melodramatic dream about dangerous Babylon. Perhaps," she thought, closing her eyes altogether, "I am in London . . . and the alarm clock will go off very soon, and I shall get up and go to Mr. Greenholtz's office—and there won't be any Edward—"

And at that last thought she opened her eyes again hastily to make sure that Edward was indeed really there (and what was it I was going to ask him at Basrah and they interrupted us and I forgot?) and it was not a dream. The sun was glaring down in a dazzling and most un-Londonlike way, and the ruins of Babylon were pale and shimmering with a background of dark palms, and sitting up with his back a little towards her was Edward. How extraordinarily nicely his hair grew down with a little twirl into his neck—and what a nice neck—bronzed red brown from the sun—with no blemishes on it—so many men had necks with cysts or pimples where their collars had rubbed—a neck like Sir Rupert's, for instance, with a boil just starting—

Suddenly with a stifled exclamation Victoria sat bolt upright and her daydreams were a thing of the past. She was wildly excited.

Edward turned an inquiring head.

"What's the matter, Charing Cross?"

"I've just remembered," said Victoria, "about Sir Rupert Crofton Lee—"

As Edward still turned a blank inquiring look upon her Victoria proceeded to elucidate her meaning which, truth to tell, she did not do very clearly.

"It was a boil," she said, "on his neck."

"A boil on his neck?" Edward was puzzled.

"Yes, in the aeroplane. He sat in front of me, you know, and that hood thing he wore fell back and I saw it—the boil."

"Why shouldn't he have a boil? Painful, but lots of people get them."

"Yes, yes, of course they do. But the point is that that morning on the balcony he hadn't."

"Hadn't what?"

"Hadn't got a boil. Oh Edward, do try and take it in. In the aeroplane he had a boil and on the balcony at the Tio he hadn't got a boil. His neck was quite smooth and unscarred—like yours now."

"Well, I suppose it had gone away."

"Oh no, Edward, it couldn't have. It was only a day later, and it was just coming up. It couldn't have gone away—not completely without a trace. So you see it means—yes, it must mean—the man at the Tio wasn't Sir Rupert at all."

She nodded her head with vehemence. Edward stared at her.

"You're crazy, Victoria. It must have been Sir Rupert. You didn't see any other difference in him."

"But don't you see, Edward, I'd never really looked at him properly—only at his—well, you might call it general effect. The hat—and the cape—and the swashbuckling attitude. He'd be a very easy man to impersonate."

"But they'd have known at the Embassy—"

"He didn't stay at the Embassy, did he? He came to the Tio. It was one of the minor secretaries or people who met him. The Ambassador's in England. Besides, he's travelled and been away from England so much."

"But why—"

"Because of Carmichael, of course. Carmichael was coming to Baghdad to meet him—to tell him what he'd found out. Only they'd never met before. So Carmichael wouldn't know he wasn't the right man—and he wouldn't be on his guard. Of course—it was Rupert Crofton Lee (the false one) who stabbed Carmichael! Oh, Edward, it all fits in."

"I don't believe a word of it. It's crazy. Don't forget Sir Rupert was killed afterwards in Cairo."

"That's where it all happened. I know now. Oh Edward, how awful. I saw it happen."

"You saw it happen—Victoria, are you quite mad?"

"No, I'm not in the least mad. Just listen, Edward. There was a knock on my door—in the Hotel in Heliopolis—at least I thought it was on my door and I looked out, but it wasn't—it was one door down, Sir Rupert Crofton Lee's. It was one of the stewardesses or Air Hostesses or whatever they call them. She asked him if he would mind coming to B.O.A.C. office—just along the corridor. I came out of my room just afterwards. I passed a door which had a notice with B.O.A.C. on it, and the door opened and he came out. I thought then that he had had some news that made him walk quite differently. Do you see, Edward? It was a trap, the substitute was waiting, all ready, and as soon as he came in, they just conked him on the head and the other one came out and took up the part. I think they probably kept him somewhere in Cairo, perhaps in the Hotel as an invalid, kept him drugged and then killed him just at the right moment when the wrong one had come back to Cairo."

"It's a magnificent story," said Edward. "But you know, Victoria, quite frankly you are making the whole thing up. There's no corroboration of it."

"There's the boil—"

"Oh, damn the boil!"

"And there are one or two other things."

"What?"

"That B.O.A.C. notice on the door. It wasn't there later. I remember being puzzled when I found the B.O.A.C. office was the other side of the entrance hall. That's one thing. And there's another. That Air stewardess, the one who knocked at his door. I've seen her since—here in Baghdad—and what's more, at the Olive Branch. The first day I went there. She came in and spoke to Catherine. I thought then I'd seen her before."

After a moment's silence, Victoria said:

"So you must admit, Edward, that it isn't all my fancy."

Edward said slowly:

"It all comes back to the Olive Branch—and to Catherine. Victoria, all ragging apart, you've got to get closer to Catherine. Flatter her, butter her up, talk Bolshie ideas to her. Somehow or other get sufficiently intimate with her to know who her friends are and where she goes and who she's in touch with outside the Olive Branch."

"It won't be easy," said Victoria, "but I'll try. What about Mr. Dakin? Ought I to tell him about this?"

"Yes, of course. But wait a day or two. We may have more to go on," Edward sighed. "I shall take Catherine to Le Select to hear the Cabaret one night."

And this time Victoria felt no pang of jealousy. Edward had spoken with a grim determination that ruled out any anticipation of pleasure in the commission he had undertaken.

II

Exhilarated by her discoveries, Victoria found it no effort to greet Catherine on the following day with an effusion of friendliness. It was so kind of Catherine, she said, to have told her of a place to have her hair washed. It needed washing terribly badly. (This was undeniable; Victoria had returned from Babylon with her dark hair the color of red rust from the clogging sand.)

"It is looking terrible, yes," said Catherine, eyeing it with a certain malicious satisfaction. "You went out then in that dust storm yesterday afternoon?"

"I hired a car and went to see Babylon," said Victoria. "It was very interesting, but on the way back, the dust-storm got up and I was nearly choked and blinded."

"It is interesting, Babylon," said Catherine, "but you should go with someone who understands it and can tell you about it properly. As for your hair, I will take you to this Armenian girl tonight. She will give you a cream shampoo. It is the best."

"I don't know how you keep your hair looking so wonderful," said Victoria, looking with what appeared to be admiring eyes at Catherine's heavy erections of greasy sausage-like curls.

A smile appeared on Catherine's usually sour face, and Victoria thought how right Edward had been about flattery.

When they left the Olive Branch that evening, the two girls were on the friendliest of terms. Catherine wove in and out of narrow passages and alleys and finally tapped on an unpromising door which gave no sign of hairdressing operations being conducted on the other side of it. They were, however, received by a plain but competent looking young woman who spoke careful slow English and who led Victoria to a spotlessly clean basin with shining taps and various bottles and lotions ranged round it. Catherine departed and Victoria surrendered her mop of hair into Miss Ankoumian's deft hands. Soon her hair was a mass of creamy lather.

"And now if you please—"

Victoria bent forward over the basin. Water streamed over her hair and gurgled down the waste pipe.

Suddenly her nose was assailed by a sweet rather sickly smell that she associated vaguely with hospitals. A wet saturated pad was clasped firmly over her nose and mouth. She struggled wildly, twisting and turning, but an iron grip kept the pad in place. She began to suffocate, her head reeled dizzily, a roaring sound came in her ears . . .

And after that, blackness, deep and profound.

Chapter 18

When Victoria regained consciousness, it was with a sense of an immense passage of time. Confused memories stirred in her—jolting in a car—high jabbering and quarrelling in Arabic—lights that flashed into her eyes—a horrible attack of nausea—then vaguely she remembered lying on a bed and someone lifting her arm—the sharp agonizing prick of a needle—then more confused dreams and darkness and behind it a mounting sense of urgency . . .

Now at last, dimly, she was herself—Victoria Jones . . . And something had happened to Victoria Jones—a long time ago—months—perhaps years . . . after all, perhaps only days.

Babylon—sunshine—dust—hair—Catherine—Catherine, of course, smiling, her eyes sly under the sausage curls—Catherine had taken her to have her hair shampooed and then—what had happened? That horrible smell—she could still smell it—nauseating—chloroform, of course. They had chloroformed her and taken her—where?

Cautiously Victoria tried to sit up. She seemed to be lying on a bed—a very hard bed—her head ached and felt dizzy—she was still drowsy, horribly drowsy . . . that prick, the prick of a hypodermic, they had been drugging her . . . she was still half drugged.

Well, anyway, they hadn't killed her (why not?). So that was all right. The best thing, thought the still half-drugged Victoria, is to go to sleep. And promptly did so.

When next she awakened she felt much more clear-headed. It was daylight now and she could see more clearly where she was.

She was in a small but very high room, distempered a depressing pale bluish grey. The floor was of beaten earth. The only furniture in the room seemed to be the bed on which she was lying, with a dirty rug thrown over her, and a rickety table with a cracked enamel basin on it and a zinc bucket underneath it. There was a window with a kind of wooden lattice work outside it. Victoria got gingerly off the bed, feeling distinctly headachy and queer, and approached the window. She could see through the lattice work quite plainly, and what she saw was a garden with palm trees beyond it. The garden was quite a pleasant one by Eastern standards, though it would have been looked down on by an English suburban householder. It had a lot of bright orange marigolds in it, and some dusty eucalyptus trees and some rather wispy tamarisks.

A small child with a face tattooed in blue and a lot of bangles on, was tumbling about with a ball and singing in a high nasal whine rather like distant bagpipes.

Victoria next turned her attention to the door which was large and massive. Without much hope she went to it and tried it. The door was locked. Victoria went back and sat on the side of the bed.

Where was she? Not in Baghdad, that was certain. And what was she going to do next?

It struck her after a minute or two that the last question did not really apply. What was more to the point was what was someone else going to do to her? With an uneasy feeling in the pit of her stomach she remembered Mr. Dakin's admonition to tell all she knew. But perhaps they had already got all that out of her while she was under the drug.

Still—Victoria returned to this one point with determined cheerfulness— she was alive. If she could manage to keep alive until Edward found her— what would Edward do when he found she had vanished? Would he go to Mr. Dakin? Would he play a lone hand? Would he put the fear of the Lord into Catherine and force her to tell—Would he suspect Catherine at all? The more Victoria tried to conjure up a reassuring picture of Edward in action, the more the image of Edward faded and became a kind of faceless abstraction. How clever was Edward? That was really what it amounted to. Edward was adorable. Edward had glamour. But had Edward got brains? Because clearly, in her present predicament, brains were going to be needed.

Mr. Dakin, now, would have the necessary brains. But would he have the impetus? Or would he merely cross off her name from a mental ledger, scoring it through, and writing after it a neat R.I.P. After all, to Mr. Dakin she was merely one of a crowd. They took their chance, and if luck failed, it was just too bad. No, she didn't see Mr. Dakin staging a rescue. After all, he had warned her.

And Dr. Rathbone had warned her. (Warned her or threatened her?)

And on her refusing to be threatened, there had not been much delay in carrying out the threat . . .

But I'm still alive, repeated Victoria, determined to look upon the bright side of things.

Footsteps approached outside and there was the grinding of a key in a rusty lock. The door staggered on its hinges and flew open. In the aperture appeared an Arab. He carried an old tin tray on which were dishes.

He appeared to be in good spirits, grinned broadly, uttered some incomprehensible remarks in Arabic, deposited the tray, opened his mouth and pointed down his throat and departed, re-locking the door behind him.

Victoria approached the tray with interest. There was a large bowl of rice, something that looked like rolled up cabbage leaves and a large flap of Arab bread. Also a jug of water and a glass.

Victoria started by drinking a large glass of water and then fell to on the rice, the bread, and the cabbage leaves which were full of rather peculiar tasting chopped meat. When she had finished everything on the tray she felt a good deal better.

She tried her best to think things out clearly. She had been chloroformed and kidnapped. How long ago? As to that, she had only the foggiest idea. From drowsy memories of sleeping and waking she judged that it was some days ago. She had been taken out of Baghdad—where? There again, she had no means of knowing. Owing to her ignorance of Arabic, it was not even possible to ask questions. She could not find out a place, or a name, or a date.

Several hours of acute boredom followed.

That evening her gaoler reappeared with another tray of food. With him this time came a couple of women. They were in rusty black with their faces hidden. They did not come into the room but stood just outside the door. One had a baby in her arms. They stood there and giggled. Through the thinness of the veil their eyes, she felt, were appraising her. It was exciting to them and highly humorous to have a European woman imprisoned here.

Victoria spoke to them in English and in French, but got only giggles in reply. It was queer, she thought, to be unable to communicate with her own sex. She said slowly and with difficulty one of the few phrases she had picked up.

"El hamdu lillah."

Its utterance was rewarded by a delighted spate of Arabic. They nodded their heads vigorously. Victoria moved towards them, but quickly the Arab servant or whatever he was, stepped back and barred her way. He motioned the two women back and went out himself, closing and locking the door again. Before he did so, he uttered one word several times over.

"Bukra—Bukra . . ."

It was a word Victoria had heard before. It meant tomorrow.

Victoria sat down on her bed to think things over. Tomorrow? Tomorrow, someone was coming or something was going to happen. Tomorrow her imprisonment would end (or wouldn't it?)—or if it did end, she herself might end too! Taking all things together, Victoria didn't much care for the idea of tomorrow. She felt instinctively that it would be much better if by tomorrow she was somewhere else.

But was that possible? For the first time, she gave this problem full attention. She went first to the door and examined it. Certainly nothing doing there. This wasn't the kind of lock you picked with a hairpin—if indeed she would have been capable of picking any lock with a hairpin, which she very much doubted.

There remained the window. The window, she soon found, was a much more hopeful proposition. The wooden lattice work that screened it was in the final stages of decrepitude. Granted she could break away sufficient of the rotten woodwork to force herself through, she could hardly do so without a good deal of noise which could not fail to attract attention. Moreover since the room in which she was confined was on an upper floor, it meant either fashioning a rope of some kind or else jumping with every likelihood of a sprained ankle or other injury. In books, thought Victoria, you make a rope of strips of bedclothes. She looked doubtfully at the thick cotton quilt and ragged blanket. Neither of them seemed at all suited to her purpose. She had nothing with which to cut the quilt in strips, and though she could probably tear the blanket, its condition of rottenness would preclude any possibility of trusting her weight to it.

"Damn," said Victoria aloud.

She was more and more enamoured of the idea of escape. As far as she could judge, her gaolers were people of very simple mentality to whom the mere fact that she was locked in a room spelt finality. They would not be expecting her to escape for the simple reason that she was a prisoner and could not. Whoever had used the hypodermic on her and presumably brought her here was not now on the premises—of that she was sure. He or she or they were expected "bukra." They had left her in some remote spot in the guardianship of simple folk who would obey instructions but who would not appreciate subtleties, and who were not, presumably, alive to the inventive faculties of a European young woman in imminent fear of extinction.

"I'm getting out of here somehow," said Victoria to herself.

She approached the table and helped herself to the new supply of food. She might as well keep her strength up. There was rice again and some oranges, and some bits of meat in a bright orange sauce.

Victoria ate everything and then had a drink of water. As she replaced the jug on the table, the table tilted slightly and some of the water went on the floor. The floor in that particular spot at once became a small puddle of liquid mud. Looking at it, an idea stirred in Miss Victoria Jones' always fertile brain.

The question was, had the key been left in the lock on the outside of the door?

The sun was setting now. Very soon it would be dark. Victoria went over to the door, knelt down and peered into the immense keyhole. She could see no light. Now what she needed was something to prod with—a pencil or the end of a fountain pen. How tiresome that her handbag had been taken away. She looked round the room frowning. The only article of cutlery on the table was a large spoon. That was no good for her immediate need, though it might come in handy later. Victoria sat down to puzzle and contrive. Presently she uttered an exclamation, took off her shoe and managed to pull out the inner leather sole. She rolled this up tightly. It was reasonably stiff. She went back to the door, squatted down and poked vigorously through the keyhole. Fortunately the immense key fitted loosely into the lock. After three or four minutes it responded to the efforts and fell out of the door on the outside. It made little noise falling on the earthen floor.

Now, Victoria thought, I must hurry, before the light goes altogether. She fetched the jug of water and poured a little carefully on a spot at the bottom of the door frame as near as possible to where she judged the key had fallen. Then, with the spoon and her fingers she scooped and scrabbled in the muddy patch that resulted. Little by little, with fresh applications of water from the jug, she scooped out a low trough under the door. Lying down she tried to peer through it but it wasn't easy to see anything. Rolling up her sleeves, she found she could get her hand and part of her arm under the door. She felt about with exploratory fingers and finally the tip of one finger touched something metallic. She had located the key, but she was unable to get her arm far enough to claw it nearer. Her next procedure was to secure the safety pin which was holding up a torn shoulder strap. Bending it into a hook, she embedded it in a wodge of Arab bread and lay down again to fish. Just as she was ready to cry with vexation the hooked safety pin caught in the key and she was able to draw it within reach of her fingers and then to pull it through the muddy trough to her side of the door.

Victoria sat back on her heels full of admiration for her own ingenuity. Grasping the key in her muddy hand, she got up and fitted it into the lock.

She waited for a moment when there was a good chorus of pi-dogs barking in the near neighbourhood and turned it. The door yielded to her push and swung open a little way. Victoria peered cautiously through the aperture. The door gave onto another small room with an open door at the end of it. Victoria waited a moment, then tiptoed out and across. This outside room had large gaping holes in the roof and one or two in the floor. The door at the end gave on the top of a flight of rough mudbrick stairs affixed to the side of the house, and which led down to the garden.

That was all Victoria wanted to see. She tiptoed back to her own place of imprisonment. There was little likelihood that anyone would come near her again tonight. She would wait until it was dark and the village or town more or less settled down to sleep and then she would go.

One other thing she had noted. A torn shapeless bit of black material lay in a heap near the outside door. It was, she thought, an old *Aba* and would come in useful to cover her Western clothes.

How long she waited Victoria did not know. It seemed to her interminable hours. Yet at last the various noises of local human kind died down. The far off blasting of a gramophone or phonograph stopped its Arab songs, the raucous voices and the spitting ceased, and there was no more far off women's high-pitched squealing laughter; no children's crying.

At last she heard only a far off howling noise which she took to be jackals, and the intermittent bursts of dog barking, which she knew would continue all through the night.

"Well, here goes!" said Victoria and stood up.

After a moment's cogitation she locked the door of her prison on the outside and left the key in the lock. Then she felt her way across the outer room, picked up the black heap of material and came out at the top of the mud stairs. There was a moon, but it was still low in the sky. It gave sufficient light for Victoria to see her way. She crept down the stairs, then paused about four stairs from the bottom. She was level here with the mudwall that enclosed the garden. If she continued down the stairs she would have to pass along the side of the house. She could hear snoring from the downstairs rooms. If she went along the top of the wall it might be better. The wall was sufficiently thick to walk along.

She chose the latter course and went swiftly and somewhat precariously to where the wall turned at right angles. Here, outside, was what seemed to be a palm garden, and at one point the wall was crumbling away. Victoria found her way there, partly jumped and partly slithered down and a few moments later was threading her way through palm trees towards a gap in the far wall. She came out upon a narrow street of a primitive nature, too small for the passage of a car, but suitable for donkeys. It ran between mudbrick walls. Victoria sped along it as fast as she could.

Now dogs began to bark furiously. Two fawn coloured pi-dogs came snarlingly out of a doorway at her. Victoria picked up a handful of rubble and brick and shied a piece at them. They yelped and ran away. Victoria sped on. She rounded a corner and came into what was evidently the main street. Narrow and heavily rutted, it ran through a village of mudbrick houses, uniformly pale in the moonlight. Palms peeped over walls, dogs snarled and barked. Victoria took a deep breath and ran. Dogs continued to bark, but no human being took any interest in this possible night marauder. Soon she came out on a wide space with a muddy stream and a decrepit humpbacked bridge over it. Beyond the road or track lay heading towards what seemed infinite space. Victoria continued to run until she was out of breath.

The village was well behind her now. The moon was high in the sky. To the left and the right and in front of her was bare stony ground, uncultivated and without a sign of human habitation. It looked flat but was really faintly contoured. It had, as far as Victoria could see, no landmarks, and she had no idea in what direction the track led. She was not learned enough in the stars to know even towards what point of the compass she was heading. There was something subtly terrifying in this large empty waste, but it was impossible to turn back. She could only go on.

Pausing a few moments to get her breath back, and assuring herself by looking back over her shoulder, that her flight had not been discovered, she set forth, walking a steady three and a half miles an hour towards the unknown.

Dawn came at last to find Victoria weary, footsore and almost on the verge of hysteria. By noting the light in the sky she ascertained that she was heading roughly south-west, but since she did not know where she was, that knowledge was of little use to her.

A little to the side of the road ahead of her was a kind of small compact hill or knob. Victoria left the track and made her way to the knob, the sides of which were quite steep, and climbed up to the top of it.

Here she was able to take a survey of the country all around and her feeling of meaningless panic returned. For everywhere there was nothing . . . The scene was beautiful in the early morning light. The ground and horizon shimmered with faint pastel shades of apricot and cream and pink on which were patterns of shadows. It was beautiful but frightening. "I know what it means now," thought Victoria, "when anyone says they are alone in the world . . ."

There was a little faint scrubby grass in dark patches here and there and some dry thorn. But otherwise there was no cultivation, and no signs of life. There was only Victoria Jones.

Of the village from which she had fled there were no signs either. The road along which she had come stretched back apparently into an infinity of waste. It seemed incredible to Victoria that she could have walked so far as to have lost the village altogether from view. For a moment she had a panic-stricken yearning to go back. Somehow or other to regain touch with human kind . . .

Then she took herself in hand. She had meant to escape, and had escaped, but her troubles were not likely to be at an end simply because she had placed several miles between her and her gaolers. A car, however old and rickety, would make short work of those miles. As soon as her escape was discovered, someone would come in search of her. And how on earth was she going to take cover or hide. There simply wasn't anywhere to hide. She still carried the ragged black *Aba* she had snatched up. Now tentatively she wrapped herself in its folds, pulling it down over her face. She had no idea what she looked like because she had no mirror with her. If she took off her European shoes and stockings and shuffled along with bare feet, she might possibly evade detection. A virtuously veiled Arab woman, however ragged and poor, had, she knew, all possible immunity. It would be the height of bad manners for any man to address her. But would that disguise fool Western eyes who might be out in a car looking for her. At any rate, it was the only chance.

She was much too tired to go on at present. She was terribly thirsty, too, but it was impossible to do anything about that. The best thing, she decided, was to lie down on the side of this hillock. She could hear a car coming and if she kept herself flattened into a little ravine which had eroded down the side of the hillock, she could get some idea of who was in the car.

She could take cover by moving round the back of the hillock so as to keep out of sight of the road.

On the other hand, what she badly needed was to get back to civilization, and the only means, as far as she could see, was to stop a car with Europeans in it and ask for a lift.

But she must be sure that the Europeans were the right Europeans. And how on earth was she to make sure of that?

Worrying over this point, Victoria quite unexpectedly fell asleep, worn out by her long trudge and her general exhaustion.

When she awoke the sun was directly overhead. She felt hot and stiff and dizzy, and her thirst was now a raging torment. Victoria gave a groan, but as the groan issued from her dry sore lips, she suddenly stiffened and listened. She heard faintly but distinctly the sound of a car. Very cautiously she raised her head. The car was not coming from the direction of the village but towards it. That meant that it was not in pursuit. It was as yet a small black dot far off on the track. Still lying as much concealed as she could, Victoria watched it come nearer. How she wished she had field glasses with her.

It disappeared for a few minutes in a depression of the landscape, then reappeared surmounting a rise not very far away. There was an Arab driver and beside him was a man in European dress.

"Now," thought Victoria, "I've got to decide." Was this her chance? Should she run down to the road and hail the car to stop?

Just as she was getting ready to do so, a sudden qualm stopped her. Suppose, just suppose, that this was the Enemy?

After all, how could she tell? The track was certainly a very deserted one. No other car had passed. No lorry. Not even a train of donkeys. This car was making, perhaps, for the village she had left last night . . .

What should she do? It was a horrible decision to have to make at a moment's notice. If it was the Enemy, it was the end. But if it wasn't the Enemy, it might be her only hope of survival. Because if she went on wandering about, she would probably die of thirst and exposure. What should she do?

And as she crouched paralysed with indecision, the note of the approaching car changed. It slackened speed, then, swerving, it came off the road and across the stony ground towards the mound on which she squatted.

It had seen her! It was looking for her!

Victoria slithered down the gully and crawled round the back of the mound away from the approaching car. She heard it come to a stop and the bang of the door as someone got out.

Then somebody said something in Arabic. After that, nothing happened. Suddenly, without any warning, a man came into view. He was walking round the mound, about half way up it. His eyes were bent on the ground and from time to time he stooped and picked something up. Whatever he was looking for, it did not seem to be a girl called Victoria Jones. Moreover, he was unmistakably an Englishman.

With an exclamation of relief Victoria struggled to her feet and came towards him. He lifted his head and stared in surprise.

"Oh please," said Victoria. "I'm so glad you've come."

He still stared.

"Who on earth," he began. "Are you English? But—"

With a spurt of laughter, Victoria cast away the enveloping *Aba*.

"Of course I'm English," she said. "And please, can you take me back to Baghdad?"

"I'm not going to Baghdad. I've just come from it. But what on earth are you doing all alone out here in the middle of the desert?"

"I was kidnapped," said Victoria breathlessly. "I went to have my hair shampooed and they gave me chloroform. And when I woke up I was in an Arab house in a village over there."

She gesticulated towards the horizon:

"In Mandali?"

"I don't know its name. I escaped last night. I walked all through the night and then I hid behind this hill in case you were an Enemy."

Her rescuer was staring at her with a very odd expression on his face. He was a man of about thirty-five, fair-haired, with a somewhat supercilious expression. His speech was academic and precise. He now put on a pair of pince-nez and stared at her through them with an expression of distaste. Victoria realised this man did not believe a word of what she was saying.

She was immediately moved to furious indignation.

"It's perfectly true," she said. "Every word of it!"

The stranger looked more disbelieving than ever.

"Very remarkable," he said in a cold tone.

Despair seized Victoria. How unfair it was that while she could always make a lie sound plausible, in recitals of stark truth she lacked the power to make herself believed. Actual facts she told baldly and without conviction.

"And if you haven't got anything to drink with you, I shall die of thirst," she said. "I shall die of thirst anyway, if you leave me here and go on without me."

"Naturally I shouldn't dream of doing that," said the stranger stiffly. "It is most unsuitable for an English-woman to be wandering about alone in the wilds. Dear me, your lips are quite cracked . . . Abdul."

"Sahib?"

The driver appeared round the side of the mound.

On receiving instructions in Arabic he ran off towards the car, to return shortly with a large Thermos flask and a bakelite cup.

Victoria drank water avidly.

"Oo!" she said. "That's better."

"My name's Richard Baker," said the Englishman.

Victoria responded.

"I'm Victoria Jones," she said. And then, in an effort to recover lost ground and to replace the disbelief she saw by a respectful attention, she added:

"Pauncefoot Jones. I'm joining my uncle, Dr. Pauncefoot Jones, on his excavation."

"What an extraordinary coincidence," said Baker, staring at her surprisedly. "I'm on my way to the Dig myself. It's only about fifteen miles from here. I'm just the right person to have rescued you, aren't I?"

To say that Victoria was taken aback is to put it mildly. She was completely flabbergasted. So much so, that she was quite incapable of saying a word of any kind. Meekly and in silence she followed Richard to the car and got in.

"I suppose you're the anthropologist," said Richard, as he settled her in the back seat and removed various impedimenta. "I heard you were coming out, but I didn't expect you so early in the season."

He stood for a moment sorting through various potsherds which he removed from his pockets and which, Victoria now realised, were what he had been picking up from the surface of the mound.

"Likely looking little *Tell*," he said, gesturing towards the mound. "But nothing out of the way on it, so far as I can see. Late Assyrian ware mostly—a little Parthian, some quite good ring bases of the Kassite period." He smiled as he added, "I'm glad to see that in spite of your troubles your archaeological instincts led you to examine a *Tell*."

Victoria opened her mouth and then shut it again. The driver let in the clutch and they started off.

What, after all, could she say? True, she would be unmasked as soon as they reached the Expedition House—but it would be infinitely better to be unmasked there and confess penitence for her inventions, than it would be to confess all to Mr. Richard Baker in the middle of nowhere. The worst they could do to her would be to send her into Baghdad. And anyway, thought Victoria, incorrigible as ever, perhaps before I get there I shall have thought of something. Her busy imagination got to work forthwith. A lapse of memory? She had travelled out with a girl who had asked her to—no really, as far as she could see, she would have to make a complete breast of it. But she infinitely preferred making a clean breast of it to Dr. Pauncefoot Jones, whatever kind of man he was, than to Mr. Richard Baker, with his supercilious way of lifting his eyebrows and his obvious disbelief of the exact and true story she had told him.

"We don't go right into Mandali," said Mr. Baker, turning in the front seat. "We branch off from the road into the desert about a mile further on. A bit difficult to hit the exact spot sometimes with no particular landmarks."

Presently he said something to Abdul and the car turned sharply off the track and made straight for the desert. With no particular landmarks to guide him, as far as Victoria could see, Richard Baker directed Abdul with gestures—he bent now to the right—now to the left. Presently Richard gave an exclamation of satisfaction.

"On the right track now," he said.

Victoria could not see any track at all. But presently she did catch sight every now and again of faintly marked tyre marks.

Once they crossed a slightly more clearly marked track and when they did so, Richard made an exclamation and ordered Abdul to stop.

"Here's an interesting sight for you," he said to Victoria. "Since you're new to this country you won't have seen it before."

Two men were advancing towards the car along the cross track. One man carried a short wooden bench on his back, the other a big wooden object about the size of an upright piano.

Richard hailed them; they greeted him with every sign of pleasure. Richard produced cigarettes and a thoroughly party spirit seemed to be developing.

Then Richard turned to her.

"Fond of the Cinema? Then you shall see a performance."

He spoke to the two men and they smiled with pleasure. They set up the bench and motioned to Victoria and Richard to sit on it. Then they set up the round contrivance on a stand of some kind. It had two eyeholes in it and as she looked at it, Victoria cried,

"It's like things on piers. *What the butler saw.*"

"That's it," said Richard. "It's a primitive form of same."

Victoria applied her eyes to the glass-fronted peephole, one man began slowly to turn a crank or handle, and the other began a monotonous kind of chant.

"What is he saying?" Victoria asked.

Richard translated as the sing-song chant continued,

"Draw near and prepare yourself for much wonder and delight. Prepare to behold the wonders of antiquity."

A crudely coloured picture of negroes reaping wheat swam into Victoria's gaze.

"Fellahin in America," announced Richard, translating.

Then came:

"The wife of the great Shah of the Western world," and the Empress Eugenie simpered and fingered a long ringlet. A picture of the King's Palace in Montenegro, another of the Great Exhibition.

An odd and varied collection of pictures followed each other, all completely unrelated and sometimes announced in the strangest terms.

The Prince Consort, Disraeli, Norwegian Fjords and Skaters in Switzerland completed this strange glimpse of olden far off days.

The showman ended his exposition with the following words,

"And so we bring to you the wonders and marvels of antiquity in other lands and far off places. Let your donation be generous to match the marvels you have seen, for all these things are true."

It was over. Victoria beamed with delight.

"That really was marvellous!" she said. "I wouldn't have believed it."

The proprietors of the travelling Cinema were smiling proudly. Victoria got up from the bench and Richard who was sitting on the other end of it was thrown to the ground in a somewhat undignified posture. Victoria apologised but was not ill pleased. Richard rewarded the Cinema men and with courteous farewells and expressions of concern for each other's welfare, and invoking the blessing of God on each other, they parted company. Richard and Victoria got into the car again and the men trudged away into the desert.

"Where are they going?" asked Victoria.

"They travel all over the country. I met them first in Trans Jordan coming up the road from the Dead Sea to Ammaan. Actually they're bound now for Kerbela, going of course by unfrequented routes so as to give shows in remote villages."

"Perhaps someone will give them a lift?"

Richard laughed.

"They probably wouldn't take it. I offered an old man a lift once who was walking from Basrah to Baghdad. I asked him how long he expected to be and he said a couple of months. I told him to get in and he would be there late that evening, but he thanked me and said no. Two months ahead would suit him just as well. Time doesn't mean anything out here. Once one gets that into one's head, one finds a curious satisfaction in it."

"Yes, I can imagine that."

"Arabs find our Western impatience for doing things quickly extraordinarily hard to understand, and our habit of coming straight to the point in conversation strikes them as extremely ill-mannered. You should always sit around and offer general observations for about an hour—or if you prefer, you need not speak at all."

"Rather odd if we did that in offices in London. One would waste a lot of time."

"Yes, but we're back again at the question: What is time? And what is waste?"

Victoria meditated on these points. The car still appeared to be proceeding to nowhere with the utmost confidence.

"Where is this place?" she said at last.

"Tell Aswad? Well out in the middle of the desert. You'll see the

Zigcurat very shortly now. In the meantime, look over to your left. There—where I'm pointing."

"Are they clouds?" asked Victoria. "They can't be mountains."

"Yes, they are. The snow-capped mountains of Kurdistan. You can only see them when it's very clear."

A dream-like feeling of contentment came over Victoria. If only she could drive on like this for ever. If only she wasn't such a miserable liar. She shrank like a child at the thought of the unpleasant denouement ahead of her. What would Dr. Pauncefoot Jones be like? Tall, with a long grey beard, and a fierce frown. Never mind, however annoyed Dr. Pauncefoot Jones might be, she had circumvented Catherine and the Olive Branch and Dr. Rathbone.

"There you are," said Richard.

He pointed ahead. Victoria made out a kind of pimple on the far horizon.

"It looks miles away."

"Oh no, it's only a few miles now. You'll see."

And, indeed, the pimple developed with astonishing rapidity into first a blob and then a hill and finally into a large and impressive *Tell*. On one side of it was a long sprawling building of mud brick.

"The Expedition House," said Richard.

They drew up with a flourish amid the barking of dogs. White robed servants rushed out to greet them, beaming with smiles.

After an interchange of greetings, Richard said:

"Apparently they weren't expecting you so soon. But they'll get your bed made. And they'll take you in hot water at once. I expect you'd like to have a wash and a rest? Dr. Pauncefoot Jones is up on the *Tell*. I'm going up to him. Ibrahim will look after you."

He strode away and Victoria followed the smiling Ibrahim into the house. It seemed dark inside at first after coming in out of the sun. They passed through a living room with some big tables and a few battered armchairs and she was then led round a courtyard and into a small room with one tiny window. It held a bed, a rough chest of drawers, a chair and a table with a jug and basin on it. Ibrahim smiled and nodded and brought her a large jug of rather muddy-looking hot water and a rough towel. Then, with an apologetic smile, he returned with a small looking glass which he carefully affixed upon a nail on the wall.

Victoria was thankful to have the chance of a wash. She was just beginning to realise how utterly weary and worn out she was and how very much encrusted with grime.

"I suppose I look simply frightful," she said to herself and approached the looking glass.

For some moments she stared at her reflection uncomprehendingly. This wasn't her—this wasn't Victoria Jones.

And then she realised that, though the features were the small neat features of Victoria Jones, her hair was now platinum blonde!

Chapter 19

Richard found Dr. Pauncefoot Jones in the excavations, squatting by the side of his foreman and tapping gently with a small pick at a section of wall.

Dr. Pauncefoot Jones greeted his colleague in a matter of fact manner.

"Hullo, Richard my boy, so you've turned up. I had an idea you were arriving on Tuesday, I don't know why."

"This is Tuesday," said Richard.

"Is it really now?" said Dr. Pauncefoot Jones without interest. "Just come down here and see what you think of this. Perfectly good walls coming out already and we're only down three feet. Seems to me there are a few traces of paint here. Come and see what you think. It looks very promising to me."

Richard leaped down into the trench and the two archaeologists enjoyed themselves in a highly technical manner for about a quarter of an hour.

"By the way," said Richard. "I've brought a girl."

"Oh, have you? What sort of girl?"

"She says she's your niece."

"My niece?" Dr. Pauncefoot Jones brought his mind back with a struggle from his contemplation of mudbrick walls. "I don't think I have a niece," he said doubtfully, as though he might have had one and forgotten about her.

"She's coming to work with you here, I gathered."

"Oh." Dr. Pauncefoot Jones' face cleared. "Of course. That will be Veronica."

"Victoria, I think she said."

"Yes, yes, Victoria. Emerson wrote to me about her from Cambridge. A very able girl, I understand. An anthropologist. Can't think why anyone wants to be an anthropologist, can you?"

"I heard you had some anthropologist girl coming out."

"There's nothing in her line so far. Of course we're only just beginning. Actually I understood she wasn't coming out for another fortnight or so, but I didn't read her letter very carefully, and then I mislaid it, so I didn't really remember what she said. My wife arrives next week—or the week after—now what have I done with her letter?—and I rather thought Venetia was coming out with her—but of course I may have got it all wrong. Well, well, I daresay we can make her useful. There's a lot of pottery coming up."

"There's nothing odd about her, is there?"

"Odd?" Dr. Pauncefoot Jones peered at him. "In what way?"

"Well, she hasn't had a nervous breakdown or anything?"

"Emerson did say, I remember, that she had been working very hard. Diploma or degree or something, but I don't think he said anything about a breakdown. Why?"

"Well, I picked her up at the side of the road, wandering about all by herself. It was on that little *Tell*, as a matter of fact, that you come to about a mile before you turn off the road—"

"I remember," said Dr. Pauncefoot Jones. "You know, I once picked up a bit of Nuzu ware on that *Tell*. Extraordinary really, to find it so far South."

Richard refused to be diverted to archaeological topics and went on firmly.

"She told me the most extraordinary story. Said she'd gone to have her hair shampooed, and they chloroformed her and kidnapped her and carried her off to Mandali and imprisoned her in a house, and she'd escaped in the middle of the night—the most preposterous rigmarole you ever heard."

Dr. Pauncefoot Jones shook his head.

"Doesn't sound at all probable," he said. "Country's perfectly quiet and well policed. It's never been safer."

"Exactly. She'd obviously made the whole thing up. That's why I asked if she'd had a breakdown. She must be one of those hysterical girls who say curates are in love with them, or that doctors assault them. She may give us a lot of trouble."

"Oh I expect she'll calm down," said Dr. Pauncefoot Jones optimistically. "Where is she now?"

"I left her to have a wash and brush up." He hesitated. "She hasn't got any luggage of any kind with her."

"Hasn't she? That really is awkward. You don't think she'll expect me to lend her pyjamas? I've only got two pairs and one of them is badly torn."

"She'll have to do the best she can until the lorry goes in next week. I must say I wonder what she can have been up to—all alone and out in the blue."

"Girls are amazing nowadays," said Dr. Pauncefoot Jones vaguely. "Turn up all over the place. Great nuisance when you want to get on with things. This place is far enough out, you'd think, to be free of visitors, but you'd be surprised how cars and people turn up when you can least do with them. Dear me, the men have stopped work. It must be lunch time. We'd better go back to the house."

II

Victoria, waiting in some trepidation, found Dr. Pauncefoot Jones wildly far from her imaginings. He was a small rotund man with a semi-bald head and a twinkling eye. To her utter amazement he came towards her with outstretched hands.

"Well, well, Venetia—I mean Victoria," he said. "This is quite a surprise. Got it into my head you weren't arriving until next month. But I'm delighted to see you. Delighted! How's Emerson? Not troubled too much by asthma, I hope?"

Victoria rallied her scattered senses and said cautiously that the asthma hadn't been too bad.

"Wraps his throat up too much," said Dr. Pauncefoot Jones. "Great mistake. I told him so. All these Academic fellows who stick around universities get far too absorbed in their health. Shouldn't think about it—that's the way to keep fit. Well, I hope you'll settle down—my wife will be out next week—or the week after—she's been seedy, you know. I really must find her letter. Richard tells me your luggage has gone astray. How are you going to manage? Can't very well send the lorry in before next week?"

"I expect I can manage until then," said Victoria. "In fact, I shall have to."

Dr. Pauncefoot Jones chuckled.

"Richard and I can't lend you much. Toothbrush will be all right. There are a dozen of them in our stores—and cotton wool if that's any good to you and—let me see—talcum powder—and some spare socks and handkerchiefs. Not much else, I'm afraid."

"I shall be all right," said Victoria and smiled happily.

"No signs of a cemetery for you," Dr. Pauncefoot Jones warned her. "Some nice walls coming up—and quantities of potsherds from the far trenches. Might get some joins. We'll keep you busy somehow or other. I forget if you do photography?"

"I know something about it," said Victoria cautiously, relieved by a mention of something that she did actually have a working knowledge of.

"Good, good. You can develop negatives? I'm old fashioned—use plates still. The dark room is rather primitive. You young people who are used to all the gadgets, often find these primitive conditions rather upsetting."

"I shan't mind," said Victoria.

From the Expedition's stores, she selected a toothbrush, toothpaste, a sponge and some talcum powder.

Her head was still in a whirl as she tried to understand exactly what her position was. Clearly she was being mistaken for a girl called Venetia Something who was coming out to join the Expedition and who was an Anthropologist. Victoria didn't even know what an anthropologist was. If there was a dictionary somewhere about, she must look it up. The other girl was presumably not arriving for at least another week. Very well then, for a week—or until such time as the car or the lorry went into Baghdad, Victoria would be Venetia Thingummy, keeping her end up as best she could. She had no fears for Dr. Pauncefoot Jones who seemed delightfully vague, but she was nervous of Richard Baker. She disliked the speculative way he looked at her, and she had an idea that unless she was careful he would soon see through her pretences. Fortunately she had been, for a brief period, a secretary typist at the Archaeological Institute in London, and she had a smattering of phrases and odds and ends that would be useful now. But she would have to be very careful not to make any real slip. Luckily, thought Victoria, men were always so superior about women that any slip she did make would be treated less as a suspicious circumstance than as a proof of how ridiculously addle-pated all women were!

This interval would give her a respite which, she felt, she badly needed. For, from the point of view of the Olive Branch, her complete disappearance would be very disconcerting. She had escaped from her prison, but what had happened to her afterwards would be very hard to trace. Richard's car had not passed through Mandali so that nobody could guess she was now at Tell Aswad. No, from their point of view, Victoria would seem to have vanished into thin air. They might conclude, very possibly they would conclude, that she was dead. That she had strayed into the desert and died of exhaustion.

Well, let them think so. Regrettably, of course, Edward would think so, too! Very well, Edward must lump it. In any case he would not have to lump it long. Just when he was torturing himself with remorse for having told her to cultivate Catherine's society—there she would be—suddenly restored to him—back from the dead—only a blonde instead of a brunette.

That brought her back to the mystery of why They (whoever they were) had dyed her hair. There must, Victoria thought, be some reason—but she could not for the life of her understand what the reason could be. As it was, she was soon going to look very peculiar when her hair started growing out black at the roots. A phoney platinum blonde, with no face powder and no lipstick! Could any girl be more unfortunately placed? Never mind, thought Victoria, I'm alive, aren't I? And I don't see at all why I shouldn't enjoy myself a good deal—at any rate for a week. It was really great fun to be on an Archaeological Expedition and see what it was like. If only she could keep her end up and not give herself away.

She did not find her role altogether easy. Reference to people, to publications, to styles of architecture and categories of pottery had to be dealt with cautiously. Fortunately a good listener is always appreciated. Victoria was an excellent listener to the two men, and warily feeling her way, she began to pick up the jargon fairly easily.

Surreptitiously, she read furiously when she was alone in the house. There was a good library of Archaeological publications. Victoria was quick to pick up a smattering of the subject. Unexpectedly, she found the life quite enchanting. Tea brought to her in the early morning, then out on the Dig. Helping Richard with camera work. Piecing together and sticking up pottery. Watching the men at work, appreciating the skill and delicacy of the pickmen—enjoying the songs and laughter of the little boys who ran to empty their baskets of earth on the dump. She mastered the periods, realised the various levels where digging was going on, and familiarised herself with the work of the previous season. The only thing she dreaded was that burials might turn up. Nothing that she read gave her any idea of what would be expected of her as a working anthropologist! "If we do get bones or a grave," said Victoria to herself, "I shall have to have a frightful cold—no, a severe bilious attack—and take to my bed."

But no graves did appear. Instead, the walls of a palace were slowly excavated. Victoria was fascinated and had no occasion to show any aptitude or special skill.

Richard Baker still looked at her quizzically sometimes and she sensed his unspoken criticism, but his manner was pleasant and friendly, and he was genuinely amused by her enthusiasm.

"It's all new to you coming out from England," he said one day. "I remember how thrilled I was my first season."

"How long ago was that?"

He smiled.

"Rather a long time. Fifteen—no, sixteen years ago."

"You must know this country very well."

"Oh, it's not only been here. Syria—and Persia as well."

"You talk Arabic very well, don't you. If you were dressed as one could you pass as an Arab?"

He shook his head.

"Oh no—that takes some doing. I doubt if any Englishman has ever been able to pass as an Arab—for any length of time, that is."

"Lawrence?"

"I don't think Lawrence ever passed as an Arab. No, the only man I know who is practically indistinguishable from the native product is a fellow who was actually born out in these parts. His father was Consul at Kashgar and other wild spots. He talked all kinds of outlandish dialects as a child and, I believe, kept them up later."

"What happened to him?"

"I lost sight of him after we left school. We were at school together. Fakir, we used to call him, because he could sit perfectly still and go into a queer sort of trance. I don't know what he's doing now—though actually I could make a pretty good guess."

"You never saw him after school?"

"Strangely enough, I ran into him only the other day—at Basrah, it was. Rather a queer business altogether."

"Queer?"

"Yes. I didn't recognise him. He was got up as an Arab, keffiyah and striped robe and an old Army coat. He had a string of those amber beads they carry sometimes and he was clicking it through his fingers in the orthodox way—only, you see, he was actually using Army code. Morse. He was clicking out a message—to me!"

"What did it say?"

"My name—or nickname, rather—and his, and then a signal to stand by, expecting trouble."

"And was there trouble?"

"Yes. As he got up and started out the door, a quiet inconspicuous commercial traveller sort of fellow tugged out a revolver. I knocked his arm up—and Carmichael got away."

"Carmichael?"

He switched his head round quickly at her tone.

"That was his real name. Why—do you know him?"

Victoria thought to herself—How odd it would sound if I said, "He died in my bed."

"Yes," she said slowly. "I knew him."

"Knew him? Why—is he—"

Victoria nodded.

"Yes," she said. "He's dead."

"When did he die?"

"In Baghdad. In the Tio Hotel." She added quickly "It was—hushed up. Nobody knows."

He nodded his head slowly.

"I see. It was that kind of business. But you—" he looked at her. "How do you know?"

"I got mixed up in it—by accident."

He gave her a long considering look.

Victoria asked suddenly,

"Your nickname at school wasn't Lucifer, was it?"

He looked surprised.

"Lucifer? no. I was called Owl—because I always had to wear shiny glasses."

"You don't know anyone who is called Lucifer—in Basrah?"

Richard shook his head.

"Lucifer, Son of the Morning—the fallen Angel."

He added, "Or an old-fashioned wax match. Its merit, if I remember rightly, was that it didn't go out in a wind."

He watched her closely as he spoke, but Victoria was frowning abstractedly.

"I wish you'd tell me," she said presently "exactly what happened at Basrah."

"I have told you."

"No. I mean where were you when all this occurred?"

"Oh I see. Actually it was in the waiting room of the Consulate. I was waiting to see Clayton, the Consul."

"And who else was there? This commercial traveller person, and Carmichael? Anyone else?"

"There were a couple of others, a thin dark Frenchman or Syrian, and an old man—a Persian, I should say."

"And the commercial traveller got the revolver out and you stopped him, and Carmichael got out—how—?"

"He turned first towards the Consul's office. It's at the other end of a passage with a garden—"

She interrupted.

"I know. I stayed there for a day or two. As a matter of fact, it was just after you left."

"It was, was it?" Once again he watched her narrowly—but Victoria was unaware of it. She was seeing the long passage at the Consulate, but with the door open at the other end—opening onto green trees and sunlight.

"Well, as I was saying, Carmichael headed that way first. Then he wheeled round and dashed the other way into the street. That's the last I saw of him."

"What about the commercial traveller?"

Richard shrugged his shoulders.

"I understand he told some garbled story about having been attacked and robbed by a man the night before and fancying he had recognised his assailant in the Arab in the Consulate. I didn't hear much more about it because I flew on to Kuwait."

"Who was staying at the Consulate just then?" Victoria asked.

"A fellow called Crosbie—one of the oil people. Nobody else. Oh yes, I believe there was someone else down from Baghdad, but I didn't meet him. Can't remember his name."

"Crosbie," thought Victoria. She remembered Captain Crosbie, his short stocky figure, his staccato conversation. A very ordinary person. A decent soul without much finesse about him. And Crosbie had been back in Baghdad the night when Carmichael came to the Tio. Could it be because he had seen Crosbie at the other end of the passage, silhouetted against the sunlight, that Carmichael had turned so suddenly and made for the street instead of attempting to reach the Consul General's office?

She had been thinking this out in some absorption. She started rather guiltily when she looked up to find Richard Baker watching her with close attention.

"Why do you want to know all this?" he asked.

"I'm just interested."

"Any more questions?"

Victoria asked:

"Do you know anybody called Lefarge?"

"No—can't say I do. Man or woman?"

"I don't know."

She was wondering again about Crosbie. Crosbie? Lucifer? Did Lucifer equal Crosbie?

That evening, when Victoria had said good night to the two men and gone to bed, Richard said to Dr. Pauncefoot Jones,

"I wonder if I might have a look at that letter from Emerson. I'd like to see just exactly what he said about this girl."

"Of course, my dear fellow, of course. It's somewhere lying around. I made some notes on the back of it, I remember. He spoke very highly of Veronica, if I remember rightly—said she was terrifically keen. She seems to me a charming girl—quite charming. Very plucky the way she's made so little fuss about the loss of her luggage. Most girls would have insisted on being motored into Baghdad the very next day to buy a new outfit. She's what I call a sporting girl. By the way, how was it that she came to lose her luggage?"

"She was chloroformed, kidnapped, and imprisoned in a native house," said Richard impassively.

"Dear, dear, yes, so you told me. I remember now. All most improbable. Reminds me—now what does it remind me of?—ah! yes, Elizabeth Canning, of course. You remember she turned up with the most impossible story after being missing a fortnight. Very interesting conflict of evidence—about some gypsies, if it's the right case I'm thinking of. And she was such a plain girl, it didn't seem likely there could be a man in the case. Now little Victoria—Veronica—I never *can* get her name right—she's a remarkably pretty little thing. Quite likely there is a man in her case."

"She'd be better looking if she didn't dye her hair," said Richard drily.

"Does she dye it? In-deed. How knowledgeable you are in these matters."

"About Emerson's letter, sir—"

"Of course—of course—I've no idea where I put it. But look anywhere you choose—I'm anxious to find it anyway because of those notes I made on the back—and a sketch of that coiled wire bead."

Chapter 20

On the following afternoon Dr. Pauncefoot Jones uttered a disgusted exclamation as the sound of a car came faintly to his ears. Presently he located it, winding across the desert towards the *Tell*.

"Visitors," he said with venom. "At the worst possible moment, too. I want to superintend the cellulosing of that painted rosette on the North East corner. Sure to be some idiots come out from Baghdad with a lot of social chatter and expecting to get shown all over the excavations."

"This is where Victoria comes in useful," said Richard. "You hear, Victoria? It's up to you to do a personally conducted tour."

"I shall probably say all the wrong things," said Victoria. "I'm really very inexperienced, you know."

"I think you're doing very well indeed," said Richard pleasantly. "Those remarks you made this morning about plano convex bricks might have come straight out of Delougaz's book."

Victoria changed colour slightly, and resolved to paraphrase her erudition more carefully. Sometimes the quizzical glance through the thick lenses made her uncomfortable.

"I'll do my best," she said meekly.

"We push all the odd jobs on to you," said Richard.

Victoria smiled.

Indeed, her activities during the last five days surprised her not a little. She had developed plates with water filtered through cotton wool and by the light of a primitive dark lantern containing a candle which always went out at the most crucial moment. The dark-room table was a packing case and to work she had to crouch or kneel—the darkroom itself being, as Richard remarked, a modern model of the famous mediaeval Little Ease. There would be more amenities in the seasons to come, Dr. Pauncefoot Jones assured her—but at the moment every penny was needed to pay workmen and get results.

The baskets of broken potsherds had at first excited her astonished derision (though this she had been careful not to display). All these broken bits of coarse stuff—what was the good of them?

Then as she found joins, stuck them and propped them up in boxes of sand, she began to take an interest. She learned to recognise shapes and even periods. And she came finally to try and reconstruct in her own mind just how and for what these vessels had been used some three thousand odd years ago. In the small area where some poor quality private houses had been dug, she pictured the houses as they had originally stood and the people who had lived in them with their wants and possessions and occupations, their hopes and their fears. Since Victoria had a lively imagination, a picture rose up easily enough in her mind. On a day when a small clay pot was found encased in a wall with a half dozen gold earrings in it, she was enthralled. Probably dowry of a daughter, Richard Baker had said smiling.

Dishes filled with grain, gold earrings saved up for a dowry, bone needles, querns and mortars, little figurines and amulets. All the everyday life and fears and hopes of a community of unimportant simple people.

"That's what I find so fascinating," said Victoria to Richard. "You see I always used to think that archaeology was just Royal Graves and Palaces.

"Kings in Babylon," she added, with a strange little smile. "But what I like so much about all this is that it's the ordinary everyday people—people like me. My St. Anthony who finds things for me when I lose them—and a lucky china pig I've got—and an awfully nice mixing bowl, blue inside and white out, that I used to make cakes in. It got broken and the new one I bought wasn't a bit the same. I can understand why these people mended up their favourite bowls or dishes so carefully with bitumen. Life's all the same really, isn't it—then or now?"

She was thinking of these things as she watched the visitors ascending the side of the *Tell*. Richard went to greet them, Victoria following behind him.

They were two Frenchmen, interested in Archaeology, who were making a tour through Syria and Iraq. After civil greetings, Victoria took them round the excavations, reciting parrot wise what was going on, but being unable to resist, being Victoria, adding sundry embellishments of her own, just, as she put it to herself, to make it more exciting.

She noticed that the second man was a very bad colour, and that he dragged himself along without much interest. Presently he said, if Mademoiselle would excuse him, he would retire to the house. He had not felt well since early that morning—and the sun was making him worse.

He departed in the direction of the Expedition House, and the other, in suitably lowered tones explained that, unfortunately, it was his estomac. The Baghdad Tummy they called it, did they not? He should not really have come out today.

The tour was completed, the Frenchman remained talking to Victoria, finally Fidos was called and Dr. Pauncefoot Jones, with a determined air of hospitality, suggested the guests should have tea before departing.

To this, however, the Frenchman demurred. They must not delay their departure until it was dark or they would never find the way. Richard Baker said immediately that this was quite right. The sick friend was retrieved from the house and the car rushed off at top speed.

"I suppose that's just the beginning," grunted Dr. Pauncefoot Jones. "We shall have visitors every day now."

He took a large flap of Arab bread and covered it thickly with apricot jam.

Richard went to his room after tea. He had letters to answer, and others to write in preparation for going into Baghdad on the following day.

Suddenly he frowned. Not a man of particular neatness to the outward view, he yet had a way of arranging his clothes and his papers that never varied. Now he saw at once that every drawer had been disturbed. It was not the servants, of that he was sure. It must be, then, that the sick visitor who had made a pretext to go down to the house, had coolly ransacked through his belongings. Nothing was missing, he assured himself of that. His money was untouched. What, then, had they been looking for? His face grew grave as he considered the implications.

He went into the Antika Room and looked into the drawer which held the seals and seal impressions. He gave a grim smile—nothing had been touched or removed. He went into the living room. Dr. Pauncefoot Jones was out in the courtyard with the foremen. Only Victoria was there, curled up with a book.

Richard said, without preamble "Somebody's been searching my room."

Victoria looked up, astonished.

"But why? And who?"

"It wasn't you?"

"Me?" Victoria was indignant. "Of course not. Why should I want to pry among your things?"

He gave her a hard stare. Then he said,

"It must have been that damned stranger—the one who shammed sick and came down to the house."

"Did he steal something?"

"No," said Richard. "Nothing was taken."

"But why on earth should someone—"

Richard cut in to say,

"I thought you might know that."

"Me?"

"Well, by your own account, rather odd things have happened to you."

"Oh that—yes." Victoria looked rather startled. She said slowly, "But I don't see why they should search your room. You've nothing to do with—"

"With what?"

Victoria did not answer for a moment or two. She seemed lost in thought.

"I'm sorry," she said at last. "What did you say? I wasn't listening."

Richard did not repeat his question. Instead he asked:

"What are you reading?"

Victoria made a slight grimace.

"You don't have much choice of light fiction here. 'Tale of Two Cities,' 'Pride and Prejudice' and 'The Mill on the Floss.' I'm reading the 'Tale of Two Cities.' "

"Never read it before?"

"Never. I always thought Dickens would be stuffy."

"What an idea!"

"I'm finding it most exciting."

"Where have you got to?" He looked over her shoulder and read out " 'And the knitting women count One.' "

"I think she's awfully frightening," said Victoria.

"Madame Defarge? Yes, a good character. Though whether you could keep a register of names in knitting has always seemed to me rather doubtful. But then, of course, I'm not a knitter."

"Oh I think you could," said Victoria, considering the point. "Plain and purl—and fancy stitches—and the wrong stitch at intervals and dropped stitches. Yes—it could be done . . . Camouflaged, of course, so that it just looked like someone who was rather bad at knitting and made mistakes . . ."

Suddenly, with a vividness like a flash of lightning, two things came together in her mind and affected her with the force of an explosion. A name—and a visual memory. The man with the ragged handknitted red scarf clasped in his hands—the scarf she had hurriedly picked up later and flung into a drawer. And together with that a name. *Defarge*—not Lefarge—*Defarge*, Madame Defarge.

She was recalled to herself by Richard saying to her courteously, "Is anything the matter?"

"No—no, that is, I just thought of something."

"I see." Richard raised his eyebrows in his most supercilious way.

Tomorrow, thought Victoria, they would all go in to Baghdad. Tomorrow her respite would be over. For over a week she had had safety, peace, time to pull herself together. And she had enjoyed that time—enjoyed it enormously. Perhaps I'm a coward, thought Victoria, perhaps that's it. She had talked gaily about adventure, but she hadn't liked it very much when it really came. She had hated that struggle against chloroform and the slow suffocation, and she had been frightened, horribly frightened, in that upper room when the ragged Arab had said "Bukra."

And now she'd got to go back to it all. Because she was employed by Mr. Dakin and paid by Mr. Dakin and she had to earn her pay and show a brave front! She might even have to go back to the Olive Branch. She shivered a little when she remembered Dr. Rathbone and that searching dark glance of his. He'd warned her . . .

But perhaps she wouldn't have to go back. Perhaps Mr. Dakin would say it was better not—now that they knew about her. But she would have to go back to her lodgings and get her things because thrust carelessly into her suitcase was the red knitted scarf . . . She had bundled everything into suitcases when she left for Basrah. Once she had put that scarf into Mr. Dakin's hands, perhaps her task would be done. He would say to her, perhaps, like on the pictures "Oh! Good show, Victoria."

She looked up to find Richard Baker watching her.

"By the way," he said, "will you be able to get hold of your passport tomorrow?"

"My passport?"

Victoria considered the position. It was characteristic of her that she had not as yet defined her plan of action as regarded the Expedition. Since the real Veronica (or Venetia) would shortly be arriving from England, a retreat in good order was necessary. But whether she would merely fade away, or confess her deception with suitable penitence, or indeed what she intended to do, had not yet presented itself as a problem to be solved. Victoria was always prone to adopt the Micawber-like attitude that Something would Turn Up.

"Well," she said temporising, "I'm not sure."

"It's needed, you see, for the police of this district," explained Richard. "They enter its number and your name and age and special distinguishing marks, etc., all the whole caboodle. As we haven't got the passport, I think we ought at any rate to send your name and description to them. By the way, what is your last name? I've always called you 'Victoria'."

Victoria rallied gallantly.

"Come now," she said. "You know my last name as well as I do."

"That's not quite true," said Richard. His smile curved upwards with a hint of cruelty. "I do know your last name. It's you, I think, who don't know it."

Through the glasses the eyes watched her.

"Of course I know my own name," snapped Victoria.

"Then I'll challenge you to tell it to me—now."

His voice was suddenly hard and curt.

"It's no good lying," he said. "The game's up. You've been very clever about it all. You've read up your subject, you've brought out very telling bits of knowledge—but it's the kind of imposture you can't keep up all the time. I've laid traps for you and you've fallen into them. I've quoted bits of sheer rubbish to you and you've accepted them." He paused. "You're not Venetia Savile. Who are you?"

"I told you who I was the first time I met you," said Victoria. "I'm Victoria Jones."

"Dr. Pauncefoot Jones' niece?"

"I'm not his niece—but my name is Jones."

"You told me a lot of other things."

"Yes, I did. And they were all true! But I could see you didn't believe me. And that made me mad, because though I do tell lies sometimes—in fact quite often—what I'd just told you wasn't a lie. And so, just to make myself more convincing, I said my name was Pauncefoot Jones—I've said that before out here, and it's always gone down frightfully well. How could I tell you were actually coming to this place?"

"It must have been a slight shock to you," said Richard grimly. "You carried it off very well—cool as a cucumber."

"Not inside," said Victoria. "I was absolutely shaking. But I felt that if I waited to explain until I got here—well at any rate I should be safe."

"Safe?" he considered the word. "Look here, Victoria, was that incredible rigmarole you told you about being chloroformed really true?"

"Of course it was true! Don't you see, if I wanted to make up a story I could make up a much better one than that, and tell it better!"

"Knowing you a little more closely now, I can see the force of that! But you must admit that, on first hearing, the story was wildly improbable."

"But you are willing to think it's possible now. Why?"

Richard said slowly.

"Because if, as you say, you were mixed up in Carmichael's death—well, then it might be true."

"That's what it all began with," said Victoria.

"You'd better tell me about it."

Victoria stared at him very hard.

"I'm wondering," she said, "if I can trust you."

"The boot is on the other leg! Do you realise that I've had grave suspicions that you'd planted yourself here under a false name in order to get information out of me? And perhaps that is what you are doing."

"Meaning that you know something about Carmichael that They would like to know?"

"Who exactly are They?"

"I shall have to tell you all about it," said Victoria. "There isn't any other way—and if you are one of Them you know it already, so it doesn't matter."

She told him of the night of Carmichael's death, of her interview with Mr. Dakin, of her journey to Basrah, her employment in the Olive Branch, of Catherine's hostility, of Dr. Rathbone and his warning and of the final denouement, including this time the enigma of the dyed hair. The only things she left out were the red scarf and Madame Defarge.

"Dr. Rathbone?" Richard seized on that point. "You think he's mixed up in this? Behind it? But my dear girl, he's a very important man. He's known all over the world. Subscriptions pour in from all over the globe for his schemes."

"Wouldn't he have to be all those things?" asked Victoria.

"I've always regarded him as a pompous ass," said Richard meditatively.

"And that's a very good camouflage, too."

"Yes—yes, I suppose it is. Who was Lefarge that you asked me about?"

"Just another name," said Victoria. "There's Anna Scheele, too," she said.

"Anna Scheele? No, I've never heard of her."

"She's important," said Victoria. "But I don't know exactly how or why. It's all so mixed up."

"Just tell me again," said Richard. "Who's the man who started you on to all this?"

"Edwar—Oh, you mean Mr. Dakin. He's in Oil, I think."

"Is he a tired, stooping, rather vacant-looking chap?"

"Yes—but he's not really. Vacant, I mean."

"Doesn't he drink?"

"People say so, but I don't think he does."

Richard sat back and looked at her.

"Phillips Oppenheim, William Le Queux and several distinguished imitators since? Is this real? Are you real? And are you the persecuted heroine, or the wicked adventuress?"

Victoria said in a practical manner,

"The real point is, what are you going to say to Dr. Pauncefoot Jones about me?"

"Nothing," said Richard. "It really won't be necessary."

Chapter 21

They started in to Baghdad early. Victoria's spirits felt curiously low. She had almost a lump in her throat as she looked back on the Expedition House. However, the acute discomfort entailed in the mad bumping of the lorry effectively distracted her mind from anything but the torture of the moment. It seemed strange to be driving along a so-called road again, passing donkeys and meeting dusty lorries. It took nearly three hours to reach the outskirts of Baghdad. The lorry decanted them at the Tio Hotel and then went off with the cook and the driver to do all necessary shopping. A large bundle of mail was awaiting Dr. Pauncefoot Jones and Richard. Marcus appeared suddenly, massive and beaming, and welcomed Victoria with his usual friendly radiance.

"Ah," he said, "it is a long time since I have seen you. You do not come to my Hotel. Not for a week—two weeks. Why is that? You lunch here today, you have everything you want? The baby chickens? The big steak? Only not the turkey stuffed very special with flavouring and rice, because for that you must let me know the day before."

It seemed clear that as far as the Tio Hotel was concerned, the kidnapping of Victoria had not been noticed. Possibly Edward, on the advice of Mr. Dakin, had not been to the police.

"Is Mr. Dakin in Baghdad, do you know, Marcus?" she asked.

"Mr. Dakin—ah yes, very nice man—of course, he is friend of yours. He was here yesterday—no, day before. And Captain Crosbie, you know him? A friend of Mr. Dakin's. He arrives today from Kermanshah."

"You know where Mr. Dakin's office is?"

"Sure I know. Everybody knows the Iraqi Iranian Oil Co."

"Well, I want to go there now. In a taxi. But I want to be sure the taxi knows where to take me."

"I tell him myself," said Marcus obligingly.

He escorted her to the head of the alleyway and yelled in his usual violent fashion. A startled minion arrived at a run. Marcus commanded him to procure a taxi. Then Victoria was escorted to the taxi and Marcus addressed the driver. Then he stepped back and waved a hand.

"And I want a room," said Victoria. "Can I have one?"

"Yes, yes. I give you a beautiful room and I order you the big steak and tonight I have—very special—some caviare. And before that we have a little drink."

"Lovely," said Victoria. "Oh Marcus, can you lend me some money?"

"Of course, my dear. Here you are. Take all you want."

The taxi started off with a violent honk and Victoria fell back onto the seat clutching an assortment of coins and notes.

Five minutes later Victoria entered the offices of the Iraqi Iranian Oil Co. and asked for Mr. Dakin.

Mr. Dakin looked up from the desk where he was writing when Victoria was shown in. He rose and shook hands with her in a formal manner.

"Miss—er—Miss Jones, isn't it? Bring coffee, Abdullah."

As the sound-proof door closed behind the clerk, he said quietly,

"You shouldn't really come here, you know."

"I had to this time," said Victoria. "There's something I've got to tell you at once—before anything more happens to me."

"Happens to you? Has anything happened to you?"

"Don't you know?" asked Victoria. "Hasn't Edward told you?"

"As far as I know, you are still working at the Olive Branch. Nobody has told me anything."

"Catherine," exclaimed Victoria.

"I beg your pardon."

"That cat Catherine! I bet she's stuffed Edward up with some tale or other and the goop has believed her."

"Well, let's hear about it," said Mr. Dakin. "Er—if I may say so," his eye went discreetly to Victoria's blonde head, "I prefer you as a brunette."

"That's only part of it," said Victoria.

There was a tap at the door and the messenger entered with two little cups of sweet coffee. When he had gone, Dakin said,

"Now take your time and tell me all about it. We can't be overheard here."

Victoria plunged into the story of her adventures. As always when she was talking to Dakin, she managed to be both coherent and concise. She finished her story with an account of the red scarf Carmichael had dropped and her association of it with Madame Defarge.

Then she looked anxiously at Dakin.

He had seemed to her when she came in, to be even more bowed and tired looking. Now she saw a new glint come into his eye.

"I should read my Dickens more often," he said.

"Then you do think I'm right? You think it was Defarge he said—and you think some message is knitted into the scarf?"

"I think," said Dakin, "that this is the first real break we've had—and we've got you to thank for it. But the important thing is the scarf. Where is it?"

"With all the rest of my things. I shoved it into a drawer that night—and when I packed I remember bundling everything in without sorting or anything."

"And you've never happened to mention to anyone—to anyone *at all*—that that scarf belonged to Carmichael?"

"No, because I'd forgotten all about it. I bundled it into a suitcase with some other things when I went to Basrah and I've never even opened the case since."

"Then it ought to be all right. Even if they've been through your things, they won't have attached any importance to an old dirty woollen scarf—unless they were tipped off to it which as far as I can see, is impossible. All we've got to do now is to have all your things collected and sent to you at—have you got anywhere to stay, by the way?"

"I've booked a room at the Tio."

Dakin nodded.

"Best place for you."

"Have I—do you want me—to go back to the Olive Branch?"

Dakin looked at her keenly.

"Scared?"

Victoria stuck her chin out.

"No," she said with defiance. "I'll go if you like."

"I don't think it's necessary—or even wise. However they learned it, I presume that someone there got wise to your activities. That being so, you wouldn't be able to find out anything more, so you'd better stay clear."

He smiled.

"Otherwise you may be a red head next time I see you."

"That's what I want to know most of all," cried Victoria. "Why did they dye my hair? I've thought and I've thought and I can't see any point in it. Can you?"

"Only the somewhat unpleasant one that your dead body might be less easy to identify."

"But if they wanted me to be a dead body, why didn't they kill me straight away?"

"That's a very interesting question, Victoria. It's the question I want answered most of all."

"And you haven't any idea?"

"I haven't got a clue," said Mr. Dakin with a faint smile.

"Talking of clues," said Victoria, "do you remember my saying that there was something about Sir Rupert Crofton Lee that didn't seem right, that morning at the Tio?"

"Yes."

"You didn't know him personally, did you?"

"I hadn't met him before, no."

"I thought not. Because, you see, he wasn't Sir Rupert Crofton Lee."

And she plunged once more into animated narrative, starting with the incipient boil on the back of Sir Rupert's neck.

"So that was how it was done," said Dakin. "I didn't see how Carmichael could have been sufficiently off his guard to be killed that night. He got safely to Crofton Lee—and Crofton Lee stabbed him, but he managed to get away and burst into your room before he collapsed. And he hung on to the scarf—literally like grim death."

"Do you think it was because I was coming to tell you this that they kidnapped me? But nobody knew except Edward."

"I think they felt they had to get you out of the picture quickly. You were tumbling to too much that was going on at the Olive Branch."

"Dr. Rathbone warned me," said Victoria. "It was—more of a threat than a warning. I think he realised that I wasn't what I pretended to be."

"Rathbone," said Dakin drily, "is no fool."

"I'm glad I haven't got to go back there," said Victoria. "I pretended to be brave just now—but really I'm scared stiff. Only if I don't go to the Olive Branch, how can I get hold of Edward?"

Dakin smiled.

"If Mohammed won't come to the mountain, the mountain must come to Mohammed. Write him a note now. Just say you're at the Tio and ask him to get your clothes and luggage and bring them along there. I'm going to consult Dr. Rathbone this morning about one of his Club Soirées. It will be easy for me to slip a note to his secretary—so there will be no danger of your enemy Catherine causing it to go astray. As for you, go back to the Tio and stay there—and, Victoria—"

"Yes?"

"If you're in a jam—of any kind—do the best you can for yourself. As far as possible you'll be watched over, but your adversaries are rather formidable, and unfortunately you know rather a lot. Once your luggage is in the Tio Hotel, your obligations to me are over. Understand that."

"I'll go straight back to the Tio now," said Victoria. "At least I shall just buy some face powder and lipstick and vanishing cream on the way. After all—"

"After all," said Mr. Dakin, "one cannot meet one's young man completely unarmoured."

"It didn't matter so much with Richard Baker, though I'd like him to know I can look quite nice if I try," said Victoria. "But Edward—"

Chapter 22

Her blonde hair carefully arranged, her nose powdered and her lips freshly painted, Victoria sat upon the balcony of the Tio, once more in the rôle of a modern Juliet, waiting for Romeo.

And in due course Romeo came. He appeared on the grass sward, looking this way and that.

"Edward," said Victoria.

Edward looked up.

"Oh, there you are. Victoria—"

"Come up here."

"Right."

A moment later he came out upon the balcony which was deserted.

"It's more peaceful up here," said Victoria. "We'll go down and let Marcus give us drinks presently."

Edward was staring at her in perplexity.

"I say, Victoria, haven't you done something to your hair?"

Victoria gave an exasperated sigh.

"If anybody mentions hair to me, I really think I shall bat them over the head."

"I think I liked it better as it was," said Edward.

"Tell Catherine so!"

"Catherine? What has she got to do with it?"

"Everything," said Victoria. "You told me to chum up to her, and I did, and I don't suppose you've any idea what it let me in for!"

"Where've you been all this time, Victoria? I've been getting quite worried."

"Oh you have, have you? Where did you think I'd been?"

"Well, Catherine gave me your message. Said you'd told her to tell me that you'd had to go off to Mosul suddenly. It was something very important and good news, and I'd hear from you in due course."

"And you believed that?" asked Victoria in an almost pitying voice.

"I thought you'd got on the track of something. Naturally, you couldn't say much to Catherine—"

"It didn't occur to you that Catherine was lying, and that I'd been knocked on the head."

"What?" Edward stared.

"Drugged, chloroformed—starved . . ."

Edward cast a sharp glance round.

"Good Lord! I never dreamed—look here, I don't like talking out here. All these windows. Can't we go to your room?"

"All right. Did you bring my luggage?"

"Yes, I dumped it all with the porter."

"Because when one hasn't had a change of clothes for a fortnight—"

"Victoria, what has been happening? I know—I've got the car here. Let's go out to Devonshire. You've never been there, have you?"

"Devonshire?" Victoria stared in surprise.

"Oh, it's just a name for a place not far out of Baghdad. It's rather lovely this time of year. Come on. I haven't had you to myself for years."

"Not since Babylon. But what will Dr. Rathbone and the Olive Branch say?"

"Blast Dr. Rathbone. I'm fed up with the old ass anyway."

They ran down the stairs and out to where Edward's car was parked. Edward drove southwards through Baghdad, along a wide avenue. Then he turned off from there; they jolted and twisted through palm groves and over irrigation bridges. Finally, with a strange unexpectedness they came to a small wooded copse surrounded and pierced by irrigation streams. The trees of the copse, mostly almond and apricot, were just coming into blossom. It was an idyllic spot. Beyond the copse, at a little distance, was the Tigris.

They got out of the car and walked together through the blossoming trees.

"This is lovely," said Victoria, sighing deeply. "It's like being back in England in Spring."

The air was soft and warm. Presently they sat down on a fallen tree trunk with pink blossom hanging down over their heads.

"Now, darling," said Edward. "Tell me what's been happening to you. I've been so dreadfully miserable."

"Have you?" she smiled dreamily.

Then she told him. Of the girl hairdresser. Of the smell of chloroform and her struggle. Of waking up drugged and sick. Of how she had escaped and of her fortuitous meeting with Richard Baker, and of how she had claimed to be Victoria Pauncefoot Jones on her way to the Excavations, and of how she had almost miraculously sustained the part of an archaeological student arriving from England.

At this point Edward shouted with laughter.

"You are marvellous, Victoria! The things you think of—and invent."

"I know," said Victoria. "My uncles. Dr. Pauncefoot Jones and before him—the Bishop."

And at that she suddenly remembered what it was she had been going to ask Edward at Basrah when Mrs. Clayton had interrupted by calling them in for drinks.

"I meant to ask you before," she said. "How did you know about the Bishop?"

She felt the hand that held hers stiffen suddenly. He said quickly, too quickly:

"Why, you told me, didn't you?"

Victoria looked at him. It was odd, she thought afterwards, that that one silly childish slip should have accomplished what it did.

For he was taken completely by surprise. He had no story ready—his face was suddenly defenceless and unmasked.

And as she looked at him, everything shifted and settled itself into a pattern, exactly as a kaleidoscope does, and she saw the truth. Perhaps it was not really sudden. Perhaps in her subconscious mind that question: How did Edward know about the Bishop? had been teasing and worrying, and she had been slowly arriving at the one, the inevitable, answer . . . Edward had not learned about the Bishop of Llangow from her, and the only other persons he could have learned it from, would have been Mr. or Mrs. Hamilton Clipp. But they could not possibly have seen Edward since her arrival in Baghdad, for Edward had been in Basrah then, so he must have learned it from them before he himself left England. He must have known all along, then, that Victoria was coming out with them—and the whole wonderful coincidence was not, after all, a coincidence. It was planned and intended . . .

And as she stared at Edward's unmasked face, she knew, suddenly, what Carmichael had meant by Lucifer. She knew what he had seen that day as he looked along the passage to the Consulate Garden. He had seen that young beautiful face that she was looking at now—for it was a beautiful face—

Lucifer, Son of the Morning, how art thou fallen?

Not Dr. Rathbone—Edward! Edward, playing a minor part, the part of the secretary, but controlling and planning and directing, using Rathbone as a figurehead—and Rathbone, warning her to go while she could . . .

As she looked at that beautiful evil face, all her silly adolescent calf love faded away, and she knew that what she felt for Edward had never been love. It had been the same feeling that she had experienced some years earlier for Humphrey Bogart, and later for the Duke of Edinburgh. It had been glamour. And Edward had never loved her. He had exerted his charm and his glamour deliberately. He had picked her up that day, using his charm so easily, so naturally, that she had fallen for it without a struggle. She'd been a sucker.

It was extraordinary how much could flash through your mind in just a few seconds. You didn't have to think it out. It just came. Full and instant knowledge. Perhaps because really, underneath, you'd known it all along. . . .

And at the same time some instinct of self preservation, quick as all Victoria's mental processes were quick, kept her face in an expression of foolish unthinking wonder. For she knew, instinctively, that she was in great danger. There was only one thing that could save her, only one card she could play. She made haste to play it.

"You knew all along!" she said. "You knew I was coming out here. You must have arranged it. Oh Edward, you are wonderful!"

Her face, that plastic impressionable face, showed one emotion only—an almost cloying adoration. And she saw the response—the faintly scornful smile, the relief. She could almost feel Edward saying to himself, "The little fool! She'll swallow anything! I can do what I like with her."

"But how did you arrange it?" she said. "You must be very powerful. You must be quite different from what you pretend to be. You're—it's like what you said the other day—you're a King in Babylon."

She saw the pride that lit up his face. She saw the power and strength and beauty and cruelty that had been disguised behind the façade of a modest likeable young man.

"And I'm only a Christian slave," thought Victoria. She said quickly and anxiously, as a final artistic touch (and what its cost was to her pride no one will ever know), "But you do love me, don't you?"

His scorn was hardly to be hidden now. This little fool—all these fools of women! So easy to make them think you loved them and that was all they cared about! They'd no conception of greatness of construction, of a new world, they just whined for love! They were slaves and you used them as slaves to further your ends.

"Of course I love you," he said.

"But what is it all about? Tell me, Edward. Make me understand."

"It's a new world, Victoria. A new world that will rise out of the muck and ashes of the old."

"Tell me."

He told her, and in spite of herself she was almost carried away, carried into the dream. The old bad things must destroy each other. There must be total war—total destruction. And then—the new Heaven and the new Earth. The small chosen band of higher beings, the scientists, the agricultural experts, the administrators—the young men like Edward— the young Siegfrieds of the New World. All young, all believing in their destiny as Supermen. When destruction had run its course, they would step in and take over.

It was madness—but it was constructive madness. It was the sort of thing that in a world, shattered and disintegrating, could happen.

"But think," said Victoria, "of all the people who will be killed first."

"You don't understand," said Edward. "That doesn't matter."

It doesn't matter—that was Edward's creed. And suddenly, for no reason, a remembrance of that three thousand years' old coarse pottery bowl mended with bitumen flashed across Victoria's mind. Surely those were the things that mattered—the little everyday things, the family to be cooked for, the four walls that enclosed the home, the one or two cherished possessions. All the thousands of ordinary people on the earth, minding their own business, and tilling that earth, and making pots and bringing up families and laughing and crying, and getting up in the morning and going to bed at night. They were the people who mattered, not these Angels with wicked faces who wanted to make a new world and who didn't care who they hurt to do it.

And carefully, feeling her way, for here in Devonshire she knew that death might be very near, she said:

"You are wonderful, Edward. But what about me? What can I do?"

"You want to—help? You believe in it?"

But she was prudent. Not sudden conversion. That would be too much.

"I think I just believe in you!" she said. "Anything you tell me to do, Edward, I'll do."

"Good girl," he said.

"Why did you arrange for me to come out here to begin with? There must have been some reason?"

"Of course there was. Do you remember I took a snap of you that day?"

"I remember," said Victoria.

(You fool, how flattered you were, how you simpered! she thought to herself.)

"I'd been struck by your profile—by your resemblance to someone. I took that snap to make sure."

"Who do I resemble?"

"A woman who's been causing us a good deal of trouble—Anna Scheele."

"Anna Scheele," Victoria stared at him in blank surprise. Whatever she had expected, it was not this. "You mean—she looks like me?"

"Quite remarkably so, side-view. The features in profile, are almost exactly the same. And there's one most extraordinary thing, you've got a tiny mark of a scar on your upper lip, left side—"

"I know. It's where I fell on a tin horse when I was a child. It had a sharp ear sticking up and it cut quite deep in. It doesn't show much—not with powder on."

"Anna Scheele has a mark in just the same place. That was a most valuable point. You're alike in height and build—she's about four or five years older than you. The real difference is the hair, you're a brunette and she's a blonde. And your style of hairdressing is quite different. Your eyes are a darker blue, but that wouldn't matter with tinted glasses."

"And that's why you wanted me to come to Baghdad? Because I looked like her."

"Yes, I thought the resemblance might—come in useful."

"So you arranged the whole thing . . . The Clipps—who are the Clipps?"

"They're not important—they just do as they're told."

Something in Edward's tone sent a faint shiver down Victoria's spine. It was as though he had said with inhuman detachment, "They are under Obedience."

There was a religious flavour about this mad project. "Edward," she thought, "is his own God. That's what's so frightening."

Aloud she said:

"You told me that Anna Scheele was the boss, the Queen Bee, in your show?"

"I had to tell you something to put you off the scent. You had already learnt too much."

"And if I hadn't happened to look like Anna Scheele that would have been the end of me," thought Victoria.

She said:

"Who is she really?"

"She's confidential secretary to Otto Morganthal, the American and international banker. But that isn't all she is. She has the most remarkable financial brain. We've reason to believe she's traced out a lot of our financial operations. Three people have been dangerous to us—Rupert

Crofton Lee, Carmichael—well, they're both wiped out. There remains Anna Scheele. She's due in Baghdad in three days' time. In the meantime, she's disappeared."

"Disappeared? Where?"

"In London. Vanished, apparently, off the face of the earth."

"And does no one know where she is?"

"Dakin may know."

But Dakin didn't know. Victoria knew that, though Edward didn't—so where was Anna Scheele?

She asked:

"You really haven't the least idea?"

"We've an idea," said Edward slowly.

"Well?"

"It's vital that Anna Scheel should be here in Baghdad for the Conference. That, as you know, is in five days' time."

"As soon as that? I'd no idea."

"We've got every entry into this country taped. She's certainly not coming here under her own name. And she's not coming in on a Government service plane. We've our means of checking that. So we've investigated all the private bookings. There's a passage booked by B.O.A.C. in the name of Grete Harden. We've traced Grete Harden back and there's no such person. It's an assumed name. The address given is a phony one. It's our idea that Grete Harden is Anna Scheele."

He added:

"Her plane will touch down at Damascus the day after tomorrow."

"And then?"

Edward's eyes looked suddenly into hers.

"That's up to you, Victoria."

"To me?"

"You'll take her place."

Victoria said slowly:

"Like Rupert Crofton Lee?"

It was almost a whisper. In the course of that substitution Rupert Crofton Lee had died. And when Victoria took her place, presumably Anna Scheele, or Grete Harden, would die . . . But even if she didn't agree, Anna Scheele would still die.

And Edward was waiting—and if for one moment Edward doubted her loyalty, then she, Victoria, would die—and die without the possibility of warning anyone.

No, she must agree and seize a chance to report to Mr. Dakin.

She drew a deep breath and said:

"I—I—oh, but Edward, I couldn't do it. I'd be found out. I can't do an American voice."

"Anna Scheele has practically no accent. In any case, you will be suffering from laryngitis. One of the best doctors in this part of the world will say so."

"They've got people everywhere," thought Victoria.

"What would I have to do?" she asked.

"Fly from Damascus to Baghdad as Grete Harden. Take to your bed immediately. Be allowed up by our reputable doctor just in time to go to the Conference. There you will lay before them the documents which you have brought with you."

Victoria asked: "The real documents?"

"Of course not. We shall substitute our version."

"What will the documents show?"

Edward smiled.

"Convincing details of the most stupendous plot in America."

Victoria thought: "How well they've got it planned."

Aloud she said:

"Do you really think I can get away with it, Edward?"

Now that she was playing a part, it was quite easy for Victoria to ask it with every appearance of anxious sincerity.

"I'm sure you can. I've noticed that your playing of a part affords you such enjoyment that it's practically impossible to disbelieve you."

Victoria said meditatively:

"I still feel an awful fool when I think of the Hamilton Clipps."

He laughed in a superior way.

Victoria, her face still a mask of adoration, thought to herself viciously, "But you were an awful fool, too, to let slip that about the Bishop at Basrah. If you hadn't I'd never have seen through you."

She said suddenly: "What about Dr. Rathbone."

"What do you mean 'What about him?' "

"Is he just a figurehead?"

Edward's lips curved in cruel amusement.

"Rathbone has got to toe the line. Do you know what he's been doing all these years? Cleverly appropriating about three quarters of the subscriptions which pour in from all over the world to his own use. It's the cleverest swindle since the time of Horatio Bottomley. Oh yes, Rathbone's completely in our hands—we can expose him at any time and he knows it."

Victoria felt a sudden gratitude to the old man with the noble domed head, and the mean acquisitive soul. He might be a swindler—but he had known pity—he had tried to get her to escape in time.

"All things work towards our new order," said Edward.

She thought to herself, "Edward, who looks so sane, is really mad! You get mad, perhaps, if you try and act the part of God. They always say humility is a Christian virtue—now I see why. Humility is what keeps you sane and a human being. . . ."

Edward got up.

"Time to be moving," he said. "We've got to get you to Damascus and our plans there worked out by the day after tomorrow."

Victoria rose with alacrity. Once she was away from Devonshire, back in Baghdad with its crowds, in the Tio Hotel with Marcus shouting and beaming and offering her a drink, the near persistent menace of Edward would be removed. Her part was to play a double game—continue to fool Edward by a sickly doglike devotion, and counter his plans secretly.

She said: "You think that Mr. Dakin knows where Anna Scheele is? Perhaps I could find that out. He might drop some hint."

"Unlikely—and in any case, you won't be seeing Dakin."

"He told me to come and see him this evening," said Victoria mendaciously, a slightly chilly feeling attacking her spine. "He'll think it odd if I don't turn up."

"It doesn't matter at this stage what he thinks," said Edward. "Our plans are made." He added, "You won't be seen in Baghdad again."

"But Edward, all my things are at the Tio! I've booked a room."

The scarf. The precious scarf.

"You won't need your things for some time to come. I've got a rig-out waiting for you. Come on."

They got in the car again. Victoria thought, "I ought to have known that Edward would never be such a fool as to let me get in touch with Mr. Dakin after I'd found him out. He believes I'm besotted about him—yes, I think he's sure of that—but all the same he isn't going to take any chances."

She said: "Won't there be a search for me if I—don't turn up?"

"We'll attend to that. Officially you'll say goodbye to me at the bridge and go off to see some friends on the West Bank."

"And actually?"

"Wait and see."

Victoria sat silent as they bumped over the rough track and twisted round palm gardens and over the little irrigation bridges.

"Lefarge," murmured Edward. "I wish we knew what Carmichael meant by that."

Victoria's heart gave a leap of anxiety.

"Oh," she said. "I forgot to tell you. I don't know if it means anything. A M. Lefarge came to the Excavations one day at Tell Aswad."

"What?" Edward almost stalled the car in his excitement. "When was this?"

"Oh! About a week ago. He said he came from some Dig in Syria. M. Parrot's, would it be?"

"Did two men called André and Juvet come while you were there?"

"Oh yes," said Victoria. "One of them had a sick stomach. He went to the house and lay down."

"They were two of our people," said Edward.

"Why did they come there? To look for me?"

"No—I'd no idea where you were. But Richard Baker was in Basrah at the same time as Carmichael. We had an idea Carmichael might have passed something on to Baker."

"He said his things had been searched. Did they find anything?"

"No—now think carefully, Victoria. Did this man Lefarge come before the other two or afterwards?"

Victoria reflected in a convincing manner, as she decided what movements to impute to the mythical M. Lefarge.

"It was—yes, the day before the other two came," she said.

"What did he do?"

"Well," said Victoria, "he went over the Dig—with Dr. Pauncefoot Jones. And then Richard Baker took him down to the house to see some of the things in the Antika Room there."

"He went to the house with Richard Baker. They talked together?"

"I suppose so," said Victoria. "I mean, you wouldn't look at things in absolute silence, would you?"

"Lefarge," murmured Edward. "Who is Lefarge? Why have we got no line on him?"

Victoria longed to say, "He's brother to Mrs. Harris," but refrained. She was pleased with her invention of M. Lefarge. She could see him quite clearly now in her mind's eye—a thin rather consumptive-looking young man with dark hair and a little moustache. Presently, when Edward asked her, she described him carefully and accurately.

They were driving now through the suburbs of Baghdad. Edward turned off down a side street of modern villas built in a pseudo European style, with balconies and gardens round them. In front of one house a big touring car was standing. Edward drew up behind it and he and Victoria got out, and went up the steps to the front door.

A thin dark woman came out to meet them and Edward spoke to her rapidly in French. Victoria's French was not sufficiently good to understand fully what was said, but it seemed to be to the effect that this was the young lady and that the change must be effected at once.

The woman turned to her and said politely in French:

"Come with me, please."

She led Victoria into a bedroom where, spread out on a bed, was the habit of a nun. The woman motioned to her, and Victoria undressed and put on the stiff wool undergarment and the voluminous mediaeval folds of dark stuff. The Frenchwoman adjusted the headdress. Victoria caught a glimpse of herself in the glass. Her small pale face under the gigantic (was it wimple?) with the white folds under her chin, looked strangely pure and unearthly. The Frenchwoman threw a Rosary of wooden beads over her head. Then, shuffling in the over-large coarse shoes, Victoria was led out to rejoin Edward.

"You look all right," he said approvingly. "Keep your eyes down, particularly when there are men about."

The Frenchwoman rejoined them a moment or two later similarly apparelled. The two nuns went out of the house and got into the touring car which now had a tall dark man in European dress in the driver's seat.

"It's up to you now, Victoria," said Edward. "Do exactly as you are told."

There was a slight steely menace behind the words.

"Aren't you coming, Edward?" Victoria sounded plaintive.

He smiled at her.

"You'll see me in three days' time," he said. And then, with a resumption of his persuasive manner, he murmured, "Don't fail me, darling. Only you could do this—I love you, Victoria. I daren't be seen kissing a nun—but I'd like to."

Victoria dropped her eyes in approved nunlike fashion, but actually to conceal the fury that showed for a moment.

"Horrible Judas," she thought.

Instead she said with an assumption of her usual manner:

"Well, I seem to be a Christian Slave all right."

"That's the girl!" said Edward. He added, "Don't worry. Your papers are in perfect order—you'll have no difficulty at the Syrian frontier. Your name in religion, by the way, is Sister Marie des Anges. Sister Thérèse who accompanies you has all the documents and is in full charge, and for God's sake obey orders—or I warn you frankly, you're for it."

He stepped back, waved his hand cheerfully, and the touring car started off.

Victoria leaned back against the upholstery and gave herself up to contemplation of possible alternatives. She could, as they were passing through Baghdad, or when they got to the frontier control, make an agitation, scream for help, explain that she was being carried off against her will—in fact, adopt one or other variants of immediate protest.

What would that accomplish? In all probability it would mean the end of Victoria Jones. She had noticed that Sister Thérèse had slipped into her sleeve a small and businesslike automatic pistol. She would be given no chance of talking.

Or she could wait until she got to Damascus? Make her protest there? Possibly, the same fate would be meted out, or her statements might be overborne by the evidence of the driver and her fellow nun. They might be able to produce papers saying that she was mentally afflicted.

The best alternative was to go through with things—to acquiesce in the plan. To come to Baghdad as Anna Scheele and to play Anna Scheele's part. For, after all, if she did so, there would come a moment, at the final climax, when Edward could no longer control her tongue or her actions. If she could continue to convince Edward that she would do anything he told her, then the moment would come when she was standing with her forged documents before the Conference—and Edward would not be there.

And no one could stop her then from saying, "I am not Anna Scheele and these papers are forged and untrue."

She wondered that Edward did not fear her doing just that. But she reflected that vanity was a strangely blinding quality. Vanity was the Achilles heel. And there was also the fact to be considered that Edward and his crowd had more or less got to have an Anna Scheele if their scheme was to succeed. To find a girl who sufficiently resembled Anna Scheele—even to the point of having a scar in the right place was extremely difficult. In the Lyons Mail, Victoria remembered, Dubosc and Lesurque had the extraordinary coincidence of both having a scar above one eyebrow and also of having a distortion, one by birth and one by accident, of the little finger of one hand. These coincidences must be very rare. No, the Supermen needed Victoria Jones, typist—and to that extent Victoria Jones had them in her power—not the other way round.

The car sped across the bridge. Victoria watched the Tigris with a nostalgic longing. Then they were speeding along a wide dusty highway. Victoria let the beads of her Rosary pass through her fingers. Their click was comforting.

"After all," thought Victoria with sudden comfort. "I am a Christian. And if you're a Christian, I suppose it's a hundred times better to be a Christian Martyr than a King in Babylon—and I must say, there seems to me a great possibility that I am going to be a Martyr. Oh! well, anyway, it won't be lions. I should have hated lions!"

Chapter 23

The Big Skymaster swooped down from the air and made a perfect landing. It taxied gently along the runway and presently came to a stop at the appointed place. The passengers were invited to descend. Those going on to Basrah were separated from those who were catching a connecting plane to Baghdad.

Of the latter there were four. A prosperous looking Iraqi business man, a young English doctor and two women. They all passed through the various controls and questioning.

A dark woman with untidy hair imperfectly bound in a scarf and a tired face came first.

"Mrs. Pauncefoot Jones? British. Yes. To join your husband. Your address in Baghdad, please? What money have you? . . ."

It went on. Then the second woman took the first one's place.

"Grete Harden. Yes. Nationality? Danish. From London. Purpose of visit? Masseuse at hospital? Address in Baghdad? What money have you?"

Grete Harden was a thin fair haired young woman wearing dark glasses. She wore neat but slightly shabby clothes.

Her French was halting—occasionally she had to have the question repeated.

Then the four passengers were told that the Baghdad plane took off that afternoon. They would be driven now to the Abbassid Hotel for a rest and lunch.

Grete Harden was sitting on her bed when a tap came on the door. She opened it and found a tall dark young woman wearing B.O.A.C. uniform.

"I'm so sorry, Miss Harden. Would you come with me to the B.O.A.C. office? A little difficulty has arisen about your ticket. This way, please."

Grete Harden followed her guide down the passage. On a door was a large board lettered in gold B.O.A.C. Office.

The Air Hostess opened the door and motioned the other inside. Then, as Grete Harden passed through, she closed the door from outside and quickly unhooked the board.

As Grete Harden came through the door, two men who had been standing behind it passed a cloth over her head. They stuffed a gag into her mouth. One of them rolled her sleeve up, and bringing out a hypodermic syringe gave her an injection.

In a few minutes her body sagged and went limp.

The young doctor said cheerfully, "That ought to take care of her for about six hours, anyway. Now then, you two, get on with it."

He nodded towards two other occupants of the room. They were nuns who were sitting immobile by the window. The men went out of the room. The elder of the two nuns went to Grete Harden and began to take the clothes off her inert body. The younger nun, trembling a little, started taking off her habit. Presently Grete Harden, dressed in a nun's habit, lay reposefully on the bed. The younger nun was now dressed in Grete Harden's clothes.

The older nun turned her attention to her companion's flaxen hair. Looking at a photograph which she propped up against the mirror, she combed and dressed the hair, bringing it back from the forehead and coiling it low on the neck.

She stepped back and said in French:

"Astonishing how it changes you. Put on the dark spectacles. Your eyes are too deep a blue. Yes—that is admirable."

There was a slight tap on the door and the two men came in again. They were grinning.

"Grete Harden is Anna Scheele all right," one said. "She'd got the papers in her luggage, carefully camouflaged between the leaves of a Danish publication on Hospital Massage. Now then, Miss Harden," he bowed with mock ceremony to Victoria, "you will do me the honour to have lunch with me."

Victoria followed him out of the room and along to the hall. The other woman passenger was trying to send off a telegram at the desk.

"No," she was saying, "P.A.U.N.C.E. foot. Dr. Pauncefoot Jones. Arriving today Tio Hotel. Good journey—"

Victoria looked at her with sudden interest. This must be Dr. Pauncefoot Jones' wife, coming out to join him. That she was a week earlier than expected did not seem to Victoria at all extraordinary since Dr. Pauncefoot

Jones had several times lamented that he had lost her letter giving the date of arrival but that he was almost certain it was the 26th!

If only she could somehow or other send a message through Mrs. Pauncefoot Jones to Richard Baker. . . .

Almost as though he read her thoughts, the man accompanying her steered her by the elbow away from the desk.

"No conversations with fellow travellers, Miss Harden," he said. "We don't want that good woman to notice that you're a different person from the one she came out from England with."

He took her out of the Hotel to a restaurant for lunch. As they came back, Mrs. Pauncefoot Jones was coming down the steps of the Hotel. She nodded without suspicion at Victoria.

"Been sightseeing?" she called. "I'm just going to the Bazaars."

"If I could slip something into her luggage—" thought Victoria.

But she was not left alone for a moment.

The Baghdad plane left at three o'clock.

Mrs. Pauncefoot Jones' seat was right up in front. Victoria's was in the tail, near the door, and across the aisle sat the fair young man who was her gaoler. Victoria had no chance of reaching the other woman or of introducing a message into any of her belongings.

The flight was not a long one. For a second time, Victoria looked down from the air and saw the city outlined below her, the Tigris dividing it like a streak of gold.

So she had seen it less than a month ago. How much had happened since then.

In two days' time the men who represented the two predominant ideologies of the world would meet here to discuss the future—

And she, Victoria Jones, would have a part to play.

II

"You know," said Richard Baker, "I'm worried about that girl."

Dr. Pauncefoot Jones said vaguely,

"What girl?"

"Victoria."

"Victoria?" Dr. Pauncefoot Jones peered about. "Where is—why, God bless me, we came back without her yesterday."

"I wondered if you'd noticed it," said Richard.

"Very remiss of me. I was so interested by that report of the Excavations at Tell Yameni. Completely unsound stratification. Didn't she know where to find the lorry?"

"There was no question of her coming back here," said Richard. "As a matter of fact, she isn't Venetia Savile."

"Not Venetia Savile? How very odd. But I thought you said her Christian name was Victoria."

"It is. But she's not an anthropologist. And she doesn't know Emerson. As a matter of fact, the whole thing has been a—well—a misunderstanding."

"Dear me. That seems very odd." Dr. Pauncefoot Jones reflected for some moments. "Very odd. I do hope—am I to blame? I know I am somewhat absent-minded. The wrong letter, perhaps?"

"I can't understand it," said Richard Baker frowning and paying no attention to Dr. Pauncefoot Jones' speculations. "She went off in a car with a young man, it seems, and she didn't come back. What's more, her baggage was there and she hadn't bothered to open it. That seems to me very strange—considering the mess she was in. I'd have thought she'd be sure to doll herself up. And we agreed to meet for lunch . . . No, I can't understand it. I hope nothing's happened to her."

"Oh, I shouldn't think so for a moment," said Dr. Pauncefoot Jones comfortably. "I shall start going down in H. tomorrow. From the general plan I should say that would be the best chance of getting a record office. That fragment of tablet was very promising."

"They've kidnapped her once," said Richard. "What's to prevent their having kidnapped her again?"

"Very improbable—very improbable," said Dr. Pauncefoot Jones. "The country's really very settled nowadays. You said so yourself."

"If I could only remember the name of that man in some oil company. Was it Deacon? Deacon, Dakin? Something like that."

"Never heard of him," said Dr. Pauncefoot Jones. "I think I shall change over Mustafa and his gang to the North East corner. Then we might extend Trench J—"

"Would you mind awfully, sir, if I went in to Baghdad again tomorrow?"

Dr. Pauncefoot Jones, suddenly giving his colleague his full attention, stared at him.

"Tomorrow? But we were there yesterday."

"I'm worried about that girl. I really am."

"Dear me, Richard, I had no idea there was anything of that kind."

"What kind?"

"That you'd formed an attachment. That's the worst of having women on a Dig—especially good looking ones. I really did think we were safe with Sybil Muirfield the year before last, a really distressingly plain girl— and see what came of it! I ought to have listened to Claude in London— these Frenchmen always hit the nail on the head. He commented on her legs at the time—was most enthusiastic about them. Of course this girl, Victoria Venetia, whatever her name is—most attractive and such a nice little thing. You've got good taste, Richard, I will admit that. Funny thing, she's the first girl I've ever known you take any interest in."

"There's nothing of that kind," said Richard, blushing and looking even more supercilious than usual. "I'm just—er—worried about her. I must go to Baghdad."

"Well, if you are going tomorrow," said Dr. Pauncefoot Jones, "you might bring back those extra picks. That fool of a driver forgot them."

Richard started into Baghdad at early dawn and went straight to the Tio Hotel. Here he learnt that Victoria had not returned.

"And it was all arranged that she was to have special dinner with me," said Marcus. "And I kept her a very nice room. It is odd, is it not?"

"Have you been to the Police?"

"Ah no, my dear, it would not be nice, that. She might not like it. And I certainly would not like it."

After a little inquiry, Richard tracked down Mr. Dakin and called upon him in his office.

His memory of the man had not played him false. He looked at the stooping figure, the indecisive face and the slight tremor of the hands. This man was no good! He apologised to Mr. Dakin if he was wasting his time, but had he seen Miss Victoria Jones.

"She called on me the day before yesterday."

"Can you give me her present address?"

"She's at the Tio Hotel, I believe."

"Her luggage is there, but she isn't."

Mr. Dakin raised his eyebrows slightly.

"She has been working with us on the Excavations at Tell Aswad," explained Richard.

"Oh I see. Well—I'm afraid I don't know anything that can help you. She has several friends in Baghdad, I believe—but I don't know her well enough to say who they are."

"Would she be at this Olive Branch?"

"I don't think so. You could ask."

Richard said: "Look here. I'm not leaving Baghdad until I find her."

He frowned angrily at Mr. Dakin and strode out of the room.

Mr. Dakin, as the door closed behind Richard, smiled and shook his head.

"Oh Victoria," he murmured reproachfully.

Fuming into the Tio Hotel, Richard was met by a beaming Marcus.

"She's come back," cried Richard eagerly.

"No, no, it is Mrs. Pauncefoot Jones. She has just arrived by plane. Dr. Pauncefoot Jones, he told me she was coming next week."

"He always gets dates wrong. What about Victoria Jones?"

Marcus's face went grave again.

"No, I have heard nothing of her. And I do not like it, Mr. Baker. It is not nice. She is so young a girl. And so pretty. And so gay and charming."

"Yes, yes," said Richard flinching. "I'd better go up and see Mrs. Pauncefoot Jones. What's her number?"

"She is in 19."

With a heavy tread, Richard went up the stairs.

III

"You!" said Victoria with undisguised hostility.

Ushered up to her room in the Babylonian Palace Hotel, the first person she saw was Catherine.

Catherine nodded her head with equal venom.

"Yes," she said. "It is I. And now please go to bed. The doctor will soon arrive."

Catherine was dressed as a hospital nurse and she took her duties seriously, being obviously quite determined never to leave Victoria's side. Victoria, lying disconsolately in bed, murmured:

"If I could get hold of Edward—"

"Edward—Edward!" said Catherine scornfully. "Edward has never cared for you, you stupid English girl. It is me whom Edward loves!"

Victoria looked at Catherine's stubborn fanatical face without enthusiasm.

Catherine went on:

"Always I have hated you from that first morning you came in and demanded to see Dr. Rathbone with such rudeness."

Searching about for an irritant, Victoria said:

"At any rate I'm much more indispensable than you are. Anybody could do your hospital nurse act. But the whole thing depends on me doing mine."

Catherine said with prim smugness:

"Nobody is indispensable. We are taught that."

"Well, I am. For goodness' sake order up a substantial meal. If I don't get something to eat, how do you expect me to give a good performance of an American banker's secretary when the time comes?"

"I suppose you might as well eat while you can," said Catherine grudgingly.

Victoria took no notice of the sinister implication.

IV

Captain Crosbie said:

"I understand you've got a Miss Harden just arrived."

The suave gentleman in the office of the Babylonian Palace inclined his head.

"Yes, sir. From England."

"She's a friend of my sister's. Will you take my card up to her."

He pencilled a few words on the card and sent it up in an envelope.

Presently the boy who had taken it returned.

"The lady is not well, sir. Very bad throat. Doctor coming soon. She has hospital nurse with her."

Crosbie turned away. He went along to the Tio where he was accosted by Marcus.

"Ah, my dear, let us have a drink. This evening my Hotel is quite full. It is for the Conference. But what a pity. Dr. Pauncefoot Jones went back to his Expedition the day before yesterday and now here is his wife who arrives and expects that he will be here to meet her. And she is not pleased, no! She says she told him she was coming on this plane. But you know what he is like, that one. Every date, every time—he always gets it wrong. But he is a very nice man," finished Marcus with his usual charity. "And I have had to squeeze her in somehow—I turn out a very important man from UNO—"

"Baghdad seems quite mad."

"All the police they have drafted in—they are taking great precautions—they say—have you heard?—there is a plot to assassinate the President! They have arrested sixty-five students! They are very suspicious of everybody. But all this is very good for trade—very good indeed."

V

The telephone bell rang and was promptly answered.

"American Embassy."

"This is the Babylonian Palace Hotel. Miss Anna Scheele is staying here."

Anna Scheele? Presently one of the Attachés was speaking. Could Miss Scheele come to the phone?

"Miss Scheele is ill in bed with laryngitis. This is Dr. Smallbrook. I am attending Miss Scheele. She has some important papers with her and would like some responsible person from the Embassy to come and fetch them. Immediately? Thank you. I will be waiting for you."

VI

Victoria turned from the mirror. She was wearing a well-cut tailored suit. Every blonde hair was in place. She felt nervous but exhilarated.

As she turned, she caught the exultant gleam in Catherine's eye and was suddenly on her guard. Why was Catherine exultant?

What was going on?

"What are you so pleased about?" she asked.

"Soon you will see."

The malice was quite unconcealed now.

"You think you are so clever," said Catherine scornfully. "You think everything depends on you. Pah, you are just a fool."

With a bound Victoria was upon her! She caught her by the shoulder and dug her fingers in.

"Tell me what you mean, you horrible girl."

"Ach—you hurt me."

"Tell me—"

A knock came on the door. A knock twice repeated and then, after a pause, a single one.

"Now you will see!" cried Catherine.

The door opened and a man slipped in. He was a tall man, dressed in the uniform of the International Police. He locked the door behind him and removed the key. Then he advanced to Catherine.

"Quickly," he said.

He took a length of thin cord from his pocket and, with Catherine's full cooperation, bound her swiftly to a chair. Then he produced a scarf and tied it over her mouth. He stood back and nodded appreciatively.

"So—that will do nicely."

Then he turned towards Victoria. She saw the heavy truncheon he was brandishing and in a moment it flashed across her brain what the real plan was. They had never intended that she should play the part of Anna Scheele at the Conference. How could they risk such a thing? Victoria was too well known in Baghdad. No, the plan was, had always been, that Anna Scheele should be attacked and killed at the last moment—killed in such a way that her features would not be too recognisable . . . Only the papers she had brought with her—those carefully forged papers—would remain.

Victoria turned away to the window—she screamed. And with a smile the man came at her—

Then several things happened—there was a crash of broken glass—a heavy hand sent her headlong down—she saw stars—and blackness . . . Then out of the blackness a voice spoke, a reassuring English voice.

"Are you all right, Miss?" it asked.

Victoria murmured something.

"What did she say?" asked a second voice.

The first man scratched his head.

"Said it was better to serve in Heaven than reign in Hell," he said doubtfully.

"That's a quotation," said the other. "But she's got it wrong," he added.

"No, I haven't," said Victoria and fainted.

VII

The telephone rang and Dakin picked up the receiver. A voice said:

"Operation Victoria successfully concluded."

"Good," said Dakin.

"We've got Catherine Serakis and the medico. The other fellow threw himself off the balcony. He's fatally injured."

"The girl's not hurt?"

"She fainted—but she's O.K."

"No news still of the real A.S.?"

"No news whatever."

Dakin laid down the receiver.

At any rate Victoria was all right—Anna herself, he thought, must be dead . . . She had insisted on playing a lone hand, had reiterated that she would be in Baghdad without fail on the 19th. Today was the 19th and there was no Anna Scheele. Perhaps she had been right not to trust the official setup—he didn't know. Certainly there had been leakages—betrayals. But apparently her own native wits had served her no better. . . .

And without Anna Scheele, the evidence was incomplete.

A messenger came in with a piece of paper on which was written Mr. Richard Baker and Mrs. Pauncefoot Jones.

"I can't see anybody now," said Dakin. "Tell them I am very sorry. I am engaged."

The messenger withdrew, but presently returned. He handed Dakin a note.

Dakin tore open the envelope and read:

"I want to see you about Henry Carmichael. R.B."

"Show him in," said Dakin.

Presently Richard Baker and Mrs. Pauncefoot Jones came in. Richard Baker said:

"I don't want to take up your time, but I was at school with a man called Henry Carmichael. We lost sight of each other for many years, but when I was at Basrah a few weeks ago I encountered him in the Consulate waiting room. He was dressed as an Arab, and without giving any overt sign of recognition, he managed to communicate with me. Does this interest you?"

"It interests me very much," said Dakin.

"I formed the idea that Carmichael believed himself to be in danger. This was very soon verified. He was attacked by a man with a revolver which I managed to knock up. Carmichael took to his heels but before he went, he slipped something into my pocket which I found later—It didn't appear to be important—it seems to be just a 'chit'—a reference for one Ahmed Mohammed. But I acted on the assumption that to Carmichael it was important.

"Since he gave me no instructions, I kept it carefully, believing that he would one day reclaim it. The other day I learnt from Victoria Jones that he was dead. From other things that she told me, I have come to the conclusion that the right person to deliver this object to is you."

He got up and placed a dirty sheet of paper with writing on it on Dakin's desk.

"Does this mean anything to you?"

Dakin drew a deep sigh.

"Yes," he said. "It means more than you can possibly imagine."

He got up.

"I'm deeply obliged to you, Baker," he said. "Forgive my cutting this interview short, but there is a lot that I have to see to without wasting a minute." He shook hands with Mrs. Pauncefoot Jones, saying, "I suppose you are joining your husband on his Dig. I hope you have a good season."

"It's a good thing Pauncefoot Jones didn't come into Baghdad with me this morning," said Richard. "Dear old John Pauncefoot Jones doesn't notice much that goes on, but he'd probably notice the difference between his wife and his wife's sister."

Dakin looked with slight surprise at Mrs. Pauncefoot Jones. She said in a low pleasant voice,

"My sister Elsie is still in England. I dyed my hair black and came out on her passport. My sister's maiden name was Elsia Scheele. *My name, Mr. Dakin, is Anna Scheele.*"

Chapter 24

Baghdad was transformed. Police lined the streets—police drafted in from outside, the International Police. At last the historic Conference had begun.

In a small anteroom certain events were taking place which might well alter the course of history. Like most momentous happenings, the proceedings were not at all dramatic.

Doctor Alan Breck of the Harwell Atomic Institute contributed his quota of information in a small precise voice.

Certain specimens had been left with him for analysis by the late Sir Rupert Crofton Lee. They had been acquired in the course of one of Sir Rupert's journeys through China and Turkestan through Kurdistan to Iraq. Dr. Breck's evidence then became severely technical. Metallic ores . . . high uranium content . . . Source of deposit not known exactly, since Sir Rupert's notes and diaries had been destroyed during the war by enemy action.

Then Mr. Dakin took up the tale. In a gentle tired voice he told the saga of Henry Carmichael, of his belief in certain rumours and wild tales of vast installations and underground laboratories functioning in a remote valley beyond the bounds of civilization. Of his search—and of the success of his search. Of how that great traveller, Sir Rupert Crofton Lee, the man who had believed Carmichael because of his own knowledge of those regions, had agreed to come to Baghdad, and of how he had died. And of how Carmichael had met his own death at the hands of Sir Rupert's impersonator.

"Sir Rupert is dead, and Henry Carmichael is dead. But there is a third witness who is alive and who is here today. I will call upon Miss Anna Scheele to give us her testimony."

Anna Scheele, as calm and composed as if she were in Mr. Morganthal's office, gave lists of names and figures. From the depths of that remarkable financial brain of hers, she outlined the vast financial network that had drained money from circulation, and poured it into the financing of activities that should tend to split the civilized world into two opposing factions. It was no mere assertion. She produced facts and figures to support her contention. To those who listened she carried a conviction that was not as yet fully accorded to Carmichael's wild tale.

Dakin spoke again.

"Henry Carmichael is dead," he said. "But he brought back with him from that hazardous journey tangible and definite proofs. He did not dare to keep those proofs on him—his enemies were too close on his track. But he was a man of many friends. By the hands of two of those friends, he sent the proofs to the safekeeping of another friend—a man whom all Iraq reveres and respects. He has courteously consented to come here today. I refer to Sheikh Hussein el Ziyara of Kerbela."

Sheikh Hussein el Ziyara was renowned, as Dakin had said, throughout the Moslem world, both as a Holy Man and a poet. He was considered by many to be a Saint. He stood up now, an imposing figure with his deep brown hennaed beard. His grey jacket edged with gold braid was covered by a flowing brown cloak of gossamer fineness. Round his head he wore a green cloth headdress which was bound with many strands of heavy gold *agal* and which gave him a patriarchal appearance. He spoke in a deep sonorous voice.

"Henry Carmichael was my friend," he said. "I knew him as a boy and he studied with me the verses of our great poets. Two men came to Kerbela, men who travel the country with a picture show. They are simple men, but good followers of the Prophet. They brought me a packet which they said they had been told to deliver into my hands from my friend the Englishman Carmichael. I was to keep this in secrecy and security and to deliver it only to Carmichael himself, or to a messenger who should repeat certain words."

Dakin said, "Sayyid, the Arabic poet Mutanabbi, called sometimes the Pretender to Prophecy, who lived just one thousand years ago, wrote an Ode to Prince Sayru 'l-Dawla at Aleppo in which these words occur: *Zid hashshi bashshi tafaddal adni surra sili*."*

With a smile Sheikh Hussein el Ziyara held out a packet to Dakin.

*Add, laugh, rejoice, bring nigh, gladden, show favour, give!

"I say, as Prince Sayru 'l-Dawla said: 'You shall have your desire' . . ."

"Gentlemen," said Dakin. "These are the microfilms brought back by Henry Carmichael in proof of his story . . ."

One more witness spoke—a tragic broken figure: an old man with a fine domed head who had once been universally admired and respected.

He spoke with a tragic dignity.

"Gentlemen," he said. "I shall shortly be arraigned as a common swindler. But there are some things that even I cannot countenance. There is a band of men, mostly young men, so evil in their hearts and aims that the truth would hardly be believed."

He lifted up his head and roared out:

"Antichrist! I say this thing must be stopped! We have got to have peace—peace to lick our wounds and make a new world—and to do that we must try to understand each other. I started a racket to make money—but, by God, I've ended in believing in what I preach—though I don't advocate the methods I've used. For God's sake, gentlemen, let's start again and try to pull together . . ."

There was a moment's silence, and then a thin official voice, with the bloodless impersonality of bureaucracy, said:

"These facts will be put forthwith before the Powers Assembled. . . ."

Chapter 25

"What bothers me," said Victoria, "is that poor Danish woman who got killed by mistake in Damascus."

"Oh! she's all right," said Mr. Dakin cheerfully. "As soon as your plane had taken off, we arrested the French woman and took Grete Harden to hospital. She came round all right. They were going to keep her drugged for a bit until they were sure the Baghdad business went off all right. She was one of our people, of course."

"Was she?"

"Yes, when Anna Scheele disappeared, we thought it might be as well to give the other side something to think about. So we booked a passage for Grete Harden and carefully didn't give her a background. They fell for it—jumped to the conclusion that Grete Harden must be Anna Scheele. We gave her a nice little set of faked papers to prove it."

"While the real Anna Scheele remained quietly in the nursing home till it was time for Mrs. Pauncefoot Jones to join her husband out here."

"Yes. Simple—but effective. Acting on the assumption that in times of stress the only people you can really trust are your own family. She's an exceedingly clever young woman."

"I really thought I was for it," said Victoria. "Were your people really keeping tabs on me?"

"All the time. Your Edward wasn't really quite so clever as he thought himself, you know. Actually we'd been investigating the activities of young Edward Goring for some time. When you told me your story, the night Carmichael was killed, I was frankly very worried about you.

"The best thing I could think of was to send you deliberately into the setup as a spy. If your Edward knew that you were in touch with me, you'd be reasonably safe, because he'd learn through you what we were up to. You'd be too valuable to kill. And he could also pass on false information to us through you. You were a link. But then you spotted the Rupert Crofton Lee impersonation, and Edward decided you'd better be kept out of it until you were needed (if you should be needed) for the impersonation of Anna Scheele. Yes, Victoria, you're very lucky to be sitting where you are now, eating all those pistachio nuts."

"I know I am."

Mr. Dakin said:

"How much do you mind—about Edward?"

Victoria looked at him steadily.

"Not at all. I was just a silly little fool. I let Edward pick me up and do his glamour act. I just had a thoroughly schoolgirl crush on him—fancying myself Juliet and all sorts of silly things."

"You needn't blame yourself too much. Edward had a wonderful natural gift for attracting women."

"Yes, and he used it."

"He certainly used it."

"Next time I fall in love," said Victoria, "it won't be looks that attract me, or glamour. I'd like a real man—not one who says pretty things to you. I shan't mind if he's bald or wears spectacles or anything like that. I'd like him to be interesting—and know about interesting things."

"About thirty-five or fifty-five?" asked Mr. Dakin.

Victoria stared.

"Oh thirty-five," she said.

"I am relieved. I thought for a moment you were proposing to me."

Victoria laughed.

"And—I know I mustn't ask questions—but was there really a message knitted into the scarf?"

"There was a name. The *tricoteuses* of whom Madame Defarge was one, knitted a register of names. The scarf and the 'chit' were the two halves of the clue. One gave us the name of Sheikh Hussein el Ziyara of Kerbela. The other when treated with iodine vapour gave us the words to induce the Sheikh to part with his trust. There couldn't have been a safer place to hide the thing, you know, than in the sacred City of Kerbela."

"And it was carried through the country by those two wandering cinema men—the ones we actually met?"

"Yes. Simple well known figures. Nothing political about them. Just Carmichael's personal friends. He had a lot of friends."

"He must have been very nice. I'm sorry he's dead."

"We've all got to die sometime," said Mr. Dakin. "And if there's another life after this which I myself fully believe, he'll have the satisfaction of knowing that his faith and his courage have done more to save this sorry old world from a fresh attack of bloodletting and misery than almost anyone that one can think of."

"It's odd, isn't it," said Victoria meditatively, "that Richard should have had one half of the secret and I should have had the other. It almost seems as though—"

"As though it were meant to be," finished Mr. Dakin with a twinkle. "And what are you going to do next, may I ask?"

"I shall have to find a job," said Victoria. "I must start looking about."

"Don't look too hard," said Mr. Dakin. "I rather think a job is coming towards you."

He ambled gently away to give place to Richard Baker.

"Look here, Victoria," said Richard. "Venetia Savile can't come out after all. Apparently she's got mumps. You were quite useful on the Dig. Would you like to come back? Only your keep, I'm afraid. And probably your passage back to England—but we'll talk about that later. Mrs. Pauncefoot Jones is coming out next week. Well, what do you say?"

"Oh, do you really want me?" cried Victoria.

For some reason Richard Baker became very pink in the face. He coughed and polished his pince-nez.

"I think," he said, "we could find you—er—quite useful."

"I'd love it," said Victoria.

"In that case," said Richard, "you'd better collect your luggage and come along back to the Dig now. You don't want to hang about Baghdad, do you?"

"Not in the least," said Victoria.

"So there you are, my dear Veronica," said Dr. Pauncefoot Jones. "Richard went off in a great state about you. Well, well—I hope you'll both be very happy."

"What does he mean?" asked Victoria bewildered, as Dr. Pauncefoot Jones pottered away.

"Nothing," said Richard. "You know what he's like. He's being—just a little—premature."

Dame Agatha Christie is the most widely published author of all time. In a career that spanned more than fifty years, Christie wrote eighty novels and short story collections, nineteen plays—one of which, *The Mousetrap*, is the longest-running play in history—and five nonfiction books, including her autobiography. In addition, she wrote six romantic novels under the pseudonym Mary Westmacott. Two of the characters she created, the ingenious Belgian Hercule Poirot and the irrepressible and relentless Miss Jane Marple, became world-famous detectives. Poirot was immortalized on television by David Suchet, and Miss Marple by both Joan Hickson and Geraldine McEwan.

Agatha Christie achieved Britain's highest honor when she was made a Dame of the British Empire. She died in 1976.